THE RETURN OF THE NATIVE

AN AUTHORITATIVE TEXT

BACKGROUND

CRITICISM

W. W. NORTON & COMPANY, INC.
also publishes

THE NORTON ANTHOLOGY OF AMERICAN LITERATURE
edited by Ronald Gottesman et al.

THE NORTON ANTHOLOGY OF ENGLISH LITERATURE
edited by M. H. Abrams et al.

THE NORTON ANTHOLOGY OF MODERN POETRY
edited by Richard Ellmann and Robert O'Clair

THE NORTON ANTHOLOGY OF POETRY
edited by Arthur M. Eastman et al.

THE NORTON ANTHOLOGY OF SHORT FICTION
edited by R. V. Cassill

THE NORTON INTRODUCTION TO LITERATURE
edited by Carl E. Bain, Jerome Beaty, and J. Paul Hunter

THE NORTON READER
edited by Arthur M. Eastman et al.

WORLD MASTERPIECES
edited by Maynard Mack et al.

THE NORTON FACSIMILE OF
THE FIRST FOLIO OF SHAKESPEARE
prepared by Charlton Hinman

A NORTON CRITICAL EDITION

THOMAS HARDY

THE RETURN OF THE NATIVE

AN AUTHORITATIVE TEXT
BACKGROUND
CRITICISM

Edited by

JAMES GINDIN
THE UNIVERSITY OF MICHIGAN

W · W · NORTON & COMPANY · INC · *New York*

ISBN 0 393 04300 2
ISBN 0 393 09791 9

Library of Congress Catalog Card No. 68-12184

PRINTED IN THE UNITED STATES OF AMERICA

9 0

Contents

Preface

The Return of the Native, Hardy's sixth novel, was written in 1877 and 1878 while he was living at Sturminster Newton, a small village in Dorset. An early version of the novel was rejected by Leslie Stephen, the editor of the *Cornhill Magazine*, which had serialized *Far from the Madding Crowd*, a novel of Hardy's published four years before *The Return of the Native*. Hardy followed Stephen's advice, making the novel more suitable for the Victorian family audience, but apparently did not submit it to the *Cornhill Magazine* again. Instead, the revised version of *The Return of the Native* was serialized in twelve issues of *Belgravia* from January through December 1878. A slightly different version was published in three volumes as the first edition by Smith, Elder & Co., London, in November 1878. Hardy later revised the novel twice: in 1895 for Osgood, McIlvaine's edition of the Wessex Novels and in 1912 for the definitive Wessex edition published by Macmillan. He added a short preface in 1895 and a postscript in 1912. The text that follows is that of the 1912 Wessex edition, containing Hardy's final revisions. I have not supplied variant readings from earlier editions of the novel, for the changes Hardy made from the 1878 edition to the 1895 to the definitive 1912 were all minor. The major and revealing differences in versions of the novel exist between the first version offered to and rejected by the *Cornhill Magazine*, the version published in *Belgravia*, and the 1878 edition. John Paterson (see Bibliography) summarizes and discusses these at length, and I have accordingly used a fairly generous selection from his work.

Hardy himself drew the map here reproduced for the first edition in 1878. This map of Egdon Heath also appeared in the first American edition, published by Henry Holt and Co. in December 1878, but in none of the principal editions thereafter.

The backgrounds of Hardy's fiction cannot easily be extrapolated from a study of his life, for Hardy was usually reticent both about himself and about his aims and methods in creating fiction. The standard biography, written by his second wife shortly after Hardy's death (see Bibliography), does, however, contain numerous quotations from his notebooks. I have selected those which seem most pertinent to *The Return of the Native* specifically and to the composition of fiction generally. Hardy stated several times during his life that his poetry was more personally significant and revealing than his prose. In selecting only twelve poems, I have tried to choose those closest to and most illuminating about the themes and atmosphere of *The Return of the Native*. Critics have frequently called attention to the prevalence of folk customs and attitudes in Hardy's fiction, particularly apparent in this novel. Since no single source I could discover discussed folk material with specific reference to *The Return of the Native*, I have written a brief essay and appended it to the background information on the novel.

When *The Return of the Native* appeared in 1878, most critics were hostile to the novel, comparing it unfavorably to *Far from the Madding Crowd*, which had been a critical success four years earlier. The few representative selections included reveal more about journalistic narrowness in the late 1870s than they do about Hardy's novel. The novel has, nevertheless, always been popular and has been generally regarded as one of Hardy's three or four best. Hardy's work has not received the wealth of twentieth-century critical attention and exegesis applied to that of Henry James or James Joyce, and there is no single standard, indispensable, or definitive critical account. Yet critics have tried, consistently since the 1890s, to explain the particular appeal and power of Hardy's fiction. The criticism of Hardy, like criticism generally, has gone through a number of changes in direction and emphasis. In a brief introduction to the critical essays, I have attempted to chart these changes. The selections from essays and books themselves, in addition to being representative, hopefully both collect the soundest and most far-reaching arguments for and against Hardy's fiction and will stimulate the student to work out his own critical interpretation and estimate. The Selected Bibliography invites expansion on the necessary narrowness of my own choices.

I am grateful to my wife for doing so much that Xerox could not do, for cutting, pasting, typing, and hunting references for footnotes. Even more centrally, I am grateful for her judgment and her willingness to discuss the most minute of editorial choices.

James Gindin

The Text of
The Return of the Native

'To sorrow
I bade good morrow,
And thought to leave her far away behind;
But cheerly, cheerly,
She loves me dearly;
She is so constant to me, and so kind.
I would deceive her,
And so leave her,
But ah! she is so constant and so kind.'

SKETCH MAP OF THE SCENE OF THE STORY

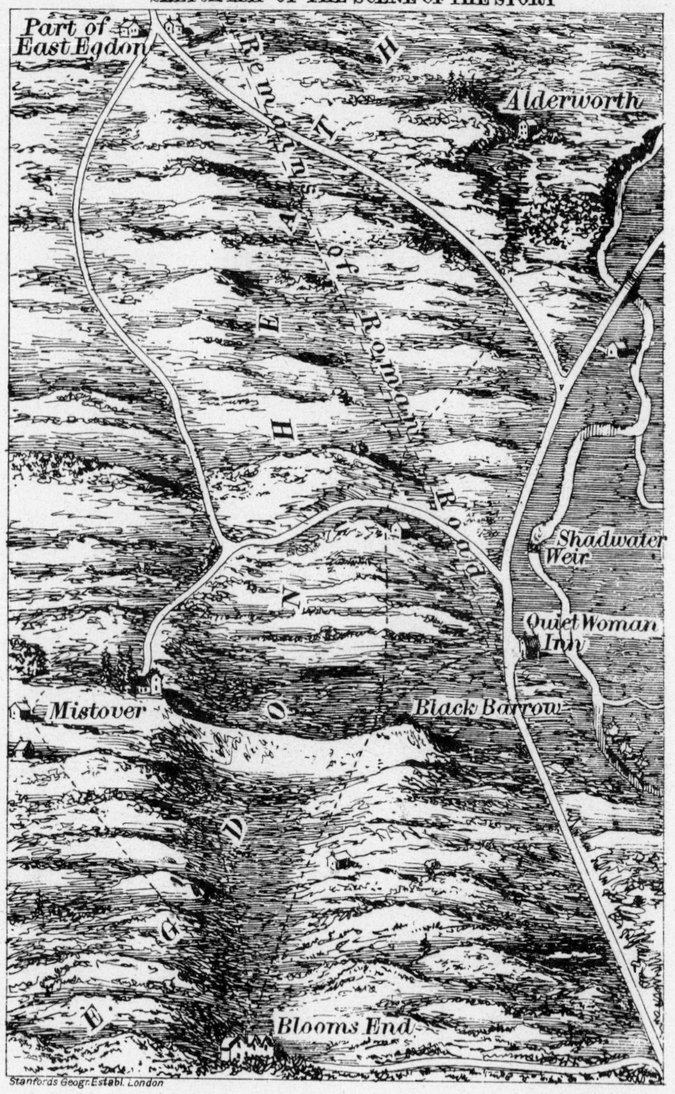

Contents of *The Return of the Native*

Book Fourth: The Closed Door

Book Fifth: The Discovery

Book Sixth: Aftercourses

AUTHOR'S PREFACE

The date at which the following events are assumed to have occurred may be set down as between 1840 and 1850, when the old watering-place herein called 'Budmouth' still retained sufficient afterglow from its Georgian gaiety and prestige to lend it an absorbing attractiveness to the romantic and imaginative soul of a lovely dweller inland.

Under the general name of 'Egdon Heath,' which has been given to the sombre scene of the story, are united or typified heaths of various real names, to the number of at least a dozen; these being virtually one in character and aspect, though their original unity, or partial unity, is now somewhat disguised by intrusive strips and slices brought under the plough with varying degrees of success, or planted to woodland.

It is pleasant to dream that some spot in the extensive tract whose south-western quarter is here described, may be the heath of that traditionary King of Wessex—Lear.

July 1895.

Postscript

To prevent disappointment to searchers for scenery it should be added that though the action of the narrative is supposed to proceed in the central and most secluded part of the heaths united into one whole, as above described, certain topographical features resembling those delineated really lie on the margin of the waste, several miles to the westward of the centre. In some other respects also there has been a bringing together of scattered characteristics.

The first edition of this novel was published in three volumes in 1878.

T.H.

April 1912.

BOOK FIRST: THE THREE WOMEN

A Face on Which Time Makes But Little Impression

I

A Saturday afternoon in November was approaching the time of twilight, and the vast tract of unenclosed wild known as Egdon Heath embrowned[1] itself moment by moment. Overhead the hollow stretch of whitish cloud shutting out the sky was as a tent which had the whole heath for its floor.

The heaven being spread with this pallid screen and the earth with the darkest vegetation, their meeting-line at the horizon was clearly marked. In such contrast the heath wore the appearance of an instalment of night which had taken up its place before its astronomical hour was come: darkness had to a great extent arrived hereon, while day stood distinct in the sky. Looking upwards, a furze-cutter[2] would have been inclined to continue work; looking down, he would have decided to finish his faggot[3] and go home. The distant rims of the world and of the firmament seemed to be a division in time no less than a division in matter. The face of the heath by its mere complexion added half an hour to evening; it could in like manner retard the dawn, sadden noon, anticipate the frowning of storms scarcely generated, and intensify the opacity of a moonless midnight to a cause of shaking and dread.

In fact, precisely at this transitional point of its nightly roll into darkness the great and particular glory of the Egdon waste began, and nobody could be said to understand the heath who had not been there at such a time. It could best be felt when it could not clearly be seen, its complete effect and explanation lying in this and the succeeding hours before the next dawn: then, and only then, did it tell its true tale. The spot was, indeed, a near relation of night, and when night showed itself an apparent tendency to gravitate together could be perceived in its shades and the scene. The sombre stretch of rounds and hollows seemed to rise and meet the evening gloom in pure sympathy, the heath exhaling darkness as

1. To become brown or dusky.
2. One who cuts furze, a spiny evergreen shrub with yellow flowers that grows abundantly on heath. Furze is sometimes called *gorse*.
3. Sticks, twigs, or small branches bound together, usually for use as fuel.

rapidly as the heavens precipitated it. And so the obscurity in the air and the obscurity in the land closed together in a black fraternization towards which each advanced half-way.

The place became full of a watchful intentness now; for when other things sank brooding to sleep the heath appeared slowly to awake and listen. Every night its Titanic form seemed to await something; but it had waited thus, unmoved, during so many centuries, through the crises of so many things, that it could only be imagined to await one last crisis—the final overthrow.

It was a spot which returned upon the memory of those who loved it with an aspect of peculiar and kindly congruity. Smiling champaigns[4] of flowers and fruit hardly do this, for they are permanently harmonious only with an existence of better reputation as to its issues than the present. Twilight combined with the scenery of Egdon Heath to evolve a thing majestic without severity, impressive without showiness, emphatic in its admonitions, grand in its simplicity. The qualifications which frequently invest the facade of a prison with far more dignity than is found in the facade of a palace double its size lent to this heath a sublimity in which spots renowned for beauty of the accepted kind are utterly wanting. Fair prospects wed happily with fair times; but alas, if times be not fair! Men have oftener suffered from the mockery of a place too smiling for their reason than from the oppression of surroundings oversadly tinged. Haggard Egdon appealed to a subtler and scarcer instinct, to a more recently learnt emotion, than that which responds to the sort of beauty called charming and fair.

Indeed, it is a question if the exclusive reign of this orthodox beauty is not approaching its last quarter. The new Vale of Tempe may be a gaunt waste in Thule:[5] human souls may find themselves in closer and closer harmony with external things wearing a sombreness distasteful to our race when it was young. The time seems near, if it has not actually arrived, when the chastened sublimity of a moor, a sea, or a mountain will be all of nature that is absolutely in keeping with the moods of the more thinking among mankind. And ultimately, to the commonest tourist, spots like Iceland may become what the vineyards and myrtle-gardens of South Europe are to him now; and Heidelberg and Baden be passed unheeded as he hastens from the Alps to the sand-dunes of Scheveningen.

The most thorough-going ascetic could feel that he had a natural right to wander on Egdon: he was keeping within the line of legitimate indulgence when he laid himself open to influences such as these. Colours and beauties so far subdued were, at least, the birth-

4. Open fields or unruffled expanses.

5. Ancient Greek and Latin name for a land six days' sail north of Britain, thought to be the most northerly region of the world. The *Vale of Tempe* is, literally, a valley in ancient Thessaly; generally used for any beautiful valley.

right of all. Only in summer days of highest feather did its mood touch the level of gaiety. Intensity was more usually reached by way of the solemn than by way of the brilliant, and such a sort of intensity was often arrived at during winter darkness, tempests, and mists. Then Egdon was aroused to reciprocity; for the storm was its lover, and the wind its friend. Then it became the home of strange phantoms; and it was found to be the hitherto unrecognized original of those wild regions of obscurity which are vaguely felt to be compassing us about in midnight dreams of flight and disaster, and are never thought of after the dream till revived by scenes like this.

It was at present a place perfectly accordant with man's nature—neither ghastly, hateful, nor ugly: neither commonplace, unmeaning, nor tame; but, like man, slighted and enduring; and withal singularly colossal and mysterious in its swarthy monotony. As with some persons who have long lived apart, solitude seemed to look out of its countenance. It had a lonely face, suggesting tragical possibilities.

This obscure, obsolete, superseded country figures in Domesday.[6] Its condition is recorded therein as that of heathy, furzy, briary wilderness—'Bruaria.' Then follows the length and breadth in leagues; and, though some uncertainty exists as to the exact extent of this ancient lineal measure, it appears from the figures that the area of Egdon down to the present day has but little diminished. 'Turbaria[7] Bruaria'—the right of cutting heath-turf—occurs in charters relating to the district. 'Overgrown with heth and mosse,' says Leland[8] of the same dark sweep of country.

Here at least were intelligible facts regarding landscape—far-reaching proofs productive of genuine satisfaction. The untameable, Ishmaelitish[9] thing that Egdon now was it always had been. Civilization was its enemy; and ever since the beginning of vegetation its soil had worn the same antique brown dress, the natural and invariable garment of the particular formation. In its venerable one coat lay a certain vein of satire on human vanity in clothes. A person on a heath in raiment of modern cut and colours has more or less an anomalous look. We seem to want the oldest and simplest human clothing where the clothing of the earth is so primitive.

To recline on a stump of thorn in the central valley of Egdon, between afternoon and night, as now, where the eye could reach

6. Book surveying the extent, value, and ownership of the lands of England, compiled by order of William the Conqueror in 1086. The name is derived from the Doomsday book, the accounts of all men at the Day of the Last Judgment.

7. Literally, peat bog.

8. John Leland (1506?-1552), famous English clergyman, poet, and antiquary who wrote a vast history and archaeology of England and Wales.

9. Outcast son of Abraham and Hagar (Genesis xvi. 11-12). Figuratively, an outcast or wanderer.

nothing of the world outside the summits and shoulders of heathland which filled the whole circumference of its glance, and to know that everything around and underneath had been from prehistoric times as unaltered as the stars overhead, gave ballast to the mind adrift on change, and harassed by the irrepressible New. The great inviolate place had an ancient permanence which the sea cannot claim. Who can say of a particular sea that it is old? Distilled by the sun, kneaded by the moon, it is renewed in a year, in a day, or in an hour. The sea changed, the fields changed, the rivers, the villages, and the people changed, yet Egdon remained. Those surfaces were neither so steep as to be destructible by weather, nor so flat as to be the victims of floods and deposits. With the exception of an aged highway, and a still more aged barrow presently to be referred to—themselves almost crystallized to natural products by long continuance—even the trifling irregularities were not caused by pickaxe, plough, or spade, but remained as the very finger-touches of the last geological change.

The above-mentioned highway traversed the lower levels of the heath, from one horizon to another. In many portions of its course it overlaid an old vicinal way,[1] which branched from the great Western road of the Romans,[2] the Via Iceniana, or Ikenild Street, hard by. On the evening under consideration it would have been noticed that though the gloom had increased sufficiently to confuse the minor features of the heath, the white surface of the road remained almost as clear as ever.

Humanity Appears upon the Scene, Hand in Hand with Trouble

II

Along the road walked an old man. He was white-headed as a mountain, bowed in the shoulders, and faded in general aspect. He wore a glazed hat, an ancient boat-cloak,[3] and shoes; his brass buttons bearing an anchor upon their face. In his hand was a silver-headed walking-stick, which he used as a veritable third leg, perseveringly dotting the ground with its point at every few inches' interval. One would have said that he had been, in his day, a naval officer of some sort or other.

Before him stretched the long, laborious road, dry, empty, and white. It was quite open to the heath on each side, and bisected

1. Byroad, local common way.
2. The road, originally built by the Romans, running due west from London to Land's End. It is also sometimes referred to as Watling Street or, by rustics, as the London Road or the Milky Way.
3. Large cloak worn by officers on duty at sea.

that vast dark surface like the parting-line on a head of black hair,[4] diminishing and bending away on the furthest horizon.

The old man frequently stretched his eyes ahead to gaze over the tract that he had yet to traverse. At length he discerned, a long distance in front of him, a moving spot, which appeared to be a vehicle, and it proved to be going the same way as that in which he himself was journeying. It was the single atom of life that the scene contained, and it only served to render the general loneliness more evident. Its rate of advance was slow, and the old man gained upon it sensibly.

When he drew nearer he perceived it to be a spring van,[5] ordinary in shape, but singular in colour, this being a lurid red. The driver walked beside it; and, like his van, he was completely red. One dye of that tincture covered his clothes, the cap upon his head, his boots, his face, and his hands. He was not temporarily overlaid with the colour: it permeated him.

The old man knew the meaning of this. The traveller with the cart was a reddleman—a person whose vocation it was to supply farmers with redding[6] for their sheep. He was one of a class rapidly becoming extinct in Wessex, filling at present in the rural world the place which, during the last century, the dodo occupied in the world of animals. He is a curious, interesting, and nearly perished link between obsolete forms of life and those which generally prevail.

The decayed officer, by degrees, came up alongside his fellow-wayfarer, and wished him good evening. The reddleman turned his head and replied in sad and occupied tones. He was young, and his face, if not exactly handsome, approached so near to handsome that nobody would have contradicted an assertion that it really was so in its natural colour. His eye, which glared so strangely through his stain, was in itself attractive—keen as that of a bird of prey, and blue as autumn mist. He had neither whisker nor moustache, which allowed the soft curves of the lower part of his face to be apparent. His lips were thin, and though, as it seemed, compressed by thought, there was a pleasant twitch at their corners now and then. He was clothed throughout in a tight-fitting suit of corduroy, excellent in quality, not much worn, and well-chosen for its purpose; but deprived of its original colour by his trade. It showed to advantage the good shape of his figure. A certain well-to-do air about the man suggested that he was not poor for his degree. The natural query of an observer would have been, Why should such a promising being as this have hidden his prepossessing exterior by adopting that singular occupation?

4. In a poem called *The Roman Road*, Hardy describes the road as "Pale as a parting-line in hair."

5. Covered wagon.

6. Red ochre widely used to mark sheep.

After replying to the old man's greeting he showed no inclination to continue in talk, although they still walked side by side, for the elder traveller seemed to desire company. There were no sounds but that of the booming wind upon the stretch of tawny herbage around them, the crackling wheels, the tread of the men, and the footsteps of the two shaggy ponies which drew the van. They were small, hardy animals, of a breed between Galloway and Exmoor, and were known as 'heath-croppers' here.

Now, as they thus pursued their way, the reddleman occasionally left his companion's side, and, stepping behind the van, looked into its interior through a small window. The look was always anxious. He would then return to the old man, who made another remark about the state of the country and so on, to which the reddleman again abstractedly replied, and then again they would lapse into silence. The silence conveyed to neither any sense of awkwardness; in these lonely places wayfarers, after a first greeting, frequently plod on for miles without speech; contiguity amounts to a tacit conversation where, otherwise than in cities, such contiguity can be put an end to on the merest inclination, and where not to put an end to it is intercourse in itself.

Possibly these two might not have spoken again till their parting, had it not been for the reddleman's visits to his van. When he returned from his fifth time of looking in the old man said, 'You have something inside there besides your load?'

'Yes.'

'Somebody who wants looking after?'

'Yes.'

Not long after this a faint cry sounded from the interior. The reddleman hastened to the back, looked in, and came away again.

'You have a child there, my man?'

'No, sir, I have a woman.'

'The deuce you have! Why did she cry out?'

'Oh, she has fallen asleep, and not being used to traveling, she's uneasy, and keeps dreaming.'

'A young woman?'

'Yes, a young woman?'

'That would have interested me forty years ago. Perhaps she's your wife?'

'My wife!' said the other bitterly. 'She's above mating with such as I. But there's no reason why I should tell you about that.'

'That's true. And there's no reason why you should not. What harm can I do to you or to her?'

The reddleman looked in the old man's face. 'Well, sir,' he said at last, 'I knew her before to-day, though perhaps it would have been better if I had not. But she's nothing to me, and I am nothing to her; and she wouldn't have been in my van if any better carriage had been there to take her.'

'Where, may I ask?'

'At Anglebury.'

'I know the town well. What was she doing there?'

'Oh, not much—to gossip about. However, she's tired to death now, and not at all well, and that's what makes her so restless. She dropped off into a nap about an hour ago, and 'twill do her good.'

'A nice-looking girl, no doubt?'

'You would say so.'

The other traveller turned his eyes with interest towards the van window, and, without withdrawing them, said, 'I presume I might look in upon her?'

'No,' said the redlleman abruptly. 'It is getting too dark for you to see much of her; and, more than that, I have no right to allow you. Thank God she sleeps so well: I hope she won't wake till she's home.'

'Who is she? One of the neighbourhood?'

' 'Tis no matter who, excuse me.'

'It is not that girl of Blooms-End, who has been talked about more or less lately? If so, I know her; and I can guess what has happened.'

' 'Tis no matter. . . . Now, sir, I am sorry to say that we shall soon have to part company. My ponies are tired, and I have further to go, and I am going to rest them under this bank for an hour.'

The elder traveller nodded his head indifferently, and the reddleman turned his horses and van in upon the turf, saying, 'Good night.' The old man replied, and proceeded on his way as before.

The reddleman watched his form as it diminished to a speck on the road and became absorbed in the thickening films of night. He then took some hay from a truss which was slung up under the van, and, throwing a portion of it in front of the horses, made a pad of the rest, which he laid on the ground beside his vehicle. Upon this he sat down, leaning his back against the wheel. From the interior a low soft breathing came to his ear. It appeared to satisfy him, and he musingly surveyed the scene, as if considering the next step that he should take.

To do things musingly, and by small degrees, seemed, indeed, to be a duty in the Egdon valleys at this transitional hour, for there was that in the condition of the heath itself which resembled protracted and halting dubiousness. It was the quality of the repose appertaining to the scene. This was not the repose of actual stagnation, but the apparent repose of incredible slowness. A condition of healthy life so nearly resembling the torpor of death is a noticeable thing of its sort; to exhibit the inertness of the desert, and at the same time to be exercising powers akin to those of the meadow, and even of the forest, awakened in those who thought of it the attentiveness usually engendered by understatement and reserve.

The scene before the reddleman's eyes was a gradual series of ascents from the level of the road backward into the heart of the heath. It embraced hillocks, pits, ridges, acclivities, one behind the other, till all was finished by a high hill cutting against the still light sky. The traveler's eye hovered about these things for a time, and finally settled upon one noteworthy object up there. It was a barrow.[7] This bossy[8] projection of earth above its natural level occupied the loftiest ground of the loneliest height that the heath contained. Although from the vale it appeared but as a wart on an Atlantean brow, its actual bulk was great. It formed the pole and axis of this heathery world.

As the resting man looked at the barrow he became aware that its summit, hitherto the highest object in the whole prospect round, was surmounted by something higher. It rose from the semi-globular mound like a spike from a helmet. The first instinct of an imaginative stranger might have been to suppose it the person of one of the Celts who built the barrow, so far had all of modern date withdrawn from the scene. It seemed a sort of last man among them, musing for a moment before dropping into eternal night with the rest of his race.

There the form stood, motionless as the hill beneath. Above the plain rose the hill, above the hill rose the barrow, and above the barrow rose the figure. Above the figure was nothing that could be mapped elsewhere than on a celestial globe.

Such a perfect, delicate, and necessary finish did the figure give to the dark pile of hills that it seemed to be the only obvious justification of their outline. Without it, there was the dome without the lantern; with it the architectural demands of the mass were satisfied. The scene was strangely homogeneous, in that the vale, the upland, the barrow, and the figure above it amounted only to unity. Looking at this or that member of the group was not observing a complete thing, but a fraction of a thing.

The form was so much like an organic part of the entire motionless structure that to see it move would have impressed the mind as a strange phenomenon. Immobility being the chief characteristic of that whole which the person formed portion of, the discontinuance of immobility in any quarter suggested confusion.

Yet that is what happened. The figure perceptibly gave up its fixity, shifted a step or two, and turned round. As if alarmed, it descended on the right side of the barrow, with the glide of a

7. High hill. A *barrow* is a prehistoric burial mound.

8. Rounded.

water-drop down a bud, and then vanished. The movement had been sufficient to show more clearly the characteristics of the figure, and that it was a woman's.

The reason of her sudden displacement now appeared. With her dropping out of sight on the right side, a new-comer, bearing a burden, protruded into the sky on the left side, ascended the tumulus[9], and deposited the burden on the top. A second followed, then a third, a fourth, a fifth, and ultimately the whole barrow was peopled with burdened figures.

The only intelligible meaning in this sky-backed pantomime of silhouettes was that the woman had no relation to the forms who had taken her place, was sedulously avoiding these, and had come thither for another object than theirs. The imagination of the observer clung by preference to that vanished, solitary figure, as to something more interesting, more important, more likely to have a history worth knowing than these new-comers, and unconsciously regarded them as intruders. But they remained, and established themselves; and the lonely person who hitherto had been queen of the solitude did not at present seem likely to return.

The Custom of the Country

III

Had a looker-on been posted in the immediate vicinity of the barrow, he would have learned that these persons were boys and men of the neighbouring hamlets. Each, as he ascended the barrow, had been heavily laden with furze-faggots, carried upon the shoulder by means of a long stake sharpened at each end for impaling them easily—two in front and two behind. They came from a part of the heath a quarter of a mile to the rear, where furze almost exclusively prevailed as a product.

Every individual was so involved in furze by his method of carrying the faggots that he appeared like a bush on legs till he had thrown them down. The party had marched in trail, like a travelling flock of sheep; that is to say, the strongest first, the weak and young behind.

The loads were all laid together, and a pyramid of furze thirty feet in circumference now occupied the crown of the tumulus, which was known as Rainbarrow for many miles round. Some made themselves busy with matches, and in selecting the driest tufts of furze, others in loosening the bramble bonds which held the faggots together. Others, again, while this was in progress, lifted their eyes and swept the vast expanse of country commanded by their position, now lying nearly obliterated by shade. In the valleys

9. Barrow, ancient burial mound.

of the heath nothing save its own wild face was visible at any time of day; but this spot commanded a horizon enclosing a tract of far extent, and in many cases lying beyond the heath country. None of its features could be seen now, but the whole made itself felt as a vague stretch of remoteness.

While the men and lads were building the pile, a change took place in the mass of shade which denoted the distant landscape. Red suns and tufts of fire one by one began to arise, flecking the whole country round. They were the bonfires of other parishes and hamlets that were engaged in the same sort of commemoration. Some were distant, and stood in a dense atmosphere, so that bundles of pale strawlike beams radiated around them in the shape of a fan. Some were large and near, glowing scarlet-red from the shade, like wounds in a black hide. Some were Maenades,[1] with winy faces and blown hair. These tinctured the silent bosom of the clouds above them and lit up their ephemeral caves, which seemed thenceforth to become scalding caldrons. Perhaps as many as thirty bonfires could be counted within the whole bounds of the district; and as the hour may be told on a clock-face when the figures themselves are invisible, so did the men recognize the locality of each fire by its angle and direction, though nothing of the scenery could be viewed.

The first tall flame from Rainbarrow sprang into the sky, attracting all eyes that had been fixed on the distant conflagrations back to their own attempt in the same kind. The cheerful blaze streaked the inner surface of the human circle—now increased by other stragglers, male and female—with its own gold livery, and even overlaid the dark turf around with a lively luminousness, which softened off into obscurity where the barrow rounded downwards out of sight. It showed the barrow to be the segment of a globe, as perfect as on the day when it was thrown up, even the little ditch remaining from which the earth was dug. Not a plough had ever disturbed a grain of that stubborn soil. In the heath's barrenness to the farmer lay its fertility to the historian. There had been no obliteration, because there had been no tending.

It seemed as if the bonfire-makers were standing in some radiant upper storey of the world, detached from and independent of the dark stretches below. The heath down there was now a vast abyss, and no longer a continuation of what they stood on; for their eyes, adapted to the blaze, could see nothing of the deeps beyond its influence. Occasionally, it is true, a more vigorous flare than usual from their faggots sent darting lights like aides-de-camp down the inclines to some distant bush, pool, or patch of white sand, kin-

1. Greek legendary figures, followers of Bacchus.

dling these to replies of the same colour, till all was lost in darkness again. Then the whole black phenomenon beneath represented Limbo as viewed from the brink by the sublime Florentine in his vision, and the muttered articulations of the wind in the hollows were as complaints and petitions from the 'souls of mighty worth' suspended therein.

It was as if these men and boys had suddenly dived into past ages, and fetched therefrom an hour and deed which had before been familiar with this spot. The ashes of the original British pyre which blazed from that summit lay fresh and undisturbed in the barrow beneath their tread. The flames from funeral piles long ago kindled there had shone down upon the lowlands as these were shining now. Festival fires to Thor and Woden[2] had followed on the same ground and duly had their day. Indeed, it is pretty well known that such blazes as this the heathmen were now enjoying are rather the lineal descendants from the jumbled Druidical rites and Saxon ceremonies than the invention of popular feeling about Gunpowder Plot.[3]

Moreover to light a fire is the instinctive and resistant act of man when, at the winter ingress, the curfew is sounded throughout Nature. It indicates a spontaneous, Promethean rebelliousness against the fiat that this recurrent season shall bring foul times, cold darkness, misery and death. Black chaos comes, and the fettered gods of the earth say, Let there be light.

The brilliant lights and sooty shades which struggled upon the skin and clothes of the persons standing round caused their lineaments and general contours to be drawn with Dureresque vigour and dash. Yet the permanent moral expression of each face it was impossible to discover, for as the nimble flames towered, nodded, and swooped through the surrounding air, the blots of shade and flakes of light upon the countenances of the group changed shape and position endlessly. All was unstable; quivering as leaves, evanescent as lightning. Shadowy eye-sockets, deep as those of a death's head, suddenly turned into pits of lustre: a lantern-jaw was cavernous, then it was shining; wrinkles were emphasized to ravines, or obliterated entirely by a changed ray. Nostrils were dark wells; sinews in old necks were guilt mouldings; things with no particular polish on them were glazed; bright objects, such as the tip

2. Chief English heathen god, appeased as the god of winter, identical with the Scandinavian Odin. *Thor* is the Scandinavian god of thunder.

3. Plot in 1605 to blow up Parliament. The central Catholic conspirator, Guy Fawkes, is burnt in effigy every November 5th over commemorative bonfires. The major portion of *The Return of the Native* begins on Guy Fawkes Night and ends a year and a night later. Modern anthropologists generally support Hardy's argument that the November 5th bonfires originated in Druid ceremonies before the conversion of the English to Christianity in the seventh century A.D.

of a furze-hook one of the men carried, were as glass; eyeballs glowed like little lanterns. Those whom Nature had depicted as merely quaint became grotesque, the grotesque became preternatural; for all was in extremity.

Hence it may be that the face of an old man, who had like others been called to the heights by the rising flames, was not really the mere nose and chin that it appeared to be, but an appreciable quantity of human countenance. He stood complacently sunning himself in the heat. With a speäker, or stake, he tossed the outlying scraps of fuel into the conflagration, looking at the midst of the pile, occasionally lifting his eyes to measure the height of the flame, or to follow the great sparks which rose with it and sailed away into darkness. The beaming sight, and the penetrating warmth, seemed to breed in him a cumulative cheerfulness, which soon amounted to delight. With his stick in his hand he began to jig a private minuet, a bunch of copper seals shining and swinging like a pendulum from under his waistcoat: he also began to sing, in the voice of a bee up a flue—

'The King′ call'd down′ his no-bles all′,
by one′, by two′, by three′;
Earl Mar′-shal, I'll′ go shrive′ the queen′,
And thou′ shalt wend′ with me′.

'A boon′, a boon′, quoth Earl′ Mar-shal′,
And fell′ on his bend′-ded knee′,
That what′-so-e'er′ the queen′ shall say′,
No harm′ there-of′ may be′.'[4]

Want of breath prevented a continuance of the song; and the breakdown attracted the attention of a firm-standing man of middle age, who kept each corner of his crescent-shaped mouth rigorously drawn back into his cheek, as if to do away with any suspicion of mirthfulness which might erroneously have attached to him.

'A fair stave,[5] Grandfer Cantle; but I am afeard 'tis too much for the mouldy weasand[6] of such a old man as you,' he said to the wrinkled reveller. 'Dostn't wish th' wast three sixes again, Grandfer, as you was when you first learnt to sing it?'

'Hey?' said Grandfer Cantle, stopping in his dance.

'Dostn't wish wast young again, I say? There's a hole in thy poor bellows nowadays seemingly.'

'But there's good art[7] in me? If I couldn't make a little wind go a long ways I should seem no younger than the most aged man, should I, Timothy?'

4. From the traditional Dorset ballad *Earl Marshal,* also known as *The Jovial Crew* and *Queen Eleanor's Confession.* This ribald ballad is still sung.

5. Verse or stanza.

6. Windpipe or throat, generally.

7. Dialect version of *heart.*

'And how about the new-married folks down there at the Quiet Woman Inn?' the other inquired, pointing towards a dim light in the direction of the distant highway, but considerably apart from where the reddleman was at that moment resting. 'What's the rights of the matter about 'em? You ought to know, being an understanding man.'

'But a little rakish, hey? I own to it. Master Cantle is that, or he's nothing. Yet 'tis a gay fault, neighbour Fairway, that age will cure.'

'I heard that they were coming home to-night. By this time they must have come. What besides?'

'The next thing is for us to go and wish 'em joy, I suppose?'

'Well, no.'

'No? Now, I thought we must. I must, or 'twould be very unlike me—the first in every spree that's going!

> "Do thou′ put on′ a fri′-ar's coat′,
> And I'll′ put on′ a-no′-ther,
> And we′ will to′ Queen Ele′anor go′,
> Like Fri′ar and′ his bro′ther."[8]

I met Mis'ess Yeobright,[1] the young bride's aunt, last night, and she told me that her son Clym was coming home a' Christmas. Wonderful clever, 'a believe—ah, I should like to have all that's under that young man's hair. Well, then, I spoke to her in my well-known merry way, and she said, "O that what's shaped so venerable should talk like a fool!"—that's what she said to me. I don't care for her, be jowned[2] if I do, and so I told her. "Be jowned if I care for 'ee," I said. I had her there—hey?'

'I rather think she had you,' said Fairway.

'No,' said Grandfer Cantle, his countenance slightly flagging. ' 'Tisn't so bad as that with me?'

'Seemingly 'tis; however, is it because of the wedding that Clym is coming home a' Christmas—to make a new arrangement because his mother is now left in the house alone?'

'Yes, yes—that's it. But, Timothy, hearken to me,' said the Grandfer earnestly. 'Though known as such a joker, I be an understanding man if you catch me serious, and I am serious now. I can tell 'ee lots about the married couple. Yes, this morning at six o'clock they went up the country to do the job, and neither vell nor mark[3] have been seen of 'em since, though I reckon that this afternoon has brought 'em home again, man and woman—wife,

8. Another verse of *Earl Marshal.*
1. Name derived from yeoman, a man born free.
2. Dialect epithet probably meaning to be struck.
3. Dialect expression for "no traces of them have been seen." The expression was originally applied to lost cattle.

that is. Isn't it spoke like a man, Timothy, and wasn't Mis'ess Yeobright wrong about me?'

'Yes, it will do. I didn't know the two had walked together since last fall, when her aunt forbad the banns. How long has this new set-to been in mangling[4] then? Do you know, Humphrey?'

'Yes, how long?' said Grandfer Cantle smartly, likewise turning to Humphrey. 'I ask that question.'

'Ever since her aunt altered her mind, and said she might hae the man after all,' replied Humphrey, without removing his eyes from the fire. He was a somewhat solemn young fellow, and carried the hook and leather gloves of a furze-cutter, his legs, by reason of that occupation, being sheathed in bulging leggings as stiff as the Philistine's greaves of brass.[5] 'That's why they went away to be married, I count. You see, after kicking up such a nunny-watch[6] and forbidding the banns 'twould have made Mis'ess Yeobright seem foolish-like to have a banging wedding in the same parish all as if she'd never gainsaid it.'

'Exactly—seem foolish-like; and that's very bad for the poor things that be so, though I only guess as much, to be sure,' said Grandfer Cantle, still strenuously preserving a sensible bearing and mien.

'Ah, well, I was at church that day,' said Fairway, 'which was a very curious thing to happen.'

'If 'twasn't my name's Simple,' said the Grandfer emphatically. 'I ha'n't been there to-year;[7] and now the winter is a-coming on I won't say I shall.'

'I ha'n't been these three years,' said Humphrey; 'for I'm so dead sleepy of a Sunday; and 'tis so terrible far to get there; and when you do get there 'tis such a mortal poor chance that you'll be chose for up above, when so many bain't, that I bide at home and don't go at all.'

'I not only happened to be there,' said Fairway, with a fresh collection of emphasis, 'but I was sitting in the same pew as Mis'ess Yeobright. And though you may not see it as such, it fairly made my blood run cold to hear her. Yes, it is a curious thing; but it made my blood run cold, for I was close at her elbow.' The speaker looked round upon the bystanders, now drawing closer to hear him, with his lips gathered tighter than ever in the rigorousness of his descriptive moderation.

' 'Tis a serious job to have things happen to 'ee there,' said a woman behind.

4. *Set-to* usually means a fight, but here it is more likely a dialect word for situation. A situation *in mangling* is one that is mixed together in a confused way. The whole expression is derogatory, suggesting that the relationship between Thomasin and Wildeve is extremely confused.

5. Armor for the leg below the knee.

6. State of excited confusion; storm.

7. This year.

' "Ye are to declare it," was the parson's words,' Fairway continuel. 'And then up stood a woman at my side—a-touching of me. "Well, be damned if there isn't Mis'ess Yeobright a-standing up," I said to myself. Yes, neighbours, though I was in the temple of prayer that's what I said. 'Tis against my conscience to curse and swear in company, and I hope any woman here will overlook it. Still what I did say I did say, and 'twould be a lie if I didn't own it.'

'So 'twould, neighbour Fairway.'

' "Be damned if there isn't Mis'ess Yeobright a-standing up," I said,' the narrator repeated, giving out the bad word with the same passionless severity of face as before, which proved how entirely necessity and not gusto had to do with the iteration. 'And the next thing I heard was, "I forbid the banns," from her. "I'll speak to you after the service," said the parson, in quite a homely way[8]—yes, turning all at once into a common man no holier than you or I. Ah, her face was pale! Maybe you can call to mind that monument in Weatherbury church—the cross-legged soldier that have had his arm knocked away by the school-children? Well, he would about have matched that woman's face, when she said, "I forbid the banns."'

The audience cleared their throats and tossed a few stalks into the fire, not because these deeds were urgent, but to give themselves time to weigh the moral of the story.

'I'm sure when I heard they'd been forbid I felt as glad as if anybody had gied me sixpence,' said an earnest voice—that of Olly Dowden, a woman who lived by making heath brooms, or besoms.[9] Her nature was to be civil to enemies as well as to friends, and grateful to all the world for letting her remain alive.

'And now the maid have married him just the same,' said Humphrey.

'After that Mis'ess Yeobright came round and was quite agreeable,' Fairway resumed, with an unheeding air, to show that his words were no appendage to Humphrey's, but the result of independent reflection.

'Supposing they were ashamed, I don't see why they shouldn't have done it here-right,' said a wide-spread woman whose stays[1] creaked like shoes whenever she stooped or turned. ' 'Tis well to call the neighbours together and to hae a good racket once now and then; and it may as well be when there's a wedding as at tide-times.[2] I don't care for close ways.'

'Ah, now, you'd hardly believe it, but I don't care for gay wed-

8. Familiar and kindly.
9. Broom made of twigs of heather or birch bound together.
1. Corset stiffened by strips of whalebone or metal.
2. Holiday times, usually those connected with church festivals.

dings,' said Timothy Fairway, his eyes again traveling round. 'I hardly blame Thomasin Yeobright and neighbour Wildeve for doing it quiet, if I must own it. A wedding at home means five and six-handed reels by the hour; and they do a man's legs no good when he's over forty.'

'True. Once at the woman's house you can hardly say nay to being one in a jig, knowing all the time that you be expected to make yourself worth your victuals.'

'You be bound to dance at Christmas because 'tis the time o' year; you must dance at weddings because 'tis the time o' life. At christenings folk will even smuggle in a reel or two, if 'tis no further on than the first or second chiel. And this is not naming the songs you've got to sing. . . . For my part I like a good hearty funeral as well as anything. You've as splendid victuals and drink as at other parties, and even better. And it don't wear your legs to stumps in talking over a poor fellow's ways as it do to stand up in hornpipes.'

'Nine folks out of ten would own 'twas going too far to dance then, I suppose?' suggested Grandfer Cantle.

' 'Tis the only sort of party a staid man can feel safe at after the mug have been round a few times.'

'Well, I can't understand a quiet lady-like little body like Tamsin Yeobright caring to be married in such a mean way,' said Susan Nunsuch, the wide woman, who preferred the original subject. ' 'Tis worse than the poorest do. And I shouldn't have cared about the man, though some may say he's good-looking.'

'To give him his due he's a clever, learned fellow in his way—a'most as clever as Clym Yeobright used to be. He was brought up to better things than keeping the Quiet Woman. An engineer—that's what the man was, as we know; but he threw away his chance, and so 'a took a public-house to live. His learning was no use to him at all.'

'Very often the case,' said Olly, the besom-maker. 'And yet how people do strive after it and get it! The class of folk that couldn't use to make a round O[3] to save their bones from the pit can write their names now without a sputter of the pen, oftentimes without a single blot: what do I say?—why, almost without a desk to lean their stomachs and elbows upon.'

'True: 'tis amazing what a polish the world have been brought to,' said Humphrey.

'Why, afore I went a soldier in the Bang-up Locals (as we was called), in the year four', chimed in Grandfer Cantle brightly, 'I didn't know no more what the world was like than the commonest

3. To write clearly.

man among ye. And now, jown it all, I won't say what I bain't fit for, hey?'

'Couldst sign the book, no doubt,' said Fairway, 'if wast young enough to join hands with a woman again, like Wildeve and Mis'ess Tamsin, which is more than Humph there could do, for he follows his father in learning. Ah, Humph, well I can mind when I was married how I zid[4] thy father's mark staring me in the face as I went to put down my name. He and your mother were the couple married just afore we were, and there stood thy father's cross with arms stretched out like a great banging scarecrow. What a terrible black cross that was—thy father's very likeness in en! To save my soul I couldn't help laughing when I zid en, though all the time I was as hot as dog-days, what with the marrying, and what with the woman a-hanging to me, and what with Jack Changley and a lot more chaps grinning at me through church window. But the next moment a strawmote[5] would have knocked me down, for I called to mind that if thy father and mother had had high words once, they'd been at it twenty times since they'd been man and wife, and I zid myself as the next poor stunpoll[6] to get into the same mess. . . . Ah—well, what a day 'twas!'

'Wildeve is older than Tamsin Yeobright by a good-few summers. A pretty maid too she is. A young woman with a home must be a fool to tear her smock[7] for a man like that.'

The speaker, a peat or turf-cutter, who had newly joined the group, carried across his shoulder the singular heart-shaped spade of large dimensions used in that species of labour; and its well-whetted edge gleamed like a silver bow in the beams of the fire.

'A hundred maidens would have had him if he'd asked 'em,' said the wide woman.

'Didst ever know a man, neighbour, that no woman at all would marry?' inquired Humphrey.

'I never did,' said the turf-cutter.

'Nor I,' said another.

'Nor I,' said Grandfer Cantle.

'Well, now, I did once,' said Timothy Fairway, adding more firmness to one of his legs. 'I did know of such a man. But only once, mind.' He gave his throat a thorough rake round, as if it were the duty of every person not to be mistaken through thickness of voice. 'Yes, I knew of such a man,' he said.

'And what ghastly gallicrow[8] might the poor fellow have been like, Master Fairway?' asked the turf-cutter.

'Well, 'a was neither a deaf man, nor a dumb man, nor a blind man. What 'a was I don't say.'

4. Saw.
5. Single stalk of straw.
6. Blockhead, dolt.
7. Break away from home (i.e., smock-bound).
8. Scarecrow.

'Is he known in these parts?' said Olly Dowden.

'Hardly,' said Timothy; 'but I name no name. . . . Come, keep the fire up there, youngsters.'

'Whatever is Christian Cantle's teeth a-chattering for?' said a boy from amid the smoke and shades on the other side of the blaze. 'Be ye a-cold, Christian?'

A thin jibbering voice was heard to reply, 'No, not at all.'

'Come forward, Christian, and show yourself. I didn't know you were here,' said Fairway, with a humane look across towards that quarter.

Thus requested, a faltering man, with reedy hair, no shoulders, and a great quantity of wrist and ankle beyond his clothes, advanced a step or two by his own will, and was pushed by the will of others half a dozen steps more. He was Grandfer Cantle's youngest son.

'What be ye quaking for, Christian?' said the turf-cutter kindly.

'I'm the man.'

'What man?'

'The man no woman will marry.'

'The deuce you be!' said Timothy Fairway, enlarging his gaze to cover Christian's whole surface and a great deal more; Grandfer Cantle meanwhile staring as a hen stares at the duck she has hatched.

'Yes, I be he; and it makes me afeard,' said Christian. 'D'ye think 'twill hurt me? I shall always say I don't care, and swear to it, though I do care all the while.'

'Well, be damned if this isn't the queerest start ever I know'd,' said Mr. Fairway. 'I didn't mean you at all. There's another in the country, then! Why did ye reveal yer misfortune, Christian?'

''Twas to be if 'twas, I suppose. I can't help it, can I?' He turned upon them his painfully circular eyes, surrounded by concentric lines like targets.

'No, that's true. But 'tis a melancholy thing, and my blood ran cold when you spoke, for I felt there were two poor fellows where I had thought only one. 'Tis a sad thing for ye, Christian. How'st know the women won't hae thee?'

'I've asked 'em.'

'Sure I should never have thought you had the face. Well, and what did the last one say to ye? Nothing that can't be got over, perhaps, after all?'

' "Get out of my sight, you slack-twisted,[9] slim-looking maphrotight[1] fool," was the woman's words to me.'

'Not encouraging, I own,' said Fairway. ' "Get out of my sight, you slack-twisted, slim-looking maphrotight fool," is rather a hard

9. Lazy, inactive.
1. Effeminate; dialect form of *hermaphrodite*.

way of saying No. But even that might be overcome by time and patience, so as to let a few grey hairs show themselves in the hussy's head. How old be you, Christian?'

'Thirty-one last tatie-digging,[2] Mister Fairway.'

'Not a boy—not a boy. Still there's hope yet.'

'That's my age by baptism, because that's put down in the great book of the Judgment that they keep in church vestry; but mother told me I was born some time afore I was christened.'

'Ah!'

'But she couldn't tell when, to save her life, except that there was no moon.'

'No moon: that's bad. Hey, neighbours, that's bad for him!'

'Yes, 'tis bad,' said Grandfer Cantle, shaking his head.

'Mother know'd 'twas no moon, for she asked another woman that had an almanac, as she did whenever a boy was born to her, because of the saying, "No moon, no man,"[3] which made her afeard every man-child she had. Do ye really think it serious, Mister Fairway, that there was no moon?'

'Yes; "No moon, no man." 'Tis one of the truest sayings ever spit out. The boy never comes to anything that's born at new moon. A bad job for thee, Christian, that you should have showed your nose then of all days in the month.'

'I suppose the moon was terrible full when you were born?' said Christian, with a look of hopeless admiration at Fairway.

'Well, 'a was not new,' Mr. Fairway replied, with a disinterested gaze.

'I'd sooner go without drink at Lammas-tide[4] than be a man of no moon,' continued Christian, in the same shattered recitative. ' 'Tis said I be only the rames[5] of a man, and no good for my race at all; and I suppose that's the cause o't.'

'Ay,' said Grandfer Cantle, somewhat subdued in spirit; 'and yet his mother cried for scores of hours when 'a was a boy, for fear he should outgrow hisself and go for a soldier.'

'Well, there's many just as bad as he,' said Fairway. 'Wethers[6] must live their time as well as other sheep, poor soul.'

'So perhaps I shall rub on? Ought I to be afeard o' nights, Master Fairway?'

'You'll have to lie alone all your life; and 'tis not to married couples but to single sleepers that a ghost shows himself when 'a do come. One has been seen lately, too. A very strange one.'

2. Potato digging.
3. Evil omen, originating in the superstition that virility is connected with the full moon.
4. Time of year observed as the harvest festival, at which, in the early English church, loaves of bread were consecrated. Lammas Day is August 1st.
5. Skeleton.
6. Castrated ram; eunuch. Through the whole conversation Christian is clearly referred to as a eunuch.

'No—don't talk about it if 'tis agreeable of ye not to! 'Twill make my skin crawl when I think of it in bed alone. But you will—ah, you will, I know, Timothy; and I shall dream all night o't! A very strange one? What sort of a spirit did ye mean when ye said, a very strange one, Timothy?—no, no—don't tell me.'

'I don't half believe in spirits myself. But I think it ghostly enough—what I was told. 'Twas a little boy that zid it.'

'What was it like?—no, don't——'

'A red one. Yes, most ghost be white; but this is as if it had been dipped in blood.'

Christian drew a deep breath without letting it expand his body, and Humphrey said, 'Where has it been seen?'

'Not exactly here; but in this same heth. But 'tisn't a thing to talk about. What do ye say,' continued Fairway in brisker tones, and turning upon them as if the idea had not been Grandfer Cantle's—'what do you say to giving the new man and wife a bit of a song to-night afore we go to bed—being their wedding-day? When folks are just married 'tis as well to look glad o't, since looking sorry won't unjoin 'em. I am no drinker, as we know, but when the womenfolk and youngsters have gone home we can drop down across to the Quiet Woman, and strike up a ballet[7] in front of the married folks' door. 'Twill please the young wife, and that's what I should like to do, for many's the skinful I've had at her hands when she lived with her aunt at Blooms-End.'

'Hey? And so we will!' said Grandfer Cantle, turning so briskly that his copper seals swung extravagantly. 'I'm as dry as a kex[8] with biding up here in the wind and I haven't seen the colour of drink since nammet-time[9] to-day. 'Tis said that the last brew at the Woman is very pretty drinking. And, neighbours, if we should be a little late in the finishing, why, to-morrow's Sunday, and we can sleep it off?'

'Grandfer Cantle! you take things very careless for an old man,' said the wide woman.

'I take things careless; I do—too careless to please the women! Klk! I'll sing the "Jovial Crew,"[1] or any other song, when a weak old man would cry his eyes out. Jown it; I am up for anything.

"The king′ look'd o′-ver his left′ shoul-der′,
And a grim′ look look′-ed hee′,
Earl Mar′-shal, he said′, but for′ my oath′
Or hang′-ed thou′ shouldst bee′." '

'Well, that's what we'll do,' said Fairway. 'We'll give 'em a song,

7. Dialect form of *ballad*, or popular song.
8. Dry hollow stem of a plant; figuratively, a dried-up, sapless person.
9. Lunchtime.
1. Another title for the traditional folk ballad *Earl Marshal*.

an' it please the Lord. What's the good of Thomasin's cousin Clym a-coming home after the deed's done? He should have come afore, if so be he wanted to stop it, and marry her himself.'

'Perhaps he's coming to bide with his mother a little time, as she must feel lonely now the maid's gone.'

'Now, 'tis very odd, but I never feel lonely—no, not at all,' said Grandfer Cantle. 'I am as brave in the night-time as a' admiral!'

The bonfire was by this time beginning to sink low, for the fuel had not been of that substantial sort which can support a blaze long. Most of the other fires within the wide horizon were also dwindling weak. Attentive observation of their brightness, colour, and length of existence would have revealed the quality of the material burnt; and through that, to some extent the natural produce of the district in which each bonfire was situate. The clear, kingly effulgence that had characterized the majority expressed a heath and furze country like their own, which in one direction extended an unlimited number of miles: the rapid flares and extinctions at other points of the compass showed the lightest of fuel—straw, beanstalks, and the usual waste from arable land. The most enduring of all—steady, unaltering eyes like planets—signified wood, such as hazel-branches, thorn-faggots, and stout billets.[2] Fires of the last-mentioned materials were rare, and, though comparatively small in magnitude beside the transient blazes, now began to get the best of them by mere long-continuance. The great ones had perished, but these remained. They occupied the remotest visible positions—sky-backed summits rising out of rich coppice and plantation districts to the north, where the soil was different, and heath foreign and strange.

Save one; and this was the nearest of any, the moon of the whole shining throng. It lay in a direction precisely opposite to that of the little window in the vale below. Its nearness was such that, notwithstanding its actual smallness, its glow infinitely transcended theirs.

This quiet eye had attracted attention from time to time; and when their own fire had become sunken and dim it attracted more; some even of the wood fires more recently lighted had reached their decline, but no change was perceptible here.

'To be sure, how near that fire is!' said Fairway. 'Seemingly, I can see a fellow of some sort walking round it. Little and good must be said of that fire, surely.'

'I can throw a stone there,' said the boy.

'And so can I!' said Grandfer Cantle.

'No, no, you can't, my sonnies. That fire is not much less than a mile off, for all that 'a seems so near.'

2. Thick pieces of wood cut for fuel.

' 'Tis in the heath, but not furze,' said the turf-cutter.

' 'Tis cleft-wood,[3] that's what 'tis.' said Timothy Fairway. 'Nothing would burn like that except clean timber. And 'tis on the knap[4] afore the old captain's house at Mistover. Such a queer mortal as that man is! To have a little fire inside your own bank and ditch, that nobody else may enjoy it or come anigh it! And what a zany an old chap must be, to light a bonfire when there's no youngsters to please.'

'Cap'n Vye has been for a long walk to-day, and is quite tired out,' said Grandfer Cantle, 'so 'tisn't likely to be he.'

'And he would hardly afford good fuel like that,' said the wide woman.

'Then it must be his grand-daughter,' said Fairway. 'Not that a body of her age can want a fire much.'

'She is very strange in her ways, living up there by herself, and such things please her,' said Susan.

'She's a well-favoured maid enough,' said Humphrey the furze-cutter; 'especially when she's got one of her dandy gowns on.'

'That's true,' said Fairway. 'Well, let her bonfire burn an't will. Ours is well-nigh out by the look o't.'

'How dark 'tis now the fire's gone down!' said Christian Cantle, looking behind him with his hare eyes. 'Don't ye think we'd better get home-along, neighbours? That heth isn't haunted, I know; but we'd better get home. . . . Ah, what was that?'

'Only the wind,' said the turf-cutter.

'I don't think Fifth-of-Novembers ought to be kept up by night except in towns. It should be by day in outstep, ill-accounted places like this!'

'Nonsense, Christian. Lift up your spirits like a man! Susy, dear, you and I will have a jig—hey, my honey?—before 'tis quite too dark to see how well-favoured you be still, though so many summers have passed since your husband, a son of a witch, snapped you up from me.'

This was addressed to Susan Nunsuch; and the next circumstance of which the beholders were conscious was a vision of the matron's broad form whisking off towards the space whereon the fire had been kindled. She was lifted bodily by Mr. Fairway's arm, which had been flung round her waist before she had become aware of his intention. The site of the fire was now merely a circle of ashes flecked with red embers and sparks, the furze having burnt completely away. Once within the circle he whirled her round and round in a dance. She was a woman noisily constructed; in addition to her enclosing framework of whalebone and lath, she wore

3. Wood purposely split for fuel.

4. Knoll or hill.

pattens[5] summer and winter, in wet weather and in dry, to preserve her boots from wear; and when Fairway began to jump about with her, the clicking of the pattens, the creaking of the stays, and her screams of surprise, formed a very audible concert.

'I'll crack thy numskull for thee, you mandy[6] chap!' said Mrs. Nunsuch, as she helplessly danced round with him, her feet playing like drumsticks among the sparks. 'My ankles were all in a fever before, from walking through that prickly furze, and now you must make 'em worse with these vlankers!'[7]

The vagary of Timothy Fairway was infectious. The turf-cutter seized old Olly Dowden, and, somewhat more gently, poussetted[8] with her likewise. The young men were not slow to imitate the example of their elders, and seized the maids; Grandfer Cantle and his stick jigged in the form of a three-legged object among the rest; and in half a minute all that could be seen on Rainbarrow was a whirling of dark shapes amid a boiling confusion of sparks, which leapt around the dancers as high as their waists. The chief noises were women's shrill cries, men's laughter, Susan's stays and pattens, Olly Dowden's 'heu-heu-heu!' and the strumming of the wind upon the furze-bushes, which formed a kind of tune to the demoniac measure they trod. Christian alone stood aloof, uneasily rocking himself as he murmured, 'They ought not to do it—how the vlankers do fly! 'tis tempting the Wicked one, 'tis.'

'What was that?' said one of the lads, stopping.

'Ah—where?' said Christian, hastily closing up to the rest.

The dancers all lessened their speed.

' 'Twas behind you, Christian, that I heard it—down there.'

'Yes—'tis behind me!' Christian said. 'Matthew, Mark, Luke, and John, bless the bed that I lie on; four angels guard—'

'Hold your tongue. What is it?' said Fairway.

'Hoi-i-i-i!' cried a voice from the darkness.

'Halloo-o-o-o!' said Fairway.

'Is there any cart-track up across here to Mis'ess Yeobright's, of Blooms-End?' came to them in the same voice, as a long, slim, indistinct figure approached the barrow.

'Ought we not to run home as hard as we can, neighbours, as 'tis getting late?' said Christian. 'Not run away from one another, you know; run close together, I mean.'

'Scrape up a few stray locks of furze, and make a blaze, so that we can see who the man is,' said Fairway.

5. Overshoes with wooden soles that raise the wearer an inch or two from the ground. *Whalebone* and *lath* are materials of a corset.

6. Obsolete form of *maundy*. Here used as an epithet suggesting a beggar, one who abases himself. Derived from one who receives alms or charity at ceremonies on Maundy Thursday, the Thursday before Easter.

7. Dialect variant of *flanker*, a spark of fire.

8. Dancer round and round with hands joined.

When the flame arose it revealed a young man in tight raiment, and red from top to toe. 'Is there a track across here to Mis'ess Yeobright's house?' he repeated.

'Ay—keep along the path down there.'

'I mean a way two horses and a van can travel over?'

'Well, yes; you can get up the vale below here with time. The track is rough, but if you've got a light your horses may pick along wi' care. Have ye brought your cart far up, neighbour reddleman?'

'I've left it in the bottom, about half a mile back. I stepped on in front to make sure of the way, as 'tis night-time, and I han't been here for so long.'

'Oh, well, you can get up,' said Fairway. 'What a turn it did give me when I saw him!' he added to the whole group, the reddleman included. 'Lord's sake, I thought, whatever fiery mommet[9] is this come to trouble us? No slight to your looks, reddleman, for ye bain't bad-looking in the groundwork, though the finish is queer. My meaning is just to say how curious I felt. I half thought it 'twas the devil or the red ghost the boy told of.'

'It gied me a turn likewise,' said Susan Nunsuch, 'for I had a dream last night of a death's head.'

'Don't ye talk o't no more,' said Christian. 'If he had a handkerchief over his head he'd look for all the world like the Devil in the picture of the Temptation.'

'Well, thank you for telling me,' said the young reddleman, smiling faintly. 'And good night t'ye all.'

He withdrew from their sight down the barrow.

'I fancy I've seen that young man's face before,' said Humphrey. 'But where, or how, or what his name is, I don't know.'

The reddleman had not been gone more than a few minutes when another person approached the partially revived bonfire. It proved to be a well-known and respected widow of the neighbourhood, of a standing which can only be expressed by the word genteel. Her face, encompassed by the blackness of the receding heath, showed whitely, and without half-lights, like a cameo.

She was a woman of middle-age, with well-formed features of the type usually found where perspicacity is the chief quality enthroned within. At moments she seemed to be regarding issues from a Nebo[1] denied to others around. She had something of an estranged mien: the solitude exhaled from the heath was concentrated in this face that had risen from it. The air with which she looked at the heathmen betokened a certain unconcern at their presence, or at what might be their opinions of her for walking in that lonely spot at such an hour, thus indirectly implying that in some respect or

9. Variant form of *mummer*.

1. Mountain from which Moses viewed the promised land. Identified as the summit of Mount Pisgah.

other they were not up to her level. The explanation lay in the fact that though her husband had been a small farmer she herself was a curate's daughter, who had once dreamt of doing better things.

Persons with any weight of character carry, like planets, their atmospheres along with them in their orbits; and the matron who entered now upon the scene could, and usually did, bring her own tone into a company. Her normal manner among the heathfolk had that reticence which results from the consciousness of superior communicative power. But the effect of coming into society and light after lonely wandering in darkness is a sociability in the comer above its usual pitch, expressed in the features even more than in the words.

'Why, 'tis Mis'ess Yeobright,' said Fairway. 'Mis'ess Yeobright, not ten minutes ago a man was here asking for you—a reddleman.'

'What did he want?' said she.

'He didn't tell us.'

'Something to sell, I suppose; what it can be I am at a loss to understand.'

'I am glad to hear that your son Mr. Clym is coming home at Christmas, ma'am,' said Sam, the turf-cutter. 'What a dog he used to be for bonfires!'

'Yes. I believe he is coming,' she said.

'He must be a fine fellow by this time,' said Fairway.

'He is a man now,' she replied quietly.

' 'Tis very lonesome for 'ee in the heth to-night, mis'ess,' said Christian, coming from the seclusion he had hitherto maintained. 'Mind you don't get lost. Egdon Heth is a bad place to get lost in, and the winds do huffle queerer to-night than ever I heard 'em afore. Them that know Egdon best have been pixy-led[2] here at times.'

'Is that you, Christian?' said Mrs. Yeobright. 'What made you hide away from me?'

' 'Twas that I didn't know you in this light, mis'ess; and being a man of the mournfullest make, I was scared a little, that's all. Oftentimes if you could see how terrible down I get in my mind, 'twould make 'ee quite nervous for fear I should die by my hand.'

'You don't take after your father,' said Mrs. Yeobright, looking towards the fire, where Grandfer Cantle, with some want of originality, was dancing by himself among the sparks, as the others had done before.

'Now, Grandfer,' said Timothy Fairway, 'we are shamed of ye. A reverent old patriarch man as you be—seventy if a day—to go hornpiping like that by yourself!'

2. The people believed that the heath was full of pixies who could lead them astray.

'A harrowing old man, Mis'ess Yeobright,' said Christian despondingly. 'I wouldn't live with him a week, so playward as he is, if I could get away.'

''Twould be more seemly in ye to stand still and welcome Mis'ess Yeobright, and you the venerablest here, Grandfer Cantle,' said the besom-woman.

'Faith, and so it would,' said the reveller, checking himself repentantly. 'I've such a bad memory, Mis'ess Yeobright, that I forget how I'm looked up to by the rest of 'em. My spirits must be wonderful good, you'll say? But not always. 'Tis a weight upon a man to be looked up to as commander, and I often feel it.'

'I'm sorry to stop the talk,' said Mrs. Yeobright. 'But I must be leaving you now. I was passing down the Anglebury Road, towards my niece's new home, who is returning to-night with her husband; and seeing the bonfire and hearing Olly's voice among the rest I came up here to learn what was going on. I should like her to walk with me, as her way is mine.'

'Ay, sure, ma'am, I'm just thinking of moving,' said Olly.

'Why, you'll be safe to meet the reddleman that I told ye of,' said Fairway. 'He's only gone back to get his van. We heard that your niece and her husband were coming straight home as soon as they were married, and we are going down there shortly, to give 'em a song o'welcome.'

'Thank you indeed,' said Mrs. Yeobright.

'But we shall take a shorter cut through the furze than you can go with long clothes; so we won't trouble you to wait.'

'Very well—are you ready, Olly?'

'Yes, ma'am. And there's a light shining from your niece's window, see. It will help to keep us in the path.'

She indicated the faint light at the bottom of the valley which Fairway had pointed out; and the two women descended the tumulus.

The Halt on the Turnpike Road

IV

Down, downward they went, and yet further down—their descent at each step seeming to outmeasure their advance. Their skirts were scratched noisily by the furze, their shoulders brushed by the ferns, which, though dead and dry, stood erect as when alive, no sufficient winter weather having as yet arrived to beat them down. Their Tartarean situation[3] might by some have been called an imprudent one for two unattended women. But these

3. Hellish or infernal, referring to Tartarus which, in Greek mythology, was either Hades or the abyss below Hades in which Zeus imprisoned the Titans.

shaggy recesses were at all seasons a familiar surrounding to Olly and Mrs. Yeobright; and the addition of darkness lends no frightfulness to the face of a friend.

'And so Tamsin has married him at last,' said Olly, when the incline had become so much less steep that their footsteps no longer required undivided attention.

Mrs. Yeobright answered slowly, 'Yes: at last.'

'How you will miss her—living with 'ee as a daughter, as she always have.'

'I do miss her.'

Olly, though without the tact to perceive when remarks were untimely, was saved by her very simplicity from rendering them offensive. Questions that would have been resented in others she could ask with impunity. This accounted for Mrs. Yeobright's acquiescence in the revival of an evidently sore subject.

'I was quite strook to hear you'd agreed to it, ma'am, that I was,' continued the besom-maker.

'You were not more struck by it than I should have been last year this time, Olly. There are a good many sides to that wedding. I could not tell you all of them, even if I tried.'

'I felt myself that he was hardly solid-going enough to mate with your family. Keeping an inn—what is it? But 'a's clever, that's true, and they say he was an engineering gentleman once, but has come down by being too outwardly given.'

'I saw that, upon the whole, it would be better she should marry where she wished.'

'Poor little thing, her feelings got the better of her, no doubt. 'Tis nature. Well, they may call him what they will—he've several acres of heth-ground broke up here, besides the public-house, and the heth-croppers, and his manners be quite like a gentleman's. And what's done cannot be undone.'

'It cannot,' said Mrs. Yeobright. 'See, here's the waggon-track at last. Now we shall get along better.'

The wedding subject was no further dwelt upon; and soon a faint diverging path was reached, where they parted company, Olly first begging her companion to remind Mr. Wildeve that he had not sent her sick husband the bottle of wine promised on the occasion of his marriage. The besom-maker turned to the left towards her own house, behind a spur of the hill, and Mrs. Yeobright followed the straight track, which further on joined the highway by the Quiet Woman Inn, whither she supposed her niece to have returned with Wildeve from their wedding at Anglebury that day.

She first reached Wildeve's Patch, as it was called, a plot of land redeemed from the heath, and after long and laborious years brought into cultivation. The man who had discovered that it could be tilled died of the labour: the man who succeeded him in possession ruined himself in fertilizing it. Wildeve came like Amerigo Vespucci, and received the honours due to those who had gone before.

When Mrs. Yeobright had drawn near to the inn, and was about to enter, she saw a horse and vehicle some two hundred yards beyond it, coming towards her, a man walking alongside with a lantern in his hand. It was soon evident that this was the reddleman who had inquired for her. Instead of entering the inn at once, she walked by it and towards the van.

The conveyance came close, and the man was about to pass her with little notice, when she turned to him and said, 'I think you have been inquiring for me? I am Mrs. Yeobright of Blooms-End.'

The reddleman started, and held up his finger. He stopped the horses, and beckoned to her to withdraw with him a few yards aside, which she did, wondering.

'You don't know me, ma'am, I suppose?' he said.

'I do not,' said she. 'Why, yes, I do! You are young Venn—your father was a dairyman somewhere here?'

'Yes; and I knew your niece, Miss Tamsin, a little. I have something bad to tell you.'

'About her—no? She has just come home, I believe, with her husband. They arranged to return this afternoon—to the inn beyond here?'

'She's not there.'

'How do you know?'

'Because she's here. She's in my van,' he added slowly.

'What new trouble has come?' murmured Mrs. Yeobright, putting her hand over her eyes.

'I can't explain much, ma'am. All I know is that, as I was going along the road this morning, about a mile out of Anglebury, I heard something trotting after me like a doe, and looking round there she was, white as death itself. "O, Diggory Venn!" she said, "I thought 'twas you: will you help me? I am in trouble." '

'How did she know your Christian name?' said Mrs. Yeobright doubtingly.

'I had met her as a lad before I went away in this trade .She asked then if she might ride, and then down she fell in a faint. I picked her up and put her in, and there she has been ever since. She has cried a good deal, but she has hardly spoke; all she has told me being that she was to have been married this morning. I tried to get her to eat something, but she couldn't; and at last she fell asleep.'

'Let me see her at once,' said Mrs. Yeobright, hastening towards the van.

The reddleman followed with the lantern, and, stepping up first, assisted Mrs. Yeobright to mount beside him. On the door being opened she perceived at the end of the van an extemporized couch, around which was hung apparently all the drapery that the reddleman possessed, to keep the occupant of the little couch from contact with the red materials of his trade. A young girl lay thereon, covered with a cloak. She was asleep, and the light of the lantern fell upon her features.

A fair, sweet, and honest country face was revealed, reposing in a nest of wavy chestnut hair. It was between pretty and beautiful. Though her eyes were closed, one could easily imagine the light necessarily shining in them as the culmination of the luminous workmanship around. The groundwork of the face was hopefulness; but over it now lay like a foreign substance a film of anxiety and grief. The grief had been there so shortly as to have abstracted nothing of the bloom, and had as yet but given a dignity to what it might eventually undermine. The scarlet of her lips had not had time to abate, and just now it appeared still more intense by the absence of the neighbouring and more transient colour of her cheek. The lips frequently parted, with a murmur of words. She seemed to belong rightly to a madrigal—to require viewing through rhyme and harmony.

One thing at least was obvious: she was not made to be looked at thus. The reddleman had appeared conscious of as much, and, while Mrs. Yeobright looked in upon her, he cast his eyes aside with a delicacy which well became him. The sleeper apparently thought so too, for the next moment she opened her own.

The lips then parted with something of anticipation, something more of doubt; and her several thoughts and fractions of thoughts, as signalled by the changes on her face, were exhibited by the light to the utmost nicety. An ingenuous, transparent life was disclosed; as if the flow of her existence could be seen passing within her. She understood the scene in a moment.

'Oh yes, it is I, aunt," she cried. 'I know how frightened you are, and how you cannot believe it; but all the same, it is I who have come home like this!'

'Tamsin, Tamsin!' said Mrs. Yeobright, stooping over the young woman and kissing her. 'O my dear girl!'

Thomasin was now on the verge of a sob; but by an unexpected self-command she uttered no sound. With a gentle panting breath she sat upright.

'I did not expect to see you in this state, any more than you me,' she went on quickly. 'Where am I, aunt?'

'Nearly home, my dear. In Egdon Bottom. What dreadful thing is it?'

'I'll tell you in a moment. So near, are we? Then I will get out and walk. I want to go home by the path.'

'But this kind man who has done so much will, I am sure, take you right on to my house?' said the aunt, turning to the reddleman, who had withdrawn from the front of the van on the awakening of the girl, and stood in the road.

'Why should you think it necessary to ask me? I will, of course,' said he.

'He is indeed kind,' murmured Thomasin. 'I was once acquainted with him, aunt, and when I saw him to-day I thought I should prefer his van to any conveyance of a stranger. But I'll walk now. Reddleman, stop the horses, please.'

The man regarded her with tender reluctance, but stopped them.

Aunt and niece then descended from the van. Mrs. Yeobright saying to its owner, 'I quite recognize you now. What made you change from the nice business your father left you?'

'Well, I did,' he said, and looked at Thomasin, who blushed a little. 'Then you'll not be wanting me any more to-night, ma'am?'

Mrs. Yeobright glanced around at the dark sky, at the hills, at the perishing bonfires, and at the lighted window of the inn they had neared. 'I think not,' she said, 'since Thomasin wishes to walk. We can soon run up the path and reach home: we know it well.'

And after a few further words they parted, the reddleman moving onwards with his van, and the two women remaining standing in the road. As soon as the vehicle and its driver had withdrawn so far as to be beyond all possible reach of her voice, Mrs. Yeobright turned to her niece.

'Now, Thomasin,' she said sternly, 'what's the meaning of this disgraceful performance?'

Perplexity among Honest People

V

Thomasin looked as if quite overcome by her aunt's change of manner. 'It means just what it seems to mean: I am—not married,' she replied faintly. 'Excuse me—for humiliating you, aunt, by this mishap: I am sorry for it. But I cannot help it.'

'Me? Think of yourself first.'

'It was nobody's fault. When we got there the parson wouldn't marry us because of some trifling irregularity in the license.'

'What irregularity?'

'I don't know. Mr. Wildeve can explain. I did not think when I went away this morning that I should come back like this.' It being dark, Thomasin allowed her emotion to escape her by the silent way of tears, which could roll down her cheek unseen.

'I could almost say that it serves you right—if I did not feel that you don't deserve it,' continued Mrs. Yeobright, who, possessing two distinct moods in close contiguity, a gentle mood and an angry, flew from one to the other without the least warning. 'Remember, Thomasin, this business was none of my seeking; from the very first, when you began to feel foolish about that man, I warned you he would not make you happy. I felt it so strongly that I did what I would never have believed myself capable of doing—stood up in the church, and made myself the public talk for weeks. But having once consented, I don't submit to these fancies without good reason. Marry him you must after this.'

'Do you think I wish to do otherwise for one moment?' said Thomasin, with a heavy sigh. 'I know how wrong it was of me to love him, but don't pain me by talking like that, aunt! You would not have had me stay there with him, would you?—and your house is the only home I have to return to. He says we can be married in a day or two.'

'I wish he had never seen you.'

'Very well; then I will be the miserablest woman in the world, and not let him see me again. No, I won't have him!'

'It is too late to speak so. Come with me. I am going to the inn to see if he has returned. Of course I shall get to the bottom of this story at once. Mr. Wildeve must not suppose he can play tricks upon me, or any belonging to me.'

'It was not that. The licence was wrong, and he couldn't get another the same day. He will tell you in a moment how it was, if he comes.'

'Why didn't he bring you back?'

'That was me!' again sobbed Thomasin. 'When I found we could not be married I didn't like to come back with him, and I was very ill. Then I saw Diggory Venn, and was glad to get him to take me home. I cannot explain it any better, and you must be angry with me if you will.'

'I shall see about that,' said Mrs. Yeobright; and they turned towards the inn, known in the neighbourhood as the Quiet Woman, the sign of which represented the figure of a matron carrying her head under her arm, beneath which gruesome design was written the couplet so well known to frequenters of the inn:—

SINCE THE WOMAN'S QUIET
LET NO MAN BREED A RIOT.[4]

4. The inn which really bore this sign and legend stood some miles to the northwest of the present scene, wherein the house more immediately referred to is now no longer an inn; and the surroundings are much changed. But another inn, some of whose features are also embodied in this description, the *Red Lion* at Winfrith, still remains as a haven for the wayfarer. [Hardy's note, 1912].

The front of the house was towards the heath and Rainbarrow, whose dark shape seemed to threaten it from the sky. Upon the door was a neglected brass plate, bearing the unexpected inscription, 'Mr. Wildeve, Engineer'—useless yet cherished relic from the time when he had been started in that profession in an office at Budmouth by those who had hoped much from him, and had been disappointed. The garden was at the back, and behind this ran a still deep stream, forming the margin of the heath in that direction, meadow-land appearing beyond the stream.

But the thick obscurity permitted only sky-lines to be visible of any scene at present. The water at the back of the house could be heard, idly spinning whirlpools in its creep between the rows of dry feather-headed reeds which formed a stockade along each bank. Their presence was denoted by sounds as of a congregation praying humbly, produced by their rubbing against each other in the slow wind.

The window, whence the candlelight had shone up the vale to the eyes of the bonfire group, was uncurtained, but the sill lay too high for a pedestrian on the outside to look over it into the room. A vast shadow, in which could be dimly traced portions of a masculine contour, blotted half the ceiling.

'He seems to be at home,' said Mrs. Yeobright.

'Must I come in, too, aunt?' asked Thomasin faintly. 'I suppose not; it would be wrong.'

'You must come, certainly—to confront him, so that he may make no false representations to me. We shall not be five minutes in the house, and then we'll walk home.'

Entering the open passage she tapped at the door of the private parlour, unfastened it, and looked in.

The back and shoulders of a man came between Mrs. Yeobright's eyes and the fire. Wildeve, whose form it was, immediately turned, arose, and advanced to meet his visitors.

He was quite a young man, and of the two properties, form and motion, the latter first attracted the eye in him. The grace of his movement was singular: it was the pantomimic expression of a lady-killing career. Next came into notice the more material qualities, among which was a profuse crop of hair impending over the top of his face, lending to his forehead the high-cornered outline of an early Gothic shield; and a neck which was smooth and round as a cylinder. The lower half of his figure was of light build. Altogether he was one in whom no man would have seen anything to admire, and in whom no woman would have seen anything to dislike.

He discerned the young girl's form in the passage, and said, 'Thomasin, then, has reached home. How could you leave me in that way, darling?' And turning to Mrs. Yeobright: 'It was useless to argue with her. She would go, and go alone.'

'But what's the meaning of it all?' demanded Mrs. Yeobright haughtily.

'Take a seat,' said Wildeve, placing chairs for the two women. 'Well, it was a very stupid mistake, but such mistakes will happen. The licence was useless at Anglebury. It was made out for Budmouth, but as I didn't read it I wasn't aware of that.'

'But you had been staying at Anglebury?'

'No. I had been at Budmouth—till two days ago—and that was where I had intended to take her; but when I came to fetch her we decided upon Anglebury, forgetting that a new licence would be necessary. There was not time to get to Budmouth afterwards.'

'I think you are very much to blame,' said Mrs. Yeobright.

'It was quite my fault we chose Anglebury,' Thomasin pleaded. 'I proposed it because I was not known there.'

'I know so well that I am to blame that you need not remind me of it,' replied Wildeve shortly.

'Such things don't happen for nothing,' said the aunt. 'It is a great slight to me and my family; and when it gets known there will be a very unpleasant time for us. How can she look her friends in the face to-morrow? It is a very great injury, and one I cannot easily forgive. It may even reflect on her character.'

'Nonsense,' said Wildeve.

Thomasin's large eyes had flown from the face of one to the face of the other during this discussion, and she now said anxiously, 'Will you allow me, aunt, to talk it over alone with Damon for five minutes? Will you, Damon?'

'Certainly, dear,' said Wildeve, 'if your aunt will excuse us.' He led her into an adjoining room, leaving Mrs. Yeobright by the fire.

As soon as they were alone, and the door closed, Thomasin said, turning up her pale, tearful face to him, 'It is killing me, this, Damon! I did not mean to part from you in anger at Anglebury this morning; but I was frightened, and hardly knew what I said. I've not let aunt know how much I have suffered to-day; and it is so hard to command my face and voice, and to smile as if it were a slight thing to me; but I try to do so, that she may not be still more indignant with you. I know you could not help it, dear, whatever aunt may think.'

'She is very unpleasant.'

'Yes,' Thomasin murmured, 'and I suppose I seem so now. . . . Damon, what do you mean to do about me?'

'Do about you?'

'Yes. Those who don't like you whisper things which at

moments make me doubt you. We mean to marry, I suppose, don't we?'

'Of course we do. We have only to go to Budmouth on Monday, and we may marry at once.'

'Then do let us go!—O Damon, what you make me say!' She hid her face in her handkerchief. 'Here am I asking you to marry me; when by rights you ought to be on your knees imploring me, your cruel mistress, not to refuse you, and saying it would break your heart if I did. I used to think it would be pretty and sweet like that; but how different!'

'Yes, real life is never at all like that.'

'But I don't care personally if it never takes place,' she added with a little dignity; 'no, I can live without you. It is aunt I think of. She is so proud, and thinks so much of her family respectability, that she will be cut down with mortification if this story should get abroad before—it is done. My cousin Clym, too, will be much wounded.'

'Then he will be very unreasonable. In fact, you are all rather unreasonable.'

Thomasin coloured a little, and not with love. But whatever the momentary feeling which caused that flush in her, it went as it came, and she humbly said, 'I never mean to be, if I can help it. I merely feel that you have my aunt to some extent in your power at last.'

'As a matter of justice it is almost due to me,' said Wildeve. 'Think what I have gone through to win her consent; the insult that it is to any man to have the banns forbidden: the double insult to a man unlucky enough to be cursed with sensitiveness, and blue demons, and Heaven knows what, as I am. I can never forget those banns. A harsher man would rejoice now in the power I have of turning upon your aunt by going no further in the business.'

She looked wistfully at him with her sorrowful eyes as he said those words, and her aspect showed that more than one person in the room could deplore the possession of sensitiveness. Seeing that she was really suffering he seemed disturbed and added, 'This is merely a reflection, you know. I have not the least intention to refuse to complete the marriage, Tamsie mine—I could not bear it.'

'You could not, I know!' said the fair girl, brightening. 'You, who cannot bear the sight of pain in even an insect, or any disagreeable sound, or unpleasant smell even, will not long cause pain to me and mine.'

'I will not, if I can help it.'

'Your hand upon it, Damon.'

He carelessly gave her his hand.

'Ah, by my crown, what's that?' he said suddenly.

There fell upon their ears the sound of numerous voices singing in front of the house. Among these, two made themselves prominent by their peculiarity: one was a very strong bass, the other a wheezy thin piping. Thomasin recognized them as belonging to Timothy Fairway and Grandfer Cantle respectively.

'What does it mean—it is not skimmity-riding,[5] I hope?' she said, with a frightened gaze at Wildeve.

'Of course not; no, it is the heath-folk have come to sing to us a welcome. This is intolerable!' He began pacing about, the men outside singing cheerily—

> 'He told' her that she' was the joy' of his life',
> And if' she'd con-sent' he would make her his wife';
> She could' not refuse' him; to church' so they went',
> Young Will was forgot', and young Sue' was content';
> And then' was she kiss'd' and set down' on his knee',
> No man' in the world' was so lov'-ing as he'!'

Mrs. Yeobright burst in from the outer room. 'Thomasin, Thomasin!' she said, looking indignantly at Wildeve; 'here's a pretty exposure! Let us escape at once. Come!'

It was, however, too late to get away by the passage. A rugged knocking had begun upon the door of the front room. Wildeve, who had gone to the window, came back.

'Stop!' he said imperiously, putting his hand upon Mrs. Yeobright's arm. 'We are regularly besieged. There are fifty of them out there if there's one. You stay in this room with Thomasin; I'll go out and face them. You must stay now, for my sake, till they are gone, so that it may seem as if all was right. Come, Tamsie dear, don't go making a scene—we must marry after this; that you can see as well as I. Sit still, that's all—and don't speak much. I'll manage them. Blundering fools!'

He pressed the agitated girl into a seat, returned to the outer room and opened the door. Immediately outside, in the passage, appeared Grandfer Cantle singing in concert with those still standing in front of the house. He came into the room and nodded abstractedly to Wildeve, his lips still parted, and his features excruciatingly strained in the emission of the chorus. This being ended, he said heartily, 'Here's welcome to the new-made couple, and God bless 'em!'

'Thank you,' said Wildeve, with dry resentment, his face as gloomy as a thunderstorm.

5. Dialect form of *skimmington,* a procession, once common in rural districts, in which an adulterous or henpecked spouse was impersonated and mocked.

At the Grandfer's heels now came the rest of the group, which included Fairway, Christian, Sam the turf-cutter, Humphrey, and a dozen others. All smiled upon Wildeve, and upon his tables and chairs likewise, from a general sense of friendliness towards the articles as well as towards their owner.

'We be not here afore Mrs. Yeobright after all,' said Fairway, recognizing the matron's bonnet through the glass partition which divided the public apartment they had entered from the room where the women sat. 'We struck down across, d'ye see, Mr. Wildeve, and she went round by the path.'

'And I see the young bride's little head!' said Grandfer, peeping in the same direction, and discerning Thomasin, who was waiting beside her aunt in a miserable and awkward way. 'Not quite settled in yet—well, well, there's plenty of time.'

Wildeve made no reply; and probably feeling that the sooner he treated them the sooner they would go, he produced a stone jar, which threw a warm halo over matters at once.

'That's a drop of the right sort, I can see,' said Grandfer Cantle, with the air of a man too well-mannered to show any hurry to taste it.

'Yes,' said Wildeve, ' 'tis some old mead. I hope you will like it.'

'O ay!' replied the guests, in the hearty tones natural when the words demanded by politeness coincide with those of deepest feeling. 'There isn't a prettier drink under the sun.'

'I'll take my oath there isn't,' added Grandfer Cantle. 'All that can be said against mead is that 'tis rather heady, and apt to lie about a man a good while. But to-morrow's Sunday, thank God.'

'I feel'd for all the world like some bold soldier after I had had some once,' said Christian.

'You shall feel so again,' said Wildeve, with condescension. 'Cups or glasses, gentlemen?'

'Well, if you don't mind, we'll have the beaker, and pass 'en round; 'tis better than heling it out in dribbles.'[6]

'Jown the slippery glasses,' said Grandfer Cantle. 'What's the good of a thing that you can't put down in the ashes to warm, hey, neighbours; that's what I ask?'

'Right, Grandfer,' said Sam; and the mead then circulated.

'Well,' said Timothy Fairway, feeling demands upon his praise in some form or other, ' 'tis a worthy thing to be married, Mr. Wildeve; and the woman you've got is a dimant, so says I. Yes,' he continued, to Grandfer Cantle, raising his voice so as to be heard through the partition; 'her father (inclining his head towards the

6. Dialect phrase indicating that pouring out the mead in small drops is petty.

inner room) was as good a feller as ever lived. He always had his great indignation ready against anything underhand.'

'Is that very dangerous?' said Christian.

'And there were few in these parts that were upsides[7] with him,' said Sam. 'Whenever a club walked he'd play the clarinet in the band that marched before 'em as if he'd never touched anything but a clarinet all his life. And then, when they got to church-door he'd throw down the clarinet, mount the gallery, snatch up the bass-viol, and rozum[8] away as if he'd never played anything but a bass-viol. Folk would say—folk that knowed what a true stave was—"Surely, surely that's never the same man that I saw handling the clarinet so masterly by now!" '

'I can mind it,' said the furze-cutter. ' 'Twas a wonderful thing that one body could hold it all and never mix the fingering.'

'There was Kingsbere church likewise,' Fairway recommenced, as one opening a new vein of the same mine of interest.

Wildeve breathed the breath of one intolerably bored, and glanced through the partition at the prisoners.

'He used to walk over there of a Sunday afternoon to visit his old acquaintance Andrew Brown, the first clarinet there; a good man enough, but rather screechy in his music, if you can mind?'

' 'A was.'

'And neighbour Yeobright would take Andrey's place for some part of the service, to let Andrey have a bit of a nap, as any friend would naturally do.'

'As any friend would,' said Grandfer Cantle, the other listeners expressing the same accord by the shorter way of nodding their heads.

'No sooner was Andrey asleep and the first whiff of neighbour Yeobright's wind had got inside Andrey's clarinet than every one in church feeled in a moment there was a great soul among 'em. All heads would turn, and they'd say, "Ah, I thought 'twas he!" One Sunday I can well mind—a bass-viol day that time, and Yeobright had brought his own. 'Twas the Hundred-and-thirty-third to "Lydia";[9] and when they'd come to "Ran down his beard and o'er his robes its costly moisture shed," neighbour Yeobright, who had just warmed to his work, drove his bow into them strings that glorious grand that he e'en a'most sawed the bass-viol into two pieces. Every winder in church rattled as if 'twere a thunderstorm. Old Pa'son Williams lifted his hands in his great holy surplice as natural as if he'd been in common clothes, and seemed to say to hisself,

7. Dialect word for *equal*.
8. Dialect variant of *rosin*, to rub the bow with rosin before playing.
9. The One Hundred and Thirty-Third Psalm, set to music, like all the other psalms, by Tate and Brady in 1696. The Tate and Brady tunes were closely allied to or actually descended from Gregorian plainsong.

"O for such a man in our parish!" But not a soul in Kingsbere could hold a candle to Yeobright.'

'Was it quite safe when the winder shook?' Christian inquired.

He received no answer; all for the moment sitting rapt in admiration of the performance described. As with *Farinelli's* singing before the princesses, Sheridan's renowned Begum Speech,[1] and other such examples, the fortunate condition of its being for ever lost to the world invested the deceased Mr. Yeobright's *tour de force* on that memorable afternoon with a cumulative glory which comparative criticism, had that been possible, might considerably have shorn down.

'He was the last you'd have expected to drop off in the prime of life,' said Humphrey.

'Ah, well: he was looking for the earth some months afore he went. At that time women used to run for smocks and gown-pieces at Greenhill Fair, and my wife that is now, being a long-legged slittering[2] maid, hardly husband-high, went with the rest of the maidens, for 'a was a good runner afore she got so heavy. When she came home I said—we were then just beginning to walk together—"What have ye got, my honey?" "I've won—well, I've won—a gown-piece," says she, her colours coming up in a moment. 'Tis a smock for a crown,[3] I thought; and so it turned out. Ay, when I think what she'll say to me now without a mossel of red in her face, it do seem strange that 'a wouldn't say such a little thing then. . . . However, then she went on, and that's what made me bring up the story, "Well, whatever clothes I've won, white or figured, for eyes to see or for eyes not to see" ('a could do a pretty stroke of modesty in those days), "I'd sooner have lost it than have seen what I have. Poor Mr. Yeobright was took bad directly he reached the fair ground, and was forced to go home again." That was the last time he ever went out of the parish.'

' 'A faltered on from one day to another, and then we heard he was gone.'

'D'ye think he had great pain when 'a died?' said Christian.

'O no: quite different. Nor any pain of mind. He was lucky enough to be God A'mighty's own man.'

'And other folk—d'ye think 'twill be much pain to 'em, Mister Fairway?'

'That depends on whether they be afeard.'

1. Richard Brinsley Sheridan, Irish dramatist and statesman (1751-1816). The Begum Speech refers to a famous oration in Parliament in 1787 defending the rights of the Princesses of Oude in India. *Begum* literally means any Mohammedan lady of high rank. Farinelli was a popular Italian male soprano (1705-1782) who performed in London for royalty in 1734.

2. Of marriageable age. *Slittering* is a dialect form of *slithering*. *Gown-pieces* are pieces of material sufficient for a dress.

3. Coin equal to five shillings (about 60¢ at current exchange), no longer minted.

'I bain't afeard at all, I thank God!' said Christian strenuously. 'I'm glad I bain't, for then 'twon't pain me. . . . I don't think I be afeard—or if I be I can't help it, and I don't deserve to suffer. I wish I was not afeard at all!'

There was a solemn silence, and looking from the window, which was unshuttered and unblinded, Timothy said, 'Well, what a fess[4] little bonfire that one is, out by Cap'n Vye's! 'Tis burning just the same now as ever, upon my life.'

All glances went through the window, and nobody noticed that Wildeve disguised a brief, tell-tale look. Far away up the sombre valley of heath, and to the right of Rainbarrow, could indeed be seen the light, small, but steady and persistent as before.

'It was lighted before ours was,' Fairway continued; 'and yet every one in the country round is out afore 'n.'

'Perhaps there's meaning in it!' murmured Christian.

'How meaning?' said Wildeve sharply.

Christian was too scattered to reply, and Timothy helped him.

'He means, sir, that the lonesome dark-eyed creature up there that some say is a witch—ever I should call a fine young woman such a name—is always up to some odd conceit or other; and so perhaps 'tis she.'

'I'd be very glad to ask her in wedlock, if she'd hae me, and take the risk of her wild dark eyes ill-wishing me,' said Grandfer Cantle staunchly.

'Don't ye say it, father!' implored Christian.

'Well, be dazed if he who do marry the maid won't hae an uncommon picture for his best parlour,' said Fairway in a liquid tone, placing down the cup of mead at the end of a good pull.

'And a partner as deep as the North Star,' said Sam, taking up the cup and finishing the little that remained.

'Well, really, now I think we must be moving,' said Humphrey, observing the emptiness of the vessel.

'But we'll gie 'em another song?' said Grandfer Cantle. 'I'm as full of notes as a bird!'

'Thank you, Grandfer,' said Wildeve. 'But we will not trouble you now. Some other day must do for that—when I have a party.'

'Be jown'd if I don't learn ten new songs for't, or I won't learn a line!' said Grandfer Cantle. 'And you may be sure I won't disappoint ye by biding away, Mr. Wildeve.'

'I quite believe you,' said that gentleman.

All then took their leave, wishing their entertainer long life and happiness as a married man, with recapitulations which occupied some time. Wildeve attended them to the door, beyond which the deep-dyed upward stretch of heath stood awaiting them, an ampli-

4. Proud.

tude of darkness reigning from their feet almost to the zenith, where a definite form first became visible in the lowering forehead of Rainbarrow. Diving into the dense obscurity in a line headed by Sam the turf-cutter, they pursued their trackless way home.

When the scratching of the furze against their leggings had fainted upon the ear, Wildeve returned to the room where he had left Thomasin and her aunt. The women were gone.

They could only have left the house in one way, by the back window; and this was open.

Wildeve laughed to himself, remained a moment thinking, and idly returned to the front room. Here his glance fell upon a bottle of wine which stood on the mantelpiece. 'Ah—old Dowden!' he murmured; and going to the kitchen door shouted, 'Is anybody here who can take something to old Dowden?'

There was no reply. The room was empty, the lad who acted as his factotum having gone to bed. Wildeve came back, put on his hat, took the bottle, and left the house, turning the key in the door, for there was no guest at the inn to-night. As soon as he was on the road the little bonfire on Mistover Knap again met his eye.

'Still waiting, are you, my lady?' he murmured.

However, he did not proceed that way just then; but leaving the hill to the left of him, he stumbled over a rutted road that brought him to a cottage which, like all other habitations on the heath at this hour, was only saved from being invisible by a faint shine from its bedroom window. This house was the home of Olly Dowden, the besom-maker, and he entered.

The lower room was in darkness; but by feeling his way he found a table, whereon he placed the bottle, and a minute later emerged again upon the heath. He stood and looked north-east at the undying little fire—high up above him, though not so high as Rainbarrow.

We have been told what happens when a woman deliberates;[5] and the epigram is not always terminable with woman, provided that one be in the case, and that a fair one. Wildeve stood, and stood longer, and breathed perplexedly, and then said to himself with resignation, 'Yes—by Heaven, I must go to her, I suppose!'

Instead of turning in the direction of home he pressed on rapidly by a path under Rainbarrow towards what was evidently a signal light.

5. "The woman that deliberates is lost." (Joseph Addison, *Cato* IV.i)

The Figure against the Sky

VI

When the whole Egdon concourse had left the site of the bonfire to its accustomed loneliness, a closely wrapped female figure approached the barrow from that quarter of the heath in which the little fire lay. Had the reddleman been watching he might have recognized her as the woman who had first stood there so singularly, and vanished at the approach of strangers. She ascended to her old position at the top, where the red coals of the perishing fire greeted her like living eyes in the corpse of day. There she stood still, around her stretching the vast night atmosphere, whose incomplete darkness in comparison with the total darkness of the heath below it might have represented a venial beside a mortal sin.

That she was tall and straight in build, that she was ladylike in her movements, was all that could be learnt of her just now, her form being wrapped in a shawl folded in the old cornerwise fashion, and her head in a large kerchief, a protection not superfluous at this hour and place. Her back was towards the wind, which blew from the north-west; but whether she had avoided that aspect because of the chilly gusts which played about her exceptional position, or because her interest lay in the south-east, did not at first appear.

Her reason for standing so dead still as the pivot of this circle of heath-country was just as obscure. Her extraordinary fixity, her conspicuous loneliness, her heedlessness of night, betokened among other things an utter absence of fear. A tract of country unaltered from that sinister condition which made Caesar anxious every year to get clear of its glooms before the autumnal equinox, a kind of landscape and weather which leads travellers from the South to describe our island as Homer's Cimmerian land,[6] was not, on the face of it, friendly to women.

It might reasonably have been supposed that she was listening to the wind, which rose somewhat as the night advanced, and laid hold of the attention. The wind, indeed, seemed made for the scene, as the scene seemed made for the hour. Part of its tone was quite special; what was heard there could be heard nowhere else. Gusts in innumerable series followed each other from the north-west, and when each one of them raced past the sound of its progress resolved into three. Treble, tenor, and bass notes were to be found therein. The general ricochet of the whole over pits and prominences had the gravest pitch of the chime. Next there could

6. The Cimmerians are a mythical people said by Homer to dwell in perpetual darkness. Figuratively, dark, gloomy.

be heard the baritone buzz of a holly tree. Below these in force, above them in pitch, a dwindled voice strove hard at a husky tune, which was the peculiar local sound alluded to. Thinner and less immediately traceable than the other two, it was far more impressive than either. In it lay what may be called the linguistic peculiarity of the heath; and being audible nowhere on earth off a heath, it afforded a shadow of reason for the woman's tenseness, which continued as unbroken as ever.

Throughout the blowing of these plaintive November winds that note bore a great resemblance to the ruins of human song which remain to the throat of fourscore and ten. It was a worn whisper, dry and papery, and it brushed so distinctly across the ear that, by the accustomed, the material minutiae in which it originated could be realized as by touch. It was the united products of infinitesimal vegetable causes, and these were neither stems, leaves, fruit, blades, prickles, lichen, nor moss.

They were the mummied heath-bells of the past summer, originally tender and purple, now washed colourless by Michaelmas[7] rains, and dried to dead skins by October suns. So low was an individual sound from these that a combination of hundreds only just emerged from silence, and the myriads of the whole declivity reached the woman's ear but as a shrivelled and intermittent recitative. Yet scarcely a single accent among the many afloat to-night could have such power to impress a listener with thoughts of its origin. One inwardly saw the infinity of those combined multitudes; and perceived that each of the tiny trumpets was seized on, entered, scoured and emerged from by the wind as thoroughly as if it were as vast as a crater.

'The spirit moved them.' A meaning of the phrase forced itself upon the attention; and an emotional listener's fetichistic mood might have ended in one of more advanced quality. It was not, after all, that the left-hand expanse of old blooms spoke, or the right-hand, or those of the slope in front; but it was the single person of something else speaking through each at once.

Suddenly, on the barrow, there mingled with all this wild rhetoric of night a sound which modulated so naturally into the rest that its beginning and ending were hardly to be distinguished. The bluffs, and the bushes, and the heather-bells had broken silence; at last, so did the woman; and her articulation was but as another phrase of the same discourse as theirs. Thrown out on the winds it became twined in with them, and with them it flew away.

What she uttered was a lengthened sighing, apparently at something in her mind which had led to her presence here. There was a

7. September 29th, the feast of St. Michael. Generally refers to autumn. *Heath-bells* are dried bell-shaped flowers.

spasmodic abandonment about it as if, in allowing herself to utter the sound, the woman's brain had authorized what it could not regulate. One point was evident in this; that she had been existing in a suppressed state, and not in one of languor, or stagnation.

Far away down the valley the faint shine from the window of the inn still lasted on; and a few additional moments proved that the window, or what was within it, had more to do with the woman's sigh than had either her own actions or the scene immediately around. She lifted her left hand, which held a closed telescope. This she rapidly extended, as if she were well accustomed to the operation, and raising it to her eye directed it towards the light beaming from the inn.

The handkerchief which had hooded her head was now a little thrown back, her face being somewhat elevated. A profile was visible against the dull monochrome of cloud around her; and it was as though side shadows from the features of Sappho and Mrs. Siddons[8] had converged upwards from the tomb to form an image like neither but suggesting both. This, however, was mere superficiality. In respect of character a face may make certain admissions by its outline; but it fully confesses only in its changes. So much is this the case that what is called the play of the features often helps more in understanding a man or woman than the earnest labours of all the other members together. Thus the night revealed little of her whose form it was embracing, for the mobile parts of her countenance could not be seen.

At last she gave up her spying attitude, closed the telescope, and turned to the decaying embers. From these no appreciable beams now radiated, except when a more than usually smart gust brushed over their faces and raised a fitful glow which came and went like the blush of a girl. She stooped over the silent circle, and selecting from the brands a piece of stick which bore the largest live coal at its end, brought it to where she had been standing before.

She held the brand to the ground, blowing the red coal with her mouth at the same time; till it faintly illuminated the sod, and revealed a small object, which turned out to be an hour-glass, though she wore a watch. She blew long enough to show that the sand had all slipped through.

'Ah!' she said, as if surprised.

The light raised by her breath had been very fitful, and a momentary irradiation of flesh was all that it had disclosed of her face. That consisted of two matchless lips and a cheek only, her head being still enveloped. She threw away the stick, took the glass in her hand, the telescope under her arm, and moved on.

8. Sarah Kemble Siddons (1775-1831), famous British actress. *Sappho* was a Greek poetess, born on the Island of Lesbos (630-570 B.C.?), who became the center of a female coterie.

Along the ridge ran a faint foot-track, which the lady followed. Those who knew it well called it a path; and, while a mere visitor would have passed it unnoticed even by day, the regular haunters of the heath were at no loss for it at midnight. The whole secret of following these incipient paths, when there was not light enough in the atmosphere to show a turnpike-road, lay in the development of the sense of touch in the feet, which comes with years of night-rambling in little-trodden spots. To a walker practised in such places a difference between impact on maiden herbage, and on the crippled stalks of a slight footway, is perceptible through the thickest boot or shoe.

The solitary figure who walked this beat took no notice of the windy tune still played on the dead heath-bells. She did not turn her head to look at a group of dark creatures further on, who fled from her presence as she skirted a ravine where they fed. They were about a score of the small wild ponies known as heath-croppers. They roamed at large on the undulations of Egdon, but in numbers too few to detract much from the solitude.

The pedestrian noticed nothing just now, and a clue to her abstraction was afforded by a trivial incident. A bramble caught hold of her skirt, and checked her progress. Instead of putting it off and hastening along, she yielded herself up to the pull, and stood passively still. When she began to extricate herself it was by turning round and round, and so unwinding the prickly switch. She was in a desponding reverie.

Her course was in the direction of the small undying fire which had drawn the attention of the men on Rainbarrow and of Wildeve in the valley below. A faint illumination from its rays began to glow upon her face, and the fire soon revealed itself to be lit, not on the level ground, but on a salient corner or redan of earth, at the junction of two converging bank fences. Outside was a ditch, dry except immediately under the fire, where there was a large pool, bearded all round by heather and rushes. In the smooth water of the pool the fire appeared upside down.

The banks meeting behind were bare of a hedge, save such as was formed by disconnected tufts of furze, standing upon stems along the top, liked impaled heads above a city wall. A white mast, fitted up with spars and other nautical tackle, could be seen rising against the dark clouds whenever the flames played brightly enough to reach it. Altogether the scene had much the appearance of a fortification upon which had been kindled a beacon fire.

Nobody was visible; but ever and anon a whitish something moved above the bank from behind, and vanished again. This was a small human hand, in the act of lifting pieces of fuel into the fire; but for all that could be seen the hand, like that which troubled Belshazzar,[9] was there alone. Occasionally an ember rolled off the bank, and dropped with a hiss into the pool.

At one side of the pool rough steps built of clods enabled any one who wished to do so to mount the bank; which the woman did. Within was a paddock in an uncultivated state, though bearing evidence of having once been tilled; but the heath and fern had insidiously crept in, and were reasserting their old supremacy. Further ahead were dimly visible an irregular dwelling-house, garden, and outbuildings, back by a clump of firs.

The young lady—for youth had revealed its presence in her buoyant bound up the bank—walked along the top instead of descending inside, and came to the corner where the fire was burning. One reason for the permanence of the blaze was now manifest: the fuel consisted of hard pieces of wood, cleft and sawn—the knotty boles of old thorn trees which grew in twos and threes about the hillsides. A yet unconsumed pile of these lay in the inner angle of the bank; and from this corner the upturned face of a little boy greeted her eyes. He was dilatorily throwing up a piece of wood into the fire every now and then, a business which seemed to have engaged him a considerable part of the evening, for his face was somewhat weary.

'I am glad you have come, Miss Eustacia,' he said, with a sigh of relief. 'I don't like biding by myself.'

'Nonsense. I have only been a little way for a walk. I have been gone only twenty minutes.'

'It seemed long,' murmured the sad boy. 'And you have been so many times.'

'Why, I thought you would be pleased to have a bonfire. Are you not much obliged to me for making you one?'

'Yes; but there's nobody here to play wi' me.'

'I suppose nobody has come while I've been away?'

'Nobody except your grandfather: he looked out of doors once for 'ee. I told him you were walking round upon the hill to look at the other bonfires.'

'A good boy.'

'I think I hear him coming again, miss.'

An old man came into the remoter light of the fire from the direction of the homestead. He was the same who had overtaken the reddleman on the road that afternoon. He looked wistfully to the top of the bank at the woman who stood there, and his teeth,

9. Son of Nebuchadnezzar who summoned Daniel to translate the handwriting on the wall. God had written "mene, mene, tekel, upharsin," meaning "God hath numbered thy kingdom, and finished it; thou art weighed in the balances and art found wanting." (Daniel v:25-27)

which were quite unimpaired, showed like parian[1] from his parted lips.

'When are you coming indoors, Eustacia?' he asked. ' 'Tis almost bedtime. I've been home these two hours, and am tired out. Surely 'tis somewhat childish of you to stay out playing at bonfires so long, and wasting such fuel. My precious thorn roots, the rarest of all firing, that I laid by on purpose for Christmas—you have burnt 'em nearly all!'

'I promised Johnny a bonfire, and it pleases him not to let it go out just yet,' said Eustacia, in a way which told at once that she was absolute queen here. 'Grandfather, you go in to bed. I shall follow you soon. You like the fire, don't you, Johnny?'

The boy looked up doubtfully at her and murmured, 'I don't think I want it any longer.'

Her grandfather had turned back again, and did not hear the boy's reply. As soon as the white-haired man had vanished she said in a tone of pique to the child, 'Ungrateful little boy, how can you contradict me? Never shall you have a bonfire again unless you keep it up now. Come, tell me you like to do things for me, and don't deny it.'

The repressed child said, 'Yes, I do, miss,' and continued to stir the fire perfunctorily.

'Stay a little longer and I will give you a crooked sixpence,'[2] said Eustacia, more gently. 'Put in one piece of wood every two or three minutes, but not too much at once. I am going to walk along the ridge a little longer, but I shall keep on coming to you. And if you hear a frog jump into the pond with a flounce like a stone thrown in, be sure you run and tell me, because it is a sign of rain.'

'Yes, Eustacia.'

'Miss Vye, sir.'

'Miss Vy—stacia.'

'That will do. Now put in one stick more.'

The little slave went on feeding the fire as before. He seemed a mere automaton, galvanized into moving and speaking by the wayward Eustacia's will. He might have been the brass statue which Albertus Magnus[3] is said to have animated just so far as to make it chatter, and move, and be his servant.

Before going on her walk again the young girl stood still on the bank for a few instants and listened. It was to the full as lonely a place as Rainbarrow, though at rather a lower level; and it was more sheltered from wind and weather on account of the few firs to the north. The bank which enclosed the homestead, and protected

1. White marble from the Island of Paros, highly valued for statuary.
2. Good luck charm, proof against witchcraft.
3. German scholastic philosopher (1206-1280), a Dominican and teacher of Thomas Aquinas.

it from the lawless state of the world without, was formed of thick square clods, dug from the ditch on the outside, and built up with a slight batter or incline, which forms no slight defence where hedges will not grow because of the wind and the wilderness, and where wall materials are unattainable. Otherwise the situation was quite open, commanding the whole length of the valley which reached to the river behind Wildeve's house. High above this to the right, and much nearer thitherward than the Quiet Woman Inn, the blurred contour of Rainbarrow obstructed the sky.

After her attentive survey of the wild slopes and hollow ravines a gesture of impatience escaped Eustacia. She vented petulant words every now and then; but there were sighs between her words, and sudden listenings between her sighs. Descending from her perch she again sauntered off towards Rainbarrow, though this time she did not go the whole way.

Twice she reappeared at intervals of a few minutes and each time she said—

'Not any flounce into the pond yet, little man?'

'No, Miss Eustacia,' the child replied.

'Well,' she said at last, 'I shall be going in, and then I will give you the crooked sixpence, and let you go home.'

'Thank'ee, Miss Eustacia,' said the tired stoker, breathing more easily. And Eustacia again strolled away from the fire, but this time not towards Rainbarrow. She skirted the bank and went round to the wicket before the house, where she stood motionless, looking at the scene.

Fifty yards off rose the corner of the two converging banks, with the fire upon it: within the bank, lifting up to the fire one stick at a time, just as before, the figure of the little child. She idly watched him as he occasionally climbed up in the nook of the bank and stood beside the brands. The wind blew the smoke, and the child's hair, and the corner of his pinafore, all in the same direction: the breeze died, and the pinafore and hair lay still, and the smoke went up straight.

While Eustacia looked on from this distance the boy's form visibly started: he slid down the bank and ran across towards the white gate.

'Well?' said Eustacia.

'A hop-frog have jumped into the pond. Yes, I heard 'en!'

'Then it is going to rain, and you had better go home. You will not be afraid?' She spoke hurriedly, as if her heart had leapt into her throat at the boy's words.

'No, because I shall hae the crooked sixpence.'

'Yes, here it is. Now run as fast as you can—not that way—

through the garden here. No other boy in the heath has had such a bonfire as yours.'

The boy, who clearly had had too much of a good thing, marched away into the shadows with alacrity. When he was gone Eustacia, leaving her telescope and hour-glass by the gate, brushed forward from the wicket towards the angle of the bank, under the fire.

Here, screened by the outwork, she waited. In a few moments a splash was audible from the pond outside. Had the child been there he would have said that a second frog had jumped in; but by most people the sound would have been likened to the fall of a stone into the water. Eustacia stepped upon the bank.

'Yes?' she said, and held her breath.

Thereupon the contour of a man became dimly visible against the low-reaching sky over the valley, beyond the outer margin of the pool. He came round it and leapt upon the bank beside her. A low laugh escaped her—the third utterance which the girl had indulged in to-night. The first, when she stood upon Rainbarrow, had expressed anxiety; the second, on the ridge, had expressed impatience; the present was one of triumphant pleasure. She let her joyous eyes rest upon him without speaking, as upon some wondrous thing she had created out of chaos.

'I have come,' said the man, who was Wildeve. 'You give me no peace. Why do you not leave me alone? I have seen your bonfire all the evening.' The words were not without emotion, and retained their level tone as if by a careful equipoise between imminent extremes.

At this unexpectedly repressing manner in her lover the girl seemed to repress herself also. 'Of course you have seen my fire,' she answered with languid calmness, artificially maintained. 'Why shouldn't I have a bonfire on the Fifth of November, like other denizens of the heath?'

'I knew it was meant for me.'

'How did you know it? I have had no word with you since you—you chose her, and walked about with her, and deserted me entirely, as if I had never been yours life and soul so irretrievably!'

'Eustacia! could I forget that last autumn at this same day of the month and at this same place you lighted exactly such a fire as a signal for me to come and see you? Why should there have been a bonfire again by Captain Vye's house if not for the same purpose?'

'Yes, yes—I own it,' she cried under her breath, with a drowsy fervour of manner and tone which was quite peculiar to her. 'Don't begin speaking to me as you did, Damon; you will drive me to say words I would not wish to say to you. I had given you up, and resolved not to think of you any more; and then I heard the news, and I came out and got the fire ready because I thought that you had been faithful to me.'

'What have you heard to make you think that?' said Wildeve, astonished.

'That you did not marry her!' she murmured exultingly. 'And I knew it was because you loved me best, and couldn't do it. . . . Damon, you have been cruel to me to go away, and I have said I would never forgive you. I do not think I can forgive you entirely, even now—it is too much for a woman of any spirit to quite overlook.'

'If I had known you wished to call me up here only to reproach me, I wouldn't have come.'

'But I don't mind it, and I do forgive you now that you have not married her, and have come back to me!'

'Who told you that I had not married her?'

'My grandfather. He took a long walk to-day, and as he was coming home he overtook some person who told him of a broken-off wedding: he thought it might be yours; and I knew it was.'

'Does anybody else know?'

'I suppose not. Now Damon, do you see why I lit my signal fire? You did not think I would have lit it if I had imagined you to have become the husband of this woman. It is insulting my pride to suppose that.'

Wildeve was silent: it was evident that he had supposed as much.

'Did you indeed think I believed you were married?' she again demanded earnestly. 'Then you wronged me; and upon my life and heart I can hardly bear to recognize that you have such ill thoughts of me! Damon, you are not worthy of me: I see it, and yet I love you. Never mind: let it go—I must bear your mean opinion as best I may. . . . It is true, is it not,' she added with ill-concealed anxiety, on his making no demonstration, 'that you could not bring yourself to give me up, and are still going to love me best of all?'

'Yes; or why should I have come?' he said touchily. 'Not that fidelity will be any great merit in me after your kind speech about my unworthiness, which should have been said by myself if by anybody, and comes with an ill grace from you. However, the curse of inflammability is upon me, and I must live under it, and take any snub from a woman. It has brought me down from engineering to innkeeping: what lower stage it has in store for me I have yet to learn.' He continued to look upon her gloomily.

She seized the moment, and throwing back the shawl so that the firelight shone full upon her face and throat, said with a smile, 'Have you seen anything better than that in your travels?'

Eustacia was not one to commit herself to such a position without good ground. He said quietly, 'No.'

'Not even on the shoulders of Thomasin?'

'Thomasin is a pleasing and innocent woman.'

'That's nothing to do with it,' she cried with quick passionateness. 'We will leave her out; there are only you and me now to think of.' After a long look at him she resumed with the old quiescent warmth: 'Must I go on weakly confessing to you things a woman ought to conceal; and own that no words can express how gloomy I have been because of that dreadful belief I held till two hours ago—that you had quite deserted me?'

'I am sorry I caused you that pain.'

'But perhaps it is not wholly because of you that I get gloomy,' she archly added. 'It is my nature to feel like that. It was born in my blood, I suppose.'

'Hypochondriasis.'

'Or else it was coming into this wild heath. I was happy enough at Budmouth. O the times, O the days at Budmouth! But Egdon will be brighter again now.'

'I hope it will,' said Wildeve moodily. 'Do you know the consequence of this recall to me, my old darling? I shall come to see you again as before, at Rainbarrow.'

'Of course you will.'

'And yet I declare that until I got here to-night I intended, after this one good-bye, never to meet you again.'

'I don't thank you for that,' she said, turning away, while indignation spread through her like subterranean heat. 'You may come again to Rainbarrow if you like, but you won't see me; and you may call, but I shall not listen; and you may tempt me, but I won't give myself to you any more.'

'You have said as much before, sweet; but such natures as yours don't so easily adhere to their words. Neither, for the matter of that, do such natures as mine.'

'This is the pleasure I have won by my trouble,' she whispered bitterly. 'Why did I try to recall you? Damon, a strange warring takes place in my mind occasionally. I think when I become calm after your woundings, "Do I embrace a cloud of common fog after all?" You are a chameleon, and now you are at your worst colour. Go home, or I shall hate you!'

He looked absently towards Rainbarrow while one might have counted twenty, and said, as if he did not much mind all this, 'Yes, I will go home. Do you mean to see me again?'

'If you own to me that the wedding is broken off because you love me best.'

'I don't think it would be good policy,' said Wildeve, smiling.

'You would get to know the extent of your power too clearly.'

'But tell me!'

'You know.'

'Where is she now?'

'I don't know. I prefer not to speak of her to you. I have not yet married her: I have come in obedience to your call. That is enough.'

'I merely lit that fire because I was dull, and thought I would get a little excitement by calling you up and triumphing over you as the Witch of Endor[4] called up Samuel. I determined you should come; and you have come! I have shown my power. A mile and half hither, and a mile and half back again to your home—three miles in the dark for me. Have I not shown my power?'

He shook his head at her. 'I know you too well, my Eustacia; I know you too well. There isn't a note in you which I don't know; and that hot little bosom couldn't play such a cold-blooded trick to save its life. I saw a woman on Rainbarrow at dusk looking down towards my house. I think I drew out you before you drew out me.'

The revived embers of an old passion glowed clearly in Wildeve now; and he leant forward as if about to put his face towards her cheek.

'O no,' she said, intractably moving to the other side of the decayed fire. 'What did you mean by that?'

'Perhaps I may kiss your hand?'

'No, you may not.'

'Then I may shake your hand?'

'No.'

'Then I wish you good-night without caring for either. Good-bye, good-bye.'

She returned no answer, and with the bow of a dancing-master he vanished on the other side of the pool as he had come.

Eustacia sighed: it was no fragile maiden sigh, but a sigh which shook her like a shiver. Whenever a flash of reason darted like an electric light upon her lover—as it sometimes would—and showed his imperfections, she shivered thus. But it was over in a second, and she loved on. She knew that he trifled with her; but she loved on. She scattered the half-burnt brands, went indoors immediately, and up to her bedroom without a light. Amid the rustles which denoted her to be undressing in the darkness other heavy breaths frequently came; and the same kind of shudder occasionally moved through her when, ten minutes later, she lay on her bed asleep.

4. King Saul, apprehensive about a battle with the Philistines, sought a medium, the Witch of Endor. The medium called up Samuel, who correctly foretold Saul's death in battle the next day. (I Samuel xxviii.7-19)

Queen of Night

VII

Eustacia Vye was the raw material of a divinity. On Olympus she would have done well with a little preparation. She had the passions and instincts which make a model goddess, that is, those which make not quite a model woman. Had it been possible for the earth and mankind to be entirely in her grasp for a while, had she handled the distaff,[5] the spindle and the shears at her own free will, few in the world would have noticed the change of government. There would have been the same inequality of lot, the same heaping up of favours here, of contumely there, the same generosity before justice, the same perpetual dilemmas, the same captious alteration of caresses and blows that we endure now.

She was in person full-limbed and somewhat heavy; without ruddiness, as without pallor; and soft to the touch as a cloud. To see her hair was to fancy that a whole winter did not contain darkness enough to form its shadow: it closed over her forehead like nightfall extinguishing the western glow.

Her nerves extended into those tresses, and her temper could always be softened by stroking them down. When her hair was brushed she would instantly sink into stillness and look like the Sphinx. If, in passing under one of the Egdon banks, any of its thick skeins were caught, as they sometimes were, by a prickly tuft of the large *Ulex Europaeus*[6]—which will act as a sort of hairbrush—she would go back a few steps, and pass against it a second time.

She had Pagan eyes, full of nocturnal mysteries, and their light, as it came and went, and came again, was partially hampered by their oppressive lids and lashes; and of these the under lid was much fuller than it usually is with English women. This enabled her to indulge in reverie without seeming to do so: she might have been believed capable of sleeping without closing them up. Assuming that the souls of men and women were visible essences, you could fancy the colour of Eustacia's soul to be flame-like. The sparks from it that rose into her dark pupils gave the same impression.

The mouth seemed formed less to speak than to quiver, less to quiver than to kiss. Some might have added, less to kiss than to curl. Viewed sideways, the closing-line of her lips formed, with almost geometric precision, the curve so well known in the arts of design as the cima-recta, or ogee. The sight of such a flexible bend

5. Staff of a spinning wheel that holds the flax to be spun. Symbolically, female authority.

6. Furze, gorse.

as that on grim Egdon was quite an apparition. It was felt at once that the mouth did not come over from Sleswig[7] with a band of Saxon pirates whose lips met like the two halves of a muffin. One had fancied that such lip-curves were mostly lurking underground in the South as fragments of forgotten marbles. So fine were the lines of her lips that, though full, each corner of her mouth was as clearly cut as the point of a spear. This keenness of corner was only blunted when she was given over to sudden fits of gloom, one of the phases of the night-side of sentiment which she knew too well for her years.

Her presence brought memories of such things as Bourbon roses, rubies, and tropical midnights; her moods recalled lotus-eaters and the march in 'Athalie';[8] her motions, the ebb and flow of the sea; her voice, the viola. In a dim light, and with a slight rearrangement of her hair, her general figure might have stood for that of either of the higher female deities. The new moon behind her head, an old helmet upon it, a diadem of accidental dewdrops round her brow, would have been adjuncts sufficient to strike the note of Artemis, Athena, or Hera respectively, with as close an approximation to the antique as that which passes muster on many respected canvases.

But celestial imperiousness, love, wrath, and fervour had proved to be somewhat thrown away on netherward Egdon. Her power was limited, and the consciousness of this limitation had biassed her development. Egdon was her Hades, and since coming there she had imbibed much of what was dark in its tone, though inwardly and eternally unreconciled thereto. Her appearance accorded well with this smouldering rebelliousness, and the shady splendour of her beauty was the real surface of the sad and stifled warmth within her. A true Tartarean dignity sat upon her brow, and not factitiously or with marks of constraint, for it had grown in her with years.

Across the upper part of her head she wore a thin fillet of black velvet, restraining the luxuriance of her shady hair, in a way which added much to this class of majesty by irregularly clouding her forehead. 'Nothing can embellish a beautiful face more than a narrow band drawn over the brow,' says Richter.[9] Some of the neighbouring girls wore coloured ribbon for the same purpose, and sported metallic ornaments elsewhere; but if any one suggested coloured ribbon and metallic ornaments to Eustacia Vye she laughed and went on.

Why did a woman of this sort live on Egdon Heath? Budmouth

7. Schleswig—now northern Germany, bounded by Denmark. Area from which the Angles, early settlers of England, migrated.

8. Tragic drama, written in 1690, by Racine. *Lotus-eaters* are Greek legendary figures who, eating the fruit called lotus, abandoned themselves to day dreaming and luxurious ease.

9. Johann Paul Friedrich Richter (1763-1825), German author, famous for his aphorisms.

was her native place, a fashionable seaside resort at that date. She was the daughter of the bandmaster of a regiment which had been quartered there—a Corfiote[1] by birth, and a fine musician—who met his future wife during her trip thither with her father the captain, a man of good family. The marriage was scarcely in accord with the old man's wishes, for the bandmaster's pockets were as light as his occupation. But the musician did his best; adopted his wife's name, made England permanently his home, took great trouble with his child's education, the expenses of which were defrayed by the grandfather, and throve as the chief local musician till her mother's death, when he left off thriving, drank, and died also. The girl was left to the care of her grandfather, who, since three of his ribs became broken in a shipwreck, had lived in this airy perch on Egdon, a spot which had taken his fancy because the house was to be had for next to nothing, and because a remote blue tinge on the horizon between the hills, visible from the cottage door, was traditionally believed to be the English Channel. She hated the change; she felt like one banished; but here she was forced to abide.

Thus it happened that in Eustacia's brain were juxtaposed the strangest assortment of ideas, from old time and from new. There was no middle distance in her perspective: romantic recollections of sunny afternoons on an esplanade, with military bands, officers, and gallants around, stood like gilded letters upon the dark tablet of surrounding Egdon. Every bizarre effect that could result from the random intertwining of watering-place glitter with the grand solemnity of a heath, was to be found in her. Seeing nothing of human life now, she imagined all the more of what she had seen.

Where did her dignity come from? By a latent vein from Alcinous' line, her father hailing from Phaeacia's isle?[2]—or from Fitzalan and De Vere,[3] her maternal grandfather having had a cousin in the peerage? Perhaps it was the gift of Heaven—a happy convergence of natural laws. Among other things opportunity had of late years been denied her of learning to be undignified, for she lived lonely. Isolation on a heath renders vulgarity well-nigh impossible. It would have been as easy for the heath-ponies, bats, and snakes to be vulgar as for her. A narrow life in Budmouth might have completely demeaned her.

The only way to look queenly without realms or hearts to queen it over is to look as if you had lost them; and Eustacia did that to a triumph. In the captain's cottage she could suggest mansions she had never seen. Perhaps that was because she frequented a vaster

1. Native of Corfu, an island off the coast of Greece.

2. Homeric Island of Scheria (now Corfu) visited by Ulysses after the fall of Troy. In Homer's *Odyssey,* Alcinous is the father of Nausicaa and king of the Phaeacians.

3. Distinguished English families of peers.

mansion than any of them, the open hills. Like the summer condition of the place around her, she was an embodiment of the phrase 'a populous solitude'—apparently so listless, void, and quiet, she was really busy and full.

To be loved to madness—such was her great desire. Love was to her the one cordial which could drive away the eating loneliness of her days. And she seemed to long for the abstraction called passionate love more than for any particular lover.

She could show a most reproachful look at times, but it was directed less against human beings than against certain creatures of her mind, the chief of these being Destiny, through whose interference she dimly fancied it arose that love alighted only on gliding youth—that any love she might win would sink simultaneously with the sand in the glass. She thought of it with an ever-growing consciousness of cruelty, which tended to breed actions of reckless unconventionality, framed to snatch a year's, a week's, even an hour's passion from anywhere while it could be won. Through want of it she had sung without being merry, possessed without enjoying, outshone without triumphing. Her loneliness deepened her desire. On Egdon, coldest and meanest kisses were at famine prices; and where was a mouth matching hers to be found?

Fidelity in love for fidelity's sake had less attraction for her than for most women: fidelity because of love's grip had much. A blaze of love, and extinction, was better than a lantern glimmer of the same which should last long years. On this head she knew by prevision what most women learn only by experience: she had mentally walked round love, told the towers thereof, considered its palaces; and concluded that love was but a doleful joy. Yet she desired it, as one in a desert would be thankful for brackish water.

She often repeated her prayers; not at particular times, but, like the unaffectedly devout, when she desired to pray. Her prayer was always spontaneous, and often ran thus, 'O deliver my heart from this fearful gloom and loneliness: send me great love from somewhere, else I shall die.'

Her high gods were William the Conqueror, Strafford,[4] and Napoleon Buonaparte, as they had appeared in the Lady's History used at the establishment in which she was educated. Had she been a mother she would have christened her boys such names as Saul or Sisera[5] in preference to Jacob or David, neither of whom she admired. At school she had used to side with the Philistines in sev-

4. Thomas Wentworth, first Earl of Strafford (1593-1641), British statesman and powerful figure in King Charles I's councils. He helped establish Irish industry and ruled dictatorially.

5. A powerful prince, leader of a confederacy of Canaanite kings, finally defeated by the judgment of the Lord. (I Samuel xii.9ff.) *Saul* was first King of Israel, warlike and powerful. (I Samuel ix.ff.)

eral battles, and had wondered if Pontius Pilate were as handsome as he was frank and fair.

Thus she was a girl of some forwardness of mind, indeed, weighed in relation to her situation among the very rereward of thinkers, very original. Her instincts towards social nonconformity were at the root of this. In the matter of holidays, her mood was that of horses who, when turned out to grass, enjoy looking upon their kind at work on the highway. She only valued rest to herself when it came in the midst of other people's labour. Hence she hated Sundays when all was at rest, and often said they would be the death of her. To see the heathmen in their Sunday condition, that is, with their hands in their pockets, their boots newly oiled, and not laced up (a particularly Sunday sign), walking leisurely among the turves[6] and furze-faggots they had cut during the week, and kicking them critically as if their use were unknown, was a fearful heaviness to her. To relieve the tedium of this untimely day she would overhaul the cupboards containing her grandfather's old charts and other rubbish, humming Saturday-night ballads of the country people the while. But on Saturday nights she would frequently sing a psalm, and it was always on a week-day that she read the Bible, that she might be unoppressed with a sense of doing her duty.

Such views of life were to some extent the natural begettings of her situation upon her nature. To dwell on a heath without studying its meanings was like wedding a foreigner without learning his tongue. The subtle beauties of the heath were lost to Eustacia; she only caught its vapours. An environment which would have made a contented woman a poet, a suffering woman a devotee, a pious woman a psalmist, even a giddy woman thoughtful, made a rebellious woman saturnine.

Eustacia had got beyond the vision of some marriage of inexpressible glory; yet, though her emotions were in full vigour, she cared for no meaner union. Thus we see her in a strange state of isolation. To have lost the godlike conceit that we may do what we will, and not to have acquired a homely zest for doing what we can, shows a grandeur of temper which cannot be objected to in the abstract, for it denotes a mind that, though disappointed, forswears compromise. But, if congenial to philosophy, it is apt to be dangerous to the commonwealth. In a world where doing means marrying, and the commonwealth is one of hearts and hands, the same peril attends the condition.

And so we see our Eustacia—for at times she was not altogether

6. Dialect form of *turf*, here pieces of sod or peat for use as fuel.

unlovable—arriving at that stage of enlightenment which feels that nothing is worth while, and filling up the spare hours of her existence by idealizing Wildeve for want of a better object. This was the sole reason of his ascendency: she knew it herself. At moments her pride rebelled against her passion for him, and she even had longed to be free. But there was only one circumstance which could dislodge him, and that was the advent of a greater man.

For the rest, she suffered much from depression of spirits, and took slow walks to recover them, in which she carried her grandfather's telescope and her grandmother's hour-glass—the latter because of a peculiar pleasure she derived from watching a material representation of time's gradual glide away. She seldom schemed, but when she did scheme, her plans showed rather the comprehensive strategy of a general than the small arts called womanish, though she could utter oracles of Delphian ambiguity when she did not choose to be direct. In heaven she will probably sit between the Héloïses and Cleopatras.

Those Who Are Found Where There Is Said to Be Nobody

VIII

As soon as the sad little boy had withdrawn from the fire he clasped the money tight in the palm of his hand, as if thereby to fortify his courage, and began to run. There was really little danger in allowing a child to go home alone on this part of Egdon Heath. The distance to the boy's house was not more than three-eighths of a mile, his father's cottage, and one other a few yards further on, forming part of the small hamlet of Mistover Knap: the third and only remaining house was that of Captain Vye and Eustacia, which stood quite away from the small cottages, and was the loneliest of lonely houses on these thinly populated slopes.

He ran until he was out of breath, and then, becoming more courageous, walked leisurely along, singing in an old voice a little song about a sailor-boy and a fair one, and bright gold in store. In the middle of this the child stopped: from a pit under the hill ahead of him shone a light, whence proceeded a cloud of floating dust and a smacking noise.

Only unusual sights and sounds frightened the boy. The shrivelled voice of the heath did not alarm him, for that was familiar. The thorn-bushes which arose in his path from time to time were less satisfactory, for they whistled gloomily, and had a ghastly habit after dark of putting on the shapes of jumping madmen, sprawling giants, and hideous cripples. Lights were not uncommon this evening, but the nature of all of them was different from this. Discretion rather than terror prompted the boy to turn back instead of passing the light, with a view of asking Miss Eustacia Vye to let her servant accompany him home.

When the boy had reascended to the top of the valley he found the fire to be still burning on the bank, though lower than before. Beside it, instead of Eustacia's solitary form, he saw two persons, the second being a man. The boy crept along under the bank to ascertain from the nature of the proceedings if it would be prudent to interrupt so splendid a creature as Miss Eustacia on his poor trivial account.

After listening under the bank for some minutes to the talk he turned in a perplexed and doubting manner and began to withdraw as silently as he had come. That he did not, upon the whole, think it advisable to interrupt her conversation with Wildeve, without being prepared to bear the whole weight of her displeasure, was obvious.

Here was a Scyllæo-Charybdean position for a poor boy. Pausing when again safe from discovery he finally decided to face the pit phenomenon as the lesser evil. With a heavy sigh he retraced the slope, and followed the path he had followed before.

The light had gone, the rising dust had disappeared—he hoped for ever. He marched resolutely along, and found nothing to alarm him till, coming within a few yards of the sandpit, he heard a slight noise in front, which led him to halt. The halt was but momentary, for the noise resolved itself into the steady bites of two animals grazing.

'Two he'th-croppers down here,' he said aloud. 'I have never known 'em come down so far afore.'

The animals were in the direct line of his path, but that the child thought little of; he had played round the fetlocks of horses from his infancy. On coming nearer, however, the boy was somewhat surprised to find that the little creatures did not run off, and that each wore a clog, to prevent his going astray; this signified that they had been broken in. He could now see the interior of the pit, which, being in the side of the hill, had a level entrance. In the innermost corner the square outline of a van appeared, with its back towards him. A light came from the interior, and threw a moving shadow upon the vertical face of gravel at the further side of the pit into which the vehicle faced.

The child assumed that this was the cart of a gipsy, and his dread of those wanderers reached but to that mild pitch which titillates rather than pains. Only a few inches of mud wall kept him and his family from being gipsies themselves. He skirted the gravel-pit at a respectful distance, ascended the slope, and came forward upon the brow, in order to look into the open door of the van and see the original of the shadow.

The picture alarmed the boy. By a little stove inside the van sat a figure red from head to heels—the man who had been Thomasin's friend. He was darning a stocking, which was red like the rest of him. Moreover, as he darned he smoked a pipe, the stem and bowl of which were red also.

At this moment one of the heath-croppers feeding in the outer shadows was audibly shaking off the clog attached to its foot. Aroused by the sound the reddleman laid down his stocking, lit a lantern which hung beside him, and came out from the van. In sticking up the candle he lifted the lantern to his face, and the light shone into the whites of his eyes and upon his ivory teeth, which, in contrast with the red surrounding, lent him a startling aspect enough to the gaze of a juvenile. The boy knew too well for his peace of mind upon whose lair he had lighted. Uglier persons than gipsies were known to cross Egdon at times, and a reddleman was one of them.

'How I wish 'twas only a gipsy!' he murmured.

The man was by this time coming back from the horses. In his fear of being seen the boy rendered detection certain by nervous motion. The heather and peat stratum overhung the brow of the pit in mats, hiding the actual verge. The boy had stepped beyond the solid ground; the heather now gave way, and down he rolled over the scarp[7] of grey sand to the very foot of the man.

The red man opened the lantern and turned it upon the figure of the prostrate boy.

'Who be ye?' he said.

'Johnny Nunsuch, master!'

'What were you doing up there?'

'I don't know.'

'Watching me, I suppose?'

'Yes, master.'

'What did you watch me for?'

'Because I was coming home from Miss Vye's bonfire.'

'Beest hurt?'

'No.'

'Why, yes, you be: your hand is bleeding. Come under my tilt[8] and let me tie it up.'

'Please let me look for my sixpence.'

'How did you come by that?'

'Miss Vye gied it to me for keeping up her bonfire.'

The sixpence was found, and the man went to the van, the boy behind, almost holding his breath.

7. Bank or slope.

8. Awning or cover for a cart or wagon.

The man took a piece of rag from a satchel containing sewing materials, tore off a strip, which, like everything else, was tinged red, and proceeded to bind up the wound.

'My eyes have got foggy-like—please may I sit down, master?' said the boy.

'To be sure, poor chap. 'Tis enough to make you feel fainty. Sit on that bundle.'

The man finished tying up the gash, and the boy said, 'I think I'll go home now, master.'

'You are rather afraid of me. Do you know what I be?'

The child surveyed his vermilion figure up and down with much misgiving, and finally said, 'Yes.'

'Well, what?'

'The reddleman!' he faltered.

'Yes, that's what I be. Though there's more than one. You little children think there's only one cuckoo, one fox, one giant, one devil, and one reddleman, when there's lots of us all.'

'Is there? You won't carry me off in your bags, will ye, master? 'Tis said that the reddleman will sometimes.'

'Nonsense. All that reddlemen do is sell reddle. You see all these bags at the back of my cart? They are not full of little boys—only full of red stuff.'

'Was you born a reddleman?'

'No, I took to it. I should be as white as you if I were to give up the trade—that is, I should be white in time—perhaps six months: not at first, because 'tis grow'd into my skin and won't wash out. Now, you'll never be afraid of a reddleman again, will ye?'

'No, never. Willy Orchard said he seed a red ghost here t'other day—perhaps that was you?'

'I was here t'other day.'

'Were you making that dusty light I saw by now?'

'O yes: I was beating out some bags. And have you had a good bonfire up there? I saw the light. Why did Miss Vye want a bonfire so bad that she should give you sixpence to keep it up?'

'I don't know. I was tired, but she made me bide and keep up the fire just the same, while she kept going up across Rainbarrow way.'

'And how long did that last?'

'Until a hopfrog jumped into the pond.'

The reddleman suddenly ceased to talk idly. 'A hopfrog?' he inquired. 'Hopfrogs don't jump into ponds this time of year.'

'They do, for I heard one.'

'Certain-sure?'

'Yes. She told me afore that I should hear'n; and so I did. They say she's clever and deep, and perhaps she charmed 'en to come.'

'And what then?'

'Then I came down here, and I was afeard, and I went back; but I didn't like to speak to her, because of the gentleman, and I came on here again.'

'A gentleman—ah! What did she say to him, my man?'

'Told him she supposed he had not married the other woman because he liked his old sweetheart best; and things like that.'

'What did the gentleman say to her, my sonny?'

'He only said he did like her best, and how he was coming to see her again under Rainbarrow o' nights.'

'Ha!' cried the reddleman, slapping his hand against the side of his van so that the whole fabric shook under the blow. 'That's the secret o't!'

The little boy jumped clean from the stool.

'My man, don't you be afraid,' said the dealer in red, suddenly becoming gentle. 'I forgot you were here. That's only a curious way reddlemen have of going mad for a moment; but they don't hurt anybody. And what did the lady say then?'

'I can't mind. Please, Master Reddleman, may I go home-along now?'

'Ay, to be sure you may. I'll go a bit of ways with you.'

He conducted the boy out of the gravel-pit and into the path leading to his mother's cottage. When the little figure had vanished in the darkness the reddleman returned, resumed his seat by the fire, and proceeded to darn again.

Love Leads a Shrewd Man into Strategy

IX

Reddlemen of the old school are now but seldom seen. Since the introduction of railways Wessex farmers have managed to do without these Mephistophelian visitants, and the bright pigment so largely used by shepherds in preparing sheep for the fair is obtained by other routes. Even those who yet survive are losing the poetry of existence which characterized them when the pursuit of the trade meant periodical journeys to the pit whence the material was dug, a regular camping out from month to month, except in the depth of winter, a peregrination among farms which could be counted by the hundred, and in spite of this Arab existence the preservation of that respectability which is insured by the never-failing production of a well-lined purse.

Reddle spreads its lively hues over everything it lights on, and stamps unmistakably, as with the mark of Cain, any person who has handled it half an hour.

A child's first sight of a reddleman was an epoch in his life. That blood-coloured figure was a sublimation of all the horrid dreams which had afflicted the juvenile spirit since imagination began. 'The reddleman is coming for you!' had been the formulated threat of Wessex mothers for many generations. He was successfully supplanted for a while, at the beginning of the present century, by Buonaparte; but as process of time rendered the latter personage stale and ineffective the older phrase resumed its early prominence. And now the reddleman has in his turn followed Buonaparte to the land of worn-out bogeys, and his place is filled by modern inventions.

The reddleman lived like a gipsy; but gipsies he scorned. He was about as thriving as travelling basket and mat makers; but he had nothing to do with them. He was more decently born and brought up than the cattle-drovers who passed and repassed him in his wanderings; but they merely nodded to him. His stock was more valuable than that of pedlars; but they did not think so, and passed his cart with eyes straight ahead. He was such an unnatural colour to look at that the men of round-abouts[9] and wax-work shows seemed gentlemen beside him; but he considered them low company, and remained aloof. Among all these squatters and folks of the road the reddleman continually found himself; yet he was not of them. His occupation tended to isolate him, and isolated he was mostly seen to be.

It was sometimes suggested that reddlemen were criminals for whose misdeeds other men had wrongfully suffered: that in escaping the law they had not escaped their own consciences, and had taken to the trade as a lifelong penance. Else why should they have chosen it? In the present case such a question would have been particularly apposite. The reddleman who had entered Egdon that afternoon was an instance of the pleasing being wasted to form the ground-work of the singular, when an ugly foundation would have done just as well for that purpose. The one point that was forbidding about this reddleman was his colour. Freed from that he would have been as agreeable a specimen of rustic manhood as one would often see. A keen observer might have been inclined to think—which was, indeed, partly the truth—that he had relinquished his proper station in life for want of interest in it. Moreover, after looking at him one would have hazarded the guess that good-nature, and an acuteness as extreme as it could be without verging on craft, formed the frame-work of his character.

While he darned the stocking his face became rigid with thought. Softer expressions followed this, and then again recurred the tender sadness which had sat upon him during his drive along the highway that afternoon. Presently his needle stopped. He laid

9. Merry-go-rounds.

down the stocking, arose from his seat, and took a leathern pouch from a hook in the corner of the van. This contained among other articles a brown-paper packet, which, to judge from the hinge-like character of its worn folds, seemed to have been carefully opened and closed a good many times. He sat down on a three-legged milking-stool that formed the only seat in the van, and, examining his packet by the light of a candle, took thence an old letter and spread it open. The writing had originally been traced on white paper, but the letter had now assumed a pale red tinge from the accident of its situation; and the black strokes of writing thereon looked like the twigs of a winter hedge against a vermilion sunset. The letter bore a date some two years previous to that time, and was signed 'Thomasin Yeobright.' It ran as follows:—

> DEAR DIGGORY VENN,—The question you put when you overtook me coming home from Pond-close gave me such a surprise that I am afraid I did not make you exactly understand what I meant. Of course, if my aunt had not met me I could have explained all then at once, but as it was there was no chance. I have been quite uneasy since, as you know I do not wish to pain you, yet I fear I shall be doing so now in contradicting what I seemed to say then. I cannot, Diggory, marry you, or think of letting you call me your sweetheart. I could not, indeed, Diggory. I hope you will not much mind my saying this, and feel in a great pain. It makes me very sad when I think it may, for I like you very much, and I always put you next to my cousin Clym in my mind. There are so many reasons why we cannot be married that I can hardly name them all in a letter. I did not in the least expect that you were going to speak on such a thing when you followed me, because I had never thought of you in the sense of a lover at all. You must not becall[1] me for laughing when you spoke; you mistook when you thought I laughed at you as a foolish man. I laughed because the idea was so odd, and not at you at all. The great reason with my own personal self for not letting you court me is, that I do not feel the things a woman ought to feel who consents to walk with you with the meaning of being your wife. It is not as you think, that I have another in my mind, for I do not encourage anybody, and never have in my life. Another reason is my aunt. She would not, I know, agree to it, even if I wished to have you. She likes you very well, but she will want me to look a little higher than a small dairy-farmer, and marry a professional man. I hope you will not set your heart against me for writing plainly, but I felt you might try to see me again, and it is better that we should not meet. I shall always think of you as a good man, and be anxious for your well-doing. I send this by Jane Orchard's little maid,—And remain Diggory, your faithful friend, THOMASIN YEOBRIGHT.
>
> TO MR. VENN, DAIRY FARMER.

1. Call someone names.

Since the arrival of that letter, on a certain autumn morning long ago, the reddleman and Thomasin had not met till to-day. During the interval he had shifted his position even further from hers than it had originally been, by adopting the reddle trade; though he was really in very good circumstances still. Indeed, seeing that his expenditure was only one-fourth of his income, he might have been called a prosperous man.

Rejected suitors take to roaming as naturally as unhived bees; and the business to which he had cynically devoted himself was in many ways congenial to Venn. But his wanderings, by mere stress of old emotions, had frequently taken an Egdon direction, though he never intruded upon her who attracted him thither. To be in Thomasin's heath, and near her, yet unseen, was the one ewe-lamb of pleasure left to him.

Then came the incident of that day, and the reddleman, still loving her well, was excited by this accidental service to her at a critical juncture to vow an active devotion to her cause, instead of, as hitherto, sighing and holding aloof. After what had happened it was impossible that he should not doubt the honesty of Wildeve's intentions. But her hope was apparently centered upon him; and dismissing his regrets Venn determined to aid her to be happy in her own chosen way. That this way was, of all others, the most distressing to himself, was awkward enough; but the reddleman's love was generous.

His first active step in watching over Thomasin's interests was taken about seven o'clock the next evening, and was dictated by the news which he had learnt from the sad boy. That Eustacia was somehow the cause of Wildeve's carelessness in relation to the marriage had at once been Venn's conclusion on hearing of the secret meeting between them. It did not occur to his mind that Eustacia's love-signal to Wildeve was the tender effect upon the deserted beauty of the intelligence which her grandfather had brought home. His instinct was to regard her as a conspirator against rather than as an antecedent obstacle to Thomasin's happiness.

During the day he had been exceedingly anxious to learn the condition of Thomasin; but he did not venture to intrude upon a threshold to which he was a stranger, particularly at such an unpleasant moment as this. He had occupied his time in moving with his ponies and load to a new point in the heath, eastward to his previous station; and here he selected a nook with a careful eye to shelter from wind and rain, which seemed to mean that his stay there was to be a comparatively extended one. After this he returned on foot some part of the way that he had come; and, it being now dark, he diverged to the left till he stood behind a holly-bush on the edge of a pit not twenty yards from Rainbarrow.

He watched for a meeting there, but he watched in vain. Nobody except himself came near the spot that night.

But the loss of his labour produced little effect upon the reddleman. He had stood in the shoes of Tantalus,[2] and seemed to look upon a certain mass of disappointment as the natural preface to all realizations, without which preface they would give cause for alarm.

The same hour the next evening found him again at the same place; but Eustacia and Wildeve, the expected trysters, did not appear.

He pursued precisely the same course yet four nights longer, and without success. But on the next, being the day-week of their previous meeting, he saw a female shape floating along the ridge and the outline of a young man ascending from the valley. They met in the little ditch encircling the tumulus—the original excavation from which it had been thrown up by the ancient British people.

The reddleman, stung with suspicion of wrong to Thomasin, was aroused to strategy in a moment. He instantly left the bush and crept forward on his hands and knees. When he had got as close as he might safely venture without discovery he found that, owing to a cross-wind, the conversation of the trysting pair could not be overheard.

Near him, as in divers places about the heath, were areas strewn with large turves, which lay edgeways and upside-down awaiting removal by Timothy Fairway, previous to the winter weather. He took two of these as he lay, and dragged them over him till one covered his head and shoulders, the other his back and legs. The reddleman would now have been quite invisible, even by daylight; the turves, standing upon him with the heather upwards, looked precisely as if they were growing. He crept along again, and the turves upon his back crept with him. Had he approached without any covering the chances are that he would not have been perceived in the dusk; approaching thus, it was as though he burrowed underground. In this manner he came quite close to where the two were standing.

'Wish to consult me on the matter?' reached his ears in the rich, impetuous accents of Eustacia Vye. 'Consult me? It is an indignity to me to talk so: I won't bear it any longer!' She began weeping. 'I have loved you, and have shown you that I loved you, much to my regret; and yet you can come and say in that frigid way that you wish to consult with me whether it would not be better to marry Thomasin. Better—of course it would be. Marry her: she is nearer to your own position in life than I am!'

2. Son of Zeus and the nymph Pluto. For revealing the secrets of the Gods, Tantalus was condemned to stand in water up to his chin, hungry and thirsty, under a tree laden with fruit.

'Yes, yes; that's very well,' said Wildeve peremptorily. 'But we must look at things as they are. Whatever blame may attach to me for having brought it about, Thomasin's position is at present much worse than yours. I simply tell you that I am in a strait.'

'But you shall not tell me! You must see that it is only harassing me. Damon, you have not acted well; you have sunk in my opinion. You have not valued my courtesy—the courtesy of a lady in loving you—who used to think of far more ambitious things. But it was Thomasin's fault. She won you away from me, and she deserves to suffer for it. Where is she staying now? Not that I care, nor where I am myself. Ah, if I were dead and gone how glad she would be! Where is she, I ask?'

'Thomasin is now staying at her aunt's shut up in a bedroom, and keeping out of everybody's sight,' he said indifferently.

'I don't think you care much about her even now,' said Eustacia with sudden joyousness; 'for if you did you wouldn't talk so coolly about her. Do you talk so coolly to her about me? Ah, I expect you do! Why did you originally go away from me? I don't think I can ever forgive you, except on one condition, that whenever you desert me, you come back again, sorry that you served me so.'

'I never wish to desert you.'

'I do not thank you for that. I should hate it to be all smooth. Indeed, I think I like you to desert me a little once now and then. Love is the dismallest thing where the lover is quite honest. O, it is a shame to say so; but it is true!' She indulged in a little laugh. 'My low spirits begin at the very idea. Don't you offer me tame love, or away you go!'

'I wish Tamsie were not such a confoundedly good little woman,' said Wildeve, 'so that I could be faithful to you without injuring a worthy person. It is I who am the sinner after all; I am not worth the little finger of either of you.'

'But you must not sacrifice yourself to her from any sense of justice,' replied Eustacia quickly. 'If you do not love her it is the most merciful thing in the long run to leave her as she is. That's always the best way. There, now I have been unwomanly, I suppose. When you have left me I am always angry with myself for things that I have said to you.'

Wildeve walked a pace or two among the heather without replying. The pause was filled up by the intonation of a pollard thorn[3] a little way to windward, the breezes filtering through its unyielding twigs as through a strainer. It was as if the night sang dirges with clenched teeth.

3. A tree or bush that has been cut back so as to produce a thick growth of young branches.

She continued, half sorrowfully, 'Since meeting you last, it has occurred to me once or twice that perhaps it was not for love of me you did not marry her. Tell me, Damon: I'll try to bear it. Had I nothing whatever to do with the matter?'

'Do you press me to tell?'

'Yes, I must know. I see I have been too ready to believe in my own power.'

'Well, the immediate reason was that the licence would not do for the place, and before I could get another she ran away. Up to that point you had nothing to do with it. Since then her aunt has spoken to me in a tone which I don't at all like.'

'Yes, yes! I am nothing in it—I am nothing in it. You only trifle with me. Heaven, what can I, Eustacia Vye, be made of to think so much of you!'

'Nonsense; do not be so passionate. . . . Eustacia, how we roved among these bushes last year, when the hot days had got cool, and the shades of the hills kept us almost invisible in the hollows!'

She remained in moody silence till she said, 'Yes; and how I used to laugh at you for daring to look up to me! But you have well made me suffer for that since.'

'Yes, you served me cruelly enough until I thought I had found some one fairer than you. A blessed find for me, Eustacia.'

'Do you still think you found somebody fairer?'

'Sometimes I do, sometimes I don't. The scales are balanced so nicely that a feather would turn them.'

'But don't you really care whether I meet you or whether I don't?' she said slowly.

'I care a little, but not enough to break my rest,' replied the young man languidly. 'No, all that's past. I find there are two flowers where I thought there was only one. Perhaps there are three, or four, or any number as good as the first. . . . Mine is a curious fate. Who would have thought that all this could happen to me?'

She interrupted with a suppressed fire of which either love or anger seemed an equally possible issue, 'Do you love me now?'

'Who can say?'

'Tell me; I will know it!'

'I do, and I do not,' said he mischievously. 'That is, I have my times and my seasons. One moment you are too tall, another moment you are too do-nothing, another too melancholy, another too dark, another I don't know what, except—that you are not the whole world to me that you used to be, my dear. But you are a pleasant lady to know, and nice to meet, and I dare say as sweet as ever—almost.'

Eustacia was silent, and she turned from him, till she said, in a voice of suspended mightiness, 'I am for a walk, and this is my way.'

'Well, I can do worse than follow you.'

'You know you can't do otherwise, for all your moods and changes!' she answered defiantly. 'Say what you will; try as you may; keep away from me all that you can—you will never forget me. You will love me all your life long. You would jump to marry me!'

'So I would!' said Wildeve. 'Such strange thoughts as I've had from time to time, Eustacia; and they come to me this moment. You hate the heath as much as ever; that I know.'

'I do,' she murmured deeply. ' 'Tis my cross, my shame, and will be my death!'

'I abhor it too,' said he. 'How mournfully the wind blows round us now!'

She did not answer. Its tone was indeed solemn and pervasive. Compound utterances addressed themselves to their senses, and it was possible to view by ear the features of the neighbourhood. Acoustic pictures were returned from the darkened scenery; they could hear where the tracts of heather began and ended; where the furze was growing stalky and tall; where it had been recently cut; in what direction the fir-clump lay, and how near was the pit in which the hollies grew; for these differing features had their voices no less than their shapes and colours.

'God, how lonely it is!' resumed Wildeve. 'What are picturesque ravines and mists to us who see nothing else? Why should we stay here? Will you go with me to America? I have kindred in Wisconsin.'

'That wants consideration.'

'It seems impossible to do well here, unless one were a wild bird or a landscape-painter. Well?'

'Give me time,' she softly said, talking his hand. 'America is so far away. Are you going to walk with me a little way?'

As Eustacia uttered the latter words she retired from the base of the barrow, and Wildeve followed her, so that the reddleman could hear no more.

He lifted the turves and arose. Their black figures sank and disappeared from against the sky. They were as two horns which the sluggish heath had put forth from its crown, like a mollusc, and had now again drawn in.

The reddleman's walk across the vale, and over into the next where his cart lay, was not sprightly for a slim young fellow of twenty-four. His spirit was perturbed to aching. The breezes that blew around his mouth in that walk carried off upon them the accents of a commination.

He entered the van, where there was a fire in a stove. Without lighting his candle he sat down at once on the three-legged stool, and pondered on what he had seen and heard touching that still loved-one of his. He uttered a sound which was neither sign nor sob, but was even more indicative than either of a troubled mind.

'My Tamsie,' he whispered heavily. 'What can be done? Yes, I will see that Eustacia Vye.'

A Desperate Attempt at Persuasion

X

The next morning, at the time when the height of the sun appeared very insignificant from any part of the heath as compared with the altitude of Rainbarrow, and when all the little hills in the lower levels were like an archipelago[4] in a fog-formed Ægean, the reddleman came from the brambled nook which he had adopted as his quarters and ascended the slopes of Mistover Knap.

Though these shaggy hills were apparently so solitary, several keen round eyes were always ready on such a wintry morning as this to converge upon a passer-by. Feathered species sojourned here in hiding which would have created wonder if found elsewhere. A bustard haunted the spot, and not many years before this five and twenty might have been seen in Egdon at one time. Marsh-harriers looked up from the valley by Wildeve's. A cream-coloured courser[5] had used to visit this hill, a bird so rare that not more than a dozen have ever been seen in England; but a barbarian rested neither night nor day till he had shot the African truant, and after that event cream-coloured coursers thought fit to enter Egdon no more.

A traveller who should walk and observe any of these visitants as Venn observed them now could feel himself to be in direct communication with regions unknown to man. Here in front of him was a wild mallard—just arrived from the home of the north wind. The creature brought within him an amplitude of Northern knowledge. Glacial catastrophes, snowstorm episodes, glittered auroral effects, Polaris in the zenith, Franklin[6] underfoot,—the category of his commonplaces was wonderful. But the bird, like many other philosophers, seemed as he looked at the reddleman to think that a present moment of comfortable reality was worth a decade of memories.

Venn passed on through these towards the house of the isolated

4. Sea containing numerous islands, originally applied to the Aegean Sea between Greece and Asia Minor.

5. A swift-running bird native to northern Africa. A *marsh-harrier* is a kind of falcon; a *bustard* is a large, powerful bird, once the largest in Europe, now almost extinct.

6. Sir John Franklin (1786-1847), English navigator who mapped and explored the Arctic regions. *Polaris* is the North Star. The *zenith* is the point in the sky directly overhead, thought of as the highest point.

beauty who lived up among them and despised them. The day was Sunday; but as going to church, except to be married or buried, was exceptional at Egdon, this made little difference. He had determined upon the bold stroke of asking for an interview with Miss Vye—to attack her position as Thomasin's rival either by art or by storm, showing therein, somewhat too conspicuously, the want of gallantry characteristic of a certain astute sort of men, from clowns to kings. The great Frederick making war on the beautiful Archduchess,[7] Napoleon refusing terms to the beautiful Queen of Prussia,[8] were not more dead to difference of sex than the reddleman was, in his peculiar way, in planning the displacement of Eustacia.

To call at the captain's cottage was always more or less an undertaking for the inferior inhabitants. Though occasionally chatty, his moods were erratic, and nobody could be certain how he would behave at any particular moment. Eustacia was reserved, and lived very much to herself. Except the daughter of one of the cotters, who was their servant, and a lad who worked in the garden and stable, scarcely any one but themselves ever entered the house. They were the only genteel people of the district except the Yeobrights, and though far from rich, they did not feel that necessity for preserving a friendly face towards every man, bird, and beast which influenced their poorer neighbours.

When the reddleman entered the garden the old man was looking through his glass at the stain of blue sea in the distant landscape, the little anchors on his buttons twinkling in the sun. He recognized Venn as his companion on the highway, but made no remark on that circumstance, merely saying, 'Ah, reddleman—you here? Have a glass of grog?'

Venn declined, on the plea of it being too early, and stated that his business was with Miss Vye. The captain surveyed him from cap to waistcoat and from waistcoat to leggings for a few moments, and finally asked him to go indoors.

Miss Vye was not to be seen by anybody just then; and the reddleman waited in the window-bench of the kitchen, his hands hanging across his divergent knees, and his cap hanging from his hands.

'I suppose the young lady is not up yet?' he presently said to the servant.

'Not quite yet. Folks never call upon ladies at this time of day.'

'Then I'll step outside,' said Venn. 'If she is willing to see me, will she please send out word, and I'll come in.'

7. Frederick the Great (1712-1786), Prussian King who took the Austrian territories from Archduchess Maria Theresa. This led to the War of the Austrian Succession in the 1740's.

8. At Tilsit (1807), where the French-Russian-Prussian war was concluded, Napoleon largely dictating the peace terms.

The reddleman left the house and loitered on the hill adjoining. A considerable time elapsed, and no request for his presence was brought. He was beginning to think that his scheme had failed, when he beheld the form of Eustacia herself coming leisurely towards him. A sense of novelty in giving audience to that singular figure had been sufficient to draw her forth.

She seemed to feel, after a bare look at Diggory Venn, that the man had come on a strange errand, and that he was not so mean as she had thought him; for her close approach did not cause him to writhe uneasily, or shift his feet, or show any of those little signs which escape an ingenuous rustic at the advent of the uncommon in womankind. On his inquiring if he might have a conversation with her she replied, 'Yes, walk beside me;' and continued to move on.

Before they had gone far it occurred to the perspicacious reddleman that he would have acted more wisely by appearing less unimpressionable, and he resolved to correct the error as soon as he could find opportunity.

'I have made so bold, miss, as to step across and tell you some strange news which has come to my ears about that man.'

'Ah! what man?'

He jerked his elbow to south-east—the direction of the Quiet Woman.

Eustacia turned quickly to him. 'Do you mean Mr. Wildeve?'

'Yes, there is trouble in a household on account of him, and I have come to let you know of it, because I believe you might have power to drive it away.'

'I? What is the trouble?'

'It is quite a secret. It is that he may refuse to marry Thomasin Yeobright after all.'

Eustacia, though set inwardly pulsing by his words, was equal to her part in such a drama as this. She replied coldly, 'I do not wish to listen to this, and you must not expect me to interfere.'

'But, miss, you will hear one word?'

'I cannot. I am not interested in the marriage, and even if I were I could not compel Mr. Wildeve to do my bidding.'

'As the only lady on the heath I think you might,' said Venn with subtle indirectness. 'This is how the case stands. Mr. Wildeve would marry Thomasin at once, and make all matters smooth, if so be there were not another woman in the case. This other woman is some person he has picked up with, and meets on the heath occasionally, I believe. He will never marry her, and yet through her he may never marry the woman who loves him dearly. Now, if you, miss, who have so much sway over us men-folk, were to insist that he should treat your young neighbour Tamsin with honourable kindness and give up the other woman, he would perhaps do it, and save her a good deal of misery.'

'Ah, my life!' said Eustacia, with a laugh which unclosed her lips so that the sun shone into her mouth as into a tulip, and lent it a similar scarlet fire. 'You think too much of my influence over men-folk indeed, reddleman. If I had such a power as you imagine I would go straight and use it for the good of anybody who has been kind to me—which Thomasin Yeobright has not particularly, to my knowledge.'

'Can it be that you really don't know of it—how much she has always thought of you?'

'I have never heard a word of it. Although we live only two miles apart I have never been inside her aunt's house in my life.'

The superciliousness that lurked in her manner told Venn that thus far he had utterly failed. He inwardly sighed and felt it necessary to unmask his second argument.

'Well, leaving that out of the question, 'tis in your power, I assure you, Miss Vye, to do a great deal of good to another woman.'

She shook her head.

'Your comeliness is law with Mr. Wildeve. It is law with all men who see 'ee. They say, "This well-favoured lady coming—what's her name? How handsome!" Handsomer than Thomasin Yeobright,' the reddleman persisted, saying to himself, 'God forgive a rascal for lying!' And she was handsomer, but the reddleman was far from thinking so. There was a certain obscurity in Eustacia's beauty, and Venn's eye was not trained. In her winter dress, as now, she was like the tiger-beetle, which, when observed in dull situations, seems to be of the quietest neutral colour, but under a full illumination blazes with dazzling splendour.

Eustacia could not help replying, though conscious that she endangered her dignity thereby. 'Many women are lovelier than Thomasin,' she said; 'so not much attaches to that.'

The reddleman suffered the wound and went on: 'He is a man who notices the looks of women, and you could twist him to your will like withywind,[9] if you only had the mind.'

'Surely what she cannot do who has been so much with him I cannot do living up here away from him.'

The reddleman wheeled and looked her in the face. 'Miss Vye!' he said.

'Why do you say that—as if you doubted me?' She spoke faintly, and her breathing was quick. 'The idea of your speaking in that

9. Bindweed, a climbing plant, easily twisted.

tone to me!' she added, with a forced smile of hauteur. 'What could have been in your mind to lead you to speak like that?'

'Miss Vye, why should you make-believe that you don't know this man?—I know why, certainly. He is beneath you, and you are ashamed.'

'You are mistaken. What do you mean?'

The reddleman had decided to play the card of truth. 'I was at the meeting by Rainbarrow last night and heard every word,' he said. 'The woman that stands between Wildeve and Thomasin is yourself.'

It was a disconcerting lift of the curtain, and the mortification of Candaules'[1] wife glowed in her. The moment had arrived when her lip would tremble in spite of herself, and when the gasp could no longer be kept down.

'I am unwell,' she said hurridly. 'No—it's not that—I am not in a humour to hear you further. Leave me, please.'

'I must speak, Miss Vye, in spite of paining you. What I would put before you is this. However it may come about—whether she is to blame, or you—her case is without doubt worse than yours. Your giving up Mr. Wildeve will be a real advantage to you, for how could you marry him? Now she cannot get off so easily—everybody will blame her if she loses him. Then I ask you—not because her right is best, but because her situation is worst—to give him up to her.'

'No—I won't, I won't!' she said impetuously, quite forgetful of her previous manner towards the reddleman as an underling. 'Nobody has ever been served so! It was going on well—I will not be beaten down—by an inferior woman like her. It is very well for you to come and plead for her, but is she not herself the cause of all her own trouble? Am I not to show favour to any person I may choose without asking permission of a parcel of cottagers? She has come between me and my inclination, and now that she finds herself rightly punished she gets you to plead for her!'

'Indeed,' said Venn earnestly, 'she knows nothing whatever about it. It is only I who ask you to give him up. It will be better for her and you both. People will say bad things if they find out that a lady secretly meets a man who has ill-used another woman.'

'I have *not* injured her: he was mine before he was hers! He came back—because—because he liked me best!' she said wildly. 'But I lose all self-respect in talking to you. What am I giving way to!'

1. Candaules was the King of Lydia who lost his throne and life in 718 B.C. According to Herodotus, Candaules bragged of his Queen's beauty to Gyges and secretly brought him into her chamber to prove his point. Indignant, the Queen incited Gyges to kill Candaules.

'I can keep secrets,' said Venn gently. 'You need not fear. I am the only man who knows of your meetings with him. There is but one thing more to speak of, and then I will be gone. I heard you say to him that you hated living here—that Egdon heath was a jail to you.'

'I did say so. There is a sort of beauty in the scenery, I know; but it is a jail to me. The man you mention does not save me from that feeling, though he lives here. I should have cared nothing for him had there been a better person near.'

The reddleman looked hopeful: after these words from her his third attempt seemed promising. 'As we have now opened our minds a bit, miss,' he said, 'I'll tell you what I have got to propose. Since I have taken to the reddle trade I travel a good deal, as you know.'

She inclined her head, and swept round so that her eyes rested in the misty vale beneath them.

'And in my travels I go near Budmouth. Now Budmouth is a wonderful place—wonderful—a great salt sheening sea bending into the land like a bow—thousands of gentlepeople walking up and down—bands of music playing—officers by sea and officers by land walking among the rest—out of every ten folk you meet nine of 'em in love.'

'I know it,' she said disdainfully. 'I know Budmouth better than you. I was born there. My father came to be a military musician there from abroad. Ah, my soul, Budmouth! I wish I was there now.'

The reddleman was surprised to see how a slow fire could blaze on occasion. 'If you were, miss,' he replied, 'in a week's time you would think no more of Wildeve than of one of those he'th-croppers that we see yond. Now, I could get you there.'

'How?' said Eustacia, with intense curiosity in her heavy eyes.

'My uncle has been for five and twenty years the trusty man of a rich widow-lady who has a beautiful house facing the sea. This lady has become old and lame, and she wants a young company-keeper to read and sing to her, but can't get one to her mind to save her life, though she've advertised in the papers, and tried half a dozen. She would jump to get you, and uncle would make it all easy.'

'I should have to work, perhaps?'

'No, not real work: you'd have a little to do, such as reading and that. You would not be wanted till New Year's Day.'

'I knew it meant work,' she said, drooping to languor again.

'I confess there would be a trifle to do in the way of amusing her; but though idle people might call it work, working people would call it play. Think of the company and the life you'd lead, miss; the gaiety you'd see, and the gentleman you'd marry. My uncle is to inquire for a trustworthy young lady from the country, as she don't like town girls.'

'It is to wear myself out to please her! and I won't go. O, if I could live in a gay town as a lady should, and go my own ways, and do my own doings, I'd give the wrinkled half of my life! Yes, reddleman, that would I.'

'Help me to get Thomasin happy, miss, and the chance shall be yours,' urged her companion.

'Chance—'tis no chance,' she said proudly. 'What can a poor man like you offer me, indeed?—I am going indoors. I have nothing more to say. Don't your horses want feeding, or your reddlebags want mending, or don't you want to find buyers for your goods, that you stay idling here like this?'

Venn spoke not another word. With his hands behind him he turned away, that she might not see the hopeless disappointment in his face. The mental clearness and power he had found in this lonely girl had indeed filled his manner with misgiving even from the first few minutes of close quarters with her. Her youth and situation had led him to expect a simplicity quite at the beck of his method. But a system of inducement which might have carried weaker country lasses along with it had merely repelled Eustacia. As a rule, the word Budmouth meant fascination on Egdon. That Royal port and watering-place, if truly mirrored in the minds of the heath-folk, must have combined, in a charming and indescribable manner, a Carthaginian bustle of building with Tarentine luxuriousness and Baian[2] health and beauty. Eustacia felt little less extravagantly about the place; but she would not sink her independence to get there.

When Diggory Venn had gone quite away, Eustacia walked to the bank and looked down the wild and picturesque vale towards the sun, which was also in the direction of Wildeve's. The mist had now so far collapsed that the tips of the trees and bushes around his house could just be discerned, as if boring upwards through a vast white cobweb which cloaked them from the day. There was no doubt that her mind was inclined thitherward; indefinitely, fancifully—twining and untwining about him as the single object within her horizon on which dreams might crystallize. The man who had begun by being merely her amusement, and would never have been more than her hobby but for his skill in deserting her at the right moments, was now again her desire. Cessation in his love-making had revivified her love. Such feeling as Eustacia had

2. Baia (now known as Baja), about 12 miles from Naples, a summer resort for wealthy Romans, famous for its baths. *Tarentine* refers to Taranto, a seaport in Southeast Italy, center of luxury in the third and fourth centuries B.C. *Carthage* is a city on Africa's Mediterranean coast, center of commerce and culture between 500 and 150 B.C.

idly given to Wildeve was dammed into a flood by Thomasin. She had used to tease Wildeve, but that was before another had favoured him. Often a drop of irony into an indifferent situation renders the whole piquant.

'I will never give him up—never!' she said impetuously.

The reddleman's hint that rumour might show her to disadvantage had no permanent terror for Eustacia. She was as unconcerned at that contingency as a goddess at a lack of linen. This did not originate in inherent shamelessness, but in her living too far from the world to feel the impact of public opinion. Zenobia[3] in the desert could hardly have cared what was said about her at Rome. As far as social ethics were concerned Eustacia approached the savage state, though in emotion she was all the while an epicure. She had advanced to the secret recesses of sensuousness, yet had hardly crossed the threshold of conventionality.

The Dishonesty of an Honest Woman

XI

The reddleman had left Eustacia's presence with desponding views on Thomasin's future happiness; but he was awakened to the fact that one channel remained untried by seeing, as he followed the way to his van, the form of Mrs. Yeobright slowly walking towards the Quiet Woman. He went across to her; and could almost perceive in her anxious face that this journey of hers to Wildeve was undertaken with the same object as his own to Eustacia.

She did not conceal the fact. 'Then,' said the reddleman, 'you may as well leave it alone, Mrs. Yeobright.'

'I half think so myself,' she said. 'But nothing else remains to be done besides pressing the question upon him.'

'I should like to say a word first,' said Venn firmly. 'Mr. Wildeve is not the only man who has asked Thomasin to marry him; and why should not another have a chance? Mrs. Yeobright, I should be glad to marry your niece, and would have done it any time these last two years. There, now it is out, and I have never told anybody before but herself.'

Mrs. Yeobright was not demonstrative, but her eyes involuntarily glanced towards his singular though shapely figure.

'Looks are not everything,' said the reddleman, noticing the glance. 'There's many a calling that don't bring in so much as mine, if it comes to money; and perhaps I am not so much worse off than Wildeve. There is nobody so poor as these professional fel-

3. Queen of Palmyra in Syria in the third century A.D., she was conquered in war by Aurelian. Her life spared, she established a prosperous and cultured kingdom in the desert.

lows who have failed; and if you shouldn't like my redness—well, I am not red by birth, you know; I only took to this business for a freak; and I might turn my hand to something else in good time.'

'I am much obliged to you for your interest in my niece; but I fear there would be objections. More than that, she is devoted to this man.'

'True; or I shouldn't have done what I have this morning.'

'Otherwise there would be no pain in the case, and you would not see me going to his house now. What was Thomasin's answer when you told her of your feelings?'

'She wrote that you would object to me; and other things.'

'She was in a measure right. You must not take this unkindly: I merely state it as a truth. You have been good to her, and we do not forget it. But as she was unwilling on her own account to be your wife, that settles the point without my wishes being concerned.'

'Yes. But there is a difference between then and now, ma'am. She is distressed now, and I have thought that if you were to talk to her about me, and think favourably of me yourself, there might be a chance of winning her round, and getting her quite independent of this Wildeve's backward and forward play, and his not knowing whether he'll have her or no.'

Mrs. Yeobright shook her head. 'Thomasin thinks, and I think with her, that she ought to be Wildeve's wife, if she means to appear before the world without a slur upon her name. If they marry soon, everybody will believe that an accident did really prevent the wedding. If not, it may cast a shade upon her character—at any rate make her ridiculous. In short, if it is anyhow possible they must marry now.'

'I thought that till half an hour ago. But, after all, why should her going off with him to Anglebury for a few hours do her any harm? Anybody who knows how pure she is will feel any such thought to be quite unjust. I have been trying this morning to help on this marriage with Wildeve—yes, I, ma'am—in the belief that I ought to do it, because she was so wrapped up in him. But I much question if I was right, after all. However, nothing came of it. And now I offer myself.'

Mrs. Yeobright appeared disinclined to enter further into the question. 'I fear I must go on,' she said. 'I do not see that anything else can be done.'

And she went on. But though this conversation did not divert Thomasin's aunt from her purposed interview with Wildeve, it made a considerable difference in her mode of conducting that interview. She thanked God for the weapon which the reddleman had put into her hands.

Wildeve was at home when she reached the inn. He showed her silently into the parlour, and closed the door. Mrs. Yeobright began—

'I have thought it my duty to call to-day. A new proposal has been made to me, which has rather astonished me. It will affect Thomasin greatly; and I have decided that it should at least be mentioned to you.'

'Yes? What is it?' he said civilly.

'It is, of course, in reference to her future. You may not be aware that another man has shown himself anxious to marry Thomasin. Now, though I have not encouraged him yet, I cannot conscientiously refuse him a chance any longer. I don't wish to be short with you; but I must be fair to him and to her.'

'Who is the man?' said Wildeve with surprise.

'One who has been in love with her longer than she has with you. He proposed to her two years ago. At that time she refused him.'

'Well?'

'He has seen her lately, and has asked me for permission to pay his addresses to her. She may not refuse him twice.'

'What is his name?'

Mrs. Yeobright declined to say. 'He is a man Thomasin likes,' she added, 'and one whose constancy she respects at least. It seems to me that what she refused then she would be glad to get now. She is much annoyed at her awkward position.'

'She never once told me of this old lover.'

'The gentlest women are not such fools as to show *every* card.'

'Well, if she wants him I suppose she must have him.'

'It is easy enough to say that; but you don't see the difficulty. He wants her much more than she wants him; and before I can encourage anything of the sort I must have a clear understanding from you that you will not interfere to injure an arrangement which I promote in the belief that it is for the best. Suppose, when they are engaged, and everything is smoothly arranged for their marriage, that you should step between them and renew your suit? You might not win her back, but you might cause much unhappiness.'

'Of course I should do no such thing,' said Wildeve. 'But they are not engaged yet. How do you know that Thomasin would accept him?'

'That's a question I have carefully put to myself; and upon the whole the probabilities are in favour of her accepting him in time. I flatter myself that I have some influence over her. She is pliable, and I can be strong in my recommendations of him.'

'And in your disparagement of me at the same time.'

'Well, you may depend upon my not praising you,' she said drily. 'And if this seems like manoeuvring, you must remember that her position is peculiar, and that she has been hardly used. I shall also be helped in making the match by her own desire to escape from the humiliation of her present state; and a woman's pride in these cases will lead her a very great way. A little managing may be required to bring her round; but I am equal to that, provided that you agree to the one thing indispensable; that is, to make a distinct declaration that she is to think no more of you as a possible husband. That will pique her into accepting him.'

'I can hardly say that just now, Mrs. Yeobright. It is so sudden.'

'And so my whole plan is interfered with! It is very inconvenient that you refuse to help my family even to the small extent of saying distinctly you will have nothing to do with us.'

Wildeve reflected uncomfortably. 'I confess I was not prepared for this,' he said. 'Of course I'll give her up if you wish, if it is necessary. But I thought I might be her husband.'

'We have heard that before.'

'Now, Mrs. Yeobright, don't let us disagree. Give me a fair time. I don't want to stand in the way of any better chance she may have; only I wish you had let me know earlier. I will write to you or call in a day or two. Will that suffice?'

'Yes,' she replied, 'provided you promise not to communicate with Thomasin without my knowledge.'

'I promise that,' he said. And the interview then terminated, Mrs. Yeobright returning homeward as she had come.

By far the greatest effect of her simple strategy on that day was, as often happens, in a quarter quite outside her view when arranging it. In the first place, her visit sent Wildeve the same evening after dark to Eustacia's house at Mistover.

At this hour the lonely dwelling was closely blinded and shuttered from the chill and darkness without. Wildeve's clandestine plan with her was to take a little gravel in his hand and hold it to the crevice at the top of the window-shutter, which was on the outside, so that it should fall with a gentle rustle, resembling that of a mouse, between shutter and glass. This precaution in attracting her attention was to avoid arousing the suspicions of her grandfather.

The soft words, 'I hear; wait for me,' in Eustacia's voice from within told him that she was alone.

He waited in his customary manner by walking round the enclosure and idling by the pool, for Wildeve was never asked into the house by his proud though condescending mistress. She showed no sign of coming out in a hurry. The time wore on, and he began to grow impatient. In the course of twenty minutes she appeared from round the corner, and advanced as if merely taking an airing.

'You would not have kept me so long had you known what I come about,' he said with bitterness. 'Still, you are worth waiting for.'

'What has happened?' said Eustacia. 'I did not know you were in trouble. I too am gloomy enough.'

'I am not in trouble,' said he. 'It is merely that affairs have come to a head, and I must take a clear course.'

'What course is that?' she asked with attentive interest.

'And can you forget so soon what I proposed to you the other night? Why, take you from this place, and carry you away with me abroad.'

'I have not forgotten. But why have you come so unexpectedly to repeat the question, when you only promised to come next Saturday? I thought I was to have plenty of time to consider.'

'Yes, but the situation is different now.'

'Explain to me.'

'I don't want to explain, for I may pain you.'

'But I must know the reason of this hurry.'

'It is simply my ardour, dear Eustacia. Everything is smooth now.'

'Then why are you so ruffled?'

'I am not aware of it. All is as it should be. Mrs. Yeobright—but she is nothing to us.'

'Ah, I knew she had something to do with it! Come, I don't like reserve.'

'No—she has nothing. She only says she wishes me to give up Thomasin because another man is anxious to marry her. The woman, now she no longer needs me, actually shows off!' Wildeve's vexation had escaped him in spite of himself.

Eustacia was silent a long while. 'You are in the awkward position of an official who is no longer wanted,' she said in a changed tone.

'It seems so. But I have not yet seen Thomasin.'

'And that irritates you. Don't deny it, Damon. You are actually nettled by this slight from an unexpected quarter.'

'Well?'

'And you come to get me because you cannot get her. This is certainly a new position altogether. I am to be a stop-gap.'

'Please remember that I proposed the same thing the other day.'

Eustacia again remained in a sort of stupefied silence. What curious feeling was this coming over her? Was it really possible that her interest in Wildeve had been so entirely the result of antagonism that the glory and the dream departed from the man with the first sound that he was no longer coveted by her rival? She was, then, secure of him at last. Thomasin no longer required him.

What a humiliating victory! He loved her best, she thought; and yet—dared she to murmur such treacherous criticism ever so softly?—what was the man worth whom a woman inferior to her self did not value? The sentiment which lurks more or less in all animate nature—that of not desiring the undesired of others—was lively as a passion in the supersubtle, epicurean heart of Eustacia. Her social superiority over him, which hitherto had scarcely ever impressed her, became unpleasantly insistent, and for the first time she felt that she had stooped in loving him.

'Well, darling, you agree?' said Wildeve.

'If it could be London, or even Budmouth, instead of America,' she murmured languidly. 'Well, I will think. It is too great a thing for me to decide off-hand. I wish I hated the heath less—or loved you more.'

'You can be painfully frank. You loved me a month ago warmly enough to go anywhere with me.'

'And you loved Thomasin.'

'Yes, perhaps that was where the reason lay,' he returned, with almost a sneer. 'I don't hate her now.'

'Exactly. The only thing is that you can no longer get her.'

'Come—no taunts, Eustacia, or we shall quarrel. If you don't agree to go with me, and agree shortly, I shall go by myself.'

'Or try Thomasin again. Damon, how strange it seems that you could have married her or me indifferently, and only have come to me because I am—cheapest! Yes, yes—it is true. There was a time when I should have exclaimed against a man of that sort, and been quite wild; but it is all past now.'

'Will you go, dearest? Come secretly with me to Bristol, marry me, and turn our backs upon this dog-hole of England for ever? Say Yes.'

'I want to get away from here at almost any cost,' she said with weariness, 'but I don't like to go with you. Give me more time to decide.'

'I have already,' said Wildeve. 'Well, I give you one more week.'

'A little longer, so that I may tell you decisively. I have to consider so many things. Fancy Thomasin being anxious to get rid of you! I cannot forget it.'

'Never mind that. Say Monday week. I will be here precisely at this time.'

'Let it be at Rainbarrow,' said she. 'This is too near home; my grandfather may be walking out.'

'Thank you, dear. On Monday week at this time I will be at the Barrow. Till then good-bye.'

'Good-bye. No, no, you must not touch me now. Shaking hands is enough till I have made up my mind.'

Eustacia watched his shadowy form till it had disappeared. She placed her hand to her forehead and breathed heavily; and then her rich, romantic lips parted under that homely impulse—a yawn. She was immediately angry at having betrayed even to herself the possible evanescence of her passion for him. She could not admit at once that she might have over-estimated Wildeve, for to perceive his mediocrity now was to admit her own great folly heretofore. And the discovery that she was the owner of a disposition so purely that of the dog in the manger, had something in it which at first made her ashamed.

The fruit of Mrs. Yeobright's diplomacy was indeed remarkable, though not as yet of the kind she had anticipated. It had appreciably influenced Wildeve, but it was influencing Eustacia far more. Her lover was no longer to her an exciting man whom many women strove for, and herself could only retain by striving with them. He was a superfluity.

She went indoors in that peculiar state of misery which is not exactly grief, and which especially attends the dawnings of reason in the latter days of an ill-judged, transient love. To be conscious that the end of the dream is approaching, and yet has not absolutely come, is one of the most wearisome as well as the most curious stages along the course between the beginning of a passion and its end.

Her grandfather had returned, and was busily engaged in pouring some gallons of newly arrived rum into the square bottles of his square cellaret. Whenever these home supplies were exhausted he would go to the Quiet Woman, and, standing with his back to the fire, grog in hand, tell remarkable stories of how he had lived seven years under the water-line of his ship, and other naval wonders, to the natives, who hoped too earnestly for a treat of ale from the teller to exhibit any doubts of his truth.

He had been there this evening. 'I suppose you have heard the Egdon news, Eustacia?' he said, without looking up from the bottles. 'The men have been talking about it at the Woman as if it were of national importance.'

'I have heard none,' she said.

'Young Clym Yeobright, as they call him, is coming home next week to spend Christmas with his mother. He is a fine fellow by this time, it seems. I suppose you remember him?'

'I never saw him in my life.'

'Ah, true; he left before you came here. I well remember him as a promising boy.'

'Where has he been living all these years?'

'In that rookery of pomp and vanity, Paris, I believe.'

BOOK SECOND: THE ARRIVAL

Tidings of the Comer

I

On fine days at this time of the year, and earlier, certain ephemeral operations were apt to disturb, in their trifling way, the majestic calm of Egdon Heath. They were activities which, beside those of a town, a village, or even a farm, would have appeared as the ferment of stagnation merely, a creeping of the flesh of somnolence. But here, away from comparisons, shut in by the stable hills, among which mere walking had the novelty of pageantry, and where any man could imagine himself to be Adam without the least difficulty, they attracted the attention of every bird within eyeshot, every reptile not yet asleep, and set the surrounding rabbits curiously watching from hillocks at a safe distance.

The performance was that of bringing together and building into a stack the furze-faggots which Humphrey had been cutting for the captain's use during the foregoing fine days. The stack was at the end of the dwelling, and the men engaged in building it were Humphrey and Sam, the old man looking on.

It was a fine and quiet afternoon, about three o'clock; but the winter solstice having stealthily come on, the lowness of the sun caused the hour to seem later than it actually was, there being little here to remind an inhabitant that he must unlearn his summer experience of the sky as a dial. In the course of many days and weeks sunrise had advanced its quarters from north-east to south-east, sunset had receded from north-west to south-west; but Egdon had hardly heeded the change.

Eustacia was indoors in the dining-room, which was really more like a kitchen, having a stone floor and a gaping chimney-corner. The air was still, and while she lingered a moment here alone sounds of voices in conversation came to her ears directly down the chimney. She entered the recess, and, listening, looked up the old irregular shaft, with its cavernous hollows, where the smoke blundered about on its way to the square bit of sky at the top, from which the daylight struck down with a pallid glare upon the tatters of soot draping the flue as sea-weed drapes a rocky fissure.

She remembered: the furze-stack was not far from the chimney, and the voices were those of the workers.

Her grandfather joined in the conversation. 'That lad ought never to have left home. His father's occupation would have suited him best, and the boy should have followed on. I don't believe in these new moves in families. My father was a sailor, so was I, and so should my son have been if I had had one.'

'The place he's been living at is Paris,' said Humphrey, 'and they tell me 'tis where the king's head was cut off years ago. My poor mother used to tell me about that business. "Hummy," she used to say, "I was a young maid then, and as I was at home ironing mother's caps one afternoon the parson came in and said, 'They've cut the king's head off, Jane; and what 'twill be next God knows.' " '

'A good many of us knew as well as He before long,' said the captain, chuckling. 'I lived seven years under water on account of it in my boyhood—in that damned surgery of the *Triumph*, seeing men brought down to the cockpit with their legs and arms blown to Jericho. . . . And so the young man has settled in Paris. Manager to a diamond merchant, or some such thing, is he not?'

'Yes, sir, that's it. 'Tis a blazing great business that he belongs to, so I've heard his mother say—like a king's palace, as far as diments go.'

'I can well mind when he left home,' said Sam.

' 'Tis a good thing for the feller,' said Humphrey. 'A sight of times better to be selling diments than nobbling[1] about here.'

'It must cost a good few shillings to deal at such a place.'

'A good few indeed, my man,' replied the captain. 'Yes, you may make away with a deal of money and be neither drunkard nor glutton.'

'They say, too, that Clym Yeobright is become a real perusing man, with the strangest notions about things. There, that's because he went to school early, such as the school was.'

'Strange notions, has he?' said the old man. 'Ah, there's too much of that sending to school in these days! It only does harm. Every gatepost and barn's door you come to is sure to have some bad word or other chalked upon it by the young rascals: a woman can hardly pass for shame some times. If they'd never been taught how to write they wouldn't have been able to scribble such villainy. Their fathers couldn't do it, and the country was all the better for it.'

'Now, I should think, cap'n, that Miss Eustacia had about as much in her head that comes from books as anybody about here?'

'Perhaps if Miss Eustacia, too, had less romantic nonsense in her head it would be better for her,' said the captain shortly; after which he walked away.

'I say, Sam,' observed Humphrey when the old man was gone, 'she and Clym Yeobright would make a very pretty pigeon-pair—hey? If they wouldn't I'll be dazed! Both of one mind about niceties for certain, and learned in print, and always thinking about

1. Dialect expression for *idling*, comes from nobbling or hobbling (i.e., laming or tampering with horses).

high doctrine—there couldn't be a better couple if they were made o' purpose. Clym's family is as good as hers. His father was a farmer, that's true; but his mother was a sort of lady, as we know. Nothing would please me better than to see them two man and wife.'

'They'd look very natty, arm-in-crook together, and their best clothes on, whether or no, if he's at all the well-favoured fellow he used to be.'

'They would, Humphrey. Well, I should like to see the chap terrible much after so many years. If I knew for certain when he was coming I'd stroll out three or four miles to meet him and help carry anything for'n; though I suppose he's altered from the boy he was. They say he can talk French as fast as a maid can eat blackberries; and if so, depend upon it we who have stayed at home shall seem no more than scroff in his eyes.'

'Coming across the water to Budmouth by steamer, isn't he?'

'Yes; but how he's coming from Budmouth I don't know.'

'That's a bad trouble about his cousin Thomasin. I wonder such a nice-notioned fellow as Clym likes to come home into it. What a nunnywatch we were in, to be sure, when we heard they weren't married at all, after singing to 'em as man and wife that night! Be dazed if I should like a relation of mine to have been made such a fool of by a man. It makes the family look small.'

'Yes. Poor maid, her heart has ached enough about it. Her health is suffering from it, I hear, for she will bide entirely indoors. We never see her out now, scampering over the furze with a face as red as a rose, as she used to do.'

'I've heard she wouldn't have Wildeve now if he asked her.'

'You have? 'Tis news to me.'

While the furze-gatherers had desultorily conversed thus Eustacia's face gradually bent to the hearth in a profound reverie, her toe unconsciously tapping the dry turf which lay burning at her feet.

The subject of their discourse had been keenly interesting to her. A young and clever man was coming into that lonely heath from, of all contrasting places in the world, Paris. It was like a man coming from heaven. More singular still, the heathmen had instinctively coupled her and this man together in their minds as a pair born for each other.

That five minutes of overhearing furnished Eustacia with visions enough to fill the whole blank afternoon. Such sudden alternations from mental vacuity do sometimes occur thus quietly. She could never have believed in the morning that her colourless inner world would before night become as animated as water under a microscope, and that without the arrival of a single visitor. The words of Sam and Humphrey on the harmony between the unknown and herself had on her mind the effect of the invading Bard's prelude in the 'Castle of Indolence,'[2] at which myriads of imprisoned shapes arose where had previously appeared the stillness of a void.

Involved in these imaginings she knew nothing of time. When she became conscious of externals it was dusk. The furze-rick was finished; the men had gone home. Eustacia went upstairs, thinking that she would take a walk at this her usual time; and she determined that her walk should be in the direction of Blooms-End, the birthplace of young Yeobright and the present home of his mother. She had no reason for walking elsewhere, and why should she not go that way? The scene of a day-dream is sufficient for a pilgrimage at nineteen. To look at the palings before the Yeobright's house had the dignity of a necessary performance. Strange that such a piece of idling should have seemed an important errand.

She put on her bonnet, and, leaving the house, descended the hill on the side towards Blooms-End, where she walked slowly along the valley for a distance of a mile and a half. This brought her to a spot in which the green bottom of the dale began to widen, the furze bushes to recede yet further from the path on each side, till they were diminished to an isolated one here and there by the increasing fertility of the soil. Beyond the irregular carpet of grass was a row of white palings, which marked the verge of the heath in this latitude. They showed upon the dusky scene that they bordered as distinctly as white lace on velvet. Behind the white palings was a little garden; behind the garden an old, irregular, thatched house, facing the heath, and commanding a full view of the valley. This was the obscure, removed spot to which was about to return a man whose latter life had been passed in the French capital—the centre and vortex of the fashionable world.

The People at Blooms-End Make Ready

II

All that afternoon the expected arrival of the subject of Eustacia's ruminations created a bustle of preparation at Blooms-End. Thomasin had been persuaded by her aunt, and by an instinctive impulse of loyalty towards her cousin Clym, to bestir herself on his account with an alacrity unusual in her during these most sorrowful days of her life. At the time that Eustacia was listening to the rick-maker's conversation on Clym's return, Thomasin was climbing into a loft over her aunt's fuel-house, where the store-apples were kept, to search out the best and largest of them for the coming holiday-time.

2. The invading Bard is a character in James Thomson's (1700-1748) long allegorical poem *The Castle of Indolence* (1748).

The loft was lighted by a semicircular hole, through which the pigeons crept to their lodgings in the same high quarters of the premises; and from this hole the sun shone in a bright yellow patch upon the figure of the maiden as she knelt and plunged her naked arms into the soft brown fern, which, from its abundance, was used on Egdon in packing away stores of all kinds. The pigeons were flying about her head with the greatest unconcern, and the face of her aunt was just visible above the floor of the loft, lit by a few stray motes of light, as she stood half-way up the ladder, looking at a spot into which she was not climber enough to venture.

'Now a few russets, Tamsin. He used to like them almost as well as ribstones.'

Thomasin turned and rolled aside the fern from another nook, where more mellow fruit greeted her with its ripe smell. Before picking them out she stopped a moment.

'Dear Clym, I wonder how your face looks now?' she said, gazing abstractedly at the pigeon-hole, which admitted the sunlight so directly upon her brown hair and transparent tissues that it almost seemed to shine through her.

'If he could have been dear to you in another way,' said Mrs. Yeobright from the ladder, 'this might have been a happy meeting.'

'Is there any use in saying what can do no good, aunt?'

'Yes,' said her aunt, with some warmth. 'To thoroughly fill the air with the past misfortune, so that other girls may take warning and keep clear of it.'

Thomasin lowered her face to the apples again. 'I am a warning to others, just as thieves and drunkards and gamblers are,' she said in a low voice. 'What a class to belong to! Do I really belong to them? 'Tis absurd! Yet why, aunt, does everybody keep on making me think that I do, by the way they behave towards me? Why don't people judge me by my acts? Now, look at me as I kneel here, picking up these apples—do I look like a lost woman? . . . I wish all good women were as good as I!' she added vehemently.

'Strangers don't see you as I do,' said Mrs. Yeobright; 'they judge from false report. Well, it is a silly job, and I am partly to blame.'

'How quickly a rash thing can be done!' replied the girl. Her lips were quivering, and tears so crowded themselves into her eyes that she could hardly distinguish apples from fern as she continued industriously searching to hide her weakness.

'As soon as you have finished getting the apples,' her aunt said, descending the ladder, 'come down, and we'll go for the holly. There is nobody on the heath this afternoon, and you need not fear being stared at. We must get some berries, or Clym will never believe in our preparations.'

Thomasin came down when the apples were collected, and

together they went through the white palings to the heath beyond. The open hills were airy and clear, and the remote atmosphere appeared, as it often appears on a fine winter day, in distinct planes of illumination independently toned, the rays which lit the nearer tracts of landscape streaming visibly across those further off; a stratum of ensaffroned light was imposed on a stratum of deep blue, and behind these lay still remoter scenes wrapped in frigid grey.

They reached the place where the hollies grew, which was in a conical pit, so that the tops of the trees were not much above the general level of the ground. Thomasin stepped up into a fork of one of the bushes, as she had done under happier circumstances on many similar occasions, and with a small chopper that they had brought she began to lop off the heavily-berried boughs.

'Don't scratch your face,' said her aunt, who stood at the edge of the pit, regarding the girl as she held on amid the glistening green and scarlet masses of the tree. 'Will you walk with me to meet him this evening?'

'I should like to. Else it would seem as if I had forgotten him,' said Thomasin, tossing out a bough. 'Not that that would matter much; I belong to one man; nothing can alter that. And that man I must marry, for my pride's sake.'

'I am afraid——' began Mrs. Yeobright.

'Ah, you think, "That weak girl—how is she going to get a man to marry her when she chooses?" But let me tell you one thing, aunt: Mr. Wildeve is not a profligate man, any more than I am an improper woman. He has an unfortunate manner, and doesn't try to make people like him if they don't wish to do it of their own accord.'

'Thomasin,' said Mrs. Yeobright quietly, fixing her eye upon her niece, 'do you think you deceive me in your defence of Mr. Wildeve?'

'How do you mean?'

'I have long had a suspicion that your love for him has changed its colour since you have found him not to be the saint you thought him, and that you act a part to me.'

'He wished to marry me, and I wish to marry him.'

'Now, I put it to you: would you at this present moment agree to be his wife if that had not happened to entangle you with him?'

Thomasin looked into the tree and appeared much disturbed. 'Aunt,' she said presently, 'I have, I think, a right to refuse to answer that question.'

'Yes, you have.'

'You may think what you choose. I have never implied to you by word or deed that I have grown to think otherwise of him, and I never will. And I shall marry him.'

'Well, wait till he repeats his offer. I think he may do it, now that hé knows—something I told him. I don't for a moment dispute that it is the most proper thing for you to marry him. Much as I have objected to him in bygone days, I agree with you now, you may be sure. It is the only way out of a false position, and a very galling one.'

'What did you tell him?'

'That he was standing in the way of another lover of yours.'

'Aunt,' said Thomasin, with round eyes, 'what do you mean?'

'Don't be alarmed; it was my duty. I can say no more about it now, but when it is over I will tell you exactly what I said, and why I said it.'

Thomasin was perforce content.

'And you will keep the secret of my would-be marriage from Clym for the present?' she next asked.

'I have given my word to. But what is the use of it? He must soon know what has happened. A mere look at your face will show him that something is wrong.'

Thomasin turned and regarded her aunt from the tree. 'Now, hearken to me,' she said, her delicate voice expanding into firmness by a force which was other than physical. 'Tell him nothing. If he finds out that I am not worthy to be his cousin, let him. But, since he loved me once, we will not pain him by telling him my trouble too soon. The air is full of the story, I know; but gossips will not dare to speak of it to him for the first few days. His closeness to me is the very thing that will hinder the tale from reaching him early. If I am not made safe from sneers in a week or two I will tell him myself.'

The earnestness with which Thomasin spoke prevented further objections. Her aunt simply said, 'Very well. He should by rights have been told at the time that the wedding was going to be. He will never forgive you for your secrecy.'

'Yes, he will, when he knows it was because I wished to spare him, and that I did not expect him home so soon. And you must not let me stand in the way of your Christmas party. Putting it off would only make matters worse.'

'Of course I shall not. I do not wish to show myself beaten before all Egdon, and the sport of a man like Wildeve. We have enough berries now, I think, and we had better take them home. By the time we have decked the house with this and hung up the mistletoe, we must think of starting to meet him.'

Thomasin came out of the tree, shook from her hair and dress the loose berries which had fallen thereon, and went down the hill with her aunt, each woman bearing half the gathered boughs. It was now nearly four o'clock, and the sunlight was leaving the vales.

When the west grew red the two relatives came again from the house and plunged into the heath in a different direction from the first, towards a point in the distant highway along which the expected man was to return.

How a Little Sound Produced a Great Dream

III

Eustacia stood just within the heath, straining her eyes in the direction of Mrs. Yeobright's house and premises. No light, sound, or movement was perceptible there. The evening was chilly; the spot was dark and lonely. She inferred that the guest had not yet come; and after lingering ten or fifteen minutes she turned again towards home.

She had not far retraced her steps when sounds in front of her betokened the approach of persons in conversation along the same path. Soon their heads became visible against the sky. They were walking slowly; and though it was too dark for much discovery of character from aspect, the gait of them showed that they were not workers on the heath. Eustacia stepped a little out of the foot-track to let them pass. They were two women and a man; and the voices of the women were those of Mrs. Yeobright and Thomasin.

They went by her, and at the moment of passing appeared to discern her dusky form. There came to her ears in a masculine voice, 'Good night!'

She murmured a reply, glided by them, and turned round. She could not, for a moment, believe that chance, unrequested, had brought into her presence the soul of the house she had gone to inspect, the man without whom her inspection would not have been thought of.

She strained her eyes to see them, but was unable. Such was her intentness, however, that it seemed as if her ears were performing the functions of seeing as well as hearing. This extension of power can almost be believed in at such moments. The deaf Dr. Kitto[3] was probably under the influence of a parallel fancy when he described his body as having become, by long endeavour, so sensitive to vibrations that he had gained the power of perceiving by it as by ears.

She could follow every word that the ramblers uttered. They were talking no secrets. They were merely indulging in the ordinary vivacious chat of relatives who have long been parted in person though not in soul. But it was not to the words that Eustacia lis-

3. John Kitto (1804-1854) was a poor English boy who had lost his hearing. Rescued from the workhouse by a philanthropist, he went to missionary college, became a Doctor of Divinity, and then a well-known editor and biblical scholar.

tened; she could not even have recalled, a few minutes later, what the words were. It was to the alternating voice that gave out about one-tenth of them—the voice that had wished her good night. Sometimes this throat uttered Yes, sometimes it uttered No; sometimes it made inquiries about a timeworn denizen of the place. Once it surprised her notions by remarking upon the friendliness and geniality written in the faces of the hills around.

The three voices passed on, and decayed and died out upon her ear. Thus much had been granted her; and all besides withheld. No event could have been more exciting. During the greater part of the afternoon she had been entrancing herself by imagining the fascination which must attend a man come direct from beautiful Paris—laden with its atmosphere, familiar with its charms. And this man had greeted her.

With the departure of the figures the profuse articulations of the women wasted away from her memory; but the accents of the other stayed on. Was there anything in the voice of Mrs. Yeobright's son—for Clym it was—startling as a sound? No: it was simply comprehensive. All emotional things were possible to the speaker of that 'good night.' Eustacia's imagination supplied the rest—except the solution to one riddle. What *could* the tastes of that man be who saw friendliness and geniality in these shaggy hills?

On such occasions as this a thousand ideas pass through a highly charged woman's head; and they indicate themselves on her face; but the changes, though actual, are minute. Eustacia's features went through a rhythmical succession of them. She glowed; remembering the mendacity of the imagination, she flagged; then she freshened; then she fired; then she cooled again. It was a cycle of aspects, produced by a cycle of visions.

Eustacia entered her own house; she was excited. Her grandfather was enjoying himself over the fire, raking about the ashes and exposing the red-hot surface of the turves, so that their lurid glare irradiated the chimney-corner with the hues of a furnace.

'Why is it that we are never friendly with the Yeobrights?' she said, coming forward and stretching her soft hands over the warmth. 'I wish we were. They seem to be very nice people.'

'Be hanged if I know why,' said the captain. 'I liked the old man well enough, though he was as rough as a hedge. But you would never have cared to go there, even if you might have, I am well sure.'

'Why shouldn't I?'

'Your town tastes would find them far too countrified. They sit in the kitchen, drink mead and elderwine, and sand the floor to keep it clean. A sensible way of life; but how would you like it?'

'I thought Mrs. Yeobright was a ladylike woman? A curate's daughter, was she not?'

'Yes; but she was obliged to live as her husband did; and I suppose she has taken kindly to it by this time. Ah, I recollect that I once accidentally offended her, and I have never seen her since.'

That night was an eventful one to Eustacia's brain, and one which she hardly ever forgot. She dreamt a dream; and few human beings, from Nebuchadnezzar to the Swaffham tinker,[4] ever dreamt a more remarkable one. Such an elaborately developed, perplexing, exciting dream was certainly never dreamed by a girl in Eustacia's situation before. It had as many ramifications as the Cretan labyrinth, as many fluctuations as the Northern Lights, as much colour as a parterre in June, and was as crowded with figures as a coronation. To Queen Scheherazade[5] the dream might have seemed not far removed from commonplace; and to a girl just returned from all the courts of Europe it might have seemed not more than interesting. But amid the circumstances of Eustacia's life it was as wonderful as a dream could be.

There was, however, gradually evolved from its transformation scenes a less extravagant episode, in which the heath dimly appeared behind the general brilliancy of the action. She was dancing to wondrous music, and her partner was the man in silver armour who had accompanied her through the previous fantastic changes, the visor of his helmet being closed. The mazes of the dance were ecstatic. Soft whispering came into her ear from under the radiant helmet, and she felt like a woman in Paradise. Suddenly these two wheeled out from the mass of dancers, dived into one of the pools of the heath, and came out somewhere beneath into an iridescent hollow, arched with rainbows. 'It must be here,' said the voice by her side, and blushingly looking up she saw him removing his casque to kiss her. At that moment there was a cracking noise, and his figure fell into fragments like a pack of cards.

She cried aloud, 'O that I had seen his face!'

Eustacia awoke. The cracking had been that of the window-shutter downstairs, which the maid-servant was opening to let in the day, now slowly increasing to Nature's meagre allowance at this sickly time of the year. 'O that I had seen his face!' she said again. ' 'Twas meant for Mr. Yeobright!'

When she became cooler she perceived that many of the phases

4. Nebuchadnezzar was a King of Babylonia (604-561? B.C.) and conqueror of Jerusalem (II Kings xxiv, xxv). *Swaffham* is a small market town near Norwich, and a *tinker* is a workman who mends pots and pans and who is generally held in low repute. Probably Hardy uses the references to cover the whole range of human beings, from the highest to the lowest.

5. In the *Arabian Nights' Entertainments*, the wife of the Sultan of India, to whom she nightly related such interesting tales that he spared her life.

of the dream had naturally arisen out of the images and fancies of the day before. But this detracted little from its interest, which lay in the excellent fuel it provided for newly kindled fervour. She was at the modulating point between indifference and love, at the stage called 'having a fancy for.' It occurs once in the history of the most gigantic passions, and it is a period when they are in the hands of the weakest will.

The perfervid woman was by this time half in love with a vision. The fantastic nature of her passion, which lowered her as an intellect, raised her as a soul. If she had had a little more self-control she would have attenuated the emotion to nothing by sheer reasoning, and so have killed it off. If she had had a little less pride she might have gone and circumambulated the Yeobright's premises at Blooms-End at any maidenly sacrifice until she had seen him. But Eustacia did neither of these things. She acted as the most exemplary might have acted, being so influenced; she took an airing twice or thrice a day upon the Egdon hills, and kept her eyes employed.

The first occasion passed, and he did not come that way.

She promenaded a second time, and was again the sole wanderer there.

The third time there was a dense fog: she looked around, but without much hope. Even if he had been walking within twenty yards of her she could not have seen him.

At the fourth attempt to encounter him it began to rain in torrents, and she turned back.

The fifth sally was in the afternoon: it was fine, and she remained out long, walking to the very top of the valley in which Blooms-End lay. She saw the white paling about half a mile off; but he did not appear. It was almost with heart-sickness that she came home, and with a sense of shame at her weakness. She resolved to look for the man from Paris no more.

But Providence is nothing if not coquettish; and no sooner had Eustacia formed this resolve than the opportunity came which, while sought, had been entirely withholden.

Eustacia Is Led on to an Adventure

IV

In the evening of this last day of expectation, which was the twenty-third of December, Eustacia was at home alone. She had passed the recent hour in lamenting over a rumour newly come to her ears—that Yeobright's visit to his mother was to be of short duration, and would end some time the next week. 'Naturally,' she said to herself. A man in the full swing of his activities in a gay city could not afford to linger long on Egdon Heath. That she would behold face to face the owner of the awakening voice within the limits of such a holiday was most unlikely, unless she were to haunt the environs of his mother's house like a robin, to do which was difficult and unseemly.

The customary expedient of provincial girls and men in such circumstances is churchgoing. In an ordinary village or country town one can safely calculate that, either on Christmas-day or the Sunday contiguous, any native home for the holidays, who has not through age or *ennui* lost the appetite for seeing and being seen, will turn up in some pew or other, shining with hope, self-consciousness, and new clothes. Thus the congregation on Christmas morning is mostly a Tussaud collection of celebrities who have been born in the neighbourhood. Hither the mistress, left neglected at home all the year, can steal and observe the development of the returned lover who has forgotten her, and think as she watches him over her prayer-book that he may throb with a renewed fidelity when novelties have lost their charm. And hither a comparatively recent settler like Eustacia may betake herself to scrutinize the person of a native son who left home before her advent upon the scene, and consider if the friendship of his parents be worth cultivating during his next absence in order to secure a knowledge of him on his next return.

But these tender schemes were not feasible among the scattered inhabitants of Egdon Heath. In name they were parishioners, but virtually they belonged to no parish at all. People who came to these few isolated houses to keep Christmas with their friends remained in their friends' chimney-corners drinking mead and other comforting liquors till they left again for good and all. Rain, snow, ice, mud everywhere around, they did not care to trudge two or three miles to sit wet-footed and splashed to the nape of their necks among those who, though in some measure neighbours, lived close to the church, and entered it clean and dry. Eustacia knew it was ten to one that Clym Yeobright would go to no church at all during his few days of leave, and that it would be a waste of labour for her to go driving the pony and gig over a bad road in hope to see him there.

It was dusk, and she was sitting by the fire in the dining-room or hall, which they occupied at this time of the year in preference to the parlour, because of its large hearth, constructed for turf-fires, a fuel the captain was partial to in the winter season. The only visible articles in the room were those on the window-sill, which showed their shapes against the low sky: the middle article being the old hour-glass, and the other two a pair of ancient British urns whch had been dug from a barrow near, and were used as flowerpots for two razor-leaved cactuses. Somebody knocked at the door. The servant was out; so was her grandfather. The person, after waiting a minute, came in and tapped at the door of the room.

'Who's there?' said Eustacia.

'Please, Cap'n Vye, will you let us——'

Eustacia arose and went to the door. 'I cannot allow you to come in so boldly. You should have waited.'

'The cap'n said I might come in without any fuss,' was answered in a lad's pleasant voice.

'Oh, did he?' said Eustacia more gently. 'What do you want, Charley?'

'Please will your grandfather lend us his fuel-house to try over our parts in, to-night at seven o'clock?'

'What, are you one of the Egdon mummers for this year?'

'Yes, miss. The cap'n used to let the old mummers practise here.'

'I know it. Yes, you may use the fuel-house if you like,' said Eustacia languidly.

The choice of Captain Vye's fuel-house as the scene of rehearsal was dictated by the fact that his dwelling was nearly in the centre of the heath. The fuel-house was as roomy as a barn, and was a most desirable place for such a purpose. The lads who formed the company of players lived at different scattered points around, and by meeting in this spot the distances to be traversed by all the comers would be about equally proportioned.

For mummers and mumming Eustacia had the greatest contempt. The mummers themselves were not afflicted with any such feeling for their art, though at the same time they were not enthusiastic. A traditional pastime is to be distinguished from a mere revival in no more striking feature than in this, that while in the revival all is excitement and fervour, the survival is carried on with a stolidity and absence of stir which sets one wondering why a thing that is done so perfunctorily should be kept up at all. Like Balaam[6] and other unwilling prophets, the agents seem moved by an inner compulsion to say and do their allotted parts whether they will or no. This unweeting[7] manner of performance is the true ring by which, in this refurbishing age, a fossilized survival may be known from a spurious reproduction.

The piece was the well-known play of 'Saint George,'[8] and all

6. Mesopotamian diviner who when commanded to curse the Israelites blessed them and uttered favorable prophecies. (Numbers xxii, xxiii)

7. Unwilling.

8. One of the best-known folk dramas performed at ancient religious festivals. After miracle plays became popular in the Middle Ages and were performed at churches, the mummers' plays were relegated to rustics and the lower classes. The word mummer is of Danish origin and signifies one "wearing a mask," and the plays all suggest their origin in ritual and dances. In the play of St. George, St. George suggests both Christianity and Summer, his adversary, the Turkish Knight, both heathenism and Winter. Hardy's version, based mainly on the memories of his elders, is less farcical and less topical (the Turkish Knight, for example, was often changed to Napoleon, St. George to King or Prince George) than most of those surviving from the early 19th century.

who were behind the scenes assisted in the preparations, including the women of each household. Without the co-operation of sisters and sweethearts the dresses were likely to be a failure; but on the other hand, this class of assistance was not without its drawbacks. The girls could never be brought to respect tradition in designing and decorating the armour; they insisted on attaching loops and bows of silk and velvet in any situation pleasing to their taste. Gorget, gusset, basinet, cuirass, gauntlet,[9] sleeve, all alike in the view of these feminine eyes were practicable spaces whereon to sew scraps of fluttering colour.

It might be that Joe, who fought on the side of Christendom, had a sweetheart, and that Jim, who fought on the side of the Moslem, had one likewise. During the making of the costumes it would come to the knowledge of Joe's sweetheart that Jim's was putting brilliant silk scallops at the bottom of her lover's surcoat, in addition to the ribbons of the visor, the bars of which, being invariably formed of coloured strips about half an inch wide hanging before the face, were mostly of that material. Joe's sweetheart straightway placed brilliant silk on the scallops of the hem in question, and, going a little further, added ribbon tufts to the shoulder pieces. Jim's, not to be outdone, would affix bows and rosettes everywhere.

The result was that in the end the Valiant Soldier, of the Christian army, was distinguished by no peculiarity of accoutrement from the Turkish Knight; and what was worse, on a casual view Saint George himself might be mistaken for his deadly enemy, the Saracen. The guisers themselves, though inwardly regretting this confusion of persons, could not afford to offend those by whose assistance they so largely profited, and the innovations were allowed to stand.

There was, it is true, a limit to this tendency to uniformity. The Leech or Doctor preserved his character intact: his darker habiliments, peculiar hat, and the bottle of physic slung under his arm, could never be mistaken. And the same might be said of the conventional figure of Father Christmas, with his gigantic club, an older man, who accompanied the band as general protector in long night journeys from parish to parish, and was bearer of the purse.

Seven o'clock, the hour of the rehearsal, came round, and in a short time Eustacia could hear voices in the fuel-house. To dissipate in some trifling measure her abiding sense of the murkiness of human life she went to the 'linhay' or lean-to shed, which formed the root-store of their dwelling and abutted on the fuel-house. Here was a small rough hole in the mud wall, originally made for

9. Glove worn as part of armor, usually made of leather covered with plates of steel. *Cuirass*: body armor, both breastplate and backplate. *Basinet*: helmet with a visor. *Gusset*: flexible piece of mail used to protect joints. *Gorget*: piece of armor for the throat.

pigeons, through which the interior of the next shed could be viewed. A light came from it now; and Eustacia stepped upon a stool to look in upon the scene.

On a ledge in the fuel-house stood three tall rushlights, and by the light of them seven or eight lads were marching about, haranguing, and confusing each other, in endeavours to perfect themselves in the play. Humphrey and Sam, the furze and turf cutters, were there looking on, so also was Timothy Fairway, who leant against the wall and prompted the boys from memory, interspersing among the set words remarks and anecdotes of the superior days when he and others were the Egdon mummers-elect that these lads were now.

'Well, ye be as well up to it as ever ye will be,' he said. 'Not that such mummering would have passed in our time. Harry as the Saracen should strut a bit more, and John needn't holler his inside out. Beyond that perhaps you'll do. Have you got all your clothes ready?'

'We shall by Monday.'

'Your first outing will be Monday night, I suppose?'

'Yes. At Mrs. Yeobright's.'

'Oh, Mrs. Yeobright's. What makes her want to see ye? I should think a middle-aged woman was tired of mumming.'

'She's got up a bit of a party, because 'tis the first Christmas that her son Clym has been home for a long time.'

'To be sure, to be sure—her party! I am going myself. I almost forgot it, upon my life.'

Eustacia's face flagged. There was to be a party at the Yeobrights'; she, naturally, had nothing to do with it. She was a stranger to all such local gatherings, and had always held them as scarcely appertaining to her sphere. But had she been going, what an opportunity would have been afforded her of seeing the man whose influence was penetrating her like summer sun! To increase that influence was coveted excitement; to cast it off might be to regain serenity; to leave it as it stood was tantalizing.

The lads and men prepared to leave the premises, and Eustacia returned to her fireside. She was immersed in thought, but not for long. In a few minutes the lad Charley, who had come to ask permission to use the place, returned with the key to the kitchen. Eustacia heard him, and opening the door into the passage said, 'Charley, come here.'

The lad was surprised. He entered the front room not without blushing; for he, like many, had felt the power of this girl's face and form.

She pointed to a seat by the fire, and entered the other side of the chimney-corner herself. It could be seen in her face that whatever motive she might have had in asking the youth indoors would soon appear.

'Which part do you play, Charley—the Turkish Knight, do you not?' inquired the beauty, looking across the smoke of the fire to him on the other side.

'Yes, miss, the Turkish Knight,' he replied diffidently.

'Is yours a long part?'

'Nine speeches, about.'

'Can you repeat them to me? If so I should like to hear them.'

The lad smiled into the glowing turf and began—

> 'Here come I, a Turkish Knight,
> Who learnt in Turkish land to fight,'

continuing the discourse throughout the scenes to the concluding catastrophe of his fall by the hand of Saint George.

Eustacia had occasionally heard the part recited before. When the lad ended she began, precisely in the same words, and ranted on without hitch or divergence till she too reached the end. It was the same thing, yet how different. Like in form, it had the added softness and finish of a Raffaelle after Perugino,[1] which, while faithfully reproducing the original subject, entirely distances the original art.

Charley's eyes rounded with surprise. 'Well, you be a clever lady!' he said, in admiration. 'I've been three weeks learning mine.'

'I have heard it before,' she quietly observed. 'Now, would you do anything to please me, Charley?'

'I'd do a good deal, miss.'

'Would you let me play your part for one night?'

'O, miss! But your woman's gown—you couldn't.'

'I can get boy's clothes—at least all that would be wanted besides the mumming dress. What should I have to give you to lend me your things, to let me take your place for an hour or two on Monday night, and on no account to say a word about who or what I am? You would, of course, have to excuse yourself from playing that night, and to say that somebody—a cousin of Miss Vye's—would act for you. The other mummers have never spoken to me in their lives, so that it would be safe enough; and if it were not, I should not mind. Now, what must I give you to agree to this? Half a crown?'

The youth shook his head.

'Five shillings?'

1. Raffaello Santi (1483-1520), now usually known as Raphael, famous Italian painter who began his career in Umbria as a pupil of Perugino, or Pietro Vannucci (1446-1524). Raffaello's early paintings are very much like those of Perugino's.

He shook his head again. 'Money won't do it,' he said, brushing the iron head of the fire-dog with the hollow of his hand.

'What will, then, Charley?' said Eustacia in a disappointed tone.

'You know what you forbade me at the maypoling, miss,' murmured the lad, without looking at her, and still stroking the fire-dog's head.

'Yes,' said Eustacia, with a little more hauteur. 'You wanted to join hands with me in the ring, if I recollect?'

'Half an hour of that, and I'll agree, miss.'

Eustacia regarded the youth steadfastly. He was three years younger than herself, but apparently not backward for his age. 'Half an hour of what?' she said, though she guessed what.

'Holding your hand in mine.'

She was silent. 'Make it a quarter of an hour,' she said.

'Yes, Miss Eustacia— I will, if I may kiss it too. A quarter of an hour. And I'll swear to do the best I can to let you take my place without anybody knowing. Don't you think somebody might know your tongue, miss?'

'It is possible. But I will put a pebble in my mouth to make it less likely. Very well; you shall be allowed to have my hand as soon as you bring the dress and your sword and staff. I don't want you any longer now.'

Charley departed, and Eustacia felt more and more interest in life. Here was something to do: here was some one to see, and a charmingly adventurous way to see him. 'Ah,' she said to herself, 'want of an object to live for—that's all is the matter with me!'

Eustacia's manner was as a rule of a slumberous sort, her passions being of the massive rather than the vivacious kind. But when aroused she would make a dash which, just for the time, was not unlike the move of a naturally lively person.

On the question of recognition she was somewhat indifferent. By the acting lads themselves she was not likely to be known. With the guests who might be assembled she was hardly so secure. Yet detection, after all, would be no such dreadful thing. The fact only could be detected, her true motive never. It would be instantly set down as the passing freak of a girl whose ways were already considered singular. That she was doing for an earnest reason what would most naturally be done in jest was at any rate a safe secret.

The next evening Eustacia stood punctually at the fuel-house door, waiting for the dusk which was to bring Charley with the trappings. Her grandfather was at home to-night, and she would be unable to ask her confederate indoors.

He appeared on the dark ridge of heathland, like a fly on a negro, bearing the articles with him, and came up breathless with his walk.

'Here are the things,' he whispered, placing them upon the threshold. 'And now, Miss Eustacia——'

'The payment. It is quite ready. I am as good as my word.'

She leant against the door-post, and gave him her hand. Charley took it in both his own with a tenderness beyond description, unless it was like that of a child holding a captured sparrow.

'Why, there's a glove on it!' he said in a deprecating way.

'I have been walking,' she observed.

'But, miss!'

'Well—it is hardly fair.' She pulled off the glove and gave him her bare hand.

They stood together minute after minute, without further speech, each looking at the blackening scene, and each thinking his and her own thoughts.

'I think I won't use it all up to-night,' said Charley devotedly, when six or eight minutes had been passed by him caressing her hand. 'May I have the other few minutes another time?'

'As you like,' said she without the least emotion. 'But it must be over in a week. Now, there is only one thing I want you to do: to wait while I put on the dress, and then to see if I do my part properly. But let me look first indoors.'

She vanished for a minute or two, and went in. Her grandfather was safely asleep in his chair. 'Now, then,' she said, on returning, 'walk down the garden a little way, and when I am ready I'll call you.'

Charley walked and waited, and presently heard a soft whistle. He returned to the fuel-house door.

'Did you whistle, Miss Vye?'

'Yes; come in,' reached him in Eustacia's voice from a back quarter. 'I must not strike a light till the door is shut, or it may be seen shining. Push your hat into the hole through to the wash-house, if you can feel your way across.'

Charley did as commanded, and she struck the light, revealing herself to be changed in sex, brilliant in colours, and armed from top to toe. Perhaps she quailed a little under Charley's vigorous gaze, but whether any shyness at her male attire appeared upon her countenance could not be seen by reason of the strips of ribbon which used to cover the face in mumming costumes, representing the barred visor of the mediaeval helmet.

'It fits pretty well,' she said, looking down at the white overalls, 'except that the tunic, or whatever you call it, is long in the sleeve. The bottom of the overalls I can turn up inside. Now pay attention.'

Eustacia then proceeded in her delivery, striking the sword against the staff or lance at the minatory phrases, in the orthodox mumming manner, and strutting up and down. Charley seasoned his admiration with criticism of the gentlest kind, for the touch of Eustacia's hand yet remained with him.

'And now for your excuse to the others,' she said. 'Where do you meet before you go to Mrs. Yeobright's?'

'We thought of meeting here, miss if you have nothing to say against it. At eight o'clock, so as to get there by nine.'

'Yes. Well, you of course must not appear. I will march in about five minutes late, ready-dressed, and tell them that you can't come. I have decided that the best plan will be for you to be sent somewhere by me, to make a real thing of the excuse. Our two heath-croppers are in the habit of straying into the meads, and to-morrow evening you can go and see if they are gone there. I'll manage the rest. Now you may leave me.'

'Yes, miss. But I think I'll have one minute more of what I am owed, if you don't mind.'

Eustacia gave him her hand as before.

'One minute,' she said, and counted on till she reached seven or eight minutes. Hand and person she then withdrew to a distance of several feet, and recovered some of her old dignity. The contract completed, she raised between them a barrier impenetrable as a wall.

'There, 'tis all gone; and I didn't mean quite all,' he said, with a sigh.

'You had good measure,' said she, turning away.

'Yes, miss. Well, 'tis over, and now I'll get home-along.'

Through the Moonlight

V

The next evening the mummers were assembled in the same spot, awaiting the entrance of the Turkish Knight.

'Twenty minutes after eight by the Quiet Woman, and Charley not come.'

'Ten minutes past by Blooms-End.'

'It wants ten minutes to, by Granfer Cantle's watch.'

'And 'tis five minutes past by the captain's clock.'

On Egdon there was no absolute hour of the day. The time at any moment was a number of varying doctrines professed by the different hamlets, some of them having originally grown up from a common root, and then become divided by secession, some having been alien from the beginning. West Egdon believed in Blooms-End time, East Egdon in the time of the Quiet Woman Inn. Grandfer Cantle's watch had numbered many followers in years gone by, but since he had grown older faiths were shaken.

Thus, the mummers having gathered hither from scattered points, each came with his own tenets on early and late; and they waited a little longer as a compromise.

Eustacia had watched the assemblage through the hole; and seeing that now was the proper moment to enter, she went from the 'linhay' and boldly pulled the bobbin of the fuel-house door. Her grandfather was safe at the Quiet Woman.

'Here's Charley at last! How late you be, Charley.'

'"Tis not Charley,' said the Turkish Knight from within his visor. ' 'Tis a cousin of Miss Vye's, come to take Charley's place from curiosity. He was obliged to go and look for the heath-croppers that have got into the meads, and I agreed to take his place, as he knew he couldn't come back here again to-night. I know the part as well as he.'

Her graceful gait, elegant figure, and dignified manner in general won the mummers to the opinion that they had gained by the exchange, if the newcomer were perfect in his part.

'It don't matter—if you be not too young,' said Saint George. Eustacia's voice had sounded somewhat more juvenile and fluty than Charley's.

'I know every word of it, I tell you,' said Eustacia decisively. Dash being all that was required to carry her triumphantly through, she adopted as much as was necessary. 'Go ahead, lads, with the try-over. I'll challenge any of you to find a mistake in me.'

The play was hastily rehearsed, whereupon the other mummers were delighted with the new knight. They extinguished the candles at half-past eight, and set out upon the heath in the direction of Mrs. Yeobright's house at Blooms-End.

There was a slight hoar-frost that night, and the moon, though not more than half full, threw a spirited and enticing brightness upon the fantastic figures of the mumming band, whose plumes and ribbons rustled in their walk like autumn leaves. Their path was not over Rainbarrow now, but down a valley which left that ancient elevation a little to the east. The bottom of the vale was green to a width of ten yards or thereabouts, and the shining facets of frost upon the blades of grass seemed to move on with the shadows of those they surrounded. The masses of furze and heath to the right and left were dark as ever; a mere half-moon was powerless to silver such sable features as theirs.

Half-an-hour of walking and talking brought them to the spot in the valley where the grass riband widened and led down to the front of the house. At sight of the place Eustacia, who had felt a few passing doubts during her walk with the youths, again was glad that the adventure had been undertaken. She had come out to see a man who might possibly have the power to deliver her soul from a most deadly oppression. What was Wildeve? Interesting, but inadequate. Perhaps she would see a sufficient hero to-night.

As they drew nearer to the front of the house the mummers became aware that music and dancing were briskly flourishing within. Every now and then a long low note from the serpent, which was the chief wind instrument played at these times, advanced further into the heath than the thin treble part, and reached their ears alone; and next a more than usually loud tread from a dancer would come the same way. With nearer approach these fragmentary sounds became pieced together, and were found to be the salient points of the tune called 'Nancy's Fancy.'[2]

He was there, of course. Who was she that he danced with? Perhaps some unknown woman, far beneath herself in culture, was by that most subtle of lures sealing his fate this very instant. To dance with a man is to concentrate a twelvemonth's regulation fire upon him in the fragment of an hour. To pass to courtship without acquaintance, to pass to marriage without courtship, is a skipping of terms reserved for those alone who tread this royal road. She would see how his heart lay by keen observation of them all.

The enterprising lady followed the mumming company through the gate in the white paling, and stood before the open porch. The house was encrusted with heavy thatchings, which dropped between the upper windows: the front, upon which the moonbeams directly played, had originally been white; but a huge pyracanth[3] now darkened the greater portion.

It became at once evident that the dance was proceeding immediately within the surface of the door, no apartment intervening. The brushing of skirts and elbows, sometimes the bumping of shoulders, could be heard against the very panels. Eustacia, though living within two miles of the place, had never seen the interior of this quaint old habitation. Between Captain Vye and the Yeobrights there had never existed much acquaintance, the former having come as a stranger and purchased the long-empty house at Mistover Knap not long before the death of Mrs. Yeobright's husband; and with that event and the departure of her son such friendship as had grown up became quite broken off.

'Is there no passage inside the door, then?' asked Eustacia as they stood within the porch.

'No,' said the lad who played the Saracen. 'The door opens right upon the front sitting-room, where the spree's going on.'

'So that we cannot open the door without stopping the dance.'

'That's it. Here we must bide till they have done, for they always bolt the back door after dark.'

2. Well-known old folk tune.
3. Thorny evergreen shrub generally trained against a house.

'They won't be much longer,' said Father Christmas.

This assertion, however, was hardly borne out by the event. Again the instruments ended the tune; again they recommenced with as much fire and pathos as if it were the first strain. The air was now that one without any particularly beginning, middle, or end, which perhaps, among all the dances which throng an inspired fiddler's fancy, best conveys the idea of the interminable—the celebrated 'Devil's Dream.'[4] The fury of personal movement that was kindled by the fury of the notes could be approximately imagined by these outsiders under the moon, from the occasional kicks of toes and heels against the door, whenever the whirl round had been of more than customary velocity.

The first five minutes of listening was interesting enough to the mummers. The five minutes extended to ten minutes, and these to a quarter of an hour; but no signs of ceasing were audible in the lively Dream. The bumping against the door, the laughter, the stamping, were all as vigorous as ever, and the pleasure in being outside lessened considerably.

'Why does Mrs. Yeobright give parties of this sort?' Eustacia asked, a little surprised to hear merriment so pronounced.

'It is not one of her bettermost parlour-parties. She's asked the plain neighbours and workpeople without drawing any lines, just to give 'em a good supper and such like. Her son and she wait upon the folks.'

'I see,' said Eustacia.

' 'Tis the last strain, I think,' said Saint George, with his ear to the panel. 'A young man and woman have just swung into this corner, and he's saying to her, "Ah, the pity; 'tis over for us this time, my own." '

'Thank God,' said the Turkish Knight, stamping, and taking from the wall the conventional lance that each of the mummers carried. Her boots being thinner than those of the young men, the hoar had damped her feet and made them cold.

'Upon my song 'tis another ten minutes for us,' said the Valiant Soldier, looking through the keyhole as the tune modulated into another without stopping. 'Grandfer Cantle is standing in this corner, waiting his turn.'

' 'Twon't be long; 'tis a six-handed reel,' said the Doctor.

'Why not go in, dancing or no? They sent for us,' said the Saracen.

'Certainly not,' said Eustacia authoritatively, as she paced smartly up and down from door to gate to warm herself. 'We should burst into the middle of them and stop the dance, and that would be unmannerly.'

4. Also known as "The Devil Among the Tailors," a famous six-handed reel air.

'He thinks himself somebody because he has had a bit more schooling than we,' said the Doctor.

'You may go to the deuce!' said Eustacia.

There was a whispered conversation between three or four of them, and one turned to her.

'Will you tell us one thing?' he said, not without gentleness. 'Be you Miss Vye? We think you must be.'

'You may think what you like,' said Eustacia slowly. 'But honourable lads will not tell tales upon a lady.'

'We'll say nothing, miss. That's upon our honour.'

'Thank you,' she replied.

At this moment the fiddles finished off with a screech, and the serpent emitted a last note that nearly lifted the roof. When, from the comparative quiet within, the mummers judged that the dancers had taken their seats, Father Christmas advanced, lifted the latch, and put his head inside the door.

'Ah, the mummers, the mummers!' cried several guests at once. 'Clear a space for the mummers.'

Hump-backed Father Christmas then made a complete entry, swinging his huge club, and in a general way clearing the stage for the actors proper, while he informed the company in smart verse that he was come, welcome or welcome not; concluding his speech with

'Make room, make room, my gallant boys,
And give us space to rhyme;
We've come to show Saint George's play,
Upon this Christmas time.'

The guests were now arranging themselves at one end of the roon, the fiddler was mending a string, the serpent-player was emptying his mouthpiece, and the play began. First of those outside the Valiant Soldier entered, in the interest of Saint George—

'Here come I, the Valiant Soldier;
Slasher is my name;'

and so on. This speech concluded with a challenge to the infidel, at the end of which it was Eustacia's duty to enter as the Turkish Knight. She, with the rest who were not yet on, had hitherto remained in the moonlight which streamed under the porch. With no apparent effort or backwardness she came in, beginning—

'Here come I, a Turkish Knight,
Who learnt in Turkish land to fight;
I'll fight this man with courage bold:
If his blood's hot I'll make it cold!'

During her declamation Eustacia held her head erect, and spoke as roughly as she could, feeling pretty secure from observation. But the concentration upon her part necessary to prevent discovery, the newness of the scene, the shine of the candles, and the confusing effect upon her vision of the ribboned visor which hid her features, left her absolutely unable to perceive who were present as spectators. On the further side of a table bearing candles she could faintly discern faces, and that was all.

Meanwhile Jim Starks, as the Valiant Soldier had come forward, and, with glare upon the Turk, replied—

> 'If, then, thou art that Turkish Knight,
> Draw out thy sword, and let us fight!'

And fight they did; the issue of the combat being that the Valiant Soldier was slain by a preternaturally inadequate thrust from Eustacia, Jim, in his ardour for genuine histrionic art, coming down like a log upon the stone floor with force enough to dislocate his shoulder. Then, after more words from the Turkish Knight, rather too faintly delivered, and statements that he'd fight Saint George and all his crew, Saint George himself magnificently entered with the well-known flourish—

> 'Here come I, Saint George, the valiant man,
> With naked sword and spear in hand,
> Who fought the dragon and brought him to the slaughter,
> And by this won fair Sabra, the King of Egypt's daughter;
> What mortal man would dare to stand
> Before me with my sword in hand?'

This was the lad who had first recognised Eustacia; and when she now, as the Turk, replied with suitable defiance, and at once began the combat, the young fellow took especial care to use his sword as gently as possible. Being wounded, the Knight fell upon one knee, according to the direction. The Doctor now entered, restored the Knight by giving him a draught from the bottle which he carried, and the fight was again resumed, the Turk sinking by degrees until quite overcome—dying as hard in this venerable drama as he is said to do at the present day.

This gradual sinking to the earth was, in fact, one reason why Eustacia had thought that the part of the Turkish Knight, though not the shortest, would suit her best. A direct fall from upright to horizontal, which was the end of the other fighting characters, was not an elegant or decorous part for a girl. But it was easy to die like a Turk, by a dogged decline.

Eustacia was now among the number of the slain, though not on the floor, for she had managed to sink into a sloping position against the clock-case, so that her head was well elevated. The play proceeded between Saint George, the Saracen, the Doctor, and Father Christmas; and Eustacia, having no more to do, for the first time found leisure to observe the scene around, and to search for the form that had drawn her hither.

The Two Stand Face to Face

VI

The room had been arranged with a view to the dancing, the large oak table having been moved back till it stood as a breastwork to the fireplace. At each end, behind, and in the chimney-corner were grouped the guests, many of them being warm-faced and panting, among whom Eustacia cursorily recognized some well-to-do persons from beyond the heath. Thomasin, as she had expected, was not visible, and Eustacia recollected that a light had shone from an upper window when they were outside—the window, probably, of Thomasin's room. A nose, chin, hands, knees, and toes projected from the seat within the chimney opening which members she found to unite in the person of Grandfer Cantle, Mrs. Yeobright's occasional assistant in the garden, and therefore one of the invited. The smoke went up from an Etna of peat in front of him, played round the notches of the chimney-crook, struck against the salt-box, and got lost among the flitches.[5]

Another part of the room soon riveted her gaze. At the other side of the chimney stood the settle,[6] which is the necessary supplement to a fire so open that nothing less than a strong breeze will carry up the smoke. It is, to the hearths of old-fashioned cavernous fireplaces, what the east belt of trees is to the exposed country estate, or the north wall to the garden. Outside the settle candles gutter, locks of hair wave, young women shiver, and old men sneeze. Inside is Paradise. Not a symptom of a draught disturbs the air; the sitters' backs are as warm as their faces, and songs and old tales are drawn from the occupants by the comfortable heat, like fruit from melon-plants in a frame.

It was, however, not with those who sat in the settle that Eustacia was concerned. A face showed itself with marked distinctness against the dark-tanned wood of the upper part. The owner, who was leaning against the settle's outer end, was Clement Yeobright, or Clym, as he was called here; she knew it could be nobody else. The spectacle constituted an area of two feet in Rembrandt's intensest manner. A strange power in the lounger's appearance lay in

5. Sides of bacon hung from hooks either in the ceiling or within the wide chimney.

6. Large bench.

the fact that, though his whole figure was visible, the observer's eye was only aware of his face.

To one of middle age the countenance was that of a young man, though a youth might hardly have seen any necessity for the term of immaturity. But it was really one of those faces which convey less the idea of so many years as its age then of so much experience as its store. The number of their years may have adequately summed up Jared, Mahalaleel,[7] and the rest of the antediluvians, but the age of a modern man is to be measured by the intensity of his history.

The face was well shaped, even excellently. But the mind within was beginning to use it as a mere waste tablet whereon to trace its idiosyncrasies as they developed themselves. The beauty here visible would in no long time be ruthlessly overrun by its parasite, thought, which might just as well have fed upon a plainer exterior where there was nothing it could harm. Had Heaven preserved Yeobright from a wearing habit of meditation, people would have said, 'A handsome man.' Had his brain unfolded under sharper contours they would have said, 'A thoughtful man.' But an inner strenuousness was preying upon an outer symmetry, and they rated his look as singular.

Hence people who began by beholding him ended by perusing him. His countenance was overlaid with legible meanings. Without being thought-worn he yet had certain marks derived from a perception of his surroundings, such as are not unfrequently found on men at the end of the four or five years of endeavour which follow the close of placid pupilage. He already showed that thought is a disease of flesh, and indirectly bore evidence that ideal physical beauty is incompatible with emotional development and a full recognition of the coil of things. Mental luminousness must be fed with the oil of life, even though there is already a physical need for it; and the pitiful sight of two demands on one supply was just showing itself here.

When standing before certain men the philosopher regrets that thinkers are but perishable tissue, the artist that perishable tissue has to think. Thus to deplore, each from his point of view, the mutually destructive interdependence of spirit and flesh would have been instinctive with these in critically observing Yeobright.

As for his look, it was a natural cheerfulness striving against depression from without, and not quite succeeding. The look suggested isolation, but it revealed something more. As is usual with

7. Father of Jared, who lived 895 years (Genesis v.12-17). Jared was patriarch of the line of Seth, who lived 962 years (Genesis v.15-20).

bright natures, the deity that lies ignominiously chained within an ephemeral human carcase shone out of him like a ray.

The effect upon Eustacia was palpable. The extraordinary pitch of excitement that she had reached beforehand would, indeed, have caused her to be influenced by the most commonplace man. She was troubled at Yeobright's presence.

The remainder of the play ended: the Saracen's head was cut off, and Saint George stood as victor. Nobody commented, any more than they would have commented on the fact of mushrooms coming in autumn or snowdrops in spring. They took the piece as phlegmatically as did the actors themselves. It was a phase of cheerfulness which was, as a matter of course, to be passed through every Christmas; and there was no more to be said.

They sang the plaintive chant which follows the play, during which all the dead men rise to their feet in a silent and awful manner, like the ghosts of Napoleon's soldiers in the Midnight Review. Afterwards the door opened, and Fairway appeared on the threshold, accompanied by Christian and another. They had been waiting outside for the conclusion of the play, as the players had waited for the conclusion of the dance.

'Come in, come in,' said Mrs. Yeobright; and Clym went forward to welcome them. 'How is it you are so late? Grandfer Cantle has been here ever so long, and we thought you'd have come with him, as you live so near one another.'

'Well, I should have come earlier,' Mr. Fairway said, and paused to look along the beam of the ceiling for a nail to hang his hat on; but, finding his accustomed one to be occupied by the mistletoe, and all the nails in the walls to be burdened with bunches of holly, he at last relieved himself of the hat by ticklishly balancing it between the candle-box and the head of the clock-case. 'I should have come earlier, ma'am,' he resumed, with a more composed air, 'but I know what parties be, and how there's none too much room in folks' houses at such times, so I thought I wouldn't come till you'd got settled a bit.'

'And I thought so too, Mrs. Yeobright,' said Christian earnestly; 'but father there was so eager that he had no manners at all, and left home almost afore 'twas dark. I told him 'twas barely decent in a' old man to come so oversoon; but words be wind.'

'Klk! I wasn't going to bide waiting about till half the game was over! I'm as light as a kite when anything's going on!' crowed Grandfer Cantle from the chimney-seat.

Fairway had meanwhile concluded a critical gaze at Yeobright. 'Now, you may not believe it,' he said to the rest of the room, 'but I should never have knowed this gentleman if I had met him anywhere off his own he'th: he's altered so much.'

'You too have altered, and for the better, I think, Timothy,' said Yeobright, surveying the firm figure of Fairway.

'Master Yeobright, look me over too. I have altered for the better, haven't I, hey?' said Grandfer Cantle, rising, and placing himself something above half a foot from Clym's eye, to induce the most searching criticism.

'To be sure we will,' said Fairway, taking the candle and moving it over the surface of the Grandfer's countenance, the subject of his scrutiny irradiating himself with light and pleasant smiles, and giving himself jerks of juvenility.

'You haven't changed much,' said Yeobright.

'If there's any difference, Grandfer is younger,' appended Fairway decisively.

'And yet not my own doing, and I feel no pride in it,' said the pleased ancient. 'But I can't be cured of my vagaries; them I plead guilty to. Yes, Master Cantle always was that, as we know. But I am nothing by the side of you, Mister Clym.'

'Nor any o' us,' said Humphrey, in a low rich tone of admiration, not intended to reach anybody's ears.

'Really, there would have been nobody here who could have stood as decent second to him, or even third, if I hadn't been a soldier in the Bang-up Locals (as we was called for our smartness),' said Grandfer Cantle. 'And even as 'tis we all look a little scammish[8] beside him. But in the year four 'twas said there wasn't a finer figure in the whole South Wessex than I, as I looked when dashing past the shop-winders with the rest of our company on the day we ran out o' Budmouth because it was thoughted that Boney had landed round the point. There was I, straight as a young poplar, wi' my firelock, and my bagnet, and my spatterdashes,[9] and my stock sawing my jaws off, and my accoutrements sheening like the seven stars! Yes, neighbours, I was a pretty sight in my soldiering days. You ought to have seen me in four!'

''Tis his mother's side where Master Clym's figure comes from, bless ye,' said Timothy. 'I know'd her brothers well. Longer coffins were never made in the whole county of South Wessex, and 'tis said that poor George's knees were crumpled up a little e'en as 'twas.'

'Coffins, where?' inquired Christian, drawing nearer. 'Have the ghost of one appeared to anybody, Master Fairway?'

'No, no. Don't let your mind so mislead your ears, Christian; and be a man,' said Timothy reproachfully.

'I will,' said Christian. 'But now I think o't my shadder last night seemed just the shape of a coffin. What is it a sign of when

8. Lean and scraggy.

9. Leather leggings to keep the trousers from being spattered. *Bagnet* is a dialect word for *bayonet*.

your shade's like a coffin, neighbours? It can't be nothing to be afeard of, I suppose?'

'Afeard, no!' said the Grandfer. 'Faith, I was never afeard of nothing except Boney, or I shouldn't ha' been the soldier I was. Yes, 'tis a thousand pities you didn't see me in four!'

By this time the mummers were preparing to leave; but Mrs. Yeobright stopped them by asking them to sit down and have a little supper. To this invitaiton Father Christmas, in the name of them all, readily agreed.

Eustacia was happy in the opportunity of staying a little longer. The cold and frosty night without was doubly frigid to her. But the lingering was not without its difficulties. Mrs. Yeobright, for want of room in the larger apartment, placed a bench for the mummers half-way through the pantry-door, which opened from the sitting-room. Here they seated themselves in a row, the door being left open: thus they were still virtually in the same apartment. Mrs. Yeobright now murmured a few words to her son, who crossed the room to the pantry-door, striking his head against the mistletoe as he passed, and brought the mummers beef and bread, cake, pastry, mead, and elder-wine, the waiting being done by him and his mother, that the little maid-servant might sit as guest. The mummers doffed their helmets, and began to eat and drink.

'But you will surely have some?' said Clym to the Turkish Knight, as he stood before that warrior, tray in hand. She had refused, and still sat covered, only the sparkle of her eyes being visible between the ribbons which covered her face.

'None, thank you,' replied Eustacia.

'He's quite a youngster,' said the Saracen apologetically, 'and you must excuse him. He's not one of the old set, but have jined us because t'other couldn't come.'

'But he will take something?' persisted Yeobright. 'Try a glass of mead or elder-wine.'

'Yes, you had better try that,' said the Saracen. 'It will keep the cold out going home-along.'

Though Eustacia could not eat without uncovering her face she could drink easily enough beneath her disguise. The elder-wine was accordingly accepted, and the glass vanished inside the ribbons.

At moments during this performance Eustacia was half in doubt about the security of her position; yet it had a fearful joy. A series of attentions paid to her, and yet not to her but to some imaginary person, by the first man she had ever been inclined to adore, complicated her emotions indescribably. She had loved him partly because he was exceptional in this scene, partly because she had determined to love him, chiefly because she was in desperate need of loving somebody after wearying of Wildeve. Believing that she must love him in spite of herself, she had been influenced after the fashion of the second Lord Lyttleton and other persons, who have dreamed that they were to die on a certain day, and by stress of a morbid imagination have actually brought about that event. Once let a maiden admit the possibility of her being stricken with love for some one at a certain hour and place, and the thing is as good as done.

Did anything at this moment suggest to Yeobright the sex of the creature whom that fantastic guise inclosed, how extended was her scope both in feeling and in making others feel, and how far her compass transcended that of her companions in the band? When the disguised Queen of Love[1] appeared before Æneas a preternatural perfume accompanied her presence and betrayed her quality. If such a mysterious emanation ever was projected by the emotions of an earthly woman upon their object, it must have signified Eustacia's presence to Yeobright now. He looked at her wistfully, then seemed to fall into a reverie, as if he were forgetting what he observed. The momentary situation ended, he passed on, and Eustacia sipped her wine without knowing what she drank. The man for whom she had predetermined to nourish a passion went into the small room, and across it to the further extremity.

The mummers, as has been stated, were seated on a bench, one end of which extended into the small apartment, or pantry, for want of space in the outer room. Eustacia, partly from shyness, had chosen the midmost seat, which thus commanded a view of the interior of the pantry as well as the room containing the guests. When Clym passed down the pantry her eyes followed him in the gloom which prevailed there. At the remote end was a door which, just as he was about to open it for himself, was opened by somebody within; and light streamed forth.

The person was Thomasin, with a candle, looking anxious, pale, and interesting. Yeobright appeared glad to see her, and pressed her hand. 'That's right, Tamsie,' he said heartily, as though recalled to himself by the sight of her: 'you have decided to come down. I am glad of it.'

'Hush—no, no,' she said quickly. 'I only came to speak to you.'

'But why not join us?'

'I cannot. At least I would rather not. I am not well enough, and we shall have plenty of time together now you are going to be home a good long holiday.'

'It isn't nearly so pleasant without you. Are you really ill?'

'Just a little, my old cousin—here,' she said, playfully sweeping her hand across her heart.

1. Venus, the mother of Aeneas, who often appeared disguised as a village maiden to warn him of difficulties.

'Ah, mother should have asked somebody else to be present to-night, perhaps?'

'O no, indeed. I merely stepped down, Clym, to ask you——' Here he followed her through the doorway into the private room beyond, and, the door closing, Eustacia and the mummer who sat next to her, the only other witness of the performance, saw and heard no more.

The heat flew to Eustacia's head and cheeks. She instantly guessed that Clym, having been home only these two or three days, had not as yet been made acquainted with Thomasin's painful situation with regard to Wildeve; and seeing her living there just as she had been living before he left home, he naturally suspected nothing. Eustacia felt a wild jealousy of Thomasin on the instant. Though Thomasin might possibly have tender sentiments towards another man as yet, how long could they be expected to last when she was shut up here with this interesting and travelled cousin of hers? There was no knowing what affection might not soon break out between the two, so constantly in each other's society, and not a distracting object near. Clym's boyish love for her might have languished, but it might easily be revived again.

Eustacia was nettled by her own contrivances. What a sheer waste of herself to be dressed thus while another was shining to advantage! Had she known the full effect of the encounter she would have moved heaven and earth to get here in a natural manner. The power of her face all lost, the charm of her emotions all disguised, the fascinations of her coquetry denied existence, nothing but a voice left to her: she had a sense of the doom of Echo[2] 'Nobody here respects me,' she said. She had overlooked the fact that, in coming as a boy among other boys, she would be treated as a boy. The slight, though of her own causing, and self-explanatory, she was unable to dismiss as unwittingly shown, so sensitive had the situation made her.

Women have done much for themselves in histrionic dress. To look far below those who, like a certain fair personator of Polly Peachum early in the last century, and another of Lydia Languish early in this,[3] have won not only love but ducal coronets into the bargain, whose shoals of them have reached to the initial satisfaction of getting love almost whence they would. But the Turkish Knight was denied even the chance of achieving this by the fluttering ribbons which she dared not brush aside.

2. According to one account, Echo, a nymph, fell in love with Narcissus. Because he didn't love her, she pined away until nothing was left but her voice.

3. Lydia Languish is a heroine in Richard Brinsley Sheridan's *The Rivals* (1775); Polly Peachum a character in John Gay's *The Beggar's Opera* (1728). Hardy, in 1912, added the note that this had been "written in 1877."

Yeobright returned to the room without his cousin. When within two or three feet of Eustacia he stopped, as if again arrested by a thought. He was gazing at her. She looked another way, disconcerted, and wondered how long this purgatory was to last. After lingering a few seconds he passed on again.

To court their own discomfiture by love is a common instinct with certain perfervid women. Conflicting sensations of love, fear, and shame reduced Eustacia to a state of the utmost uneasiness. To escape was her great and immediate desire. The other mummers appeared to be in no hurry to leave; and murmuring to the lad who sat next to her that she preferred waiting for them outside the house, she moved to the door as imperceptibly as possible, opened it, and slipped out.

The calm, lone scene reassured her. She went forward to the palings and leant over them, looking at the moon. She had stood thus but a little time when the door again opened. Expecting to see the remainder of the band Eustacia turned; but no—Clym Yeobright came out as softly as she had done, and closed the door behind him.

He advanced and stood beside her. 'I have an odd opinion,' he said,'and should like to ask you a question. Are you a woman—or am I wrong?'

'I am a woman.'

His eyes lingered on her with great interest. 'Do girls often play as mummers now? They never used to.'

'They don't now.'

'Why did you?'

'To get excitement and shake off depression,' she said in low tones.

'What depressed you?'

'Life.'

'That's a cause of depression a good many have to put up with.'

'Yes.'

A long silence. 'And do you find excitement?' asked Clym at last.

'At this moment, perhaps.'

'Then you are vexed at being discovered?'

'Yes; though I thought I might be.'

'I would gladly have asked you to our party had I known you wished to come. Have I ever been acquainted with you in my youth?'

'Never.'

'Won't you come in again, and stay as long as you like?'

'No. I wish not to be further recognized.'

'Well, you are safe with me.' After remaining in thought a

minute he added gently, 'I will not intrude upon you longer. It is a strange way of meeting, and I will not ask why I find a cultivated woman playing such a part as this.'

She did not volunteer the reason which he seemed to hope for, and he wished her good night, going thence round to the back of the house, where he walked up and down by himself for some time before re-entering.

Eustacia, warmed with an inner fire, could not wait for her companions after this. She flung back the ribbons from her face, opened the gate, and at once struck into the heath. She did not hasten along. Her grandfather was in bed at this hour, for she so frequently walked upon the hills on moonlight nights that he took no notice of her comings and goings, and, enjoying himself in his own way, left her to do likewise. A more important subject than that of getting indoors now engrossed her. Yeobright, if he had the least curiosity, would infallibly discover her name. What then? She first felt a sort of exultation at the way in which the adventure had terminated, even though at moments between her exultations she was abashed and blushful. Then this consideration recurred to chill her: What was the use of her exploit? She was at present a total stranger to the Yeobright family. The unreasonable nimbus of romance with which she had encircled that man might be her misery. How could she allow herself to become so infatuated with a stranger? And to fill the cup of her sorrow there would be Thomasin, living day after day in inflammable proximity to him; for she had just learnt that, contrary to her first belief, he was going to stay at home some considerable time.

She reached the wicket at Mistover Knap, but before opening it she turned and faced the heath once more. The form of Rainbarrow stood above the hills, and the moon stood above Rainbarrow. The air was charged with silence and frost. The scene reminded Eustacia of a circumstance which till that moment she had totally forgotten. She had promised to meet Wildeve by the Barrow this very night at eight, to give a final answer to his pleading for an elopement.

She herself had fixed the evening and the hour. He had probably come to the spot, waited there in the cold, and been greatly disappointed.

'Well, so much the better: it did not hurt him,' she said serenely. Wildeve had at present the rayless outline of the sun through smoked glass, and she could say such things as that with the greatest facility.

She remained deeply pondering; and Thomasin's winning manner towards her cousin arose again upon Eustacia's mind.

'O that she had been married to Damon before this!' she said. 'And she would if it hadn't been for me! If I had only known—if I had only known!'

Eustacia once more lifted her deep stormy eyes to the moonlight, and, sighing that tragic sigh of hers which was so much like a shudder, entered the shadow of the roof. She threw off her trappings in the out-house, rolled them up, and went indoors to her chamber.

A Coalition between Beauty and Oddness

VII

The old captain's prevailing indifference to his granddaughter's movements left her free as a bird to follow her own courses; but it so happened that he did take upon himself the next morning to ask her why she had walked out so late.

'Only in search of events, grandfather,' she said, looking out of the window with that drowsy latency of manner which discovered so much force behind it whenever the trigger was pressed.

'Search of events—one would think you were one of the bucks I knew at one-and-twenty.'

'It is so lonely here.'

'So much the better. If I were living in a town my whole time would be taken up in looking after you. I fully expected you would have been home when I returned from the Woman.'

'I won't conceal what I did. I wanted an adventure, and I went with the mummers. I played the part of the Turkish Knight.'

'No, never? Ha, ha! Good gad! I didn't expect it of you, Eustacia.'

'It was my first performance, and it certainly will be my last. Now I have told you—and remember it is a secret.'

'Of course. But, Eustacia, you never did—ha! ha! Dammy, how 'twould have pleased me forty years ago! But remember, no more of it, my girl. You may walk on the heath night or day, as you choose, so that you don't bother me; but no figuring in breeches again.'

'You need have no fear for me, grandpapa.'

Here the conversation ceased, Eustacia's moral training never exceeding in severity a dialogue of this sort, which, if it ever became profitable to good works, would be a result not dear at the price. But her thoughts soon strayed far from her own personality; and, full of a passionate and indescribable solicitude for one to whom she was not even a name, she went forth into the amplitude of tanned wild around her, restless as Ahasuerus the Jew.[4] She was

4. The Wandering Jew of the legend popular in the Middle Ages. Ahasuerus was doomed to wander the earth, finding no resting place.

about half a mile from her residence when she beheld a sinister redness arising from a ravine a little way in advance—dull and lurid like a flame in sunlight, and she guessed it to signify Diggory Venn.

When the farmers who had wished to buy in a new stock of reddle during the last month had inquired where Venn was to be found, people replied, 'On Egdon Heath.' Day after day the answer was the same. Now, since Egdon was populated with heath-croppers and furze-cutters rather than with sheep and shepherds, and the downs where most of the latter were to be found lay some to the north, some to the west of Egdon, his reason for camping about there like Israel in Zin[5] was not apparent. The position was central and occasionally desirable. But the sale of reddle was not Diggory's primary object in remaining on the heath, particularly at so late a period of the year, when most travellers of his class had gone into winter quarters.

Eustacia looked at the lonely man. Wildeve had told her at their last meeting that Venn had been thrust forward by Mrs. Yeobright as one ready and anxious to take his place as Thomasin's betrothed. His figure was perfect, his face young and well outlined, his eye bright, his intelligence keen, and his position one which he could readily better if he chose. But in spite of possibilities it was not likely that Thomasin would accept this Ishmaelitish creature while she had a cousin like Yeobright at her elbow, and Wildeve at the same time not absolutely indifferent. Eustacia was not long in guessing that poor Mrs. Yeobright, in her anxiety for her niece's future, had mentioned this lover to stimulate the zeal of the other. Eustacia was on the side of the Yeobrights now, and entered into the spirit of the aunt's desire.

'Good morning, miss,' said the reddleman, taking off his cap of hareskin, and apparently bearing her no ill-will from recollection of their last meeting.

'Good morning, reddleman,' she said, hardly troubling to lift her heavily shaded eyes to his. 'I did not know you were so near. Is your van here too?'

Venn moved his elbow towards a hollow in which a dense brake of purple-stemmed brambles had grown to such vast dimensions as almost to form a dell. Brambles, though churlish when handled, are kindly shelter in early winter, being the latest of the deciduous bushes to lose their leaves. The roof and chimney of Venn's caravan showed behind the tracery and tangles of the brake.

'You remain near this part?' she asked with more interest.

'Yes, I have business here.'

'Not altogether the selling of reddle?'

5. The Wilderness of Zin through which the Israelites passed on the journey to Canaan. (Numbers xiii.20)

'It has nothing to do with that.'

'It has to do with Miss Yeobright?'

Her face seemed to ask for an armed peace, and he therefore said frankly, 'Yes, miss; it is on account of her.'

'On account of your approaching marriage with her?'

Venn flushed through his stain. 'Don't make sport of me, Miss Vye,' he said.

'It isn't true?'

'Certainly not.'

She was thus convinced that the reddleman was a mere *pis aller*[6] in Mrs. Yeobright's mind; one, moreover, who had not even been informed of his promotion to that lowly standing. 'It was a mere notion of mine,' she said quietly; and was about to pass by without further speech, when, looking round to the right, she saw a painfully well-known figure serpentining upwards by one of the little paths which led to the top where she stood. Owing to the necessary windings of his course his back was at present towards them. She glanced quickly round; to escape that man there was only one way. Turning to Venn, she said, 'Would you allow me to rest a few minutes in your van? The banks are damp for sitting on.'

'Certainly, miss; I'll make a place for you.'

She followed him behind the dell of brambles to his wheeled dwelling, into which Venn mounted, placing the three-legged stool just within the door.

'That is the best I can do for you,' he said, stepping down and retiring to the path, where he resumed the smoking of his pipe as he walked up and down.

Eustacia bounded into the vehicle and sat on the stool, ensconced from view on the side towards the trackway. Soon she heard the brushing of other feet than the reddleman's, a not very friendly 'Good day' uttered by two men in passing each other, and then the dwindling of the footfall of one of them in a direction onwards. Eustacia stretched her neck forward till she caught a glimpse of a receding back and shoulders; and she felt a wretched twinge of misery, she knew not why. It was the sickening feeling which, if the changed heart has any generosity at all in its composition, accompanies the sudden sight of a once-loved one who is beloved no more.

When Eustacia descended to proceed on her way the reddleman came near. 'That was Mr. Wildeve who passed, miss,' he said slowly, and expressed by his face that he expected her to feel vexed at having been sitting unseen.

'Yes, I saw him coming up the hill,' replied Eustacia. 'Why

6. French, literally, "go worst." Idiomatically, what one accepts when he can do no better.

should you tell me that?' It was a bold question, considering the reddleman's knowledge of her past love; but her undemonstrative manner had power to repress the opinions of those she treated as remote from her.

'I am glad to hear that you can ask it,' said the reddleman bluntly. 'And, now I think of it, it agrees with what I saw last night.'

'Ah—what was that?' Eustacia wished to leave him, but wished to know.

'Mr. Wildeve stayed at Rainbarrow a long time waiting for a lady who didn't come.'

'You waited too, it seems?'

'Yes, I always do. I was glad to see him disappointed. He will be there again to-night.'

'To be again disappointed. The truth is, reddleman, that that lady, so far from wishing to stand in the way of Thomasin's marriage with Mr. Wildeve, would be very glad to promote it.'

Venn felt much astonishment at this avowal, though he did not show it clearly; that exhibition may greet remarks which are one remove from expectation, but it is usually withheld in complicated cases of two removes and upwards. 'Indeed, miss,' he replied.

'How do you know that Mr. Wildeve will come to Rainbarrow again to-night?' she asked.

'I heard him say to himself that he would. He's in a regular temper.'

Eustacia looked for a moment what she felt, and she murmured, lifting her deep dark eyes anxiously to his, 'I wish I knew what to do. I don't want to be uncivil to him; but I don't wish to see him again; and I have some few little things to return to him.'

'If you choose to send 'em by me, miss, and a note to tell him that you wish to say no more to him, I'll take it for you quite privately. That would be the most straightforward way of letting him know your mind.'

'Very well,' said Eustacia. 'Come towards my house, and I will bring it out to you.'

She went on, and as the path was an infinitely small parting in the shaggy locks of the heath, the reddleman followed exactly in her trail. She saw from a distance that the captain was on the bank sweeping the horizon with his telescope; and bidding Venn to wait where he stood she entered the house alone.

In ten minutes she returned with a parcel and a note, and said, in placing them in his hand, 'Why are you so ready to take these for me?'

'Can you ask that?'

'I suppose you think to serve Thomasin in some way by it. Are you as anxious as ever to help on her marriage?'

Venn was a little moved. 'I would sooner have married her myself,' he said in a low voice. 'But what I feel is that if she cannot be happy without him I will do my duty in helping her to get him, as a man ought.'

Eustacia looked curiously at the singular man who spoke thus. What a strange sort of love, to be entirely free from that quality of selfishness which is frequently the chief constituent of the passion, and sometimes its only one! The reddleman's disinterestedness was so well deserving of respect that it overshot respect by being barely comprehended; and she almost thought it absurd.

'Then we are both of one mind at last,' she said.

'Yes,' replied Venn gloomily. 'But if you would tell me, miss, why you take such an interest in her, I should be easier. It is so sudden and strange.'

Eustacia appeared at a loss. 'I cannot tell you that, reddleman,' she said coldly.

Venn said no more. He pocketed the letter, and, bowing to Eustacia, went away.

Rainbarrow had again become blended with night when Wildeve ascended the long acclivity at its base. On his reaching the top a shape grew up from the earth immediately behind him. It was that of Eustacia's emissary. He slapped Wildeve on the shoulder. The feverish young innkeeper and ex-engineer started like Satan at the touch of Ithuriel's spear.[7]

'The meeting is always at eight o'clock, at this place,' said Venn, 'and here we are—we three.'

'We three?' said Wildeve, looking quickly round.

'Yes; you, and I, and she. This is she.' He held up the letter and parcel.

Wildeve took them wonderingly. 'I don't quite see what this means,' he said. 'How do you come here? There must be some mistake.'

'It will be cleared from your mind when you have read the letter. Lanterns for one.' The reddleman struck a light, kindled an inch of tallow-candle which he had brought, and sheltered it with his cap.

'Who are you?' said Wildeve, discerning by the candle-light an obscure rubicundity of person in his companion. 'You are the reddleman I saw on the hill this morning—why, you are the man who——'

'Please read the letter.'

'If you had come from the other one I shouldn't have been surprised,' murmured Wildeve as he opened the letter and read. His face grew serious.

7. An angel in Milton's *Paradise Lost* who guarded Adam and Eve in Paradise. With his sword he lightly touched Satan, who had been tempting Eve through a dream, and Satan immediately assumed his natural grisly shape. (*Paradise Lost* IV.788-822)

To Mr. Wildeve.

After some thought I have decided once and for all that we must hold no further communication. The more I consider the matter the more I am convinced that there must be an end to our acquaintance. Had you been uniformly faithful to me throughout these two years you might now have some ground for accusing me of heartlessness; but if you calmly consider what I bore during the period of your desertion, and how I passively put up with your courtship of another without once interfering, you will, I think, own that I have a right to consult my own feelings when you come back to me again. That these are not what they were towards you may, perhaps, be a fault in me, but it is one which you can scarcely reproach me for when you remember how you left me for Thomasin.

The little articles you gave me in the early part of our friendship are returned by the bearer of this letter. They should rightly have been sent back when I first heard of your engagement to her.

Eustacia.

By the time that Wildeve reached her name the blankness with which he had read the first half of the letter intensified to mortification. 'I am made a great fool of, one way and another,' he said pettishly. 'Do you know what is in this letter?'

The reddleman hummed a tune.

'Can't you answer me?' asked Wildeve warmly.

'Ru-um-tum-tum, 'sang the reddleman.

Wildeve stood looking on the ground beside Venn's feet, till he allowed his eyes to travel upwards over Diggory's form, as illuminated by the candle, to his head and face. 'Ha-ha! Well, I suppose I deserve it, considering how I have played with them both,' he said at last, as much to himself as to Venn. 'But of all the odd things that ever I knew, the oddest is that you should so run counter to your own interests as to bring this to me.'

'My interests?'

'Certainly. 'Twas your interest not to do anything which would send me courting Thomasin again, now she has accepted you—or something like it. Mrs. Yeobright says you are to marry her. 'Tisn't true, then?'

'Good Lord! I heard of this before, but didn't believe it. When did she say so?'

Wildeve began humming as the reddleman had done.

'I don't believe it now,' cried Venn.

'Ru-um-tum-tum,' sang Wildeve.

'O Lord—how we can imitate!' said Venn contemptuously. 'I'll have this out. I'll go straight to her.'

Diggory withdrew with an emphatic step, Wildeve's eye passing over his form in withering derision, as if he were no more than a heath-cropper. When the reddleman's figure could no longer be seen, Wildeve himself descended and plunged into the rayless hollow of the vale.

To lose the two women—he who had been the well-beloved of both—was too ironical an issue to be endured. He could only decently save himself by Thomasin; and once he became her husband, Eustacia's repentance, he thought, would set in for a long and bitter term. It was no wonder that Wildeve, ignorant of the new man at the back of the scene, should have supposed Eustacia to be playing a part. To believe that the letter was not the result of some momentary pique, to infer that she really gave him up to Thomasin, would have required previous knowledge of her transfiguration by that man's influence. Who was to know that she had grown generous in the greediness of a new passion, that in coveting one cousin she was dealing liberally with another, that in her eagerness to appropriate she gave way?

Full of this resolve to marry in haste, and wring the heart of the proud girl, Wildeve went his way.

Meanwhile Diggory Venn had returned to his van, where he stood looking thoughtfully into the stove. A new vista was opened up to him. But, however promising Mrs. Yeobright's views of him might be as a candidate for her niece's hand, one condition was indispensable to the favour of Thomasin herself, and that was a renunciation of his present wild mode of life. In this he saw little difficulty.

He could not afford to wait till the next day before seeing Thomasin and detailing his plan. He speedily plunged himself into toilet operations, pulled a suit of cloth clothes from a box, and in about twenty minutes stood before the van-lantern as a reddleman in nothing but his face, the vermilion shades of which were not to be removed in a day. Closing the door and fastening it with a padlock Venn set off towards Blooms-End.

He had reached the white palings and laid his hand upon the gate when the door of the house opened, and quickly closed again. A female form had glided in. At the same time a man, who had seemingly been standing with the woman in the porch, came forward from the house till he was face to face with Venn. It was Wildeve again.

'Man alive, you've been quick at it,' said Diggory sarcastically.

'And you slow, as you will find,' said Wildeve. 'And,' lowering his voice, 'you may as well go back again now. I've claimed her, and got her. Good night, reddleman!' Thereupon Wildeve walked away.

Venn's heart sank within him, though it had not risen unduly high. He stood leaning over the palings in an indecisive mood for nearly a quarter of an hour. Then he went up the garden-path, knocked, and asked for Mrs. Yeobright.

Instead of requesting him to enter she came to the porch. A discourse was carried on between them in low measured tones for the space of ten minutes or more. At the end of the time Mrs. Yeobright went in, and Venn sadly retraced his steps into the heath. When he had again regained his van he lit the lantern, and with an apathetic face at once began to pull off his best clothes, till in the course of a few minutes he reappeared as the confirmed and irretrievable reddleman that he had seemed before.

Firmness Is Discovered in a Gentle Heart

VIII

On that evening the interior of Blooms-End, though cosy and comfortable, had been rather silent. Clym Yeobright was not at home. Since the Christmas party he had gone on a few days' visit to a friend about ten miles off.

The shadowy form seen by Venn to part from Wildeve in the porch, and quickly withdraw into the house, was Thomasin's. On entering she threw down a cloak which had been carelessly wrapped round her, and came forward to the light, where Mrs. Yeobright sat at her work-table, drawn up within the settle, so that part of it projected into the chimney-corner.

'I don't like your going out after dark alone, Tamsin,' said her aunt quietly, without looking up from her work.

'I have only been just outside the door.'

'Well?' inquired Mrs. Yeobright, struck by a change in the tone of Thomasin's voice, and observing her. Thomasin's cheek was flushed to a pitch far beyond that which it had reached before her troubles, and her eyes glittered.

'It was *he* who knocked,' she said.

'I thought as much.'

'He wishes the marriage to be at once.'

'Indeed! What—is he anxious?' Mrs. Yeobright directed a searching look upon her niece. 'Why did not Mr. Wildeve come in?'

'He did not wish to. You are not friends with him, he says. He would like the wedding to be the day after to-morrow, quite privately; at the church of his parish—not at ours.'

'Oh! And what did you say?'

'I agreed to it,' Thomasin answered firmly. 'I am a practical woman now. I don't believe in hearts at all. I would marry him under any circumstances since—since Clym's letter.'

A letter was lying on Mrs. Yeobright's work-basket, and at Thomasin's words her aunt reopened it, and silently read for the tenth time that day:—

> What is the meaning of this silly story that people are circulating about Thomasin and Mr. Wildeve? I should call such a scandal humiliating if there was the least chance of its being true. How could such a gross falsehood have arisen? It is said that one should go abroad to hear news of home, and I appear to have done it. Of course I contradict the tale everywhere; but it is very vexing, and I wonder how it could have originated. It is too ridiculous that such a girl as Thomasin could so mortify us as to get jilted on the wedding-day. What has she done?

'Yes,' Mrs. Yeobright said sadly, putting down the letter. 'If you think you can marry him, do so. And since Mr. Wildeve wishes it to be unceremonious, let it be that too, I can do nothing. It is all in your own hands now. My power over your welfare came to an end when you left this house to go with him to Anglebury.' She continued, half in bitterness, 'I may almost ask, why do you consult me in the matter at all? If you had gone and married him without saying a word to me, I could hardly have been angry—simply because, poor girl, you can't do a better thing.'

'Don't say that and dishearten me.'

'You are right: I will not.'

'I do not plead for him, aunt. Human nature is weak, and I am not a blind woman to insist that he is perfect. I did think so, but I don't now. But I know my course, and you know that I know it. I hope for the best.'

'And so do I, and we will both continue to,' said Mrs. Yeobright, rising and kissing her. 'Then the wedding, if it comes off, will be on the morning of the very day Clym comes home?'

'Yes. I decided that it ought to be over before he came. After that you can look him in the face, and so can I. Our concealments will matter nothing.'

Mrs. Yeobright moved her head in thoughtful assent, and presently said, 'Do you wish me to give you away? I am willing to undertake that, you know, if you wish, as I was last time. After once forbidding the banns I think I can do no less.'

'I don't think I will ask you to come,' said Thomasin reluctantly, but with decision. 'It would be unpleasant, I am almost sure. Better let there be only strangers present, and none of my relations at all. I would rather have it so. I do not wish to do anything which may touch your credit, and I feel that I should be uncomfortable if you were there, after what has passed. I am only your niece, and there is no necessity why you should concern yourself more about me.'

'Well, he has beaten us,' her aunt said. 'It really seems as if he had been playing with you in this way in revenge for my humbling him as I did by standing up against him at first.'

'O no, aunt,' murmured Thomasin.

They said no more on the subject then. Diggory Venn's knock came soon after; and Mrs. Yeobright, on returning from her interview with him on the porch, carelessly observed, 'Another lover has come to ask for you.'

'No?'

'Yes; that queer young man Venn.'

'Asks to pay his addresses to me?'

'Yes; and I told him he was too late.'

Thomasin looked silently into the candle-flame. 'Poor Diggory!' she said, and then aroused herself to other things.

The next day was passed in mere mechanical deeds of preparation, both the women being anxious to immerse themselves in these to escape the emotional aspect of the situation. Some wearing apparel and other articles were collected anew for Thomasin, and remarks on domestic details were frequently made, so as to obscure any inner misgivings about her future as Wildeve's wife.

The appointed morning came. The arrangement with Wildeve was that he should meet her at the church to guard against any unpleasant curiosity which might have affected them had they been seen walking off together in the usual country way.

Aunt and niece stood together in the bedroom where the bride was dressing. The sun, where it could catch it, made a mirror of Thomasin's hair, which she always wore braided. It was braided according to a calendric system: the more important the day the more numerous the strands in the braid. On ordinary working-days she braided it in threes; on ordinary Sundays in fours; at May-polings, gipsyings, and the like, she braided it in fives. Years ago she had said that when she married she would braid it in sevens. She had braided it in sevens to-day.

'I have been thinking that I will wear my blue silk after all,' she said. 'It *is* my wedding day, even though there may be something sad about the time. I mean,' she added, anxious to correct any wrong impression, 'not sad in itself, but in its having had great disappointment and trouble before it.'

Mrs. Yeobright breathed in a way which might have been called a sigh. 'I almost wish Clym had been at home.' she said. 'Of course you chose the time because of his absence.'

'Partly. I have felt that I acted unfairly to him in not telling him all; but, as it was done not to grieve him, I thought I would carry out the plan to its end, and tell the whole story when the sky was clear.'

'You are a practical little woman,' said Mrs. Yeobright, smiling. 'I wish you and he—no, I don't wish anything. There, it is nine o'clock,' she interrupted, hearing a whizz and a dinging downstairs.

'I told Damon I would leave at nine,' said Thomasin, hastening out of the room.

Her aunt followed. When Thomasin was going up the little walk from the door to the wicket-gate, Mrs. Yeobright looked reluctantly at her, and said, 'It is a shame to let you go alone.'

'It is necessary,' said Thomasin.

'At any rate,' added her aunt with forced cheerfulness, 'I shall call upon you this afternoon, and bring the cake with me. If Clym has returned by that time he will perhaps come too. I wish to show Mr. Wildeve that I bear him no ill-will. Let the past be forgotten. Well, God bless you! There, I don't believe in old superstitions, but I'll do it.' She threw a slipper at the retreating figure of the girl, who turned, smiled, and went on again.

A few steps further, and she looked back. 'Did you call me, aunt?' she tremulously inquired. 'Good-bye!'

Moved by an uncontrollable feeling as she looked upon Mrs. Yeobright's worn, wet face, she ran back, when her aunt came forward, and they met again. 'O—Tamsie,' said the elder, weeping, 'I don't like to let you go.'

'I——I am———' Thomasin began, giving way likewise. But, quelling her grief, she said 'Good-bye!' again and went on.

Then Mrs. Yeobright saw a little figure wending its way between the scratching furze-bushes, and diminishing far up the valley—a pale-blue spot in a vast field of neutral brown, solitary and undefended except by the power of her own hope.

But the worst feature in the case was one which did not appear in the landscape; it was the man.

The hour chosen for the ceremony by Thomasin and Wildeve had been so timed as to enable her to escape the awkwardness of meeting her cousin Clym, who was returning the same morning. To own to the partial truth of what he had heard would be distressing as long as the humiliating position resulting from the event was unimproved. It was only after a second and successful journey to the altar that she could lift up her head and prove the failure of the first attempt a pure accident.

She had not been gone from Blooms-End more than half an hour when Yeobright came by the meads from the other direction and entered the house.

'I had an early breakfast,' he said to his mother after greeting her. 'Now I could eat a little more.'

They sat down to the repeated meal, and he went on in a low, anxious voice, apparently imagining that Thomasin had not yet come downstairs, 'What's this I have heard about Thomasin and Mr. Wildeve?'

'It is true in many points,' said Mrs. Yeobright quietly; 'but it is all right now, I hope.' She looked at the clock.

'True?'

'Thomasin is gone to him to-day.'

Clym pushed away his breakfast. 'Then there is a scandal of some sort, and that's what's the matter with Thomasin. Was it this that made her ill?'

'Yes. Not a scandal: a misfortune. I will tell you all about it, Clym. You must not be angry, but you must listen, and you'll find that what we have done has been done for the best.'

She then told him the circumstances. All that he had known of the affair before he returned from Paris was that there had existed an attachment between Thomasin and Wildeve, which his mother had at first discountenanced, but had since, owing to the arguments of Thomasin, looked upon in a little more favourable light. When she, therefore, proceeded to explain all he was greatly surprised and troubled.

'And she determined that the wedding should be over before you came back,' said Mrs. Yeobright, 'that there might be no chance of her meeting you, and having a very painful time of it. That's why she has gone to him; they have arranged to be married this morning.'

'But I can't understand it,' said Yeobright, rising. ' 'Tis so unlike her. I can see why you did not write to me after her unfortunate return home. But why didn't you let me know when the wedding was going to be—the first time?'

'Well, I felt vexed with her just then. She seemed to me to be obstinate; and when I found that you were nothing in her mind I vowed that she should be nothing in yours. I felt that she was only my niece after all; I told her she might marry, but that I should take no interest in it, and should not bother you about it either.'

'It wouldn't have been bothering me. Mother, you did wrong.'

'I thought it might disturb you in your business, and that you might throw up your situation, or injure your prospects in some way because of it, so I said nothing. Of course, if they had married at that time in a proper manner, I should have told you at once.'

'Tamsin actually being married while we are sitting here!'

'Yes. Unless some accident happens again, as it did the first time. It may, considering he's the same man.'

'Yes, and I believe it will. Was it right to let her go? Suppose Wildeve is really a bad fellow?'

'Then he won't come, and she'll come home again.'

'You should have looked more into it.'

'It is useless to say that,' his mother answered with an impatient look of sorrow. 'You don't know how bad it has been here with us all these weeks, Clym. You don't know what a mortification anything of that sort is to a woman. You don't know the sleepless nights we've had in this house, and the almost bitter words that have passed between us since that Fifth of November. I hope never to pass seven such weeks again. Tamsin has not gone outside the door, and I have been ashamed to look anybody in the face; and now you blame me for letting her do the only thing that can be done to set that trouble straight.'

'No,' he said slowly. 'Upon the whole I don't blame you. But just consider how sudden it seems to me. Here was I, knowing nothing; and then I am told all at once that Tamsie is gone to be married. Well, I suppose there was nothing better to do. Do you know, mother,' he continued after a moment or two, looking suddenly interested in his own past history. 'I once thought of Tamsin as a sweetheart? Yes, I did. How odd boys are! And when I came home and saw her this time she seemed so much more affectionate than usual, that I was quite reminded of those days, particularly on the night of the party, when she was unwell. We had the party just the same—was not that rather cruel to her?'

'It made no difference. I had arranged to give one, and it was not worth while to make more gloom than necessary. To begin by shutting ourselves up and telling you of Tamsin's misfortunes would have been a poor sort of welcome.'

Clym remained thinking. 'I almost wish you had not had that party,' he said; 'and for other reasons. But I will tell you in a day or two. We must think of Tamsin now.'

They lapsed into silence. 'I'll tell you what,' said Yeobright again, in a tone which showed some slumbering feeling still. 'I don't think it kind to Tamsin to let her be married like this, and neither of us there to keep up her spirits or care a bit about her. She hasn't disgraced herself, or done anything to deserve that. It is bad enough that the wedding should be so hurried and unceremonious, without our keeping away from it in addition. Upon my soul, 'tis almost a shame. I'll go.'

'It is over by this time,' said his mother with a sigh; 'unless they were late, or he——'

'Then I shall be soon enough to see them come out. I don't quite like your keeping me in ignorance, mother, after all. Really, I half hope he has failed to meet her!'

'And ruined her character?'

'Nonsense: that wouldn't ruin Thomasin.'

He took up his hat and hastily left the house. Mrs. Yeobright looked rather unhappy, and sat still, deep in thought. But she was not long left alone. A few minutes later Clym came back again, and in his company came Diggory Venn.

'I find there isn't time for me to get there,' said Clym.

'Is she married?' Mrs. Yeobright inquired, turning to the reddleman a face in which a strange strife of wishes, for and against, was apparent.

Venn bowed. 'She is, ma'am.'

'How strange it sounds,' murmured Clym.

'And he didn't disappoint her this time?' said Mrs. Yeobright.

'He did not. And there is now no slight on her name. I was hastening arth'art[8] to tell you at once, as I saw you were not there.'

'How came you to be there? How did you know it?' she asked.

'I have been in that neighbourhood for some time, and I saw them go in,' said the reddleman. 'Wildeve came up to the door, punctual as the clock. I didn't expect it of him.' He did not add, as he might have added, that how he came to be in that neighbourhood was not by accident; that, since Wildeve's resumption of his right to Thomasin, Venn, with the thoroughness which was part of his character, had determined to see the end of the episode.

'Who was there?' said Mrs. Yeobright.

'Nobody hardly. I stood right out of the way, and she did not see me.' The reddleman spoke huskily, and looked into the garden.

'Who gave her away?'

'Miss Vye.'

'How very remarkable! Miss Vye! It is to be considered an honour, I suppose?'

'Who's Miss Vye?' said Clym.

'Captain Vye's granddaughter, of Mistover Knap.'

'A proud girl from Budmouth,' said Mrs. Yeobright. 'One not much to my liking. People say she's a witch, but of course that's absurd.'

The reddleman kept to himself his acquaintance with that fair personage, and also that Eustacia was there because he went to fetch her, in accordance with a promise he had given as soon as he learnt that the marriage was to take place. He merely said, in continuation of the story—

'I was sitting on the churchyard-wall when they came up, one from one way, the other from the other; and Miss Vye was walking thereabouts, looking at the head-stones. As soon as they had gone in I went to the door, feeling I should like to see it, as I knew her so well. I pulled off my boots because they were so noisy, and went up into the gallery. I saw then that the parson and clerk were already there.'

8. Athwart—dialect word for across, so as to meet or fall in with. In other words, "I was coming to see you."

'How came Miss Vye to have anything to do with it, if she was only on a walk that way?'

'Because there was nobody else. She had gone into the church just before me, not into the gallery. The parson looked round before beginning, and as she was the only one near he beckoned to her, and she went up to the rails. After that, when it came to signing the book, she pushed up her veil and signed; and Tamsin seemed to thank her for her kindness.' The reddleman told the tale thoughtfully, for there lingered upon his vision the changing colour of Wildeve, when Eustacia lifted the thick veil which had concealed her from recognition and looked calmly into his face. 'And then,' said Diggory sadly, 'I came away, for her history as Tamsin Yeobright was over.'

'I offered to go,' said Mrs. Yeobright regretfully. 'But she said it was not necessary.'

'Well, it is no matter,' said the reddleman. 'The thing is done at last as it was meant to be at first, and God send her happiness. Now I'll wish you good morning.'

He placed his cap on his head and went out.

From that instant of leaving Mrs. Yeobright's door, the reddleman was seen no more in or about Egdon Heath for a space of many months. He vanished entirely. The nook among the brambles where his van had been standing was as vacant as ever the next morning, and scarcely a sign remained to show that he had been there, excepting a few straws, and a little redness on the turf, which was washed away by the next storm of rain.

The report that Diggory had brought of the wedding, correct as far as it went, was deficient in one significant particular, which had escaped him through his being at some distance back in the church. When Thomasin was tremblingly engaged in signing her name Wildeve had flung towards Eustacia a glance that said plainly, 'I have punished you now.' She had replied in a low tone—and he little thought how truly—'You mistake; it gives me sincerest pleasure to see her your wife to-day.'

BOOK THIRD: THE FASCINATION

'My Mind to Me a Kingdom Is'

I

In Clym Yeobright's face could be dimly seen the typical countenance of the future. Should there be a classic period to art hereafter, its Pheidias[1] may produce such faces. The view of life as a thing

1. Phidias (500-432 B.C.), Greek sculptor and architect in the age of Pericles.

to be put up with, replacing that zest for existence which was so intense in early civilizations, must ultimately enter so thoroughly into the constitution of the advanced races that its facial expression will become accepted as a new artistic departure. People already feel that a man who lives without disturbing a curve of feature, or setting a mark of mental concern anywhere upon himself, is too far removed from modern perceptiveness to be a modern type. Physically beautiful men—the glory of the race when it was young—are almost an anachronism now; and we may wonder whether, at some time or other, physically beautiful women may not be an anachronism likewise.

The truth seems to be that a long line of disillusive centuries has permanently displaced the Hellenic idea of life, or whatever it may be called. What the Greeks only suspected we know well; what their Aeschylus imagined our nursery children feel. That old-fashioned revelling in the general situation grows less and less possible as we uncover the defects of natural laws, and see the quandary that man is in by their operation.

The lineaments which will get embodied in ideals based upon this new recognition will probably be akin to those of Yeobright. The observer's eye was arrested, not by his face as a picture, but by his face as a page; not by what it was, but by what it recorded. His features were attractive in the light of symbols, as sounds intrinsically common become attractive in language, and as shapes intrinsically simple become interesting in writing.

He had been a lad of whom something was expected. Beyond this all had been chaos. That he would be successful in an original way, or that he would go to the dogs in an original way, seemed equally probable. The only absolute certainty about him was that he would not stand still in the circumstances amid which he was born.

Hence, when his name was casually mentioned by neighbouring yeomen, the listener said, 'Ah, Clym Yeobright: what is he doing now?' When the instinctive question about a person is, What is he doing? it is felt that he will not be found to be, like most of us, doing nothing in particular. There is an indefinite sense that he must be invading some region of singularity, good or bad. The devout hope is that he is doing well. The secret faith is that he is making a mess of it. Half a dozen comfortable market-men, who were habitual callers at the Quiet Woman as they passed by in their carts, were partial to the topic. In fact, though they were not Egdon men, they could hardly avoid it while they sucked their long clay tubes and regarded the heath through the window. Clym had been so inwoven with the heath in his boyhood that hardly anybody could look upon it without thinking of him. So the subject recurred: if he were making a fortune and a name, so much the better for him; if he were making a tragical figure in the world, so much the better for a narrative.

The fact was that Yeobright's fame had spread to an awkward extent before he left home. 'It is bad when your fame outruns your means,' said the Spanish Jesuit Gracian. At the age of six he had asked a Scripture riddle: 'Who was the first man known to wear breeches?' and applause had resounded from the very verge of the heath. At seven he painted the Battle of Waterloo with tiger-lily pollen and black-currant juice, in the absence of water-colours. By the time he reached twelve he had in this manner been heard of as artist and scholar for at least two miles round. An individual whose fame spreads three or four thousand yards in the time taken by the fame of others similarly situated to travel six or eight hundred, must of necessity have something in him. Possibly Clym's fame, like Homer's, owed something to the accidents of his situation; nevertheless famous he was.

He grew up and was helped out in life. That waggery of fate which started Clive as a writing clerk, Gay[2] as a linen-draper, Keats as a surgeon, and a thousand others in a thousand other odd ways, banished the wild and ascetic heath lad to a trade whose sole concern was with the especial symbols of self-indulgence and vainglory.

The details of this choice of a business for him it is not necessary to give. At the death of his father a neighbouring gentleman had kindly undertaken to give the boy a start; and this assumed the form of sending him to Budmouth. Yeobright did not wish to go there, but it was the only feasible opening. Thence he went to London; and thence, shortly after, to Paris, where he had remained till now.

Something being expected of him, he had not been at home many days before a great curiosity as to why he stayed on so long began to arise in the heath. The natural term of a holiday had passed, yet he still remained. On the Sunday morning following the week of Thomasin's marriage a discussion on this subject was in progress at a hair-cutting before Fairway's house. Here the local barbering was always done at this hour on this day; to be followed by the great Sunday wash of the inhabitants at noon, which in its turn was followed by the great Sunday dressing an hour later. On Egdon Heath Sunday proper did not begin till dinner-time, and even then it was a somewhat battered specimen of the day.

These Sunday-morning hair-cuttings were performed by Fairway; the victim sitting on a chopping-block in front of the house, with-

2. John Gay (1685-1732), poet and playwright, author of *The Beggar's Opera*. In his youth, he was apprenticed to a drygoods merchant. *Clive* is a reference to Robert, Baron Clive (1725-1774), soldier and statesman who began a distinguished career in India as a writing clerk for the East India Company.

out a coat, and the neighbours gossiping around, idly observing the locks of hair as they rose upon the wind after the snip, and flew away out of sight to the four quarters of the heavens. Summer and winter the scene was the same, unless the wind were more than usually blusterous, when the stool was shifted a few feet round the corner. To complain of cold in sitting out of doors, hatless and coatless, while Fairway told true stories between the cuts of the scissors, would have been to pronounce yourself no man at once. To flinch, exclaim, or move a muscle of the face at the small stabs under the ear received from those instruments, or at scarifications of the neck by the comb, would have been thought a gross breach of good manners, considering that Fairway did it all for nothing. A bleeding about the poll on Sunday afternoons was amply accounted for by the explanation, 'I have had my hair cut, you know.'

The conversation on Yeobright had been started by a distant view of the young man rambling leisurely across the heath before them.

'A man who is doing well elsewhere wouldn't bide here two or three weeks for nothing,' said Fairway. 'He's got some project in 's head—depend upon that.'

'Well, 'a can't keep a diment shop here,' said Sam.

'I don't see why he should have had them two heavy boxes home if he had not been going to bide; and what there is for him to do here the Lord in heaven knows.'

Before many more surmises could be indulged in Yeobright had come near; and seeing the hair-cutting group he turned aside to join them. Marching up, and looking critically at their faces for a moment, he said, without introduction, 'Now, folks, let me guess what you have been talking about.'

'Ay, sure, if you will,' said Sam.

'About me.'

'Now, it is a thing I shouldn't have dreamed of doing, otherwise,' said Fairway in a tone of integrity; 'but since you have named it, Master Yeobright, I'll own that we was talking about 'ee. We were wondering what could keep you home here mollyhorning[3] about when you have made such a world-wide name for yourself in the nick-nack trade—now, that's the truth o't.'

'I'll tell you,' said Yeobright, with unexpected earnestness. 'I am not sorry to have the opportunity. I've come home because, all things considered, I can be a trifle less useless here than anywhere else. But I have only lately found this out. When I first got away from home I thought this place was not worth troubling about. I thought our life here was contemptible. To oil your boots instead

3. Dialect version of *blatantly idling* (from molly as idle and horning as trumpeting).

of blacking them, to dust your coat with a switch instead of a brush: was there ever anything more ridiculous? I said.'

'So 'tis; so 'tis!'

'No, no—you are wrong; it isn't.'

'Beg your pardon, we thought that was your maning?'[4]

'Well, as my views changed my course became very depressing. I found that I was trying to be like people who had hardly anything in common with myself. I was endeavouring to put off one sort of life for another sort of life, which was not better than the life I had known before. It was simply different.'

'True; a sight different,' said Fairway.

'Yes, Paris must be a taking place,' said Humphrey. 'Grand shop-winders, trumpets, and drums; and here be we out of doors in all winds and weathers——'

'But you mistake me,' pleaded Clym. 'All this was very depressing. But not so depressing as something I next perceived—that my business was the idlest, vainest, most effeminate business that ever a man could be put to. That decided me: I would give it up and try to follow some rational occupation among the people I knew best, and to whom I could be of most use. I have come home; and this is how I mean to carry out my plan. I shall keep a school as near to Egdon as possible, so as to be able to walk over here and have a night-school in my mother's house. But I must study a little at first, to get properly qualified. Now, neighbours, I must go.'

And Clym resumed his walk across the heath.

'He'll never carry it out in the world,' said Fairway. 'In a few weeks he'll learn to see things otherwise.'

' 'Tis good-hearted of the young man,' said another. 'But, for my part, I think he had better mind his business.'

The New Course Causes Disappointment

II

Yeobright loved his kind. He had a conviction that the want of most men was knowledge of a sort which brings wisdom rather than affluence. He wished to raise the class at the expense of individuals rather than individuals at the expense of the class. What was more, he was ready at once to be the first unit sacrificed.

In passing from the bucolic to the intellectual life the intermediate stages are usually two at least, frequently many more; and one of these stages is almost sure to be worldly advance. We can hardly imagine bucolic placidity quickening to intellectual aims without imagining social aims as the transitional phase. Yeobright's local peculiarity was that in striving at high thinking he still cleaved to

4. Meaning.

plain living—nay, wild and meagre living in many respects, and brotherliness with clowns.

He was a John the Baptist who took ennoblement rather than repentance for his text. Mentally he was in a provincial future, that is, he was in many points abreast with the central town thinkers of his date. Much of this development he may have owed to his studious life in Paris, where he had become acquainted with ethical systems popular at the time.

In consequence of this relatively advanced position, Yeobright might have been called unfortunate. The rural world was not ripe for him. A man should be only partially before his time: to be completely to the vanward in aspirations is fatal to fame. Had Philip's warlike son been intellectually so far ahead as to have attempted civilization without bloodshed, he would have been twice the godlike hero that he seemed, but nobody would have heard of an Alexander.

In the interests of renown the forwardness should lie chiefly in the capacity to handle things. Successful propagandists have succeeded because the doctrine they bring into form is that which their listeners have for some time felt without being able to shape. A man who advocates aesthetic effort and deprecates social effort is only likely to be understood by a class to which social effort has become a stale matter. To argue upon the possibility of culture before luxury to the bucolic world may be to argue truly, but it is an attempt to disturb a sequence to which humanity has been long accustomed. Yeobright preaching to the Egdon eremites[5] that they might rise to a serene comprehensiveness without going through the process of enriching themselves, was not unlike arguing to ancient Chaldeans[6] that in ascending from earth to the pure empyrean it was not necessary to pass first into the intervening heaven of ether.

Was Yeobright's mind well-proportioned? No. A well-proportioned mind is one which shows no particular bias; one of which we may safely say that it will never cause its owner to be confined as a madman, tortured as a heretic, or crucified as a blasphemer. Also, on the other hand, that it will never cause him to be applauded as a prophet, revered as a priest, or exalted as a king. Its usual blessings are happiness and mediocrity. It produces the poetry of Rogers, the paintings of West, the statecraft of North,[7]

5. Hermits.

6. In the biblical book of Daniel, a group of people in Babylon specially learned in occult science, magic, and astrology.

7. Lord Frederick North, Second Earl of Guilford, (1732-1792), became Prime Minister under George III. Widely regarded as simply the King's tool, he was neither a great statesman nor a great orator. *Benjamin West* (1738-1820) was an American artist who became a highly popular portrait painter in England. He was President of the Royal Academy after Joshua Reynolds died. Modern criticism finds him dull and unimaginative. *Samuel Rogers* (1763-1855), an English poet, was recognized so widely in his own day that he was offered (but declined) the Laureateship when Wordsworth died. Now, he is dismissed as a poet of carefully finished and graceful trivia.

the spiritual guidance of Tomline;[8] enabling its possessors to find their way to wealth, to wind up well, to step with dignity off the stage, to die comfortably in their beds, and to get the decent monument which, in many cases, they deserve. It never would have allowed Yeobright to do such a ridiculous thing as throw up his business to benefit his fellow-creatures.

He walked along towards home without attending to paths. If any one knew the heath well it was Clym. He was permeated with its scenes, with its substance, and with its odours. He might be said to be its product. His eyes had first opened theron; with it appearance all the first images of his memory were mingled; his estimate of life had been coloured by it; his toys had been the flint knives and arrow-heads which he found there, wondering why stones should 'grow' to such odd shapes; his flowers, the purple bells and yellow furze; his animal kingdom, the snakes and croppers; his society, its human haunters. Take all the varying hates felt by Eustacia Vye towards the heath, and translate them into loves, and you have the heart of Clym. He gazed upon the wide prospect as he walked, and was glad.

To many persons this Egdon was a place which had slipped out of its century generations ago, to intrude as an uncouth object into this. It was an obsolete thing, and few cared to study it. How could this be otherwise in the days of square fields, plashed hedges, and meadows watered on a plan so rectangular that on a fine day they look like silver gridirons? The farmer, in his ride, who could smile at artificial grasses, look with solicitude at the coming corn, and sigh with sadness at the fly-eaten turnips, bestowed upon the distant upland of heath nothing better than a frown. But as for Yeobright, when he looked from the heights on his way he could not help indulging in a barbarous satisfaction at observing that, in some of the attempts at reclamation from the waste, tillage, after holding on for a year or two, had receded again in despair, the ferns and furze-tufts stubbornly reasserting themselves.

He descended into the valley, and soon reached his home at Blooms-End. His mother was snipping dead leaves from the window-plants. She looked up at him as if she did not understand the meaning of his long stay with her; her face had worn that look for several days. He could perceive that the curiosity which had been shown by the hair-cutting group amounted in his mother to concern. But she had asked no question with her lips, even when the arrival of his trunks suggested that he was not going to leave her soon. Her silence besought an explanation of him more loudly than words.

'I am not going back to Paris again, mother,' he said. 'At least, in my old capacity. I have given up the business.'

8. Sir George Tomline (1750-1827), Bishop of Winchester and tutor and spiritual adviser to William Pitt, the younger.

Mrs. Yeobright turned in pained surprise. 'I thought something was amiss, because of the boxes. I wonder you did not tell me sooner.'

'I ought to have done it. But I have been in doubt whether you would be pleased with my plan. I was not quite clear on a few points myself. I am going to take an entirely new course.'

'I am astonished, Clym. How can you want to do better than you've been doing?'

'Very easily. But I shall not do better in the way you mean; I suppose it will be called doing worse. But I hate that business of mine, and I want to do some worthy thing before I die. As a schoolmaster I think to do it—a schoolmaster to the poor and ignorant, to teach them what nobody else will.'

'After all the trouble that has been taken to give you a start, and when there is nothing to do but to keep straight on towards affluence, you say you will be a poor man's schoolmaster. Your fancies will be your ruin, Clym.'

Mrs. Yeobright spoke calmly, but the force of feeling behind the words was but too apparent to one who knew her as well as her son did. He did not answer. There was in his face that hopelessness of being understood which comes when the objector is constitutionally beyond the reach of a logic that, even under favouring conditions, is almost too coarse a vehicle for the subtlety of the argument.

No more was said on the subject till the end of dinner. His mother then began, as if there had been no interval since the morning. 'It disturbs me, Clym, to find that you have come home with such thoughts as those. I hadn't the least idea that you meant to go backward in the world by your own free choice. Of course, I have always supposed you were going to push straight on, as other men do—all who deserve the name—when they have been put in a good way of doing well.'

'I cannot help it,' said Clym, in a troubled tone. 'Mother, I hate the flashy business. Talk about men who deserve the name, can any man deserving the name waste his time in that effeminate way, when he sees half the world going to ruin for want of somebody to buckle to and teach them how to breast the misery they are born to? I get up every morning and see the whole creation groaning and travailing in pain, as St. Paul says, and yet there am I, trafficking in glittering splendours with wealthy women and titled libertines, and pandering to the meanest vanities—I, who have health and strength enough for anything. I have been troubled in my mind about it all the year, and the end is that I cannot do it any more.'

'Why can't you do it as well as others?'

'I don't know, except that there are many things other people care for which I don't; and that's partly why I think I ought to do this. For one thing, my body does not require much of me. I cannot enjoy delicacies; good things are wasted upon me. Well, I ought to turn that defect to advantage, and by being able to do without what other people require I can spend what such things cost upon anybody else.'

Now, Yeobright, having inherited some of these very instincts from the woman before him, could not fail to awaken a reciprocity in her through her feelings, if not by arguments, diguise it as she might for his good. She spoke with less assurance. 'And yet you might have been a wealthy man if you had only persevered. Manager to that large diamond establishment—what better can a man wish for? What a post of trust and respect! I suppose you will be like your father; like him, you are getting weary of doing well.'

'No,' said her son; 'I am not weary of that, though I am weary of what you mean by it. Mother, what is doing well?'

Mrs. Yeobright was far too thoughtful a woman to be content with ready definitions, and, like the 'What is wisdom?' of Plato's Socrates, and the 'What is truth?' of Pontius Pilate, Yeobright's burning question received no answer.

The silence was broken by the clash of the garden gate, a tap at the door, and its opening. Christian Cantle appeared in the room in his Sunday clothes.

It was the custom on Egdon to begin the preface to a story before absolutely entering the house, so as to be well in for the body of the narrative by the time visitor and visited stood face to face. Christian had been saying to them while the door was leaving its latch, 'To think that I, who go from home but once in a while, and hardly then, should have been there this morning!'

' 'Tis news you have brought us, then, Christian?' said Mrs. Yeobright.

'Ay, sure, about a witch, and ye must overlook my time o' day; for, says I, "I must go and tell 'em, though they won't have half done dinner." I assure ye it made me shake like a driven leaf. Do ye think any harm will come o't?'

'Well—what?'

'This morning at church we was all standing up, and the pa'son said, "Let us pray." "Well," thinks I, "one may as well kneel as stand;" so down I went; and, more than that, all the rest were as willing to oblige the man as I. We hadn't been hard at it for more than a minute when a most terrible screech sounded through church, as if somebody had just gied up their heart's blood. All the folk jumped up, and then we found that Susan Nunsuch had pricked Miss Vye with a long stocking-needle, as she had threatened to do as soon as ever she could get the young lady to church, where she don't come very often. She've waited for this chance for weeks, so as to draw her blood and put an end to the bewitching of Susan's children that has been carried on so long. Sue followed her into church, sat next to her, and as soon as she could find a chance in went the stocking-needle into my lady's arm.'

'Good heaven, how horrid!' said Mrs. Yeobright.

'Sue pricked her that deep that the maid fainted away; and as I was afeard there might be some tumult among us, I got behind the bass-viol and didn't see no more. But they carried her out into the air, 'tis said; but when they looked round for Sue she was gone. What a scream that girl gied, poor thing! There were the pa'son in his surplice holding up his hand and saying, "Sit down, my good people, sit down!" But the deuce a bit would they sit down. O, and what d'ye think I found out, Mrs. Yeobright? The pa'son wears a suit of clothes under his surplice!—I could see his black sleeve when he held up his arm.'

' 'Tis a cruel thing,' said Yeobright.

'Yes,' said his mother.

'The nation ought to look into it,' said Christian. 'Here's Humphrey coming, I think.'

In came Humphrey. 'Well, have ye heard the news? But I see you have. 'Tis a very strange thing that whenever one of Egdon folk goes to church some rum job or other is sure to be doing. The last time one of us was there was when neighbour Fairway went in the fall; and that was the day you forbad the banns, Mrs. Yeobright.'

'Has this cruelly treated girl been able to walk home?' said Clym.

'They say she got better, and went home very well. And now I've told it I must be moving homeward myself.'

'And I,' said Humphrey. 'Truly now we shall see if there's anything in what folks say about her.'

When they were gone into the heath again Yeobright said quietly to his mother, 'Do you think I have turned teacher too soon?'

'It is right that there should be schoolmasters, and missionaries, and all such men,' she replied. 'But it is right, too, that I should try to lift you out of this life into something richer, and that you should not come back again, and be as if I had not tried at all.'

Later in the day Sam, the turf-cutter, entered. 'I've come a-borrowing, Mrs. Yeobright. I suppose you have heard what's been happening to the beauty on the hill?'

'Yes, Sam: half a dozen have been telling us.'

'Beauty?' said Clym.

'Yes, tolerably well-favoured,' Sam replied. 'Lord! all the country owns that 'tis one of the strangest things in the world that such a woman should have come to live up there.'

'Dark or fair?'

'Now, though I've seen her twenty times, that's a thing I cannot call to mind.'

'Darker than Tamsin,' murmured Mrs. Yeobright.

'A woman who seems to care for nothing at all, as you may say.'

'She is melancholy, then?' inquired Clym.

'She mopes about by herself, and don't mix in with the people.'

'Is she a young lady inclined for adventures?'

'Not to my knowledge.'

'Doesn't join in with the lads in their games, to get some sort of excitement in this lonely place?'

'No.'

'Mumming, for instance?'

'No. Her notions be different. I should rather say her thoughts were far away from here, with lords and ladies she'll never know, and mansions she'll never see again.'

Observing that Clym appeared singularly interested Mrs. Yeobright said rather uneasily to Sam, 'You see more in her than most of us do. Miss Vye is to my mind too idle to be charming. I have never heard that she is of any use to herself or to other people. Good girls don't get treated as witches even on Egdon.'

'Nonsense—that proves nothing either way,' said Yeobright.

'Well, of course I don't understand such niceties,' said Sam, withdrawing from a possibly unpleasant argument; 'and what she is we must wait for time to tell us. The business that I have really called about is this, to borrow the longest and strongest rope you have. The captain's bucket has dropped into the well, and they are in want of water; and as all the chaps are at home to-day we think we can get it out for him. We have three cart-ropes already, but they won't reach to the bottom.'

Mrs. Yeobright told him that he might have whatever ropes he could find in the outhouse, and Sam went out to search. When he passed by the door Clym joined him, and accompanied him to the gate.

'Is this young witch-lady going to stay long at Mistover?' he asked.

'I should say so.'

'What a cruel shame to ill-use her! She must have suffered greatly—more in mind than in body.'

''Twas a graceless trick—such a handsome girl, too. You ought to see her, Mr. Yeobright, being a young man come from far, and with a little more to show for your years than most of us.'

'Do you think she would like to teach children?' said Clym.

Sam shook his head. 'Quite a different sort of body from that, I reckon.'

'O, it was merely something which occurred to me. It would of course be necessary to see her and talk it over—not an easy thing, by the way, for my family and hers are not very friendly.'

'I'll tell you how you mid see her, Mr. Yeobright,' said Sam. 'We are going to grapple for the bucket at six o'clock to-night at her house, and you could lend a hand. There's five or six coming, but the well is deep, and another might be useful, if you don't mind appearing in that shape. She's sure to be walking round.'

'I'll think of it,' said Yeobright; and they parted.

He thought of it a good deal; but nothing more was said about Eustacia inside the house at that time. Whether this romantic martyr to superstition and the melancholy mummer he had conversed with under the full moon were one and the same person remained as yet a problem.

The First Act in a Timeworn Drama

III

The afternoon was fine, and Yeobright walked on the heath for an hour with his mother. When they reached the lofty ridge which divided the valley of Blooms-End from the adjoining valley they stood still and looked round. The Quiet Woman Inn was visible on the low margin of the heath in one direction, and afar on the other hand rose Mistover Knap.

'You mean to call on Thomasin?' he inquired.

'Yes. But you need not come this time,' said his mother.

'In that case I'll branch off here, mother. I am going to Mistover.'

Mrs. Yeobright turned to him inquiringly.

'I am going to help them get the bucket out of the captain's well,' he continued. 'As it is so very deep I may be useful. And I should like to see this Miss Vye—not so much for her good looks as for another reason.'

'Must you go?' his mother asked.

'I thought to.'

And they parted. 'There is no help for it,' murmured Clym's mother gloomily as he withdrew. 'They are sure to see each other. I wish Sam would carry his news to other houses than mine.'

Clym's retreating figure got smaller and smaller as it rose and fell over the hillocks on his way. 'He is tender-hearted,' said Mrs. Yeobright to herself while she watched him; 'otherwise it would matter little. How he's going on!'

He was, indeed, walking with a will over the furze, as straight as a line, as if his life depended upon it. His mother drew a long breath, and, abandoning the visit to Thomasin, turned back. The evening films began to make nebulous pictures of the valleys, but the high lands still were raked by the declining rays of the winter sun, which glanced on Clym as he walked forward, eyed by every rabbit and fieldfare around, a long shadow advancing in front of him.

On drawing near to the furze-covered bank and ditch which fortified the captain's dwelling he could hear voices within, signifying that operations had been already begun. At the side-entrance gate he stopped and looked over.

Half a dozen able-bodied men were standing in a line from the well-mouth, holding a rope which passed over the well-roller into the depths below. Fairway, with a piece of smaller rope round his body, made fast to one of the standards, to guard against accidents, was leaning over the opening, his right hand clasping the vertical rope that descended into the well.

'Now, silence, folks,' said Fairway.

The talking ceased, and Fairway gave a circular motion to the rope, as if he were stirring batter. At the end of a minute a dull splashing reverberated from the bottom of the well; the helical twist he had imparted to the rope had reached the grapnel[9] below.

'Haul!' said Fairway; and the men who held the rope began to gather it over the wheel.

'I think we've got sommat,' said one of the haulers-in.

'Then pull steady,' said Fairway.

They gathered up more and more, till a regular dripping into the well could be heard below. It grew smarter with the increasing height of the bucket, and presently a hundred and fifty feet of rope had been pulled in.

Fairway then lit a lantern, tied it to another cord, and began lowering it into the well beside the first. Clym came forward and looked down. Strange humid leaves, which knew nothing of the seasons of the year, and quaint-natured mosses were revealed on the well-side as the lantern descended; till its rays fell upon a confused mass of rope and bucket dangling in the dank, dark air.

'We've only got en by the edge of the hoop—steady, for God's sake!' said Fairway.

They pulled with the greatest gentleness, till the wet bucket appeared about two yards below them, like a dead friend come to earth again. Three or four hands were stretched out, then jerk went the rope, whizz went the wheel, the two foremost haulers fell backward, the beating of a falling body was heard, receding down the

9. Instrument with iron claws made to seize or hold a rope or an object. *Helical twist* is a spiral.

sides of the well, and a thunderous uproar arose at the bottom. The bucket was gone again.

'Damn the bucket!' said Fairway.

'Lower again,' said Sam.

'I'm as stiff as a ram's horn stooping so long,' said Fairway, standing up and stretching himself till his joints creaked.

'Rest a few minutes, Timothy,' said Yeobright. 'I'll take your place.'

The grapnel was again lowered. Its smart impact upon the distant water reached their ears like a kiss, whereupon Yeobright knelt down, and leaning over the well began dragging the grapnel round and round as Fairway had done.

'Tie a rope round him—it is dangerous!' cried a soft and anxious voice somewhere above them.

Everybody turned. The speaker was a woman, gazing down upon the group from an upper window, whose panes blazed in the ruddy glare from the west. Her lips were parted and she appeared for the moment to forget where she was.

The rope was accordingly tied round his waist, and the work proceeded. At the next haul the weight was not heavy, and it was discovered that they had only secured a coil of the rope detached from the bucket. The tangled mass was thrown into the background. Humphrey took Yeobright's place, and the grapnel was lowered again.

Yeobright retired to the heap of recovered rope in a meditative mood. Of the identity between the lady's voice and that of the melancholy mummer he had not a moment's doubt. 'How thoughtful of her!' he said to himself.

Eustacia, who had reddened when she perceived the effect of her exclamation upon the group below, was no longer to be seen at the window, though Yeobright scanned it wistfully. While he stood there the men at the well succeeded in getting up the bucket without a mishap. One of them then went to inquire for the captain, to learn what orders he wished to give for mending the well-tackle. The captain proved to be away from home; and Eustacia appeared at the door and came out. She had lapsed into an easy and dignified calm, far removed from the intensity of life in her words of solicitude for Clym's safety.

'Will it be possible to draw water here to-night?' she inquired.

'No, miss; the bottom of the bucket is clean knocked out. And as we can do no more now we'll leave off, and come again to-morrow morning.'

'No water,' she murmured, turning away.

'I can send you up some from Blooms-End,' said Clym, coming forward and raising his hat as the men retired.

Yeobright and Eustacia looked at each other for one instant, as if each had in mind those few moments during which a certain moonlight scene was common to both. With the glance the calm fixity of her features sublimed itself to an expression of refinement and warmth: it was like garish noon rising to the dignity of sunset in a couple of seconds.

'Thank you; it will hardly be necessary,' she replied.

'But if you have no water?'

'Well, it is what I call no water,' she said, blushing, and lifting her long-lashed eyelids as if to lift them were a work requiring consideration. 'But my grandfather calls it water enough. I'll show you what I mean.'

She moved away a few yards, and Clym followed. When she reached the corner of the enclosure, where the steps were formed for mounting the boundary bank, she sprang up with a lightness which seemed strange after her listless movement towards the well. It incidentally showed that her apparent languor did not arise from lack of force.

Clym ascended behind her, and noticed a circular burnt patch at the top of the bank. 'Ashes?' he said.

'Yes,' said Eustacia. 'We had a little bonfire here last Fifth of November, and those are the marks of it.'

On that spot had stood the fire she had kindled to attract Wildeve.

'That's the only kind of water we have,' she continued, tossing a stone into the pool, which lay on the outside of the bank like the white of an eye without its pupil. The stone fell with a flounce, but no Wildeve appeared on the other side, as on a previous occasion there. 'My grandfather says he lived for more than twenty years at sea on water twice as bad as that,' she went on, 'and considers it quite good enough for us here on an emergency.'

'Well, as a matter of fact there are no impurities in the water of these pools at this time of the year. It has only just rained into them.'

She shook her head. 'I am managing to exist in a wilderness, but I cannot drink from a pond,' she said.

Clym looked towards the well, which was now deserted, the men having gone home. 'It is a long way to send for spring-water,' he said, after a silence. 'But since you don't like this in the pond, I'll try to get you some myself.' He went back to the well. 'Yes, I think I could do it by tying on this pail.'

'But, since I would not trouble the men to get it, I cannot in conscience let you.'

'I don't mind the trouble at all.'

He made fast the pail to the long coil of rope, put it over the wheel, and allowed it to descend by letting the rope slip through his hands. Before it had gone far, however, he checked it.

'I must make fast the end first, or we may lose the whole,' he said to Eustacia, who had drawn near. 'Could you hold this a moment, while I do it—or shall I call your servant?'

'I can hold it,' said Eustacia; and he placed the rope in her hands, going then to search for the end.

'I suppose I may let it slip down?' she inquired.

'I would advise you not to let it go far,' said Clym. 'It will get much heavier, you will find.'

However, Eustacia had begun to pay out. While he was tying she cried, 'I cannot stop it!'

Clym ran to her side, and found he could only check the rope by twisting the loose part round the upright post, when it stopped with a jerk. 'Has it hurt you?'

'Yes,' she replied.

'Very much?'

'No; I think not.' She opened her hands. One of them was bleeding; the rope had dragged off the skin. Eustacia wrapped it in her handkerchief.

'You should have let go,' said Yeobright. 'Why didn't you?'

'You said I was to hold on. . . . This is the second time I have been wounded to-day.'

'Ah, yes; I have heard of it. I blush for my native Egdon. Was it a serious injury you received in church, Miss Vye?'

There was such an abundance of sympathy in Clym's tone that Eustacia slowly drew up her sleeve and disclosed her round white arm. A bright red spot appeared on its smooth surface, like a ruby on Parian marble.

'There it is,' she said, putting her finger against the spot.

'It was dastardly of the woman,' said Clym. 'Will not Captain Vye get her punished?'

'He is gone from home on that very business. I did not know that I had such a magic reputation.'

'And you fainted?' said Clym, looking at the scarlet little puncture as if he would like to kiss it and make it well.

'Yes, it frightened me. I had not been to church for a long time. And now I shall not go again for ever so long—perhaps never. I cannot face their eyes after this. Don't you think it dreadfully humiliating? I wished I was dead for hours after, but I don't mind now.'

'I have come to clean away these cobwebs,' said Yeobright. 'Would you like to help me—by high class teaching? We might benefit them much.'

'I don't quite feel anxious to. I have not much love for my fellow-creatures. Sometimes I quite hate them.'

'Still I think that if you were to hear my scheme you might take an interest in it. There is no use in hating people—if you hate anything, you should hate what produced them.'

'Do you mean Nature? I hate her already. But I shall be glad to hear your scheme at any time.'

The situation had now worked itself out, and the next natural thing was for them to part. Clym knew this well enough, and Eustacia made a move of conclusion; yet he looked at her as if he had one word more to say. Perhaps if he had not lived in Paris it would never have been uttered.

'We have met before,' he said, regarding her with rather more interest than was necessary.

'I do not own it,' said Eustacia, with a repressed, still look.

'But I may think what I like.'

'Yes.'

'You are lonely here.'

'I cannot endure the heath, except in its purple season. The heath is a cruel taskmaster to me.'

'Can you say so?' he asked. 'To my mind it is most exhilarating, and strengthening, and soothing. I would rather live on these hills than anywhere else in the world.'

'It is well enough for artists; but I never would learn to draw.'

'And there is a very curious Druidical stone just out there.' He threw a pebble in the direction signified. 'Do you often go to see it?'

'I was not even aware that there existed any such curious Druidical stone. I am aware that there are Boulevards in Paris.'

Yeobright looked thoughtfully on the ground. 'That means much,' he said.

'It does indeed,' said Eustacia.

'I remember when I had the same longing for town bustle. Five years of a great city would be a perfect cure for that.'

'Heaven send me such a cure! Now, Mr. Yeobright, I will go indoors and plaster my wounded hand.'

They separated, and Eustacia vanished in the increasing shade. She seemed full of many things. Her past was a blank, her life had begun. The effect upon Clym of this meeting he did not fully discover till some time after. During his walk home his most intelligible sensation was that his scheme had somehow become glorified. A beautiful woman had been intertwined with it.

On reaching the house he went up to the room which was to be made his study, and occupied himself during the evening in unpacking his books from the boxes and arranging them on shelves. From another box he drew a lamp and a can of oil. He trimmed the lamp, arranged his table, and said, 'Now, I am ready to begin.'

He rose early the next morning, read two hours before breakfast by the light of his lamp—read all the morning, all the afternoon. Just when the sun was going down his eyes felt weary, and he leant back in his chair.

His room overlooked the front of the premises and the valley of the heath beyond. The lowest beams of the winter sun threw the shadow of the house over the palings, across the grass margin of the heath, and far up the vale, where the chimney outlines and those of the surrounding tree-tops stretched forth in long dark prongs. Having been seated at work all day, he decided to take a turn upon the hills before it got dark; and, going out forthwith, he struck across the heath towards Mistover.

It was an hour and a half later when he again appeared at the garden gate. The shutters of the house were closed, and Christian Cantle, who had been wheeling manure about the garden all day, had gone home. On entering he found that his mother, after waiting a long time for him, had finished her meal.

'Where have you been, Clym?' she immediately said. 'Why didn't you tell me that you were going away at this time?'

'I have been on the heath.'

'You'll meet Eustacia Vye if you go up there.'

Clym paused a minute. 'Yes, I met her this evening,' he said, as though it were spoken under the sheer necessity of preserving honesty.

'I wondered if you had.'

'It was no appointment.'

'No; such meetings never are.'

'But you are not angry, mother?'

'I can hardly say that I am not. Angry? No. But when I consider the usual nature of the drag which causes men of promise to disappoint the world I feel uneasy.'

'You deserve credit for the feeling, mother. But I can assure you that you need not be disturbed by it on my account.'

'When I think of you and your new crotchets,' said Mrs. Yeobright, with some emphasis, 'I naturally don't feel so comfortable as I did a twelvemonth ago. It is incredible to me that a man accustomed to the attractive women of Paris and elsewhere should be so easily worked upon by a girl in a heath. You could just as well have walked another way.'

'I had been studying all day.'

'Well, yes,' she added more hopefully, 'I have been thinking that you might get on as a schoolmaster, and rise that way, since you really are determined to hate the course you were pursuing.'

Yeobright was unwilling to disturb this idea, though his scheme was far enough removed from one wherein the education of youth should be made a mere channel of social ascent. He had no desires of that sort. He had reached the stage in a young man's life when the grimness of the general human situation first becomes clear; and the realization of this causes ambition to halt awhile. In France it is not uncustomary to commit suicide at this stage; in England we do much better, or much worse, as the case may be.

The love between the young man and his mother was strangely invisible now. Of love it may be said, the less earthly the less demonstrative. In its absolutely indestructible form it reaches a profundity in which all exhibition of itself is painful. It was so with these. Had conversations between them been overheard, people would have said, 'How cold they are to each other!'

His theory and his wishes about devoting his future to teaching had made an impression on Mrs. Yeobright. Indeed, how could it be otherwise when he was a part of her—when their discourses were as if carried on between the right and the left hands of the same body? He had despaired of reaching her by argument; and it was almost as a discovery to him that he could reach her by a magnetism which was as superior to words as words are to yells.

Strangely enough he began to feel now that it would not be so hard to persuade her who was his best friend that comparative poverty was essentially the higher course for him, as to reconcile to his feelings the act of persuading her. From every provident point of view his mother was so undoubtedly right, that he was not without a sickness of heart in finding he could shake her.

She had a singular insight into life, considering that she had never mixed with it. There are instances of persons who, without clear ideas of the things they criticize, have yet had clear ideas of the relations of those things. Blacklock, a poet blind from his birth, could describe visual objects with accuracy; Professor Sanderson,[1] who was also blind, gave excellent lectures on colour, and taught others the theory of ideas which they had and he had not. In the social sphere these gifted ones are mostly women; they can watch a world which they never saw, and estimate forces of which they have only heard. We call it intuition.

What was the great world to Mrs. Yeobright? A multitude whose tendencies could be perceived, though not its essences. Communities were seen by her as from a distance; she saw them as

1. Nicholas Sanderson (or Saunderson) (1682-1739), lost his eyes from smallpox at the age of one. He became a mathematician and scientist at Cambridge, and was described by Lord Chesterfield as one who, without the use of his own eyes, taught others to use theirs. *Thomas Blacklock* (1721-1791) was a Scottish poet who became blind from an attack of smallpox at the age of 6 months. He was patronized by David Hume.

we see the throngs which cover the canvases of Sallaert, Van Alsloot,[2] and others of that school—vast masses of beings, jostling, zigzagging, and processioning in definite directions, but whose features are indistinguishable by the very comprehensiveness of the view.

One could see that, as far as it had gone, her life was very complete on its reflective side. The philosophy of her nature, and its limitation by circumstances, was almost written in her movements. They had a majestic foundation, though they were far from being majestic; and they had a groundwork of assurance, but they were not assured. As her once elastic walk had become deadened by time, so had her natural pride of life been hindered in its blooming by her necessities.

The next slight touch in the shaping of Clym's destiny occurred a few days after. A barrow was opened on the heath, and Yeobright attended the operation, remaining away from his study during several hours. In the afternoon Christian returned from a journey in the same direction, and Mrs. Yeobright questioned him.

'They have dug a hole, and they have found things like flowerpots upside down, Mis'ess Yeobright; and inside these be real charnel bones. They have carried 'em off to men's houses; but I shouldn't like to sleep where they will bide. Dead folks have been known to come and claim their own. Mr. Yeobright had got one pot of the bones, and was going to bring 'em home—real skellington bones—but 'twas ordered otherwise. You'll be relieved to hear that he gave away his, pot and all, on second thoughts; and a blessed thing for ye, Mis'ess Yeobright, considering the wind o' nights.'

'Gave it away?'

'Yes. To Miss Vye. She has a cannibal taste for such churchyard furniture seemingly.'

'Miss Vye was there too?'

'Ay, 'a b'lieve she was.'

When Clym came home, which was shortly after, his mother said, in a curious tone, 'The urn you had meant for me you gave away.'

Yeobright made no reply; the current of her feeling was too pronounced to admit it.

The early weeks of the year passed on. Yeobright certainly studied at home, but he also walked much abroad, and the direction of his walk was always towards some point of a line between Mistover and Rainbarrow.

2. Denis Van Alsloot, court painter to Archduke Albert, Governor of the Netherlands about 1600. *Anthonie Sallaert* (1590?-1648?) was a Flemish painter often employed by Rubens.

The month of March arrived, and the heath showed its first faint signs of awakening from winter trance. The awakening was almost feline in its stealthiness. The pool outside the bank by Eustacia's dwelling, which seemed as dead and desolate as ever to an observer who moved and made noises in his observation, would gradually disclose a state of great animation when silently watched awhile. A timid animal world had come to life for the season. Little tadpoles and efts began to bubble up through the water, and to race along beneath it; toads made noises like very young ducks, and advanced to the margin in twos and threes; overhead, bumble-bees flew hither and thither in the thickening light, their drone coming and going like the sound of a gong.

On an evening such as this Yeobright descended into the Blooms-End valley from beside that very pool, where he had been standing with another person quite silently and quite long enough to hear all this puny stir of resurrection in nature; yet he had not heard it. His walk was rapid as he came down, and he went with a springy tread. Before entering upon his mother's premises he stopped and breathed. The light which shone forth on him from the window revealed that his face was flushed and his eye bright. What it did not show was something which lingered upon his lips like a seal set there. The abiding presence of this impress was so real that he hardly dared to enter the house, for it seemed as if his mother might say, 'What red spot is that glowing upon your mouth so vividly?'

But he entered soon after. The tea was ready, and he sat down opposite his mother. She did not speak many words; and as for him, something had been just done and some words had been just said on the hill which prevented him from beginning a desultory chat. His mother's taciturnity was not without ominousness, but he appeared not to care. He knew why she said so little, but he could not remove the cause of her bearing towards him. These half-silent sittings were far from uncommon with them now. At last Yeobright made a beginning of what was intended to strike at the whole root of the matter.

'Five days have we sat like this at meals with scarcely a word. What's the use of it, mother?'

'None,' said she, in a heart-swollen tone. 'But there is only too good a reason.'

'Not when you know all. I have been wanting to speak about this, and I am glad the subject is begun. The reason, of course, is Eustacia Vye. Well, I confess I have seen her lately, and have seen her a good many times.'

'Yes, yes; and I know what that amounts to. It troubles me, Clym. You are wasting your life here; and it is solely on account of her. If it had not been for that woman you would never have entertained this teaching scheme at all.'

Clym looked hard at his mother. 'You know that is not it,' he said.

'Well, I know you had decided to attempt it before you saw her; but that would have ended in intentions. It was very well to talk of, but ridiculous to put in practice. I fully expected that in the course of a month or two you would have seen the folly of such self-sacrifice, and would have been by this time back again to Paris in some business or other. I can understand objections to the diamond trade—I really was thinking that it might be inadequate to the life of a man like you even though it might have made you a millionaire. But now I see how mistaken you are about this girl I doubt if you could be correct about other things.'

'How am I mistaken in her?'

'She is lazy and dissatisfied. But that is not all of it. Supposing her to be as good a woman as any you can find, which she certainly is not, why do you wish to connect yourself with anybody at present?'

'Well, there are practical reasons,' Clym began, and then almost broke off under an overpowering sense of the weight of argument which could be brought against his statement. 'If I take a school an educated woman would be invaluable as a help to me.'

'What! you really mean to marry her?'

'It would be premature to state that plainly. But consider what obvious advantages there would be in doing it. She——'

'Don't suppose she has any money. She hasn't a farthing.'

'She is excellently educated, and would make a good matron in a boarding-school. I candidly own that I have modified my views a little, in deference to you; and it should satisfy you. I no longer adhere to my intention of giving with my own mouth rudimentary education to the lowest class. I can do better. I can establish a good private school for farmers' sons, and without stopping the school I can manage to pass examinations. By this means, and by the assistance of a wife like her——'

'O, Clym!'

'I shall ultimately, I hope, be at the head of one of the best schools in the country.'

Yeobright had enunciated the word 'her' with a fervour which, in conversation with a mother, was absurdly indiscreet. Hardly a maternal heart within the four seas could, in such circumstances, have helped being irritated at that ill-timed betrayal of feeling for a new woman.

'You are blinded, Clym,' she said warmly. 'It was a bad day for you when you first set eyes on her. And you scheme is merely a castle in the air built on purpose to justify this folly which has seized you, and to salve your conscience on the irrational situation you are in.'

'Mother, that's not true,' he firmly answered.

'Can you maintain that I sit and tell untruths, when all I wish to do is to save you from sorrow? For shame, Clym! But it is all through that woman—a hussy!'

Clym reddened like fire and rose. He placed his hand upon his mother's shoulder and said, in a tone which hung strangely between entreaty and command, 'I won't hear it. I may be led to answer you in a way which we shall both regret.'

His mother parted her lips to begin some other vehement truth, but on looking at him she saw that in his face which led her to leave the words unsaid. Yeobright walked once or twice across the room, and then suddenly went out of the house. It was eleven o'clock when he came in, though he had not been further than the precincts of the garden. His mother was gone to bed. A light was left burning on the table, and supper was spread. Without stopping for any food he secured the doors and went upstairs.

An Hour of Bliss and Many Hours of Sadness

IV

The next day was gloomy enough at Blooms-End. Yeobright remained in his study, sitting over the open books; but the work of those hours was miserably scant. Determined that there should be nothing in his conduct towards his mother resembling sullenness, he had occasionally spoken to her on passing matters, and would take no notice of the brevity of her replies. With the same resolve to keep up a show of conversation he said, about seven o'clock in the evening, 'There's an eclipse of the moon to-night. I am going out to see it.' And, putting on his overcoat, he left her.

The low moon was not as yet visible from the front of the house, and Yeobright climbed out of the valley until he stood in the full flood of her light. But even now he walked on, and his steps were in the direction of Rainbarrow.

In half an hour he stood at the top. The sky was clear from verge to verge, and the moon flung her rays over the whole heath, but without sensibly lighting it, except where paths and water-courses had laid bare the white flints and glistening quartz sand, which made streaks upon the general shade. After standing awhile he stooped and felt the heather. It was dry, and he flung himself down upon the barrow, his face towards the moon, which depicted a small image of herself in each of his eyes.

He had often come up here without stating his purpose to his mother; but this was the first time that he had been ostensibly frank as to his purpose while really concealing it. It was a moral situation which, three months earlier, he could hardly have credited of himself. In returning to labour in this sequestered spot he had anticipated an escape from the chafing of social necessities; yet behold they were here also. More than ever he longed to be in some world where personal ambition was not the only recognized form of progress—such, perhaps, as might have been the case at some time or other in the silvery globe then shining upon him. His eye travelled over the length and breadth of that distant country—over the Bay of Rainbows, the sombre Sea of Crises, the Ocean of Storms, the Lake of Dreams, the vast Walled Plains, and the wondrous Ring Mountains[3]— till he almost felt himself to be voyaging bodily through its wild scenes, standing on its hollow hills, traversing its deserts, descending its vales and old sea bottoms, or mounting to the edges of its craters.

While he watched the far-removed landscape a tawny stain grew into being on the lower verge: the eclipse had begun. This marked a preconcerted moment: for the remote celestial phenomenon had been pressed into sublunary service as a lover's signal. Yeobright's mind flew back to earth at the sight; he arose, shook himself, and listened. Minute after minute passed by, perhaps ten minutes passed, and the shadow on the moon perceptibly widened. He heard a rustling on his left hand, a cloaked figure with an upturned face appeared at the base of the Barrow, and Clym descended. In a moment the figure was in his arms, and his lips upon hers.

'My Eustacia!'

'Clym dearest!'

Such a situation had less than three months brought forth.

They remained long without a single utterance, for no language could reach the level of their condition: words were as the rusty implements of a by-gone barbarous epoch, and only to be occasionally tolerated.

'I began to wonder why you did not come,' said Yeobright, when she had withdrawn a little from his embrace.

'You said ten minutes after the first mark of shade on the edge of the moon; and that's what it is now.'

'Well, let us only think that here we are.'

Then, holding each other's hand, they were again silent, and the shadow on the moon's disc grew a little larger.

'Has it seemed long since you last saw me?' she asked.

3. Fanciful names for areas on the surface of the moon, listed along with many other names in an 1836 book by Beer and Madler. Their description of the moon's surface became the standard means for denoting areas of the moon in literary allusions and popular references throughout the nineteenth century.

'It has seemed sad.'

'And not long? That's because you occupy yourself, and so blind yourself to my absence. To me, who can do nothing, it has been like living under stagnant water.'

'I would rather bear tediousness, dear, than have time made short by such means as have shortened mine.'

'In what way is that? You have been thinking you wished you did not love me.'

'How can a man wish that, and yet love on? No, Eustacia.'

'Men can, women cannot.'

'Well, whatever I may have thought, one thing is certain—I do love you—past all compass and description. I love you to oppressiveness—I, who have never before felt more than a pleasant passing fancy for any woman I have ever seen. Let me look right into your moonlit face, and dwell on every line and curve in it! Only a few hair-breadths make the difference between this face and faces I have seen many times before I knew you; yet what a differnce—the difference between everything and nothing at all. One touch on that mouth again! there, and there, and there. Your eyes seem heavy, Eustacia.'

'No, it is my general way of looking. I think it arises from my feeling sometimes an agonizing pity for myself that I ever was born.'

'You don't feel it now?'

'No. Yet I know that we shall not love like this always. Nothing can ensure the continuance of love. It will evaporate like a spirit, and so I feel full of fears.'

'You need not.'

'Ah, you don't know. You have seen more than I, and have been into cities and among people that I have only heard of, and have lived more years than I; but yet I am older at this than you. I loved another man once, and now I love you.'

'In God's mercy don't talk so, Eustacia!'

'But I do not think I shall be the one who wearies first. It will, I fear, end in this way: your mother will find out that you meet me, and she will influence you against me!'

'That can never be. She knows of these meeting already.'

'And she speaks against me?'

'I will not say.'

'There, go away! Obey her. I shall ruin you. It is foolish of you to meet me like this. Kiss me, and go away for ever. For ever—do you hear?—for ever!'

'Not I.'

'It is your only chance. Many a man's love has been a curse to him.'

'You are desperate, full of fancies, and wilful; and you misunderstand. I have an additional reason for seeing you to-night besides love of you. For though, unlike you, I feel our affection may be eternal, I feel with you in this, that our present mode of existence cannot last.'

'Oh! 'tis your mother. Yes, that's it! I knew it.'

'Never mind what it is. Believe this, I cannot let myself lose you. I must have you always with me. This very evening I do not like to let you go. There is only one cure for this anxiety, dearest—you must be my wife.'

She started: then endeavoured to say calmly, 'Cynics say that cures the anxiety by curing the love.'

'But you must answer me. Shall I claim you some day—I don't mean at once?'

'I must think,' Eustacia murmured. 'At present speak of Paris to me. Is there any place like it on earth?'

'It is very beautiful. But will you be mine?'

'I will be nobody else's in the world—does that satisfy you?'

'Yes, for the present.'

'Now tell me of the Tuileries, and the Louvre,' she continued evasively.

'I hate talking of Paris! Well, I remember one sunny room in the Louvre which would make a fitting place for you to live in—the Galerie d'Apollon. Its windows are mainly east; and in the early morning, when the sun is bright, the whole apartment is in a perfect blaze of splendour. The rays bristle and dart from the encrustations of gilding to the magnificent inlaid coffers, from the coffers to the gold and silver plate, from the plate to the jewels and precious stones, from these to the enamels, till there is a perfect network of light which quite dazzles the eye. But now, about our marriage——'

'And Versailles—the King's Gallery is some such gorgeous room, is it not?'

'Yes. But what's the use of talking of gorgeous rooms? By the way, the Little Trianon would suit us beautifully to live in, and you might walk in the gardens in the moonlight and think you were in some English shrubbery; it is laid out in English fashion.'

'I should hate to think that!'

'Then you could keep to the lawn in front of the Grand Palace. All about there you would doubtless feel in a world of historical romance.'

He went on, since it was all new to her, and described Fontainebleau, St. Cloud, the Bois, and many other familiar haunts of the Parisians; till she said—

'When used you to go to these places?'

'On Sundays.'

'Ah, yes. I dislike English Sundays. How I should chime in with their manners over there! Dear Clym, you'll go back again?'

Clym shook his head, and looked at the eclipse.

'If you'll go back again I'll—be something,' she said tenderly, putting her head near his breast. 'If you'll agree I'll give my promise, without making you wait a minute longer.'

'How extraordinary that you and my mother should be of one mind about this!' said Yeobright. 'I have vowed not to go back, Eustacia. It is not the place I dislike; it is the occupation.'

'But you can go in some other capacity.'

'No. Besides, it would interfere with my scheme. Don't press that, Eustacia. Will you marry me?'

'I cannot tell.'

'Now—never mind Paris; it is no better than other spots. Promise, sweet!'

'You will never adhere to your education plan, I am quite sure; and then it will be all right for me; and so I promise to be yours for ever and ever.'

Clum brought her face towards his by a gentle pressure of the hand, and kissed her.

'Ah! but you don't know what you have got in me,' she said. 'Sometimes I think there is not that in Eustacia Vye which will make a good homespun wife. Well, let it go—see how our time is slipping, slipping, slipping!' She pointed towards the half eclipsed moon.

'You are too mournful.'

'No. Only I dread to think of anything beyond the present. What is, we know. We are together now, and it is unknown how long we shall be so: the unknown always fills my mind with terrible possibilities, even when I may reasonably expect it to be cheerful. . . . Clym, the eclipsed moonlight shines upon your face with a strange foreign colour, and shows its shape as if it were cut out in gold. That means that you should be doing better things than this.'

'You are ambitious, Eustacia—no, not exactly ambitious, luxurious. I ought to be of the same vein, to make you happy, I suppose. And yet, far from that, I could live and die in a hermitage here, with proper work to do.'

There was that in his tone which implied distrust of his position as a solicitous lover, a doubt if he were acting fairly towards one whose tastes touched his own only at rare and infrequent points. She saw his meaning, and whispered, in a low, full accent of eager assurance, 'Don't mistake me, Clym: though I should like Paris, I love you for yourself alone. To be your wife and live in Paris would be heaven to me; but I would rather live with you in a hermitage here than not be yours at all. It is gain to me either way, and very great gain. There's my too candid confession.'

'Spoken like a women. And now I must soon leave you. I'll walk with you towards your house.'

'But must you go home yet?' she asked. 'Yes, the sand has nearly slipped away, I see, and the eclipse is creeping on more and more. Don't go yet! Stop till the hour has run itself out; then I will not press you any more. You will go home and sleep well; I keep sighing in my sleep! Do you ever dream of me?'

'I cannot recollect a clear dream of you.'

'I see your face in every scene of my dreams, and hear your voice in every sound. I wish I did not. It is too much what I feel. They say such love never lasts. But it must! And yet once, I remember, I saw an officer of the Hussars ride down the street at Budmouth, and though he was a total stranger and never spoke to me, I loved him till I thought I should really die of love—but I didn't die, and at last I left off caring for him. How terrible it would be if a time should come when I could not love you, my Clym!'

'Please don't say such reckless things. When we see such a time at hand we will say, "I have outlived my faith and purpose," and die. There, the hour has expired: now let us walk on.'

Hand in hand they went along the path towards Mistover. When they were near the house he said, 'It is too late for me to see your grandfather to-night. Do you think he will object to it?'

'I will speak to him. I am so accustomed to be my own mistress that it did not occur to me that we should have to ask him.'

Then they lingeringly separated, and Clym descended towards Blooms-End.

And as he walked further and further from the charmed atmosphere of his Olympian girl his face grew sad with a new sort of sadness. A perception of the dilemma in which his love had placed him came back in full force. In spite of Eustacia's apparent willingness to wait through the period of an unpromising engagement, till he should be established in his new pursuit, he could not but perceive at moments that she loved him rather as a visitant from a gay world to which she rightly belonged than as a man with a purpose opposed to that recent past of his which so interested her. Often at their meetings a word or a sigh escaped her. It meant that, though she made no conditions as to his return to the French capital, this was what she secretly longed for in the event of marriage; and it robbed him of many an otherwise pleasant hour. Along with that came the widening breach between himself and his mother. Whenever any little occurrence had brought into more prominence than usual the disappointment that he was causing her it had sent him on lone and moody walks; or he was kept awake a great part of the night by the turmoil of spirit which such a recognition created. If Mrs. Yeobright could only have been led to see what a sound and worthy purpose this purpose of his was and how little it was being affected by his devotion to Eustacia, how differently would she regard him!

Thus as his sight grew accustomed to the first blinding halo kindled about him by love and beauty, Yeobright began to perceive what a strait he was in. Sometimes he wished that he had never known Eustacia, immediately to retract the wish as brutal. Three antagonistic growths had to be kept alive: his mother's trust in him, his plan for becoming a teacher, and Eustacia's happiness. His fervid nature could not afford to relinquish one of these, though two of the three were as many as he could hope to preserve. Though his love was as chaste as that of Petrarch for his Laura, it had made fetters of what previously was only a difficulty. A position which was not too simple when he stood whole-hearted had become indescribably complicated by the addition of Eustacia. Just when his mother was beginning to tolerate one scheme he had introduced another still bitterer than the first, and the combination was more than she could bear.

Sharp Words Are Spoken and a Crisis Ensues

V

When Yeobright was not with Eustacia he was sitting slavishly over his books; when he was not reading he was meeting her. These meetings were carried on with the greatest secrecy.

One afternoon his mother came home from a morning visit to Thomasin. He could see from a disturbance in the lines of her face that something had happened.

'I have been told an incomprehensible thing,' she said mournfully. 'The captain has let out at the Woman that you and Eustacia Vye are engaged to be married.'

'We are,' said Yeobright. 'But it may not be yet for a very long time.'

'I should hardly think it *would* be yet for a very long time! You will take her to Paris, I suppose?' She spoke with weary hopelessness.

'I am not going back to Paris.'

'What will you do with a wife, then?'

'Keep a school in Budmouth, as I have told you.'

'That's incredible! The place is overrun with schoolmasters. You have no special qualifications. What possible chance is there for such as you?'

'There is no chance of getting rich. But with my system of education, which is as new as it is true, I shall do a great deal of good to my fellow-creatures.'

'Dreams, dreams! If there had been any system left to be invented they would have found it out at the universities long before this time.'

'Never, mother. They cannot find it out, because their teachers don't come in contact with the class which demands such a system—that is, those who have had no preliminary training. My plan is one for instilling high knowledge into empty minds without first cramming them with what has to be uncrammed again before true study begins.'

'I might have believed you if you had kept yourself free from entanglements; but this woman—if she had been a good girl it would have been bad enough; but being——'

'She is a good girl.'

'So you think. A Corfu bandmaster's daughter! What has her life been? Her surname even is not her true one.'

'She is Captain Vye's granddaughter, and her father merely took her mother's name. And she is a lady by instinct.'

'They call him "captain," but anybody is captain.'

'He was in the Royal Navy!'

'No doubt he has been to sea in some tub or other. Why doesn't he look after her? No lady would rove about the heath at all hours of the day and night as she does. But that's not all of it. There was something queer between her and Thomasin's husband at one time—I am as sure of it as that I stand here.'

'Eustacia has told me. He did pay her a little attention a year ago; but there's no harm in that. I like her all the better.'

'Clym,' said his mother with firmness, 'I have no proofs against her, unfortunately. But if she makes you a good wife, there has never been a bad one.'

'Believe me, you are almost exasperating,' said Yeobright vehemently. 'And this very day I had intended to arrange a meeting between you. But you give me no peace; you try to thwart my wishes in everything.'

'I hate the thought of any son of mine marrying badly! I wish I had never lived to see this; it is too much for me—it is more than I dreamt!' She turned to the window. Her breath was coming quickly, and her lips were pale, parted, and trembling.

'Mother,' said Clym, 'whatever you do, you will always be dear to me—that you know. But one thing I have a right to say, which is, that at my age I am old enough to know what is best for me.'

Mrs. Yeobright remained for some time silent and shaken, as if she could say no more. Then she replied, 'Best? Is it best for you to injure your prospects for such a voluptuous, idle woman as that?

Don't you see that by the very fact of your choosing her you prove that you do not know what is best for you? You give up your whole thought—you set your whole soul—to please a woman.'

'I do. And that woman is you.'

'How can you treat me so flippantly!' said his mother, turning again to him with a tearful look. 'You are unnatural, Clym, and I did not expect it.'

'Very likely,' said he cheerlessly. 'You did not know the measure you were going to mete me, and therefore did not know the measure that would be returned to you again.'

'You answer me; you think only of her. You stick to her in all things.'

'That proves her to be worthy. I have never yet supported what is bad. And I do not care only for her. I care for you and for myself, and for anything that is good. When a woman once dislikes another she is merciless!'

'O Clym! please don't go setting down as my fault what is your obstinate wrong-headedness. If you wished to connect yourself with an unworthy person why did you come home here to do it? Why didn't you do it in Paris?—it is more the fashion there. You have come only to distress me, a lonely woman, and shorten my days! I wish that you would bestow your presence where you bestow your love!'

Clym said huskily, 'You are my mother. I will say no more—beyond this, that I beg your pardon for having thought this my home. I will no longer inflict myself upon you; I'll go.' And he went out with tears in his eyes.

It was a sunny afternoon at the beginning of summer, and the moist hollows of the heath had passed from their brown to their green stage. Yeobright walked to the edge of the basin which extended down from Mistover and Rainbarrow. By this time he was calm, and he looked over the landscape. In the minor valleys, between the hillocks which diversified the contour of the vale, the fresh young ferns were luxuriantly growing up, ultimately to reach a height of five or six feet. He descended a little way, flung himself down in a spot where a path emerged from one of the small hollows, and waited. Hither it was that he had promised Eustacia to bring his mother this afternoon, that they might meet and be friends. His attempt had utterly failed.

He was in a nest of vivid green. The ferny vegetation round him, though so abundant, was quite uniform: it was a grove of machine-made foliage, a world of green triangles with saw-edges, and not a single flower. The air was warm with a vaporous warmth, and the stillness was unbroken. Lizards, grasshoppers, and ants were the only living things to be beheld. The scene seemed to belong to the ancient world of the carboniferous period, when the forms of plants were few, and of the fern kind; when there was neither bud nor blossom, nothing but a monotonous extent of leafage, amid which no bird sang.

When he had reclined for some considerable time, gloomily pondering, he discerned above the ferns a drawn bonnet of white silk approaching from the left, and Yeobright knew directly that it covered the head of her he loved. His heart awoke from its apathy to a warm excitement, and, jumping to his feet, he said aloud, 'I knew she was sure to come.'

She vanished in a hollow for a few moments, and then her whole form unfolded itself from the brake.

'Only you here?' she exclaimed, with a disappointed air, whose hollowness was proved by her rising redness and her half-guilty low laugh. 'Where is Mrs. Yeobright?'

'She has not come,' he replied in a subdued tone.

'I wish I had known that you would be here alone,' she said seriously, 'and that we were going to have such an idle, pleasant time as this. Pleasure not known beforehand is half wasted; to anticipate it is to double it. I have not thought once to-day of having you all to myself this afternoon, and the actual moment of a thing is so soon gone.'

'It is indeed.'

'Poor Clym!' she continued, looking tenderly into his face. 'You are sad. Something has happened at your home. Never mind what is—let us only look at what seems.'

'But, darling, what shall we do?' said he.

'Still go on as we do now—just live on from meeting to meeting, never minding about another day. You, I know, are always thinking of that—I can see you are. But you must not—will you, dear Clym?'

'You are just like all women. They are ever content to build their lives on any incidental position that offers itself; whilst men would fain make a globe to suit them. Listen to this, Eustacia. There is a subject I have determined to put off no longer. Your sentiment on the wisdom of *Carpe diem* does not impress me to-day. Our present mode of life must shortly be brought to an end.'

'It is your mother!'

'It is. I love you none the less in telling you; it is only right you should know.'

'I have feared my bliss,' she said, with the merest motion of her lips. 'It has been too intense and consuming.'

'There is hope yet. There are forty years of work in me yet, and why should you despair? I am only at an awkward turning. I wish people wouldn't be so ready to think that there is no progress without uniformity.'

'Ah—your mind runs off to the philosophical side of it. Well, these sad and hopeless obstacles are welcomed in one sense, for they enable us to look with indiffrence upon the cruel satires that Fate loves to indulge in. I have heard of people, who, upon coming suddenly into happiness, have died from anxiety lest they should not live to enjoy it. I felt myself in that whimsical state of uneasiness lately; but I shall be spared it now. Let us walk on.'

Clym took the hand which was already bared for him—it was a favourite way with them to walk bare hand in bare hand—and led her through the ferns. They formed a very comely picture of love at full flush, as they walked along the valley that late afternoon, the sun sloping down on their right, and throwing their thin spectral shadows, tall as poplar trees, far out across the furze and fern. Eustacia went with her head thrown back fancifully, a certain glad and voluptuous air of triumph pervading her eyes at having won by her own unaided self a man who was her perfect complement in attainments, appearance, and age. On the young man's part, the paleness of face which he had brought with him from Paris, and the incipient marks of time and thought, were less perceptible than when he returned, the healthful and energetic sturdiness which was his by nature having partially recovered its original proportions. They wandered onward till they reached the nether margin of the heath, where it became marshy, and merged in moorland.

'I must part from you here, Clym,' said Eustacia.

They stood still and prepared to bid each other farewell. Everything before them was on a perfect level. The sun, resting on the horizon line, streamed across the ground from between copper-coloured and lilac clouds, stretched out in flats beneath a sky of pale soft green. All dark objects on the earth that lay towards the sun were overspread by a purple haze, against which groups of wailing gnats shone out, rising upwards and dancing about like sparks of fire.

'O! this leaving you is too hard to bear!' exclaimed Eustacia in a sudden whisper of anguish. 'Your mother will influence you too much; I shall not be judged fairly, it will get afloat that I am not a good girl, and the witch story will be added to make me blacker!'

'They cannot. Nobody dares to speak disrespectfully of you or of me.'

'O how I wish I was sure of never losing you—that you could not be able to desert me anyhow!'

Clym stood silent a moment. His feelings were high, the moment was passionate, and he cut the knot.

'You shall be sure of me, darling,' he said, folding her in his arms. 'We will be married at once.'

'O Clym!'

'Do you agree to it?'

'If—if we can.'

'We certainly can, both being of full age. And I have not followed my occupation all these years without having accumulated money; and if you will agree to live in a tiny cottage somewhere on the heath, until I take a house in Budmouth for the school, we can do it at a very little expense.'

'How long shall we have to live in the tiny cottage, Clym?'

'About six months. At the end of that time I shall have finished my reading—yes, we will do it, and this heart-aching will be over. We shall, of course, live in absolute seclusion, and our married life will only begin to outward view when we take the house in Budmouth, where I have already addressed a letter on the matter. Would your grandfather allow you?'

'I think he would—on the understanding that it should not last longer than six months.'

'I will guarantee that, if no misfortune happens.'

'If no misfortune happens,' she repeated slowly.

'Which is not likely. Dearest, fix the exact day.'

And then they consulted on the question, and the day was chosen. It was to be a fortnight from that time.

This was the end of their talk, and Eustacia left him. Clym watched her as she retired towards the sun. The luminous rays wrapped her up with her increasing distance, and the rustle of her dress over the sprouting sedge and grass died away. As he watched, the dead flat of the scenery overpowered him, though he was fully alive to the beauty of that untarnished early summer green which was worn for the nonce by the poorest blade. There was something in its oppressive horizontality which too much reminded him of the arena of life; it gave him a sense of bare equality with, and no superiority to, a single living thing under the sun.

Eustacia was now no longer the goddess but the woman to him, a being to fight for, support, help, be maligned for. Now that he had reached a cooler moment he would have preferred a less hasty marriage; but the card was laid, and he determined to abide by the game. Whether Eustacia was to add one other to the list of those who love too hotly to love long and well, the forthcoming event was certainly a ready way of proving.

Yeobright Goes, and the Breach Is Complete

VI

All that evening smart sounds denoting an active packing up came from Yeobright's room to the ears of his mother downstairs.

Next morning he departed from the house and again proceeded

across the heath. A long day's march was before him, his object being to secure a dwelling to which he might take Eustacia when she became his wife. Such a house, small, secluded, and with its windows boarded up, he had casually observed a month earlier, about two miles beyond the village of East Egdon, and six miles distant altogether; and thither he directed his steps to-day.

The weather was far different from that of the evening before. The yellow and vapoury sunset which had wrapped up Eustacia from his parting gaze had presaged change. It was one of those not infrequent days of an English June which are as wet and boisterous as November. The cold clouds hastened on in a body, as if painted on a moving slide. Vapours from other continents arrived upon the wind, which curled and parted round him as he walked on.

At length Clym reached the margin of a fir and beech plantation that had been enclosed from heath land in the year of his birth. Here the trees, laden heavily with their new and humid leaves, were now suffering more damage than during the highest winds of winter, when the boughs are specially disencumbered to do battle with the storm. The wet young beeches were undergoing amputations, bruises, cripplings, and harsh lacerations, from which the wasting sap would bleed for many a day to come, and which would leave scars visible till the day of their burning. Each stem was wrenched at the root, where it moved like a bone in its socket, and at every onset of the gale convulsive sounds came from the branches, as if pain were felt. In a neighbouring brake a finch was trying to sing; but the wind blew under his feathers till they stood on end, twisted round his little tail, and made him give up his song.

Yet a few yards to Yeobright's left, on the open heath, how ineffectively gnashed the storm! Those gusts which tore the trees merely waved the furze and heather in a light caress. Egdon was made for such times as these.

Yeobright reached the empty house about mid-day. It was almost as lonely as that of Eustacia's grandfather, but the fact that it stood near a heath was disguised by a belt of firs which almost enclosed the premises. He journeyed on about a mile further to the village in which the owner lived, and, returning with him to the house, arrangements were completed, and the man undertook that one room at least should be ready for occupation the next day. Clym's intention was to live there alone until Eustacia should join him on their wedding-day.

Then he turned to pursue his way homeward through the drizzle that had so greatly transformed the scene. The ferns, among which he had lain in comfort yesterday, were dripping moisture from every frond, wetting his legs through as he brushed past; and the fur of the rabbits leaping before him was clotted into dark locks by the same watery surrounding.

He reached home damp and weary enough after his ten-mile walk. It had hardly been a propitious beginning, but he had chosen his course, and would show no swerving. The evening and the following morning were spent in concluding arrangements for his departure. To stay at home a minute longer than necessary after having once come to his determination would be, he felt, only to give new pain to his mother by some word, look, or deed.

He had hired a conveyance and sent off his goods by two o'clock that day. The next step was to get some furniture, which, after serving for temporary use in the cottage, would be available for the house at Budmouth when increased by goods of a better description. A mart extensive enough for the purpose existed at Anglebury, some miles beyond the spot chosen for his residence, and there he resolved to pass the coming night.

It now only remained to wish his mother good-bye. She was sitting by the window as usual when he came downstairs.

'Mother, I am going to leave you,' he said, holding out his hand.

'I thought you were, by your packing,' replied Mrs. Yeobright in a voice from which every particle of emotion was painfully excluded.

'And you will part friends with me?'

'Certainly, Clym.'

'I am going to be married on the twenty-fifth.'

'I thought you were going to be married.'

'And then—and then you must come and see us. You will understand me better after that, and our situation will not be so wretched as it is now.'

'I do not think it likely I shall come to see you.'

'Then it will not be my fault or Eustacia's, mother. Good-bye!'

He kissed her cheek, and departed in great misery, which was several hours in lessening itself to a controllable level. The position had been such that nothing more could be said without, in the first place, breaking down a barrier; and that was not to be done.

No sooner had Yeobright gone from his mother's house than her face changed its rigid aspect for one of blank despair. After a while she wept, and her tears brought some relief. During the rest of the day she did nothing but walk up and down the garden path in a state bordering on stupefaction. Night came, and with it but little rest. The next day, with an instinct to do something which should reduce prostration to mournfulness, she went to her son's room, and with her own hands arranged it in order, for an imaginary time when he should return again. She gave some attention to her flowers, but it was perfunctorily bestowed, for they no longer charmed her.

It was a great relief when, early in the afternoon, Thomasin paid her an unexpected visit. This was not the first meeting between the relatives since Thomasin's marriage; and past blunders having been in a rough way rectified, they could always greet each other with pleasure and ease.

The oblique band of sunlight which followed her through the door became the young wife well. It illuminated her as her presence illuminated the heath. In her movements, in her gaze, she reminded the beholder of the feathered creatures who lived around her home. All similes and allegories concerning her began and ended with birds. There was as much variety in her motions as in their flight. When she was musing she was a kestrel, which hangs in the air by an invisible motion of its wings. When she was in a high wind her light body was blown against trees and banks like a heron's. When she was frightened she darted noiselessly like a kingfisher. When she was serene she skimmed like a swallow, and that is how she was moving now.

'You are looking very blithe, upon my word, Tamsie,' said Mrs. Yeobright with a sad smile. 'How is Damon?'

'He is very well.'

'Is he kind to you, Thomasin?' And Mrs. Yeobright observed her narrowly.

'Pretty fairly.'

'Is that honestly said?'

'Yes, aunt. I would tell you if he were unkind.' She added, blushing, and with hesitation, 'He—I don't know if I ought to complain to you about this, but I am not quite sure what to do. I want some money, you know, aunt—some to buy little things for myself—and he doesn't give me any. I don't like to ask him; and yet, perhaps, he doesn't give it me because he doesn't know. Ought I to mention it to him, aunt?'

'Of course you ought. Have you never said a word on the matter?'

'You see, I had some of my own,' said Thomasin evasively; 'and I have not wanted any of his until lately. I did just say something about it last week; but he seems—not to remember.'

'He must be made to remember. You are aware that I have a little box full of spade-guineas, which your uncle put into my hands to divide between yourself and Clym whenever I chose. Perhaps the time has come when it should be done. They can be turned into sovereigns at any moment.'

'I think I should like to have my share—that is, if you don't mind.'

'You shall, if necessary. But it is only proper that you should first tell your husband distinctly that you are without any, and see what he will do.'

'Very well, I will. . . . Aunt, I have heard about Clym. I know you are in trouble about him, and that's why I have come.'

Mrs. Yeobright turned away, and her features worked in her attempt to conceal her feelings. Then she ceased to make any attempt, and said, weeping, 'O Thomasin, do you think he hates me? How can he bear to grieve me so, when I have lived only for him through all these years?'

'Hate you—no,' said Thomasin soothingly. 'It is only that he loves her too well. Look at it quietly—do. It is not so very bad of him. Do you know, I thought it not the worst match he could have made. Miss Vye's family is a good one on her mother's side; and her father was a romantic wanderer—a sort of Greek Ulysses.'

'It is no use, Thomasin; it is no use. Your intention is good; but I will not trouble you to argue. I have gone through the whole that can be said on either side times, and many times. Clym and I have not parted in anger; we have parted in a worse way. It is not a passionate quarrel that would have broken my heart; it is the steady opposition and persistence in going wrong that he has shown. O Thomasin, he was so good as a little boy—so tender and kind!'

'He was, I know.'

'I did not think one whom I called mine would grow up to treat me like this. He spoke to me as if I opposed him to injure him. As though I could wish him ill!'

'There are worse women in the world than Eustacia Vye.'

'There are too many better; that's the agony of it. It was she, Thomasin, and she only, who led your husband to act as he did: I would swear it!'

'No,' said Thomasin eagerly. 'It was before he knew me that he thought of her, and it was nothing but a mere flirtation.'

'Very well; we will let it be so. There is little use in unravelling that now. Sons must be blind if they will. Why is it that a woman can see from a distance what a man cannot see close? Clym must do as he will—he is nothing more to me. And this is maternity—to give one's best years and best love to ensure the fate of being despised!'

'You are too unyielding. Think how many mothers there are whose sons have brought them to public shame by real crimes before you feel so deeply a case like this.'

'Thomasin, don't lecture me—I can't have it. It is the excess above what we expect that makes the force of the blow, and that may not be greater in their case than in mine: they may have foreseen the worst. . . . I am wrongly made, Thomasin,' she added, with a mournful smile. 'Some widows can guard against the wounds their children give them by turning their hearts to another husband and beginning life again. But I always was a poor, weak, one-idea'd creature—I had not the compass of heart nor the enterprise for that. Just as forlorn and stupefied as I was when my husband's spirit flew away I have sat ever since—never attempting to mend matters at all. I was comparatively a young woman then, and I might have had another family by this time, and have been comforted by them for the failure of this one son.

'It is more noble in you that you did not.'

'The more noble, the less wise.'

'Forget it, and be soothed, dear aunt. And I shall not leave you alone for long. I shall come and see you every day.'

And for one week Thomasin literally fulfilled her word. She endeavoured to make light of the wedding; and brought news of the preparations, and that she was invited to be present. The next week she was rather unwell, and did not appear. Nothing had as yet been done about the guineas, for Thomasin feared to address her husband again on the subject, and Mrs. Yeobright had insisted upon this.

One day just before this time Wildeve was standing at the door of the Quiet Woman. In addition to the upward path through the heath to Rainbarrow and Mistover, there was a road which branched from the highway a short distance below the inn, and ascended to Mistover by a circuitous and easy incline. This was the only route on that side for vehicles to the captain's retreat. A light cart from the nearest town descended the road, and the lad who was driving pulled up in front of the inn for something to drink.

'You come from Mistover?' said Wildeve.

'Yes. They are taking in good things up there. Going to be a wedding.' And the driver buried his face in his mug.

Wildeve had not received an inkling of the fact before, and a sudden expression of pain overspread his face. He turned for a moment into the passage to hide it. Then he came back again.

'Do you mean Miss Vye?' he said. 'How is it—that she can be married so soon?'

'By the will of God and a ready young man, I suppose.'

'You don't mean Mr. Yeobright?'

'Yes. He has been creeping about with her all the spring.'

'I suppose—she was immensely taken with him?'

'She is crazy about him, so their general servant of all work tells me. And that lad Charley that looks after the horse is all in a daze about it. The stun-poll has got fond-like of her.'

'Is she lively—is she glad? Going to be married so soon—well!'

'It isn't so very soon.'

'No; not so very soon.'

Wildeve went indoors to the empty room, a curious heart-ache within him. He rested his elbow upon the mantelpiece and his face upon his hand. When Thomasin entered the room he did not tell her of what he had heard. The old longing for Eustacia had reappeared in his soul: and it was mainly because he had discovered that it was another man's intention to possess her.

To be yearning for the difficult, to be weary of that offered; to care for the remote, to dislike the near; it was Wildeve's nature always. This is the true mark of the man of sentiment. Though Wildeve's fevered feeling had not been elaborated to real poetical compass, it was of the standard sort. He might have been called the Rousseau of Egdon.

The Morning and the Evening of a Day

VII

The wedding morning came. Nobody would have imagined from appearances that Blooms-End had any interest in Mistover that day. A solemn stillness prevailed around the house of Clym's mother, and there was no more animation indoors. Mrs. Yeobright, who had declined to attend the ceremony, sat by the breakfast-table in the old room which communicated immediately with the porch, her eyes listlessly directed towards the open door. It was the room in which, six months earlier, the merry Christmas party had met, to which Eustacia came secretly and as a stranger. The only living thing that entered now was a sparrow; and seeing no movements to cause alarm, he hopped boldly round the room, endeavoured to go out by the window, and fluttered among the pot-flowers. This roused the lonely sitter, who got up, released the bird, and went to the door. She was expecting Thomasin, who had written the night before to state that the time had come when she would wish to have the money, and that she would if possible call this day.

Yet Thomasin occupied Mrs. Yeobright's thoughts but slightly as she looked up the valley of the heath, alive with butterflies, and with grasshoppers whose husky noises on every side formed a whispered chorus. A domestic drama, for which the preparations were now being made a mile or two off, was but little less vividly present to her eyes than if enacted before her. She tried to dismiss the vision, and walked about the garden-plot; but her eyes ever and anon sought out the direction of the parish church to which Mistover belonged, and her excited fancy clove the hills which divided the building from her eyes. The morning wore away. Eleven o'clock struck: could it be that the wedding was then in progress? It must be so. She went on imagining the scene at the church, which he had by this time approached with his bride. She pictured the little group of children by the gate as the pony-carriage drove up, in which, as Thomasin had learnt, they were going to perform the short journey. Then she saw them enter and proceed to the chancel and kneel; and the service seemed to go on.

She covered her face with her hands. 'O, it is a mistake!' she groaned. 'And he will rue it some day, and think of me!'

While she remained thus, overcome by her forebodings, the old clock indoors whizzed forth twelve strokes. Soon after, faint sounds floated to her ear from afar over the hills. The breeze came from that quarter, and it had brought with it the notes of distant bells, gaily starting off in a peal: one, two, three, four, five. The ringers at East Egdon were announcing the nuptials of Eustacia and her son.

'Then it is over,' she murmured. 'Well, well! and life too will be over soon. And why should I go on scalding my face like this? Cry about one thing in life, cry about all; one thread runs through the whole piece. And yet we say, "a time to laugh!" '

Towards evening Wildeve came. Since Thomasin's marriage Mrs. Yeobright had shown towards him that grim friendliness which at last arises in all such cases of undesired affinity. The vision of what ought to have been is thrown aside in sheer weariness, and browbeaten human endeavour listlessly makes the best of the fact that is. Wildeve, to do him justice, had behaved very courteously to his wife's aunt; and it was with no surprise that she saw him enter now.

'Thomasin has not been able to come, as she promised to do,' he replied to her inquiry, which had been anxious, for she knew that her niece was badly in want of money. 'The captain came down last night and personally pressed her to join them to-day. So, not to be unpleasant, she determined to go. They fetched her in the pony-chaise, and are going to bring her back.'

"Then it is done,' said Mrs. Yeobright. 'Have they gone to their new home?'

'I don't know. I have had no news from Mistover since Thomasin left to go.'

'You did not go with her?' said she, as if there might be good reasons why.

'I could not,' said Wildeve, reddening slightly. 'We could not both leave the house; it was rather a busy morning, on account of Anglebury Great Market. I believe you have something to give to Thomasin? If you like, I will take it.'

Mrs. Yeobright hesitated, and wondered if Wildeve knew what the something was. 'Did she tell you of this?' she inquired.

'Not particularly. She casually dropped a remark about having arranged to fetch some article or other.'

'It is hardly necessary to send it. She can have it whenever she chooses to come.'

'That won't be yet. In the present state of her health she must not go on walking so much as she has done.' He added, with a faint twang of sarcasm, 'What wonderful thing is it that I cannot be trusted to take?'

'Nothing worth troubling you with.'

'One would think you doubted my honesty,' he said, with a laugh, though his colour rose in a quick resentfulness frequent with him.

'You need think no such thing,' said she drily. 'It is simply that I, in common with the rest of the world, feel that there are certain things which had better be done by certain people than by others.'

'As you like, as you like,' said Wildeve laconically. 'It is not worth arguing about. Well, I think I must turn homeward again, as the inn must not be left long in charge of the lad and the maid only.'

He went his way, his farewell being scarcely so courteous as his greeting. But Mrs. Yeobright knew him thoroughly by this time, and took little notice of his manner, good or bad.

When Wildeve was gone Mrs. Yeobright stood and considered what would be the best course to adopt with regard to the guineas, which she had not liked to entrust to Wildeve. It was hardly credible that Thomasin had told him to ask for them, when the necessity for them had arisen from the difficulty of obtaining money at his hands. At the same time Thomasin really wanted them, and might be unable to come to Blooms-End for another week at least. To take or send the money to her at the inn would be impolitic, since Wildeve would pretty surely be present, or would discover the transaction; and if, as her aunt suspected, he treated her less kindly than she deserved to be treated, he might then get the whole sum out of her gentle hands. But on this particular evening Thomasin was at Mistover, and anything might be conveyed to her there without the knowledge of her husband. Upon the whole the opportunity was worth taking advantage of.

Her son, too, was there, and was now married. There could be no more proper moment to render him his share of the money than the present. And the chance that would be afforded her, by sending him this gift, of showing how far she was from bearing him ill-will, cheered the sad mother's heart.

She went upstairs and took from a locked drawer a little box, out of which she poured a hoard of broad unworn guineas that had lain there many a year. There were a hundred in all, and she divided them into two heaps, fifty in each. Tying up these in small canvas bags, she went down to the garden and called to Christian Cantle, who was loitering about in hope of a supper which was not really owed him. Mrs. Yeobright gave him the money-bags, charged him to go to Mistover, and on no account to deliver them into any one's hands save her son's and Thomasin's. On further thought she deemed it advisable to tell Christian precisely what the two bags contained, that he might be fully impressed with their importance. Christian pocketed the money-bags, promised the greatest carefulness, and set out on his way.

'You need not hurry,' said Mrs. Yeobright. 'It will be better not to get there till after dusk, and then nobody will notice you. Come back here to supper, if it is not too late.'

It was nearly nine o'clock when he began to ascend the vale towards Mistover; but the long days of summer being at their climax, the first obscurity of evening had only just begun to tan the landscape. At this point of his journey Christian heard voices, and found that they proceeded from a company of men and women who were traversing a hollow ahead of him, the tops only of their heads being visible.

He paused and thought of the money he carried. It was almost too early even for Christian seriously to fear robbery; nevertheless he took a precaution which ever since his boyhood he had adopted whenever he carried more than two or three shillings upon his person—a precaution somewhat like that of the owner of the Pitt Diamond[4] when filled with similar misgivings. He took off his boots, untied the guineas, and emptied the contents of one little bag into the right boot, and of the other into the left, spreading them as flatly as possible over the bottom of each, which was really a spacious coffer by no means limited to the size of the foot. Pulling them on again and lacing them to the very top, he proceeded on his way, more easy in his head than under his soles.

His path converged towards that of the noisy company, and on coming nearer he found to his relief that they were several Egdon people whom he knew very well, while with them walked Fairway, of Blooms-End.

'What! Christian going too?' said Fairway as soon as he recognized the new-comer. 'You've got no young woman nor wife to your name to gie a gown-piece to, I'm sure.'

4. Pitt Diamond, also known as the Regent Diamond, brought from India and made part of the French crown jewels. During the French Revolution it was cut to about one-third of its size in order to escape detection, but still was stolen, along with the other crown jewels, from the Tuileries in 1792. It was later recovered.

'What d'ye mean?' said Christian.

'Why, the raffle. The one we go to every year. Going to the raffle as well as ourselves?'

'Never knew a word o't. Is it like cudgel-playing or other sportful forms of bloodshed? I don't want to go, thank you, Mister Fairway, and no offence.'

'Christian don't know the fun o't, and 'twould be a fine sight for him,' said a buxom woman. 'There's no danger at all, Christian. Every man puts in a shilling apiece, and one wins a gown-piece for his wife or sweetheart if he's got one.'

'Well, as that's not my fortune there's no meaning in it to me. But I should like to see the fun, if there's nothing of the black art in it, and if a man may look on without cost or getting into any dangerous wrangle?'

'There will be no uproar at all,' said Timothy. 'Sure, Christian, if you'd like to come we'll see there's no harm done.'

'And no ba'dy gaieties, I suppose? You see, neighbours, if so, it would be setting father a bad example, as he is so light moral'd. But a gown-piece for a shilling, and no black art—'tis worth looking in to see, and it wouldn't hinder me half an hour. Yes, I'll come, if you'll step a little way towards Mistover with me afterwards, supposing night should have closed in, and nobody else is going that way?'

One or two promised; and Christian, diverging from his direct path, turned round to the right with his companons towards the Quiet Woman.

When they entered the large common room of the inn they found assembled there about ten men from among the neighbouring population, and the group was increased by the new contingent to double that number. Most of them were sitting round the room in seats divided by wooden elbows like those of crude cathedral stalls, which were carved with the initials of many an illustrious drunkard of former times who had passed his days and his nights between them, and now lay as an alcoholic cinder in the nearest churchyard. Among the cups on the long table before the sitters lay an open parcel of light drapery—the gown-piece, as it was called—which was to be raffled for. Wildeve was standing with his back to the fireplace, smoking a cigar; and the promoter of the raffle, a packman from a distant town, was expatiating upon the value of the fabric as material for a summer dress.

'Now, gentlemen,' he continued, as the new-comers drew up to the table, 'there's five have entered, and we want four more to make up the number. I think, by the faces of those gentlemen who have just come in, that they are shrewd enough to take advantage of this rare opportunity of beautifying their ladies at a very trifling expense.'

Fairway, Sam, and another placed their shillings on the table, and the man turned to Christian.

'No, sir,' said Christian, drawing back, with a quick gaze of misgiving. 'I am only a poor chap come to look on, an it please ye, sir. I don't so much as know how you do it. If so be I was sure of getting it I would put down the shilling; but I couldn't otherwise.'

'I think you might almost be sure,' said the pedlar. 'In fact, now I look into your face, even if I can't say you are sure to win, I can say that I never saw anything look more like winning in my life.'

'You'll anyhow have the same chance as the rest of us,' said Sam.

'And the extra luck of being the last comer,' said another.

'And I was born wi' a caul,[5] and perhaps can be no more ruined than drowned?' Christian added, beginning to give way.

Ultimately Christian laid down his shilling, the raffle began, and the dice went round.[6] When it came to Christian's turn he took the box with a trembling hand, shook it fearfully, and threw a pair-royal. Three of the others had thrown common low pairs, and all the rest mere points.

'The gentleman looked like winning, as I said,' observed the chapman blandly. 'Take it, sir; the article is yours.'

'Haw-haw-haw!' said Fairway. 'I'm damned if this isn't the quarest start that ever I knowed!'

'Mine?' asked Christian, with a vacant stare from his target eyes. 'I—I haven't got neither maid, wife, nor widder belonging to me at all, and I'm afeard it will make me laughed at to ha'e it, Master Traveller. What with being curious to join in I never thought of that! What shall I do wi' a woman's clothes in my bedroom, and not lose my decency!'

'Keep 'em, to be sure,' said Fairway, 'if it is only for luck. Perhaps 'twill tempt some woman that thy poor carcase had no power over when standing empty-handed.'

'Keep it, certainly,' said Wildeve, who had idly watched the scene from a distance.

The table was then cleared of the articles, and the men began to drink.

'Well, to be sure!' said Christian, half to himself. 'To think I should have been born so lucky as this, and not have found it out until now! What curious creatures these dice be—powerful rulers of us all, and yet at my command! I am sure I never need be afeard of anything after this.' He handled the dice fondly one by one. 'Why, sir,' he said in a confidential whisper to Wildeve, who was near his left hand, 'if I could only use this power that's in me of multiplying money I might do some good to a near relation of yours,

5. Membrane enclosing the fetus. Sometimes part of the caul envelops the head of the infant at birth. Old superstitions regard this as a good omen, a protection against drowning.

6. They are playing poker dice, evaluated in the same way as poker with cards.

seeing what I've got about me of hers—eh?' He tapped one of his money-laden boots upon the floor.

'What do you mean?' said Wildeve.

'That's a secret. Well, I must be going now.' He looked anxiously towards Fairway.

'Where are you going?' Wildeve asked.

'To Mistover Knap. I have to see Mrs. Thomasin there—that's all.'

'I am going there, too, to fetch Mrs. Wildeve. We can walk together.'

Wildeve became lost in thought, and a look of inward illumination came into his eyes. It was money for his wife that Mrs. Yeobright could not trust him with. 'Yet she could trust this fellow,' he said to himself. 'Why doesn't that which belongs to the wife belong to the husband too?'

He called to the pot-boy[7] to bring him his hat, and said, 'Now, Christian, I am ready.'

'Mr. Wildeve,' said Christian timidly, as he turned to leave the room, 'would you mind lending me them wonderful little things that carry my luck inside 'em, that I might practise a bit by myself, you know?' He looked wistfully at the dice and box lying on the mantelpiece.

'Certainly,' said Wildeve carelessly. 'They were only cut out by some lad with his knife, and are worth nothing.' And Christian went back and privately pocketed them.

Wildeve opened the door and looked out. The night was warm and cloudy. 'By Gad! 'tis dark,' he continued. 'But I suppose we shall find our way.'

'If we should lose the path it might be awkward,' said Christian. 'A lantern is the only shield that will make it safe for us.'

'Let's have a lantern by all means.' The stable-lantern was fetched and lighted. Christian took up his gown-piece, and the two set out to ascend the hill.

Within the room the men fell into chat till their attention was for a moment drawn to the chimney-corner. This was large, and, in addition to its proper recess, contained within its jambs, like many on Egdon, a receding seat, so that a person might sit there absolutely unobserved, provided there was no fire to light him up, as was the case now and throughout the summer. From the niche a single object protruded into the light from the candles on the table. It was a clay pipe, and its colour was reddish. The men had been attracted to this object by a voice behind the pipe asking for a light.

7. Servant at a pub.

'Upon my life, it fairly startled me when the man spoke!' said Fairway, handing a candle. 'Oh—'tis the reddleman! You've kept a quiet tongue, young man.'

'Yes, I had nothing to say,' observed Venn. In a few minutes he arose and wished the company good night.

Meanwhile Wildeve and Christian had plunged into the heath.

It was a stagnant, warm, and misty night, full of all the heavy perfumes of new vegetation not yet dried by hot sun, and among these particularly the scent of the fern. The lantern, dangling from Christian's hand, brushed the feathery fronds in passing by, disturbing moths and other winged insects, which flew out and alighted upon its horny panes.

'So you have money to carry to Mrs. Wildeve?' said Christian's companion, after a silence. 'Don't you think it very odd that it shouldn't be given to me?'

'As man and wife be one flesh, 'twould have been all the same, I should think,' said Christian. 'But my strict documents was, to give the money into Mrs. Wildeve's hand: and 'tis well to do things right.'

'No doubt,' said Wildeve. Any person who had known the circumstances might have perceived that Wildeve was mortified by the discovery that the matter in transit was money, and not, as he had supposed when at Blooms-End, some fancy nick-nack which only interested the two women themselves. Mrs. Yeobright's refusal implied that his honour was not considered to be of sufficiently good quality to make him a safe bearer of his wife's property.

'How very warm it is to-night, Christian!' he said, panting, when they were nearly under Rainbarrow. 'Let us sit down for a few minutes, for Heaven's sake.'

Wildeve flung himself down on the soft ferns; and Christian, placing the lantern and parcel on the ground, perched himself in a cramped position hard by, his knees almost touching his chin. He presently thrust one hand into his coat-pocket and began shaking it about.

'What are you rattling in there?' said Wildeve.

'Only the dice, sir,' said Christian, quickly withdrawing his hand. 'What magical machines these little things be, Mr. Wildeve! 'Tis a game I should never get tired of. Would you mind my taking 'em out and looking at 'em for a minute, to see how they are made? I didn't like to look close before the other men, for fear they should think it bad manners in me.' Christian took them out and examined them in the hollow of his hand by the lantern light. 'That these little things should carry such luck, and such charm, and such a spell, and such power in 'em, passes all I ever heard or zeed,' he went on, with a fascinated gaze at the dice, which, as is frequently the case in country places, were made of wood, the points being burnt upon each face with the end of a wire.

'They are a great deal in a small compass, you think?'

'Yes. Do ye suppose they really be the devil's playthings, Mr. Wildeve? If so, 'tis no good sign that I be such a lucky man.'

'You ought to win some money, now that you've got them. Any woman would marry you then. Now is your time, Christian, and I would recommend you not to let it slip. Some men are born to luck, some are not. I belong to the latter class.'

'Did you ever know anybody who was born to it besides myself?'

'O yes. I once heard of an Italian, who sat down at a gaming-table with only a louis (that's a foreign sovereign) in his pocket. He played on for twenty-four hours, and won ten thousand pounds, stripping the bank he had played against. Then there was another man who had lost a thousand pounds, and went to the broker's next day to sell stock, that he might pay the debt. The man to whom he owned the money went with him in a hackney-coach; and to pass the time they tossed who should pay the fare. The ruined man won, and the other was tempted to continue the game, and they played all the way. When the coachman stopped he was told to drive home again: the whole thousand pounds had been won back by the man who was going to sell.'

'Ha—ha—splendid!' exclaimed Christian. 'Go on—go on!'

'Then there was a man of London, who was only a waiter at White's club-house. He began playing first half-crown stakes, and then higher and higher, till he became very rich, got an appointment in India, and rose to be Governor of Madras. His daughter married a member of parliament, and the Bishop of Carlisle stood godfather to one of the children.'

'Wonderful! wonderful!'

'And once there was a young man in America who gambled till he had lost his last dollar. He staked his watch and chain; and lost as before: staked his umbrella; lost again: staked his hat; lost again: staked his coat and stood in his shirt-sleeves; lost again. Began taking off his breeches, and then a looker-on gave him a trifle for his pluck. With this he won. Won back his coat, won back his hat, won back his umbrella, his watch, his money, and went out of the door a rich man.'

'O, 'tis too good—it takes away my breath! Mr. Wildeve, I think I will try another shilling with you, as I am one of that sort; no danger can come o't, and you can afford to lose.'

'Very well,' said Wildeve, rising. Searching about with the lantern, he found a large flat stone, which he placed between himself and Christian, and sat down again. The lantern was opened to give more light, and its rays directed upon the stone. Christian put down a shilling, Wildeve another, and each threw. Christian won. They played for two. Christian won again.

'Let us try four,' said Wildeve. They played for four. This time the stakes were won by Wildeve.

'Ah, those little accidents will, of course, sometimes happen to the luckiest man,' he observed.

'And now I have no more money!' exclaimed Christian excitedly. 'And yet, if I could go on, I should get it back again, and more. I wish this was mine.' He struck his boot upon the ground, so that the guineas chinked within.

'What! you have not put Mrs. Wildeve's money there?'

'Yes. 'Tis for safety. Is it any harm to raffle with a married lady's money when, if I win, I shall keep my winnings, and give her her own all the same; and if t'other man wins, her money will go to the lawful owner?'

'None at all.'

Wildeve had been brooding ever since they started on the mean estimation in which he was held by his wife's friends; and it cut his heart severely. As the minutes passed he had gradually drifted into a revengeful intention without knowing the precise moment of forming it. This was to teach Mrs. Yeobright a lesson, as he considered it to be; in other words, to show her if he could, that her niece's husband was the proper guardian of her niece's money.

'Well, here goes!' said Christian, beginning to unlace one boot. 'I shall dream of it nights and nights, I suppose; but I shall always swear my flesh don't crawl when I think o't!'

He thrust his hand into the boot and withdrew one of poor Thomasin's precious guineas, piping hot. Wildeve had already placed a sovereign on the stone. The game was then resumed. Wildeve won first, and Christian ventured another, winning himself this time. The game fluctuated, but the average was in Wildeve's favour. Both men became so absorbed in the game that they took no heed of anything but the pigmy objects immediately beneath their eyes; the flat stone, the open lantern, the dice, and the few illuminated fern-leaves which lay under the light, were the whole world to them.

At length Christian lost rapidly; and presently, to his horror, the whole fifty guineas belonging to Thomasin had been handed over to his adversary.

'I don't care—I don't care!' he moaned, and desperately set about untying his left boot to get at the other fifty. 'The devil will toss me into the flames on his three-pronged fork for this night's work, I know! But perhaps I shall win yet, and then I'll get a wife to sit up with me o'nights, and I won't be afeard, I won't! Here's another for'ee, my man!' He slapped another guinea down upon the stone, and the dice-box was rattled again.

Time passed on. Wildeve began to be as excited as Christian himself. When commencing the game his intention had been nothing further than a bitter practical joke on Mrs. Yeobright. To win the money, fairly or otherwise, and to hand it contemptuously to Thomasin in her aunt's presence, had been the dim outline of his purpose. But men are drawn from their intentions even in the course of carrying them out, and it was extremely doubtful, by the time the twentieth guinea had been reached, whether Wildeve was conscious of any other intention than that of winning for his own personal benefit. Moreover, he was now no longer gambling for his wife's money, but for Yeobright's; though of this fact Christian, in his apprehensiveness, did not inform him till afterwards.

It was nearly eleven o'clock, when, with almost a shriek, Christian placed Yeobright's last gleaming guinea upon the stone. In thirty seconds it had gone the way of its companions.

Christian turned and flung himself on the ferns in a convulsion of remorse. 'O, what shall I do with my wretched self?' he groaned. 'What shall I do? Will any good Heaven hae mercy upon my wicked soul?'

'Do? Live on just the same.'

'I won't live on just the same! I'll die! I say you are a—a——'

'A man sharper than my neighbour.'

'Yes, a man sharper than my neighbour; a regular sharper!'

'Poor chips-in-porridge,[8] you are very unmannerly.'

'I don't know about that! And I say you be unmannerly. You've got money that isn't your own. Half the guineas are poor Mr. Clym's.'

'How's that?'

'Because I had to gie fifty of 'em to him. Mrs. Yeobright said so.'

'Oh? . . . Well, 'twould have been more graceful of her to have given them to his wife Eustacia. But they are in my hands now.'

Christian pulled on his boots, and with heavy breathings, which could be heard to some distance, dragged his limbs together, arose, and tottered away out of sight. Wildeve set about shutting the lantern to return to the house, for he deemed it too late to go to Mistover to meet his wife, who was to be driven home in the captain's four-wheel. While he was closing the little horn door a figure rose from behind a neighbouring bush and came forward into the lantern light. It was the reddleman approaching.

8. Dialect expression for an absolutely insignificant person. The term originated in the folk practice of putting a chip, a medicinal or magical herb, in porridge so that its taste would be disguised. The chip had no discernible effect on the porridge.

A New Force Disturbs the Current

VIII

Wildeve stared. Venn looked coolly towards Wildeve, and, without a word being spoken, he deliberately sat himself down where Christian had been seated, thrust his hand into his pocket, drew out a sovereign, and laid it on the stone.

'You have been watching us from behind that bush?' said Wildeve.

The reddleman nodded. 'Down with your stake,' he said. 'Or haven't you pluck enough to go on?'

Now, gambling is a species of amusement which is much more easily begun with full pockets than left off with the same; and though Wildeve in a cooler temper might have prudently declined this invitation, the excitement of his recent success carried him completely away. He placed one of the guineas on the slab beside the reddleman's sovereign. 'Mine is a guinea,' he said.

'A guinea that's not your own,' said Venn sarcastically.

'It is my own,' answered Wildeve haughtily. 'It is my wife's, and what is hers is mine.'

'Very well; let's make a beginning.' He shook the box, and threw eight, ten, and nine; the three casts amounted to twenty-seven.

This encouraged Wildeve. He took the box; and his three casts amounted to forty-five.[9]

Down went another of the reddleman's sovereigns against his first one which Wildeve laid. This time Wildeve threw fifty-one points, but no pair. The reddleman looked grim, threw a raffle of aces, and pocketed the stakes.

'Here you are again,' said Wildeve contemptuously. 'Double the stakes.' He laid two of Thomasin's guineas, and the reddleman his two pounds. Venn won again. New stakes were laid on the stone, and the gamblers proceeded as before.

Wildeve was a nervous and excitable man; and the game was beginning to tell upon his temper. He writhed, fumed, shifted his seat; and the beating of his heart was almost audible. Venn sat with lips impassively closed and eyes reduced to a pair of unimportant twinkles; he scarcely appeared to breathe. He might have been an Arab, or an automaton; he would have been like a red-sandstone statue but for the motion of his arm with the dice-box.

The game fluctuated, now in favour of one, now in favour of the

9. They are still playing poker dice. If neither player has a pair, the points rolled are added and the highest total wins. Later, in this scene, as dice are lost, the game simplifies into rolling a single die for the highest or the lowest point.

other, without any great advantage on the side of either. Nearly twenty minutes were passed thus. The light of the candle had by this time attracted heath-flies, moths, and other winged creatures of night, which floated round the lantern, flew into the flame, or beat about the faces of the two players.

But neither of the men paid much attention to these things, their eyes being concentrated upon the little flat stone, which to them was an area vast and important as a battle-field. By this time a change had come over the game; the reddleman won continually. At length sixty guineas—Thomasin's fifty, and ten of Clym's—had passed into his hands. Wildeve was reckless, frantic, exasperated.

' "Won back his coat," ' said Venn slily.

Another throw, and the money went the same way.

' "Won back his hat," ' continued Venn.

'Oh, oh!' said Wildeve.

' "Won back his watch, won back his money, and went out of the door a rich man," ' added Venn sentence by sentence, as stake after stake passed over to him.

'Five more!' shouted Wildeve, dashing down the money. 'And three casts be hanged—one shall decide.'

The red automaton opposite lapsed into silence, nodded, and followed his example. Wildeve rattled the box, and threw a pair of sixes and five points. He clapped his hands; 'I have done it this time—hurrah!'

'There are two playing, and only one has thrown,' said the reddleman, quietly bringing down the box. The eyes of each were then so intently converged upon the stone that one could fancy their beams were visible, like rays in a fog.

Venn lifted the box, and behold a triplet of sixes was disclosed.

Wildeve was full of fury. While the reddleman was grasping the stakes Wildeve seized the dice and hurled them, box and all, into the darkness, uttering a fearful imprecation. Then he arose and began stamping up and down like a madman.

'It is all over, then?' said Venn.

'No, No!' cried Wildeve. 'I mean to have another chance yet. I must!'

'But, my good man what have you done with the dice?'

'I threw them away—it was a momentary irritation. What a fool I am! Here—come and help me to look for them—we must find them again.'

Wildeve snatched up the lantern and began anxiously prowling among the furze and fern.

'You are not likely to find them there,' said Venn, following. 'What did you do such a crazy thing as that for? Here's the box. The dice can't be far off.'

Wildeve turned the light eagerly upon the spot where Venn had found the box, and mauled the herbage right and left. In the course of a few minutes one of the dice was found. They searched on for some time, but no other was to be seen.

'Never mind,' said Wildeve; 'let's play with one.'

'Agreed,' said Venn.

Down they sat again, and recommenced with single guinea stakes; and the play went on smartly. But Fortune had unmistakably fallen in love with the reddleman to-night. He won steadily, till he was the owner of fourteen more of the gold pieces. Seventy-nine of the hundred guineas were his, Wildeve possessing only twenty-one. The aspect of the two opponents was not singular. Apart from motions, a complete diorama of the fluctuations of the game went on in their eyes. A diminutive candle-flame was mirrored in each pupil, and it would have been possible to distinguish therein between the moods of hope and the moods of abandonment, even as regards the reddleman, though his facial muscles betrayed nothing at all. Wildeve played on with the recklessness of despair.

'What's that?' he suddenly exclaimed, hearing a rustle; and they both looked up.

They were surrounded by dusky forms between four and five feet high, standing a few paces beyond the rays of the lantern. A moment's inspection revealed that the encircling figures were heath-croppers, their heads being all towards the players, at whom they gazed intently.

'Hoosh!' said Wildeve; and the whole forty or fifty animals at once turned and galloped away. Play was again resumed.

Ten minutes passed away. Then a large death's head moth advanced from the obscure outer air, wheeled twice round the lantern, flew straight at the candle, and extinguished it by the force of the blow. Wildeve had just thrown, but had not lifted the box to see what he had cast; and now it was impossible.

'What the infernal!' he shrieked. 'Now, what shall we do? Perhaps I have thrown six—have you any matches?'

'None,' said Venn.

'Christian had some—I wonder where he is. Christian!'

But there was no reply to Wildeve's shout, save a mournful whining from the herons which were nesting lower down the vale. Both men looked blankly round without rising. As their eyes grew accustomed to the darkness they perceived faint greenish points of light among the grass and fern. These lights dotted the hillside like stars of a low magnitude.

'Ah—glowworms,' said Wildeve. 'Wait a minute. We can continue the game.'

Venn sat still, and his companion went hither and thither till he had gathered thirteen glowworms—as many as he could find in a space of four or five minutes—upon a foxglove leaf which he pulled for the purpose. The reddleman vented a low humorous laugh when he saw his adversary return with these. 'Determined to go on, then?' he said drily.

'I always am!' said Wildeve angrily. And shaking the glowworms from the leaf he ranged them with a trembling hand in a circle on the stone, leaving a space in the middle for the descent of the dice-box, over which the thirteen tiny lamps threw a pale phosphoric shine. The game was again renewed. It happened to be that season of the year at which glowworms put forth their greatest brilliancy, and the light they yielded was more than ample for the purpose, since it is possible on such nights to read the handwriting of a letter by the light of two or three.

The incongruity between the men's deeds and their environment was great. Amid the soft juicy vegetation of the hollow in which they sat, the motionless and the uninhabited solitude, intruded the chink of guineas, the rattle of dice, the exclamations of the reckless players.

Wildeve had lifted the box as soon as the lights were obtained, and the solitary die proclaimed that the game was still against him.

'I won't play any more: you've been tampering with the dice,' he shouted.

'How—when they were your own?' said the reddleman.

'We'll change the game: the lowest point shall win the stake—it may cut off my ill luck. Do you refuse?'

'No—go on,' said Venn.

'O, there they are again—damn them!' cried Wildeve, looking up. The heath-croppers had returned noiselessly and were looking on with erect heads just as before, their timid eyes fixed upon the scene, as if they were wondering what mankind and candle-light could have to do in these haunts at this untoward hour.

'What a plague those creatures are—staring at me so!' he said, and flung a stone, which scattered them; when the game was continued as before.

Wildeve had now ten guineas left; and each laid five. Wildeve threw three points; Venn two, and raked in the coins. The other seized the die, and clenched his teeth upon it in sheer rage, as if he would bite it in pieces. 'Never give in—here are my last five!' he cried, throwing them down. 'Hang the glowworms—they are going out. Why don't you burn, you little fools? Stir them up with a thorn.'

He probed the glowworms with a bit of stick, and rolled them over, till the bright side of their tails was upwards.

'There's light enough. Throw on,' said Venn.

Wildeve brought down the box within the shining circle and looked eagerly. He had thrown ace. 'Well done!—I said it would turn, and it has turned.' Venn said nothing; but his hand shook slightly.

He threw ace also.

'O!' said Wildeve. 'Curse me!'

The die smacked the stone a second time. It was ace again. Venn looked gloomy, threw: the die was seen to be lying in two pieces, the cleft sides uppermost.

'I've thrown nothing at all,' he said.

'Serves me right—I split the die with my teeth. Here—take your money. Blank is less than one.'

'I don't wish it.'

'Take it, I say—you've won it!' And Wildeve threw the stakes against the reddleman's chest. Venn gathered them up, arose, and withdrew from the hollow, Wildeve sitting stupefied.

When he had come to himself he also arose, and, with the extinguished lantern in his hand, went towards the high-road. On reaching it he stood still. The silence of night pervaded the whole heath except in one direction; and that was towards Mistover. There he could hear the noise of light wheels, and presently saw two carriage-lamps descending the hill. Wildeve screened himself under a bush and waited.

The vehicle came on and passed before him. It was a hired carriage, and behind the coachman were two persons whom he knew well. There sat Eustacia and Yeobright, the arm of the latter being round her waist. They turned the sharp corner at the bottom towards the temporary home which Clym had hired and furnished, about five miles to the eastward.

Wildeve forgot the loss of the money at the sight of his lost love, whose preciousness in his eyes was increasing in geometrical progression with each new incident that reminded him of their hopeless division. Brimming with the subtilized misery that he was capable of feeling, he followed the opposite way towards the inn.

About the same moment that Wildeve stepped into the highway Venn also had reached it at a point a hundred yards further on; and he, hearing the same wheels, likewise waited till the carriage should come up. When he saw who sat therein he seemed to be disappointed. Reflecting a minute or two, during which interval the carriage rolled on, he crossed the road, and took a short cut through the furze and heath to a point where the turnpike-road bent round in ascending a hill. He was now again in front of the carriage, which presently came up at a walking pace. Venn stepped forward and showed himself.

Eustacia started when the lamp shone upon him, and Clym's

arm was involuntarily withdrawn from her waist. He said, 'What, Diggory? You are having a lonely walk.'

'Yes—I beg your pardon for stopping you,' said Venn. 'But I am waiting about for Mrs. Wildeve: I have something to give her from Mrs. Yeobright. Can you tell me if she's gone home from the party yet?'

'No. But she will be leaving soon. You may possibly meet her at the corner.'

Venn made a farewell obeisance, and walked back to his former position, where the by-road from Mistover joined the highway. Here he remained fixed for nearly half an hour; and then another pair of lights came down the hill. It was the old-fashioned wheeled nondescript belonging to the captain, and Thomasin sat in it alone, driven by Charley.

The reddleman came up as they slowly turned the corner. 'I beg pardon for stopping you, Mrs. Wildeve,' he said. 'But I have something to give you privately from Mrs. Yeobright.' He handed a small parcel; it consisted of the hundred guineas he had just won, roughly twisted up in a piece of paper.

Thomasin recovered from her surprise, and took the packet. 'That's all, ma'am—I wish you good-night,' he said, and vanished from her view.

Thus Venn, in his anxiety to rectify matters, had placed in Thomasin's hands not only the fifty guineas which rightly belonged to her, but also the fifty intended for her cousin Clym. His mistake had been based upon Wildeve's words at the opening of the game, when he indignantly denied that the guinea was not his own. It had not been comprehended by the reddleman that at half-way through the performance the game was continued with the money of another person; and it was an error which afterwards helped to cause more misfortune than treble the loss in money value could have done.

The night was now somewhat advanced; and Venn plunged deeper into the heath, till he came to a ravine where his van was standing—a spot not more than two hundred yards from the site of the gambling bout. He entered this movable home of his, lit his lantern, and, before closing his door for the night, stood reflecting on the circumstances of the preceding hours. While he stood the dawn grew visible in the north-east quarter of the heavens, which, the clouds having cleared off, was bright with a soft sheen at this midsummer time, though it was only between one and two o'clock. Venn, thoroughly weary, then shut his door and flung himself down to sleep.

BOOK FOURTH: THE CLOSED DOOR

The Rencounter by the Pool

I

The July sun shone over Egdon and fired its crimson heather to scarlet. It was the one season of the year, and the one weather of the season, in which the heath was gorgeous. This flowering period represented the second or noontide division in the cycle of those superficial changes which alone were possible here; it followed the green or young-fern period, representing the morn, and preceded the brown period, when the heath-bells and ferns would wear the russet tinges of evening; to be in turn displaced by the dark hue of the winter period, representing night.

Clym and Eustacia, in their little house at Alderworth, beyond East Egdon, were living on with a monotony which was delightful to them. The heath and changes of weather were quite blotted out from their eyes for the present. They were enclosed in a sort of luminous mist, which hid from them surroundings of any inharmonious colour, and gave to all things the character of light. When it rained they were charmed, because they could remain indoors together all day with such a show of reason; when it was fine they were charmed, because they could sit together on the hills. They were like those double stars which revolve round and round each other, and from a distance appear to be one. The absolute solitude in which they lived intensified their reciprocal thoughts; yet some might have said that it had the disadvantage of consuming their mutual affections at a fearfully prodigal rate. Yeobright did not fear for his own part; but recollection of Eustacia's old speech about the evanescence of love, now apparently forgotten by her, sometimes caused him to ask himself a question; and he recoiled at the thought that the quality of finiteness was not foreign to Eden.

When three or four weeks had been passed thus, Yeobright resumed his reading in earnest. To make up for lost time he studied indefatigably, for he wished to enter his new profession with the least possible delay.

Now, Eustacia's dream had always been that, once married to Clym, she would have the power of inducing him to return to Paris. He had carefully withheld all promise to do so; but would he be proof against her coaxing and argument? She had calculated to such a degree on the probability of success that she had represented Paris, and not Budmouth, to her grandfather as in all likelihood their future home. Her hopes were bound up in this dream. In the quiet days since their marriage, when Yeobright had been poring over her lips, her eyes, and the lines of her face, she had mused and mused on the subject, even while in the act of returning his gaze; and now the sight of the books, indicating a future which was antagonistic to her dream, struck her with positively painful jar. She was hoping for the time when, as the mistress of some pretty establishment, however small, near a Parisian Boulevard, she would be passing her days on the skirts at least of the gay world, and catching stray wafts from those town pleasures she was so well fitted to enjoy. Yet Yeobright was as firm in the contrary intention as if the tendency of marriage were rather to develop the fantasies of young philanthropy than to sweep them away.

Her anxiety reached a high pitch; but there was something in Clym's undeviating manner which made her hesitate before sounding him on the subject. At this point in their experience, however, an incident helped her. It occurred one evening about six weeks after their union, and arose entirely out of the unconscious misapplication by Venn of the fifty guineas intended for Yeobright.

A day or two after the receipt of the money Thomasin had sent a note to her aunt to thank her. She had been surprised at the largeness of the amount; but as no sum had ever been mentioned she set that down to her late uncle's generosity. She had been strictly charged by her aunt to say nothing to her husband of this gift; and Wildeve, as was natural enough, had not brought himself to mention to his wife a single particular of the midnight scene in the heath. Christian's terror, in like manner, had tied his tongue on the share he took in that proceeding; and hoping that by some means or other the money had gone to its proper destination, he simply asserted as much, without giving details.

Therefore, when a week or two had passed away, Mrs. Yeobright began to wonder why she never heard from her son of the receipt of the present; and to add gloom to her perplexity came the possibility that resentment might be the cause of his silence. She could hardly believe as much, but why did he not write? She questioned Christian, and the confusion in his answers would at once have led her to believe that something was wrong, had not one-half of his story been corroborated by Thomasin's note.

Mrs. Yeobright was in this state of uncertainty when she was informed one morning that her son's wife was visiting her grandfather at Mistover. She determined to walk up the hill, see Eustacia, and ascertain from her daughter-in-law's lips whether the family guineas, which were to Mrs. Yeobright what family jewels are to wealthier dowagers, had miscarried or not.

When Christian learnt where she was going his concern reached its height. At the moment of her departure he could prevaricate no longer, and, confessing to the gambling, told her the truth as far as he knew it—that the guineas had been won by Wildeve.

'What, is he going to keep them?' Mrs. Yeobright cried.

'I hope and trust not!' moaned Christian. 'He's a good man, and perhaps will do right things. He said you ought to have gied Mr. Clym's share to Eustacia, and that's perhaps what he'll do himself.'

To Mrs. Yeobright, as soon as she could calmly reflect, there was much likelihood in this, for she could hardly believe that Wildeve would really appropriate money belonging to her son. The intermediate course of giving it to Eustacia was the sort of thing to please Wildeve's fancy. But it filled the mother with anger none the less. That Wildeve should have got command of the guineas after all, and should rearrange the disposal of them, placing Clym's share in Clym's wife's hands, because she had been his own sweetheart, and might be so still, was as irritating a pain as any that Mrs. Yeobright had ever borne.

She instantly dismissed the wretched Christian from her employ for his conduct in the affair; but, feeling quite helpless and unable to do without him, told him afterwards that he might stay a little longer if he chose. Then she hastened off to Eustacia, moved by a much less promising emotion towards her daughter-in-law than she had felt half an hour earlier, when planning her journey. At that time it was to inquire in a friendly spirit if there had been any accidental loss; now it was to ask plainly if Wildeve had privately given her money which had been intended as a sacred gift to Clym.

She started at two o'clock, and meeting with Eustacia was hastened by the appearance of the young lady beside the pool and bank which bordered her grandfather's premises, where she stood surveying the scene, and perhaps thinking of the romantic enactments it had witnessed in past days. When Mrs. Yeobright approached, Eustacia surveyed her with the calm stare of a stranger.

The mother-in-law was the first to speak. 'I was coming to see you,' she said.

'Indeed!' said Eustacia with surprise, for Mrs. Yeobright, much to the girl's mortification, had refused to be present at the wedding. 'I did not at all expect you.'

'I was coming on business only,' said the visitor, more coldly than at first. 'Will you excuse my asking this—Have you received a gift from Thomasin's husband?'

'A gift?'

'I mean money!'

'What—I myself?'

'Well, I meant yourself, privately—though I was not going to put it in that way.'

'Money from Mr. Wildeve? No—never! Madam, what do you mean by that?' Eustacia fired up all too quickly, for her own consciousness of the old attachment between her self and Wildeve led her to jump to the conclusion that Mrs. Yeobright also knew of it, and might have come to accuse her of receiving dishonourable presents from him now.

'I simply ask the question,' said Mrs. Yeobright. 'I have been——'

'You ought to have better opinions of me—I feared you were against me from the first!' exclaimed Eustacia.

'No. I was simply for Clym,' replied Mrs. Yeobright, with too much emphasis in her earnestness. 'It is the instinct of every one to look after their own.'

'How can you imply that he required guarding against me?' cried Eustacia, passionate tears in her eyes. 'I have not injured him by marrying him! What sin have I done that you should think so ill of me? You had no right to speak against me to him when I have never wronged you.'

'I only did what was fair under the circumstances,' said Mrs. Yeobright more softly. 'I would rather not have gone into this question at present, but you compel me. I am not ashamed to tell you the honest truth. I was firmly convinced that he ought not to marry you—therefore I tried to dissuade him by all the means in my power. But it is done now, and I have no idea of complaining any more. I am ready to welcome you.'

'Ah, yes, it is very well to see things in that business point of view,' murmured Eustacia with a smothered fire of feeling. 'But why should you think there is anything between me and Mr. Wildeve? I have a spirit as well as you. I am indignant; and so would any woman be. It was a condescension in me to be Clym's wife, and not a manoeuvre, let me remind you; and therefore I will not be treated as a schemer whom it becomes necessary to bear with because she has crept into the family.'

'Oh!' said Mrs. Yeobright, vainly endeavouring to control her anger. 'I have never heard anything to show that my son's lineage is not as good as the Vyes'—perhaps better. It is amusing to hear you talk of condescension.'

'It was condescension, nevertheless,' said Eustacia vehemently. 'And if I had known then what I know now, that I should be living in this wild heath a month after my marriage, I—I should have thought twice before agreeing.'

'It would be better not to say that; it might not sound truthful. I am not aware that any deception was used on his part—I know there was not—whatever might have been the case on the other side.'

'This is too exasperating!' answered the younger woman huskily, her face crimsoning, and her eyes darting light. 'How can you dare to speak to me like that? I insist upon repeating to you that had I known that my life would from my marriage up to this time have been as it is, I should have said *No.* I don't complain. I have never uttered a sound of such a thing to him; but it is true. I hope therefore that in the future you will be silent on my eagerness. If you injure me now you injure yourself.'

'Injure you? Do you think I am an evil-disposed person?'

'You injured me before my marriage, and you have now suspected me of secretly favouring another man for money!'

'I could not help what I thought. But I have never spoken of you outside my house.'

'You spoke of me within it, to Clym, and you could not do worse.'

'I did my duty.'

'And I'll do mine.'

'A part of which will possibly be to set him against his mother. It is always so. But why should I not bear it as others have borne it before me!'

'I understand you,' said Eustacia, breathless with emotion. 'You think me capable of every bad thing. Who can be worse than a wife who encourages a lover, and poisons her husband's mind against his relative? Yet that is now the character given to me. Will you not come and drag him out of my hands?'

Mrs. Yeobright gave back heat for heat.

'Don't rage at me, madam! It ill becomes your beauty, and I am not worth the injury you may do it on my account, I assure you. I am only a poor old woman who has lost a son.'

'If you had treated me honourably you would have had him still,' Eustacia said, while scalding tears trickled from her eyes. 'You have brought yourself to folly; you have caused a division which can never be healed!'

'I have done nothing. This audacity from a young woman is more than I can bear.'

'It was asked for: you have suspected me, and you have made me speak of my husband in a way I would not have done. You will let him know that I have spoken thus, and it will cause misery between us. Will you go away from me? You are no friend!'

'I will go when I have spoken a word. If any one says I have come here to question you without good grounds for it, that person speaks untruly. If any one says that I attempted to stop your marriage by any but honest means, that person, too, does not speak the truth. I have fallen on an evil time; God has been unjust to me in letting you insult me! Probably my son's happiness does not lie on this side of the grave, for he is a foolish man who neglects the advice of his parent. You, Eustacia, stand on the edge of a precipice without knowing it. Only show my son one-half the temper you have shown me to-day—and you may before long—and you will find that though he is as gentle as a child with you now, he can be as hard as steel!'

The excited mother then withdrew, and Eustacia, panting, stood looking into the pool.

He Is Set Upon by Adversities but He Sings a Song

II

The result of that unpropitious interview was that Eustacia, instead of passing the afternoon with her grandfather, hastily returned home to Clym, where she arrived three hours earlier than she had been expected.

She came indoors with her face flushed, and her eyes still showing traces of her recent excitement. Yeobright looked up astonished; he had never seen her in any way approaching to that state before. She passed him by, and would have gone upstairs unnoticed, but Clym was so concerned that he immediately followed her.

'What is the matter, Eustacia?' he said. She was standing on the hearthrug in the bedroom, looking upon the floor, her hands clasped in front of her, her bonnet yet unremoved. For a moment she did not answer; and then she replied in a low voice—

'I have seen your mother; and I will never see her again!'

A weight fell like a stone upon Clym. That same morning, when Eustacia had arranged to go and see her grandfather, Clym had expressed a wish that she would drive down to Blooms-End and inquire for her mother-in-law, or adopt any other means she might think fit to bring about a reconciliation. She had set out gaily; and he had hoped for much.

'Why is this?' he asked.

'I cannot tell—I cannot remember. I met your mother. And I will never meet her again.'

'Why?'

'What do I know about Mr. Wildeve now? I won't have wicked opinions passed on me by anybody. O! it was too humiliating to be asked if I had received any money from him, or encouraged him, or something of the sort—I don't exactly know what!'

'How could she have asked you that?'

'She did.'

'Then there must have been some meaning in it. What did my mother say besides?'

'I don't know what she said, except in so far as this, that we both said words which can never be forgiven!'

'O, there must be some misapprehension. Whose fault was it that her meaning was not made clear?'

'I would rather not say. It may have been the fault of the circumstances, which were awkward at the very least. O Clym—I cannot help expressing it—this is an unpleasant position that you have placed me in. But you must improve it—yes, say you will—for I hate it all now! Yes, take me to Paris, and go on with your old occupation, Clym! I don't mind how humbly we live there at first, if it can only be Paris, and not Egdon Heath.'

'But I have quite given up that idea,' said Yeobright, with surprise. 'Surely I never led you to expect such a thing?'

'I own it. Yet there are thoughts which cannot be kept out of mind, and that one was mine. Must I not have a voice in the matter, now I am your wife and the sharer of your doom?'

'Well, there are things which are placed beyond the pale of discussion; and I thought this was specially so, and by mutual agreement.'

'Clym, I am unhappy at what I hear,' she said in a low voice; and her eyes drooped, and she turned away.

This indication of an unexpected mine of hope in Eustacia's bosom disconcerted her husband. It was the first time that he had confronted the fact of the indirectness of a woman's movement towards her desire. But his intention was unshaken, though he loved Eustacia well. All the effect that her remark had upon him was a resolve to chain himself more closely than ever to his books, so as to be the sooner enabled to appeal to substantial results from another course in arguing against her whim.

Next day the mystery of the guineas was explained. Thomasin paid them a hurried visit, and Clym's share was delivered up to him by her own hands. Eustacia was not present at the time.

'Then this is what my mother meant,' exclaimed Clym. 'Thomasin, do you know that they have had a bitter quarrel?'

There was a little more reticence now than formerly in Thomasin's manner towards her cousin. It is the effect of marriage to engender in several directions some of the reserve it annihilates in one. 'Your mother told me,' she said quietly. 'She came back to my house after seeing Eustacia.'

'The worst thing I dreaded has come to pass. Was mother much disturbed when she came to you, Thomasin?'

'Yes.'

'Very much indeed?'

'Yes.

Clym leant his elbow upon the post of the garden gate, and covered his eyes with his hand.

'Don't trouble about it, Clym. They may get to be friends.'

He shook his head. 'Not two people with inflammable natures like theirs. Well, what must be will be.'

'One thing is cheerful in it—the guineas are not lost.'

'I would rather have lost them twice over than have had this happen.'

Amid these jarring events Yeobright felt one thing to be indispensable—that he should speedily make some show of progress in his scholastic plans. With this view he read far into the small hours during many nights.

One morning, after a severer strain than usual, he awoke with a strange sensation in his eyes. The sun was shining directly upon the window-blind, and at his first glance thitherward a sharp pain obliged him to close his eyelids quickly. At every new attempt to look about him the same morbid sensibility to light was manifested, and excoriating tears ran down his cheeks. He was obliged to tie a bandage over his brow while dressing; and during the day it could not be abandoned. Eustacia was thoroughly alarmed. On finding that the case was no better the next morning they decided to send to Anglebury for a surgeon.

Towards evening he arrived, and pronounced the disease to be acute inflammation induced by Clym's night studies, continued in spite of a cold previously caught, which had weakened his eyes for the time.

Fretting with impatience at this interruption to a task he was so anxious to hasten, Clym was transformed into an invalid. He was shut up in a room from which all light was excluded, and his condition would have been one of absolute misery had not Eustacia read to him by the glimmer of a shaded lamp. He hoped that the worst would soon be over; but at the surgeon's third visit he learnt to his dismay that although he might venture out of doors with shaded eyes in the course of a month, all thought of pursuing his work, or of reading print of any description, would have to be given up for a long time to come.

One week and another week wore on, and nothing seemed to lighten the gloom of the young couple. Dreadful imaginings occurred to Eustacia, but she carefully refrained from uttering them to her husband. Suppose he should become blind, or, at all events, never recover sufficient strength of sight to engage in an occupation which would be congenial to her feelings, and conduce to her removal from this lonely dwelling among the hills? That dream of beautiful Paris was not likely to cohere into substance in the presence of this misfortune. As day after day passed by, and he got no better, her mind ran more and more in this mournful groove, and she would go away from him into the garden and weep despairing tears.

Yeobright thought he would send for his mother; and then he thought he would not. Knowledge of his state could only make her the more unhappy; and the seclusion of their life was such that she would hardly be likely to learn the news except through a special messenger. Endeavouring to take the trouble as philosophically as possible, he waited on till the third week had arrived, when he went into the open air for the first time since the attack. The surgeon visited him again at this stage, and Clym urged him to express a distinct opinion. The young man learnt with added surprise that the date at which he might expect to resume his labours was as uncertain as ever, his eyes being in that peculiar state which, though affording him sight enough for walking about, would not admit of their being strained upon any definite object without incurring the risk of reproducing ophthalmia in its acute form.

Clym was very grave at the intelligence, but not despairing. A quiet firmness, and even cheerfulness, took possession of him. He was not to be blind; that was enough. To be doomed to behold the world through smoked glass for an indefinite period was bad enough, and fatal to any kind of advance; but Yeobright was an absolute stoic in the face of mishaps which only affected his social standing; and, apart from Eustacia, the humblest walk of life would satisfy him if it could be made to work in with some form of his culture scheme. To keep a cottage night-school was one such form; and his affliction did not master his spirit as it might otherwise have done.

He walked through the warm sun westward into those tracts of Egdon with which he was best acquainted, being those lying nearer to his old home. He saw before him in one of the valleys the gleaming of whetted iron, and advancing, dimly perceived that the shine came from the tool of a man who was cutting furze. The worker recognized Clym, and Yeobright learnt from the voice that the speaker was Humphrey.

Humphrey expressed his sorrow at Clym's condition; and added, 'Now, if yours was low-class work like mine, you could go on with it just the same.'

'Yes; I could,' said Yeobright musingly. 'How much do you get for cutting these faggots?'

'Half-a-crown a hundred, and in these long days I can live very well on the wages.'

During the whole of Yeobright's walk home to Alderworth he was lost in reflections which were not of an unpleasant kind. On his coming up to the house Eustacia spoke to him from the open window, and he went across to her.

'Darling,' he said, 'I am much happier. And if my mother were reconciled to me and to you I should, I think, be happy quite.'

'I fear that will never be,' she said, looking afar with her beautiful stormy eyes. 'How *can* you say "I am happier," and nothing changed?'

'It arises from my having at last discovered something I can do, and get a living at, in this time of misfortune.'

'Yes?'

'I am going to be a furze and turf cutter.'

'No, Clym!' she said, the slight hopefulness previously apparent in her face going off again, and leaving her worse than before.

'Surely I shall. Is it not very unwise in us to go on spending the little money we've got when I can keep down expenditure by an honest occupation? The outdoor exercise will do me good, and who knows but that in a few months I shall be able to go on with my reading again?'

'But my grandfather offers to assist us, if we require assistance?'

'We don't require it. If I go furze-cutting we shall be fairly well off.'

'In comparison with slaves, and the Israelites in Egypt, and such people!' A bitter tear rolled down Eustacia's face, which he did not see. There had been *nonchalance* in his tone, showing her that he felt no absolute grief at a consummation which to her was a positive horror.

The very next day Yeobright went to Humphrey's cottage, and borrowed of him leggings, gloves, a whet-stone, and a hook, to use till he should be able to purchase some for himself. Then he sallied forth with his new fellow-labourer and old acquaintance, and selecting a spot where the furze grew thickest he struck the first blow in his adopted calling. His sight, like the wings in 'Rasselas,'[1] though useless to him for his grand purpose, sufficed for this strait, and he found that when a little practice should have hardened his palms against blistering he would be able to work with ease.

Day after day he rose with the sun, buckled on his leggings, and went off to the rendezvous with Humphrey. His custom was to work from four o'clock in the morning till noon; then, when the heat of the day was at its highest, to go home and sleep for an hour or two; afterwards coming out again and working till dusk at nine.

This man from Paris was now so disguised by his leather accoutrements, and by the goggles he was obliged to wear over his eyes, that his closest friend might have passed by without recognizing

1. A 1759 prose work by Samuel Johnson (1709-1784). Rasselas the Prince, eager to leave the luxurious valley in which he is confined, meets an inventor who promises to make wings to enable him to fly over the mountains. The experiment fails, but the mental activity expended by Rasselas eventually helps him escape to see the world.

him. He was a brown spot in the midst of an expanse of olive-green gorse, and nothing more. Though frequently depressed in spirit when not actually at work, owing to thoughts of Eustacia's position and his mother's estrangement, when in the full swing of labour he was cheerfully disposed and calm.

His daily life was of a curious microscopic sort, his whole world being limited to a circuit of a few feet from his person. His familiars were creeping and winged things, and they seemed to enroll him in their band. Bees hummed around his ears with an intimate air, and tugged at the heath and furze-flowers at his side in such numbers as to weigh them down to the sod. The strange amber-coloured butterflies which Egdon produced, and which were never seen elsewhere, quivered in the breath of his lips, alighted upon his bowed back, and sported with the glittering point of his hook as he flourished it up and down. Tribes of emerald-green grasshoppers leaped over his feet, falling awkwardly on their backs, heads, or hips, like unskilful acrobats, as chance might rule; or engaged themselves in noisy flirtations under the fern-fronds with silent ones of homely hue. Huge flies, ignorant of larders and wire-netting, and quite in savage state, buzzed about him without knowing that he was a man. In and out of the fern-dells snakes glided in their most brilliant blue and yellow guise, it being the season immediately following the shedding of their old skins, when their colours are brightest. Litters of young rabbits came out from their forms to sun themselves upon hillocks, the hot beams blazing through the delicate tissue of each thin-fleshed ear, and firing it to a blood-red transparency in which the veins could be seen. None of them feared him.

The monotony of his occupation soothed him, and was in itself a pleasure. A forced limitation of effort offered a justification of homely courses to an unambitious man, whose conscience would hardly have allowed him to remain in such obscurity while his powers were unimpeded. Hence Yeobright sometimes sang to himself, and when obliged to accompany Humphrey in search of brambles for faggot-bonds he would amuse his companion with sketches of Parisian life and character, and so while away the time.

On one of these warm afternoons Eustacia walked out alone in the direction of Yeobright's place of work. He was busily chopping away at the furze, a long row of faggots which stretched downward from his position representing the labour of the day. He did not observe her approach, and she stood close to him, and heard his undercurrent of song. It shocked her. To see him there, a poor afflicted man, earning money by the sweat of his brow, had at first moved her to tears; but to hear him sing and not at all rebel against an occupation which, however satisfactory to himself, was degrading to her, as an educated lady-wife, wounded her through. Unconscious of her presence, he still went on singing:—

"Le point du jour
À nos bosquets rend toute leur parure;
Flore est plus belle à son retour;
L'oiseau reprend doux chant d'amour;
Tout célèbre dans la nature
Le point du jour.

"Le point du jour
Cause parfois, cause douleur extrême;
Que l'espace des nuits est court
Pour le berger brûlant d'amour,
Forcé de quitter ce qu'il aime
Au point du jour!"[2]

It was bitterly plain to Eustacia that he did not care much about social failure; and the proud fair woman bowed her head and wept in sick despair at thought of the blasting effect upon her own life of that mood and condition in him. Then she came forward.

'I would starve rather than do it!' she exclaimed vehemently. 'And you can sing! I will go and live with my grandfather again!'

'Eustacia! I did not see you, though I noticed something moving,' he said gently. He came forward, pulled off his huge leather glove, and took her hand. 'Why do you speak in such a strange way? It is only a little old song which struck my fancy when I was in Paris, and now just applies to my life with you. Has your love for me all died, then, because my appearance is no longer that of a fine gentleman?'

'Dearest, you must not question me unpleasantly, or it may make me not love you.'

'Do you believe it possible that I would run the risk of doing that?'

'Well, you follow out your own ideas, and won't give in to mine when I wish you to leave off this shameful labour. Is there anything you dislike in me that you act so contrarily to my wishes? I am your wife, and why will you not listen? Yes, I am your wife indeed!'

'I know what that tone means.'

'What tone?'

'The tone in which you said, "Your wife indeed." It meant, "Your wife, worse luck." '

'It is hard in you to probe me with that remark. A woman may have reason, though she is not without heart, and if I felt "worse luck," it was no ignoble feeling—it was only too natural. There,

2. This song, about the coming of dawn, describes both the beauty and sadness of the change from night to day.

you see that at any rate I do not attempt untruths. Do you remember how, before we were married, I warned you that I had not good wifely qualities?'

'You mock me to say that now. On that point at least the only noble course would be to hold your tongue, for you are still queen of me, Eustacia, though I may no longer be king of you.'

'You are my husband. Does not that content you?'

'Not unless you are my wife without regret.'

'I cannot answer you. I remember saying that I should be a serious matter on your hands.'

'Yes, I saw that.'

'Then you were too quick to see! No true lover would have seen any such thing; you are too severe upon me, Clym—I don't like your speaking so at all.'

'Well, I married you in spite of it, and don't regret doing so. How cold you seem this afternoon! and yet I used to think there never was a warmer heart than yours.'

'Yes, I fear we are cooling—I see it as well as you,' she sighed mournfully. 'And how madly we loved two months ago! You were never tired of contemplating me, nor I of contemplating you. Who could have thought then that by this time my eyes would not seem so very bright to yours, nor your lips so very sweet to mine? Two months—is it possible? Yes, 'tis too true!'

'You sigh, dear, as if you were sorry for it; and that's a hopeful sign.'

'No. I don't sigh for that. There are other things for me to sigh for, or any other woman in my place.'

'That your chances in life are ruined by marrying in haste an unfortunate man?'

'Why will you force me, Clym, to say bitter things? I deserve pity as much as you. As much?—I think I deserve it more. For you can sing! It would be a strange hour which should catch me singing under such a cloud as this! Believe me, sweet, I could weep to a degree that would astonish and confound such an elastic mind as yours. Even had you felt careless about your own affliction, you might have refrained from singing out of sheer pity for mine. God! if I were a man in such a position I would curse rather than sing.'

Yeobright placed his hand upon her arm. 'Now, don't you suppose, my inexperienced girl, that I cannot rebel, in high Promethean fashion, against the gods and fate as well as you. I have felt more steam and smoke of that sort than you have ever heard of. But the more I see of life the more do I perceive that there is nothing particularly great in its greatest walks, and therefore nothing particularly small in mine of furze-cutting. If I feel that the greatest blessings vouchsafed to us are not very valuable, how can I feel it to be any great hardship when they are taken away? So I sing to pass the time. Have you indeed lost all tenderness for me, that you begrudge me a few cheerful moments?'

'I have still some tenderness left for you.'

'Your words have no longer their old flavour. And so love dies with good fortune!'

'I cannot listen to this, Clym—it will end bitterly,' she said in a broken voice. 'I will go home.'

She Goes Out to Battle against Depression

III

A few days later, before the month of August had expired, Eustacia and Yeobright sat together at their early dinner.

Eustacia's manner had become of late almost apathetic. There was a forlorn look about her beautiful eyes which, whether she deserved it or not, would have excited pity in the breast of any one who had known her during the full flush of her love for Clym. The feelings of husband and wife varied, in some measure, inversely with their positions. Clym, the afflicted man, was cheerful; and he even tried to comfort her, who had never felt a moment of physical suffering in her whole life.

'Come, brighten up, dearest; we shall be all right again. Some day perhaps I shall see as well as ever. And I solemnly promise that I'll leave off cutting furze as soon as I have the power to do anything better. You cannot seriously wish me to stay idling at home all day?'

'But it is so dreadful—a furze-cutter! and you a man who have lived about the world, and speak French, and German, and who are fit for what is so much better than this.'

'I suppose when you first saw me and heard about me I was wrapped in a sort of golden halo to your eyes—a man who knew glorious things, and had mixed in brilliant scenes—in short, an adorable, delightful, distracting hero?'

'Yes,' she said, sobbing.

'And now I am a poor fellow in brown leather.'

'Don't taunt me. But enough of this. I will not be depressed any more. I am going from home this afternoon, unless you greatly object. There is to be a village picnic—a gipsying, they call it—at East Egdon, and I shall go.'

'To dance?'

'Why not? You can sing.'

'Well, well, as you will. Must I come to fetch you?'

'If you return soon enough from your work. But do not inconvenience yourself about it. I know the way home, and the heath has no terror for me.'

'And can you cling to gaiety so eagerly as to walk all the way to a village festival in search of it?'

'Now, you don't like my going alone! Clym, you are not jealous?'

'No. But I would come with you if it could give you any pleasure; though, as things stand, perhaps you have too much of me already. Still, I somehow wish that you did not want to go. Yes, perhaps I am jealous; and who could be jealous with more reason than I, a half-blind man, over such a woman as you?'

'Don't think like it. Let me go, and don't take all my spirits away!'

'I would rather lose all my own, my sweet wife. Go and do whatever you like. Who can forbid your indulgence in any whim? You have all my heart yet, I believe; and because you bear with me, who am in truth a drag upon you, I owe you thanks. Yes, go alone and shine. As for me, I still stick to my doom. At that kind of meeting people would shun me. My hook and gloves are like the St. Lazarus rattle of the leper, warning the world to get out of the way of a sight that would sadden them.' He kissed her, put on his leggings, and went out.

When he was gone she rested her head upon her hands and said to herself, 'Two wasted lives—his and mine. And I am come to this! Will it drive me out of my mind?'

She cast about for any possible course which offered the least improvement on the existing state of things, and could find none. She imagined how all those Budmouth ones who should learn what had become of her would say, 'Look at the girl for whom nobody was good enough!' To Eustacia the situation seemed such a mockery of her hopes that death appeared the only door of relief if the satire of Heaven should go much further.

Suddenly she aroused herself and exclaimed, 'But I'll shake it off. Yes, I *will* shake it off! No one shall know my suffering. I'll be bitterly merry, and ironically gay, and I'll laugh in derision! And I'll begin by going to this dance on the green.'

She ascended to her bedroom and dressed herself with scrupulous care. To an onlooker her beauty would have made her feelings almost seem reasonable. The gloomy corner into which accident as much as indiscretion had brought this woman might have led even a moderate partisan to feel that she had cogent reasons for asking the Supreme Power by what right a being of such exquisite finish had been placed in circumstances calculated to make of her charms a curse rather than a blessing.

It was five in the afternoon when she came out from the house ready for her walk. There was material enough in the picture for twenty new conquests. The rebellious sadness that was rather too apparent when she sat indoors without a bonnet was cloaked and softened by her outdoor attire, which always had a sort of nebulousness about it, devoid of harsh edges anywhere; so that her face looked from its environment as from a cloud, with no noticeable lines of demarcation between flesh and clothes. The heat of the day had scarcely declined as yet, and she went along the sunny hills at a leisurely pace, there being ample time for her idle expedition. Tall ferns buried her in their leafage whenever her path lay through them, which now formed miniature forests, though not one stem of them would remain to bud the next year.

The site chosen for the village festivity was one of the lawn-like oases which were occasionally, yet not often, met with on the plateaux of the heath district. The brakes of furze and fern terminated abruptly round the margin, and the grass was unbroken. A green cattle-track skirted the spot, without, however, emerging from the screen of fern, and this path Eustacia followed, in order to reconnoitre the group before joining it. The lusty notes of the East Egdon band had directed her unerringly, and she now beheld the musicians themselves, sitting in a blue waggon with red wheels scrubbed as bright as new, and arched with sticks, to which boughs and flowers were tied. In front of this was the grand central dance of fifteen or twenty couples, flanked by minor dances of inferior individuals whose gyrations were not always in strict keeping with the tune.

The young men wore blue and white rosettes, and with a flush on their faces footed it to the girls, who, with the excitement and the exercise, blushed deeper than the pink of their numerous ribbons. Fair ones with long curls, fair ones with short curls, fair ones with love-locks, fair ones with braids, flew round and round; and a beholder might well have wondered how such a prepossessing set of young women of like size, age, and disposition, could have been collected together where there were only one or two villages to choose from. In the background was one happy man dancing by himself, with closed eyes, totally oblivious of all the rest. A fire was burning under a pollard thorn a few paces off, over which three kettles hung in a row. Hard by was a table where elderly dames prepared tea, but Eustacia looked among them in vain for the cattle-dealer's wife who had suggested that she should come, and had promised to obtain a courteous welcome for her.

This unexpected absence of the only local resident whom Eustacia knew considerably damaged her scheme for an afternoon of reckless gaiety. Joining in became a matter of difficulty, notwithstanding that, were she to advance, cheerful dames would come forward with cups of tea and make much of her as a stranger of superior grace and knowledge to themselves. Having watched the company through the figures of two dances, she decided to walk a little further, to a cottage where she might get some refreshment, and then return homeward in the shady time of evening.

This she did; and by the time that she retraced her steps towards the scene of the gipsying, which it was necessary to repass on her way to Alderworth, the sun was going down. The air was now so still that she could hear the band afar off, and it seemed to be playing with more spirit, if that were possible, than when she had come away. On reaching the hill the sun had quite disappeared; but this made little difference either to Eustacia or to the revellers, for a round yellow moon was rising before her, though its rays had not yet outmastered those from the west. The dance was going on just the same, but strangers had arrived and formed a ring around the figure, so that Eustacia could stand among these without a chance of being recognized.

A whole village-full of sensuous emotion, scattered abroad all the year long, surged here in a focus for an hour. The forty hearts of those waving couples were beating as they had not done since, twelve months before, they had come together in similar jollity. For the time Paganism was revived in their hearts, the pride of life was all in all, and they adored none other than themselves.

How many of those impassioned but temporary embraces were destined to become perpetual was possibly the wonder of some of those who indulged in them, as well as of Eustacia who looked on. She began to envy those pirouetters, to hunger for the hope and happiness which the fascination of the dance seemed to engender within them. Desperately fond of dancing herself, one of Eustacia's expectations of Paris had been the opportunity it might afford her of indulgence in this favourite pastime. Unhappily, that expectation was now extinct within her for ever.

Whilst she abstractedly watched them spinning and fluctuating in the increasing moonlight she suddenly heard her name whispered by a voice over her shoulder. Turning in surprise, she beheld at her elbow one whose presence instantly caused her to flush to the temples.

It was Wildeve. Till this moment he had not met her eye since the morning of his marriage, when she had been loitering in the church, and had startled him by lifting her veil and coming forward to sign the register as witness. Yet why the sight of him should have instigated that sudden rush of blood she could not tell.

Before she could speak he whispered, 'Do you like dancing as much as ever?'

'I think I do,' she replied in a low voice.

'Will you dance with me?'

'It would be a great change for me; but will it not seem strange?'

'What strangeness can there be in relations dancing together?'

'Ah—yes, relations. Perhaps none.'

'Still, if you don't like to be seen, pull down your veil; though there is not much risk of being known by this light. Lots of strangers are here.'

She did as he suggested; and the act was a tacit acknowledgment that she accepted his offer.

Wildeve gave her his arm and took her down on the outside of the ring to the bottom of the dance, which they entered. In two minutes more they were involved in the figure and began working their way upwards to the top. Till they had advanced halfway thither Eustacia wished more than once that she had not yielded to his request; from the middle to the top she felt that, since she had come out to seek pleasure, she was only doing a natural thing to obtain it. Fairly launched into the ceaseless glides and whirls which their new position as top couple opened up to them, Eustacia's pulses began to move too quickly for longer rumination of any kind.

Through the length of five-and-twenty couples they threaded their giddy way, and a new vitality entered her form. The pale ray of evening lent a fascination to the experience. There is a certain degree and tone of light which tends to disturb the equilibrium of the senses, and to promote dangerously the tenderer moods; added to movement, it drives the emotions to rankness, the reason becoming sleepy and unperceiving in inverse proportion; and this light fell now upon these two from the disc of the moon. All the dancing girls felt the symptoms, but Eustacia most of all. The grass under their feet became trodden away, and the hard, beaten surface of the sod, when viewed aslant towards the moonlight, shone like a polished table. The air became quite still; the flag above the waggon which held the musicians clung to the pole, and the players appeared only in outline against the sky; except when the circular mouths of the trombone, ophicleide,[3] and French horn gleamed out like huge eyes from the shade of their figures. The pretty dresses of the maids lost their subtler day colours and showed more or less of a misty white. Eustacia floated round and round on Wildeve's arm, her face rapt and statuesque; her soul had passed away from and forgotten her features, which were left empty and quiescent, as they always are when feeling goes beyond their register.

How near she was to Wildeve! it was terrible to think of. She could feel his breathing, and he, of course, could feel hers. How badly she had treated him! yet, here they were treading one measure. The enchantment of the dance surprised her. A clear line of

3. Eleven-keyed wind instrument, consisting of conical brass tube bent double. Now superseded by the bass tuba.

difference divided like a tangible fence her experience within this maze of motion from her experience without it. Her beginning to dance had been like a change of atmosphere; outside, she had been steeped in arctic frigidity by comparison with the tropical sensations here. She had entered the dance from the troubled hours of her late life as one might enter a brilliant chamber after a night walk in a wood. Wildeve by himself would have been merely an agitation; Wildeve added to the dance, and the moonlight, and the secrecy, began to be a delight. Whether his personality supplied the greater part of this sweetly compounded feeling, or whether the dance and the scene weighed the more therein, was a nice point upon which Eustacia herself was entirely in a cloud.

People began to say 'Who are they?' but no invidious inquiries were made. Had Eustacia mingled with the other girls in their ordinary daily walks the case would have been different: here she was not inconvenienced by excessive inspection, for all were wrought to their brightest grace by the occasion. Like the planet Mercury surrounded by the lustre of sunset, her permanent brilliancy passed without much notice in the temporary glory of the situation.

As for Wildeve, his feelings are easy to guess. Obstacles were a ripening sun to his love, and he was at this moment in a delirium of exquisite misery. To clasp as his for five minutes what was another man's through all the rest of the year was a kind of thing he of all men could appreciate. He had long since begun to sigh again for Eustacia; indeed, it may be asserted that signing the marriage register with Thomasin was the natural signal to his heart to return to its first quarters, and that the extra complication of Eustacia's marriage was the one addition required to make that return compulsory.

Thus, for different reasons, what was to the rest an exhilarating movement was to these two a riding upon the whirlwind. The dance had come like an irresistible attack upon whatever sense of social order there was in their minds, to drive them back into old paths which were now doubly irregular. Through three dances in succession they spun their way; and then, fatigued with the incessant motion, Eustacia turned to quit the circle in which she had already remained too long. Wildeve led her to a grassy mound a few yards distant, where she sat down, her partner standing beside her. From the time that he addressed her at the beginning of the dance till now they had not exchanged a word.

'The dance and the walking have tired you?' he said tenderly.

'No; not greatly.'

'It is strange that we should have met here of all places, after missing each other so long.'

'We have missed because we tried to miss, I suppose.'

'Yes. But you began that proceeding—by breaking a promise.'

'It is scarcely worth while to talk of that now. We have formed other ties since then—you no less than I.'

'I am sorry to hear that your husband is ill.'

'He is not ill—only incapacitated.'

'Yes: that is what I mean. I sincerely sympathize with you in your trouble. Fate has treated you cruelly.'

She was silent awhile. 'Have you heard that he has chosen to work as a furze-cutter?' she said in a low, mournful voice.

'It has been mentioned to me,' answered Wildeve hesitatingly. 'But I hardly believed it.'

'It is true. What do you think of me as a furze-cutter's wife?'

'I think the same as ever of you, Eustacia. Nothing of the sort can degrade you: you ennoble the occupation of your husband.'

'I wish I could feel it.'

'Is there any chance of Mr. Yeobright getting better?'

'He thinks so. I doubt it.'

'I was quite surprised to hear that he had taken a cottage. I thought, in common with other people, that he would have taken you off to a home in Paris immediately after you had married him. "What a gay, bright future she has before her!" I thought. He will, I suppose, return there with you, if his sight gets strong again?'

Observing that she did not reply he regarded her more closely. She was almost weeping. Images of a future never to be enjoyed, the revived sense of her bitter disappointment, the picture of the neighbours' suspended ridicule which was raised by Wildeve's words, had been too much for proud Eustacia's equanimity.

Wildeve could hardly control his own too forward feelings when he saw her silent perturbation. But he affected not to notice this, and she soon recovered her calmness.

'You did not intend to walk home by yourself?' he asked.

'O yes,' said Eustacia. 'What could hurt me on this heath, who have nothing?'

'By diverging a little I can make my way home the same as yours. I shall be glad to keep you company as far as Throope Corner.' Seeing that Eustacia sat on in hesitation he added, 'Perhaps you think it unwise to be seen in the same road with me after the events of last summer?'

'Indeed I think no such thing,' she said haughtily. 'I shall accept whose company I choose, for all that may be said by the miserable inhabitants of Egdon.'

'Then let us walk on—if you are ready. Our nearest way is towards that holly-bush with the dark shadow that you see down there.'

Eustacia arose, and walked beside him in the direction signified, brushing her way over the damping heath and fern, and followed by the strains of the merrymakers, who still kept up the dance. The moon had now waxed bright and silvery, but the heath was proof against such illumination, and there was to be observed the striking scene of a dark, rayless tract of country under an atmosphere charged from its zenith to its extremities with whitest light. To an eye above them their two faces would have appeared amid the expanse like two pearls on a table of ebony.

On this account the irregularities of the path were not visible, and Wildeve occasionally stumbled; whilst Eustacia found it necessary to perform some graceful feats of balancing whenever a small tuft of heather or root of furze protruded itself through the grass of the narrow track and entangled her feet. At these junctures in her progress a hand was invariably stretched forward to steady her, holding her firmly until smooth ground was again reached, when the hand was again withdrawn to a respectful distance.

They performed the journey for the most part in silence, and drew near to Throope Corner, a few hundred yards from which a short path branched away to Eustacia's house. By degrees they discerned coming towards them a pair of human figures, apparently of the male sex.

When they came a little nearer Eustacia broke the silence by saying, 'One of those men is my husband. He promised to come to meet me.'

'And the other is my greatest enemy,' said Wildeve.

'It looks like Diggory Venn.'

'That is the man.'

'It is an awkward meeting,' said she; 'but such is my fortune. He knows too much about me, unless he could know more, and so prove to himself that what he now knows counts for nothing. Well, let it be: you must deliver me up to them.'

'You will think twice before you direct me to do that. Here is a man who has not forgotten an item in our meetings at Rainbarrow: he is in company with your husband. Which of them, seeing us together here, will believe that our meeting and dancing at the gipsy-party was by chance?'

'Very well,' she whispered gloomily. 'Leave me before they come up.'

Wildeve bade her a tender farewell, and plunged across the fern and furze, Eustacia slowly walking on. In two or three minutes she met her husband and his companion.

'My journey ends here for to-night, reddleman,' said Yeobright as soon as he perceived her. 'I turn back with this lady. Good night.'

'Good night, Mr. Yeobright,' said Venn. 'I hope to see you better soon.'

The moonlight shone directly upon Venn's face as he spoke, and revealed all its lines to Eustacia. He was looking suspiciously at her. That Venn's keen eye had discerned what Yeobright's feeble vision had not—a man in the act of withdrawing from Eustacia's side—was within the limits of the probable.

If Eustacia had been able to follow the reddleman she would soon have found striking confirmation of her thought. No sooner had Clym given her his arm and led her off the scene than the reddleman turned back from the beaten track towards East Egdon, whither he had been strolling merely to accompany Clym in his walk, Diggory's van being again in the neighbourhood. Stretching out his long legs he crossed the pathless portion of the heath somewhat in the direction which Wildeve had taken. Only a man accustomed to nocturnal rambles could at this hour have descended those shaggy slopes with Venn's velocity without falling headlong into a pit, or snapping off his leg by jamming his foot into some rabbit-burrow. But Venn went on without much inconvenience to himself, and the course of his scamper was towards the Quiet Woman Inn. This place he reached in about half an hour, and he was well aware that no person who had been near Throope Corner when he started could have got down here before him.

The lonely inn was not yet closed, though scarcely an individual was there, the business done being chiefly with travellers who passed the inn on long journeys, and these had now gone on their way. Venn went to the public room, called for a mug of ale, and inquired of the maid in an indifferent tone if Mr. Wildeve was at home.

Thomasin sat in an inner room and heard Venn's voice. When customers were present she seldom showed herself, owing to her inherent dislike for the business; but perceiving that no one else was there to-night she came out.

'He is not at home yet, Diggory,' she said pleasantly. 'But I expected him sooner. He has been to East Egdon to buy a horse.'

'Did he wear a light wideawake?'[4]

'Yes.'

'Then I saw him at Throope Corner, leading one home,' said Venn drily. 'A beauty, with a white face and a mane as black as night. He will soon be here, no doubt.' Rising and looking for a moment at the pure, sweet face of Thomasin, over which a shadow of sadness had passed since the time when he had last seen her, he ventured to add, 'Mr. Wildeve seems to be often away at this time.'

4. Soft felt hat with a broad brim and a low crown.

'Oh yes,' cried Thomasin in what was intended to be a tone of gaiety. 'Husbands will play the truant, you know. I wish you could tell me of some secret plan that would help me to keep him home at my will in the evenings.'

'I will consider if I know of one,' replied Venn in that same light tone which meant no lightness. And then he bowed in a manner of his own invention and moved to go. Thomasin offered him her hand; and without a sigh, though with food for many, the reddleman went out.

When Wildeve returned, a quarter of an hour later, Thomasin said simply, and in the abashed manner usual with her now, 'Where is the horse, Damon?'

'O, I have not bought it, after all. The man asks too much.'

'But somebody saw you at Throope Corner leading it home—a beauty, with a white face and a mane as black as night.'

'Ah!' said Wildeve, fixing his eyes upon her; 'who told you that?'

'Venn the reddleman.'

The expression of Wildeve's face became curiously condensed. 'That is a mistake—it must have been some one else,' he said slowly and testily, for he perceived that Venn's counter-moves had begun again.

Rough Coercion Is Employed

IV

Those words of Thomasin, which seemed so little, but meant so much, remained in the ears of Diggory Venn: 'Help me to keep him home in the evenings.'

On this occasion Venn had arrived on Egdon Heath only to cross to the other side: he had no further connection with the interests of the Yeobright family, and he had a business of his own to attend to. Yet he suddenly began to feel himself drifting into the old track of manoeuvring on Thomasin's account.

He sat in his van and considered. From Thomasin's words and manner he had plainly gathered that Wildeve neglected her. For whom could he neglect her if not for Eustacia? Yet it was scarcely credible that things had come to such a head as to indicate that Eustacia systematically encouraged him. Venn resolved to reconnoitre somewhat carefully the lonely road which led along the vale from Wildeve's dwelling to Clym's house at Alderworth.

At this time, as has been seen, Wildeve was quite innocent of any predetermined act of intrigue, and except at the dance on the green he had not once met Eustacia since her marriage. But that the spirit of intrigue was in him had been shown by a recent romantic habit of his: a habit of going out after dark and strolling towards Alderworth, there looking at the moon and stars, looking at Eustacia's house, and walking back at leisure.

Accordingly, when watching on the night after the festival, the reddleman saw him ascend by the little path, lean over the front gate of Clym's garden, sigh, and turn to go back again. It was plain that Wildeve's intrigue was rather ideal than real. Venn retreated before him down the hill to a place where the path was merely a deep groove between the heather; here he mysteriously bent over the ground for a few minutes, and retired. When Wildeve came on to that spot his ankle was caught by something, and he fell headlong.

As soon as he had recovered the power of respiration he sat up and listened. There was not a sound in the gloom beyond the spiritless stir of the summer wind. Feeling about for the obstacle which had flung him down, he discovered that two turfs of heath had been tied together across the path, forming a loop, which to a traveller was certain overthrow. Wildeve pulled off the string that bound them, and went on with tolerable quickness. On reaching home he found the cord to be of a reddish colour. It was just what he had expected.

Although his weaknesses were not specially those akin to physical fear, this species of *coup-de-Jarnac*[5] from one he knew too well troubled the mind of Wildeve. But his movements were unaltered thereby. A night or two later he again went along the vale to Alderworth, taking the precaution of keeping out of any path. The sense that he was watched, that craft was employed to circumvent his errant tastes, added piquancy to a journey so entirely sentimental, so long as the danger was of no fearful sort. He imagined that Venn and Mrs. Yeobright were in league, and felt that there was a certain legitimacy in combating such a coalition.

The heath to-night appeared to be totally deserted; and Wildeve, after looking over Eustacia's garden gate for some little time, with a cigar in his mouth, was tempted by the fascination that emotional smuggling had for his nature to advance towards the window, which was not quite closed, the blind being only partly drawn down. He could see into the room, and Eustacia was sitting there alone. Wildeve contemplated her for a minute, and then retreating into the heath beat the ferns lightly, whereupon moths flew out alarmed. Securing one, he returned to the window, and holding the moth to the chink, opened his hand. The moth made towards the candle upon Eustacia's table, hovered round it two or three times, and flew into the flame.

Eustacia started up. This had been a well-known signal in old times when Wildeve had used to come secretly wooing to Mistover.

5. Stab in the back.

She at once knew that Wildeve was outside, but before she could consider what to do her husband came in from upstairs. Eustacia's face burnt crimson at the unexpected collision of incidents, and filled it with an animation that it too frequently lacked.

'You have a very high colour, dearest,' said Yeobright, when he came close enough to see it. 'Your appearance would be no worse if it were always so.'

'I am warm,' said Eustacia. 'I think I will go into the air for a few minutes.'

'Shall I go with you?'

'O no. I am only going to the gate.'

She arose, but before she had time to get out of the room a loud rapping began upon the front door.

'I'll go—I'll go,' said Eustacia in an unusually quick tone for her; and she glanced eagerly towards the window whence the moth had flown; but nothing appeared there.

'You had better not at this time of the evening,' he said. Clym stepped before her into the passage, and Eustacia waited, her somnolent manner covering her inner heat and agitation.

She listened, and Clym opened the door. No words were uttered outside, and presently he closed it and came back, saying, 'Nobody was there. I wonder what that could have meant?'

He was left to wonder during the rest of the evening, for no explanation offered itself, and Eustacia said nothing, the additional fact that she knew of only adding more mystery to the performance.

Meanwhile a little drama had been acted outside which saved Eustacia from all possibility of compromising herself that evening at least. Whilst Wildeve had been preparing his moth-signal another person had come behind him up to the gate. This man, who carried a gun in his hand, looked on for a moment at the other's operation by the window, walked up to the house, knocked at the door, and then vanished round the corner and over the hedge.

'Damn him!' said Wildeve. 'He has been watching me again.'

As his signal had been rendered futile by this uproarious rapping Wildeve withdrew, passed out at the gate, and walked quickly down the path without thinking of anything except getting away unnoticed. Half-way down the hill the path ran near a knot of stunted hollies, which in the general darkness of the scene stood as the pupil in a black eye. When Wildeve reached this point a report startled his ear, and a few spent gunshots fell among the leaves around him.

There was no doubt that he himself was the cause of that gun's discharge; and he rushed into the clump of hollies, beating the bushes furiously with his stick; but nobody was there. This attack was a more serious matter than the last, and it was some time before Wildeve recovered his equanimity. A new and most unpleasant system of menace had begun, and the intent appeared to be to do him grievous bodily harm. Wildeve had looked upon Venn's first attempt as a species of horse-play, which the reddleman had indulged in for want of knowing better; but now the boundary-line was passed which divides the annoying from the perilous.

Had Wildeve known how thoroughly in earnest Venn had become he might have been still more alarmed. The reddleman had been almost exasperated by the sight of Wildeve outside Clym's house, and he was prepared to go to any lengths short of absolutely shooting him, to terrify the young innkeeper out of his recalcitrant impulses. The doubtful legitimacy of such rough coercion did not disturb the mind of Venn. It troubles few such minds in such cases, and sometimes this is not to be regretted. From the impeachment of Strafford[6] to Farmer Lynch's short way with the scamps of Virginia there have been many triumphs of justice which are mockeries of law.

About half a mile below Clym's secluded dwelling lay a hamlet where lived one of the two constables who preserved the peace in the parish of Alderworth, and Wildeve went straight to the constable's cottage. Almost the first thing that he saw on opening the door was the constable's truncheon hanging to a nail, as if to assure him that here were the means to his purpose. On inquiry, however, of the constable's wife he learnt that the constable was not at home. Wildeve said he would wait.

The minutes ticked on, and the constable did not arrive. Wildeve cooled down from his state of high indignation to a restless dissatisfaction with himself, the scene, the constable's wife, and the whole set of circumstances. He arose and left the house. Altogether, the experience of that evening had had a cooling, not to say a chilling, effect on misdirected tenderness, and Wildeve was in no mood to ramble again to Alderworth after nightfall in hope of a stray glance from Eustacia.

Thus far the reddleman had been tolerably successful in his rude contrivances for keeping down Wildeve's inclination to rove in the evening. He had nipped in the bud the possible meeting between Eustacia and her old lover this very night. But he had not anticipated that the tendency of his action would be to divert Wildeve's

6. Thomas Wentworth, first Earl of Strafford (see note on p. 80). Charged with treason, for which there was no evidence, Strafford was impeached in 1640. He himself urged King Charles I to ratify these charges in order to assuage anti-Royalist sentiment. After his execution, Strafford became a famous martyr for the Royalist cause. Farmer Lynch caught a thief and flogged him himself, one version of the origin of the term "lynch law" or "lynching."

movement rather than to stop it. The gambling with the guineas had not conduced to make him a welcome guest to Clym; but to call upon his wife's relative was natural, and he was determined to see Eustacia. It was necessary to choose some less untoward hour than ten o'clock at night. 'Since it is unsafe to go in the evening,' he said, 'I'll go by day.'

Meanwhile Venn had left the heath and gone to call upon Mrs. Yeobright, with whom he had been on friendly terms since she had learnt what a providential counter-move he had made towards the restitution of the family guineas. She wondered at the lateness of his call, but had no objection to see him.

He gave her a full account of Clym's affliction, and of the state in which he was living; then, referring to Thomasin, touched gently upon the apparent sadness of her days. 'Now, ma'am, depend upon it,' he said, 'you couldn't do a better thing for either of 'em than to make yourself at home in their houses, even if there should be a little rebuff at first.'

'Both she and my son disobeyed me in marrying; therefore I have no interest in their households. Their troubles are of their own making.' Mrs. Yeobright tried to speak severely; but the account of her son's state had moved her more than she cared to show.

'Your visits would make Wildeve walk straighter than he is inclined to do, and might prevent unhappiness down the heath.'

'What do you mean?'

'I saw something to-night out there which I didn't like at all. I wish your son's house and Mr. Wildeve's were a hundred miles apart instead of four or five.'

'Then there *was* an understanding between him and Clym's wife when he made a fool of Thomasin!'

'We'll hope there's no understanding now.'

'And our hope will probably be very vain. O Clym! O Thomasin!'

'There's no harm done yet. In fact, I've persuaded Wildeve to mind his own business.'

'How?'

'O, not by talking—by a plan of mine called the silent system.'

'I hope you'll succeed.'

'I shall if you help me by calling and making friends with your son. You'll have a chance then of using your eyes.'

'Well, since it has come to this,' said Mrs. Yeobright sadly, 'I will own to you, reddleman, that I thought of going. I should be much happier if we were reconciled. The marriage is unalterable, my life may be cut short, and I should wish to die in peace. He is my only son; and since sons are made of such stuff I am not sorry I have no other. As for Thomasin, I never expected much from her; and she has not disappointed me. But I forgave her long ago; and I forgive him now. I'll go.'

At this very time of the reddleman's conversation with Mrs. Yeobright at Blooms-End another conversation on the same subject was languidly proceeding at Alderworth.

All the day Clym had borne himself as if his mind were too full of its own matter to allow him to care about outward things, and his words now showed what had occupied his thoughts. It was just after the mysterious knocking that he began the theme. 'Since I have been away to-day, Eustacia, I have considered that something must be done to heal up this ghastly breach between my dear mother and myself. It troubles me.'

'What do you propose to do?' said Eustacia abstractedly, for she could not clear away from her the excitement caused by Wildeve's recent manoeuvre for an interview.

'You seem to take a very mild interest in what I propose, little or much,' said Clym, with tolerable warmth.

'You mistake me,' she answered, reviving at his reproach. 'I am only thinking.'

'What of?'

'Partly of that moth whose skeleton is getting burnt up in the wick of the candle,' she said slowly. 'But you know I always take an interest in what you say.'

'Very well, dear. Then I think I must go and call upon her.' . . . He went on with tender feeling: 'It is a thing I am not at all too proud to do, and only a fear that I might irritate her has kept me away so long. But I must do something. It is wrong in me to allow this sort of thing to go on.'

'What have you to blame yourself about?'

'She is getting old, and her life is lonely, and I am her only son.'

'She has Thomasin.'

'Thomasin is not her daughter; and if she were that would not excuse me. But this is beside the point. I have made up my mind to go to her, and all I wish to ask you is whether you will do your best to help me—that is, forget the past; and if she shows her willingness to be reconciled, meet her half-way by welcoming her to our house, or by accepting a welcome to hers?'

At first Eustacia closed her lips as if she would rather do anything on the whole globe than what he suggested. But the lines of her mouth softened with thought, though not so far as they might have softened; and she said, 'I will put nothing in your way; but after what has passed it is asking too much that I go and make advances.'

'You never distinctly told me what did pass between you.'

'I could not do it then, nor can I now. Sometimes more bitterness is sown in five minutes than can be got rid of in a whole life; and that may be the case here.' She paused a few moments, and added, 'If you had never returned to your native place, Clym, what a blessing it would have been for you! . . . It has altered the destinies of——'

'Three people.'

'Five,' Eustacia thought; but she kept that in.

The Journey across the Heath

V

Thursday, the thirty-first of August, was one of a series of days during which snug houses were stifling, and when cool draughts were treats; when cracks appeared in clayey gardens, and were called 'earthquakes' by apprehensive children; when loose spokes were discovered in the wheels of carts and carriages; and when stinging insects haunted the air, the earth, and every drop of water that was to be found.

In Mrs. Yeobright's garden large-leaved plants of a tender kind flagged by ten o'clock in the morning; rhubarb bent downward at eleven; and even stiff cabbages were limp by noon.

It was about eleven o'clock on this day that Mrs. Yeobright started across the heath towards her son's house, to do her best in getting reconciled with him and Eustacia, in conformity with her words to the reddleman. She had hoped to be well advanced in her walk before the heat of the day was at its highest, but after setting out she found that this was not to be done. The sun had branded the whole heath with his mark, even the purple heath-flowers having put on a brownness under the dry blazes of the few preceding days. Every valley was filled with air like that of a kiln, and the clean quartz sand of the winter water-courses, which formed summer paths, had undergone a species of incineration since the drought had set in.

In cool, fresh weather Mrs. Yeobright would have found no inconvenience in walking to Alderworth, but the present torrid attack made the journey a heavy undertaking for a woman past middle age; and at the end of the third mile she wished that she had hired Fairway to drive her a portion at least of the distance. But from the point at which she had arrived it was as easy to reach Clym's house as to get home again. So she went on, the air around her pulsating silently, and oppressing the earth with lassitude. She looked at the sky overhead, and saw that the sapphirine hue of the zenith in spring and early summer had been replaced by a metallic violet.

Occasionally she came to a spot where independent worlds of

ephemerons were passing their time in mad carousal, some in the air, some on the hot ground and vegetation, some in the tepid and stringy water of a nearly dried pool. All the shallower ponds had decreased to a vaporous mud amid which the maggoty shapes of innumerable obscure creatures could be indistinctly seen, heaving and wallowing with enjoyment. Being a woman not disinclined to philosophize she sometimes sat down under her umbrella to rest and to watch their happiness, for a certain hopefulness as to the result of her visit gave ease to her mind, and between important thoughts left it free to dwell on any infinitesimal matter which caught her eyes.

Mrs. Yeobright had never before been to her son's house, and exact position was unknown to her. She tried one ascending path and another, and found that they led her astray. Retracing her steps she came again to an open level, where she perceived at a distance a man at work. She went towards him and inquired the way.

The labourer pointed out the direction, and added, 'Do you see that furze-cutter, ma'am, going up that footpath yond?'

Mrs. Yeobright strained her eyes, and at last said that she did perceive him.

'Well, if you follow him you can make no mistake. He's going to the same place, ma'am.'

She followed the figure indicated. He appeared of a russet hue, not more distinguishable from the scene around him than the green caterpillar from the leaf it feeds on. His progress when actually walking was more rapid than Mrs. Yeobright's; but she was enabled to keep at an equable distance from him by his habit of stopping whenever he came to a brake of brambles, where he paused awhile. On coming in her turn to each of these spots she found half a dozen long limp brambles which he had cut from the bush during his halt and laid out straight beside the path. They were evidently intended for furze-faggot bonds which he meant to collect on his return.

The silent being who thus occupied himself seemed to be of no more account in life than an insect. He appeared as a mere parasite of the heath, fretting its surface in his daily labour as a moth frets a garment, entirely engrossed with its products, having no knowledge of anything in the world but fern, furze, heath, lichens, and moss.

The furze-cutter was so absorbed in the business of his journey that he never turned his head; and his leather-legged and gauntleted form at length became to her as nothing more than a moving handpost to show her the way. Suddenly she was attracted to his individuality by observing peculiarities in his walk. It was a gait she had seen somewhere before; and the gait revealed the man to her, as the gait of Ahimaaz[7] in the distant plain made him known to the watchman of the king. 'His walk is exactly as my husband's used to be,' she said; and then the thought burst upon her that the furze-cutter was her son.

She was scarcely able to familiarize herself with this strange reality. She had been told that Clym was in the habit of cutting furze, but she had supposed that he occupied himself with the labour only at odd times, by way of useful pastime; yet she now beheld him as a furze-cutter and nothing more—wearing the regulation dress of the craft, and thinking the regulation thoughts, to judge by his motions. Planning a dozen hasty schemes for at once preserving him and Eustacia from this mode of life she throbbingly followed the way, and saw him enter his own door.

At one side of Clym's house was a knoll, and on the top of the knoll a clump of fir trees so highly thrust up into the sky that their foliage from a distance appeared as a black spot in the air above the crown of the hill. On reaching this place Mrs. Yeobright felt distressingly agitated, weary, and unwell. She ascended, and sat down under their shade to recover herself, and to consider how best to break the ground with Eustacia, so as not to irritate a woman underneath whose apparent indolence lurked passions even stronger and more active than her own.

The trees beneath which she sat were singularly battered, rude, and wild, and for a few minutes Mrs. Yeobright dismissed thoughts of her own storm-broken and exhausted state to contemplate theirs. Not a bough in the nine trees which composed the group but was splintered, lopped, and distorted by the fierce weather that there held them at its mercy whenever it prevailed. Some were blasted and split as if by lightning, black stains as from fire marking their sides, while the ground at their feet was strewn with dead fir-needles and heaps of cones blown down in the gales of past years. The place was called the Devil's Bellows, and it was only necessary to come there on a March or November night to discover the forcible reasons for that name. On the present heated afternoon, when no perceptible wind was blowing, the trees kept up a perpetual moan which one could hardly believe to be caused by the air.

Here she sat for twenty minutes or more ere she could summon resolution to go down to the door, her courage being lowered to zero by her physical lassitude. To any other person than a mother it might have seemed a little humiliating that she, the elder of the two women, should be the first to make advances. But Mrs. Yeobright had well considered all that, and she only thought how best to make her visit appear to Eustacia not abject but wise.

7. King's councilor who brought the news of Absalom's defeat and death to King David. He was recognized by the King's watchman from the way he ran. (II Samuel xviii.19-33)

From her elevated position the exhausted woman could perceive the roof of the house below, and the garden and the whole enclosure of the little domicile. And now, at the moment of rising, she saw a second man approaching the gate. His manner was peculiar, hesitating, and not that of a person come on business or by invitation. He surveyed the house with interest, and then walked round and scanned the outer boundary of the garden, as one might have done had it been the birthplace of Shakespeare, the prison of Mary Stuart, or the Château of Hougomont.[8] After passing round and again reaching the gate he went in. Mrs. Yeobright was vexed at this, having reckoned on finding her son and his wife by themselves; but a moment's thought showed her that the presence of an acquaintance would take off the awkwardness of her first appearance in the house, by confining the talk to general matters until she had begun to feel comfortable with them. She came down the hill to the gate, and looked into the hot garden.

There lay the cat asleep on the bare gravel of the path, as if beds, rugs, and carpets were unendurable. The leaves of the hollyhocks hung like half-closed umbrellas, the sap almost simmered in the stems, and foliage with a smooth surface glared like metallic mirrors. A small apple tree, of the sort called Ratheripe, grew just inside the gate, the only one which throve in the garden, by reason of the lightness of the soil; and among the fallen apples on the ground beneath were wasps rolling drunk with the juice, or creeping about the little caves in each fruit which they had eaten out before stupefied by its sweetness. By the door lay Clym's furze-hook and the last handful of faggot-bonds she had seen him gather; they had plainly been thrown down there as he entered the house.

A Conjuncture, and Its Result upon the Pedestrian

VI

Wildeve, as has been stated, was determined to visit Eustacia boldly, by day, and on the easy terms of a relation, since the reddleman had spied out and spoilt his walks to her by night. The spell that she had thrown over him in the moonlight dance made it impossible for a man having no strong puritanic force within him to keep away altogether. He merely calculated on meeting her and her husband in an ordinary manner, chatting a little while, and leaving again. Every outward sign was to be conventional; but the one great fact would be there to satisfy him: he would see her. He did not even desire Clym's absence, since it was just possible that

8. Mansion on the farm near Waterloo, the base of the Duke of Wellington's right wing, against which the first French attack was launched (1815).

Eustacia might resent any situation which could compromise her dignity as a wife, whatever the state of her heart towards him. Women were often so.

He went accordingly; and it happened that the time of his arrival coincided with that of Mrs. Yeobright's pause on the hill near the house. When he had looked round the premises in the manner she had noticed he went and knocked at the door. There was a few minutes' interval, and then the key turned in the lock, the door opened, and Eustacia herself confronted him.

Nobody could have imagined from her bearing now that here stood the woman who had joined with him in the impassioned dance of the week before, unless indeed he could have penetrated below the surface and gauged the real depth of that still stream.

'I hope you reached home safely?' said Wildeve.

'O yes,' she carelessly returned.

'And were you not tired the next day? I feared you might be.'

'I was rather. You need not speak low—nobody will overhear us. My small servant is gone on an errand to the village.'

'Then Clym is not at home?'

'Yes, he is.'

'O! I thought that perhaps you had locked the door because you were alone and were afraid of tramps.'

'No—here is my husband.'

They had been standing in the entry. Closing the front door and turning the key, as before, she threw open the door of the adjoining room and asked him to walk in. Wildeve entered, the room appearing to be empty; but as soon as he had advanced a few steps he started. On the hearthrug lay Clym asleep. Beside him were the leggings, thick boots, leather gloves, and sleeve-waistcoat in which he worked.

'You may go in; you will not disturb him,' she said, following behind. 'My reason for fastening the door is that he may not be intruded upon by any chance comer while lying here, if I should be in the garden or upstairs.'

'Why is he sleeping there?' said Wildeve in low tones.

'He is very weary. He went out at half-past four this morning, and has been working ever since. He cuts furze because it is the only thing he can do that does not put any strain upon his poor eyes.' The contrast between the sleeper's appearance and Wildeve's at this moment was painfully apparent to Eustacia, Wildeve being elegantly dressed in a new summer suit and light hat; and she continued: 'Ah! you don't know how differently he appeared when I first met him, though it is such a little while ago. His hands were as white and soft as mine; and look at them now, how rough and brown they are! His complexion is by nature fair, and that rusty look he has now, all of a colour with his leather clothes, is caused by the burning of the sun.'

'Why does he go out at all?' Wildeve whispered.

'Because he hates to be idle; though what he earns doesn't add much to our exchequer. However, he says that when people are living upon their capital they must keep down current expenses by turning a penny where they can.'

'The fates have not been kind to you, Eustacia Yeobright.'

'I have nothing to thank them for.'

'Nor has he—except for their one great gift to him.'

'What's that?'

Wildeve looked her in the eyes.

Eustacia blushed for the first time that day. 'Well, I am a questionable gift,' she said quietly. 'I thought you meant the gift of content—which he has, and I have not.'

'I can understand content in such a case—though how the outward situation can attract him puzzles me.'

'That's because you don't know him. He's an enthusiast about ideas, and careless about outward things. He often reminds me of the Apostle Paul.'

'I am glad to hear that he's so grand in character as that.'

'Yes; but the worst of it is that though Paul was excellent as a man in the Bible he would hardly have done in real life.'

Their voices had instinctively dropped lower, though at first they had taken no particular care to avoid awakening Clym. 'Well, if that means that your marriage is a misfortune to you, you know who is to blame,' said Wildeve.

'The marriage is no misfortune in itself,' she retorted with some little petulance. 'It is simply the accident which has happened since that has been the cause of my ruin. I have certainly got thistles for figs[9] in a worldly sense, but how could I tell what time would bring forth?'

'Sometimes, Eustacia, I think it is a judgment upon you. You rightly belonged to me, you know; and I had no idea of losing you.'

'No, it was not my fault! Two could not belong to you; and remember that, before I was aware, you turned aside to another woman. It was cruel levity in you to do that. I never dreamt of playing such a game on my side till you began it on yours.'

'I meant nothing by it,' replied Wildeve. 'It was a mere interlude. Men are given to the trick of having a passing fancy for somebody else in the midst of a permanent love, which reasserts itself afterwards just as before. On account of your rebellious manner to me I was tempted to go further than I should have done; and when you still would keep playing the same tantalizing part I went fur-

9. Dialect expression for receiving thorns instead of the fruit expected.

ther still, and married her.' Turning and looking again at the unconscious form of Clym he murmured, 'I am afraid that you don't value your prize, Clym. . . . He ought to be happier than I in one thing at least. He may know what it is to come down in the world, and to be afflicted with a great personal calamity; but he probably doesn't know what it is to lose the woman he loved.'

'He is not ungrateful for winning her,' whispered Eustacia, 'and in that respect he is a good man. Many women would go far for such a husband. But do I desire unreasonably much in wanting what is called life—music, poetry, passion, war, and all the beating and pulsing that is going on in the great arteries of the world? That was the shape of my youthful dream; but I did not get it. Yet I thought I saw the way to it in my Clym.'

'And you only married him on that account?'

'There you mistake me. I married him because I loved him, but I won't say that I didn't love him partly because I thought I saw a promise of that life in him.'

'You have dropped into your old mournful key.'

'But I am not going to be depressed,' she cried perversely. 'I began a new system by going to that dance, and I mean to stick to it. Clym can sing merrily; why should not I?'

Wildeve looked thoughtfully at her. 'It is easier to say you will sing than to do it; though if I could I would encourage you in your attempt. But as life means nothing to me, without one thing which is now impossible, you will forgive me for not being able to encourage you.'

'Damon, what is the matter with you, that you speak like that?' she asked, raising her deep shady eyes to his.

'That's a thing I shall never tell plainly; and perhaps if I try to tell you in riddles you will not care to guess them.'

Eustacia remained silent for a minute, and she said, 'We are in a strange relationship to-day. You mince matters to an uncommon nicety. You mean, Damon, that you still love me. Well, that gives me sorrow, for I am not made so entirely happy by my marriage that I am willing to spurn you for the information, as I ought to do. But we have said too much about this. Do you mean to wait until my husband is awake?'

'I thought to speak to him; but it is unnecessary, Eustacia, if I offend you by not forgetting you, you are right to mention it; but do not talk of spurning.'

She did not reply, and they stood looking musingly at Clym as he slept on in that profound sleep which is the result of physical labour carried on in circumstances that wake no nervous fear.

'God, how I envy him that sweet sleep!' said Wildeve. 'I have not slept like that since I was a boy—years and years ago.'

While they thus watched him a click at the gate was audible, and a knock came to the door. Eustacia went to a window and looked out.

Her countenance changed. First she became crimson, and then the red subsided till it even partially left her lips.

'Shall I go away?' said Wildeve, standing up.

'I hardly know.'

'Who is it?'

'Mrs. Yeobright. O, what she said to me that day! I cannot understand this visit—what does she mean? And she suspects that past time of ours.'

'I am in your hands. If you think she had better not see me here I'll go into the next room.'

'Well, yes: go.'

Wildeve at once withdrew; but before he had been half a minute in the adjoining apartment Eustacia came after him.

'No,' she said, 'we won't have any of this. If she comes in she must see you—and think if she likes there's something wrong! But how can I open the door to her, when she dislikes me—wishes to see not me, but her son? I won't open the door!'

Mrs. Yeobright knocked again more loudly.

'Her knocking will, in all likelihood, awaken him,' continued Eustacia; 'and then he will let her in himself. Ah—listen.'

They could hear Clym moving in the other room, as if disturbed by the knocking, and he uttered the word 'Mother.'

'Yes—he is awake—he will go to the door,' she said, with a breath of relief. 'Come this way. I have a bad name with her, and you must not be seen. Thus I am obliged to act by stealth, not because I do ill, but because others are pleased to say so.'

By this time she had taken him to the back door, which was open, disclosing a path leading down the garden. 'Now, one word, Damon,' she remarked as he stepped forth. 'This is your first visit here; let it be your last. We have been hot lovers in our time, but it won't do now. Good-bye.'

'Good-bye,' said Wildeve. 'I have had all I came for, and I am satisfied.'

'What was it?'

'A sight of you. Upon my eternal honour I came for no more.'

Wildeve kissed his hand to the beautiful girl he addressed, and passed into the garden, where she watched him down the path, over the stile at the end, and into the ferns outside, which brushed his hips as he went along till he became lost in their thickets. When he had quite gone she slowly turned, and directed her attention to the interior of the house.

But it was possible that her presence might not be desired by Clym and his mother at this moment of their first meeting, or that it would be superfluous. At all events, she was in no hurry to meet Mrs. Yeobright. She resolved to wait till Clym came to look for her, and glided back into the garden. Here she idly occupied herself for a few minutes, till finding no notice was taken of her she retraced her steps through the house to the front, where she listened for voices in the parlour. But hearing none she opened the door and went in. To her astonishment Clym lay precisely as Wildeve and herself had left him, his sleep apparently unbroken. He had been disturbed and made to dream and murmur by the knocking, but he had not awakened. Eustacia hastened to the door, and in spite of her reluctance to open it to a woman who had spoken of her so bitterly, she unfastened it and looked out. Nobody was to be seen. There, by the scraper, lay Clym's hook and the handful of faggot-bonds he had brought home; in front of her were the empty path, the garden gate standing slightly ajar; and, beyond, the great valley of purple heath thrilling silently in the sun. Mrs. Yeobright was gone.

Clym's mother was at this time following a path which lay hidden from Eustacia by a shoulder of the hill. Her walk thither from the garden gate had been hasty and determined, as of a woman who was now no less anxious to escape from the scene than she had previously been to enter it. Her eyes were fixed on the ground; within her two sights were graven—that of Clym's hook and brambles at the door, and that of a woman's face at a window. Her lips trembled, becoming unnaturally thin as she murmured, ''Tis too much—Clym, how can he bear to do it! He is at home; and yet he lets her shut the door against me!'

In her anxiety to get out of the direct view of the house she had diverged from the straightest path homeward, and while looking about to regain it she came upon a little boy gathering whortleberries in a hollow. The boy was Johnny Nunsuch, who had been Eustacia's stoker at the bonfire, and, with the tendency of a minute body to gravitate towards a greater, he began hovering round Mrs. Yeobright as soon as she appeared, and trotted on beside her without perceptible consciousness of his act.

Mrs. Yeobright spoke to him as one in a mesmeric sleep. ''Tis a long way home, my child, and we shall not get there till evening.'

'I shall,' said her small companion. 'I am going to play marnels[1] afore supper, and we go to supper at six o'clock, because father comes home. Does your father come home at six too?'

'No: he never comes; nor my son either, nor anybody.'

1. A Dorset game played with nine white and nine black stones on a board or a lined piece of turf. Closer to checkers than to marbles. Also spelled marnull or marnhill.

'What have made you so down? Have you seen a ooser?'[2]

'I have seen what's worse—a woman's face looking at me through a window-pane.'

'Is that a bad sight?'

'Yes. It is always a bad sight to see a woman looking out at a weary wayfarer and not letting her in.'

'Once when I went to Throope Great Pond to catch effets[3] I seed myself looking up at myself, and I was frightened and jumped back like anything.'

. . . 'If they had only shown signs of meeting my advances half-way how well it might have been done! But there is no chance. Shut out! She must have set him against me. Can there be beautiful bodies without hearts inside? I think so. I would not have done it against a neighbour's cat on such a fiery day as this!'

'What is it you say?'

'Never again—never! Not even if they send for me!'

'You must be a very curious woman to talk like that.'

'O no, not at all,' she said, returning to the boy's prattle. 'Most people who grow up and have children talk as I do. When you grow up your mother will talk as I do too.'

'I hope she won't; because 'tis very bad to talk nonsense.'

'Yes, child; it is nonsense, I suppose. Are you not nearly spent with the heat?'

'Yes. But not so much as you be.'

'How do you know?'

'Your face is white and wet, and your head is hanging-down-like.'

'Ah, I am exhausted from inside.'

'Why do you, every time you take a step, go like this?' The child in speaking gave to his motion the jerk and limp of an invalid.

'Because I have a burden which is more than I can bear.'

The little boy remained silently pondering, and they tottered on side by side until more than a quarter of an hour had elapsed, when Mrs. Yeobright, whose weakness plainly increased, said to him, 'I must sit down here to rest.'

When she had seated herself he looked long in her face and said, 'How funny you draw your breath—like a lamb when you drive him till he's nearly done for. Do you always draw your breath like that?'

'Not always.' Her voice was now so low as to be scarcely above a whisper.

'You will go to sleep there, I suppose, won't you? You have shut your eyes already.'

2. A grotesque devil mask worn at Christmas revels in Dorset or, less likely, a headless ghost.

3. Dialect form of *eft*, a newt or small lizardlike animal.

'No. I shall not sleep much till—another day, and then I hope to have a long, long one—very long. Now can you tell me if Rimsmoor Pond is dry this summer?'

'Rimsmoor Pond is, but Oker's Pool isn't, because he is deep, and is never dry—'tis just over there.'

'Is the water clear?'

'Yes, middling—except where the heath-croppers walk into it.'

'Then, take this, and go as fast as you can, and dip me up the clearest you can find. I am very faint.'

She drew from the small willow reticule that she carried in her hand an old-fashioned china teacup without a handle; it was one of half a dozen of the same sort lying in the reticule, which she had preserved ever since her childhood, and had brought with her to-day as a small present for Clym and Eustacia.

The boy started on his errand, and soon came back with the water, such as it was. Mrs. Yeobright attempted to drink, but it was so warm as to give her nausea, and she threw it away. Afterwards she still remained sitting, with her eyes closed.

The boy waited, played near her, caught several of the little brown butterflies which abounded, and then said as he waited again, 'I like going on better than biding still. Will you soon start again?'

'I don't know.'

'I wish I might go on by myself,' he resumed, fearing, apparently, that he was to be pressed into some unpleasant service. 'Do you want me any more, please?'

Mrs. Yeobright made no reply.

'What shall I tell mother?' the boy continued.

'Tell her you have seen a broken-hearted woman cast off by her son.'

Before quite leaving her he threw upon her face a wistful glance, as if he had misgivings on the generosity of forsaking her thus. He gazed into her face in a vague, wondering manner, like that of one examining some strange old manuscript the key to whose characters is undiscoverable. He was not so young as to be absolutely without a sense that sympathy was demanded, he was not old enough to be free from the terror felt in childhood at beholding misery in adult quarters hitherto deemed impregnable; and whether she were in a position to cause trouble or to suffer from it, whether she and her affliction were something to pity or something to fear, it was beyond him to decide. He lowered his eyes and went on without another word. Before he had gone half a mile he had forgotten all about her, except that she was a woman who had sat down to rest.

Mrs. Yeobright's exertions, physical and emotional, had well-nigh prostrated her; but she continued to creep along in short stages with long breaks between. The sun had now got far to the west of south and stood directly in her face, like some merciless incendiary, brand in hand, waiting to consume her. With the departure of the boy all visible animation disappeared from the landscape, though the intermittent husky notes of the male grasshoppers from every tuft of furze were enough to show that amid the prostration of the larger animal species an unseen insect world was busy in all the fulness of life.

In two hours she reached a slope about three-fourths the whole distance from Alderworth to her own home, where a little patch of shepherd's-thyme intruded upon the path; and she sat down upon the perfumed mat it formed there. In front of her a colony of ants had established a thoroughfare across the way, where they toiled a never-ending and heavy-laden throng. To look down upon them was like observing a city street from the top of a tower. She remembered that this bustle of ants had been in progress for years at the same spot—doubtless those of the old times were the ancestors of these which walked there now. She leant back to obtain more thorough rest, and the soft eastern portion of the sky was as great a relief to her eyes as the thyme was to her head. While she looked a heron arose on that side of the sky and flew on with his face towards the sun. He had come dripping wet from some pool in the valleys, and as he flew the edges and lining of his wings, his thighs, and his breast were so caught by the bright sunbeams that he appeared as if formed of burnished silver. Up in the zenith where he was seemed a free and happy place, away from all contact with the earthly ball to which she was pinioned; and she wished that she could arise uncrushed from its surface and fly as he flew then.

But, being a mother, it was inevitable that she should soon cease to ruminate upon her own condition. Had the track of her next thought been marked by a streak in the air, like the path of a meteor, it would have shown a direction contrary to the heron's, and have descended to the eastward upon the roof of Clym's house.

The Tragic Meeting of Two Old Friends

VII

He in the meantime had aroused himself from sleep, sat up, and looked around. Eustacia was sitting in a chair hard by him, and though she held a book in her hand she had not looked into it for some time.

'Well, indeed!' said Clym, brushing his eyes with his hands. 'How soundly I have slept! I have had such a tremendous dream, too: one I shall never forget.'

'I thought you had been dreaming,' said she.

'Yes. It was about my mother. I dreamt that I took you to her house to make up differences, and when we got there we couldn't get in, though she kept on crying to us for help. However, dreams are dreams. What o'clock is it, Eustacia?'

'Half-past two.'

'So late, is it? I didn't mean to stay so long. By the time I have had something to eat it will be after three.'

'Ann is not come back from the village, and I thought I would let you sleep on till she returned.'

Clym went to the window and looked out. Presently he said, musingly, 'Week after week passes, and yet mother does not come. I thought I should have heard something from her long before this.'

Misgiving, regret, fear, resolution, ran their swift course of expression in Eustacia's dark eyes. She was face to face with a monstrous difficulty, and she resolved to get free of it by postponement.

'I must certainly go to Blooms-End soon,' he continued, 'and I think I had better go alone.' He picked up his leggings and gloves, threw them down again, and added, 'As dinner will be so late to-day I will not go back to the heath, but work in the garden till the evening, and then, when it will be cooler, I will walk to Blooms-End. I am quite sure that if I make a little advance mother will be willing to forget all. It will be rather late before I can get home, as I shall not be able to do the distance either way in less than an hour and a half. But you will not mind for one evening, dear? What are you thinking of to make you look so abstracted?'

'I cannot tell you,' she said heavily. 'I wish we didn't live here, Clym. The world seems all wrong in this place.'

'Well—if we make it so. I wonder if Thomasin has been to Blooms-End lately. I hope so. But probably not, as she is, I believe, expecting to be confined in a month or so. I wish I had thought of that before. Poor mother must indeed be very lonely.'

'I don't like you going to-night.'

'Why not to-night?'

'Something may be said which will terribly injure me.'

'My mother is not vindictive,' said Clym, his colour faintly rising.

'But I wish you would not go,' Eustacia repeated in a low tone. 'If you agree not to go to-night I promise to go by myself to her house to-morrow, and make it up with her, and wait till you fetch me.'

'Why do you want to do that at this particular time, when at every previous time that I have proposed it you have refused?'

'I cannot explain further than that I should like to see her alone before you go,' she answered, with an impatient move of her head, and looking at him with an anxiety more frequently seen upon those of a sanguine temperament than upon such as herself.

'Well, it is very odd that just when I had decided to go myself you should want to do what I proposed long ago. If I wait for you to go to-morrow another day will be lost; and I know I shall be unable to rest another night without having been. I want to get this settled, and will. You must visit her afterwards: it will be all the same.'

'I could even go with you now?'

'You could scarcely walk there and back without a longer rest than I shall take. No, not to-night, Eustacia.'

'Let it be as you say, then,' she replied in the quiet way of one who, though willing to ward off evil consequences by a mild effort, would let events fall out as they might sooner than wrestle hard to direct them.

Clym then went into the garden; and a thoughtful languor stole over Eustacia for the remainder of the afternoon, which her husband attributed to the heat of the weather.

In the evening he set out on the journey. Although the heat of summer was yet intense the days had considerably shortened, and before he had advanced a mile on his way all the heath purples, browns, and greens had merged in a uniform dress without airiness or gradation, and broken only by touches of white where the little heaps of clean quartz sand showed the entrance to a rabbit-burrow, or where the white flints of a footpath lay like a thread over the slopes. In almost every one of the isolated and stunted thorns which grew here and there a night-hawk revealed his presence by whirring like the clack of a mill as long as he could hold his breath, then stopping, flapping his wings, wheeling round the bush, alighting, and after a silent interval of listening beginning to whirr again. At each brushing of Clym's feet white miller-moths flew into the air just high enough to catch upon their dusty wings the mellowed light from the west, which now shone across the depressions and levels of the ground without falling thereon to light them up.

Yeobright walked on amid this quiet scene with a hope that all would soon be well. Three miles on he came to a spot where a soft perfume was wafted across his path, and he stood still for a moment to inhale the familiar scent. It was the place at which, four hours earlier, his mother had sat down exhausted on the knoll covered with shepherd's-thyme. While he stood a sound between a breathing and a moan suddenly reached his ears.

He looked to where the sound came from; but nothing appeared there save the verge of the hillock stretching against the sky in an unbroken line. He moved a few steps in that direction, and now he perceived a recumbent figure almost close at his feet.

Among the different possibilities as to the person's individuality there did not for a moment occur to Yeobright that it might be one of his own family. Sometimes furze-cutters had been known to sleep out of doors at these times, to save a long journey homeward and back again; but Clym remembered the moan and looked closer, and saw that the form was feminine; and a distress came over him like cold air from a cave. But he was not absolutely certain that the woman was his mother till he stooped and beheld her face, pallid, and with closed eyes.

His breath went, as it were, out of his body and the cry of anguish which would have escaped him died upon his lips. During the momentary interval that elapsed before he became conscious that something must be done all sense of time and place left him, and it seemed as if he and his mother were as when he was a child with her many years ago on this heath at hours similar to the present. Then he awoke to activity; and bending yet lower he found that she still breathed, and that her breath though feeble was regular, except when disturbed by an occasional gasp.

'O, what is it! Mother, are you very ill—you are not dying?' he cried, pressing his lips to her face. 'I am your Clym. How did you come here? What does it all mean?'

At that moment the chasm in their lives which his love for Eustacia had caused was not remembered by Yeobright, and to him the present joined continuously with that friendly past that had been their experience before the division.

She moved her lips, appeared to know him, but could not speak; and then Clym strove to consider how best to move her, as it would be necessary to get her away from the spot before the dews were intense. He was able-bodied, and his mother was thin. He clasped his arms round her, lifted her a little, and said, 'Does that hurt you?'

She shook her head, and he lifted her up; then, at a slow pace, went onward with his load. The air was now completely cool; but whenever he passed over a sandy patch of ground uncarpeted with vegetation there was reflected from its surface into his face the heat which it had imbibed during the day. At the beginning of his undertaking he had thought but little of the distance which yet would have to be traversed before Blooms-End could be reached; but though he had slept that afternoon he soon began to feel the weight of his burden. Thus he proceeded, like Æneas with his father;[4] the bats circling round his head, nightjars flapping their wings within a yard of his face, and not a human being within call.

While he was yet nearly a mile from the house his mother exhib-

4. Aeneas carried his father, Anchises, on his shoulders to safety after the fall of Troy.

ited signs of restlessness under the constraint of being borne along, as if his arms were irksome to her. He lowered her upon his knees and looked around. The point they had now reached, though far from any road, was not more than a mile from the Blooms-End cottages occupied by Fairway, Sam, Humphrey, and the Cantles. Moreover, fifty yards off stood a hut, built of clods and covered with thin turves, but now entirely disused. The simple outline of the lonely shed was visible, and thither he determined to direct his steps. As soon as he arrived he laid her down carefully by the entrance, and then ran and cut with his pocket-knife an armful of the dryest fern. Spreading this within the shed, which was entirely open on one side, he placed his mother thereon: then he ran with all his might towards the dwelling of Fairway.

Nearly a quarter of an hour had passed, disturbed only by the broken breathing of the sufferer, when moving figures began to animate the line between heath and sky. In a few moments Clym arrived with Fairway, Humphrey, and Susan Nunsuch; Olly Dowden, who had chanced to be at Fairway's, Christian and Grandfer Cantle following helter-skelter behind. They had brought a lantern and matches, water, a pillow, and a few other articles which had occurred to their minds in the hurry of the moment. Sam had been despatched back again for brandy, and a boy brought Fairway's pony, upon which he rode off to the nearest medical man, with directions to call at Wildeve's on his way, and inform Thomasin that her aunt was unwell.

Sam and the brandy soon arrived, and it was administered by the light of the lantern; after which she became sufficiently conscious to signify by signs that something was wrong with her foot. Olly Dowden at length understood her meaning, and examined the foot indicated. It was swollen and red. Even as they watched the red began to assume a more livid colour, in the midst of which appeared a scarlet speck, smaller than a pea, and it was found to consist of a drop of blood, which rose above the smooth flesh of her ankle in a hemisphere.

'I know what it is,' cried Sam. 'She has been stung by an adder!'

'Yes,' said Clym instantly. 'I remember when I was a child seeing just such a bite. O, my poor mother!'

'It was my father who was bit,' said Sam. 'And there's only one way to cure it. You must rub the place with the fat of other adders, and the only way to get that is by frying them. That's what they did for him.'

''Tis an old remedy,' said Clym distrustfully, 'and I have doubts about it. But we can do nothing else till the doctor comes.'

' 'Tis a sure cure,' said Olly Dowden, with emphasis. 'I've used it when I used to go out nursing.'

'Then we must pray for daylight, to catch them,' said Clym gloomily.

'I will see what I can do,' said Sam.

He took a green hazel which he had used as a walking-stick, split it at the end, inserted a small pebble, and with the lantern in his hand went out into the heath. Clym had by this time lit a small fire, and despatched Susan Nunsuch for a frying-pan. Before she had returned Sam came in with three adders, one briskly coiling and uncoiling in the cleft of the stick, and the other two hanging dead across it.

'I have only been able to get one alive and fresh as he ought to be,' said Sam. 'These limp ones are two I killed to-day at work; but as they don't die till the sun goes down they can't be very stale meat.'

The live adder regarded the assembled group with a sinister look in its small black eye, and the beautiful brown and jet pattern on its back seemed to intensify with indignation. Mrs. Yeobright saw the creature, and the creature saw her: she quivered throughout, and averted her eyes.

'Look at that,' murmured Christian Cantle. 'Neighbours, how do we know but that something of the old serpent in God's garden, that gied the apple to the young woman with no clothes, lives on in adders and snakes still? Look at his eye—for all the world like a villainous sort of black currant. 'Tis to be hoped he can't ill-wish us! There's folks in heath who've been overlooked already. I will never kill another adder as long as I live.'

'Well, 'tis right to be afeard of things, if folks can't help it,' said Grandfer Cantle. ''Twould have saved me many a brave danger in my time.'

'I fancy I heard something outside the shed,' said Christian. 'I wish troubles would come in the daytime, for then a man could show his courage, and hardly beg for mercy of the most broomstick old woman he should see, if he was a brave man, and able to run out of her sight!'

'Even such an ignorant fellow as I should know better than do that,' said Sam.

'Well, there's calamities where we least expect it, whether or no. Neighbours, if Mrs. Yeobright were to die, d'ye think we should be took up and tried for the manslaughter of a woman?'

'No, they couldn't bring it in as that,' said Sam, 'unless they could prove we had been poachers at some time of our lives. But she'll fetch round.'

'Now, if I had been stung by ten adders I should hardly have lost a day's work for't,' said Grandfer Cantle. 'Such is my spirit when I am on my mettle. But perhaps 'tis natural in a man trained for war. Yes, I've gone through a good deal; but nothing ever came amiss to me after I joined the Locals in four.' He shook his head and smiled at a mental picture of himself in uniform. 'I was always first in the most galliantest scrapes in my younger days!'

'I suppose that was because they always used to put the biggest fool afore,' said Fairway from the fire, beside which he knelt, blowing it with his breath.

'D'ye think so, Timothy?' said Grandfer Cantle, coming forward to Fairway's side with sudden depression in his face. 'Then a man may feel for years that he is good solid company, and be wrong about himself after all?'

'Never mind that question, Grandfer. Stir your stumps and get some more sticks. 'Tis very nonsense of an old man to prattle so when life and death's in mangling.'

'Yes, yes,' said Grandfer Cantle, with melancholy conviction. 'Well, this is a bad night altogether for them that have done well in their time; and if I were ever such a dab at the hautboy or tenor-viol, I shouldn't have the heart to play tunes upon 'em now.'

Susan now arrived with the frying-pan, when the live adder was killed and the heads of the three taken off. The remainders, being cut into lengths and split open, were tossed into the pan, which began hissing and crackling over the fire. Soon a rill of clear oil trickled from the carcases, whereupon Clym dipped the corner of his handkerchief into the liquid and anointed the wound.

Eustacia Hears of Good Fortune and Beholds Evil

VIII

In the meantime Eustacia, left alone in her cottage at Alderworth, had become considerably depressed by the posture of affairs. The consequences which might result from Clym's discovery that his mother had been turned from his door that day were likely to be disagreeable, and this was a quality in events which she hated as much as the dreadful.

To be left to pass the evening by herself was irksome to her at any time, and this evening it was more irksome than usual by reason of the excitements of the past hours. The two visits had stirred her into restlessness. She was not wrought to any great pitch of uneasiness by the probability of appearing in an ill light in the discussion between Clym and his mother, but she was wrought to vexation; and her slumbering activities were quickened to the extent of wishing that she had opened the door. She had certainly believed that Clym was awake, and the excuse would be an honest one as far as it went; but nothing could save her from censure in refusing to answer at the first knock. Yet, instead of blaming herself for the issue she laid the fault upon the shoulders of some indistinct, colossal Prince of the World, who had framed her situation and ruled her lot.

At this time of the year it was pleasanter to walk by night than by day, and when Clym had been absent about an hour she suddenly resolved to go out in the direction of Blooms-End, on the chance of meeting him on his return. When she reached the garden gate she heard wheels approaching, and looking round beheld her grandfather coming up in his car.

'I can't stay a minute, thank ye,' he answered to her greeting. 'I am driving to East Egdon; but I came round here just to tell you the news. Perhaps you have heard—about Mr. Wildeve's fortune?'

'No,' said Eustacia blankly.

'Well, he has come into a fortune of eleven thousand pounds—uncle died in Canada, just after hearing that all his family, whom he was sending home, had gone to the bottom in the *Cassiopeia*; so Wildeve has come into everything, without in the least expecting it.'

Eustacia stood motionless awhile. 'How long has he known of this?' she asked.

'Well, it was known to him this morning early, for I knew it at ten o'clock, when Charley came back. Now, he is what I call a lucky man. What a fool you were, Eustacia!'

'In what way?' she said, lifting here eyes in apparent calmness.

'Why, in not sticking to him when you had him.'

'Had him, indeed!'

'I did not know there had ever been anything between you till lately; and, faith, I should have been hot and strong against it if I had known; but since it seems that there was some sniffing between ye, why the deuce didn't you stick to him?'

Eustacia made no reply, but she looked as if she could say as much upon that subject as he if she chose.

'And how is your poor purblind husband?' continued the old man. 'Not a bad fellow either, as far as he goes.'

'He is quite well.'

'It is a good thing for his cousin what-d'ye-call-her? By George, you ought to have been in that galley, my girl! Now I must drive on. Do you want any assistance? What's mine is yours, you know.'

'Thank you, grandfather, we are not in want at present,' she said coldly. 'Clym cuts furze, but he does it mostly as a useful pastime, because he can do nothing else.'

'He is paid for his pastime, isn't he? Three shillings a hundred, I heard.'

'Clym has money,' she said, colouring; 'but he likes to earn a little.'

'Very well; good night.' And the captain drove on.

When her grandfather was gone Eustacia went on her way mechanically; but her thoughts were no longer concerning her mother-in-law and Clym. Wildeve, notwithstanding his complaints against his fate, had been seized upon by destiny and placed in the sunshine once more. Eleven thousand pounds! From every Egdon point of view he was a rich man. In Eustacia's eyes, too, it was an ample sum—one sufficient to supply those wants of hers which had been stigmatized by Clym in his more austere moods as vain and luxurious. Though she was no lover of money she loved what money could bring; and the new accessories she imagined around him clothed Wildeve with a great deal of interest. She recollected now how quietly well-dressed he had been that morning: he had probably put on his newest suit, regardless of damage by briars and thorns. And then she thought of his manner towards herself.

'O I see it, I see it,' she said. 'How much he wishes he had me now, that he might give me all I desire!'

In recalling the details of his glances and words—at the time scarcely regarded—it became plain to her how greatly they had been dictated by his knowledge of this new event. 'Had he been a man to bear a jilt ill-will he would have told me of his good fortune in crowing tones; instead of doing that he mentioned not a word, in deference to my misfortunes, and merely implied that he loved me still, as one superior to him.'

Wildeve's silence that day on what had happened to him was just the kind of behaviour calculated to make an impression on such a woman. Those delicate touches of good taste were, in fact, one of the strong points in his demeanour towards the other sex. The peculiarity of Wildeve was that, while at one time passionate, upbraiding, and resentful towards a woman, at another he would treat her with such unparalleled grace as to make previous neglect appear as no discourtesy, injury as no insult, interference as a delicate attention, and the ruin of her honour as excess of chivalry. This man, whose admiration to-day Eustacia had disregarded, whose good wishes she had scarcely taken the trouble to accept, whom she had shown out of the house by the back door, was the possessor of eleven thousand pounds—a man of fair professional education, and one who had served his articles with a civil engineer.

So intent was Eustacia upon Wildeve's fortunes that she forgot how much closer to her own course were those of Clym; and instead of walking on to meet him at once she sat down upon a stone. She was disturbed in her reverie by a voice behind, and turning her head beheld the old lover and fortunate inheritor of wealth immediately beside her.

She remained sitting, though the fluctuation in her look might have told any man who knew her so well as Wildeve that she was thinking of him.

'How did you come here?' she said in her clear low tone. 'I thought you were at home.'

'I went on to the village after leaving your garden; and now I have come back again: that's all. Which way are you walking, may I ask?'

She waved her hand in the direction of Blooms-End. 'I am going to meet my husband. I think I may possibly have got into trouble whilst you were with me to-day.'

'How could that be?'

'By not letting in Mrs. Yeobright.'

'I hope that visit of mine did you no harm.'

'None. It was not your fault,' she said quietly.

By this time she had risen; and they involuntarily sauntered on together, without speaking, for two or three minutes; when Eustacia broke silence by saying, 'I assume I must congratulate you.'

'On what? O yes; on my eleven thousand pounds, you mean. Well, since I didn't get something else, I must be content with getting that.'

'You seem very indifferent about it. Why didn't you tell me to-day when you came?' she said in the tone of a neglected person. 'I heard of it quite by accident.'

'I did mean to tell you,' said Wildeve. 'But I—well, I will speak frankly—I did not like to mention it when I saw, Eustacia, that your star was not high. The sight of a man lying wearied out with hard work, as your husband lay, made me feel that to brag of my own fortune to you would be greatly out of place. Yet, as you stood there beside him, I could not help feeling too that in many respects he was a richer man than I.'

At this Eustacia said, with slumbering mischievousness, 'What, would you exchange with him—your fortune for me?'

'I certainly would,' said Wildeve.

'As we are imagining what is impossible and absurd, suppose we change the subject?'

'Very well; and I will tell you of my plans for the future, if you care to hear them. I shall permanently invest nine thousand pounds, keep one thousand as ready money, and with the remaining thousand travel for a year or so.'

'Travel? What a bright idea! Where will you go to?'

'From here to Paris, where I shall pass the winter and spring. Then I shall go to Italy, Greece, Egypt, and Palestine, before the hot weather comes on. In the summer I shall go to America; and then, by a plan not yet settled, I shall go to Australia and round to India. By that time I shall have begun to have had enough of it. Then I shall probably come back to Paris again, and there I shall stay as long as I can afford to.'

'Back to Paris again,' she murmured in a voice that was nearly a sigh. She had never once told Wildeve of the Parisian desires which Clym's description had sown in her; yet here was he involuntarily in a position to gratify them. 'You think a good deal of Paris?' she added.

'Yes. In my opinion it is the central beauty-spot of the world.'

'And in mine! And Thomasin will go with you?'

'Yes, if she cares to. She may prefer to stay at home.'

'So you will be going about, and I shall be staying here!'

'I suppose you will. But we know whose fault that is.'

'I am not blaming you,' she said quickly.

'Oh, I thought you were. If ever you *should* be inclined to blame me, think of a certain evening by Rainbarrow, when you promised to meet me and did not. You sent me a letter; and my heart ached to read that as I hope yours never will. That was one point of divergence. I then did something in haste. . . . But she is a good woman, and I will say no more.'

'I know that the blame was on my side that time,' said Eustacia. 'But it had not always been so. However, it is my misfortune to be too sudden in feeling. O Damon, don't reproach me any more—I can't bear that.'

They went on silently for a distance of two or three miles, when Eustacia said suddenly, 'Haven't you come out of your way, Mr. Wildeve?'

'My way is anywhere to-night. I will go with you as far as the hill on which we can see Blooms-End, as it is getting late for you to be alone.'

'Don't trouble. I am not obliged to be out at all. I think I would rather you did not accompany me further. This sort of thing would have an odd look if known.'

'Very well, I will leave you.' He took her hand unexpectedly, and kissed it—for the first time since her marriage. 'What light is that on the hill?' he added, as it were to hide the caress.

She looked, and saw a flickering firelight proceeding from the open side of a hovel a little way before them. The hovel, which she had hitherto always found empty, seemed to be inhabited now.

'Since you have come so far,' said Eustacia, 'will you see me safely past that hut? I thought I should have met Clym somewhere about here, but as he doesn't appear I will hasten on and get to Blooms-End before he leaves.'

They advanced to the turf-shed, and when they got near it the firelight and the lantern inside showed distinctly enough the form of a woman reclining on a bed of fern, a group of heath men and women standing around her. Eustacia did not recognize Mrs. Yeobright in the reclining figure, nor Clym as one of the standers-by till she came close. Then she quickly pressed her hand upon Wildeve's arm and signified to him to come back from the open side of the shed into the shadow.

'It is my husband and his mother,' she whispered in an agitated voice. 'What can it mean? Will you step forward and tell me?'

Wildeve left her side and went to the back wall of the hut. Presently Eustacia perceived that he was beckoning to her, and she advanced and joined him.

'It is a serious case,' said Wildeve.

From their position they could hear what was proceeding inside.

'I cannot think where she could have been going,' said Clym to some one. 'She had evidently walked a long way, but even when she was able to speak just now she would not tell me where. What do you really think of her?'

'There is a great deal to fear,' was gravely answered, in a voice which Eustacia recognized as that of the only surgeon in the district. 'She has suffered somewhat from the bite of the adder; but it is exhaustion which has overpowered her. My impression is that her walk must have been exceptionally long.'

'I used to tell her not to overwalk herself this weather,' said Clym, with distress. 'Do you think we did well in using the adder's fat?'

'Well, it is a very ancient remedy—the old remedy of the viper-catchers, I believe,' replied the doctor. 'It is mentioned as an infallible ointment by Hoffman, Mead, and I think the Abbé Fontana. Unboubtedly it was as good a thing as you could do; though I question if some other oils would not have been equally efficacious.'

'Come here, come here!' was then rapidly said in anxious female tones; and Clym and the doctor could be heard rushing forward from the back part of the shed to where Mrs. Yeobright lay.

'O, what is it?' whispered Eustacia.

''Twas Thomasin who spoke,' said Wildeve. 'Then they have fetched her. I wonder if I had better go in—yet it might do harm.'

For a long time there was utter silence among the group within; and it was broken at last by Clym saying, in an agonized voice, 'O doctor, what does it mean?'

The doctor did not reply at once; ultimately he said, 'She is sinking fast. Her heart was previously affected, and physical exhaustion has dealt the finishing blow.'

Then there was a weeping of women, then waiting, then hushed exclamations, then a strange gasping sound, then a painful stillness.

'It is all over,' said the doctor.

Further back in the hut the cotters whispered, 'Mrs. Yeobright is dead.'

Almost at the same moment the two watchers observed the form of a small old-fashioned child entering at the open side of the shed. Susan Nunsuch, whose boy it was, went forward to the opening and silently beckoned to him to go back.

'I've got something to tell 'ee, mother,' he cried in a shrill tone. 'That woman asleep there walked along with me to-day; and she said I was to say that I had seed her, and she was a broken-hearted woman and cast off by her son, and then I came on home.'

A confused sob as from a man was heard within, upon which Eustacia gasped faintly, 'That's Clym—I must go to him—yet dare I do it? No: come away!'

When they had withdrawn from the neighbourhood of the shed she said huskily, 'I am to blame for this. There is evil in store for me.'

'Was she not admitted to your house after all?' Wildeve inquired.

'No; and that's where it all lies! O, what shall I do! I shall not intrude upon them: I shall go straight home. Damon, good-bye! I cannot speak to you any more now.'

They parted company; and when Eustacia had reached the next hill she looked back. A melancholy procession was wending its way by the light of the lantern from the hut towards Blooms-End. Wildeve was nowhere to be seen.

BOOK FIFTH: THE DISCOVERY

'Wherefore Is Light Given to Him That Is in Misery'

I

One evening, about three weeks after the funeral of Mrs. Yeobright, when the silver face of the moon sent a bundle of beams directly upon the floor of Clym's house at Alderworth, a woman came forth from within. She reclined over the garden gate as if to refresh herself awhile. The pale lunar touches which make beauties of hags lent divinity to this face, already beautiful.

She had not long been there when a man came up the road and with some hesitation said to her, 'How is he to-night, ma'am, if you please?'

'He is better, though still very unwell, Humphrey,' replied Eustacia.

'Is he light-headed, ma'am?'

'No. He is quite sensible now.'

'Do he rave about his mother just the same, poor fellow?' continued Humphrey.

'Just as much, though not quite so wildly,' she said in a low voice.

'It was very unfortunate, ma'am, that the boy Johnny should ever ha' told him his mother's dying words, about her being broken-hearted and cast off by her son. 'Twas enough to upset any man alive.'

Eustacia made no reply beyond that of a slight catch in her breath, as of one who fain would speak but could not; and Humphrey, declining her invitation to come in, went away.

Eustacia turned, entered the house, and ascended to the front bedroom, where a shaded light was burning. In the bed lay Clym, pale, haggard, wide awake, tossing to one side and to the other, his eyes lit by a hot light, as if the fire in their pupils were burning up their substance.

'Is it you, Eustacia?' he said as she sat down.

'Yes, Clym. I have been down to the gate. The moon is shining beautifully, and there is not a leaf stirring.'

'Shining, is it? What's the moon to a man like me? Let it shine—let anything be, so that I never see another day! . . . Eustacia, I don't know where to look: my thoughts go through me like swords. O, if any man wants to make himself immortal by painting a picture of wretchedness, let him come here!'

'Why do you say so?'

'I cannot help feeling that I did my best to kill her.'

'No, Clym.'

'Yes, it was so; it is useless to excuse me! My conduct to her was too hideous—I made no advances; and she could not bring herself to forgive me. Now she is dead! If I had only shown myself willing to make it up with her sooner, and we had been friends, and then she had died, it wouldn't be so hard to bear. But I never went near her house, so she never came near mine, and didn't know how welcome she would have been—that's what troubles me. She did not know I was going to her house that very night, for she was too insensible to understand me. If she had only come to see me! I longed that she would. But it was not to be.'

There escaped from Eustacia one of those shivering sighs which used to shake her like a pestilent blast. She had not yet told.

But Yeobright was too deeply absorbed in the ramblings incidental to his remorseful state to notice her. During his illness he had been continually talking thus. Despair had been added to his original grief by the unfortunate disclosure of the boy who had received the last words of Mrs. Yeobright—words too bitterly uttered in an hour of misapprehension. Then his distress had overwhelmed him, and he longed for death as a field labourer longs for the shade. It was the pitiful sight of a man standing in the very focus of sorrow. He continually bewailed his tardy journey to his mother's house, because it was an error which could never be rectified, and insisted that he must have been horribly perverted by some fiend not to have thought before that it was his duty to go to her, since she did not come to him. He would ask Eustacia to agree with him in his self-condemnation; and when she, seared inwardly by a secret she dared not tell, declared that she could not give an opinion, he would say, 'That's because you didn't know my mother's nature. She was always ready to forgive if asked to do so; but I seemed to her to be as an obstinate child, and that made her unyielding. Yet not unyielding: she was proud and reserved, no more. . . . Yes, I can understand why she held out against me so long. She was waiting for me. I dare say she said a hundred times in her sorrow, "What a return he makes for all the sacrifices I have made for him!" I never went to her! When I set out to visit her it was too late. To think of that is nearly intolerable!'

Sometimes his condition had been one of utter remorse, unsoftened by a single tear of pure sorrow: and then he writhed as he lay, fevered far more by thought than by physical ills. 'If I could only get one assurance that she did not die in a belief that I was resentful,' he said one day when in this mood, 'it would be better to think of than a hope of heaven. But that I cannot do.'

'You give yourself up too much to this wearying despair,' said Eustacia. 'Other men's mothers have died.'

'That doesn't make the loss of mine less. Yet it is less the loss than the circumstances of the loss. I sinned against her, and on that account there is no light for me.'

'She sinned against you, I think.'

'No: she did not. I committed the guilt; and may the whole burden be upon my head!'

'I think you might consider twice before you say that,' Eustacia replied. 'Single men have, no doubt, a right to curse themselves as much as they please; but men with wives involve two in the doom they pray down.'

'I am in too sorry a state to understand what you are refining on,' said the wretched man. 'Day and night shout at me, "You have helped to kill her." But in loathing myself I may, I own, be unjust to you, my poor wife. Forgive me for it, Eustacia, for I scarcely know what I do.'

Eustacia was always anxious to avoid the sight of her husband in such a state as this, which had become as dreadful to her as the trial scene was to Judas Iscariot. It brought before her eyes the spectre of a worn-out woman knocking at a door which she would not open; and she shrank from contemplating it. Yet it was better for Yeobright himself when he spoke openly of his sharp regret, for in silence he endured infinitely more, and would sometimes remain so long in a tense, brooding mood, consuming himself by the gnawing of his thought, that it was imperatively necessary to make him talk aloud, that his grief might in some degree expend itself in the effort.

Eustacia had not been long indoors after her look at the moonlight when a soft footstep came up to the house, and Thomasin was announced by the woman downstairs.

'Ah, Thomasin! Thank you for coming to-night,' said Clym when she entered the room. 'Here am I, you see. Such a wretched spectacle am I, that I shrink from being seen by a single friend, and almost from you.'

'You must not shrink from me, dear Clym,' said Thomasin earnestly, in that sweet voice of hers which came to a sufferer like fresh air into a Black Hole. 'Nothing in you can ever shock me or drive me away. I have been here before, but you don't remember it.'

'Yes, I do; I am not delirious, Thomasin, nor have I been so at all. Don't you believe that if they say so. I am only in great misery at what I have done: and that, with the weakness, makes me seem mad. But it has not upset my reason. Do you think I should remember all about my mother's death if I were out of my mind? No such good luck. Two months and a half, Thomasin, the last of her life, did my poor mother live alone, distracted and mourning because of me; yet she was unvisited by me, though I was living only six miles off. Two months and a half—seventy-five days did the sun rise and set upon her in that deserted state which a dog didn't deserve! Poor people who had nothing in common with her would have cared for her, and visited her had they known her sickness and loneliness; but I, who should have been all to her, stayed away like a cur. If there is any justice in God let Him kill me now. He has nearly blinded me, but that is not enough. If He would only strike me with more pain I would believe in Him for ever!'

'Hush, hush! O, pray, Clym, don't, don't say it!' implored Thomasin, affrighted into sobs and tears; while Eustacia, at the other side of the room, though her pale face remained calm, writhed in her chair. Clym went on without heeding his cousin.

'But I am not worth receiving further proof even of Heaven's reprobation. Do you think, Thomasin, that she knew me—that she did not die in that horrid mistaken notion about my not forgiving her, which I can't tell you how she acquired? If you could only assure me of that! Do you think so, Eustacia? Do speak to me.'

'I think I can assure you that she knew better at last,' said Thomasin. The pallid Eustacia said nothing.

'Why didn't she come to my house? I would have taken her in and showed her how I loved her in spite of all. But she never came;

and I didn't go to her, and she died on the heath like an animal kicked out, nobody to help her till it was too late. If you could have seen her, Thomasin, as I saw her—a poor dying woman, lying in the dark upon the bare ground, moaning, nobody near, believing she was utterly deserted by all the world, it would have moved you to anguish, it would have moved a brute. And this poor woman my mother! No wonder she said to the child, "You have seen a broken-hearted woman." What a state she must have been brought to, to say that! and who can have done it but I? It is too dreadful to think of, and I wish I could be punished more heavily than I am. How long was I what they called out of my senses?'

'A week, I think.'

'And then I became calm.'

'Yes, for four days.'

'And now I have left off being calm.'

'But try to be quiet: please do, and you will soon be strong. If you could remove that impression from your mind——'

'Yes, yes,' he said impatiently. 'But I don't want to get strong. What's the use of my getting well? It would be better for me if I die, and it would certainly be better for Eustacia. Is Eustacia there?'

'Yes.'

'It would be better for you, Eustacia, if I were to die?'

'Don't press such a question, dear Clym.'

'Well, it really is but a shadowy supposition; for unfortunately I am going to live. I feel myself getting better. Thomasin, how long are you going to stay at the inn, now that all this money has come to your husband?'

'Another month or two, probably; until my illness is over. We cannot get off till then. I think it will be a month or more.'

'Yes, yes. Of course. Ah, Cousin Tamsie, you will get over your trouble—one little month will take you through it, and bring something to console you; but I shall never get over mine, and no consolation will come!'

'Clym, you are unjust to yourself. Depend upon it, aunt thought kindly of you. I know that, if she had lived, you would have been reconciled with her.'

'But she didn't come to see me, though I asked her, before I married, if she would come. Had she come, or had I gone there, she would never have died saying, "I am a broken-hearted woman, cast off by my son." My door has always been open to her—a welcome here has always awaited her. But that she never came to see.'

'You had better not talk any more now, Clym,' said Eustacia faintly from the other part of the room, for the scene was growing intolerable to her.

'Let me talk to you instead for the little time I shall be here,' Thomasin said soothingly. 'Consider what a one-sided way you have of looking at the matter, Clym, When she said that to the little boy you had not found her and taken her into your arms: and it might have been uttered in a moment of bitterness. It was rather like aunt to say things in haste. She sometimes used to speak so to me. Though she did not come I am convinced that she thought of coming to see you. Do you suppose a man's mother could live two or three months without one forgiving thought? She forgave me; and why should she not have forgiven you?'

'You laboured to win her round; I did nothing. I, who was going to teach people the higher secrets of happiness, did not know how to keep out of that gross misery which the most untaught are wise enough to avoid.'

'How did you get here to-night, Thomasin? said Eustacia.

'Damon set me down at the end of the lane. He has driven into East Egdon on business, and he will come and pick me up by-and-by.'

Accordingly they soon after heard the noise of wheels. Wildeve had come, and was waiting outside with his horse and gig.

'Send out and tell him I will be down in two minutes,' said Thomasin.

'I will run down myself,' said Eustacia.

She went down. Wildeve had alighted, and was standing before the horse's head when Eustacia opened the door. He did not turn for a moment, thinking the comer Thomasin. Then he looked, started ever so little, and said one word :'Well?'

'I have not yet told him,' she replied in a whisper.

'Then don't do so till he is well—it will be fatal. You are ill yourself.'

'I am wretched . . . O Damon,' she said, bursting into tears, 'I—I can't tell you how unhappy I am! I can hardly bear this. I can tell nobody my trouble—nobody knows of it but you.'

'Poor girl!' said Wildeve, visibly affected at her distress, and at last led on so far as to take her hand. 'It is hard, when you have done nothing to deserve it, that you should have got involved in such a web as this. You were not made for these sad scenes. I am to blame most. If I could only have saved you from it all!'

'But, Damon, please pray tell me what I must do? To sit by him hour after hour, and hear him reproach himself as being the cause of her death, and to know that I am the sinner, if any human being is at all, drives me into cold despair. I don't know what to do. Should I tell him or should I not tell him? I always am asking myself that. O, I want to tell him; and yet I am afraid. If he finds it out he must surely kill me, for nothing else will be in proportion to his feelings now. "Beware the fury of a patient man" sounds day by day in my ears as I watch him.'

'Well, wait till he is better, and trust to chance. And when you tell, you must only tell part—for his own sake.'

'Which part should I keep back?'

Wildeve paused. 'That I was in the house at the time,' he said in a low tone.

'Yes; it must be concealed, seeing what has been whispered. How much easier are hasty actions than speeches that will excuse them!'

'If he were only to die——' Wildeve murmured.

'Do not think of it! I would not buy hope of immunity by so cowardly a desire even if I hated him. Now I am going up to him again. Thomasin bade me tell you she would be down in a few minutes. Good-bye.'

She returned, and Thomasin soon appeared. When she was seated in the gig with her husband, and the horse was turning to go off, Wildeve lifted his eyes to the bedroom windows. Looking from one of them he could discern a pale, tragic face watching him drive away. It was Eustacia's.

A Lurid Light Breaks In upon a Darkened Understanding

II

Clym's grief became mitigated by wearing itself out. His strength returned, and a month after the visit of Thomasin he might have been seen walking about the garden. Endurance and despair, equanimity and gloom, the tints of health and the pallor of death, mingled weirdly in his face. He was now unnaturally silent upon all of the past that related to his mother; and though Eustacia knew that he was thinking of it none the less, she was only too glad to escape the topic ever to bring it up anew. When his mind had been weaker his heart had led him to speak out; but reason having now somewhat recovered itself he sank into taciturnity.

One evening when he was thus standing in the garden, abstractedly spudding up a weed with his stick, a bony figure turned the corner of the house and came up to him.

'Christian, isn't it?' said Clym. 'I am glad you have found me out. I shall soon want you to go to Blooms-End and assist me in putting the house in order. I suppose it is all locked up as I left it?'

'Yes, Mister Clym.'

'Have you dug up the potatoes and other roots?"

'Yes, without a drop o' rain, thank God. But I was coming to tell 'ee of something else which is quite different from what we have lately had in the family. I am sent by the rich gentleman at the Woman, that we used to call the landlord, to tell 'ee that Mrs. Wildeve is doing well of a girl, which was born punctually at one o'clock at noon, or a few minutes more or less; and 'tis said that expecting of this increase is what have kept 'em there since they came into their money.'

'And she is getting on well, you say?'

'Yes, sir. Only Mr. Wildeve is twanky[1] because 'tisn't a boy—that's what they say in the kitchen, but I was not supposed to notice that.'

'Christian, now listen to me.'

'Yes, sure, Mr. Yeobright.'

'Did you see my mother the day before she died?'

'No, I did not.'

Yeobright's face expressed disappointment.

'But I zeed her the morning of the same day she died.'

Clym's look lighted up. 'That's nearer still to my meaning,' he said.

'Yes, I know 'twas the same day; for she said, "I be going to see him, Christian; so I shall not want any vegetables brought in for dinner." '

'See whom?'

'See you. She was going to your house, you understand.'

Yeobright regarded Christian with intense surprise. 'Why did you never mention this?' he said. 'Are you sure it was my house she was coming to?'

'O yes. I didn't mention it because I've never zeed you lately. And as she didn't get there it was all nought, and nothing to tell.'

'And I have been wondering why she should have walked in the heath on that hot day! Well, did she say what she was coming for? It is a thing, Christian, I am very anxious to know.'

'Yes, Mister Clym. She didn't say it to me, though I think she did to one here and there.'

'Do you know one person to whom she spoke of it?'

'There is one man, please, sir, but I hope you won't mention my name to him, as I have seen him in strange places, particular in dreams. One night last summer he glared at me like Famine and Sword, and it made me feel so low that I didn't comb out my few hairs for two days. He was standing, as it might be, Mister Yeobright, in the middle of the path to Mistover, and your mother came up, looking as pale——'

'Yes, when was that?'

'Last summer, in my dream.'

'Pooh! Who's the man?'

1. Peevish, complaining—though with some cause.

'Diggory, the reddleman. He called upon her and sat with her the evening before she set out to see you. I hadn't gone home from work when he came up to the gate.'

'I must see Venn—I wish I had known it before,' said Clym anxiously. 'I wonder why he has not come to tell me?'

'He went out of Egdon Heath the next day, so would not be likely to know you wanted him.'

'Christian,' said Clym, 'you must go and find Venn. I am otherwise engaged, or I would go myself. Find him at once, and tell him I want to speak to him.'

'I am a good hand at hunting up folk by day,' said Christian, looking dubiously round at the declining light; 'but as to night-time, never is such a bad hand as I, Mister Yeobright.'

'Search the heath when you will, so that you bring him soon. Bring him to-morrow, if you can.'

Christian then departed. The morrow came, but no Venn. In the evening Christian arrived, looking very weary. He had been searching all day, and had heard nothing of the reddleman.

'Inquire as much as you can to-morrow without neglecting your work,' said Yeobright. 'Don't come again till you have found him.'

The next day Yeobright set out for the old house at Blooms-End, which, with the garden, was now his own. His severe illness had hindered all preparations for his removal thither; but it had become necessary that he should go and overlook its contents, as administrator to his mother's little property; for which purpose he decided to pass the next night on the premises.

He journeyed onward, not quickly or decisively, but in the slow walk of one who has been awakened from a stupefying sleep. It was early afternoon when he reached the valley. The expression of the place, the tone of the hour, were precisely those of many such occasions in days gone by; and these antecedent similarities fostered the illusion that she, who was there no longer, would come out to welcome him. The garden gate was locked and the shutters were closed, just as he himself had left them on the evening after the funeral. He unlocked the gate, and found that a spider had already constructed a large web, tying the door to the lintel, on the supposition that it was never to be opened again. When he had entered the house and flung back the shutters he set about his task of overhauling the cupboards and closets, burning papers, and considering how best to arrange the place for Eustacia's reception, until such time as he might be in a position to carry out his long-delayed scheme, should that time ever arrive.

As he surveyed the rooms he felt strongly disinclined for the alterations which would have to be made in the time-honoured furnishing of his parents and grandparents, to suit Eustacia's modern ideas. The gaunt oak-cased clock, with the picture of the Ascension on the door-panel and the Miraculous Draught of Fishes[2] on the base; his grandmother's corner cupboard with the glass door, through which the spotted china was visible; the dumb-waiter; the wooden tea-trays; the hanging fountain with the brass tap—whither would these venerable articles have to be banished?

He noticed that the flowers in the window had died for want of water, and he placed them out upon the ledge, that they might be taken away. While thus engaged he heard footsteps on the gravel without, and somebody knocked at the door.

Yeobright opened it, and Venn was standing before him.

'Good morning,' said the reddleman. 'Is Mrs. Yeobright at home?'

Yeobright looked upon the ground. 'Then you have not seen Christian or any of the Egdon folks?' he said.

'No. I have only just returned after a long stay away. I called here the day before I left.'

'And you have heard nothing?'

'Nothing.'

'My mother is—dead.'

'Dead!' said Venn mechanically.

'Her home now is where I shouldn't mind having mine.'

Venn regarded him, and then said, 'If I didn't see your face I could never believe your words. Have you been ill?'

'I had an illness.'

'Well, the change! When I parted from her a month ago everything seemed to say that she was going to begin a new life.'

'And what seemed came true.'

'You say right, no doubt. Trouble has taught you a deeper vein of talk than mine. All I meant was regarding her life here. She has died too soon.'

'Perhaps through my living too long. I have had a bitter experience on that score this last month, Diggory. But come in; I have been wanting to see you.'

He conducted the reddleman into the large room where the dancing had taken place the previous Christmas; and they sat down in the settle together. 'There's the cold fireplace, you see,' said Clym. 'When that half-burnt log and those cinders were alight she was alive! Little has been changed here yet. I can do nothing. My life creeps like a snail.'

'How came she to die?' said Venn.

Yeobright gave him some particulars of her illness and death,

2. The story in the New Testament in which Jesus, after his resurrection, revealed himself to his disciples by having them haul in a large net filled with fish when they had been unable to catch any before. In most versions, the catching of fish is a metaphor for the catching of souls. (Luke v.1ff.; John xxi.1ff.)

and continued: 'After this no kind of pain will ever seem more than an indisposition to me—I began saying that I wanted to ask you something, but I stray from subjects like a drunken man. I am anxious to know what my mother said to you when she last saw you. You talked with her a long time, I think?'

'I talked with her more than half an hour.'

'About me?'

'Yes. And it must have been on account of what we said that she was on the heath. Without question she was coming to see you.'

'But why should she come to see me if she felt so bitterly against me? There's the mystery.'

'Yet I know she quite forgave 'ee.'

'But, Diggory—would a woman, who had quite forgiven her son, say, when she felt herself ill on the way to his house, that she was broken-hearted because of his ill-usage? Never!'

'What I know is that she didn't blame you at all. She blamed herself for what had happened, and only herself. I had it from her own lips.'

'You had it from her lips that I had *not* ill-treated her; and at the same time another had it from her lips that I *had* ill-treated her? My mother was no impulsive woman who changed her opinion every hour without reason. How can it be, Venn, that she should have told such different stories in close succession?"

'I cannot say. It is certainly odd, when she had forgiven you, and had forgiven your wife, and was going to see ye on purpose to make friends.'

'If there was one thing wanting to bewilder me it was this incomprehensible thing! . . . Diggory, if we, who remain alive, were only allowed to hold conversation with the dead—just once, a bare minute, even through a screen of iron bars, as with persons in prison—what we might learn! How many who now ride smiling would hide their heads! And this mystery—I should then be at the bottom of it at once. But the grave has for ever shut her in; and how shall it be found out now?'

No reply was returned by his companion, since none could be given; and when Venn left, a few minutes later, Clym had passed from the dulness of sorrow to the fluctuation of carking incertitude.

He continued in the same state all the afternoon. A bed was made up for him in the same house by a neighbour, that he might not have to return again the next day; and when he retired to rest in the deserted place it was only to remain awake hour after hour thinking the same thoughts. How to discover a solution to this riddle of death seemed a query of more importance than highest problems of the living. There was housed in his memory a vivid picture of the face of a little boy as he entered the hovel where

Clym's mother lay. The round eyes, eager gaze, the piping voice which enunciated the words, had operated like stilettos on his brain.

A visit to the boy suggested itself as a means of gleaning new particulars; though it might be quite unproductive. To probe a child's mind after the lapse of six weeks, not for facts which the child had seen and understood, but to get at those which were in their nature beyond him, did not promise much; yet when every obvious channel is blocked we grope towards the small and obscure. There was nothing else left to do; after that he would allow the enigma to drop into the abyss of undiscoverable things.

It was about daybreak when he had reached this decision, and he at once arose. He locked up the house and went out into the green patch which merged in heather further on. In front of the white garden-palings the path branched into three like a broad-arrow. The road to the right led to the Quiet Woman and its neighbourhood; the middle track led to Mistover Knap; the left-hand track led over the hill to another part of Mistover, where the child lived. On inclining into the latter path Yeobright felt a creeping chilliness, familiar enough to most people, and probably caused by the unsunned morning air. In after days he thought of it as a thing of singular significance.

When Yeobright reached the cottage of Susan Nunsuch, the mother of the boy he sought, he found that the inmates were not yet astir. But in upland hamlets the transition from a-bed to abroad is surprisingly swift and easy. There no dense partition of yawns and toilets divides humanity by night from humanity by day. Yeobright tapped at the upper window-sill, which he could reach with his walking-stick; and in three or four minutes the woman came down.

It was not till this moment that Clym recollected her to be the person who had behaved so barbarously to Eustacia. It partly explained the insuavity with which the woman greeted him. Moreover, the boy had been ailing again; and Susan now, as ever since the night when he had been pressed into Eustacia's service at the bonfire, attributed his indispositions to Eustacia's influence as a witch. It was one of those sentiments which lurk like moles underneath the visible surface of manners, and may have been kept alive by Eustacia's entreaty to the captain, at the time that he had intended to prosecute Susan for the pricking in church, to let the matter drop; which he accordingly had done.

Yeobright overcame his repugnance, for Susan had at least borne his mother no ill-will. He asked kindly for the boy; but her manner did not improve.

'I wish to see him,' continued Yeobright, with some hesitation;

'to ask him if he remembers anything more of his walk with my mother than what he has previously told.'

She regarded him in a peculiar and criticizing manner. To anybody but a half-blind man it would have said, 'You want another of the knocks which have already laid you so low.'

She called the boy downstairs, asked Clym to sit down on a stool, and continued, 'Now, Johnny, tell Mr. Yeobright anything you can call to mind.'

'You have not forgotten how you walked with the poor lady on that hot day?' said Clym.

'No,' said the boy.

'And what she said to you?'

The boy repeated the exact words he had used on entering the hut. Yeobright rested his elbow on the table and shaded his face with his hand; and the mother looked as if she wondered how a man could want more of what had stung him so deeply.

'She was going to Alderworth when you first met her?'

'No; she was coming away.'

'That can't be.'

'Yes; she walked along with me. I was coming away, too.'

'Then where did you first see her?'

'At your house.'

'Attend, and speak the truth!' said Clym sternly.

'Yes, sir; at your house was where I seed her first.'

Clym started up, and Susan smiled in an expectant way which did not embellish her face; it seemed to mean, 'Something sinister is coming!'

'What did she do at my house?'

'She went and sat under the trees at the Devil's Bellows.'

'Good God! this is all news to me!'

'You never told me this before?' said Susan.

'No, mother; because I didn't like to tell 'ee I had been so far. I was picking black-hearts,[3] and went further than I meant.'

'What did she do then?' said Yeobright.

'Looked at a man who came up and went into your house.'

'That was myself—a furze-cutter, with brambles in his hand.'

'No; 'twas not you. 'Twas a gentleman. You had gone in afore.'

'Who was he?'

'I don't know.'

'Now tell me what happened next.'

'The poor lady went and knocked at your door, and the lady with black hair looked out of the side-window at her.'

3. Usually a kind of cherry, although Johnny was earlier described (p. 223) as picking whortleberries, or wild blackberries.

The boy's mother turned to Clym and said, 'This is something you didn't expect?'

Yeobright took no more notice of her than if he had been of stone. 'Go on, go on,' he said hoarsely to the boy.

'And when she saw the young lady look out of the window the old lady knocked again; and when nobody came she took up the furze-hook and looked at it, and put it down again, and then she looked at the faggot-bonds; and then she went away, and walked across to me, and blowed her breath very hard, like this. We walked on together, she and I, and I talked to her and she talked to me a bit, but not much, because she couldn't blow her breath.'

'O!' murmured Clym, in a low tone, and bowed his head. 'Let's have more,' he said.

'She couldn't talk much, and she couldn't walk; and her face was, O so queer!'

'How was her face?'

'Like yours is now.'

The woman looked at Yeobright, and beheld him colourless, in a cold sweat. 'Isn't there meaning in it?' she said stealthily. 'What do you think of her now?'

'Silence!' said Clym fiercely. And, turning to the boy, 'And then you left her to die?'

'No,' said the woman, quickly and angrily. 'He did not leave her to die! She sent him away. Whoever says he forsook her says what's not true.'

'Trouble no more about that,' answered Clym, with a quivering mouth. 'What he did is a trifle in comparison with what he saw. Door kept shut, did you say? Kept shut, she looking out of window? Good heart of God!—what does it mean?'

The child shrank away from the gaze of his questioner.

'He said so,' answered the mother, 'and Johnny's a God-fearing boy and tells no lies.'

' "Cast off by my son!" No, by my best life, dear mother, it is not so! But by your son's, your son's——May all murderesses get the torment they deserve!'

With these words Yeobright went forth from the little dwelling. The pupils of his eyes, fixed steadfastly on blankness, were vaguely lit with an icy shine; his mouth had passed into the phase more or less imaginatively rendered in studies of Oedipus. The strangest deeds were possible to his mood. But they were not possible to his situation. Instead of there being before him the pale face of Eustacia, and a masculine shape unknown, there was only the imperturbable countenance of the heath, which, having defied the cataclysmal onsets of centuries, reduced to insignificance by its seamed and antique features the wildest turmoil of a single man.

Eustacia Dresses Herself on a Black Morning

III

A consciousness of a vast impassivity in all which lay around him took possession even of Yeobright in his wild walk towards Alderworth. He had once before felt in his own person this overpowering of the fervid by the inanimate; but then it had tended to enervate a passion far sweeter than that which at present pervaded him. It was once when he stood parting from Eustacia in the moist still levels beyond the hills.

But dismissing all this he went onward home, and came to the front of his house. The blinds of Eustacia's bedroom were still closely drawn, for she was no early riser. All the life visible was in the shape of a solitary thrust cracking a small snail upon the doorstone for his breakfast, and his tapping seemed a loud noise in the general silence which prevailed; but on going to the door Clym found it unfastened, the young girl who attended upon Eustacia being astir in the back part of the premises. Yeobright entered and went straight to his wife's room.

The noise of his arrival must have aroused her, for when he opened the door she was standing before the looking-glass in her night-dress, the ends of her hair gathered into one hand, with which she was coiling the whole mass round her head, previous to beginning toilette operations. She was not a woman given to speaking first at a meeting, and she allowed Clym to walk across in silence, without turning her head. He came behind her, and she saw his face in the glass. It was ashy, haggard, and terrible. Instead of starting towards him in sorrowful surprise, as even Eustacia, undemonstrative wife as she was, would have done in days before she burdened herself with a secret, she remained motionless, looking at him in the glass. And while she looked the carmine flush with which warmth and sound sleep had suffused her cheeks and neck, dissolved from view, and the death-like pallor in his face flew across into hers. He was close enough to see this, and the sight instigated his tongue.

'You know what is the matter,' he said huskily. 'I see it in your face.'

Her hand relinquished the rope of hair and dropped to her side, and the pile of tresses, no longer supported, fell from the crown of her head about her shoulders and over the white night-gown. She made no reply.

'Speak to me,' said Yeobright peremptorily.

The blanching process did not cease in her, and her lips now became as white as her face. She turned to him and said, 'Yes,

Clym, I'll speak to you. Why do you return so early? Can I do anything for you?'

'Yes, you can listen to me. It seems that my wife is not very well?'

'Why?'

'Your face, my dear; your face. Or perhaps it is the pale morning light which takes your colour away? Now I am going to reveal a secret to you. Ha-ha!'

'O, that is ghastly!'

'What?'

'Your laugh.'

'There's reason for ghastliness. Eustacia, you have held my happiness in the hollow of your hand, and like a devil you have dashed it down.'

She started back from the dressing-table, retreated a few steps from him, and looked him in the face. 'Ah! you think to frighten me,' she said, with a slight laugh. 'Is it worth while? I am undefended, and alone.'

'How extraordinary!'

'What do you mean?'

'As there is ample time I will tell you, though you know well enough. I mean that it is extraordinary that you should be alone in my absence. Tell me, now, where is he who was with you on the afternoon of the thirty-first of August? Under the bed? Up the chimney?'

A shudder overcame her and shook the light fabric of her night-dress throughout. 'I do not remember dates so exactly,' she said. 'I cannot recollect that anybody was with me besides yourself.'

'The day I mean,' said Yeobright, his voice growing louder and harsher, 'was the day you shut the door against my mother and killed her. O, it is too much—too bad!' He leant over the footpiece of the bedstead for a few moments, with his back towards her; then rising again: 'Tell me, tell me! tell me—do you hear?' he cried, rushing up to her and seizing her by the loose folds of her sleeve.

The superstratum of timidity which often overlies those who are daring and defiant at heart had been passed through, and the mettlesome substance of the woman was reached. The red blood inundated her face, previously so pale.

'What are you going to do?' she said in a low voice, regarding him with a proud smile. 'You will not alarm me by holding on so; but it would be a pity to tear my sleeve.'

Instead of letting go he drew her closer to him. 'Tell me the particulars of—my mother's death,' he said in a hard, panting whisper; 'or—I'll—I'll——'

'Clym,' she answered slowly, 'do you think you dare do anything to me that I dare not bear? But before you strike me listen. You will get nothing from me by a blow, even though it should kill me, as it probably will. But perhaps you do not wish me to speak—killing may be all you mean?'

'Kill you! Do you expect it?'

'I do.'

'Why?'

'No less degree of rage against me will match your previous grief for her.'

'Phew—I shall not kill you,' he said contemptuously, as if under a sudden change of purpose. 'I did think of it; but—I shall not. That would be making a martyr of you, and sending you to where she is; and I would keep you away from her till the universe come to an end, if I could.'

'I almost wish you would kill me,' said she with gloomy bitterness. 'It is with no strong desire, I assure you, that I play the part I have lately played on earth. You are no blessing, my husband.'

'You shut the door—you looked out of the window upon her—you had a man in the house with you—you sent her away to die. The inhumanity—the treachery—I will not touch you—stand away from me—and confess every word!'

'Never! I'll hold my tongue like the very death that I don't mind meeting, even though I can clear myself of half you believe by speaking. Yes. I will! Who of any dignity would take the trouble to clear cobwebs from a wild man's mind after such language as this? No; let him go on, and think his narrow thoughts, and run his head into the mire. I have other cares.'

' 'Tis too much—but I must spare you.'

'Poor charity.'

'By my wretched soul you sting me, Eustacia! I can keep it up, and hotly too. Now, then, madam, tell me his name!'

'Never, I am resolved.'

'How often does he write to you? Where does he put his letters—when does he meet you? Ah, his letters! Do you tell me his name?'

'I do not.'

'Then I'll find it myself.' His eye had fallen upon a small desk that stood near, on which she was accustomed to write her letters. He went to it. It was locked.

'Unlock this!'

'You have no right to say it. That's mine.'

Without another word he seized the desk and dashed it to the floor. The hinge burst open, and a number of letters tumbled out.

'Stay!' said Eustacia, stepping before him with more excitement than she had hitherto shown.

'Come, come! stand away! I must see them.'

She looked at the letters as they lay, checked her feeling, and moved indifferently aside; when he gathered them up, and examined them.

By no stretch of meaning could any but a harmless construction be placed upon a single one of the letters themselves. The solitary exception was an empty envelope directed to her, and the handwriting was Wildeve's. Yeobright held it up. Eustacia was doggedly silent.

'Can you read, madam? Look at this envelope. Doubtless we shall find more soon, and what was inside them. I shall no doubt be gratified by learning in good time what a well-finished and full-blown adept in a certain trade my lady is.'

'Do you say it to me—do you?' she gasped.

He searched further, but found nothing more. 'What was in this letter?' he said.

'Ask the writer. Am I your hound that you should talk to me in this way?'

'Do you brave me? do you stand me out, mistress? Answer. Don't look at me with those eyes as if you would bewitch me again! Sooner than that I die. You refuse to answer?'

'I wouldn't tell you after this, if I were as innocent as the sweetest babe in heaven!'

'Which you are not.'

'Certainly I am not absolutely,' she replied. 'I have not done what you suppose; but if to have done no harm at all is the only innocence recognized, I am beyond forgiveness. But I require no help from your conscience.'

'You can resist, and resist again! Instead of hating you I could, I think, mourn for and pity you, if you were contrite, and would confess all. Forgive you I never can. I don't speak of your lover—I will give you the benefit of the doubt in that matter, for it only affects me personally. But the other: had you half-killed *me*, had it been that you willfully took the sight away from these feeble eyes of mine, I could have forgiven you. But *that's* too much for nature!'

'Say no more. I will do without your pity. But I would have saved you from uttering what you will regret.'

'I am going away now. I shall leave you.'

'You need not go, as I am going myself. You will keep just as far from me by staying here.'

'Call her to mind—think of her—what goodness there was in her: it showed in every line of her face! Most women, even when but slightly annoyed, show a flicker of evil in some curl of the mouth or some corner of the cheek; but as for her, never in her angriest moments was there anything malicious in her look. She was angered quickly, but she forgave just as readily, and underneath her pride there was the meekness of a child. What came of it?—what cared you? You hated her just as she was learning to love you. O! couldn't you see what was best for you, but must bring a curse upon me, and agony and death upon her, by doing that cruel deed! What was the fellow's name who was keeping you company and causing you to add cruelty to her to your wrong to me? Was it Wildeve? Was it poor Thomasin's husband? Heaven, what wickedness! Lost your voice, have you? It is natural after detection of that most noble trick. . . . Eustacia, didn't any tender thought of your own mother lead you to think of being gentle to mine at such a time of weariness? Did not one grain of pity enter your heart as she turned away? Think what a vast opportunity was then lost of beginning a forgiving and honest course. Why did not you kick him out, and let her in, and say, I'll be a honest wife and a noble woman from this hour? Had I told you to go and quench eternally our last flickering chance of happiness here you could have done no worse. Well, she's asleep now; and have you a hundred gallants, neither they nor you can insult her any more.'

'You exaggerate fearfully,' she said in a faint, weary voice: 'but I cannot enter into my defence—it is not worth doing. You are nothing to me in future, and the past side of the story may as well remain untold. I have lost all through you, but I have not complained. Your blunders and misfortunes may have been a sorrow to you, but they have been a wrong to me. All persons of refinement have been scared away from me since I sank into the mire of marriage. Is this your cherishing—to put me into a hut like this, and keep me like the wife of a hind? You deceived me—not by words, but by appearances, which are less seen through than words. But the place will serve as well as any other—as somewhere to pass from—into my grave.' Her words were smothered in her throat, and her head drooped down.

'I don't know what you mean by that. Am I the cause of your sin?' (Eustacia made a trembling motion towards him.) 'What, you can begin to shed tears and offer me your hand? Good God! can you? No, not I. I'll not commit the fault of taking that.' (The hand she had offered dropped nervelessly, but the tears continued flowing.) 'Well, yes, I'll take it, if only for the sake of my own foolish kisses that were wasted there before I knew what I cherished. How bewitched I was! How could there be any good in a woman that everybody spoke ill of?'

'O, O, O!' she cried, breaking down at last; and, shaking with sobs which choked her, she sank upon her knees. 'O, will you have done! O, you are too relentless—there's a limit to the cruelty of savages! I have held out long—but you crush me down. I beg for mercy—I cannot bear this any longer—it is inhuman to go further with this! If I had—killed your—mother with my own hand—I should not deserve such a scourging to the bone as this. O, O! God have mercy upon a miserable woman! . . . You have beaten me in this game—I beg you to stay your hand in pity! . . . I confess that I—willfully did not undo the door the first time she knocked—but—I—should have unfastened it the second—if I had not thought you had gone to do it yourself. When I found you had not I opened it, but she was gone. That's the extent of my crime—towards *her*. Best natures commit bad faults sometimes, don't they?—I think they do. Now I will leave you—for ever and ever!'

'Tell all, and I *will* pity you. Was the man in the house with you Wildeve?'

'I cannot tell,' she said desperately through her sobbing. 'Don't insist further—I cannot tell. I am going from this house. We cannot both stay here.'

'You need not go: I will go. You can stay here.'

'No, I will dress, and then I will go.'

'Where?'

'Where I came from, or *else*where.'

She hastily dressed herself, Yeobright moodily walking up and down the room the whole of the time. At last all her things were on. Her little hands quivered so violently as she held them to her chin to fasten her bonnet that she could not tie the strings, and after a few moments she relinquished the attempt. Seeing this he moved forward and said, 'Let me tie them.'

She assented in silence, and lifted her chin. For once at least in her life she was totally oblivious of the charm of her attitude. But he was not, and he turned his eyes aside, that he might not be tempted to softness.

The strings were tied; she turned from him. 'Do you still prefer going away yourself to my leaving you?' he inquired again.

'I do.'

'Very well—let it be. And when you will confess to the man I may pity you.'

She flung her shawl about her and went downstairs, leaving him standing in the room.

Eustacia had not long been gone when there came a knock at the door of the bedroom; and Yeobright said, 'Well?'

It was the servant; and she replied, 'Somebody from Mrs. Wildeve's have called to tell 'ee that the mis'ess and the baby are getting on wonderful well, and the baby's name is to be Eustacia Clementine.' And the girl retired.

'What a mockery!' said Clym. 'This unhappy marriage of mine to be perpetuated in that child's name!'

The Ministrations of a Half-Forgotten One

IV

Eustacia's journey was at first as vague in direction as that of thistledown on the wind. She did not know what to do. She wished it had been night instead of morning, that she might at least have borne her misery without the possibility of being seen. Tracing mile after mile along between the dying ferns and the wet white spiders' webs, she at length turned her steps towards her grandfather's house. She found the front door closed and locked. Mechanically she went round to the end where the stable was, and on looking in at the stable-door she saw Charley standing within.

'Captain Vye is not at home?' she said.

'No, ma'am,' said the lad in a flutter of feeling; 'he's gone to Weatherbury, and won't be home till night. And the servant is gone home for a holiday. So the house is locked up.'

Eustacia's face was not visible to Charley as she stood at the doorway, her back being to the sky, and the stable but indifferently lighted; but the wildness of her manner arrested his attention. She turned and walked away across the enclosure to the gate, and was hidden by the bank.

When she had disappeared Charley, with misgiving in his eyes, slowly came from the stable-door, and going to another point in the bank he looked over. Eustacia was leaning against it on the outside, her face covered with her hands, and her head pressing the dewy heather which bearded the bank's outer side. She appeared to be utterly indifferent to the circumstance that her bonnet, hair, and garments were becoming wet and disarranged by the moisture of her cold, harsh pillow. Clearly something was wrong.

Charley had always regarded Eustacia as Eustacia had regarded Clym when she first beheld him—as a romantic and sweet vision, scarcely incarnate. He had been so shut off from her by the dignity of her look and the pride of her speech, except at that one blissful interval when he was allowed to hold her hand, that he had hardly deemed her a woman, wingless and earthly, subject to household conditions and domestic jars. The inner details of her life he had only conjectured. She had been a lovely wonder, predestined to an orbit in which the whole of his own was but a point; and this sight of her leaning like a helpless, despairing creature against a wild wet bank, filled him with an amazed horror. He could no longer remain where he was. Leaping over, he came up, touched her with his finger, and said tenderly, 'You are poorly, ma'am. What can I do?'

Eustacia started up, and said, 'Ah, Charley—you have followed me. You did not think when I left home in the summer that I should come back like this!'

'I did not, dear ma'am. Can I help you now?'

'I am afraid not. I wish I could get into the house. I feel giddy—that's all.'

'Lean on my arm, ma'am, till we get to the porch; and I will try to open the door.'

He supported her to the porch, and there depositing her on a seat hastened to the back, climbed to a window by the help of a ladder, and descending inside opened the door. Next he assisted her into the room, where there was an old-fashioned horsehair settee as large as a donkey-waggon. She lay down here, and Charley covered her with a cloak he found in the hall.

'Shall I get you something to eat and drink?' he said.

'If you please, Charley. But I suppose there is no fire?'

'I can light it, ma'am.'

He vanished, and she heard a splitting of wood and a blowing of bellows; and presently he returned, saying, 'I have lighted a fire in the kitchen, and now I'll light one here.'

He lit the fire, Eustacia dreamily observing him from her couch. When it was blazing up he said, 'Shall I wheel you round in front of it, ma'am, as the morning is chilly?'

'Yes, if you like.'

'Shall I go and bring the victuals now?'

'Yes, do,' she murmured languidly.

When he had gone, and the dull sounds occasionally reached her ears of his movements in the kitchen, she forgot where she was, and had for a moment to consider by an effort what the sounds meant. After an interval which seemed short to her whose thoughts were elsewhere, he came in with a tray on which steamed tea and toast, though it was nearly lunch-time.

'Place it on the table,' she said. 'I shall be ready soon.'

He did so, and retired to the door: when, however, he perceived that she did not move he came back a few steps.

'Let me hold it to you, if you don't wish to get up,' said Charley. He brought the tray to the front of the couch, where he knelt down, adding, 'I will hold it for you.'

Eustacia sat up and poured out a cup of tea. 'You are very kind to me, Charley,' she murmured as she sipped.

'Well, I ought to be,' said he diffidently, taking great trouble not to rest his eyes upon her, though this was their only natural position, Eustacia being immediately before him. 'You have been kind to me.'

'How have I?' said Eustacia.

'You let me hold your hand when you were a maiden at home.'

'Ah, so I did. Why did I do that? My mind is lost—it had to do with the mumming, had it not?'

'Yes, you wanted to go in my place.'

'I remember. I do indeed remember—too well!'

She again became utterly downcast; and Charley, seeing that she was not going to eat or drink any more, took away the tray.

Afterwards he occasionally came in to see if the fire was burning, to ask her if she wanted anything, to tell her that the wind had shifted from south to west, to ask her if she would like him to gather her some blackberries; to all which inquiries she replied in the negative or with indifference.

She remained on the settee some time longer, when she aroused herself and went upstairs. The room in which she had formerly slept still remained much as she had left it, and the recollection that this forced upon her of her own greatly changed and infinitely worsened situation again set on her face the undetermined and formless misery which it had worn on her first arrival. She peeped into her grandfather's room, through which the fresh autumn air was blowing from the open window. Her eye was arrested by what was a familiar sight enough, though it broke upon her now with a new significance.

It was a brace of pistols, hanging near the head of her grandfather's bed, which he always kept there loaded, as a precaution against possible burglars, the house being very lonely. Eustacia regarded them long, as if they were the page of a book in which she read a new and a strange matter. Quickly, like one afraid of herself, she returned downstairs and stood in deep thought.

'If I could only do it!' she said. 'It would be doing much good to myself and all connected with me, and no harm to a single one.'

The idea seemed to gather force within her, and she remained in a fixed attitude nearly ten minutes, when a certain finality was expressed in her gaze, and no longer the blankness of indecision.

She turned and went up the second time—softly and stealthily now—and entered her grandfather's room, her eyes at once seeking the head of the bed. The pistols were gone.

The instant quashing of her purpose by their absence affected her brain as a sudden vacuum affects the body: she nearly fainted. Who had done this? There was only one person on the premises besides herself. Eustacia involuntarily turned to the open window which overlooked the garden as far as the bank that bounded it. On the summit of the latter stood Charley, sufficiently elevated by its height to see into the room. His gaze was directed eagerly and solicitously upon her.

She went downstairs to the door and beckoned to him.

'You have taken them away?'

'Yes, ma'am.'

'Why did you do it?'

'I saw you looking at them too long.'

'What has that to do with it?'

'You have been heart-broken all the morning, as if you did not want to live.'

'Well?'

'And I could not bear to leave them in your way. There was meaning in your look at them.'

'Where are they now?'

'Locked up.'

'Where?'

'In the stable.'

'Give them to me.'

'No, ma'am.'

'You refuse?'

'I do. I care too much for you to give 'em up.'

She turned aside, her face for the first time softening from the stony immobility of the earlier day, and the corners of her mouth resuming something of that delicacy of cut which was always lost in her moments of despair. At last she confronted him again.

'Why should I not die if I wish?' she said tremulously. 'I have made a bad bargain with life, and I am weary of it—weary. And now you have hindered my escape. O, why did you, Charley! What makes death painful except the thought of others' grief?—and that is absent in my case, for not a sigh would follow me!'

'Ah, it is trouble that has done this! I wish in my very soul that he who brought it about might die and rot, even if 'tis transportation to say it!'

'Charley, no more of that. What do you mean to do about this you have seen?'

'Keep it close as night, if you promise not to think of it again.'

'You need not fear. The moment has passed. I promise.' She then went away, entered the house, and lay down.

Later in the afternoon her grandfather returned. He was about to question her categorically; but on looking at her he withheld his words.

'Yes, it is too bad to talk of,' she slowly returned in answer to his glance. 'Can my old room be got ready for me to-night, grandfather? I shall want to occupy it again.'

He did not ask what it all meant, or why she had left her husband, but ordered the room to be prepared.

An Old Move Inadvertently Repeated

V

Charley's attentions to his former mistress were unbounded. The only solace to his own trouble lay in his attempts to relieve hers. Hour after hour he considered her wants: he thought of her presence there with a sort of gratitude, and, while uttering imprecations on the cause of her unhappiness, in some measure blessed the result. Perhaps she would always remain there, he thought, and then he would be as happy as he had been before. His dread was lest she should think fit to return to Alderworth, and in that dread his eyes, with all the inquisitiveness of affection, frequently sought her face when she was not observing him, as he would have watched the head of a stockdove to learn if it contemplated flight. Having once really succoured her, and possibly preserved her from the rashest of acts, he mentally assumed in addition a guardian's responsibility for her welfare.

For this reason he busily endeavoured to provide her with pleasant distractions, bringing home curious objects which he found in the heath, such as white trumpet-shaped mosses, red-headed lichens, stone arrow-heads used by the old tribes on Egdon, and faceted crystals from the hollows of flints. These he deposited on the premises in such positions that she should see them as if by accident.

A week passed, Eustacia never going out of the house. Then she walked into the enclosed plot and looked through her grandfather's spy-glass, as she had been in the habit of doing before her marriage. One day she saw, at a place where the high-road crossed the distant valley, a heavily laden waggon passing along. It was piled with household furniture. She looked again and again, and recognized it to be her own. In the evening her grandfather came indoors with a rumour that Yeobright had removed that day from Alderworth to the old house at Blooms-End.

On another occasion when reconnoitring thus she beheld two female figures walking in the vale. The day was fine and clear; and the persons not being more than half a mile off she could see their every detail with the telescope. The woman walking in front carried a white bundle in her arms, from one end of which hung a long appendage of drapery; and when the walkers turned, so that the sun fell more directly upon them, Eustacia could see that the object was a baby. She called Charley, and asked him if he knew who they were, though she well guessed.

'Mrs. Wildeve and the nurse-girl,' said Charley.

'The nurse is carrying the baby?' said Eustacia.

'No, 'tis Mrs. Wildeve carrying that,' he answered, 'and the nurse walks behind carrying nothing.'

The lad was in good spirits that day, for the fifth of November had again come round, and he was planning yet another scheme to divert her from her too absorbing thoughts. For two successive years his mistress had seemed to take pleasure in lighting a bonfire on the bank overlooking the valley; but this year she had apparently quite forgotten the day and the customary deed. He was careful not to remind her, and went on with his secret preparations for a cheerful surprise, the more zealously that he had been absent last time and unable to assist. At every vacant minute he hastened to gather furze-stumps, thorn-tree roots, and other solid materials from the adjacent slopes, hiding them from cursory view.

The evening came, and Eustacia was still seemingly unconscious of the anniversary. She had gone indoors after her survey through the glass, and had not been visible since. As soon as it was quite dark Charley began to build the bonfire, choosing precisely that spot on the bank which Eustacia had chosen at previous times.

When all the surrounding bonfires had burst into existence Charley kindled his, and arranged its fuel so that it should not require tending for some time. He then went back to the house, and lingered round the door and windows till she should by some means or other learn of his achievement and come out to witness it. But the shutters were closed, the door remained shut, and no heed whatever seemed to be taken of his performance. Not liking to call her he went back and replenished the fire, continuing to do this for more than half an hour. It was not till his stock of fuel had greatly diminished that he went to the back door and sent in to beg that Mrs. Yeobright would open the window-shutters and see the sight outside.

Eustacia, who had been sitting listlessly in the parlour, started up at the intelligence and flung open the shutters. Facing her on the bank blazed the fire, which at once sent a ruddy glare into the room where she was, and overpowered the candles.

'Well done, Charley!' said Captain Vye from the chimney-corner. 'But I hope it is not my wood that he's burning. . . . Ah, it was this time last year that I met with that man Venn, bringing home Thomasin Yeobright—to be sure it was! Well, who would have thought that girl's troubles would have ended so well? What a snipe you were in that matter, Eustacia! Has your husband written to you yet?'

'No,' said Eustacia, looking vaguely through the window at the fire, which just then so much engaged her mind that she did not resent her grandfather's blunt opinion. She could see Charley's form on the bank, shovelling and stirring the fire; and there flashed upon her imagination some other form which that fire might call up.

She left the room, put on her garden-bonnet and cloak, and went out. Reaching the bank she looked over with a wild curiosity and misgiving, when Charley said to her, with a pleased sense of himself, 'I made it o' purpose for you, ma'am.'

'Thank you,' she said hastily. 'But I wish you to put it out now.'

'It will soon burn down,' said Charley, rather disappointed. 'Is it not a pity to knock it out?'

'I don't know,' she musingly answered.

They stood in silence, broken only by the crackling of the flames, till Charley, perceiving that she did not want to talk to him, moved reluctantly away.

Eustacia remained within the bank looking at the fire, intending to go indoors, yet lingering still. Had she not by her situation been inclined to hold in indifference all things honoured of the gods and of men she would probably have come away. But her state was so hopeless that she could play with it. To have lost is less disturbing than to wonder if we may possibly have won: and Eustacia could now, like other people at such a stage, take a standing-point outside herself, observe herself as a disinterested spectator, and think what a sport for Heaven this woman Eustacia was.

While she stood she heard a sound. It was the splash of a stone in the pond.

Had Eustacia received the stone full in the bosom her heart could not have given a more decided thump. She had thought of the possibility of such a signal in answer to that which had been unwittingly given by Charley; but she had not expected it yet. How prompt Wildeve was! Yet how could he think her capable of deliberately wishing to renew their assignations now? An impulse to leave the spot, a desire to stay, struggled within her; and the desire held its own. More than that it did not do, for she refrained even from ascending the bank and looking over. She remained motionless, not disturbing a muscle of her face or raising her eyes; for were she to turn up her face the fire on the bank would shine upon it, and Wildeve might be looking down.

There was a second splash into the pond.

Why did he stay so long without advancing and looking over? Curiosity had its way: she ascended one or two of the earth-steps in the bank and glanced out.

Wildeve was before her. He had come forward after throwing the last pebble, and the fire now shone into each of their faces from the bank stretching breast-high between them.

'I did not light it!' cried Eustacia quickly. 'It was lit without my knowledge. Don't, don't come over to me!'

'Why have you been living here all these days without telling me? You have left your home. I fear I am something to blame in this?'

'I did not let in his mother; that's how it is!'

'You do not deserve what you have got, Eustacia; you are in great misery; I see it in your eyes, your mouth, and all over you.

My poor, poor girl!' He stepped over the bank. 'You are beyond everything unhappy!'

'No, no; not exactly——'

'It has been pushed too far—it is killing you: I do think it!'

Her usually quiet breathing had grown quicker with his words. 'I—I——' she began, and then burst into quivering sobs, shaken to the very heart by the unexpected voice of pity—a sentiment whose existence in relation to herself she had almost forgotten.

This outbreak of weeping took Eustacia herself so much by surprise that she could not leave off, and she turned aside from him in some shame, though turning hid nothing from him. She sobbed on desperately; then the outpour lessened, and she became quieter. Wildeve had resisted the impulse to clasp her, and stood without speaking.

'Are you not ashamed of me, who used never to be a crying animal?' she asked in a weak whisper as she wiped her eyes. 'Why didn't you go away? I wish you had not seen quite all that; it reveals too much by half.'

'You might have wished it, because it makes me as sad as you,' he said with emotion and deference. 'As for revealing—the word is impossible between us two.'

'I did not send for you—don't forget it, Damon; I am in pain, but I did not send for you! As a wife, at least, I've been straight.'

'Never mind—I came. O, Eustacia, forgive me for the harm I have done you in these two past years! I see more and more that I have been your ruin.'

'Not you. This place I live in.'

'Ah, your generosity may naturally make you say that. But I am the culprit. I should either have done more or nothing at all.'

'In what way?'

'I ought never to have hunted you out; or, having done it, I ought to have persisted in retaining you. But of course I have no right to talk of that now. I will only ask this: can I do anything for you? Is there anything on the face of the earth that a man can do to make you happier than you are at present? If there is, I will do it. You may command me, Eustacia, to the limit of my influence; and don't forget that I am richer now. Surely something can be done to save you from this! Such a rare plant in such a wild place it grieves me to see. Do you want anything bought? Do you want to go anywhere? Do you want to escape the place altogether? Only say it, and I'll do anything to put an end to those tears, which but for me would never have been at all.'

'We are each married to another person,' she said faintly; 'and assistance from you would have an evil sound—after—after——'

'Well, there's no preventing slanderers from having their fill at any time; but you need not be afraid. Whatever I may feel I promise you on my word of honour never to speak to you about—or act upon—until you say I may. I know my duty to Thomasin quite as well as I know my duty to you as a woman unfairly treated. What shall I assist you in?'

'In getting away from here.'

'Where do you wish to go to?'

'I have a place in my mind. If you could help me as far as Budmouth I can do all the rest. Steamers sail from there across the Channel, and so I can get to Paris, where I want to be. Yes,' she pleaded earnestly, 'help me to get to Budmouth harbour without my grandfather's or my husband's knowledge, and I can do all the rest.'

'Will it be safe to leave you there alone?'

'Yes, yes. I know Budmouth well.'

'Shall I go with you? I am rich now.'

She was silent.

'Say yes, sweet!'

She was silent still.

'Well, let me know when you wish to go. We shall be at our present house till December; after that we remove to Casterbridge. Command me in anything till that time.'

'I will think of this,' she said hurriedly. 'Whether I can honestly make use of you as a friend, or must close with you as a lover—that is what I must ask myself. If I wish to go and decide to accept your company I will signal to you some evening at eight o'clock punctually, and this will mean that you are to be ready with a horse and trap at twelve o'clock the same night to drive me to Budmouth harbour in time for the morning boat.'

'I will look out every night at eight, and no signal shall escape me.'

'Now please go away. If I decide on this escape I can only meet you once more unless—I cannot go without you. Go—I cannot bear it longer. Go—go!'

Wildeve slowly went up the steps and descended into the darkness on the other side; and as he walked he glanced back, till the bank blotted out her form from his further view.

Thomasin Argues with Her Cousin, and He Writes a Letter

VI

Yeobright was at this time at Blooms-End, hoping that Eustacia would return to him. The removal of furniture had been accomplished only that day, though Clym had lived in the old house for more than a week. He had spent the time in working about the premises, sweeping leaves from the garden-paths, cutting dead stalks from the flower-beds, and nailing up creepers which had been displaced by the autumn winds. He took no particular pleasure in these deeds, but they formed a screen between himself and despair. Moreover, it had become a religion with him to preserve in good condition all that had lapsed from his mother's hands to this own.

During these operations he was constantly on the watch for Eustacia. That there should be no mistake about her knowing where to find him he had ordered a notice-board to be affixed to the garden gate at Alderworth, signifying in white letters whither he had removed. When a leaf floated to the earth he turned his head, thinking it might be her footfall. A bird searching for worms in the mould of the flower-beds sounded like her hand on the latch of the gate; and at dusk, when soft, strange ventriloquisms came from holes in the ground, hollow stalks, curled dead leaves, and other crannies wherein breezes, worms, and insects can work their will, he fancied that they were Eustacia, standing without and breathing wishes of reconciliation.

Up to this hour he had persevered in his resolve not to invite her back. At the same time the severity with which he had treated her lulled the sharpness of his regret for his mother, and awoke some of his old solicitude for his mother's supplanter. Harsh feelings produce harsh usage, and this by reaction quenches the sentiments that gave it birth. The more he reflected the more he softened. But to look upon his wife as innocence in distress was impossible, though he could ask himself whether he had given her quite time enough—if he had not come a little too suddenly upon her on that sombre morning.

Now that the first flush of his anger had paled he was disinclined to ascribe to her more than an indiscreet friendship with Wildeve, for there had not appeared in her manner the signs of dishonour. And this once admitted, an absolutely dark interpretation of her act towards his mother was no longer forced upon him.

On the evening of the fifth November his thoughts of Eustacia were intense. Echoes from those past times when they had exchanged tender words all the day long came like the diffused murmur of a seashore left miles behind. 'Surely,' he said, 'she might have brought herself to communicate with me before now, and confess honestly what Wildeve was to her.'

Instead of remaining at home that night he determined to go and see Thomasin and her husband. If he found opportunity he would allude to the cause of the separation between Eustacia and himself, keeping silence, however, on the fact that there was a third person in his house when his mother was turned away. If it proved that Wildeve was innocently there he would doubtless openly mention it. If he were there with unjust intentions Wildeve, being a man of quick feeling, might possibly say something to reveal the extent to which Eustacia was compromised.

But on reaching his cousin's house he found that only Thomasin was at home, Wildeve being at that time on his way towards the bonfire innocently lit by Charley at Mistover. Thomasin then, as always, was glad to see Clym, and took him to inspect the sleeping baby, carefully screening the candlelight from the infant's eyes with her hand.

'Tamsin, have you heard that Eustacia is not with me now?' he said when they had sat down again.

'No,' said Thomasin, alarmed.

'And not that I have left Alderworth?'

'No. I never hear tidings from Alderworth unless you bring them. What is the matter?'

Clym in a disturbed voice related to her his visit to Susan Nunsuch's boy, the revelation he had made, and what had resulted from his charging Eustacia with having wilfully and heartlessly done the deed. He suppressed all mention of Wildeve's presence with her.

'All this, and I not knowing it!' murmured Thomason in an awe-struck tone. 'Terrible! What could have made her——O, Eustacia! And when you found it out you went in hot haste to her? Were you too cruel?—or is she really so wicked as she seems?'

'Can a man be too cruel to his mother's enemy?'

'I can fancy so.'

'Very well, then—I'll admit that he can. But now what is to be done?'

'Make it up again—if a quarrel so deadly can ever be made up. I almost wish you had not told me. But do try to be reconciled. There are ways, after all, if you both wish to.'

'I don't know that we do both wish to make it up,' said Clym. 'If she had wished it, would she not have sent to me by this time?'

'You seem to wish to, and yet you have not sent to her.'

'True; but I have been tossed to and fro in doubt if I ought, after such strong provocation. To see me now, Thomasin, gives you no idea of what I have been; of what depths I have descended to in these few last days. O, it was a bitter shame to shut out my mother like that! Can I ever forget it, or even agree to see her again?'

'She might not have known that anything serious would come of it, and perhaps she did not mean to keep aunt out altogether.'

'She says herself that she did not. But the fact remains that keep her out she did.'

'Believe her sorry, and send for her.'

'How if she will not come?'

'It will prove her guilty, by showing that it is her habit to nourish enmity. But I do not think that for a moment.'

'I will do this. I will wait for a day or two longer—not longer than two days certainly; and if she does not send to me in that time I will indeed send to her. I thought to have seen Wildeve here to-night. Is he from home?'

Thomasin blushed a little. 'No,' she said. 'He is merely gone out for a walk.'

'Why didn't he take you with him? The evening is fine. You want fresh air as well as he.'

'O, I don't care for going anywhere; besides, there is baby.'

'Yes, yes. Well, I have been thinking whether I should not consult your husband about this as well as you,' said Clym steadily.

'I fancy I would not,' she quickly answered. 'It can do no good.'

Her cousin looked her in the face. No doubt Thomasin was ignorant that her husband had any share in the events of that tragic afternoon; but her countenance seemed to signify that she concealed some suspicion or thought of the reputed tender relations between Wildeve and Eustacia in days gone by.

Clym, however, could make nothing of it, and he rose to depart, more in doubt than when he came.

'You will write to her in a day or two?' said the young woman earnestly. 'I do so hope the wretched separation may come to an end.'

'I will,' said Clym; 'I don't rejoice in my present state at all.'

And he left her and climbed over the hill to Blooms-End. Before going to bed he sat down and wrote the following letter:—

> 'My dear Eustacia,—I must obey my heart without consulting my reason too closely. Will you come back to me? Do so, and the past shall never be mentioned. I was too severe; but O, Eustacia, the provocation! You don't know, you never will know, what those words of anger cost me which you drew down upon yourself. All that an honest man can promise you I promise now, which is that from me you shall never suffer anything on this score again. After all the vows we have made, Eustacia, I think we had better pass the remainder of our lives in trying to keep them. Come to me, then, even if you reproach me. I have thought of your sufferings that morning on which I parted from you; I know they were genuine, and they are as much as you ought to bear. Our love must still continue. Such hearts as ours would never have been given us but to be concerned with each other. I could not ask you back at first, Eustacia, for I was unable to persuade myself that he who was with you was not there as a lover. But if you will come and explain distracting appearances I do not question that you can show your honesty to me. Why have you not come before? Do you think I will not listen to you?

Surely not, when you remember the kisses and vows we exchanged under the summer moon. Return then, and you shall be warmly welcomed. I can no longer think of you to your prejudice—I am but too much absorbed in justifying you.—Your husband as ever,

CLYM

'There,' he said, as he laid it in his desk, 'that's a good thing done. If she does not come before to-morrow night I will send it to her.'

Meanwhile, at the house he had just left Thomasin sat sighing uneasily. Fidelity to her husband had that evening induced her to conceal all suspicion that Wildeve's interest in Eustacia had not ended with his marriage. But she knew nothing positive; and though Clym was her well-beloved cousin there was one nearer to her still.

When a little later, Wildeve returned from his walk to Mistover, Thomasin said, 'Damon, where have you been? I was getting quite frightened, and thought you had fallen into the river. I dislike being in the house by myself.'

'Frightened?' he said, touching her cheek as if she were some domestic animal. 'Why, I thought nothing could frighten you. It is that you are getting proud, I am sure, and don't like living here since we have risen above our business. Well, it is a tedious matter, this getting a new house; but I couldn't have set about it sooner, unless our ten thousand pounds had been a hundred thousand, when we could have afforded to despise caution.'

'No—I don't mind waiting—I would rather stay here twelve months longer than run any risk with baby. But I don't like your vanishing so in the evenings. There's something on your mind—I know there is, Damon. You go about so gloomily, and look at the heath as if it were somebody's gaol instead of a nice wild place to walk in.'

He looked towards her with pitying surprise. 'What, do you like Egdon Heath?' he said.

'I like what I was born near to; I admire its grim old face.'

'Pooh, my dear. You don't know what you like.'

'I am sure I do. There's only one thing unpleasant about Egdon.'

'What's that?'

'You never take me with you when you walk there. Why do you wander so much in it yourself if you so dislike it?'

The inquiry, though a simple one, was plainly disconcerting, and he sat down before replying. 'I don't think you often see me there. Give an instance.'

'I will,' she answered triumphantly. 'When you went out this evening I thought that as baby was asleep I would see where you were going to so mysteriously without telling me. So I ran out and followed behind you. You stopped at the place where the road forks, looked round at the bonfires, and then said, "Damn it, I'll go!" And you went quickly up the left-hand road. Then I stood and watched you.'

Wildeve frowned, afterwards saying, with a forced smile, 'Well, what wonderful discovery did you make?'

'There—now you are angry, and we won't talk of this any more.' She went across to him, sat on a footstool, and looked up in his face.

'Nonsense!' he said; 'that's how you always back out. We will go on with it now we have begun. What did you next see? I particularly want to know.'

'Don't be like that, Damon!' she murmured. 'I didn't see anything. You vanished out of sight, and then I looked round at the bonfires and came in.'

'Perhaps this is not the only time you have dogged my steps. Are you trying to find out something bad about me?'

'Not at all! I have never done such a thing before, and I shouldn't have done it now if words had not sometimes been dropped about you.'

'What *do* you mean?' he impatiently asked.

'They say—they say you used to go to Alderworth in the evenings, and it puts into my mind what I have heard about——'

Wildeve turned angrily and stood up in front of her. 'Now,' he said, flourishing his hand in the air, 'just out with it, madam! I demand to know what remarks you have heard.'

'Well, I heard that you used to be very fond of Eustacia—nothing more than that, though dropped in a bit-by-bit way. You ought not to be angry!'

He observed that her eyes were brimming with tears. 'Well,' he said, 'there is nothing new in that, and of course I don't mean to be rough towards you, so you need not cry. Now, don't let us speak of the subject any more.'

And no more was said, Thomasin being glad enough of a reason for not mentioning Clym's visit to her that evening, and his story.

The Night of the Sixth of November

VII

Having resolved on flight Eustacia at times seemed anxious that something should happen to thwart her own intention. The only event that could really change her position was the appearance of Clym. The glory which had encircled him as her lover was departed now; yet some good simple quality of his would occasionally return to her memory and stir a momentary throb of hope that he would again present himself before her. But calmly considered it was not likely that such a severance as now existed would ever close up: she would have to live on as a painful object, isolated, and out of place. She had used to think of the heath alone as an uncongenial spot to be in; she felt it now of the whole world.

Towards evening on the sixth her determination to go away again revived. About four o'clock she packed up anew the few small articles she had brought in her flight from Alderworth, and also some belonging to her which had been left here: the whole formed a bundle not too large to be carried in her hand for a distance of a mile or two. The scene without grew darker; mud-coloured clouds bellied downwards from the sky like vast hammocks slung across it, and with the increase of night a stormy wind arose; but as yet there was no rain.

Eustacia could not rest indoors, having nothing more to do, and she wandered to and fro on the hill, not far from the house she was soon to leave. In these desultory ramblings she passed the cottage of Susan Nunsuch, a little lower down than her grandfather's. The door was ajar, and a riband of bright firelight fell over the ground without. As Eustacia crossed the firebeams she appeared for an instant as distinct as a figure in a phantasmagoria—a creature of light surrounded by an area of darkness: the moment passed, and she was absorbed in night again.

A woman who was sitting inside the cottage had seen and recognized her in that momentary irradiation. This was Susan herself, occupied in preparing a posset for her little boy, who, often ailing, was now seriously unwell. Susan dropped the spoon, shook her fist at the vanished figure, and then proceeded with her work in a musing, absent way.

At eight o'clock, the hour at which Eustacia had promised to signal to Wildeve if ever she signalled at all, she looked around the premises to learn if the coast was clear, went to the furze-rick, and pulled thence a long-stemmed bough of that fuel. This she carried to the corner of the bank, and, glancing behind to see if the shutters were all closed, she struck a light, and kindled the furze. When it was thoroughly ablaze Eustacia took it by the stem and waved it in the air above her head till it had burned itself out.

She was gratified, if gratification were possible to such a mood, by seeing a similar light in the vicinity of Wildeve's residence a minute or two later. Having agreed to keep watch at this hour every night, in case she should require assistance, this promptness proved how strictly he had held to his word. Four hours after the present time, that is, at midnight, he was to be ready to drive her to Budmouth, as prearranged.

Eustacia returned to the house. Supper having been got over she retired early, and sat in her bedroom waiting for the time to go by. The night being dark and threatening Captain Vye had not strolled out to gossip in any cottage or to call at the inn, as was sometimes his custom on these long autumn nights; and he sat sipping grog alone downstairs. About ten o'clock there was a knock at the door. When the servant opened it the rays of the candle fell upon the form of Fairway.

'I was a-forced to go to Lower Mistover to-night,' he said; 'and Mr. Yeobright asked me to leave this here on my way; but, faith, I put it in the lining of my hat, and thought no more about it till I got back and was hasping my gate before going to bed. So I have run back with it at once.'

He handed in a letter and went his way. The girl brought it to the captain, who found that it was directed to Eustacia. He turned it over and over, and fancied that the writing was her husband's, though he could not be sure. However, he decided to let her have it at once if possible, and took it upstairs for that purpose; but on reaching the door of her room and looking in at the keyhole he found there was no light within, the fact being that Eustacia, without undressing, had flung herself upon the bed, to rest and gather a little strength for her coming journey. Her grandfather concluded from what he saw that he ought not to disturb her; and descending again to the parlour he placed the letter on the mantelpiece to give it to her in the morning.

At eleven o'clock he went to bed himself, smoked for some time in his bedroom, put out his light at half-past eleven, and then, as was his invariable custom, pulled up the blind before getting into bed, that he might see which way the wind blew on opening his eyes in the morning, his bedroom window commanding a view of the flagstaff and vane. Just as he had lain down he was surprised to observe the white pole of the staff flash into existence like a streak of phosphorus drawn downwards across the shade of night without. Only one explanation met this—a light had been suddenly thrown upon the pole from the direction of the house. As everybody had retired to rest the old man felt it necessary to get out of bed, open the window softly, and look to the right and left. Eustacia's bedroom was lighted up, and it was the shine from her window which had lighted the pole. Wondering what had aroused her he remained undecided at the window, and was thinking of fetching the letter to slip it under her door, when he heard a slight brushing of garments on the partition dividing his room from the passage.

The captain concluded that Eustacia, feeling wakeful, had gone for a book, and would have dismissed the matter as unimportant if he had not also heard her distinctly weeping as she passed.

'She is thinking of that husband of hers,' he said to himself. 'Ah, the silly goose! she had no business to marry him. I wonder if that letter is really his?'

He arose, threw his boat-cloak round him, opened the door, and said, 'Eustacia!' There was no answer. 'Eustacia!' he repeated louder, 'there is a letter on the mantelpiece for you.'

But no response was made to this statement save an imaginary one from the wind, which seemed to gnaw at the corners of the house, and the stroke of a few drops of rain upon the windows.

He went on to the landing, and stood waiting nearly five minutes. Still she did not return. He went back for a light, and prepared to follow her; but first he looked into her bedroom. There, on the outside of the quilt, was the impression of her form, showing that the bed had not been opened; and, what was more significant, she had not taken her candlestick downstairs. He was now thoroughly alarmed; and hastily putting on his clothes he descended to the front door, which he himself had bolted and locked. It was now unfastened. There was no longer any doubt that Eustacia had left the house at this midnight hour; and whither could she have gone? To follow her was almost impossible. Had the dwelling stood in an ordinary road, two persons setting out, one in each direction, might have made sure of overtaking her; but it was a hopeless task to seek for anybody on a heath in the dark, the practicable directions for flight across it from any point being as numerous as the meridians radiating from the pole. Perplexed what to do he looked into the parlour, and was vexed to find that the letter still lay there untouched.

At half-past eleven, finding that the house was silent, Eustacia had lighted her candle, put on some warm outer wrappings, taken her bag in her hand, and, extinguishing the light again, descended the staircase. When she got into the outer air she found that it had begun to rain, and as she stood pausing at the door it increased, threatening to come on heavily. But having committed herself to this line of action there was no retreating for bad weather. Even the receipt of Clym's letter would not have stopped her now. The gloom of the night was funereal; all nature seemed clothed in crape. The spiky points of the fir trees behind the house rose into the sky like the turrets and pinnacles of an abbey. Nothing below the horizon was visible save a light which was still burning in the cottage of Susan Nunsuch.

Eustacia opened her umbrella and went out from the enclosure by the steps over the bank, after which she was beyond all danger of being perceived. Skirting the pool she followed the path towards Rainbarrow, occasionally stumbling over twisted furze-roots, tufts of rushes, or oozing lumps of fleshy fungi, which at this season lay scattered about the heath like the rotten liver and lungs of some colossal animal. The moon and stars were closed up by cloud and rain to the degree of extinction. It was a night which led the traveller's thoughts instinctively to dwell on nocturnal scenes of disaster in the chronicles of the world, on all that is terrible and dark in history and legend—the last plague of Egypt, the destruction of Sennacherib's host, the agony in Gethsemane.

Eustacia at length reached Rainbarrow, and stood still there to think. Never was harmony more perfect than that between the chaos of her mind and the chaos of the world without. A sudden recollection had flashed on her this moment: she had not money enough for undertaking a long journey. Amid the fluctuating sentiments of the day her unpractical mind had not dwelt on the necessity of being well-provided, and now that she thoroughly realized the conditions she sighed bitterly and ceased to stand erect, gradually crouching down under the umbrella as if she were drawn into the Barrow by a hand from beneath. Could it be that she was to remain a captive still? Money: she had never felt its value before. Even to efface herself from the country means were required. To ask Wildeve for pecuniary aid without allowing him to accompany her was impossible to a woman with a shadow of pride left in her: to fly as his mistress—and she knew that he loved her—was of the nature of humiliation.

Any one who had stood by now would have pitied her, not so much on account of her exposure to weather, and isolation from all of humanity except the mouldered remains inside the tumulus; but for that other form of misery which was denoted by the slightly rocking movement that her feelings imparted to her person. Extreme unhappiness weighed visibly upon her. Between the drippings of the rain from her umbrella to her mantle, from her mantle to the heather, from the heather to the earth, very similar sounds could be heard coming from her lips; and the tearfulness of the outer scene was repeated upon her face. The wings of her soul were broken by the cruel obstructiveness of all about her; and even had she seen herself in a promising way of getting to Budmouth, entering a steamer, and sailing to some opposite port, she would have been but little more buoyant, so fearfully malignant were other things. She uttered words aloud. When a woman in such a situation, neither old, deaf, crazed, nor whimsical, takes upon herself to sob and soliloquize aloud there is something grievous the matter.

'Can I go, can I go?' she moaned. 'He's not *great* enough for me to give myself to—he does not suffice for my desire! . . . If he had been a Saul or a Bonaparte—ah! But to break my marriage vow for him—it is too poor a luxury! . . . And I have no money to go alone! And if I could, what comfort to me? I must drag on next year, as I have dragged on this year, and the year after that as before. How I have tried and tried to be a splendid woman, and how destiny has been against me! . . . I do not deserve my lot!' she cried in a frenzy of bitter revolt. 'O, the cruelty of putting me into this ill-conceived world! I was capable of much; but I have been injured and blighted and crushed by things beyond my control! O, how hard it is of Heaven to devise such tortures for me, who have done no harm to Heaven at all?'

The distant light which Eustacia had cursorily observed in leaving the house came, as she had divined, from the cottage-window of Susan Nunsuch. What Eustacia did not divine was the occupation of the woman within at that moment. Susan's sight of her passing figure earlier in the evening, not five minutes after the sick boy's exclamation, 'Mother, I do feel so bad!' persuaded the matron that an evil influence was certainly exercised by Eustacia's propinquity.

On this account Susan did not go to bed as soon as the evening's work was over, as she would have done at ordinary times. To counteract the malign spell which she imagined poor Eustacia to be working, the boy's mother busied herself with a ghastly invention of superstition, calculated to bring powerlessness, atrophy, and annihilation on any human being against whom it was directed. It was a practice well known on Egdon at that date, and one that is not quite extinct at the present day.

She passed with her candle into an inner room, where, among other utensils, were two large brown pans, containing together perhaps a hundredweight of liquid honey, the produce of the bees during the foregoing summer. On a shelf over the pans was a smooth and solid yellow mass of a hemispherical form, consisting of beeswax from the same take of honey. Susan took down the lump, and, cutting off several thin slices, heaped them in an iron ladle, with which she returned to the living-room, and placed the vessel in the hot ashes of the fireplace. As soon as the wax had softened to the plasticity of dough she kneaded the pieces together. And now her face became more intent. She began moulding the wax; and it was evident from her manner of manipulation that she was endeavouring to give it some preconceived form. The form was human.

By warming and kneading, cutting and twisting, dismembering and re-joining the incipient image she had in about a quarter of an hour produced a shape which tolerably well resembled a woman, and was about six inches high. She laid it on the table to get cold and hard. Meanwhile she took the candle and went upstairs to where the little boy was lying.

'Did you notice, my dear, what Mrs. Eustacia wore this afternoon besides the dark dress?'

'A red ribbon round her neck.'

'Anything else?'

'No—except sandal-shoes.'

'A red ribbon and sandal-shoes,' she said to herself.

Mrs. Nunsuch went and searched till she found a fragment of the narrowest red ribbon, which she took downstairs and tied round the neck of the image. Then fetching ink and a quill from the rickety bureau by the window, she blackened the feet of the image to the extent presumably covered by shoes; and on the instep of each foot marked cross-lines in the shape taken by the sandal-strings of those days. Finally she tied a bit of black thread round the upper part of the head, in faint resemblance to a snood worn for confining the hair.

Susan held the object at arm's length and contemplated it with a satisfaction in which there was no smile. To anybody acquainted with the inhabitants of Egdon Heath the image would have suggested Eustacia Yeobright.

From her work-basket in the window-seat the woman took a paper of pins, of the old long and yellow sort, whose heads were disposed to come off at their first usage. These she began to thrust into the image in all directions, with apparently excruciating energy. Probably as many as fifty were thus inserted, some into the head of the wax model, some into the shoulders, some into the trunk, some upwards through the soles of the feet, till the figure was completely permeated with pins.

She turned to the fire. It had been of turf; and though the high heap of ashes which turf fires produce was somewhat dark and dead on the outside, upon raking it abroad with the shovel the inside of the mass showed a glow of red heat. She took a few pieces of fresh turf from the chimney-corner and built them together over the flow, upon which the fire brightened. Seizing with the tongs the image that she had made of Eustacia, she held it in the heat, and watched it as it began to waste slowly away. And while she stood thus engaged there came from between her lips a murmur of words.

It was a strange jargon—the Lord's Prayer repeated backwards—the incantation usual in proceedings for obtaining unhallowed assistance against an enemy. Susan uttered the lugubrious discourse three times slowly, and when it was completed the image had considerably diminished. As the wax dropped into the fire a long flame arose from the spot, and curling its tongue round the figure eat still further into its substance. A pin occasionally dropped with the wax, and the embers heated it red as it lay.

Rain, Darkness, and Anxious Wanderers

VIII

While the effigy of Eustacia was melting to nothing, and the fair woman herself was standing on Rainbarrow, her soul in an abyss of desolation seldom plumbed by one so young, Yeobright sat lonely at Blooms-End. He had fulfilled his word to Thomasin by sending off Fairway with the letter to his wife, and now waited with increased impatience for some sound or signal of her return. Were Eustacia still at Mistover the very least he expected was that she would send him back a reply to-night by the same hand; though, to leave all to her inclination, he had cautioned Fairway not to ask for an answer. If one were handed to him he was to bring it immediately; if not, he was to go straight home without troubling to come round to Blooms-End again that night.

But secretly Clym had a more pleasing hope. Eustacia might possibly decline to use her pen—it was rather her way to work silently—and surprise him by appearing at his door. How fully her mind was made up to do otherwise he did not know.

To Clym's regret it began to rain and blow hard as the evening advanced. The wind rasped and scraped at the corners of the house, and filliped the eavesdroppings like peas against the panes. He walked restlessly about the untenanted rooms, stopping strange noises in windows and doors by jamming splinters of wood into the casements and crevices, and pressing together the lead-work of the quarries where it had become loosened from the glass. It was one of those nights when cracks in the walls of old churches widen, when ancient stains on the ceilings of decayed manor-houses are renewed and enlarged from the size of a man's hand to an area of many feet. The little gate in the palings before his dwelling continually opened and clicked together again, but when he looked out eagerly nobody was there; it was as if invisible shapes of the dead were passing in on their way to visit him.

Between ten and eleven o'clock, finding that neither Fairway nor anybody else came to him, he retired to rest, and despite his anxieties soon fell asleep. His sleep, however, was not very sound, by reason of the expectancy he had given way to, and he was easily awakened by a knocking which began at the door about an hour after. Clym arose and looked out of the window. Rain was still falling heavily, the whole expanse of heath before him emitting a subdued hiss under the downpour. It was too dark to see anything at all.

'Who's there?' he cried.

Light footsteps shifted their position in the porch, and he could just distinguish in a plaintive female voice the words, 'O Clym, come down and let me in!'

He flushed hot with agitation. 'Surely it is Eustacia!' he murmured. If so, she had indeed come to him unawares.

He hastily got a light, dressed himself, and went down. On his flinging open the door the rays of the candle fell upon a woman closely wrapped up, who at once came forward.

'Thomasin!' he exclaimed in an indescribable tone of disappointment. 'It is Thomasin, and on such a night as this! O, where is Eustacia?'

Thomasin it was, wet, frightened, and panting.

'Eustacia? I don't know, Clym; but I can think,' she said with much perturbation. 'Let me come in and rest—I will explain this. There is a great trouble brewing—my husband and Eustacia!'

'What, what?'

'I think my husband is going to leave me or do something dreadful—I don't know what—Clym, will you go see? I have nobody to help me but you! Eustacia has not yet come home?'

'No.'

She went on breathlessly: 'Then they are going to run off together! He came indoors to-night about eight o'clock and said in an off-hand way, "Tamsie, I have just found that I must go a journey." "When?" I said. "To-night," he said. "Where?" I asked him. "I cannot tell you at present," he said; "I shall be back again to-morrow." He then went and busied himself in looking up his things, and took no notice of me at all. I expected to see him start, but he did not, and then it came to be ten o'clock, when he said, "You had better go to bed." I didn't know what to do, and I went to bed. I believe he thought I fell asleep, for half an hour after that he came up and unlocked the oak chest we keep money in when we have much in the house and took out a roll of something which I believe was bank-notes, though I was not aware that he had 'em there. These he must have got from the bank when he went there the other day. What does he want bank-notes for, if he is only going off for a day? When he had gone down I thought of Eustacia, and how he had met her the night before—I know he did meet her, Clym, for I followed him part of the way; but I did not like to tell you when you called, and so make you think ill of him, as I did not think it was so serious. Then I could not stay in bed: I got up and dressed myself, and when I heard him out in the stable I thought I would come and tell you. So I came downstairs without any noise and slipped out.'

'Then he was not absolutely gone when you left?'

'No. Will you, dear Cousin Clym, go and try to persuade him not to go? He takes no notice of what I say, and puts me off with the story of his going on a journey, and will be home to-morrow, and all that; but I don't believe it. I think you could influence him.'

'I'll go,' said Clym. 'O, Eustacia!'

Thomasin carried in her arms a large bundle; and having by this time seated herself she began to unroll it, when a baby appeared as the kernel to the husks—dry, warm, and unconscious of travel or rough weather. Thomasin briefly kissed the baby, and then found time to begin crying as she said, 'I brought baby, for I was afraid what might happen to her. I suppose it will be her death, but I couldn't leave her with Rachel!'

Clym hastily put together the logs on the hearth, raked abroad the embers, which were scarcely yet extinct, and blew up a flame with the bellows.

'Dry yourself,' he said. 'I'll go and get some more wood.'

'No, no—don't stay for that. I'll make up the fire. Will you go at once—please will you?'

Yeobright ran upstairs to finish dressing himself. While he was gone another rapping came to the door. This time there was no delusion that it might be Eustacia's: the footsteps just preceding it had been heavy and slow. Yeobright, thinking it might possibly be Fairway with a note in answer, descended again and opened the door.

'Captain Vye?' he said to a dripping figure.

'Is my grand-daughter here?' said the captain.

'No.'

'Then where is she?'

'I don't know.'

'But you ought to know—you are her husband.'

'Only in name apparently,' said Clym with rising excitement. 'I believe she means to elope to-night with Wildeve. I am just going to look to it.'

'Well, she has left my house; she left about half an hour ago. Who's sitting there?'

'My cousin Thomasin.'

The captain bowed in a preoccupied way to her. 'I only hope it is no worse than an elopement,' he said.

'Worse? What's worse than the worst a wife can do?'

'Well, I have been told a strange tale. Before starting in search of her I called up Charley, my stable-lad. I missed my pistols the other day.'

'Pistols?'

'He said at the time that he took them down to clean. He has now owned that he took them because he saw Eustacia looking curiously at them; and she afterwards owned to him that she was thinking of taking her life, but bound him to secrecy, and promised never to think of such a thing again. I hardly suppose she will ever have bravado enough to use one of them; but it shows what has been lurking in her mind; and people who think of that sort of thing once think of it again.'

'Where are the pistols?'

'Safely locked up. O no, she won't touch them again. But there are more ways of letting out life than through a bullet-hole. What did you quarrel about so bitterly with her to drive her to all this? You must have treated her badly indeed. Well, I was always against the marriage, and I was right.'

'Are you going with me?' said Yeobright, paying no attention to the captain's latter remark. 'If so I can tell you what we quarrelled about as we walk along.'

'Where to?'

'To Wildeve's—that was her destination, depend upon it.'

Thomasin here broke in, still weeping: 'He said he was only going on a sudden short journey; but if so why did he want so much money? O, Clym, what do you think will happen? I am afraid that you, my poor baby, will soon have no father left to you!'

'I am off now,' said Yeobright, stepping into the porch.

'I would fain go with 'ee,' said the old man doubtfully. 'But I begin to be afraid that my legs will hardly carry me there such a night as this. I am not so young as I was. If they are interrupted in their flight she will be sure to come back to me, and I ought to be at the house to receive her. But be it as 'twill I can't walk to the Quiet Woman, and that's an end on't. I'll go straight home.'

'It will perhaps be best,' said Clym. 'Thomasin, dry yourself, and be as comfortable as you can.'

With this he closed the door upon her, and left the house in company with Captain Vye, who parted from him outside the gate, taking the middle path, which led to Mistover. Clym crossed by the right-hand track towards the inn.

Thomasin, being left alone, took off some of her wet garments, carried the baby upstairs to Clym's bed, and then came down to the sitting-room again, where she made a larger fire, and began drying herself. The fire soon flared up the chimney, giving the room an appearance of comfort that was doubled by contrast with the drumming of the storm without, which snapped at the window-panes and breathed into the chimney strange low utterances that seemed to be the prologue to some tragedy.

But the least part of Thomasin was in the house, for her heart being at ease about the little girl upstairs she was mentally following Clym on his journey. Having indulged in this imaginary peregrination for some considerable interval, she became impressed with a sense of the intolerable slowness of time. But she sat on. The moment then came when she could scarcely sit longer; and it was like a satire on her patience to remember that Clym could hardly have reached the inn as yet. At last she went to the baby's bedside. The child was sleeping soundly; but her imagination of possibly disastrous events at her home, the predominance within her of the unseen over the seen, agitated her beyond endurance. She could not refrain from going down and opening the door. The rain still continued, the candlelight falling upon the nearest drops and making glistening darts of them as they descended across the throng of invisible ones behind. To plunge into that medium was to plunge into water slightly diluted with air. But the difficulty of returning to her house at this moment made her all the more desirous of doing so: anything was better than suspense. 'I have come here well enough,' she said, 'and why shouldn't I go back again? It is a mistake for me to be away.'

She hastily fetched the infant, wrapped it up, cloaked herself as before, and shovelling the ashes over the fire, to prevent accidents, went into the open air. Pausing first to put the door-key in its old place behind the shutter, she resolutely turned her face to the confronting pile of firmamental darkness beyond the palings, and stepped into its midst. But Thomasin's imagination being so actively engaged elsewhere, the night and the weather had for her no terror beyond that of their actual discomfort and difficulty.

She was soon ascending Blooms-End valley and traversing the undulations on the side of the hill. The noise of the wind over the heath was shrill, and as if it whistled for joy at finding a night so congenial as this. Sometimes the path led her to hollows between thickets of tall and dripping bracken, dead, though not yet prostrate, which enclosed her like a pool. When they were more than usually tall she lifted the baby to the top of her head, that it might be out of the reach of their drenching fronds. On higher ground, where the wind was brisk and sustained, the rain flew in a level flight without sensible descent, so that it was beyond all power to imagine the remoteness of the point at which it left the bosoms of the clouds. Here self-defence was impossible, and individual drops stuck into her like the arrows into Saint Sebastian. She was enabled to avoid puddles by the nebulous paleness which signified their presence, though beside anything less dark than the heath they themselves would have appeared as blackness.

Yet in spite of all this Thomasin was not sorry that she had started. To her there were not, as to Eustacia, demons in the air, and malice in every bush and bough. The drops which lashed her face were not scorpions, but prosy rain; Egdon in the mass was no monster whatever, but impersonal open ground. Her fears of the place were rational, her dislikes of its worst moods reasonable. At this time it was in her view a windy, wet place, in which a person might experience much discomfort, lose the path without care, and possibly catch cold.

If the path is well known the difficulty at such times of keeping therein is not altogether great, from its familiar feel to the feet; but once lost it is irrecoverable. Owing to her baby, who somewhat impeded Thomasin's view forward and distracted her mind, she did at last lose the track. This mishap occurred when she was descending an open slope about two-thirds home. Instead of attempting, by wandering hither and thither, the hopeless task of finding such a mere thread, she went straight on, trusting for guidance to her general knowledge of the contours, which was scarcely surpassed by Clym's or by that of the heath-croppers themselves.

At length Thomasin reached a hollow and began to discern through the rain a faint blotted radiance, which presently assumed the oblong form of an open door. She knew that no house stood hereabouts, and was soon aware of the nature of the door by its height above the ground.

'Why, it is Diggory Venn's van, surely!' she said.

A certain secluded spot near Rainbarrow was, she knew, often Venn's chosen centre when staying in this neighbourhood; and she guessed at once that she had stumbled upon this mysterious retreat. The question arose in her mind whether or not she should ask him to guide her into the path. In her anxiety to reach home she decided that she would appeal to him, notwithstanding the strangeness of appearing before his eyes at this place and season. But when, in pursuance of this resolve, Thomasin reached the van and looked in she found it to be untenanted; though there was no doubt that it was the reddleman's. The fire was burning in the stove, the lantern hung from the nail. Round the doorway the floor was merely sprinkled with rain, and not saturated, which told her that the door had not long been opened.

While she stood uncertainly looking in Thomasin heard a footstep advancing from the darkness behind her; and turning, beheld the well-known form in corduroy, lurid from head to foot, the lantern beams falling upon him through an intervening gauze of raindrops.

'I thought you went down the slope,' he said, without noticing her face. 'How do you come back here again?'

'Diggory?' said Thomasin faintly.

'Who are you?' said Venn, still unperceiving. 'And why were you crying so just now?'

'O, Diggory! don't you know me?' said she. 'But of course you don't, wrapped up like this. What do you mean? I have not been crying here, and I have not been here before.'

Venn then came nearer till he could see the illuminated side of her form.

'Mrs. Wildeve!' he exclaimed, starting. 'What a time for us to meet! And the baby too! What dreadful thing can have brought you out on such a night as this?'

She could not immediately answer; and without asking her permission he hopped into his van, took her by the arm, and drew her up after him.

'What is it?' he continued when they stood within.

'I have lost my way coming from Blooms-End, and I am in a great hurry to get home. Please show me as quickly as you can! It is so silly of me not to know Egdon better, and I cannot think how I came to lose the path. Show me quickly, Diggory, please.'

'Yes, of course. I will go with 'ee. But you came to me before this, Mrs. Wildeve?'

'I only came this minute.'

'That's strange. I was lying down here asleep about five minutes ago, with the door shut to keep out the weather, when the brushing of a woman's clothes over the heath-bushes just outside woke me up (for I don't sleep heavy), and at the same time I heard a sobbing or crying from the same woman. I opened my door and held out my lantern, and just as far as the light would reach I saw a woman: she turned her head when the light sheened on her, and then hurried on downhill. I hung up the lantern, and was curious enough to pull on my things and dog her a few steps, but I could see nothing of her any more. That was where I had been when you came up; and when I saw you I thought you were the same one.'

'Perhaps it was one of the heath-folk going home?'

'No, it couldn't be. 'Tis too late. The noise of her gown over the he'th was of a whistling sort that nothing but silk will make.'

'It wasn't I, then. My dress is not silk, you see. . . . Are we anywhere in a line between Mistover and the inn?'

'Well, yes; not far out.'

'Ah, I wonder if it was she! Diggory, I must go at once!'

She jumped down from the van before he was aware, when Venn unhooked the lantern and leaped down after her. 'I'll take the baby, ma'am,' he said. 'You must be tired out by the weight.'

Thomasin hesitated a moment, and then delivered the baby into Venn's hands. 'Don't squeeze her, Diggory,' she said, 'or hurt her little arm; and keep the cloak close over her like this, so that the rain may not drop in her face.'

'I will,' said Venn earnestly. 'As if I could hurt anything belonging to you!'

'I only meant accidentally,' said Thomasin.

'The baby is dry enough, but you are pretty wet,' said the reddleman when, in closing the door of his cart to padlock it, he noticed on the floor a ring of water-drops where her cloak had hung from her.

Thomasin followed him as he wound right and left to avoid the larger bushes, stopping occasionally and covering the lantern, while he looked over his shoulder to gain some idea of the position of Rainbarrow above them, which it was necessary to keep directly behind their backs to preserve a proper course.

'You are sure the rain does not fall upon baby?'

'Quite sure. May I ask how old he is, ma'am?'

'He!' said Thomasin reproachfully. 'Anybody can see better than that in a moment. She is nearly two months old. How far is it now to the inn?'

'A little over a quarter of a mile.'

'Will you walk a little faster?'

'I was afraid you could not keep up.'

'I am very anxious to get there. Ah, there is a light from the window!'

''Tis not from the window. That's a gig-lamp, to the best of my belief.'

'O!' said Thomasin in despair. 'I wish I had been there sooner—give me the baby, Diggory—you can go back now.'

'I must go all the way,' said Venn. 'There is a quag between us and that light, and you will walk into it up to your neck unless I take you round.'

'But the light is at the inn, and there is no quag in front of that.'

'No, the light is below the inn some two or three hundred yards.'

'Never mind,' said Thomasin hurriedly. 'Go towards the light, and not towards the inn.'

'Yes,' answered Venn, swerving round in obedience; and, after a pause, 'I wish you would tell me what this great trouble is. I think you have proved that I can be trusted.'

'There are some things that cannot be—cannot be told to——' And then her heart rose into her throat, and she could say no more.

Sights and Sounds Draw the Wanderers Together

IX

Having seen Eustacia's signal from the hill at eight o'clock, Wildeve immediately prepared to assist her in her flight, and, as he hoped, accompany her. He was somewhat perturbed, and his manner of informing Thomasin that he was going on a journey was in itself sufficient to rouse her suspicions. When she had gone to bed he collected the few articles he would require, and went upstairs to the money-chest, whence he took a tolerably bountiful sum in notes, which had been advanced to him on the property he was so soon to have in possession, to defray expenses incidental to the removal.

He then went to the stable and coach-house to assure himself that the horse, gig, and harness were in a fit condition for a long drive. Nearly half an hour was spent thus, and on returning to the house Wildeve had no thought of Thomasin being anywhere but in bed. He had told the stable-lad not to stay up, leading the boy to understand that his departure would be at three or four in the morning; for this, though an exceptional hour, was less strange than midnight, the time actually agreed on, the packet from Budmouth sailing between one and two.

At last all was quiet, and he had nothing to do but to wait. By no effort could he shake off the oppression of spirits which he had experienced ever since his last meeting with Eustacia, but he hoped there was that in his situation which money could cure. He had persuaded himself that to act not ungenerously towards his gentle wife by settling on her the half of his property, and with chivalrous devotion towards another and greater woman by sharing her fate, was possible. And though he meant to adhere to Eustacia's instructions to the letter, to deposit her where she wished and to leave her, should that be her will, the spell that she had cast over him intensified, and his heart was beating fast in the anticipated futility of such commands in the face of a mutual wish that they should throw in their lot together.

He would not allow himself to dwell long upon these conjectures, maxims, and hopes, and at twenty minutes to twelve he again went softly to the stable, harnessed the horse, and lit the lamps; whence, taking the horse by the head, he led him with the covered car out of the yard to a spot by the roadside some quarter of a mile below the inn.

Here Wildeve waited, slightly sheltered from the driving rain by a high bank that had been cast up at this place. Along the surface of the road where lit by the lamps the loosened gravel and small stones scudded and clicked together before the wind, which, leaving them in heaps, plunged into the heath and boomed across the bushes into darkness. Only one sound rose above this din of weather, and that was the roaring of a ten-hatch weir[4] to the southward, from a river in the meads which formed the boundary of the heath in this direction.

He lingered on in perfect stillness till he began to fancy that the midnight hour must have struck. A very strong doubt had arisen in his mind if Eustacia would venture down the hill in such weather; yet knowing her nature he felt that she might. 'Poor thing! 'tis like her ill-luck,' he murmured.

At length he turned to the lamp and looked at his watch. To his surprise it was nearly a quarter past midnight. He now wished that he had driven up the circuitous road to Mistover, a plan not adopted because of the enormous length of the route in proportion to that of the pedestrian's path down the open hillside, and the consequent increase of labour for the horse.

At this moment a footstep approached; but the light of the lamp being in a different direction the comer was not visible. The step paused, then came on again.

'Eustacia?' said Wildeve.

The person came forward, and the light fell upon the form of Clym, glistening with wet, whom Wildeve immediately recognized; but Wildeve, who stood behind the lamp, was not at once recognized by Yeobright.

He stopped as if in doubt whether this waiting vehicle could have anything to do with the flight of his wife or not. The sight of Yeobright at once banished Wildeve's sober feelings, who saw him again as the deadly rival from whom Eustacia was to be kept at all hazards. Hence Wildeve did not speak, in the hope that Clym would pass by without particular inquiry.

While they both hung thus in hesitation a dull sound became audible above the storm and wind. Its origin was unmistakable—it was the fall of a body into the stream in the adjoining mead, apparently at a point near the weir.

Both started. 'Good God! can it be she?' said Clym.

'Why should it be she?' said Wildeve, in his alarm forgetting that he had hitherto screened himself.

'Ah!—that's you, you traitor, is it?' cried Yeobright. 'Why should it be she? Because last week she would have put an end to her life if she had been able. She ought to have been watched! Take one of the lamps and come with me.'

4. A dam to retain the water and regulate its flow.

Yeobright seized the one on his side and hastened on; Wildeve did not wait to unfasten the other, but followed at once along the meadow-track to the weir, a little in the rear of Clym.

Shadwater Weir had at its foot a large circular pool, fifty feet in diameter, into which the water flowed through ten huge hatches, raised and lowered by a winch and cogs in the ordinary manner. The sides of the pool were of masonry, to prevent the water from washing away the bank; but the force of the stream in winter was sometimes such as to undermine the retaining wall and precipitate it into the hole. Clym reached the hatches, the framework of which was shaken to its foundations by the velocity of the current. Nothing but the froth of the waves could be discerned in the pool below. He got upon the plank bridge over the race, and holding to the rail, that the wind might not blow him off, crossed to the other side of the river. There he leant over the wall and lowered the lamp, only to behold the vortex formed at the curl of the returning current.

Wildeve meanwhile had arrived on the former side, and the light from Yeobright's lamp shed a flecked and agitated radiance across the weir-pool, revealing to the ex-engineer the tumbling courses of the currents from the hatches above. Across this gashed and puckered mirror a dark body was slowly borne by one of the backward currents.

'Oh, my darling!' exclaimed Wildeve in an agonized voice; and, without showing sufficient presence of mind even to throw off his great-coat, he leaped into the boiling caldron.

Yeobright could now also discern the floating body, though but indistinctly; and imagining from Wildeve's plunge that there was life to be saved he was about to leap after. Bethinking himself of a wiser plan he placed the lamp against a post to make it stand upright, and running round to the lower part of the pool, where there was no wall, he sprang in and boldly waded upwards towards the deeper portion. Here he was taken off his legs, and in swimming was carried round into the centre of the basin, where he perceived Wildeve struggling.

While these hasty actions were in progress here, Venn and Thomasin had been toiling through the lower corner of the heath in the direction of the light. They had not been near enough to the river to hear the plunge, but they saw the removal of the carriage-lamp, and watched its motion into the mead. As soon as they reached the car and horse Venn guessed that something new was amiss, and hastened to follow in the course of the moving light. Venn walked faster than Thomasin, and came to the weir alone.

The lamp placed against the post by Clym still shone across the water, and the reddleman observed something floating motionless.

Being encumbered with the infant he ran back to meet Thomasin.

'Take the baby, please, Mrs. Wildeve,' he said hastily. 'Run home with her, call the stable-lad, and make him send down to me any men who may be living near. Somebody has fallen into the weir.'

Thomasin took the child and ran. When she came to the covered car the horse, though fresh from the stable, was standing perfectly still, as if conscious of misfortune. She saw for the first time whose it was. She nearly fainted, and would have been unable to proceed another step but that the necessity of preserving the little girl from harm nerved her to an amazing self-control. In this agony of suspense she entered the house, put the baby in a place of safety, woke the lad and the female domestic, and ran out to give the alarm at the nearest cottage.

Diggory, having returned to the brink of the pool, observed that the small upper hatches or floats were withdrawn. He found one of these lying upon the grass, and taking it under one arm, and with his lantern in his hand, entered at the bottom of the pool as Clym had done. As soon as he began to be in deep water he flung himself across the hatch; thus supported he was able to keep afloat as long as he chose, holding the lantern aloft with his disengaged hand. Propelled by his feet he steered round and round the pool, ascending each time by one of the back streams and descending in the middle of the current.

At first he could see nothing. Then amidst the glistening of the whirlpools and the white clots of foam he distinguished a woman's bonnet floating alone. His search was now under the left wall, when something came to the surface almost close beside him. It was not, as he had expected, a woman, but a man. The reddleman put the ring of the lantern between his teeth, seized the floating man by the collar, and, holding on to the hatch with his remaining arm, struck out into the strongest race, by which the unconscious man, the hatch, and himself were carried down the stream. As soon as Venn found his feet dragging over the pebbles of the shallower part below he secured his footing and waded towards the brink. There, where the water stood at about the height of his waist, he flung away the hatch, and attempted to drag forth the man. This was a matter of great difficulty, and he found as the reason that the legs of the unfortunate stranger were tightly embraced by the arms of another man, who had hitherto been entirely beneath the surface.

At this moment his heart bounded to hear footsteps running towards him, and two men, roused by Thomasin, appeared at the brink above. They ran to where Venn was, and helped him in lifting out the apparently drowned persons, separating them, and laying them out upon the grass. Venn turned the light upon their faces. The one who had been uppermost was Yeobright; he who had been completely submerged was Wildeve.

'Now we must search the hole again,' said Venn. 'A woman is in there somewhere. Get a pole.'

One of the men went to the foot-bridge and tore off the hand-rail. The reddleman and the two others then entered the water together from below as before, and with their united force probed the pool forwards to where it sloped down to its central depth. Venn was not mistaken in supposing that any person who had sunk for the last time would be washed down to this point, for when they had examined to about half-way across something impeded their thrust.

'Pull it forward,' said Venn, and they raked it in with the pole till it was close to their feet.

Venn vanished under the stream, and came up with an armful of wet drapery enclosing a woman's cold form, which was all that remained of the desperate Eustacia.

When they reached the bank there stood Thomasin, in a stress of grief, bending over the two unconscious ones who already lay there. The horse and car were brought to the nearest point in the road, and it was the work of a few minutes only to place the three in the vehicle, Venn led on the horse, supporting Thomasin upon his arm, and the two men followed, till they reached the inn.

The woman who had been shaken out of her sleep by Thomasin had hastily dressed herself and lighted a fire, the other servant being left to snore on in peace at the back of the house. The insensible forms of Eustacia, Clym, and Wildeve were then brought in and laid on the carpet, with their feet to the fire, when such restorative processes as could be thought of were adopted at once, the stableman being in the meantime sent for a doctor. But there seemed to be not a whiff of life left in either of the bodies. Then Thomasin, whose stupor of grief had been thrust off awhile by frantic action, applied a bottle of hartshorn to Clym's nostrils, having tried it in vain upon the other two. He sighed.

'Clym's alive!' she exclaimed.

He soon breathed distinctly, and again and again did she attempt to revive her husband by the same means; but Wildeve gave no sigh. There was too much reason to think that he and Eustacia both were for ever beyond the reach of stimulating perfumes. Their exertions did not relax till the doctor arrived, when, one by one, the senseless three were taken upstairs and put into warm beds.

Venn soon felt himself relieved from further attendance, and went to the door, scarcely able yet to realize the strange catastrophe that had befallen the family in which he took so great an interest. Thomasin surely would be broken down by the sudden and overwhelming nature of this event. No firm and sensible Mrs. Yeobright lived now to support the gentle girl through the ordeal; and, whatever an unimpassioned spectator might think of her loss of such a husband as Wildeve, there could be no doubt that for the moment she was distracted and horrified by the blow. As for himself, not being privileged to go to her and comfort her, he saw no reason for waiting longer in a house where he remained only as a stranger.

He returned across the heath to his van. The fire was not yet out, and everything remained as he had left it. Venn now bethought himself of his clothes, which were saturated with water to the weight of lead. He changed them, spread them before the fire, and lay down to sleep. But it was more than he could do to rest here while excited by a vivid imagination of the turmoil they were in at the house he had quitted, and, blaming himself for coming away, he dressed in another suit, locked up the door, and again hastened across to the inn. Rain was still falling heavily when he entered the kitchen. A bright fire was shining from the hearth, and two women were bustling about, one of whom was Olly Dowden.

'Well, how is it going on now?' said Venn in a whisper.

'Mr. Yeobright is better; but Mrs. Yeobright and Mr. Wildeve are dead and cold. The doctor says they were quite gone before they were out of the water.'

'Ah! I thought as much when I hauled 'em up. And Mrs. Wildeve?'

'She is as well as can be expected. The doctor had her put between blankets, for she was almost as wet as they that had been in the river, poor young thing. You don't seem very dry, reddleman.'

'O, 'tis not much. I have changed my things. This is only a little dampness I've got coming through the rain again.'

'Stand by the fire. Mis'ess says you be to have whatever you want, and she was sorry when she was told that you'd gone away.'

Venn drew near to the fireplace, and looked into the flames in an absent mood. The steam came from his leggings and ascended the chimney with the smoke, while he thought of those who were upstairs. Two were corpses, one had barely escaped the jaws of death, another was sick and a widow. The last occasion on which he had lingered by that fireplace was when the raffle was in progress; when Wildeve was alive and well; Thomasin active and smiling in the next room; Yeobright and Eustacia just made husband and wife, and Mrs. Yeobright living at Blooms-End. It had seemed at that time that the then position of affairs was good for at least twenty years to come. Yet, of all the circle, he himself was the only one whose situation had not materially changed.

While he ruminated a footstep descended the stairs. It was the nurse, who brought in her hand a rolled mass of wet paper. The woman was so engrossed with her occupation that she hardly saw Venn. She took from a cupboard some pieces of twine, which she strained across the fireplace, tying the end of each piece to the firedog, previously pulled forward for the purpose, and, unrolling the wet papers, she began pinning them one by one to the strings in a manner of clothes on a line.

'What be they?' said Venn.

'Poor master's bank-notes,' she answered. 'They were found in his pocket when they undressed him.'

'Then he was not coming back again for some time?' said Venn.

'That we shall never know,' said she.

Venn was loth to depart, for all on earth that interested him lay under this roof. As nobody in the house had any more sleep that night, except the two who slept for ever, there was no reason why he should not remain. So he retired into the niche of the fireplace where he had used to sit, and there he continued, watching the steam from the double row of bank-notes as they waved backwards and forwards in the draught of the chimney till their flaccidity was changed to dry crispness throughout. Then the woman came and unpinned them, and, folding them together, carried the handful upstairs. Presently the doctor appeared from above with the look of a man who could do no more, and, pulling on his gloves, went out of the house, the trotting of his horse soon dying away upon the road.

At four o'clock there was a gentle knock at the door. It was from Charley, who had been sent by Captain Vye to inquire if anything had been heard of Eustacia. The girl who admitted him looked in his face as if she did not know what answer to return, and showed him in to where Venn was seated, saying to the reddleman, 'Will you tell him, please?'

Venn told. Charley's only utterance was a feeble, indistinct sound. He stood quite still; then he burst out spasmodically, 'I shall see her once more?'

'I dare say you may see her,' said Diggory gravely. 'But hadn't you better run and tell Captain Vye?'

'Yes, yes. Only I do hope I shall see her just once again.'

'You shall,' said a low voice behind; and starting round they beheld by the dim light a thin, pallid, almost spectral form, wrapped in a blanket, and looking like Lazarus coming from the tomb.

It was Yeobright. Neither Venn nor Charley spoke, and Clym continued: 'You shall see her. There will be time enough to tell the captain when it gets daylight. You would like to see her too—would you not, Diggory? She looks very beautiful now.'

Venn assented by rising to his feet, and with Charley he followed Clym to the foot of the staircase, where he took off his boots; Charley did the same. They followed Yeobright upstairs to the landing, where there was a candle burning, which Yeobright took in his hand, and with it led the way into an adjoining room. Here he went to the bedside and folded back the sheet.

They stood silently looking upon Eustacia, who, as she lay there still in death, eclipsed all her living phases. Pallor did not include all the quality of her complexion, which seemed more than whiteness; it was almost light. The expression of her finely carved mouth was pleasant, as if a sense of dignity had just compelled her to leave off speaking. Eternal rigidity had seized upon it in a momentary transition between fervour and resignation. Her black hair was looser now than either of them had ever seen it before, and surrounded her brow like a forest. The stateliness of look which had been almost too marked for a dweller in a country domicile had at last found an artistically happy background.

Nobody spoke, till at length Clym covered her and turned aside. 'Now come here,' he said.

They went to a recess in the same room, and there, on a smaller bed, lay another figure—Wildeve. Less repose was visible in his face than in Eustacia's, but the same luminous youthfulness overspread it, and the least sympathetic observer would have felt at sight of him now that he was born for a higher destiny than this. The only sign upon him of his recent struggle for life was in his finger-tips, which were worn and scarified in his dying endeavours to obtain a hold on the face of the weir-wall.

Yeobright's manner had been so quiet, he had uttered so few syllables since his reappearance, that Venn imagined him resigned. It was only when they had left the room and stood upon the landing that the true state of his mind was apparent. Here he said, with a wild smile, inclining his head towards the chamber in which Eustacia lay, 'She is the second woman I have killed this year. I was a great cause of my mother's death; and I am the chief cause of hers.'

'How?' said Venn.

'I spoke cruel words to her, and she left my house. I did not invite her back till it was too late. It is I who ought to have drowned myself. It would have been a charity to the living had the river overwhelmed me and borne her up. But I cannot die. Those who ought to have lived lie dead; and here am I alive!'

'But you can't charge yourself with crimes in that way,' said

Venn. 'You may as well say that the parents be the cause of a murder by the child, for without the parents the child would never have been begot.'

'Yes, Venn, that is very true; but you don't know all the circumstances. If it had pleased God to put an end to me it would have been a good thing for all. But I am getting used to the horror of my existence. They say that a time comes when men laugh at misery through long acquaintance with it. Surely that time will soon come to me!'

'Your aim has always been good,' said Venn. 'Why should you say such desperate things?'

'No, they are not desperate. They are only hopeless; and my great regret is that for what I have done no man or law can punish me!'

BOOK SIXTH: AFTERCOURSES

The Inevitable Movement Onward

I

The story of the deaths of Eustacia and Wildeve was told throughout Egdon, and far beyond, for many weeks and months. All the known incidents of their love were enlarged, distorted, touched up, and modified, till the original reality bore but a slight resemblance to the counterfeit presentation by surrounding tongues. Yet, upon the whole, neither the man nor the woman lost dignity by sudden death. Misfortune had struck them gracefully, cutting off their erratic histories with a catastrophic dash, instead of, as with many, attenuating each life to an uninteresting meagreness, through long years of wrinkles, neglect, and decay.

On those most nearly concerned the effect was somewhat different. Strangers who had heard of many such cases now merely heard of one more; but immediately where a blow falls no previous imaginings amount to appreciable preparation for it. The very suddenness of her bereavement dulled, to some extent, Thomasin's feelings; yet, irrationally enough, a consciousness that the husband she had lost ought to have been a better man did not lessen her mourning at all. On the contrary, this fact seemed at first to set off the dead husband in his young wife's eyes, and to be the necessary cloud to the rainbow.

But the horrors of the unknown had passed. Vague misgivings about her future as a deserted wife were at an end. The worst had once been matter of trembling conjecture; it was now matter of reason only, a limited badness. Her chief interest, the little Eustacia, still remained. There was humility in her grief, no defiance in her attitude; and when this is the case a shaken spirit is apt to be stilled.

Could Thomasin's mournfulness now and Eustacia's serenity during life have been reduced to common measure, they would have touched the same mark nearly. But Thomasin's former brightness made shadow of that which in a sombre atmosphere was light itself.

The spring came and calmed her; the summer came and soothed her; the autumn arrived, and she began to be comforted, for her little girl was strong and happy, growing in size and knowledge every day. Outward events flattered Thomasin not a little. Wildeve had died intestate, and she and the child were his only relatives. When administration had been granted, all the debts paid, and the residue of her husband's uncle's property had come into her hands, it was found that the sum waiting to be invested for her own and the child's benefit was little less than ten thousand pounds.

Where should she live? The obvious place was Blooms-End. The old rooms, it is true, were not much higher than the between-decks of a frigate, necessitating a sinking in the floor under the new clock-case she brought from the inn, and the removal of the handsome brass knobs on its head, before there was height for it to stand; but, such as the rooms were, there were plenty of them, and the place was endeared to her by every early recollection. Clym very gladly admitted her as a tenant, confining his own existence to two rooms at the top of the back staircase, where he lived on quietly, shut off from Thomasin and the three servants she had thought fit to indulge in now that she was a mistress of money, going his own ways, and thinking his own thoughts.

His sorrows had made some change in his outward appearance; and yet the alteration was chiefly within. It might have been said that he had a wrinkled mind. He had no enemies, and he could get nobody to reproach him, which was why he so bitterly reproached himself.

He did sometimes think he had been ill-used by fortune, so far as to say that to be born is a palpable dilemma, and that instead of men aiming to advance in life with glory they should calculate how to retreat out of it without shame. But that he and his had been sarcastically and pitilessly handled in having such irons thrust into their souls he did not maintain long. It is usually so, except with the sternest of men. Human beings, in their generous endeavour to construct a hypothesis that shall not degrade a First Cause, have always hesitated to conceive a dominant power of lower moral quality than their own; and, even while they sit down and weep by the waters of Babylon, invent excuses for the oppression which prompts their tears.

Thus, though words of solace were vainly uttered in his presence, he found relief in a direction of his own choosing when left to himself. For a man of his habits the house and the hundred and twenty pounds a year which he had inherited from his mother were enough to supply all worldly needs. Resources do not depend upon gross amounts, but upon the proportion of spendings to takings.

He frequently walked the heath alone, when the past seized upon him with its shadowy hand, and held him there to listen to its tale. His imagination would then people the spot with its ancient inhabitants: forgotten Celtic tribes trod their tracks about him, and he could almost live among them, look in their faces, and see them standing beside the barrows which swelled around, untouched and perfect as at the time of their erection. Those of the dyed barbarians who had chosen the cultivable tracts were, in comparison with those who had left their marks here, as writers on paper beside writers on parchment. Their records had perished long ago by the plough, while the works of these remained. Yet they all had lived and died unconscious of the different fates awaiting their relics. It reminded him that unforeseen factors operate in the evolution of immortality.

Winter again came round, with its winds, frosts, tame robins, and sparkling starlight. The year previous Thomasin had hardly been conscious of the season's advance; this year she laid her heart open to external influences of every kind. The life of this sweet cousin, her baby, and her servants, came to Clym's senses only in the form of sounds through a wood partition as he sat over books of exceptionally large type; but his ear became at last so accustomed to these slight noises from the other part of the house that he almost could witness the scenes they signified. A faint beat of half-seconds conjured up Thomasin rocking the cradle, a wavering hum meant that she was singing the baby to sleep, a crunching of sand as between millstones raised the picture of Humphrey's, Fairway's, or Sam's heavy feet crossing the stone floor of the kitchen; a light boyish step, and a gay tune in a high key, betokened a visit from Grandfer Cantle; a sudden break-off in the Grandfer's utterances implied the application to his lips of a mug of small beer; a bustling and slamming of doors meant starting to go to market; for Thomasin, in spite of her added scope for gentility, led a ludicrously narrow life, to the end that she might save every possible pound for her little daughter.

One summer day Clym was in the garden, immediately outside the parlour-window, which was as usual open. He was looking at the pot-flowers on the sill; they had been revived and restored by

Thomasin to the state in which his mother had left them. He heard a slight scream from Thomasin, who was sitting inside the room.

'O, how you frightened me!' she said to some one who had entered. 'I thought you were the ghost of yourself.'

Clym was curious enough to advance a little further and look in at the window. To his astonishment there stood within the room Diggory Venn, no longer a reddleman, but exhibiting the strangely altered hues of an ordinary Christian countenance, white shirt-front, light flowered waistcoat, blue-spotted neckerchief, and bottle-green coat. Nothing in this appearance was at all singular but the fact of its great difference from what he had formerly been. Red, and all approach to red, was carefully excluded from every article of clothes upon him; for what is there that persons just out of harness dread so much as reminders of the trade which has enriched them?

Yeobright went round to the door and entered.

'I was so alarmed!' said Thomasin, smiling from one to the other. 'I couldn't believe that he had got white of his own accord! It seemed supernatural.'

'I gave up dealing in reddle last Christmas,' said Venn. 'It was a profitable trade, and I found that by that time I had made enough to take the dairy of fifty cows that my father had in his lifetime. I always thought of getting to that place again if I changed at all; and now I am there.'

'How did you manage to become white, Diggory?' Thomasin asked.

'I turned so by degrees, ma'am.'

'You look much better than ever you did before.'

Venn appeared confused; and Thomasin, seeing how inadvertently she had spoken to a man who might possibly have tender feelings for her still, blushed a little. Clym saw nothing of this, and added good-humouredly—

'What shall we have to frighten Thomasin's baby with, now you have become a human being again?'

'Sit down, Diggory,' said Thomasin, 'and stay to tea.'

Venn moved as if he would retire to the kitchen, when Thomasin said with pleasant pertness as she went on with some sewing, 'Of course you must sit down here. And where does your fifty-cow dairy lie, Mr. Venn?'

'At Stickleford—about two miles to the right of Alderworth, ma'am, where the meads begin. I have thought that if Mr. Yeobright would like to pay me a visit sometimes he shouldn't stay away for want of asking. I'll not bide to tea this afternoon, thank'ee, for I've got something on hand that must be settled. 'Tis Maypole-day to-morrow, and the Shadwater folk have clubbed with a few of your neighbours here to have a pole just outside your palings in the heath, as it is a nice green place.' Venn waved his elbow towards the patch in front of the house. 'I have been talking to Fairway about it,' he continued, 'and I said to him that before we put up the pole it would be as well to ask Mrs. Wildeve.'

'I can say nothing against it,' she answered. 'Our property does not reach an inch further than the white palings.'

'But you might not like to see a lot of folk going crazy round a stick, under your very nose?'

'I shall have no objection at all.'

Venn soon after went away, and in the evening Yeobright strolled as far as Fairway's cottage. It was a lovely May sunset, and the birch trees which grew on this margin of the vast Egdon wilderness had put on their new leaves, delicate as butterflies' wings, and diaphanous as amber. Beside Fairway's dwelling was an open space recessed from the road, and here were now collected all the young people from within a radius of a couple of miles. The pole lay with one end supported on a trestle, and women were engaged in wreathing it from the top downwards with wild-flowers. The instincts of merry England lingered on here with exceptional vitality, and the symbolic customs which tradition has attached to each season of the year were yet a reality on Egdon. Indeed, the impulses of all such outlandish hamlets are pagan still: in these spots homage to nature, self-adoration, frantic gaieties, fragments of Teutonic rites to divinities whose names are forgotten, seem in some way or other to have survived mediaeval doctrine.

Yeobright did not interrupt the preparations, and went home again. The next morning, when Thomasin withdrew the curtains of her bedroom window, there stood the Maypole in the middle of the green, its top cutting into the sky. It had sprung up in the night, or rather early morning, like Jack's bean-stalk. She opened the casement to get a better view of the garlands and posies that adorned it. The sweet perfume of the flowers had already spread into the surrounding air, which, being free from every taint, conducted to her lips a full measure of the fragrance received from the spire of blossom in its midst. At the top of the pole were crossed hoops decked with small flowers; beneath these came a milk-white zone of Maybloom; then a zone of bluebells, then of cowslips, then of lilacs, then of ragged-robins, daffodils, and so on, till the lowest stage was reached. Thomasin noticed all these, and was delighted that the May-level was to be so near.

When afternoon came people began to gather on the green, and Yeobright was interested enough to look out upon them from the open window of his room. Soon after this Thomasin walked out from the door immediately below and turned her eyes up to her cousin's face. She was dressed more gaily than Yeobright had ever seen her dress since the time of Wildeve's death, eighteen months before; since the day of her marriage even she had not exhibited herself to such advantage.

'How pretty you look to-day, Thomasin!' he said. 'Is it because of the Maypole?'

'Not altogether.' And then she blushed and dropped her eyes, which he did not specially observe, though her manner seemed to him to be rather peculiar, considering that she was only addressing himself. Could it be possible that she had put on her summer clothes to please him?

He recalled her conduct towards him throughout the last few weeks, when they had often been working together in the garden, just as they had formerly done when they were boy and girl under his mother's eye. What if her interest in him were not so entirely that of a relative as it had formerly been? To Yeobright any possibility of this sort was a serious matter; and he almost felt troubled at the thought of it. Every pulse of loverlike feeling which had not been stilled during Eustacia's lifetime had gone into the grave with her. His passion for her had occurred too far on in his manhood to leave fuel enough on hand for another fire of that sort, as may happen with more boyish loves. Even supposing him capable of loving again, that love would be a plant of slow and laboured growth, and in the end only small and sickly, like an autumn-hatched bird.

He was so distressed by this new complexity that when the enthusiastic brass band arrived and struck up, which it did about five o'clock, with apparently wind enough among its members to blow down his house, he withdrew from his rooms by the back door, went down the garden, through the gate in the hedge, and away out of sight. He could not bear to remain in the presence of enjoyment to-day, though he had tried hard.

Nothing was seen of him for four hours. When he came back by the same path it was dusk, and the dews were coating every green thing. The boisterous music had ceased; but, entering the premises as he did from behind, he could not see if the May party had all gone till he had passed through Thomasin's division of the house to the front door. Thomasin was standing within the porch alone.

She looked at him reproachfully. 'You went away just when it began, Clym,' she said.

'Yes. I felt I could not join in. You went out with them, of course?'

'No, I did not.'

'You appeared to be dressed on purpose.'

'Yes, but I could not go out alone; so many people were there. One is there now.'

Yeobright strained his eyes across the dark-green patch beyond the paling, and near the black form of the Maypole he discerned a shadowy figure, sauntering idly up and down. 'Who is it?' he said.

'Mr. Venn,' said Thomasin.

'You might have asked him to come in, I think, Tamsie. He has been very kind to you first and last.'

'I will now,' she said; and, acting on the impulse, went through the wicket to where Venn stood under the Maypole.

'It is Mr. Venn, I think?' she inquired.

Venn started as if he had not seen her—artful man that he was—and said, 'Yes.'

'Will you come in?'

'I am afraid that I——'

'I have seen you dancing this evening, and you had the very best of the girls for your partners. Is it that you won't come in because you wish to stand here, and think over the past hours of enjoyment?'

'Well, that's partly it,' said Mr. Venn, with ostentatious sentiment. 'But the main reason why I am biding here like this is that I want to wait till the moon rises.'

'To see how pretty the Maypole looks in the moonlight?'

'No. To look for a glove that was dropped by one of the maidens.'

Thomasin was speechless with surprise. That a man who had to walk some four or five miles to his home should wait here for such a reason pointed to only one conclusion: the man must be amazingly interested in that glove's owner.

'Were you dancing with her, Diggory?' she asked, in a voice which revealed that he had made himself considerably more interesting to her by this disclosure.

'No,' he sighed.

'And you will not come in, then?'

'Not to-night, thank you, ma'am.'

'Shall I lend you a lantern to look for the young person's glove, Mr. Venn?'

'O no; it is not necessary, Mrs. Wildeve, thank you. The moon will rise in a few minutes.'

Thomasin went back to the porch. 'Is he coming in?' said Clym, who had been waiting where she had left him.

'He would rather not to-night,' she said, and then passed by him into the house; whereupon Clym too retired to his own rooms.

When Clym was gone Thomasin crept upstairs in the dark, and, just listening by the cot, to assure herself that the child was asleep, she went to the window, gently lifted the corner of the white curtain, and looked out. Venn was still there. She watched the growth of the faint radiance appearing in the sky by the eastern hill, till presently the edge of the moon burst upwards and flooded the valley with light. Diggory's form was now distinct on the green; he was moving about in a bowed attitude, evidently scanning the grass for the precious missing article, walking in zigzags right and left till he should have passed over every foot of the ground.

'How very ridiculous!' Thomasin murmured to herself, in a tone which was intended to be satirical. 'To think that a man should be so silly as to go mooning about like that for a girl's glove! A respectable dairyman, too, and a man of money as he is now. What a pity!'

At last Venn appeared to find it; whereupon he stood up and raised it to his lips. Then placing it in his breast-pocket—the nearest receptacle to a man's heart permitted by modern raiment—he ascended the valley in a mathematically direct line towards his distant home in the meadows.

Thomasin Walks in a Green Place by the Roman Road

II

Clym saw little of Thomasin for several days after this; and when they met she was more silent than usual. At length he asked her what she was thinking of so intently.

'I am thoroughly perplexed,' she said candidly. 'I cannot for my life think who it is that Diggory Venn is so much in love with. None of the girls at the Maypole were good enough for him, and yet she must have been there.'

Clym tried to imagine Venn's choice for a moment; but ceasing to be interested in the question he went on again with his gardening.

No clearing up of the mystery was granted her for some time. But one afternoon Thomasin was upstairs getting ready for a walk, when she had occasion to come to the landing and call 'Rachel.' Rachel was a girl about thirteen, who carried the baby out for airings; and she came upstairs at the call.

'Have you seen one of my last new gloves about the house, Rachel?' inquired Thomasin. 'It is the fellow to this one.'

Rachel did not reply.

'Why don't you answer?' said her mistress.

'I think it is lost, ma'am.'

'Lost? Who lost it? I have never worn them but once.'

Rachel appeared as one dreadfully troubled, and at last began to cry. 'Please, ma'am, on the day of the Maypole I had none to wear, and I seed yours on the table, and I thought I would borrow 'em. I did not mean to hurt 'em at all, but one of them got lost. Somebody gave me some money to buy another pair for you, but I have not been able to go anywhere to get 'em.'

'Who's somebody?'

'Mr. Venn.'

'Did he know it was my glove?'

'Yes. I told him.'

Thomasin was so surprised by the explanation that she quite forgot to lecture the girl, who glided silently away. Thomasin did not move further than to turn her eyes upon the grass-plat where the Maypole had stood. She remained thinking, then said to herself that she would not go out that afternoon, but would work hard at the baby's unfinished lovely plaid frock, cut on the cross in the newest fashion. How she managed to work hard, and yet do no more than she had done at the end of two hours, would have been a mystery to any one not aware that the recent incident was of a kind likely to divert her industry from a manual to a mental channel.

Next day she went her ways as usual, and continued her custom of walking in the heath with no other companion than little Eustacia, now of the age when it is a matter of doubt with such characters whether they are intended to walk through the world on their hands or on their feet; so that they get into painful complications by trying both. It was very pleasant to Thomasin, when she had carried the child to some lonely place, to give her a little private practice on the green turf and shepherd's-thyme, which formed a soft mat to fall headlong upon when equilibrium was lost.

Once, when engaged in this system of training, and stooping to remove bits of stick, fern-stalks, and other such fragments from the child's path, that the journey might not be brought to an untimely end by some insuperable barrier a quarter of an inch high, she was alarmed by discovering that a man on horseback was almost close beside her, the soft natural carpet having muffled the horse's tread. The rider, who was Venn, waved his hat in the air and bowed gallantly.

'Diggory, give me my glove,' said Thomasin, whose manner it was under any circumstances to plunge into the midst of a subject which engrossed her.

Venn immediately dismounted, put his hand in his breast-pocket, and handed the glove.

'Thank you. It was very good of you to take care of it.'

'It is very good of you to say so.'

'O no. I was quite glad to find you had it. Everybody gets so indifferent that I was surprised to know you thought of me.'

'If you had remembered what I was once you wouldn't have been surprised.'

'Ah, no,' she said quickly. 'But men of your character are mostly so independent.'

'What is my character?' he asked.

'I don't exactly know,' said Thomasin simply, 'except it is to cover up your feelings under a practical manner, and only to show them when you are alone.'

'Ah, how do you know that?' said Venn strategically.

'Because,' said she, stopping to put the little girl, who had managed to get herself upside down, right end up again, 'because I do.'

'You mustn't judge by folks in general,' said Venn. 'Still I don't know much what feelings are now-a-days. I have got so mixed up with business of one sort and t'other that my soft sentiments are gone off in vapour like. Yes, I am given up body and soul to the making of money. Money is all my dream.'

'Oh Diggory, how wicked!' said Thomasin reproachfully, and looking at him in exact balance between taking his words seriously and judging them as said to tease her.

'Yes, 'tis rather a rum course,' said Venn, in the bland tone of one comfortably resigned to sins he could no longer overcome.

'You, who used to be so nice!'

'Well, that's an argument I rather like, because what a man has once been he may be again.' Thomasin blushed. 'Except that it is rather harder now,' Venn continued.

'Why?' she asked.

'Because you be richer than you were at that time.'

'O no—not much. I have made it nearly all over to the baby, as it was my duty to do, except just enough to live on.'

'I am rather glad of that,' said Venn softly, and regarding her from the corner of his eye, 'for it makes it easier for us to be friendly.'

Thomasin blushed again, and, when a few more words had been said of a not unpleasing kind, Venn mounted his horse and rode on.

This conversation had passed in a hollow of the heath near the old Roman road, a place much frequented by Thomasin. And it might have been observed that she did not in future walk that way less often from having met Venn there now. Whether or not Venn abstained from riding thither because he had met Thomasin in the same place might easily have been guessed from her proceedings about two months later in the same year.

The Serious Discourse of Clym with His Cousin

III

Throughout this period Yeobright had more or less pondered on his duty to his cousin Thomasin. He could not help feeling that it would be a pitiful waste of sweet material if the tender-natured thing should be doomed from this early stage of her life onwards to dribble away her winsome qualities on lonely gorse and fern. But he felt this as an economist merely, and not as a lover. His passion for Eustacia had been a sort of conserve of his whole life, and he had nothing more of that supreme quality left to bestow. So far the obvious thing was not to entertain any idea of marriage with Thomasin, even to oblige her.

But this was not all. Years ago there had been in his mother's mind a great fancy about Thomasin and himself. It had not positively amounted to a desire, but it had always been a favourite dream. That they should be man and wife in good time, if the happiness of neither were endangered thereby, was the fancy in question. So that what course save one was there now left for any son who reverenced his mother's memory as Yeobright did? It is an unfortunate fact that any particular whim of parents, which might have been dispersed by half an hour's conversation during their lives, becomes sublimated by their deaths into a fiat the most absolute, with such results to conscientious children as those parents, had they lived, would have been the first to decry.

Had only Yeobright's own future been involved he would have proposed to Thomasin with a ready heart. He had nothing to lose by carrying out a dead mother's hope. But he dreaded to contemplate Thomasin wedded to the mere corpse of a lover that he now felt himself to be. He had but three activities alive in him. One was his almost daily walk to the little graveyard wherein his mother lay; another, his just as frequent visits by night to the more distant enclosure, which numbered his Eustacia among its dead; the third was self-preparation for a vocation which alone seemed likely to satisfy his cravings—that of an itinerant preacher of the eleventh commandment. It was difficult to believe that Thomasin would be cheered by a husband with such tendencies as these.

Yet he resolved to ask her, and let her decide for herself. It was even with a pleasant sense of doing his duty that he went downstairs to her one evening for this purpose, when the sun was printing on the valley the same long shadow of the housetop that he had seen lying there times out of number while his mother lived.

Thomasin was not in her room, and he found her in the front garden. 'I have long been wanting, Thomasin,' he began, 'to say something about a matter that concerns both our futures.'

'And are you going to say it now?' she remarked quickly, colouring as she met his gaze. 'Do stop a minute, Clym, and let me speak first, for oddly enough, I have been wanting to say something to you.'

'By all means say on, Tamsie.'

'I suppose nobody can overhear us?' she went on, casting her eyes around and lowering her voice. 'Well, first you will promise me this—that you won't be angry and call me anything harsh if you disagree with what I propose?'

Yeobright promised, and she continued: 'What I want is your advice, for you are my relation—I mean, a sort of guardian to me—aren't you, Clym?'

'Well, yes, I suppose I am; a sort of guardian. In fact, I am, of course,' he said, altogether perplexed as to her drift.

'I am thinking of marrying,' she then observed blandly. 'But I shall not marry unless you assure me that you approve of such a step. Why don't you speak?'

'I was taken rather by surprise. But, nevertheless, I am very glad to hear such news. I shall approve, of course, dear Tamsie. Who can it be? I am quite at a loss to guess. No, I am not—'tis the old doctor!—not that I mean to call him old, for he is not very old after all. Ah—I noticed when he attended you last time!'

'No, no,' she said hastily. ''Tis Mr. Venn.'

Clym's face suddenly became grave.

'There, now, you don't like him, and I wish I hadn't mentioned him!' she exclaimed almost petulantly. 'And I shouldn't have done it, either, only he keeps on bothering me so till I don't know what to do!'

Clym looked at the heath. 'I like Venn well enough,' he answered at last. 'He is a very honest and at the same time astute man. He is clever too, as is proved by his having got you to favour him. But really, Thomasin, he is not quite——'

'Gentleman enough for me? That is just what I feel. I am sorry now that I asked you, and I won't think any more of him. At the same time I must marry him if I marry anybody—that I *will* say!'

'I don't see that,' said Clym, carefully concealing every clue to his own interrupted intention, which she plainly had not guessed. 'You might marry a professional man, or somebody of that sort, by going into the town to live and forming acquaintances there.'

'I am not fit for town life—so very rural and silly as I always have been. Do not you yourself notice my countrified ways?'

'Well, when I came home from Paris I did, a little; but I don't now.'

'That's because you have got countrified too. O, I couldn't live in a street for the world! Egdon is a ridiculous old place; but I have got used to it, and I couldn't be happy anywhere else at all.'

'Neither could I,' said Clym.

'Then how could you say that I should marry some town man? I am sure, say what you will, that I must marry Diggory, if I marry at all. He has been kinder to me than anybody else, and has helped me in many ways that I don't know of!' Thomasin almost pouted now.

'Yes, he has,' said Clym in a neutral tone. 'Well, I wish with all my heart that I could say, marry him. But I cannot forget what my mother thought on that matter, and it goes rather against me not to respect her opinion. There is too much reason why we should do the little we can to respect it now.'

'Very well, then,' sighed Thomasin. 'I will say no more.'

'But you are not bound to obey my wishes. I merely say what I think.'

'O no—I don't want to be rebellious in that way,' she said sadly. 'I had no business to think of him—I ought to have thought of my family. What dreadfully bad impulses there are in me!' Her lip trembled, and she turned away to hide a tear.

Clym, though vexed at what seemed her unaccountable taste, was in a measure relieved to find that at any rate the marriage question in relation to himself was shelved. Through several succeeding days he saw her at different times from the window of his room moping disconsolately about the garden. He was half angry with her for choosing Venn; then he was grieved at having put himself in the way of Venn's happiness, who was, after all, as honest and persevering a young fellow as any on Egdon, since he had turned over a new leaf. In short, Clym did not know what to do.

When next they met she said abruptly, 'He is much more respectable now than he was then!'

'Who? O yes—Diggory Venn.'

'Aunt only objected because he was a reddleman.'

'Well, Thomasin, perhaps I don't know all the particulars of my mother's wish. So you had better use your own discretion.'

'You will always feel that I slighted your mother's memory.'

'No, I will not. I shall think you are convinced that, had she seen Diggory in his present position, she would have considered him a fitting husband for you. Now, that's my real feeling. Don't consult me any more, but do as you like, Thomasin. I shall be content.'

It is to be supposed that Thomasin was convinced; for a few days after this, when Clym strayed into a part of the heath that he had not lately visited, Humphrey, who was at work there, said to him, 'I am glad to see that Mrs. Wildeve and Venn have made it up again, seemingly.'

'Have they?' said Clym abstractedly.

'Yes; and he do contrive to stumble upon her whenever she walks out on fine days with the chiel. But, Mr. Yeobright, I can't help feeling that your cousin ought to have married you. 'Tis a pity to make two chimley-corners where there need be only one. You could get her away from him now, 'tis my belief, if you were only to set about it.'

'How can I have the conscience to marry after having driven two women to their deaths? Don't think such a thing, Humphrey. After my experience I should consider it too much of a burlesque to go to church and take a wife. In the words of Job, "I have made a covenant with mine eyes; why then should I think upon a maid?" '

'No, Mr. Clym, don't fancy that about driving two women to their deaths. You shouldn't say it.'

'Well, we'll leave that out,' said Yeobright. 'But anyhow God has set a mark upon me which wouldn't look well in a love-making scene. I have two ideas in my head, and no others. I am going to keep a night-school; and I am going to turn preacher. What have you got to say to that, Humphrey?'

'I'll come and hear 'ee with all my heart.'

'Thanks. 'Tis all I wish.'

As Clym descended into the valley Thomasin came down by the other path, and met him at the gate. 'What do you think I have to tell you, Clym?' she said, looking archly over her shoulder at him.

'I can guess,' he replied.

She scrutinized his face. 'Yes, you guess right. It is going to be after all. He thinks I may as well make up my mind, and I have got to think so too. It is to be on the twenty-fifth of next month, if you don't object.'

'Do what you think right, dear. I am only too glad that you see your way clear to happiness again. My sex owes you every amends for the treatment you received in days gone by.'[5]

Cheerfulness Again Asserts Itself at Blooms-End, and Clym Finds His Vocation

IV

Anybody who had passed through Blooms-End about eleven o'clock on the morning fixed for the wedding would have found

5. The writer may state here that the original conception of the story did not design a marriage between Thomasin and Venn. He was to have retained his isolation and weird character to the last, and to have disappeared mysteriously from the heath, nobody knowing whither—Thomasin remaining a widow. But certain circumstances of serial publication led to a change of intent.

Readers can therefore choose between the endings, and those with an austere artistic code can assume the more consistent conclusion to be the true one [Hardy's note].

that, while Yeobright's house was comparatively quiet, sounds denoting great activity came from the dwelling of his nearest neighbour, Timothy Fairway. It was chiefly a noise of feet, briskly crunching hither and thither over the sanded floor within. One man only was visible outside, and he seemed to be later at an appointment than he had intended to be, for he hastened up to the door, lifted the latch, and walked in without ceremony.

The scene within was not quite the customary one. Standing about the room was the little knot of men who formed the chief part of the Egdon coterie, there being present Fairway himself, Grandfer Cantle, Humphrey, Christian, and one or two turf-cutters. It was a warm day, and the men were as a matter of course in their shirt-sleeves, except Christian, who had always a nervous fear of parting with a scrap of his clothing when in anybody's house but his own. Across the stout oak table in the middle of the room was thrown a mass of striped linen, which Grandfer Cantle held down on one side, and Humphrey on the other, while Fairway rubbed its surface with a yellow lump, his face being damp and creased with the effort of the labour.

'Waxing a bed-tick, souls?' said the new-comer.

'Yes, Sam,' said Grandfer Cantle, as a man too busy to waste words. 'Shall I stretch this corner a shade tighter, Timothy?'

Fairway replied, and the waxing went on with unabated vigour. ' 'Tis going to be a good bed, by the look o't,' continued Sam, after an interval of silence. 'Who may it be for?'

' 'Tis a present for the new folks that's going to set up housekeeping,' said Christian, who stood helpless and overcome by the majesty of the proceedings.

'Ah, to be sure; and a valuable one, 'a b'lieve.'

'Beds be dear to fokes that don't keep geese, bain't they, Mister Fairway?' said Christian, as to an omniscient being.

'Yes,' said the furze-dealer, standing up, giving his forehead a thorough mopping, and handing the beeswax to Humphrey, who succeeded at the rubbing forthwith. 'Not that this couple be in want of one, but 'twas well to show 'em a bit of friendliness at this great racketing vagary of their lives. I set up both my own daughters in one when they was married, and there have been feathers enough for another in the house the last twelve months. Now then, neighbours, I think we have laid on enough wax. Grandfer Cantle, you turn the tick the right way outwards, and then I'll begin to shake in the feathers.'

When the bed was in proper trim Fairway and Christian brought forward vast paper bags, stuffed to the full, but light as balloons, and began to turn the contents of each into the receptacle just prepared. As bag after bag was emptied, airy tufts of down and feathers floated about the room in increasing quantity till, through a mishap of Christian's, who shook the contents of one bag outside the tick, the atmosphere of the room became dense with gigantic flakes, which descended upon the workers like a windless snowstorm.

'I never saw such a clumsy chap as you, Christian,' said Grandfer Cantle severely. 'You might have been the son of a man that's never been outside Blooms-End in his life for all the wit you have. Really all the soldiering and smartness in the world in the father seems to count for nothing in forming the nater of the son. As far as that chiel Christian is concerned I might as well have stayed at home and seed nothing, like all the rest of ye here. Though, as far as myself is concerned, a dashing spirit has counted for sommat, to be sure!'

'Don't ye let me down so, father; I feel no bigger than a ninepin after it. I've made but a bruckle hit,[6] I'm afeared.'

'Come, come. Never pitch yerself in such a low key as that, Christian; you should try more,' said Fairway.

'Yes, you should try more,' echoed the Grandfer with insistence, as if he had been the first to make the suggestion. 'In common conscience every man ought either to marry or go for a soldier. 'Tis a scandal to the nation to do neither one nor t'other. I did both, thank God! Neither to raise men nor to lay 'em low—that shows a poor do-nothing spirit indeed.'

'I never had the nerve to stand fire,' faltered Christian. 'But as to marrying, I own I've asked here and there, though without much fruit from it. Yes, there's some house or other that might have had a man for a master—such as he is—that's now ruled by a woman alone. Still it might have been awkward if I had found her; for, d'ye see, neighbours, there'd have been nobody left at home to keep down father's spirits to the decent pitch that becomes a old man.'

'And you've your work cut out to do that, my son,' said Grandfer Cantle smartly. 'I wish that the dread of infirmities was not so strong in me!—I'd start the very first thing to-morrow to see the world over again! But seventy-one, though nothing at home, is a high figure for a rover. . . . Ay, seventy-one last Candlemas-day. Gad, I'd sooner have it in guineas than in years!' And the old man sighed.

'Don't you be mournful, Grandfer,' said Fairway. 'Empt some more feathers into the bed-tick, and keep up yer heart. Though rather lean in the stalks you be a green-leaved old man still. There's time enough left to ye yet to fill whole chronicles.'

'Begad, I'll go to 'em, Timothy—to the married pair!' said

6. Weak, shaky impact.

Grandfer Cantle in an encouraged voice, and starting round briskly. 'I'll go to 'em to-night and sing a wedding song, hey? 'Tis like me to do so, you know; and they'd see it as such. My "Down in Cupid's Gardens"[7] was well liked in four; still, I've got others as good, and even better. What do you say to my

"She cal'-led to' her love'
From the lat'-ice a-bove,
'O, come in' from the fog'-gy fog'-gy dew'.' "[8]

'Twould please 'em well at such a time! Really, now I come to think of it, I haven't turned my tongue in my head to the shape of a real good song since Old Midsummer night, when we had the "Barley Mow"[9] at the Woman; and 'tis a pity to neglect your strong point where there's few that have the compass for such things!'

'So 'tis, so 'tis,' said Fairway. 'Now gie the bed a shake down. We've put in seventy pound of best feathers, and I think that's as many as the tick will fairly hold. A bit and a drap wouldn't be amiss now, I reckon. Christian, maul down the victuals from corner-cupboard if canst reach, man, and I'll draw a drap o'sommat to wet it with.'

They sat down to a lunch in the midst of their work, feathers around, above, and below them; the original owners of which occasionally came to the open door and cackled begrudgingly at sight of such a quantity of their old clothes.

'Upon my soul I shall be chokt,' said Fairway when, having extracted a feather from his mouth, he found several others floating on the mug as it was handed round.

'I've swallered several; and one had a tolerable quill,' said Sam placidly from the corner.

'Hullo—what's that—wheels I hear coming?' Grandfer Cantle exclaimed, jumping up and hastening to the door. 'Why, 'tis they back again: I didn't expect 'em yet this half-hour. To be sure, how quick marrying can be done when you are in the mind for't!'

'O yes, it can soon be *done*,' said Fairway, as if something should be added to make the statement complete.

He arose and followed the Grandfer, and the rest also went to the door. In a moment an open fly was driven past, in which sat Venn and Mrs. Venn, Yeobright, and a grand relative of Venn's who had come from Budmouth for the occasion. The fly had been hired at the nearest town, regardless of distance and cost, there being nothing on Egdon Heath, in Venn's opinion, dignified

7. Famous old folk song, used more centrally in *Tess of the D'Urbervilles*.
8. Bawdy song, still popular in many versions.
9. Famous cumulative folk song sung at harvest festivals, with choruses punctuated by drink.

enough for such an event when such a woman as Thomasin was the bride; and the church was too remote for a walking bridal-party.

As the fly passed the group which had run out from the homestead they shouted 'Hurrah!' and waved their hands; feathers and down floating from their hair, their sleeves, and the folds of their garments at every motion, and Grandfer Cantle's seals dancing merrily in the sunlight as he twirled himself about. The driver of the fly turned a supercilious gaze upon them; he even treated the wedded pair themselves with something like condescension; for in what other state than heathen could people, rich or poor, exist who were doomed to abide in such a world's end as Egdon? Thomasin showed no such superiority to the group at the door, fluttering her hand as quickly as a bird's wing towards them, and asking Diggory, with tears in her eyes, if they ought not to alight and speak to these kind neighbours. Venn, however, suggested that, as they were all coming to the house in the evening, this was hardly necessary.

After this excitement the saluting party returned to their occupation, and the stuffing and sewing was soon afterwards finished, when Fairway harnessed a horse, wrapped up the cumbrous present, and drove off with it in the cart to Venn's house at Stickleford.

Yeobright, having filled the office at the wedding service which naturally fell to his hands, and afterwards returned to the house with the husband and wife, was indisposed to take part in the feasting and dancing that wound up the evening. Thomasin was disappointed.

'I wish I could be there without dashing your spirits,' he said. 'But I might be too much like the skull at the banquet.'

'No, no.'

'Well, dear, apart from that, if you would excuse me, I should be glad. I know it seems unkind; but, dear Thomasin, I fear I should not be happy in the company—there, that's the truth of it. I shall always be coming to see you at your new home, you know, so that my absence now will not matter.'

'Then I give in. Do whatever will be most comfortable to yourself.'

Clym retired to his lodging at the housetop much relieved, and occupied himself during the afternoon in noting down the heads of a sermon, with which he intended to initiate all that really seemed practicable of the scheme that had originally brought him hither, and that he had so long kept in view under various modifications, and through evil and good report. He had tested and weighed his convictions again and again, and saw no reason to alter them, though he had considerably lessened his plan. His eyesight, by long humouring in his native air, had grown stronger, but not sufficiently strong to warrant his attempting his extensive educational project. Yet he did not repine: there was still more than enough of an unambitious sort to tax all his energies and occupy all his hours.

Evening drew on, and sounds of life and movement in the lower part of the domicile became more pronounced, the gate in the palings clicking incessantly. The party was to be an early one, and all the guests were assembled long before it was dark. Yeobright went down the back staircase and into the heath by another path than that in front, intending to walk in the open air till the party was over, when he would return to wish Thomasin and her husband good-bye as they departed. His steps were insensibly bent towards Mistover by the path that he had followed on that terrible morning when he learnt the strange news from Susan's boy.

He did not turn aside to the cottage, but pushed on to an eminence, whence he could see over the whole quarter that had once been Eustacia's home. While he stood observing the darkening scene somebody came up. Clym, seeing him but dimly, would have let him pass by silently, had not the pedestrian, who was Charley, recognized the young man and spoken to him.

'Charley, I have not seen you for a length of time,' said Yeobright. 'Do you often walk this way?'

'No,' the lad replied. 'I don't often come outside the bank.'

'You were not at the Maypole.'

'No,' said Charley, in the same listless tone. 'I don't care for that sort of thing now.'

'You rather liked Miss Eustacia, didn't you?' Yeobright gently asked. Eustacia had frequently told him of Charley's romantic attachment.

'Yes, very much. Ah, I wish——'

'Yes?'

'I wish, Mr. Yeobright, you could give me something to keep that once belonged to her—if you don't mind.'

'I shall be very happy to. It will give me very great pleasure, Charley. Let me think what I have of hers that you would like. But come with me to the house, and I'll see.'

They walked towards Blooms-End together. When they reached the front it was dark, and the shutters were closed, so that nothing of the interior could be seen.

'Come round this way,' said Clym. 'My entrance is at the back for the present.'

The two went round and ascended the crooked stair in darkness till Clym's sitting-room on the upper floor was reached, where he lit a candle, Charley entering gently behind. Yeobright searched his desk, and taking out a sheet of tissue-paper unfolded from it two or three undulating locks of raven hair, which fell over the paper like black streams. From these he selected one, wrapped it up, and gave it to the lad, whose eyes had filled with tears. He kissed the packet, put it in his pocket, and said in a voice of emotion, 'O, Mr. Clym, how good you are to me!'

'I will go a little way with you,' said Clym. And amid the noise of merriment from below they descended. Their path to the front led them close to a little side-window, whence the rays of candles streamed across the shrubs. The window, being screened from general observation by the bushes, had been left unblinded, so that a person in this private nook could see all that was going on within the room which contained the wedding-guests, except in so far as vision was hindered by the green antiquity of the panes.

'Charley, what are they doing?' said Clym. 'My sight is weaker again to-night, and the glass of this window is not good.'

Charley wiped his own eyes, which were rather blurred with moisture, and stepped closer to the casement. 'Mr. Venn is asking Christian Cantle to sing,' he replied; 'and Christian is moving about in his chair as if he were much frightened at the question, and his father has struck up a stave instead of him.'

'Yes, I can hear the old man's voice,' said Clym. 'So there's to be no dancing, I suppose. And is Thomasin in the room? I see something moving in front of the candles that resembles her shape, I think.'

'Yes. She do seem happy. She is red in the face, and laughing at something Fairway has said to her. O my!'

'What noise was that?' said Clym.

'Mr. Venn is so tall that he has knocked his head against the beam in gieing a skip as he passed under. Mrs. Venn has run up quite frightened and now she's put her hand to his head to feel if there's a lump. And now they be all laughing again as if nothing had happened.'

'Do any of them seem to care about my not being there?' Clym asked.

'No, not a bit in the world. Now they are all holding up their glasses and drinking somebody's health.'

'I wonder if it is mine?'

'No, 'tis Mr. and Mrs. Venn's, because he is making a hearty sort of speech. There—now Mrs. Venn has got up, and is going away to put on her things, I think.'

'Well, they haven't concerned themselves about me, and it is quite right they should not. It is all as it should be, and Thomasin at least is happy. We will not stay any longer now, as they will soon be coming out to go home.'

He accompanied the lad into the heath on his way home, and, returning alone to the house a quarter of an hour later, found Venn and Thomasin ready to start, all the guests having departed in his absence. The wedded pair took their seats in the four-wheeled dogcart which Venn's head milker and handy man had driven from Stickleford to fetch them in; little Eustacia and the nurse were packed securely upon the open flap behind; and the milker, on an ancient overstepping pony, whose shoes clashed like cymbals at every tread, rode in the rear, in the manner of a body-servant of the last century.

'Now we leave you in absolute possession of your own house again,' said Thomasin as she bent down to wish her cousin good-night. 'It will be rather lonely for you, Clym, after the hubbub we have been making.'

'O, that's no inconvenience,' said Clym, smiling rather sadly. And then the party drove off and vanished in the night-shades, and Yeobright entered the house. The ticking of the clock was the only sound that greeted him, for not a soul remained; Christian, who acted as cook, valet, and gardener to Clym, sleeping at his father's house. Yeobright sat down in one of the vacant chairs, and remained in thought a long time. His mother's old chair was opposite; it had been sat in that evening by those who had scarcely remembered that it ever was hers. But to Clym she was almost a presence there, now as always. Whatever she was in other people's memories, in his she was the sublime saint whose radiance even his tenderness for Eustacia could not obscure. But his heart was heavy; that mother had *not* crowned him in the day of his espousals and in the day of the gladness of his heart. And events had borne out the accuracy of her judgment, and proved the devotedness of her care. He should have heeded her for Eustacia's sake even more than for his own. 'It was all my fault,' he whispered. 'O, my mother, my mother! would to God that I could live my life again, and endure for you what you endured for me!'

On the Sunday after this wedding an unusual sight was to be seen on Rainbarrow. From a distance there simply appeared to be a motionless figure standing on the top of the tumulus, just as Eustacia had stood on that lonely summit some two years and a half before. But now it was fine warm weather, with only a summer breeze blowing, and early afternoon instead of dull twilight. Those who ascended to the immediate neighbourhood of the Barrow perceived that the erect form in the centre, piercing the sky, was not really alone. Round him upon the slopes of the Barrow a number of heathmen and women were reclining or sitting at their ease. They listened to the words of the man in their midst, who was preaching, while they abstractedly pulled heather, stripped ferns, or tossed pebbles down the slope. This was the first of a series of moral lectures or Sermons on the Mount, which were to be delivered from the same place every Sunday afternoon as long as the fine weather lasted.

The commanding elevation of Rainbarrow had been chosen for two reasons: first, that it occupied a central position among the remote cottages around; secondly, that the preacher thereon could be seen from all adjacent points as soon as he arrived at his post, the view of him being thus a convenient signal to those stragglers who wished to draw near. The speaker was bareheaded, and the breeze at each waft gently lifted and lowered his hair, somewhat too thin for a man of his years, these still numbering less than thirty-three. He wore a shade over his eyes, and his face was pensive and lined; but, though these bodily features were marked with decay there was no defect in the tones of his voice, which were rich, musical, and stirring. He stated that his discourses to people were to be sometimes secular, and sometimes religious, but never dogmatic; and that his texts would be taken from all kinds of books. This afternoon the words were as follows:—

'"And the king rose up to meet her, and bowed himself unto her, and sat down on his throne, and caused a seat to be set for the king's mother; and she sat on his right hand. Then she said, I desire one small petition of thee; I pray thee say me not nay. And the king said unto her, Ask on, my mother: for I will not say thee nay."'[1]

Yeobright had, in fact, found his vocation in the career of an itinerant open-air preacher and lecturer on morally unimpeachable subjects; and from this day he laboured incessantly in that office, speaking not only in simple language on Rainbarrow and in the hamlets round, but in a more cultivated strain elsewhere—from the steps and porticoes of town-halls, from market-crosses, from conduits, on esplanades and on wharves, from the parapets of bridges, in barns and outhouses, and all other such places in the neighbouring Wessex towns and villages. He left alone creeds and systems of philosophy, finding enough and more than enough to occupy his tongue in the opinions and actions common to all good men. Some believed him, and some believed not; some said that his words were commonplace, others complained of his want of theological doctrine; while others again remarked that it was well enough for a man to take to preaching who could not see to do anything else. But everywhere he was kindly received, for the story of his life had become generally known.

1. King Solomon's mother, Bathsheba, interceded for Adonijah, who was requesting permission to marry (I Kings ii.19–20).

THE END

Background

Composition, Publication, and Scholarship

RICHARD L. PURDY

[Publication of the Novel]†

THE / RETURN OF THE NATIVE / BY / THOMAS HARDY / AUTHOR OF / 'FAR FROM THE MADDING CROWD' 'A PAIR OF BLUE EYES [' *in VOLS. II and III*] ETC. / 'To sorrow / I bade good morrow, / And thought to leave her far away behind; / But cheerly, cheerly, / She loves me dearly; / She is so constant to me, and so kind. / I would deceive her, / And so leave her, / But ah! she is so constant and so kind ['*in VOLS. II and III*] / IN THREE VOLUMES—VOL. I. [*II.*] [*III.*] / LONDON / SMITH, ELDER, & CO., 15 WATERLOO PLACE / 1878 / [*All rights reserved*]

* * *

Illustration. Inserted in Vol. I as frontispiece is a 'Sketch map of the scene of the story', drawn by Hardy himself and separately printed.[1]

Binding. Brown diagonal-fine-ribbed cloth; blocked in black on front with conventional panel design, in blind on back with 2-rule border; lettered on spine in gold and blind with bands and ornaments blocked in black and gold: The / Return / of / the / Native / Thomas / Hardy / Vol. I. [*II*] [*Vol III.*] / Smith Elder & Co. /

Cream-white end-papers; top uncut, fore-edge and tail cut; leaves measure 5″x7⅜″.

Secondary Binding. Cloth usually a slightly redder shade of brown; blocked in blind on back with 3-rule border; imprint on spine (caps. ⅛″ instead of 3/16″): Smith, Elder & Co. / ; leaves measure 4⅞″x7¼″; conforms in all other respects to the description above.

† From Richard L. Purdy, *Thomas Hardy: A Bibliographical Study* (Oxford, 1954), pp. 24–27, 279–86. Reprinted by permission of Oxford University Press and the author.

1. See *Early Life*, p. 160. In his own copy of the novel (Dorset County Museum) Hardy has identified Mistover on the map as 'Troytown?' and Blooms End as 'Thornicombe?'.

There are a number of reasons for considering this a secondary binding, though it is immediately distinguishable only by its 3-rule border: it is very much less common than the 2-rule binding, which appears on the British Museum, Cambridge, and Bodleian copies (accession dates '19 De 78', '1 Jan 79', and 'Aug 1879' respectively) and Hardy's own copy (though it must be noted that not all the first editions at Max Gate were of contemporary acquisition); copies in the 3-rule binding almost invariably lack the frontispiece in Vol. I; an identical situation prevails in the case of *The Trumpet-Major*, and Smith, Elder records show that 100 quires of *The Return of the Native* and 250 quires of *The Trumpet-Major* were remaindered to W. Glaisher, wholesale bookseller, in the same year, 1882. It seems reasonable to suggest that this is a secondary binding dating from that sale. There were no Smith, Elder binding orders after December 1878.

Serial Issue. The Return of the Native was first printed serially in *Belgravia* from January to December 1878. The monthly instalments ran as follows: January, Bk. I, Chaps. 1–4; February, Bk. I, Chaps. 5–7; March, Bk. I. Chaps. 8–11; April, Bk. II, Chaps. 1–5; May, Bk. II, Chaps. 6–8; June, Bk. III, Chaps. 1–4; July, Bk. III, Chaps. 5–8; August, Bk. IV, Chaps. 1–4; September, Bk. IV, Chaps. 5–8; October, Bk. V, Chaps. 1–4; November, Bk. V, Chaps. 5–8; December, Bk. V, Chap. 9–Bk. VI, Chap. 4. The Books are here untitled but provided with brief arguments, not reprinted. Several chapters were retitled before the novel was published in book form, and there were a number of deletions and additions, notably in Bk. III, Chap. 8 and Bk. IV, Chap. 1.

With each of the 12 instalments appeared 1 full-page illustration by A[rthur] Hopkins.[2] The interest Hardy took in these illustrations, though they were not reproduced in book form, is revealed in his correspondence with the artist, a portion of which has survived. He warned Hopkins that 'the scenes are somewhat outlandish, and may be unduly troublesome to you' and offered rough sketches wherever there might be difficulty with accessories, as in the case of the mummers' dress (in the May illustration), which he drew in detail for the artist. He provided a sketch of Eustacia, but when she first appeared (in the February illustration) he felt that Hopkins had failed and wrote to him, 8 February, 'It is rather ungenerous to criticise;

2. Arthur Hopkins was the brother of the poet Gerard Manley Hopkins [*Editor*].

but since you invite me to do so I will say that I think Eustacia should have been represented as more youthful in face, supple in figure, and, in general, with a little more roundness and softness than have been given her. . . . Perhaps it is well for me to give you the following ideas of the story as a guide—Thomasin, as you have divined, is the *good* heroine, and she ultimately marries the reddleman, and lives happily. Eustacia is the wayward and erring heroine—She marries Yeobright, the son of Mrs. Yeobright, is unhappy, and dies. The order of importance of the characters is as follows—1 Clym Yeobright 2 Eustacia 3 Thomasin and the reddleman 4 Wildeve 5 Mrs Yeobright.' When Eustacia appeared again in the August illustration (it had been thought unsafe to introduce her in boy's clothes in the mumming scene), Hardy wrote to Hopkins, 3 August, 'I think Eustacia is charming—she is certainly just what I imagined her to be, and the rebelliousness of her nature is precisely caught in your drawing.' Of Clym, who first appears conspicuously in the May illustration, Hardy wrote, 20 February, 'I should prefer to leave Clym's face entirely to you. A thoughtful young man of 25 is all that can be shown, as the particulars of his appearance given in the story are too minute to be represented in a small drawing.'

The novel was also published serially in America in *Harper's New Monthly Magazine* from February 1878 to January 1879. It had been planned to use the Hopkins illustrations, but apparently electrotypes could not be dispatched in time, so after falling a month behind with illustrations for the second and third instalments of the story and publishing two with the fourth instalment *Harper's* abandoned them altogether.

Manuscript. The MS. of *The Return of the Native* is written on 439 leaves, measuring 6½"x8", though some are fragmentary. The leaves have been numbered 1–429 by Hardy, but there are 13 scattered supplementary leaves and 3 bear double numbers (e.g. 130–131) suggesting excisions. The MS. is divided for use in *Belgravia*, and corrections and additions are not numerous. Portions of it, to an unusual extent, are fair copy (e.g. Chap. 1), and 7 pages are in Mrs. Hardy's hand. The arguments are marked 'For Magazine only' or 'Omit in Vols', and the 'Sketch map of the scene of the story', a late addition, is not present.

The MS., now in a black grained morocco binding with a printed title-page, was given by Hardy to Clement Shorter in 1908 in return for his having had a number of Hardy's MSS. bound. At Shorter's death in 1926 it was bequeathed to the 'Royal University of Dublin' and is now in the Library of University College, Dublin (National University of Ireland).

Notes on Composition and Publication. The Return of the Native was written at 'Riverside Villa', Sturminster Newton, though it must have been concluded at Upper Tooting where the Hardys took a house in March 1878. We have no evidence as to when it was commenced or finished, but the first 7 chapters were written by 28 August 1877 and the first 2 books by 8 November, and publication was begun in Chatto & Windus's *Belgravia* in January of 1878. The novel had been offered Leslie Stephen for the *Cornhill*, 'but, though he liked the opening, he feared that the relations between Eustacia, Wildeve, and Thomasin might develop into something "dangerous" for a family magazine, and he refused to have anything to do with it unless he could see the whole.'[3] This was not possible, and Hardy's profitable association with Stephen as editor was ended, though Smith, Elder agreed on 20 September 1878 to publish the finished novel.

The Return of the Native was published at 31s. 6*d*. in an edition of 1,000 copies on 4 November 1878. The reviews were not flattering, and in 1882 there were 100 quires and 22 copies in cloth to be remaindered.

Subsequent Editions (*see also* COLLECTED EDITIONS). *The Return of the Native* was never reprinted in its original three-volume form. In 1880 it passed to Kegan Paul and in 1884 to Sampson Low. Hardy added a Preface in July 1895, when he revised the novel for Osgood, McIlvaine's edition of the Wessex Novels, and a Postscript in April 1912, for Macmillan's definitive Wessex Edition. In the latter edition the provocative note on the original conception of the story was inserted at p. 473. The novel was published in America by Henry Holt & Co. in their Leisure Hour Series in December 1878.

* * *

[1895 edition]

Notes on Revision and Publication. Osgood, McIlvaine & Co. had become Hardy's publishers with the appearance of *A Group of Noble Dames* in 1891. On the expiration of Sampson Low's rights in the earlier novels in June 1894 these passed into Osgood, McIlvaine's hands, and they immediately undertook the publication of the first uniform and complete edition of Hardy's works. Though Sampson Low had bought up (largely from Smith, Elder) the plates and the rights of 8 novels and

3. Hardy, in F. W. Maitland, *The Life and Letters of Leslie Stephen* (London, 1906), pp. 276–77.

issued them in frequent popular impressions between 1881 and 1893, 4 books were controlled elsewhere (*Desperate Remedies* by Heinemann, *Under the Greenwood Tree* by Chatto & Windus, and *The Woodlanders* and *Wessex Tales* by Macmillan) and there had been no attempt at such an edition before.

Osgood, McIlvaine's edition is an important one. The text of every novel was thoroughly and carefully revised, the topography (names and distances) corrected where necessary, chapters frequently retitled, and much rewriting done. In addition Hardy prepared a special preface for each volume (prefaces which have a peculiar interest when read consecutively as the work of 1895–6) and assumed the drudgery of proof-reading. The first volume of the edition was published at 6*s*., 4 April 1895, and subsequent volumes followed at monthly intervals, the last appearing in September 1896.

Sheets of the Osgood, McIlvaine edition of the Wessex Novels with an altered title-page were published in America by Harper & Brothers, except for the copyright volumes they already had in type. The plates were used for a number of impressions by Osgood, McIlvaine, their successors Harper & Brothers (London), and after 1902 by Macmillan & Co. for their Uniform Edition.

* * *

[1912 edition]

Notes on Revision and Publication. Macmillan & Co. became the publishers of Hardy's works on the expiration of his agreements with Osgood, McIlvaine & Co. and Harper & Brothers in 1902. As he wrote to Frederick Macmillan, 'The unexpected vicissitudes of the firm [the taking over in 1897 of Osgood, McIlvaine & Co. by Harper & Brothers, whose London representatives they had been], owing to which it befalls that my publisher here has become only a subordinate member of a New York house, make it necessary—from obvious considerations of convenience—that I transfer the English edition of the books to a publisher whose headquarters are London.' Macmillan's had held Hardy's colonial rights since 1894 and were quick to accept his new offer. At first they printed the Wessex Novels from Osgood, McIlvaine's plates, * * * but in 1912 they undertook a new and definitive edition, called (at Frederick Macmillan's suggestion) the 'Wessex Edition'.

For this edition Hardy revised his novels throughout for the last time, correcting a few errors and adding an occasional footnote or brief postscript to the earlier prefaces. The task was a fairly exacting one (see *Later Years*, pp. 151–2). The revisions and notes, with a few exceptions, are by no means so important, however, as those of 1895–6. In a 'General Preface to the Novels and Poems', dated October 1911 and printed in Vol. I, he explained the classification of his novels here adopted for the first time (revealing his estimate of their relative merits) and offered a brief *apologia* for his work. This is an essay of primary importance. The revise of these pages (in the Bliss collection) shows it was much worked over.

The first 2 volumes of the Wessex Edition were published at 7*s*. 6*d*., 30 April 1912, and 2 volumes were issued monthly until the original 20 had appeared. Four volumes were published at irregular intervals thereafter (the last, posthumously) to complete the series. Later impressions incorporate the slight revisions made for the Mellstock Edition in 1919 and some 4 pages of trifling corrections submitted in April 1920. The Wessex Edition is in every sense the definitive edition of Hardy's work and the last authority in questions of text.

American Edition. Harper & Brothers issued the first 21 volumes of the Wessex Edition in America as the 'Autograph Edition' in 1915. This edition, limited to 153 sets with Hardy's signature on an inserted leaf, was in 20 volumes (*The Well-Beloved* and *A Group of Noble Dames* being combined in a single volume) and was partly printed from the English plates and partly reset in America (in the case of volumes already copyright there). The 'Map of the Wessex of the Novels and Poems' appears in Vol. I only, and the illustrations (4 to a volume) are derived from Lea's *Thomas Hardy's Wessex*. Hardy inscribed his own set to his wife, June 1915.

The edition was reissued in 1920 as the 'Anniversary Edition' (recalling Hardy's eightieth year), limited to 1,250 sets.

JOHN PATERSON

[Composition and Revision of the Novel]†

The most striking revelation of the manuscript is that *The Return of the Native* had its origin in what is best described as an

† From John Paterson, *The Making of* The Return of the Native, *English Studies*, 19 (Berkeley, 1960), 8-9, 17-19, 21-25, 35-40, 42, 45-55, 59-66, 75-80, 89-94, 129-30, 163-68. Reprinted by permission of the publishers, the University of California Press.

Ur-novel. After completing a portion of the novel, perhaps as many as sixteen chapters, Hardy subjected it to a basic reorganization. The existence of the Ur-novel is first of all betrayed by an irregularity in the physical structure of the manuscript, by a discrepancy between the numerical order of the leaves and the actual order of their composition: although the names of the principal characters appear unrevised and in their final form on the majority of the leaves, they have been changed on a number of others. Thus on fol. 18, "Clym" is antedated by "*Hugh*"; on fols. 19, 20, 21, 23, 52, 53, and 149, "Yeobright" is antedated by "*Britton*" or "*Bretton*"; on fols. 21, 23, and 150, "Wildeve" is antedated by "*Toogood*" [?]; and on as many as twenty-six leaves between fols. 64 and 206, "Eustacia" is antedated by "*Avice*," the name that was to identify the "heroines" of Hardy's last-published novel, *The Well-Beloved* (1897).[1] These leaves are significant not in themselves but in the irregularity of their appearance. Scattered as they are throughout the first half of the manuscript and juxtaposed with leaves which, by virtue of the stability of the proper names, are identifiable as later in date of composition, they suggest an earlier phase in the history of the novel and, specifically, an Ur-version.

This version is even more dramatically betrayed, however, by the existence of leaves whose texts reveal radical changes in the relation between the major characters. At one point on fol. 89, the reddleman, whose antecedents and associations are appropriately obscure in the finished form of the novel, was regarded as the "grandchild" of Grandfer Cantle and the "nephew" of Christian Cantle:

> ~~Grandfer~~ ~~grandchild~~ *who had*
> The reddleman ~~who was Christian Cantle's nephew had discov-~~
> *entered Egdon that afternoon*
> ~~ered on Egdon~~ was an instance of the pleasing being wasted to form the groundwork of the singular . . .[2] [fols. 89-90]

The boy Johnny, who is eventually designated the son of Susan Nunsuch, was originally named "Orchard" on fols. 46^{v} and 85 and hence was not affiliated with her at all. Eustacia Vye, in the novel as it now stands the granddaughter of an aging Captain Drew

1. Although written in 1892, *The Well-Beloved* may well have been conceived in the period of *The Return of the Native*. It was sketched, Hardy was to acknowledge, many years before the date of its composition. Florence Hardy, *The Later Years of Thomas Hardy* (London, 1930), p. 59.

2. In all quotations from the manuscript, cancelled words and phrases will be run through, the indecipherable portions being left blank (———). Where there is the slightest element of doubt as to the reading of a cancellation, the word or words in question will be followed by a question mark [?]. All interlinear elements—i.e., substitutions and interpolations—will be distinguished from the original text by italics. Unless otherwise indicated, all italics may be assumed to be mine. Hardy did not always put quotation marks around the speeches of his characters in the manuscript: I did not add them if they were missing, even though they appeared in the printed editions.

(Vye),[3] formerly was projected on fols. 64, 65, and 78 as the "daughter" of "Lieutenant" Drew: "My *father's* [love] is not enough for me," she was to have declaimed [fol. 78]. And Thomasin Yeobright, in the final terms of the novel Mrs. Yeobright's niece and Clym's cousin, initially figured on fols. 18, 28, and 91 as their "daughter" and "sister" respectively. "What's the good of Thomasin's *brother* a coming home," Timothy Fairway was to have asked, "now the deed's done" [fol. 28].

* * *

Hardy may well have conceived Thomasin Yeobright the figure of the pure woman caught in the toils of social law and convention and in her story the grounds for a direct attack upon the institution of marriage.[4] For if her honor was, implausibly enough, to have survived the week of her absence undamaged, appearances were to compel her, nevertheless, to marry a man she could no longer love. The hostile tone of the Ur-novel may be gauged by the fact that the present title of the chapter in which she is finally married to Wildeve, "Firmness is discovered in a gentle heart," was antedated by, "*Happiness must needs be sacrificed to propriety*" (fol. 181). Indeed, the possibility that Thomasin might even rebel against the tyranny of the marriage law was at least momentarily considered:

> ~~*refusal*~~ [?] ~~*to marry*~~
> On the Sunday morning following the week of Thomasin's ~~mar-~~
> *marriage*
> ~~riage,~~ a discussion on this subject was in progress . . . [fol. 196]

So far as it took the form of a bowdlerization, the revision of the novel must have been inspired by an editorial directive. Whether this directive came from the *Cornhill* or from *Belgravia* is not known. The circumstantial evidence points, however, to the influence of Leslie Stephen, who had inspected, as has been seen, a fragment of the novel roughly approximating the length of the Ur-version ("he refused to have anything to do with it unless he could see the whole") and who, for reasons which the special character of the Ur-novel may explain, had refused to approve it ("he feared that the relations between Eustacia, Wildeve, and Thomasin

3. Eustacia's grandfather, called Captain Drew in the texts of the manuscript, serial, and first edition, was not given the surname "Vye" until the Uniform Edition of 1895.

4. It may be worth pointing out, in this connection, that Hardy was to exploit in the serial version of *Tess* roughly the same situation exploited in the Ur-version of *The Return of the Native*. For Tess was to be compromised, as Thomasin had been compromised, by a false marriage ceremony. She was not permitted, that is, to succumb to the blandishments of her seducer without first undergoing what she considered a *bona fide* marriage ceremony, the ceremony turning out, of course, to have been a hoax nourished in the wicked imagination of Alex D'Urberville. See Mary Ellen Chase, *Thomas Hardy from Serial to Novel* (Minneapolis, 1927), pp. 77-82.

might develop into something 'dangerous' for a family magazine"). Stephen could, perhaps, have objected on these grounds to the manuscript as it now stands—to the manuscript accepted and published by *Belgravia.* It is unlikely, however, that *Belgravia's* criteria of what was safe for a family magazine were more liberal than those of an editor notable for his liberalism. It is therefore easier to believe that the "dangerous" situation to which Stephen referred was exactly the situation, with all its critical social and moral implications, in which Thomasin and Wildeve were originally involved; that the provisional novel first seen and rejected by him was the Ur-novel itself; and that his serious misgivings prompted Hardy to bowdlerize it before sending it elsewhere—i.e., to *Belgravia.*

* * *

II

At the very last, however, Hardy's reappraisal of the Ur-version went far beyond the narrow requirements of a bowdlerization. Whatever his original intentions may have been, he eventually made changes which were artistic rather than editorial in motivation. Of this fact the almost total transfiguration of Eustacia Vye offers the most dramatic proof: the splendid creature who now dominates the novel as the "erring" heroine to Thomasin's "pure" heroine earlier recalled not the romantic protagonist but the wicked and even disreputable antagonist. In her initial appearance, indeed, she was to have suggested a satanic creature supernatural in origin.

In the novel as it now stands, Eustacia's more sinister possibilities are not, of course, meant to go unregarded. If she is not literally a witch, she is metaphorically one, the metaphor objectifying the satanism implicit in the Byronism of her character. In the special context of the Ur-novel, however, she was evidently intended to play the witch in a more than merely metaphorical sense. She was evidently intended to play the part in something like Susan Nunsuch's literal understanding of the term. Thus at the scene of the bonfiring, she is at present described as "a well-favoured maid enough," though "very strange in her ways" (fol. 30). She was originally described, however—and this, significantly, represents the novel's first reference to her by name—in more pejorative terms: in the opinion of the peasant chorus, "Avice Vye [was] a *witch*" (fol. 31).[5]

That they had good grounds for suspecting the purity of her humanity becomes apparent in the textual transformations of the sixth chapter, the occasion of Eustacia's first major appearance in

5. This comes out in one of the four cancelled lines at the head of fol. 31, all the evidence suggesting that the writing of this page antedated that of fol. 30 and that it represents, therefore, a survival from the Ur-version.

the novel. In the final form of this chapter, she yields passively to the bramble that has caught in her skirt and, instead of hastening along, stands perfectly still in a mood of "desponding reverie" before slowly unwinding herself. This image of a rich and sensuous womanhood was antedated, however, by another image altogether, an image more evocative of the demon than the woman. Instead of surrendering herself to the bramble, Eustacia was to have "*uttered hot words of passion*[?]." And her mood was identified not as "desponding reverie" but as "*anger, which there found a temporary leak*" (fol. 62).

Certainly, the girlish imperiousness, almost humorous in its effect, with which she now manages Johnny Nunsuch in the same chapter, earlier resembled satanic pride and willfulness. She now addresses him "in a tone of pique," chides him as an "ungrateful little boy," and subdues him with, "Come, tell me you like to do things for me, & don't deny it," but the original version suggested a less sympathetic young woman:

> *in a tone of pique*
> As soon as the white-haired man had vanished she said ~~angrily~~ to
> *boy*
> the child, "Ungrateful little ~~scamp~~ [?], how can you contradict me! Never shall you have a bonfire again unless you keep it up
> *to do things for me*
> now. Come, tell me you like ~~a bonfire~~, & don't deny it." [fol. 65]

Again, in the chapter as it now stands, Eustacia's sighs and petulant words express the divine dissatisfaction and melancholia of the romantic heroine: "She vented petulant words every now & then; but there were sighs between her words, & sudden listenings between her sighs." In the original rendering of the passage, however, she was to have given vent to less agreeable emotions. She was to have broken into a laughter which, under the circumstances—the darkness of the heath, and her complete soltitude—could only have had an evil significance:

> *petulant* ~~*broken*~~ *words every now & then;*
> She vented ~~laughs at herself~~, but there were sighs between
> *words*
> her ~~laughs~~, & sudden listenings between her sighs. [fol. 66]

In fact, so far as Egdon Heath was persistently identified, in the Ur-version as in the final version, with the Tartarean underworld of the ancients,[6] Eustacia may well have suggested at this point the image of the restless and ominously unhappy ghost at large in the regions of hell and night.

6. The heath is represented, for example, as a "Titanic form," creates for Mrs. Yeobright and her companion a "Tartarean situation," and is later defined as Eustacia's "Hades."

The diabolism basic to Eustacia's original conception discloses itself even more explicitly in the cancellations and interlineations of the "Queen of Night" chapter. Even in her final development, she is pictured as formidable as well as grand. "Had it been possible for the earth & mankind to be entirely in her grasp for a while . . . ," according to the manuscript as it now stands, "there would have been . . . the same perpetual dilemmas, the same captious interchange of caresses & blows as those we notice now." At one point in the chapter's development, however, a creature more formidable than grand and as much witch as woman could be suggested: i.e., she could bring to mind the grisly incantations of the three witches in *Macbeth*.

> . . . there would have been . . . the same perpetual dilemmas, the
> ~~*sudden changes from fair to foul, from foul to fair*~~ *captious*
> same ~~the same cutting wrongs as we notice now sudden~~ inter-
> *caresses & blows as those*
> change of ~~foul & fair~~ as we notice now. [fol. 73]

Moreover, the soul which is now described as "flame-like" earlier evoked an image more Plutonean than Promethean: it was described as "*a lurid red*"—

> *Eustacia's* *flame-like*
> . . you could fancy the colour of ~~Avice's~~ soul to be ~~a lurid red.~~
> [fol. 73]

The underlid of her eyes, which empowers her, in her final romantic impression, "to indulge in reverie without seeming to do so," previously empowered her to create a positively weird effect: i.e., "to *watch* without seeming to *watch*"—

> *indulge in reverie* *do so*
> This enabled her to ~~watch~~ [?] without seeming to ~~watch~~ [?].
> [fol. 73]

And where Eustacia's mouth seems formed "less to speak than to quiver, less to quiver than to kiss . . . less to kiss than to curl," Avice's, evidently more predatory than amorous, seemed formed "*less to speak than to taste, less to taste than to quiver, less to quiver than to curl*":

> ~~*kiss*~~ *quiver, less to*
> The mouth seemed formed less to speak than to ~~taste, less to~~
> *quiver than to kiss. Some——might have added, less to kiss*
> ~~taste than to quiver, less to quiver~~ than to curl. [fol. 73]

* * *

Her high gods were William the Conqueror, Strafford, & Napoleon Bonaparte, as they had appeared in the Lady's History used at the establishment in which she was educated. Her chief-priest was Byron; her antichrist a well-meaning polemical preacher at Cresmouth, of the name of Slatters.[7] . . [fol. 78^v]

Eustacia's satanism derives, however, from a source older and more rudimentary than the cult of Lord Byron. It derives from the unsophisticated folk imagination with its genius for the occult and the marvellous, for the imagery of ghosts and ogres and demons.[8] For if Eustacia now belongs to Nature, she formerly belonged, as the local witch of the Ur-version, to Supernature. Vestiges of this primitive conception occasionally survive in the definitive text of the novel. The significance of the crooked sixpence she gives to Johnny Nunsuch—"Stay a little longer and I will give you a crooked sixpence"—is not registered in the context of the novel as it now stands. According to folk tradition, however, it was a charm against witchcraft[9] and in the context of the Ur-version would have been emblematical of her membership in a dark fraternity.

When, in the same chapter, she summons the reluctant Wildeve to her bonfire, she now exercises nothing more irresistible than the power of a woman. There are signs, however, that at one time she may have exercised a less legitimate, less honorable power. For when Wildeve answers her summons, she gazes upon him, in a manner reminiscent of Milton's Satan, "as upon some wondrous thing she had created out of chaos" and, in exulting over him, employs terms and metaphors which frankly express a demoniacal nature: "I thought," she tells him, "I would get a little excitement by calling you up and triumphing over you as the Witch of Endor called up Samuel. I determined you should come; and you have come! I have shown my power. . . ." * * *

An even more convincing evidence of her one-time satanism presents itself in the earlier reading of the pricking-in-church episode. In the final form of the manuscript text, Susan Nunsuch drives the knitting needle into Eustacia's arm and extracts from her one womanly screech. In his original form, however, this episode had still more lurid implications: the needle was driven "into my lady's *side*[?]" [fol. 207], and the victim uttered, in the immemorial fashion of evil creatures in pain, "*three* most terrible screeches" [fol. 206]. In other words, where Susan's act of persecution is, in the final form of the novel, the measure of her own delusion, it was, in the unfamiliar form of the Ur-novel, the measure of Eustacia's almost literal, and clearly more than metaphorical, demonism.

7. These allusions to Lord Byron will later be removed.

8. The primitive supernaturalistic element in Hardy is variously documented in Ruth A. Firor, *Folkways in Thomas Hardy* (Philadelphia, 1931); J. O. Bailey, "Hardy's 'Mephistophelian Visitants'" in *PMLA*, LXI (1946), 1146-1184; and Donald Davidson, "The Traditional Basis of Thomas Hardy's Fiction" in *The Southern Review*, VI (1940), 162–178.

9. Firor, *Folkways in Thomas Hardy*, p. 91.

* * *

Clym Yeobright himself did not, in the initial formulation of the scene, stand out from his neighbors. "Grandfer Cantle has been here ever so long," he tells Timothy Fairway in the manuscript's final form, "& we thought you'd come with him as you live so near one another." In the original form of the text, Clym used the dialect of his guests:

> *have* *near*
> . . . we thought you'd ~~ha~~' come with him as you live so ~~handy~~ one another. [fol. 160]

"Master Yeobright," cries Grandfer Cantle on this occasion, "—look me over too. I have altered for the better, haven't I—hey?" "To be sure we will," Fairway replies, examining the Grandfer's countenance. In the early version of the scene, however, Clym Yeobright, not Timothy Fairway, was called upon to serve the purposes of comedy:

> *we* *Fairway*
> "To be sure ~~I~~ will," said ~~Yeobright~~, taking the candle & moving it over the surface of the Grandfer's countenance . . . [fol. 161]

Moreover, where Clym is finally addressed by Timothy as "this *gentleman*," he was earlier addressed, less reverently, as "this young man" [fol. 160] and where he is now approached by Grandfer Cantle as "*Mister* Clym," he was approached in the original version as plain "Clym" [fol. 161].

Under these circumstances, it is not surprising that the dimensions of Clym's world were formerly not imagined as exceeding the boundaries of Wessex. The manuscript now reads:

> At the death of his father, a neighbouring gentleman had kindly undertaken to give the boy a start; & this assumed the form of sending him to the shop in Budmouth above-mentioned. Yeobright did not wish to go there, but it was the only feasible opening. Thence he went to London; & thence, shortly after, to Paris where he had remained till now. [fol. 196]

According to the original rendering of the passage, however, Clym was not to have gone as far abroad as godless and exotic Paris. Budmouth was to have sufficed, in the narrower field of Ur-version, as the symbol of the great Babylonian outer world. Furthermore, Clym's patron and benefactor was to have been not a gentleman but, to illustrate the essential provincialism of his experience as well as the prose-scale of the Ur-novel, a country parson:

> At the death of his father, a neighbouring *clergyman* had kindly undertaken to give the boy a start; & this took the form of sending him to the shop in Budmouth above-mentioned, *the owner of which was a relative of the parson's wife*. Yeobright did not

> wish to go but it was the only possible arrangement, & there he had remained till now. [fol. 196]

Hence, in the original version of his quarrel with his mother, Clym refused to return, not to Paris, but to Budmouth:

> *Paris* ~~*Cresmouth*~~
> "I am not going back to ~~Budmouth~~ again, mother," he said. [fol. 203]

It is a question, in fact, whether the world beyond Wessex was invoked anywhere in the Ur-version of the novel. Even Eustacia and her grandfather, who are finally represented as romantic strangers, were once imagined as natives of the heath. Thus Captain Drew (Vye) initially was not differentiated from the country bumpkins about him. Eventually called upon to remark, as a man of high station and wide interests, upon the state of the country, he was originally called upon to comment in a country fashion upon the state of the weather:

> He would then return to the old man, who made another remark
> *state of the country*
> about the ~~weather~~ . . . [fol. 8]

And the dialogue that now suggests the knowledgeability of a man of the world earlier suggested the blunt curiosity of a local worthy: e.g.,

> Why did she cry out? *The deuce you have.*
> ~~H'm.~~ Perhaps she's your wife. *That would have interested me forty years ago.*
> What was she doing there? *I know the town well.* [fol. 8-9]

Indeed, in the original form of the scene, Diggory Venn approached the Captain as a social equal. For where he now addresses him as "Sir," he earlier addressed him as "*neighbour*" and was himself addressed with the same familiarity [fols. 9-10]. At one point, the old man was so little conscious of any superiority on his part, that he could feel "*his presence was no more desired*" by the reddleman:

> *nodded his head indifferently, and*
> The elder traveller ~~that his presence was no more desired &~~
> *horses &* *saying*
> ~~as~~ the reddleman turned his ^ van in upon the turf, ~~he said~~ goodnight . . . (fol. 10)

Certainly, the Captain's language was not distinguishable, originally, from the dialect of his country neighbors. "It is not that damsel of Blooms-End" was antedated by "'*Tisn't* that *young* damsel of Blooms-End" (fol. 9), and where he now describes Thomasin as a "girl," he formerly described her as a "*maid*" (fol. 9). "When are you coming indoors, Eustacia?" he asks in the final form of the manuscript text. " 'Tis almost bedtime. . . . Surely 'tis somewhat childish of you to stay out playing at bonfires so long . . ." In the earlier form of the passage, however, he was to have used the local dialect.

> *are you* *Eustacia*
> "When ~~be ye a~~ coming indoors, ~~Avice~~?" he asked. 'Tis almost
>
> *I've been home these two hours, & am tired out* *you* *stay*
> bedtime.——∧Surely 'tis somewhat childish of ~~us~~[?] to ~~bide~~[?]
> *playing at bonfires*
> out ~~bonfiring~~ so long . . . [fol. 65]

If this image of Eustacia's grandfather contradicts the image of the retired naval officer depicted in the novel as it now stands, the manuscript suggests that he was not at first conceived as the naval officer at all. "In these lonely places, wayfarers . . . frequently plod on for miles without speech," the author eventually observes with reference to Diggory and the old man, but in the original form of the text the noun "wayfarers" was qualified by the adjective "native":

> The silence conveyed to neither any sense of awkwardness: in
> *after a first greeting*
> these lonely places ~~native~~ wayfarers ∧ frequently plod on for
> miles without speech . . . [fol. 8]

Unless the appearance of the adjective was inadvertent, the author must have regarded Captain Vye at this time as, with Diggory Venn, a native of the heath. More significantly still, those elements which establish him as a retired naval officer and hence as a stranger to Egdon entered the novel as interlinear additions to the text. Such is the status of the physical description by which he is introduced in the first paragraph of the novel's second chapter, "*He wore a glazed hat, an ancient boatcloak, & shoes, his brass buttons bearing an anchor upon their face,*" and of the sentence which concludes the same paragraph, "*One would have said that he had been, in his day, a naval officer of some order or other*" [fol. 6]. And such is the status of a significant reference in the "Queen of Night" chapter to his "*old charts & other rubbish*" [fol. 79]. Although the material displaced by these interlineations cannot be entirely deciphered, the few words that can be made out make it clear that a radical alteration in sense did take place. They suggest that the Captain's status as a retired naval officer was an entirely new departure and that he and his "daughter" were, in the context of the Ur-novel, not romantic strangers but natives of the heath.

Nothing in the manuscript specifically establishes Eustacia herself as an Egdonite born and bred. At an early stage of the novel's development, however, both she and her grandfather were discussed in terms which did not distinguish them from the ordinary population of the heath. They were identified casually and informally as plain "Avice" and "Jonathan Drew." "Who gave her away?" Mrs. Yeobright asks Diggory, who had come to report on Thomasin's marriage to Wildeve:

> *Miss*
> "~~Avice~~ Vye."
>
> *Miss*
> "How very remarkable. ~~Avice~~ Vye. It is to considered an honour, I suppose."
>
> *Miss*
> "Who's ~~Avice~~ Vye?" said Clym.
>
> *Captain*
> "~~Jonathan~~ Drew's grand-daughter, of Mistover Knap."
>
> "A proud girl from Budmouth," said Mrs. Yeobright. . . . [fol. 190]

Furthermore, where in the serial text the time is told "by *the Captain's* clock,"[1] in the manuscript text it was told—and the note of complete familiarity is unmistakable—"by *Jonathan's* clock" [fol. 147*a*]. At one time, then, the line separating the Vyes from their country cousins could not have been very marked.

That Eustacia herself was as indigenous to the heath as Diggory Venn or Christian Cantle is most dramatically testified by an important discrepancy between the texts of the first edition of 1878 and the Uniform Edition of 1895. Where did her dignity come from? In the 1895 edition, a high and foreign lineage is evoked:

> By a latent vein from Alcinous' line, her father hailing from Phaeacia's isle?—or from Fitzalan and De Vere, her maternal grandfather having had a cousin in the peerage? Perhaps it was the gift of Heaven—a happy convergence of natural laws. Among other things opportunity had of late years been denied her of learning to be undignified, for she lived lonely. Isolation on a heath renders vulgarity well-nigh impossible. It would have been as easy for the heathponies, bats, and snakes to be vulgar as for her. . . .[2]

In the text of the first edition, however, a background of natural simplicity rather than aristocratic splendor was evoked: "Where did her dignity come from? By *no* side passage from Fitzalan or De Vere. It was the gift of heaven—a happy convergence of natural

1. *Belgravia,* XXXV (1878), 249.
2. *The Return of the Native* (New York, Harper & Brothers [1895], pp. 80-81.

laws. . . ."[3] The aristocratic girl of the novel in its final form would appear, then, to have had her genesis in the primitive child of nature. Indeed, as a creature of supernatural malice, as the black witch of local tradition, she could not really have been anything else.

* * *

The course that the Ur-novel was to have taken cannot now be made out. The original relationships between the main characters and the original terms of Clym's response to Eustacia's pricking-in-church do suggest, however, that it was not to have been dominated, as it now is, by themes of romantic love and aspiration, but that a rural melodrama of crime and passion unrelieved by images of romantic exaltation was projected.

Thus the adjustment in Eustacia's relation to the Captain must have accompanied her transition from Satanic antagonist to Promethean protagonist. In being converted from daughter to granddaughter, she achieved the fatherlessness, and in effect the isolation from conventional law and authority, that ultimately distinguishes her as a type of the romantic individual. As the demoniacal Avice Vye, certainly, she scarcely qualified as the heroine of the novel in the romantic sense that she now does. Although she was evidently to have desired a greater love than Wildeve could offer and to have chosen Clym Yeobright as the agent of that love, she suggested the demon rather than the human lover and hence was not likely to have authorized the romantic death which now marks the climax of the novel.

* * *

The hypothesis that the original emphasis of the novel was not romantic is corroborated by Thomasin's translation from daughter to niece, from sister to cousin. For this change could only have been made to permit the development of a sentimental connection between Clym and Thomasin.

To begin with, it was evidently one of Clym's functions in the Ur-novel, if not his only function, to perform as the brother to a sister in trouble. Thus, where in the novel's final form he is not called upon to deliver an opinion on the merits of Thomasin's marriage, in the Ur-novel he was apparently to have joined Mrs. Yeobright in opposing it:

> his mother had at first discountenanced [it] ~~but equally with himself~~, but had since . . . looked upon [it] in a little more favourable light. [fol. 186]

3. *The Return of the Native* [First edition] (London, Smith, Elder & Co., 1878), I, p. 152.

A specific allusion elsewhere to this opposition appeared in the serial version, although it was deleted from the text of the first edition.

> Seeing [Thomasin] living there just as she had been living before he left home, [Eustacia conjectured], Clym naturally suspected nothing more about her than a possible love-affair. *Having, with his mother, been opposed originally to Wildeve's courtship of Thomasin,* he was clearly at present ignorant that Mrs. Yeobright had latterly assented to their union, and to its being privately performed away from home because of the sensation previously excited by her forbidding the banns. Eustacia felt a wild jealousy of Thomasin on the instant.[4]

In the text of the first edition, however, this allusion to a brotherly concern that was once, but is now no longer, significant was omitted entirely. "Seeing her living there just as she had been living before he left home," it recorded simply, "he naturally suspected nothing. Eustacia felt a wild jealousy of Thomasin on the instant."[5]

If, as Thomasin's brother, Clym was to have opposed her marriage and to have returned to see, perhaps, that justice was done, as her cousin he could play an entirely new role: he could return now to suggest that he had felt and still felt the stirrings of a more-than-brotherly affection. "What's the good of Thomasin's *brother* a coming home now the deed's done," Timothy Fairway had declared originally. "He should have come afore if so be he wanted to stop it." With Clym's emergence as Thomasin's cousin, Timothy's dialogue could infer something more than a desire to stop a marriage:

> *cousin Clym* *after*
> What's the good of Thomasin's ~~brother~~ a coming home ~~now~~ the
> *so*
> deed's done. He should have come afore if ^ be he wanted to stop it, *& marry her himself*[6] [fol. 28]

"I'll tell you what," Yeobright was at one time to have said to his mother. "I don't think it kind to Tamsin to let her be married like this . . ." An interlinear addition to the text was, however, to disclose that his solicitude was something more than fraternal:

> *in a tone which showed some slumbering feeling still*
> "I'll tell you what," said Yeobright again./"I don't think it kind to Tamsin to let her be married like this . . ." [fol. 188]

4. *Belgravia,* XXXV (1878), 263.
5. *The Return of the Native* [First edition] II, p. 20.
6. The very evident condensation of the script would testify that the last clause of Timothy's sentence was a postscript addition to the text.

Thomasin's transition from sister to cousin had the effect, then, of opening up a whole new dimension not envisaged in the Ur-program of the novel. Indeed, the ramifications of this change are not limited to the relations of Clym and Thomasin but extend to the novel as a whole. Eustacia's infatuation with Clym Yeobright is partly stimulated by her anxiety over the rivalry of his cousin, Thomasin. This motive could not have been operative, of course, while the terms of the Ur-version were in force. Again, the architecture of the novel ultimately rests on an elaborate and paradoxical situation involving four lovers who assume precisely those combinations most likely to produce their unhappiness. In a novel in which Thomasin figured as Clym's sister, however, this structural irony would manifestly not be possible.

It is hard, then, to believe that the Ur-version was to have followed the course of the novel in its present form. What Hardy had in mind cannot now be made out. He may have conceived Thomasin as the central figure of a drama of seduction and later replaced her domestic tragedy with Eustacia's cosmic tragedy. But there is no warrant for believing that Eustacia Vye, however ambiguous she may have been as heroine, was ever confined to the background of the novel.

* * *

Diggory Venn may be said to have passed, in his evolution, through three distinct phases. In the first, he was the blood-relation of the Cantles, the rude member of the peasant community, and the unsuccessful suitor of an entirely countrified Thomasin Yeobright. In a second and dominant phase that linked him more to Supernature than to Nature, he assumed as the reddleman the character of the romantic outcast. In a third and final phase, however, the mysterious creature in red was domesticated. For when, contrary to his original intention, Hardy added a sixth book providing for Diggory's marriage to the widowed Thomasin, the Ishmaelite had necessarily to give way to the citizen-dairy-farmer . . . . The image of Diggory Venn represents a complex, then, of three clearly irreconcileable elements: the yokel, the reddleman, and the ordinary citizen.

Hardy was anxious, of course, to emphasize the creature of magic and mystery. In the manuscript . . . he separated him from the low-born Cantle tribe and, at a stroke, extended the range of his possibilities as a creature of romance; he replaced the epithet, "red," by the more sensational "*blood-coloured*" [fol. 88]; and later underlined his weird propensity for preternaturally sudden appearances by having him rise, as Eustacia's emissary, behind rather than in front of Wildeve:

On his——reaching the top
. . . when Wildeve ascended the long acclivity at its base. ^ A
behind
shape grew up from the earth immediately ~~in front of~~ him. . . .
[fol. 175]

Diggory's identification with the supernatural was to be reinforced, furthermore, by revisions made for the first edition. In the serial, he had hailed the heath folk at the scene of the bonfire and evoked the following response:

> ' 'Twas behind you, Christian, that I heard it—down there.'
> 'Hoi-i-i-i!' cried a voice from the darkness. (B, XXXIV, 280)

In the first edition, however, he evoked a more dramatic response. He recalled, as the pious nature of Christian's counterspell should indicate, the figure of the evil one:

> ' 'Twas behind you, Christian, that I heard it—down there.'
> *'Yes—'tis behind me!' Christian said. 'Matthew, Mark, Luke, and John; bless the bed that I lie on; four angels guard——'*
> *'Hold your tongue. What is it?' said Fairway.*
> 'Hoi-i-i-i' cried a voice from the darkness. (F, 1, 64-65)

Again, on the same occasion, Christian, terrified by the superstitious talk of his neighbors, had cried out in the serial version, "Don't ye talk o't no more" (B, XXXIV, 280). In the text of the first edition, he went on to say, "*If he had a handkerchief over his head he'd look for all the world like the Devil in the picture of the Temptation.*" (F, 1,67). As the visible emanation of the weird secular spirit of the heath or, in the more melodramatic terms of Christian's Christian imagination, as the Devil himself, Diggory Venn was evidently intended to acquire an at least shadowy symbolism.

Certainly, as a creature of vaguely supernatural origins, his psychology was evidently to have been, during the early stages of the novel's development, a dim and enigmatical one. At two points in the manuscript, at least, substantial passages were interpolated ascribing to him specific motives and emotions where none had been ascribed to him before. He was originally to have received without comment Johnny Nunsuch's report that Wildeve and Eustacia had met clandestinely:

"What did the gentleman say to her, my sonny?"
did *best*
"He only said he ^ like~~d~~ her ^ & how he was coming to see her again under Blackbarrow o'nights ——"
"And what did she say?"
"I can't mind. Please Master Reddleman may I go home along now?"

> "Ay, to be sure you may. I'll go a bit of ways with you."
>
> He conducted the boy out of the gravel-pit & into the path leading to his *father's* cottage. When the little figure had vanished in the darkness the reddleman returned, resumed his seat by the fire, & proceeded to darn again. [fol. 87]

Eight lines of a dialogue were subsequently added, however, providing for a less inscrutable response—for a response more recognizably human:

> "What did the gentleman say to her, my sonny?"
>
> *did* *best*
>
> "He only said he ∧ like~~d~~ her ∧ & how he was coming to see her again under Blackbarrow o'nights—"
>
> *"Ha!" cried the reddleman, slapping his hand against the side of his van so that the whole fabric shook under the blow. "That's the secret o't!"*
>
> *The little boy jumped clean from the stool.*
>
> *"My man—don't you be afraid," said the dealer in red, suddenly becoming gentle. "I forgot you were here. That's only a curious way reddlemen have of going mad for a moment; but they don't hurt anybody.* And what did the lady say then?"
>
> "I can't mind. Please, Master Reddleman may I go home along now?"
>
> "Ay, to be sure you may, I'll go a bit of ways with you."
>
> He conducted the boy out of the gravel-pit & into the path leading to his *mother's*[7] cottage. . . . [fols. 87-87*a*]

Originally, too, Diggory's magical appearance on the heath and his recovery of the guineas in a weird game of dice with Wildeve were not specifically accounted for. His appearance was to have been, presumably, all the more uncanny, all the more supernatural, in being neither foreshadowed nor motivated. But a substantial passage was subsequently entered, establishing that, unknown to Wildeve, the reddleman had been present at the Quiet Woman during the raffle scene and hence had not only witnessed his departure with Christian but had guessed that he had designs on the guineas:

> *Within the room* [which Wildeve and Christian have just quitted] *the men fell into chat till their attention was for a moment drawn to the chimney corner. This was large, & in addition to its proper recess contained within its jambs, like many on Egdon, a receding seat, so that a person might sit there absolutely unobserved, provided there was no fire to light him up, as was the case now & throughout the summer. From the niche a single object protruded into the light from the candles on the table. It was a clay pipe, & its colour was crimson red. The men had been attracted to this object by a voice behind the pipe asking for a light.*

7. This change would of course support the hypothesis that Johnny was not originally cast as Susan Nunsuch's son.

> *"Upon my life it fairly startled me when you spoke," said Fairway, handing a candle. "Oh—'tis the reddleman. You've kept a quiet tongue, young man."*
>
> *"Yes, I had nothing to say," observed Venn. In a few minutes he arose, & wished the company Good-night.* [fol. 254^{v}]

As a result of this interpolation, what had once been conceived as an apparition was converted to a mere appearance.

If Hardy originally saw Diggory Venn as a creature of magic and mystery, as a creature whose movements had no rational explanation, he was eventually committed, in the extraneous sixth book, to the conventional figure of the prosperous bridegroom—to such an image of Diggory Venn as flatly contradicted the image and the symbol earlier created. Hardy's perplexity and embarrassment at this unlooked-for turn of events are plain to see in the manuscript of Book Sixth. He was hard-put, for example, to account for the sudden worldly prosperity of his one-time weirdly supernatural creature:

> I gave up dealing in reddle last Christmas, said Venn. It was a profitable trade, & I found that by that time I had made enough
> ~~stone quarries~~ *large dairy of eighty cows that*
> to take the ~~farm~~ my father had in his lifetime. [fol. 405]

Hardy had Thomasin exclaim,

> To think that a man should be so silly as to go mooning about
> *& a man of money, as he is now.*
> like that for a girl's glove. A respectable dairy-man, too. ^ What a pity! [fol. 410]

Before the last page of the novel was written, in fact, Diggory was supplied not only with land, money, and eighty cows, but also with grand connections:

> In a moment an open fly was driven past, in which sat Venn &
> *grand*
> Mrs. Venn, Yeobright, & a ^ relative of Venn's who had come from Budmouth for the occasion. [fol. 422]

And he was, furthermore, in an ironic reversal of form, to be able to present for all these happy occasions a distinctly Christian countenance:

> . . . there stood within the room Diggory Venn, no longer a reddleman, but exhibiting the strangely altered hues of an
> *Christian*
> ordinary ^ countenance . . . [fol. 405]

In the last analysis, Hardy's major problem in dealing with the figure of Diggory Venn turned out to be as much the opposition between the citizen and the peasant as the opposition between the citizen and the reddleman. For, in the hasty preparation of the manuscript for serial publication, the terms of Diggory's rehabilitation in Book Sixth, obviously not contemplated or provided for in the original program of the novel, were not everywhere carried out, and hence he tended frequently to betray a closer affinity with the proletarian Cantles than with the genteel Yeobrights. The alterations made in the text of the first edition sought, therefore, to bring the obsolescent Diggory up to date, to suppress all evidences of his humble peasanthood and so provide for his middle-class apotheosis in Book Sixth.

* * *

The instability of the reddleman as a character-image is ultimately traceable to fluctuations in the conception of the novel over which, as has been seen, the author had no control. For the radical failure of Clym Yeobright, however, Hardy himself was in large measure responsible.

Clym was finally conceived as a hero of almost mythical proportions. As the agonized conscience of his time and place, he was called upon to evoke the titanic forms of Prometheus and Oedipus. Between the image of the character and the almost religious emotion it was meant to inspire, however, a persistent discrepancy eventually makes itself felt. For one thing, Hardy could not produce that impression of physical force or magnitude that distinguishes the tragic figures of classical drama. He could not make concrete in terms of gesture and dialogue the alleged mental or spiritual greatness of his hero. For another, he could never convincingly pass Clym off as an aristocratic hero like Oedipus or Prometheus. The ghost of the provincial boy who, in the Ur-novel, had gone to Budmouth to be a shopkeeper, could never completely be laid, and it returned to frustrate the consummation Hardy had in mind. Finally, Clym's true analogy would appear to have been less with Oedipus and Prometheus than with Hamlet. But to such an analogy Hardy was apparently unable or unwilling to consent.

What was intended in the figure of Clym Yeobright and the difficulties that put themselves in the way are variously identified in the manuscript. During the scene of the Christmas party, for instance, he was visualized as crossing the room and "striking his great head against the mistletoe . . ." [fol. 162]. The physical grandeur of the traditional hero was clearly incompatible, however, with the nature of Clym's sensibility and hence the adjective was—regretfully, no doubt—withdrawn. Clym steadily resisted, in fact, all attempts to conceive him in physical terms. When he addressed the indifferent citizenry of Egdon Heath on the subject of his scholastic program, he was at one time required to place himself against a convenient tree:

> *with unexpected earnestness*
> "I'll tell you, said Yeobright ^. I am not sorry to have the opportunity. ~~He leant his back against a tree, & went on.~~ "I've come home because . . ." [fol. 198]

This physical attitude was patently artificial, however, and hence was not allowed to remain. Significantly, when Hardy sought to objectify the meaning legible in Clym's face, he had to resort to the artificial device of an analogue in painting:

> . . . it could be nobody else. ~~A strange power~~
> *The spectacle constituted*
> *intensest*
> *an area of two feet in Rembrandt's* ~~best~~ *manner.* A strange power in the ~~you~~ man's appearance . . . [fol. 157]

If Hardy found it difficult to objectify the grandeur of his hero in terms of physical detail, he also found it difficult to objectify that grandeur in terms of dialogue. He could not devise a noble or elevated style of speech that did not expose Clym's unreality as a hero in the grand manner. Indeed, Clym's natural accents, as Hardy apparently realized, tended more to the schoolmasterish than to the heroic:

> *little*
> Is it not very unwise in us to go on spending the ^ money ~~we~~
> *we've got* *keep down* *an*
> ~~already possess~~ when I can ~~diminish~~ expenditure by ^ honest
> *do me good*
> occupation? The out-door exercise will ~~be beneficial~~ & who
> *go on with*
> knows but that in a few months I shall be able to ~~resume~~ my reading again? [fol. 278]

Elsewhere, in situations where emotions of a generally heroic nature are called for, he lapsed too easily into feeble imitations of Jacoban rhetoric. "I don't know where to look," he had said at the moment of his greatest anguish, "my thoughts go through me like swords." To this already literary expression of guilt and grief, Hardy was dubiously inspired to add, "*O if any man wants to make himself immortal by painting a picture of wretchedness, let him come here!*" [fol. 333].

Hardy's attempt to celebrate Clym as a hero of almost mythical proportions was perhaps most obvious in the scene of the Christmas party where he sought to draw attention to the reverential emotion of the peasant community:

> ~~*none of us*~~
> "Master Cantle always was that, as we know. But ~~I am nothing~~
> ~~*be anything*~~ ~~*Really*~~
> ~~by the side of you, Clym.~~ ^ ~~There would ha' been nobody here~~

~~——— who could have stood as decent second to 'ee, or even third if I hadn't been in the militia. But I am nothing by the~~ I
Mister
am nothing by the side of you, ^ Clym."

"*Nor any o' us*," *said Humphrey, in a low rich tone of admiration, not intended to reach anybody's ears.*

"Really, there would have been nobody here who could have stood as decent second to him, or even third, if I hadn't
a sojer *Bang-up Locals, as we was called*
been ^ in the ~~militia~~, said Grandfer Cantle. And even as 'tis
all
we ^ look a little scammish beside him. . . ." [fol. 161]

However, the antiheroic mediocrity of Clym's station in the world—at this point in the novel's development, he was imagined as assistant to a jeweler in Budmouth—rendered the hero worship of the peasant community plainly gratuitous.

Hardy hoped to deal with this disparity between the image and the emotion evoked by moving the scene of Clym's operations from provincial Budmouth to metropolitan Paris. But his hero's essential provinciality was not perceptibly affected by the Parisian experience. Challenged by Eustacia to give his impressions of the great city, he could only refer to such commonplaces as the Louvre, the Galerie d'Apollon, and Versailles; and even when he was permitted, by an interlinear addition to the text, to expatiate on the subject, could produce nothing more convincing in the way of credentials than "*Fontainebleau, St. Cloud, the Bois, & many other familiar haunts of the Parisians*" [fol. 229]. Clym's Paris was, in other words, the Paris of Baedeker.

The superficiality of his cosmopolitanism became most apparent when Hardy contrived, in the manuscript and serial, to wrap him in a "faded Parisian dressing-gown":

> Beside him were the leggings, thick boots, leather gloves, and sleeve-waistcoat in which he worked: [these he had thrown off for comfort, *and had wrapped himself in a faded Parisian dressing-gown.*] (B, XXXVI, 261-262)

The triviality of the image must have been sufficiently obvious, however, for it was deleted in the text of the first edition (F, 3, 32).

* * *

Equally unsuccessful were Hardy's attempts to make Clym's "hero-as-thinker" more convincing. In the serial text of the novel, Clym had been described as "in many points synchronous with the central town thinkers of his date" (B,XXXV, 484). To this the first edition was able to add, on the basis of Clym's dubious Parisian experience, "*Much of this development he may have owed to his studious life in Paris, where he had become acquainted* with *ethical systems popular at the time*" (F, 2, 85). "But it is so dreadful," Eustacia had protested in the magazine version, "—a furze-cutter; and you a man who have lived about the world, and speak French, and who are fit for what is so much better than this" (B, XXXVI, 241). His range as a scholar and thinker was broadened in the first edition, where he was said to "*know the classics,*" too (F, 2, 272). Finally, in an unguarded moment in the serial, Clym had betrayed the fundamental orthodoxy of his thinking and feeling: ". . . I could keep you away from her," he told Eustacia, "till heaven and hell came to an end if I could" (B,XXXVI, 500). As a man who had learned at Paris the "ethical systems popular at the time," however, he was ready in the first edition to keep her away from his mother, "till the *universe* come to an end" (F, 3, 136). Once again, it should be obvious that these revisions tended to disclose rather than to solve Hardy's problem. Clym's heroism as thinker continued everywhere to be celebrated, but was seldom convincingly presented.

In the last analysis, Clym's failure, the discrepancy between the image created and the emotion evoked, originated in Hardy's reluctance to acknowledge that his hero's true analogy was not with King Oedipus but with Lord Hamlet. With reference to the dance at East Egdon, Clym had remarked in the manuscript:

> *hook & gloves are*
> At that kind of meeting people would shun me. My ~~affliction is~~
> like the St. Lazarus rattle of the leper . . . [fol. 285]

Quite clearly, however, neither his affliction nor his book and gloves, neither his blindness nor his fall from prosperity, justified the grimness of the analogy. Clym assumed in effect, without in the least having earned it, the sublime insight and humility of King Oedipus at the last station of his tragic progress. Indeed, his emotion at this point was so clearly gratuitous, so clearly greater than the facts would warrant, and Hardy himself was so clearly uncertain how to account for it, that one is tempted to reject both the "affliction" and the hook and gloves and to look for its source in that disaffection from life, that corruption of spirit or failure of nerve, which is more characteristic of Hamlet than of Oedipus.

There is some evidence, certainly, that the role of the humanitarian reformer that Clym was called upon to play was not an altogether natural extension of his personality. "The humblest walk of life would satisfy him," Hardy was to report, "if it could be made to work in with some form of his culture scheme." Originally, however, he ascribed to him a markedly different motive, a motive less suggestive of the humanitarian than of Hamlet—Clym wanted to be free not to educate the masses but "*to think his own thoughts*":

> *walk*
> . . . the humblest ~~way~~ of life would ~~have satisfied him, could he be free to think his own thoughts~~ satisfy him if it ~~did not~~ could
> *culture*
> be made to work in with some form of his ~~education~~ scheme.
> [fol. 277]

Again, according to the serial text, Clym Yeobright "showed that thought [was] a disease of flesh, and indirectly bore evidence that ideal physical beauty [was] incompatible with *emotional development and wide recognitions*" (B, XXXV, 258). In the text of the first edition, however, he was once again required to assume the humanitarian mask: he was required to bear evidence "that ideal physical beauty [was] incompatible with *growth of fellow-feeling and a full sense of the coil of things*" (F, 2, 7). Some seventeen years later Hardy apparently recognized that "fellow-feeling," albeit an excellent thing in a young man, was not in harmony with the essential, if unspoken, gloom of his hero. For in the Uniform Edition of 1895 Clym was once again permitted to bear evidence "that ideal physical beauty [was] incompatible with *emotional development and a full recognition of the coil of things.*"

Hardy preferred, of course, to regard himself as a meliorist. He was offended in his later years by the critical tendency to describe him as a pessimist. Yet his very indignation on the subject should indicate that there was more truth in the charge than he cared to admit. He was, after all, as anxious to be cheerful as the age in which he lived, and, in this sense, his profession of meliorism was a gesture as much of self-assurance as of fellow-feeling. Clym's failure as a character may be said to originate, then, in Hardy's reluctance to articulate the pessimistic conclusions which the image of the character plainly justified. The alienation of the intelligent and sensitive individual from life and society, the theme that was increasingly to dominate modern fiction, was suppressed in favor of a basically irrelevant and superficial humanitarianism, and hence Clym came to express not what Hardy deeply and truly believed, but what, as a citizen of his time and place, he preferred to believe.

* * *

Perhaps the most alarming aspect of Thomasin's plight in the special terms of the Ur-version was the sinister nature of her antagonists. For, like Eustacia Vye, Damon Wildeve was originally to have presented a very different image from that which he now presents. In the first place, the obliquity of his conduct was not to have been redeemed by the lucky accident of his youth. In the manuscript and serial, he was conceived, not as the quixotic young man, but, more darkly, as the *adult* philanderer:

> [*He appeared to have reached the stage of life at which fervour and phlegm, impulse and reflection, balance like a pair of wrestlers, previous to passion's final abandonment of its early sway. In truth,*] *he was about thirty-five*; and of the two properties, form and motion, the latter first attracted the eye in him. (B, XXXIV, 483)

In the first edition, however, the first sentence was deleted and the reference to his thirty-five years displaced: "*He was quite a young man*," the novel now reported simply, "and of the two properties, form and motion, the latter first attracted the eye in him" (F, 1, 90). Where, then, in the serial publication, the reddleman had beheld "a male figure ascending from the valley" (B, XXXV, 9), in the first edition he beheld "*the outline of a young man* ascending from the valley" (F, 1, 182).[8]

Wildeve's conversion from near middle age to young manhood must of course have been the index of a radical transformation in his image: without his youth to excuse him, he must have resembled the squalid and disreputable roué. Certainly, there are strong indications in the manuscript that he was to have been guilty not simply of the moral irresolution of the romantic lover but, more seriously, of the calculated evil of the romantic criminal. For one thing, the invalid marriage of the Ur-version may not have been invalid by accident. Thomasin may have been the victim, not of an innocent oversight on Wildeve's part, but of a deliberate deception. Such, at any rate, was Mrs. Yeobright's understanding at one time, for she could notify Clym in Chapter VII of Book Second that Thomasin was at that moment marrying Wildeve,

> unless ~~he disappoints her again~~ some accident happens again as it did the first time. [fol. 187]

the substitution and the clause substituted suggesting that, originally, Wildeve's failure at Anglebury was more intentional than accidental. A cancelled passage in the manuscript of the same chapter corroborates this view:

> Her aunt was very far from thinking that under no circumstances would Thomasin come back to that house again that day. What she meant to do *if the man were to deceive her the*

8. In the novel in its present form, the old image of a Wildeve somewhat soiled by time and experience occasionally survives. Certainly, he has lived long enough to have failed as an engineer and to have made a going concern of the Quiet Woman Inn. More specifically, he can still be described as "older than Tamsin Yeobright by a good-few summers" (p. 25).

> *second time* she had not clearly decided, but what she would not do was clear enough in her mind . . .[9] [fol. 184]

For the phrasing, "*deceive her the second time*," implies that originally Wildeve was guilty of something more serious than a naive failure to secure the proper marriage license.

The hypothesis that Thomasin had someone more dangerous to contend with than the rudderless young man who finally emerges would be supported by a later development of the manuscript. In the final version he is not held responsible for the misappropriation of Mrs. Yeobright's guineas and the tragic events that follow. Although he elects to accompany Christian to Mistover Knap, it is clear that he has not designed the seizure of the money in Christian's charge in the game of dice that follows:

> "Where are you going?" Wildeve asked.
>
> "To Mistover Knap. I have to see Mrs. Thomasin there—that's all."
>
> "I am going there, too, to fetch Mrs. Wildeve. We can walk together."
>
> Wildeve became lost in thought, and a look of inward illumination came into his eyes. It was money for his wife that Mrs. Yeobright could not trust him with. "Yet she could trust this fellow," he said to himself. "Why doesn't that which belongs to the wife belong to the husband too?"

Originally, however, the implications were that Wildeve's seduction of the simpleton Christian was the deliberate resolution of a villain and not the vagary of a weak-willed man:

> Where are you going! ~~said~~ Wildeve asked.
>
> To Mistover Knap. I have to see Mrs. Thomasin there—that's all. *I am going there too, to fetch Mrs. Wildeve. We can walk together*
>
> Wildeve became lost in thought, & a look of inward illumina-
>
> *for his wife*
>
> tion came into his eyes. It was money ^ that Mrs. Yeobright could not trust him with. "Yet she could trust this fellow," he
>
> *Why doesn't that which*
>
> said to himself. "~~We will see if what~~ belongs to the wife ~~doesn't~~ belong to the husband too? [fol. 254]

Certainly, the rather ominous threat, "*We will see if what belongs to the wife doesn't belong to the husband too*," taken together with the introduction of his motive for joining Christian, suggests that Wildeve was previously to have engineered the seizure of the money. The point of an interpolation on the verso of fol. 253 may

9. It should be noted, however, that at the time when this was written, Mrs. Yeobright was designated as Thomasin's aunt and not as her mother.

have been, precisely, to diffuse the blame, to make Christian as responsible for the miscarriage of the guineas as Wildeve:

> *as he ~~stood~~ turned to leave the room;*
> *Mr. Wildeve, said Christian timidly,* ^ *would you mind lending me them wonderful little things that carry my luck inside 'em, that I might practise a bit by myself, you know. He looked*
> *lying*
> *wistfully at the dice & box ~~as they~~ stood on the mantelpiece.*
> *Certainly, said Wildeve. And Christian went back & privately pocketed them.* [fol. 253^{v}]

In the chapter that followed, at any rate, Hardy made a point of relieving Wildeve of any suspicion of having predetermined the seizure of the money:

> *drifted into a revengeful*
> As the minutes had passed he had gradually ~~formed an angry~~ intention without knowing the precise moment of forming it. [fol. 257]

The substitution of "drifted" for "formed" makes all the difference.

* * *

The Return of the Native had its genesis in what may loosely be defined as a pastoral novel. Naturalistic in the sense that, like *Tess of the D'Urbervilles*, it focussed on the theme of the ruined maid, it also permitted, like *The Romantic Adventures of a Milkmaid*, the intervention of the supernatural, i.e., the demonism of Avice Vye. This novel was before long suspended, however: other interests materialized to direct and control its development.

The first of these interests was, as has already been seen, external or editorial in origin. If the program of the novel was not determined by necessities arising out of a narrow public conception of morality, it was clearly conditioned by them. The abandonment of the Ur-version was evidently inspired, for one thing, by the editorial anxieties of Leslie Stephen. And even when the novel was pushed in a new and presumably safer direction, the irresistible tendency of Hardy's imagination to veer towards dangerous moral territory had once again, this time by *Belgravia's* editor, to be checked. Hence the addition of the extraneous sixth book and hence, too, the suppression of the sexual connotations of the Wildeve-Eustacia relationship.

The effect of these restrictive conditions on the form and substance of the novel cannot, of course, be fully or finally reckoned. It could scarcely have been, however, much less than immense. In the later novels, *Tess of the D'Urbervilles* and *Jude the Obscure*, the artistic transaction was completed with relatively little interference of an editorial nature. *Tess* was written in its entirety before it became apparent that it would have to be modified for serial publication; *Jude* was written, through a special arrangement with Harper, with publication as a book in mind and was then emasculated for its appearance as a serial. *The Return of the Native*, however, was intended for serial publication and hence was exposed to the pressures of censorship not subsequent to, but in the course of, the act of composition. Its primary text was not, therefore, like that of *Tess* and *Jude*, a faithful transcript of an imagination freely exercised, but the record of an imagination acting under straitened circumstances.

The revisions made for the first and Uniform editions did much, of course, to repair the original damage. They sought to release what in the manuscript of a novel meant for serial publication had necessarily to be repressed. However, in having operated as a basic condition of the act of composition, the editorial censorship must have inflicted damage that no amount of readjustment or reorganization could possibly have corrected. In this light, *The Return of the Native* must stand as a classic instance of the miscarriage, in the interests of a fastidious public morality, of the creative act.

The second major influence in the making of the novel, however, originated in a source within, rather than outside, its own proper boundaries and hence had a vitalizing, where the first had had a demoralizing, effect on its development. For although *The Return of the Native* had its inception in a novel not different in subject and treatment from *Far From the Madding Crowd* and *The Woodlanders*, it underwent, in a process of dynamic growth to which the revisions bear witness, what may be identified as a classical transvaluation.

The classical influence is first of all apparent in the frequency of the novel's references to Homer, Virgil, Sophocles, and Aeschylus as well as to more modern practitioners of epic and tragic form: e.g., Dante, Shakespeare, Milton and, through Handel, Racine.[1] It

1. Eustacia's moods are said to recall "the march in 'Athalie'" (p. 76). Other references to classical literature or to classical forms were for one reason or another suspended at various stages in the novel's progress. An allusion to the Cid was made in the manuscript but was promptly cancelled: Wildeve could "be chivalrous as the Cid while compromising [a woman's] honour" [fol. 327]. The names of Plautus and Martial came up in the manuscript and serial version but not in the first and subsequent editions (F, 1, 150): "When [Eustacia] saw less sophisticated maidens with their decoctions of lavender and boy's-love she laughed and went on; unwittingly chiming in with Plautus, Martial, Ben Jonson, and others, in holding that, though rather than smell sour a woman's robe should smell sweet, better even than smelling sweet is that it should not smell at all" (B, XXIV, 504). Finally, a reference made in the manuscript, serial, and first edition to the Stoic philosophers was expunged from the Uniform Edition: "One familiar with the Stoic philosophy would have fancied that he saw the delicate tissue of her soul, extricating itself from her body and leaving it a simple heap of cold clay" (F, 3, 132-133).

would appear, however, to have entered the novel more especially as a dramatic influence. For one thing, although Hardy failed finally to actualize his subject as drama, it was as drama, nevertheless, that he chose to define it: Eustacia was equal, he reported, "to her part in such a *drama* as this" (W, 103); the husky noises of the grasshoppers formed "a whispered *chorus*" (W, 255); the marriage preparations of Clym and Eustacia suggested "a domestic *drama*" (W, 256); and in the final scenes, Thomasin heard the sound of the wind in the chimney as "*the prologue to some tragedy*" (W, 431).

Still more specifically, Hardy evidently had in mind a formal and structural analogy with Greek tragedy. In Eustacia's moments of high passion, for example, he used the convention of the set speech and the soliloquy. In isolating the Yeobrights and the Vyes from the community of humble peasants, he paid at least token respect to the traditional separation of the principals of the action from the chorus. In planning to organize the novel in five books, he doubtless intended an analogy with the five acts identified with classical drama, and in confining the action to the heath and the time to a year and a day, he sought to preserve, as he would later acknowledge,[2] the unities of time and place. As has already been pointed out, however, the classical motive signified by these formal and structural features was not likely to have presided at the birth of the novel. The five-"act" division and the differentiation of the principals from the ordinary citizenry of the heath were established well after the novel was launched and, all the evidence suggests, simultaneously with the suppression of the Ur-version and the transfiguration of Eustacia Vye.

Notwithstanding the classical revaluation of the materials, the Ur-version continued, of course, to assert itself. Such arbitrary formal and structural impositions as the five-"act" organization and the preservation of the unities were powerless to conceal the romance-conception, the traditional ballad tale, in which *The Return of the Native* originated. The novel is open, first of all, to infiltrations of subjective feeling altogether foreign to the incorruptible vision of the ancient tragedians. Unpersuaded of the essential justice of the divine administration, it ultimately fails to command the splendid detachment and equanimity of the classical imagination. Furthermore, the claims of the main characters to aristocratic standing are not always convincing: they qualify at best as a species of provincial gentility and elsewhere carry with them into the world of the new novel something of their rusticity in the world of the old. Again, the stress of the novel falls not on one major figure but

2. Florence Hardy, *The Later Years*, p. 235.

on several: although the image of Eustacia Vye does come to dominate, it is only after a debilitating struggle with the competing images of Thomasin, Clym, and Mrs. Yeobright, and at the very last Hardy can rank Clym, in spite of Eustacia's clear priority, as first in order of importance. The instability of the novel's center of gravity is indeed such that its interest is eventually dispersed and the intensity of its effect correspondingly weakened. In the complication of the plot, certainly, its kinship is more with the loosely structured ballad romance in which it originated than with the severely imagined classical drama to which it aspired. The traditional ballad tale with its imagery of witches and distressed country maidens shows through the more sophisticated and more ambitious conception that was to displace it.

However, if Hardy did not quite manage to produce a formal and structural parallel with Greek tragedy, he did manage, perhaps without wholly premeditating it, to achieve a reasonable artistic equivalent. By a virtually systematic accumulation of classical allusions, he evoked the atmosphere or background of Greek tragedy and, by so doing, framed and transfigured, as he had not done in *Far From the Madding Crowd* and as he would not do in *The Woodlanders*, his purely pastoral narrative. By a perceptibly cumulative movement that began with the decision to incorporate certain formal features of classical drama, that continued with the proliferation of such classical allusions as those to Parian marble, Sappho, and Oedipus, and that culminated in Eustacia's designation in the Uniform Edition as the lineal descendant of Homeric kings, Hardy created the illusion of a world larger than Wessex, a world capable of suggesting and supporting actions of an epic-tragic dimension. He evoked, furthermore, by a proliferation of the imagery of fire, the major theme of the Prometheus legend and thereby gave to the substance of the novel a still more specific and significant frame.

If, then, the action of *The Return of the Native* is intrinsically less an action of antique nobility and grandeur than a domestic action peculiar to ballad and pastoral romance, it is placed in a medium of analogy, a frame of reference, that creates the illusion of antique nobility and grandeur. It puts on, in the incorporation of classical allusions and in the establishment of a Promethean frame of reference, the imposing air of classical tragedy. Indeed, as the richness of its linguistic and stylistic resources may already have suggested, *The Return of the Native* obeys not so much the architectural concept of form favored by the Greek tragedians as the harmonic or poetic—i.e., less clearly rational—concept of form favored by modern novelists. It derives its form and meaning not from such flourishes as the five-book division and the preservation of the unities but from the play, at a level well beneath that of plot and character, of what may be called classical theme and image and allusion.

The Return of the Native emerges, then, out of both freedom and necessity. If it is worked on from without by an editorial censorship that circumscribes and distorts its form and meaning, it is increasingly worked on from within by a creative force, a vision, a theme, that animates and transmutes that form and meaning. The first expresses the journeyman novelist unwilling to be more than a good hand at a serial; the second expresses the poet who becomes, in spite of his theoretical contempt for the medium, an artist in prose fiction.

CARL J. WEBER

[Scholarship on the Novel]†

The active publishing house of Chatto & Windus in London had offered to buy Hardy's next novel for use in their magazine *Belgravia*, and before the end of 1877 *The Return of the Native* was ready. * * *

Toward the end of 1878 the novel was published by Smith, Elder & Co., in three volumes, bound in brown cloth. The world did not acknowledge it, but a masterpiece of English literature had appeared. It is Hardy's most nearly perfect work of art. There is no reason to think that this was his own opinion at the time; but, in view of the care he had lavished upon his novel, he cannot have been other than shocked and discouraged at the reception the reading public gave the book. It was called "distinctly inferior" to anything he had written. One reviewer was content to remark that in it the reader would find himself taken farther from the madding crowd than ever. Sir James M. Barrie afterward related: "In an old library copy of *The Return of the Native* I have been shown, in the handwriting of different ladies, 'What a horrid book!'—'Eustacia is a libel on noble womankind,' and 'Oh, how I *hate* Thomas Hardy!' " The author was rapidly discovering that the rose of literary fame carries many a thorn with it, and it took only a slight scratch to cause pain to his sensitive nature. He came to feel that he "was living in a world where nothing bears out in practice what it promises incipiently." Clym's view that life is "a thing to be put up with, replacing that zest for existence which was so intense in early civilizations," settled more permanently than ever upon Hardy.

† From Carl J. Weber, *Hardy of Wessex: His Life and Literary Career* (New York, 1940), pp. 72-75. Reprinted by permission of the publishers, Columbia University Press.

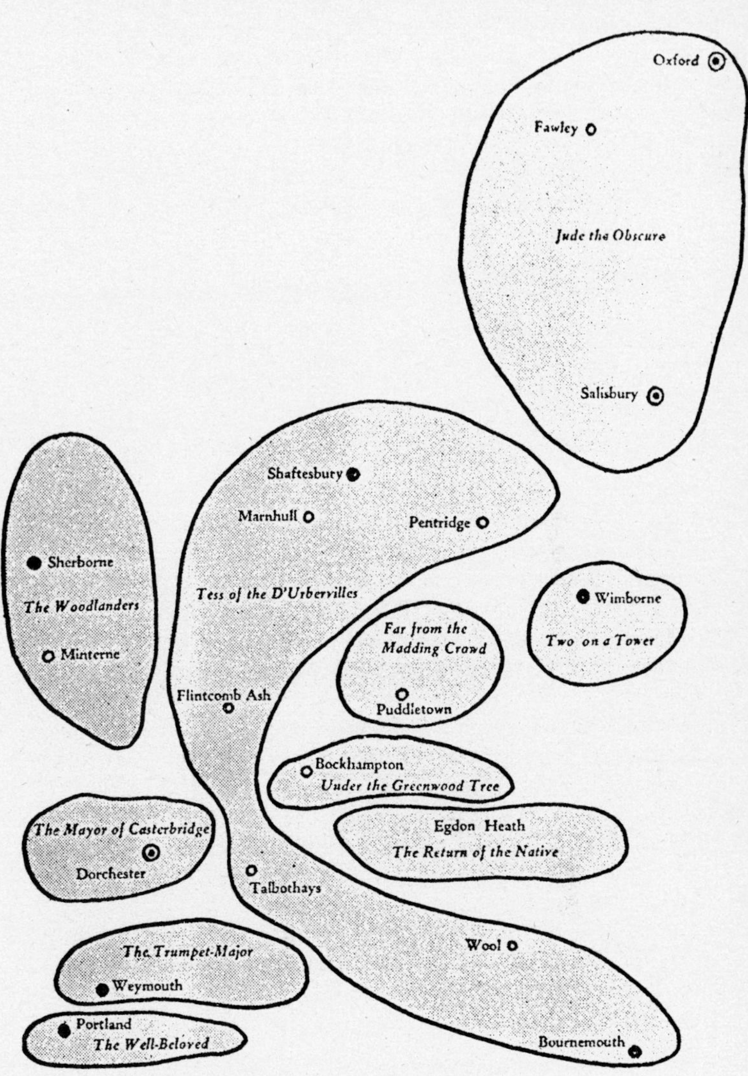

The Country of Ten of the Wessex Novels[1]

1. The map, by Carl J. Weber, covers Hardy's fictional Wessex: the south-west of England (not including the south-west tip of Devon and Cornwall). The counties roughly included are: Somerset, Dorset, Wiltshire, Hampshire, parts of Berkshire and Oxfordshire.

The same ten novels show that Hardy was equally alert to the possibilities of historical atmosphere. The periods of time are kept just as distinct as are the geographical regions. In one of the earliest magazine articles on Hardy, Barrie called him the "historian of Wessex." That Hardy covered almost the entire nineteenth century is made clear by examining a list of the ten novels in the order of the historical decades to which they refer. The action of the stories is dated as follows:

The Trumpet-Major	1800–1808
Under the Greenwood Tree	1835–1836
The Return of the Native	1842–1843
The Mayor of Casterbridge	1846–1849
The Well-Beloved	1852–1892
Jude the Obscure	1855–1874
Two on a Tower	1858–1863
Far from the Madding Crowd	1869–1873
The Woodlanders	1876–1879
Tess of the D'Urbervilles	1884–1889

After their initial edition, Smith, Elder & Co. had nothing more to do with the *Native*. The novel was issued in one volume at six shillings in December, 1879, by Kegan, Paul & Co., and in May, 1884, a third edition was published in London by Sampson Low & Co. Tauchnitz issued an edition in two volumes at Leipzig in 1879, and there have been two French translations, one of them greatly abridged.

Editorial discussion and annotation have been provided in the following editions: by J. W. Cunliffe (New York, Scribners, 1917), by Warner Taylor (New York, Harpers, 1922), by Albert C. Baugh (New York, Macmillan, 1928), by Irene M. Haworth (Boston, Ginn & Co., 1931), by Carl Van Doren (New York, Literary Guild, 1931), and by Cyril Aldred (London, Macmillan, 1935).

For the text of the entire Mummers' Play, as Hardy late in life wrote it down from memory, see *The Play of Saint George*, by Roger S. Loomis, New York, Samuel French, 1928.

* * *

Hardy once confessed that in Mrs. Yeobright he had drawn something of the character of his own mother. She died April 3, 1904.

Hardy's Life and Opinions

Thomas Hardy was born at Bockhampton, a small village near Dorchester, on June 2, 1840. He was the eldest of four children born to a respectable but not wealthy master mason and builder. A studious and quiet lad who, by his own account, matured slowly, Hardy was educated in a village school, then in Dorchester. His formal schooling ended at age sixteen when he became a pupil of John Hicks, an architect, in Dorchester. After six years there, Hardy went to London, where he worked as an architect and began writing poems and stories. In 1867, as an architect specializing in church restoration, he returned to Dorset and lived with his parents. Although later he frequently stayed in or near London for weeks or months at a time, Dorset remained his home. From 1885 until his death in 1928, he lived at Max Gate, a house he built near Dorchester.

Hardy's first novel, *The Poor Man and The Lady*, was finished in 1869, but never accepted for publication. George Meredith, the novelist, was the publisher's reader; he encouraged Hardy, but also advised him to tone down his social satire and to provide plots that were more complicated. Hardy's first published novel was *Desperate Remedies* in 1871. *Far from The Madding Crowd*, published in 1874, established him as a popular novelist, and he gave up architecture. After the critical outcry against his fourteenth novel, *Jude The Obscure* (1895), in which the book was denounced as immoral and unpleasant, Hardy stopped writing fiction and returned to poetry, which he had always contended was the superior form of literature.

In 1870, while on a visit to Cornwall to plan the restoration of an old church, Hardy met the vicar's sister-in-law, Emma Lavinia Gifford (1840-1912). They were married in 1874. In 1914, two years after his first wife's death, Hardy married his long-time secretary, Florence Emily Dugdale (1879-1937). Both marriages were childless. Hardy died on January 11, 1928. His heart was buried at Stinsford, Dorset, in the grave of his first wife, and his ashes were placed next to those of Charles Dickens in the Poets' Corner in Westminster Abbey.

The standard biography is in two volumes: *The Early Life of Thomas Hardy, 1840-1891* (New York, 1928) and *The Later Years of Thomas Hardy, 1892-1928* (New York, 1930). Although "by Florence Emily Hardy," his second wife, both volumes were largely compiled from notes, letters, and diaries that Hardy himself wrote. All critics have agreed that Mrs. Hardy really served as the editor of an autobiography, and she herself never claimed more. At times, she simply quoted Hardy's notebooks or letters; at other times, she synthesized Hardy's writing and provided necessary background.

Most of the following selections are taken from the autobiographical volumes. At the end of this section are a few selections from other essays or notes that Hardy wrote and that are not included in the autobiography. Quotation marks within the selections indicate a passage directly quoted from Hardy's notebooks or letters.

FROM HARDY'S AUTOBIOGRAPHY†

[On *The Return of the Native*]

* * * But his main occupation at Riverside Villa (or "River-cliff" as they sometimes called it) was writing *The Return of the Native*. The only note he makes of its progress is that, on November 8 [1877], parts 3, 4, and 5 of the story were posted to Messrs. Chatto and Windus for publication in (of all places) *Belgravia*—a monthly magazine then running. Strangely enough, the rich alluvial district of Sturminster Newton in which the author was now living was not used by him at this time as a setting for the story he was constructing there, but the heath country twenty miles off. It may be mentioned here that the name "Eustacia" which he gave to his heroine was that of the wife of the owner of the manor of Ower Moigne in the reign of Henry IV., which parish includes part of the "Edgon" Heath of the story (*vide* Hutchin's Dorset); and that "Clement", the name of the hero, was suggested by its being borne by one of his supposed ancestors, Clement le Hardy, of Jersey, whose family migrated from that isle to the west of England at the beginning of the sixteenth century.

* * *

"September 20, [1878]. Returned and called on G. Smith. Agreed to his terms for publishing *The Return of the Native*."

Shortly after he wrote to Messrs Smith and Elder:

"I enclose a sketch-map of the supposed scene in which *The Return of the Native* is laid, copied from the one I used in writing the story; and my suggestion is that we place an engraving of it as frontispiece to the first volume. Unity of place is so seldom preserved in novels that a map of the scene of action is as a rule quite impracticable. But since the present story affords an opportunity of doing so I am of opinion that it would be a desirable novelty." The publishers fell in with the idea and the map was made.

A peculiarity in the local descriptions running through all Hardy's writings may be instanced here—that he never uses the

† *The Life of Thomas Hardy*, 1840-1928 (London, 1962). Selections reprinted by permission of the publisher, Macmillan & Co. Ltd.

word "Dorset", never names the county at all (except possibly in an explanatory footnote), but obliterates the names of the six counties, whose area he traverses in his scenes, under the general appellation of "Wessex"—an old word that became quite popular after the date of *Far from the Madding Crowd,* where he first introduced it. So far did he carry this idea of the unity of Wessex that he used to say he had grown to forget the crossing of county boundaries within the ancient kingdom—in this respect being quite unlike the poet Barnes, who was "Dorset" emphatically.

* * *

The Return of the Native was published by Messrs Smith and Elder in November [1878], *The Times*' remark upon the book being that the reader found himself taken farther from the madding crowd than ever. Old Mrs. Procter's amusing criticism in a letter was "Poor Eustacia. I so fully understood her longing for the Beautiful. I love the Common; but still one may wish for something else. I rejoice that Venn [a character] is happy. A man is never cured when he loves a stupid woman [Thomasin]. Beauty fades, and intelligence and wit grow irritating; but your dear Dulness is always the same."

* * *

The year 1912, which was to advance and end in such gloom for Hardy,[1] began serenely. In January he went to London for a day or two and witnessed the performance of *Oedipus* at Covent Garden. But in February he learnt of the death of his friend General Henniker, and in April occurred the disaster to the *Titanic* steamship, upon which he wrote the poem called "The Convergence of the Twain" in aid of the fund for the sufferers.

On the 22nd April Hardy was correcting proofs for a new edition of his works, the Wessex Edition, concerning which he wrote to a friend:

". . . I am now on to p. 140 of *The Woodlanders* (in copy I mean, not in proofs, of course). That is vol. vi. Some of the later ones will be shorter. I read ten hours yesterday—finishing the *proofs* of the *Native* (wh. I have thus got rid of). I got to like the character of Clym before I had done with him. I think he is the nicest of all my heroes, and *not a bit* like me. On taking up *The Woodlanders* and reading it after many years I think I like it, *as a story*, the best of all.

* * *

On the 13th [November, 1920], the Dorchester Amateurs performed *The Return of the Native* in Dorchester, as dramatized by Mr. Tilley.

1. Hardy's first wife died in November of that year.

"More interested than I expected to be. The dancing was just as it used to be at Higher Bockhampton in my childhood."

* * *

On Christmas night [1920] the carol singers and mummers came to Max Gate as they had promised, the latter performing the *Play of Saint George*, just as he had seen it performed in his childhood.

* * *

On November 15th [1923] the poetic drama *The Famous Tragedy of the Queen of Cornwall* was published. Hardy's plan in writing this is clearly given in a letter to Mr. Harold Child:

"The unities are strictly preserved, whatever virtue there may be in that. (I, myself, am old-fashioned enough to think there *is* a virtue in it, if it can be done without artificiality. The only other case I remember attempting it in was *The Return of the Native.*) The original events could have been enacted in the time taken up by the performance, and they continue unbroken throughout. The change of persons on the stage is called a change of scene, there being no change of background.

"My temerity in pulling together into the space of an hour events that in the traditional stories covered a long time will doubtless be criticized, if it is noticed. But there are so many versions of the famous romance that I felt free to adapt it to my purpose in any way—as, in fact, the Greek dramatists did in their plays—notably Euripides.

"Wishing it to be thoroughly English I have dropped the name of Chorus for the conventional onlookers, and called them Chanters, though they play the part of a Greek Chorus to some extent. I have also called them Ghosts (I don't for the moment recall an instance of this in a Greek play). . . . Whether the lady ghosts in our performance will submit to have their faces whitened I don't know! . . .

"I have tried to avoid turning the rude personages of, say, the fifth century into respectable Victorians, as was done by Tennyson, Swinburne, Arnold, etc.

[Philosophical Ideas in Fiction]

" 'All is vanity',[2] said the Preacher. But if all were only vanity, who would mind? Alas, it is too often worse than vanity; agony, darkness, death also."

"A man would never laugh were he not to forget his situation, or were he not one who never has learnt it. After risibility from comedy, how often does the thoughtful mind reproach itself for

2. Ecclesiastes i.2.

forgetting the truth? Laughter always means blindness—either from defect, choice, or accident."[3]

* * *

" '*June* 25 [1876] The irritating necessity of conforming to rules which in themselves have no virtue.

" '*June* 26. If it be possible to compress into a sentence all that a man learns between 20 and 40, it is that all things merge in one another—good into evil, generosity into justice, religion into politics, the year into the ages, the world into the universe. With this in view the evolution of species seems but a minute and obvious process in the same movement."

* * *

"1879. *January* 1. New Year's thought. A perception of the FAILURE of THINGS to be what they are meant to be, lends them, in place of the intended interest, a new and greater interest of an unintended kind."

* * *

"Arnold is wrong about provincialism, if he means anything more than a provincialism of style and manner in exposition. A certain provincialism of feeling is invaluable. It is of the essence of individuality, and is largely made up of that crude enthusiasm without which no great thoughts are thought, no great deeds done."

Some days later he writes:

"Romanticism will exist in human nature as long as human nature itself exists. The point is (in imaginative literature) to adopt that form of romanticism which is the mood of the age."[4]

* * *

"History is rather a stream than a tree. There is nothing organic in its shape, nothing systematic in its development. It flows on like a thunderstorm-rill by a road side; now a straw turns it this way, now a tiny barrier of sand that. The offhand decision of some commonplace mind high in office at a critical moment influences the course of events for a hundred years. Consider the evenings at Lord Carnarvon's,[5] and the intensely average conversation on politics held there by average men who two or three weeks later were members of the Cabinet. A row of shopkeepers in Oxford Street[6] taken just as they came would conduct the affairs of the nation as ably as these.

"Thus, judging by bulk of effect, it becomes impossible to estimate the intrinsic value of ideas, acts, material things: we are

3. From Hardy's notebooks of 1876.

4. From Hardy's notebooks, winter, 1880-81.

5. Henry H. M. Herbert, fourth Earl of Carnarvon (1831-1890), was a scholarly Conservative, twice in the Cabinet as Colonial Secretary.

6. Street of large middle-class stores on the northern edge of London's largest shopping district.

forced to appraise them by the curves of their career. There were more beautiful women in Greece than Helen; but what of them?

"What Ruskin says as to the cause of the want of imagination in works of the present age is probably true—that it is the flippant sarcasm of the time. 'Men dare not open their hearts to us if we are to broil them on a thorn fire.' "[7]

* * *

"In an article on Ibsen in the *Fortnightly* the writer says that his manner is wrong. That the drama, like the novel, should not be for edification. In this I think the writer errs. It should be so, but the edified should not perceive the edification. Ibsen's edifying is too obvious."[8]

* * *

"[April] 15. *Good Friday* [1892]. Read review *of Tess* in *The Quarterly*. A smart and amusing article; but it is easy to be smart and amusing if a man will forgo veracity and sincerity. . . . How strange that one may write a book without knowing what one puts into it—or rather, the reader reads into it. Well, if this sort of thing continues no more novel-writing for me. A man must be a fool to deliberately stand up to be shot at."

Moreover, the repute of the book was spreading not only through England, and America, and the Colonies, but through the European Continent and Asia; and during this year translations appeared in various languages, its publication in Russia exciting great interest. On the other hand, some local libraries in English-speaking countries "suppressed" the novel—with what effect was not ascertained.

* * *

"Poetry. Perhaps I can express more fully in verse ideas and emotions which run counter to the inert crystallized opinion—hard as a rock—which the vast body of men have vested interests in supporting. To cry out in a passionate poem that (for instance) the Supreme Mover or Movers, the Prime Force or Forces, must be either limited in power, unknowing, or cruel—which is obvious enough, and has been for centuries—will cause them merely a shake of the head; but to put it in argumentative prose will make them sneer, or foam, and set all the literary contortionists jumping upon me, a harmless agnostic, as if I were a clamorous atheist, which in their crass illiteracy they seem to think is the same thing. . . . If Galileo had said in verse that the world moved, the Inquisition might have let him alone."[9]

7. From Hardy's notebooks of 1885.

8. From Hardy's notebooks, Easter, 1890.

9. From Hardy's notebooks, October 17, 1896.

* * *

In a letter on Rationalism written about this time [1901] but apparently not sent, he remarks:

"My own interest lies largely in non-rationalistic subjects, since non-rationality seems, so far as one can perceive, to be the principle of the Universe. By which I do not mean foolishness, but rather a principle for which there is no exact name, lying at the indifference point between rationality and irrationality."

* * *

On the last day of the year [1901] he makes the following reflection: "After reading various philosophic systems, and being struck with their contradictions and futilities, I have come to this: *Let every man make a philosophy for himself out of his own experience.* He will not be able to escape using terms and phraseology from earlier philosophers, but let him avoid adopting their theories if he values his own mental life. Let him remember the fate of Coleridge,[1] and save years of labour by working out his own views as given him by his surroundings."

"*January* 1 (1902). A Pessimist's apology. Pessimism (or rather what is called such) is, in brief, playing the sure game. You cannot lose at it; you may gain. It is the only view of life in which you can never be disappointed. Having reckoned what to do in the worst possible circumstances, when better arise, as they may, life becomes child's play."

* * *

June 2 [1907]. Hardy's birthday, which he kept by dining at Lady St. Helier's.

On the same day he wrote to Mr. Edward Wright:

"Your interesting letter on the philosophy of The Dynasts[2] has reached me here. I will try to answer some of your inquiries.

"I quite agree with you in holding that the word 'Will' does not perfectly fit the idea to be conveyed—a vague thrusting or urging internal force in no predetermined direction. But it has become accepted in philosophy for want of a better, and is hardly likely to be supplanted by another, unless a highly appropriate one could be found, which I doubt. The word that you suggest—Impulse—seems to me to imply a driving power behind it; also a spasmodic

1. Hardy here is probably referring to the legend that Coleridge was desultory about his work and wasted years in idleness and vague reading. Coleridge helped to generate this legend himself. Modern biographers and critics, however, point out that Coleridge was plagued by ill health, personal and financial difficulties, and addiction to opium. In spite of this, he managed to finish a considerable amount of critical work and his reading was profoundly relevant to his great *Biographia Literaria*.

2. *The Dynasts* was Hardy's dramatic epic on the Napoleonic Wars, published in three parts, 1903, 1906, and 1908.

movement unlike that of, say, the tendency of an ape to become a man and other such processes.

"In a dramatic epic—which I may perhaps assume *The Dynasts* to be—some philosophy of life was necessary, and I went on using that which I had denoted in my previous volumes of verse (and to some extent prose) as being a generalized form of what the thinking world had gradually come to adopt, myself included. That the Unconscious Will of the Universe is growing aware of Itself I believe I may claim as my own idea solely—at which I arrived by reflecting that what has already taken place in a fraction of the whole (i.e. so much of the world as has become conscious) is likely to take place in the mass; and there being no Will outside the mass—that is, the Universe—the whole Will becomes conscious thereby: and ultimately, it is to be hoped, sympathetic.

"I believe, too, that the Prime Cause, this Will, has never before been called 'It' in any poetical literature, English or foreign.

"This theory, too, seems to me to settle the question of Free-will v. Necessity. The will of a man is, according to it, neither wholly free nor wholly unfree. When swayed by the Universal Will (which he mostly must be as a subservient part of it) he is not individually free; but whenever it happens that all the rest of the Great Will is in equilibrium the minute portion called one person's will is free, just as a performer's fingers are free to go on playing the pianoforte of themselves when he talks or thinks of something else and the head does not rule them.

"In the first edition of a drama of the extent of *The Dynasts* there may be, of course, accidental discrepancies and oversights which seem not quite to harmonize with these principles; but I hope they are not many.

"The third part will probably not be ready till the end of this or the beginning of next year; so that I have no proofs as yet. I do not think, however, that they would help you much in your proposed article. The first and second parts already published, and some of the poems in *Poems of the Past and the Present*, exhibit fairly enough the whole philosophy."

* * *

"You will see how much I want to have the pleasure of being a Bergsonian.[3] But I fear his theory is, in the bulk, only our old friend Dualism in a new suit of clothes—an ingenious fancy without real foundation, and more complicated than the fancies he endeavours to overthrow.

"You must not think me a hard-headed rationalist for all this. Half my time—particularly when writing verse—I 'believe' (in the

3. Henri Bergson (1859–1941), French philosopher and writer.

modern sense of the word) not only in the things Bergson believes in, but in spectres, mysterious voices, intuitions, omens, dreams, haunted places, etc., etc. But I do not believe in them in the old sense of the word any more for that. . . .

"By the way, how do you explain the following from the *Cambridge Magazine*, by a writer whom I imagine to be of a school of thinkers akin to your own, concerning Herbert Spencer's doctrine of the Unknowable?[4]

" 'We doubt if there is a single philosopher alive to-day who would subscribe to it. Even men of science are gradually discarding it in favour of Realism and Pragmatism.'

"I am utterly bewildered to understand how the doctrine that, beyond the knowable, there must always be an unknown, can be displaced."[5]

* * *

To Mr. Alfred Noyes

"DORCHESTER, 13TH DECEMBER 1920

"Dear Mr. Noyes,

"Somebody has sent me an article from the *Morning Post* of December 9 entitled 'Poetry and Religion', which reports you as saying, in a lecture, that mine is 'a philosophy which told them (readers) that the Power behind the Universe was an imbecile jester'.

"As I hold no such 'philosophy', and, to the best of my recollection, never could have done so, I should be glad if you would inform me whereabouts I have seriously asserted such to be my opinion.

"Yours truly,

"Th. Hardy"

It should be stated that Mr. Noyes had always been a friendly critic of Hardy's writings, and one with whom he was on good terms, which was probably Hardy's reason for writing to him, who would be aware there was no personal antagonism in his letter.

Mr. Noyes replied that he was sorry the abbreviated report of his address did not contain the tribute he had paid Hardy as a writer with artistic mastery and at the head of living authors, although he did disagree with his pessimistic philosophy; a philosophy which, in his opinion, led logically to the conclusion that the Power behind the Universe was malign; and he referred to various passages in Hardy's poems that seemed to bear out his belief that their writer

4. Herbert Spencer (1820-1903), English philosopher.

5. From a letter written in 1916

held the views attributed to him in the lecture; offering, however, to revise it when reprinted, if he had misinterpreted the aforesaid passages.

To Mr. Alfred Noyes

"DECEMBER 19TH, 1920

"I am much obliged for your reply, which I really ought not to have troubled you to write. I may say for myself that I very seldom do give critics such trouble, usually letting things drift, though there have been many occasions when a writer who has been so much abused for his opinions as I have been would perhaps have done well not to hold his peace.

"I do not know that there can be much use in my saying more than I did say. It seems strange that I should have to remind a man of letters of what, I should have supposed, he would have known as well as I—of the very elementary rule of criticism that a writer's works should be judged as a whole, and not from picked passages that contradict them as a whole—and this especially when they are scattered over a period of fifty years.

"Also that I should have to remind him of the vast difference between the expression of fancy and the expression of belief. My imagination may have often run away with me; but all the same, my sober opinion—so far as I have any definite one—of the Cause of Things, has been defined in scores of places, and is that of a great many ordinary thinkers: that the said Cause is neither moral nor immoral, but *un*moral: 'loveless and hateless' I have called it, 'which neither good nor evil knows'—etc., etc.—(you will find plenty of these definitions in *The Dynasts* as well as in short poems, and I am surprised that you have not taken them in). This view is quite in keeping with what you call a Pessimistic philosophy (a mere nickname with no sense in it), which I am quite unable to see as 'leading logically to the conclusion that the Power behind the universe is malign'.

"In my fancies, or poems of the imagination, I have of course called this Power all sorts of names—never supposing they would be taken for more than fancies. I have even in prefaces warned readers to take them as such—as mere impressions of the moment, exclamations in fact. But it has always been my misfortune to presuppose a too intelligent reading public, and no doubt people will go on thinking that I really believe the Prime Mover to be a malignant old gentleman, a sort of King of Dahomey[6]—an idea which,

6. Dahomey, a country in West Africa on the western border of Nigeria, was formerly a Negro kingdom ruled by an absolute monarch. Conquered by the French in the 1890's, Dahomey became part of French West Africa. It has been an independent republic since 1960.

so far from my holding it, is to me irresistibly comic. 'What a fool one must have been to write for such a public!' is the inevitable reflection at the end of one's life.

"The lines you allude to, 'A Young Man's Epigram', dated 1866, I remember finding in a drawer, and printed them merely as an amusing instance of early cynicism. The words 'Time's Laughing-stocks' are legitimate imagery all of a piece with such expressions as 'Life, Time's fool', and thousands in poetry and I am amazed that you should see any *belief* in them. * * * "

[On Fiction and Art]

You have no right to say you are not connected with art. Everybody is to a certain extent; the only difference between a professor and an amateur being that the former has the (often disagreeable) necessity of making it his means of earning bread and cheese—and thus often rendering what is a pleasure to other people a "bore" to himself.

About Thackeray. You must read something of his. He is considered to be the greatest novelist of the day—looking at novel writing of the highest kind as a perfect and truthful representation of actual life—which is no doubt the proper view to take. Hence, because his novels stand so high as works of Art or Truth, they often have anything but an elevating tendency, and on that account are particularly unfitted for young people—from their very truthfulness. People say that it is beyond Mr. Thackeray to paint a perfect man or woman—a great fault if novels are intended to instruct, but just the opposite if they are to be considered merely as Pictures. *Vanity Fair* is considered one of his best.

I expect to go home about Tuesday or Wednesday after Xmas and then shall find you there of course—We must have a "bit of a lark."

Ever affectionately

Tom

I am able to write 40 words a minute. The average rate of a speaker is from 100 to 120 and occasionally 140; so I have much more to do yet.[7]

Another incident which added to his dubiety was the arrival of a letter from Coventry Patmore,[8] a total stranger to him, expressing the view that *A Pair of Blue Eyes* was in its nature not a conception for prose, and that he "regretted at almost every page that such unequalled beauty and power should not have assured themselves the immortality which would have been impressed upon them

7. From Hardy's letter to his sister Mary, December 19, 1863.

8. Coventry Patmore (1823-1896) was a poet who had earlier studied as a painter. He was loosely associated with the Pre-Raphaelite movement.

by the form of verse". Hardy was much struck by this opinion from Patmore. However, finding himself committed to prose, he renewed his consideration of a prose style, as it is evident from the following note [1874]:

"Read again Addison, Macaulay, Newman, Sterne, Defoe, Lamb, Gibbon, Burke, Times Leaders, etc., in a study of style. Am more and more confirmed in an idea I have long held, as a matter of commonsense, before I thought of any old aphorism bearing on the subject: 'Ars est celare artem'.[9] The whole secret of a living style and the difference between it and a dead style, lies in not having too much style—being—in fact, a little careless, or rather seeming to be, here and there. It brings wonderful life into the writing:

> A sweet disorder in the dress . . .
> A careless shoe-string, in whose tie
> I see a wild civility,
> Do more bewitch me than when art
> Is too precise in every part.[1]

"Otherwise your style is like worn half-pence—all the fresh images rounded off by rubbing, and no crispness or movement at all.

"It is, of course, simply a carrying into prose the knowledge I have acquired in poetry—that inexact rhymes and rhythms now and then are far more pleasing than correct ones."

"*April* [1878]—Note. A Plot, or Tragedy, should arise from the gradual closing in of a situation that comes of ordinary human passions, prejudices, and ambitions, by reason of the characters taking no trouble to ward off the disastrous events produced by the said passions, prejudices, and ambitions."

"The advantages of the letter-system of telling a story (passing over the disadvantages) are that, hearing what one side has to say, you are led constantly to the imagination of what the other side must be feeling, and at last are anxious to know if the other side does really feel what you imagine."

* * *

In July [1881] he jots down some notes on fiction, possibly for an article that was never written:

"The real, if unavowed, purpose of fiction is to give pleasure by gratifying the love of the uncommon in human experience, mental or corporeal.

"This is done all the more perfectly in proportion as the reader is illuded to believe the personages true and real like himself.

"Solely to this latter end a work of fiction should be a precise transcript of ordinary life: but,

9. "Art is to conceal art."
1. Robert Herrick, "Delight in Disorder," (1648).

"The uncommon would be absent and the interest lost. Hence,

"The writer's problem is, how to strike the balance between the uncommon and the ordinary so as on the one hand to give interest, on the other to give reality.

"In working out this problem, human nature must never be made abnormal, which is introducing incredibility. The uncommonness must be in the events, not in the characters; and the writer's art lies in shaping that uncommonness while disguising its unlikelihood, if it be unlikely."

* * *

"*June* 3 [1882]. . . . As, in looking at a carpet, by following one colour a certain pattern is suggested, by following another colour, another; so in life the seer should watch that pattern among general things which his idiosyncrasy moves him to observe, and describe that alone. This is, quite accurately, a going to Nature; yet the result is no mere photograph, but purely the product of the writer's own mind."

* * *

"*April* 19 [1885]. The business of the poet and novelist is to show the sorriness underlying the grandest things, and the grandeur underlying the sorriest things."

* * *

"*Easter Sunday* [1885]. Evidences of art in Bible narratives. They are written with a watchful attention (though disguised) as to their effect on their reader. Their so-called simplicity is, in fact, the simplicity of the highest cunning. And one is led to inquire, when even in these latter days artistic development and arrangement are the qualities least appreciated by readers, who was there likely to appreciate the art in these chronicles at that day?

"Looking round on a well-selected shelf of fiction or history, how few stories of any length does one recognize as well told from beginning to end! The first half of this story, the last half of that, the middle of another. . . . The modern art of narration is yet in its infancy.

"But in these Bible lives and adventures there is the spherical completeness of perfect art. And our first, and second, feeling that they must be true because they are so impressive, becomes, as a third feeling, modified to, 'Are they so very true, after all?' Is not the fact of their being so convincing an argument, not for their actuality, but for the actuality of a consummate artist who was no more content with what Nature offered than Sophocles[2] and Pheidias[3] were content?"

2. Sophocles (c. 496-406 B.C.), famous Greek tragedian, most of whose plays are now lost.

3. Pheidias (500-432 B.C.), Greek sculptor and architect.

* * *

"Tragedy. It may be put thus in brief: a tragedy exhibits a state of things in the life of an individual which unavoidably causes some natural aim or desire of his to end in a catastrophe when carried out."[4]

* * *

"*March* 4 [1886]. Novel-writing as an art cannot go backward. Having reached the analytic stage it must transcend it by going still further in the same direction. Why not by rendering as visible essences, spectres, etc. the abstract thoughts of the analytic school?"

This notion was approximately carried out, not in a novel, but through the much more appropriate medium of poetry, in the supernatural framework of *The Dynasts* as also in smaller poems. And a further note of the same date enlarges the same idea:

"The human race to be shown as one great network or tissue which quivers in every part when one point is shaken, like a spider's web if touched. Abstract realisms to be in the form of Spirits, Spectral figures, etc.

"The Realities to be the true realities of life, hitherto called abstractions. The old material realities to be placed behind the former, as shadowy accessories."

* * *

January 1887 was uneventful at Max Gate, and the only remark its occupier makes during the month is the following:

"After looking at the landscape ascribed to Bonington[5] in our drawing-room I feel that Nature is played out as a Beauty, but not as a Mystery. I don't want to see landscapes, *i.e.*, scenic paintings of them, because I don't want to see the original realities—as optical effects, that is. I want to see the deeper reality underlying the scenic, the expression of what are sometimes called abstract imaginings.

"The 'simply natural' is interesting no longer. The much decried, mad, late-Turner rendering is now necessary to create my interest. The exact truth as to material fact ceases to be of importance in art—it is a student's style—the style of a period when the mind is serene and unawakened to the tragical mysteries of life; when it does not bring anything to the object that coalesces with and translates the qualities that are already there,—half hidden, it may be—and the two united are depicted as the All."

* * *

"*March–April* [1890]:

"Altruism, or The Golden Rule, or whatever 'Love your Neighbour as Yourself' may be called, will ultimately be brought about I

4. From Hardy's notebooks, November, 1885.

5. Richard Parkes Bonington, (1801-1828), English landscape painter.

think by the pain we see in others reacting on ourselves, as if we and they were a part of one body. Mankind, in fact, may be and possibly will be viewed as members of one corporeal frame."

"Tories will often do by way of exception to their principles more extreme acts of democratism or broad-mindedness than Radicals do by rule—such as help on promising plebeians, tolerate wild beliefs, etc."

"Art consists in so depicting the common events of life as to bring out the features which illustrate the author's idiosyncratic mode of regard; making old incidents and things seem as new."

* * *

"*August* 5 [1890]. Reflections on Art. Art is a changing of the actual proportions and order of things, so as to bring out more forcibly than might otherwise be done that feature in them which appeals most strongly to the idiosyncrasy of the artist. The changing, or distortion, may be of two kinds: (1) The kind which increases the sense of vraisemblance: (2) That which diminishes it. (1) is high art: (2) is low art.

"High art may choose to depict evil as well as good, without losing its quality. Its choice of evil, however, must be limited by the sense of worthiness." A continuation of the same note was made a little later, and can be given here:

"Art is a disproportioning—(*i.e.*, distorting, throwing out of proportion)—of realities, to show more clearly the features that matter in those realities, which, if merely copied or reported inventorially, might possibly be observed, but would more probably be overlooked. Hence 'realism' is not Art."

* * *

"*October* 30 [1891]. Howells[6] and those of his school forget that a story *must* be striking enough to be worth telling. Therein lies the problem—to reconcile the average with that uncommonness which alone makes it natural that a tale or experience would dwell in the memory and induce repetition."

* * *

"*February* 23 [1893]. A story must be exceptional enough to justify its telling. We tale-tellers are all Ancient Mariners and none of us is warranted in stopping Wedding Guests[7] (in other words, the hurrying public) unless he has something more unusual to relate than the ordinary experience of every average man and woman.

"The whole secret of fiction and the drama—in the constructional part—lies in the adjustment of things unusual to things eter-

6. William Dean Howells (1837-1920), American realistic novelist and prominent literary critic.

7. The ancient mariner stopped one of the wedding guests in Samuel Taylor Coleridge's poem, "The Rime of the Ancient Mariner" (1798).

nal and universal. The writer who knows exactly how exceptional, and how non-exceptional, his events should be made, possesses the key to the art."

* * *

The misrepresentations of the last two or three years [1895–97] affected but little, if at all, the informed appreciation of Hardy's writings, being heeded almost entirely by those who had not read him; and turned out ultimately to be the best thing that could have happened; for they wellnigh compelled him, in his own judgement at any rate, if he wished to retain any shadow of self-respect, to abandon at once a form of literary art he had long intended to abandon at some indefinite time, and resume openly that form of it which had always been more instinctive with him, and which he had just been able to keep alive from his early years, half in secrecy, under the pressure of magazine writing. He abandoned it with all the less reluctance in that the novel was, in his own words, "gradually losing artistic form, with a beginning, middle, and end, and becoming a spasmodic inventory of items, which has nothing to do with art".

The change, after all, was not so great as it seemed. It was not as if he had been a writer of novels proper, and as more specifically understood, that is, stories of modern artificial life and manners showing a certain smartness of treatment. He had mostly aimed at keeping his narratives close to natural life and as near to poetry in their subject as the conditions would allow, and had often regretted that those conditions would not let him keep them nearer still.

* * *

"*September* 15 [1913]. Thoughts on the recent school of novel-writers. They forget in their insistence on life, and nothing but life, in a plain slice, that a story *must be worth the telling,* that a good deal of life is not worth any such thing, and that they must not occupy a reader's time with what he can get at first hand anywhere around him."

* * *

"*January* 6 [1917]. I find I wrote in 1888 that 'Art is concerned with seemings only', which is true."

* * *

An article in the April [1917] *Fortnightly* by Mr. Courtney, the editor, on Hardy's writings, especially *The Dynasts,* interested him not only by its appreciativeness, but also by the aspect some features of the drama assumed in the reviewer's mind:

"Like so many critics, Mr. Courtney treats my works of art as if they were a scientific system of philosophy, although I have repeatedly stated in prefaces and elsewhere that the views in them are *seemings*, provisional impressions only, used for artistic purposes because they represent approximately the impressions of the age, and are plausible, till somebody produces better theories of the universe.

"As to his winding up about a God of Mercy, etc.—if I wished to make a smart retort, which I really should hate doing, I might say that the Good-God theory having, after some thousands of years of trial, produced the present infamous and disgraceful state of Europe—that most Christian Continent!—a theory of a Goodless-and-Badless God (as in *The Dynasts*) might perhaps be given a trial with advantage."

FROM LIFE AND ART BY THOMAS HARDY†

The Profitable Reading of Fiction[1]

* * *

If we speak of deriving good from a story, we usually mean something more than the gain of pleasure during the hours of its perusal. Nevertheless, to get pleasure out of a book is a beneficial and profitable thing, if the pleasure be of a kind which, while doing no moral injury, affords relaxation and relief when the mind is overstrained or sick of itself. The prime remedy in such cases is change of scene, by which change of the material scene is not necessarily implied. A sudden shifting of the mental perspective into a fictitious world, combined with rest, is well known to be often as efficacious for renovation as a corporeal journey afar.

In such a case the shifting of scene should manifestly be as complete as if the reader had taken the hind seat on a witch's broomstick. The town man finds what he seeks in novels of the country, the countryman in novels of society, the indoor class generally in outdoor novels, the villager in novels of the mansion, the aristocrat in novels of the cottage.

The narrative must be of a somewhat absorbing kind, if not absolutely fascinating. To discover a book or books which shall possess, in addition to the special scenery, the special action required, may be a matter of some difficulty, though not always of such difficulty as to be insuperable; and it may be asserted that after every variety of spiritual fatigue there is to be found refreshment, if

† The articles in this section, written by Hardy for various magazines and journals, were collected and reprinted in the volume entitled *Life and Art by Thomas Hardy*, edited by Ernest Brennecke Jr. (Greenberg Publishers, New York, 1925), pp. 56-58, 61-67, 72-73, 78-83, 85-90, 120, 130.

1. This selection originally appeared in an essay of the same title, first published in *The Forum* (New York), in March, 1888.

not restoration, in some antithetic realm of ideas which lies waiting in the pages of romance.

In reading for such hygienic purposes it is, of course, of the first consequence that the reader be not too critical. In other words, his author should be swallowed whole, like any other alterative pill. He should be believed in slavishly, implicitly. However profusely he may pour out his coincidences, his marvelous juxtapositions, his catastrophes, his conversions of bad people into good people at a stroke, and *vice versa,* let him never be doubted for a moment. When he exhibits people going out of their way and spending their money on purpose to act consistently, or taking a great deal of trouble to move in a curious and roundabout manner when a plain, straight course lies open to them; when he shows that heroes are never faithless in love, and that the unheroic always are so, there should arise a conviction that this is precisely according to personal experience. Let the invalid reverse the attitude of a certain class of critics—now happily becoming less numerous—who only allow themselves to be interested in a novel by the defeat of every attempt to the contrary. The aim should be the exercise of a generous imaginativeness, which shall find in a tale not only all that was put there by the author, put he it never so awkwardly, but which shall find there what was never inserted by him, never foreseen, never contemplated. Sometimes these additions which are woven around a work of fiction by the intensitive power of the reader's own imagination are the finest parts of the scenery.

It is not altogether necessary to this tonic purpose that the stories chosen should be 'of most disastrous chances, of moving accidents by flood and field.' As stated above, the aim should be contrast. Directly the circumstances begin to resemble those of the reader, a personal connection, an interest other than an imaginative one, is set up, which results in an intellectual stir that is not in the present case to be desired. It sets his serious thoughts at work, and he does not want them stimulated just now; he wants to dream.

So much may be said initially upon alleviating the effects of over-work and carking care by a course of imaginative reading. But I will assume that benefit of this sort is not that which is primarily contemplated when we speak of getting good out of novels, but intellectual or moral profit to active and undulled spirits.

It is obvious that choice in this case, though more limited than in the former, is by no means limited to compositions which touch the highest level in the essential constituents of a novel—those without which it would be no novel at all—the plot and the characters. Not only may the book be read for these main features—the presentation, as they may collectively be called—but for the accidents and appendages of narrative; and such are of more kinds than one. Excursions into various philosophies, which vary or delay narrative proper, may have more attraction than the regular course of the enactment; the judicious inquirer may be on the look-out for didactic reflection, such as is found in large lumps in 'Rasselas';[2] he may be a picker-up of trifles of useful knowledge, statistics, queer historic fact, such as sometimes occur in the pages of Hugo;[3] he may search for specimens of the manners of good or bad society, such as are to be obtained from the fashionable writers; or he may even wish to brush up his knowledge of quotations from ancient and other authors by studying some chapters of 'Pelham,'[4] and the disquisitions of Parson Adams in 'Joseph Andrews.'[5]

* * *

Good fiction may be defined here as that kind of imaginative writing which lies nearest to the epic, dramatic, or narrative masterpieces of the past. One fact is certain: in fiction there can be no intrinsically new thing at this stage of the world's history. New methods and plans may arise and come into fashion, as we see them do; but the general theme can neither be changed, nor (what is less obvious) can the relative importance of its various particulars be greatly interfered with. The higher passions must ever rank above the inferior—intellectual tendencies above animal, and moral above intellectual—whatever the treatment, realistic or ideal. Any system of inversion which should attach more importance to the delineation of man's appetites than to the delineation of his aspirations, affections, or humors, would condemn the old masters of imaginative creation from Æschylus to Shakespeare. Whether we hold the arts which depict mankind to be, in the words of Mr. Matthew Arnold, a criticism of life, or, in those of Mr. Addington Symonds, a revelation of life, the material remains the same, with its sublimities, its beauties, its uglinesses, as the case may be. The finer manifestations must precede in importance the meaner, without such a radical change in human nature as we can hardly conceive as pertaining to an even remote future of decline, and certainly do not recognize now.

In pursuance of his quest for a true exhibition of man, the reader will naturally consider whether he feels himself under the guidance of a mind who sees further into life than he himself has seen; or, at least, who can throw a stronger irradiation over subjects already within his ken than he has been able to do unaided. The new light needs not to be set off by a finish of phraseology or incisive sentences of subtle definition. The treatment may be baldly incidental,

2. A 1759 prose work by Samuel Johnson (1709-1784).
3. Victor Hugo (1802-1885), French novelist.
4. *Pelham* or *The Adventures of a Gentleman* was an 1828 novel by Edward Bulwer-Lytton (1803-1873).
5. Parson Adams was a character in *Joseph Andrews*, a 1742 novel by Henry Fielding (1707-1754).

without inference or commentary. Many elaborate reflections, for example, have been composed by moralizing chroniclers on the effect of prosperity in blunting men's recollection of those to whom they have sworn friendship when they shared a hard lot in common. But the writer in Genesis who tells his legend of certain friends in such adverse circumstances, one of whom, a chief butler, afterward came to good fortune, and ends the account of this good fortune with the simple words, 'Now the chief butler did not remember Joseph, but forgat him,[6] brings out a dramatic sequence on ground prepared for assent, shows us the general principle in the particular case, and hence writes with a force beyond that of aphorism or argument. It is the force of an appeal to the emotional reason rather than to the logical reason; for by their emotions men are acted upon, and act upon others.

If it be true, as is frequently asserted, that young people nowadays go to novels for their sentiments, their religion, and their morals, the question as to the wisdom or folly of those young people hangs upon their methods of acquisition in each case. A deduction from what these works exemplify by action that bears evidence of being a counterpart of life, has a distinct educational value; but an imitation of what may be called the philosophy of the personages—the doctrines of the actors, as shown in their conversation—may lead to surprising results. They should be informed that a writer whose story is not a tract in disguise has as his main object that of characterizing the people of his little world. A philosophy which appears between the inverted commas of a dialogue may, with propriety, be as full of holes as a sieve if the person or persons who advance it gain any reality of humanity thereby.

These considerations only bring us back again to the vital question how to discriminate the best in fiction. Unfortunately the two hundred years or so of the modern novel's development have not left the world so full of fine examples as to make it particularly easy to light upon them when the first obvious list has been run through. The, at first sight, high-piled granary sifts down to a very small measure of genuine corn. The conclusion cannot be resisted, notwithstanding what has been stated to the contrary in so many places, that the scarcity of perfect novels in any language is because the art of writing them is as yet in its youth, if not in its infancy. Narrative art is neither mature in its artistic aspect, nor in its ethical or philosophical aspect; neither in form nor in substance. To me, at least, the difficulties of perfect presentation in both these kinds appear of such magnitude that the utmost which each generation can be expected to do is to add one or two strokes toward the selection and shaping of a possible ultimate perfection.

6. Genesis xl.23.

In this scarcity of excellence in novels as wholes the reader must content himself with excellence in parts; and his estimate of the degree to which any given modern instance approximates to greatness will, of course, depend not only upon the proportion that the finer characteristics bear to the mass, but upon the figure cut by those finer characteristics beside those of the admitted masterpieces as yet. In this process he will go with the professed critic so far as to inquire whether the story forms a regular structure of incident, accompanied by an equally regular development of character—a composition based on faithful imagination, less the transcript than the similitude of material fact. But the appreciative, perspicacious reader will do more than this. He will see what his author is aiming at, and by affording full scope to his own insight, catch the vision which the writer has in his eye, and is endeavoring to project upon the paper, even while it half eludes him.

He will almost invariably discover that, however numerous the writer's excellencies, he is what is called unequal; he has a specialty. This especial gift being discovered, he fixes his regard more particularly thereupon. It is frequently not that feature in an author's work which common repute has given him credit for; more often it is, while co-existent with his popular attribute, overshadowed by it lurking like a violet in the shade of the more obvious, possibly more vulgar, talent, but for which it might have received high attention. Behind the broad humor of one popular pen he discerns startling touches of weirdness; amid the colossal fancies of another he sees strokes of the most exquisite tenderness; and the unobtrusive quality may grow to have more charm for him than the palpable one.

It must always be borne in mind, despite the claims of realism, that the best fiction, like the highest artistic expression in other modes, is more true, so to put it, than history or nature can be. In history occur from time to time monstrosities of human action and character explicable by no known law which appertains to sane beings; hitches in the machinery of existence, wherein we have not yet discovered a principle, which the artist is therefore bound to regard as accidents, hinderances to clearness of presentation, and hence, weakeners of the effect. To take an example from sculpture: no real gladiator ever died in such perfect harmony with normal nature as is represented in the well-known Capitoline marble. There was always a jar somewhere, a jot or tittle of something foreign in the real death-scene, which did not essentially appertain to the situation, and tended toward neutralizing its pathos; but this the sculptor omitted, and so consecrated his theme. In drama likewise. Observe the characters of any sterling play. No dozen persons who were capable of being animated by the profound reasons and truths thrown broadcast over 'Hamlet' or 'Othello,' of feeling the pulse of life so accurately, ever met together in one place in this world to shape an end. And, to come to fiction, nobody ever met an Uncle Toby[7] who was Uncle Toby all around; no historian's Queen Elizabeth was ever so perfectly a woman as the fictitious Elizabeth of 'Kenilworth.'[8] What is called the idealization of characters is, in truth, the making of them too real to be possible.

It may seem something of a paradox to assert that the novels which most conduce to moral profit are likely to be among those written without a moral purpose. But the truth of the statement may be realized if we consider that the didactic novel is so generally devoid of *vraisemblance* as to teach nothing but the impossibility of tampering with natural truth to advance dogmatic opinions. Those, on the other hand, which impress the reader with the inevitableness of character and environment in working out destiny, whether that destiny be just or unjust, enviable or cruel, must have a sound effect, if not what is called a good effect, upon a healthy mind.

Of the effects of such sincere presentation on weak minds, when the courses of the characters are not exemplary, and the rewards and punishments ill adjusted to deserts, it is not our duty to consider too closely. A novel which does moral injury to a dozen imbeciles, and has bracing results upon a thousand intellects of normal vigor, can justify its existence; and probably a novel was never written by the purest-minded author for which there could not be found some moral invalid or other whom it was capable of harming.

To distinguish truths which are temporary from truths which are eternal, the accidental from the essential, accuracies as to custom and ceremony from accuracies as to the perennial procedure of humanity, is of vital importance in our attempts to read for something more than amusement. There are certain novels, both among the works of living and the works of deceased writers, which give convincing proof of much exceptional fidelity, and yet they do not rank as great productions; for what they are faithful in is life garniture and not life. You are fully persuaded that the personages are clothed precisely as you see them clothed in the street, in the drawing-room, at the assembly. Even the trifling accidents of their costume are rendered by the honest narrator. They use the phrases of the season, present or past, with absolute accuracy as to idiom, expletive, slang. They lift their tea-cups or fan themselves to date. But what of it, after our first sense of its photographic curiousness is past? In aiming at the trivial

7. A character in the novel *Tristram Shandy* (1759-67) by Laurence Sterne (1713-1768).

8. An 1821 novel by Sir Walter Scott (1771-1832).

and the ephemeral they have almost surely missed better things.

* * *

Considerations as to the rank or station in life from which characters are drawn can have but little value in regulating the choice of novels for literary reasons, and the reader may thus leave much to the mood of the moment. I remember reading a lecture on novels by a young and ingenious, though not very profound, critic, some years ago, in which the theory was propounded that novels which depict life in the upper walks of society must, in the nature of things, be better reading than those which exhibit the life of any lower class, for the reason that the subjects of the former represent a higher stage of development than their less fortunate brethren. At the first blush this was a plausible theory; but when practically tested it is found to be based on such a totally erroneous conception of what a novel is, and where it comes from, as not to be worth a moment's consideration. It proceeds from the assumption that a novel is the thing, and not a view of the thing. It forgets that the characters, however they may differ, express mainly the author, his largeness of heart or otherwise, his culture, his insight, and very little of any other living person, except in such an inferior kind of procedure as might occasionally be applied to dialogue, and would take the narrative out of the category of fiction: *i.e.*, verbatim reporting without selective judgment.

But there is another reason, disconnected entirely from methods of construction, why the physical condition of the characters rules nothing of itself one way or the other. All persons who have thoughtfully compared class with class—and the wider their experience the more pronounced their opinion—are convinced that education has as yet but little broken or modified the waves of human impulse on which deeds and words depend. So that in the portraiture of scenes in any way emotional or dramatic—the highest province of fiction—the peer and the peasant stand on much the same level; the woman who makes the satin train and the woman who wears it. In the lapse of countless ages, no doubt, improved systems of moral education will considerably and appreciably elevate even the involuntary instincts of human nature; but at present culture has only affected the surface of those lives with which it has come in contact, binding down the passions of those predisposed to turmoil as by a silken thread only, which the first ebullition suffices to break. With regard to what may be termed the minor key of action and speech—the unemotional, every-day doings of men—social refinement operates upon character in a way which is oftener than not prejudicial to vigorous portraiture, by making the exteriors of men their screen rather than their index, as with untutored mankind.

* * *

Candour in English Fiction[9]

* * *

The popular vehicles for the introduction of a novel to the public have grown to be, from one cause and another, the magazine and the circulating library; and the object of the magazine and circulating library is not upward advance but lateral advance; to suit themselves to what is called household reading, which means, or is made to mean, the reading of the majority in a household or of the household collectively. The number of adults, even in a large household, being normally two, and these being the members which, as a rule, have least time on their hands to bestow on current literature, the taste of the majority can hardly be, and seldom is, tempered by the ripe judgment which desires fidelity. However, the immature members of a household often keep an open mind, and they might, and no doubt would, take sincere fiction with the rest but for another condition, almost generally co-existent: which is that adults who would desire true views for their own reading insist, for a plausible but questionable reason, upon false views for the reading of their young people.

As a consequence, the magazine in particular and the circulating library in general do not foster the growth of the novel which reflects and reveals life. They directly tend to exterminate it by monopolising all literary space. Cause and effect were never more clearly conjoined, though commentators upon the result, both French and English, seem seldom if ever to trace their connection. A sincere and comprehensive sequence of the ruling passions, however moral in its ultimate bearings, must not be put on paper as the foundation of imaginative works, which have to claim notice through the above-named channels, though it is extensively welcomed in the form of newspaper reports. That the magazine and library have arrogated to themselves the dispensation of fiction is not the fault of the authors, but of circumstances over which they, as representatives of Grub Street,[1] have no control.

What this practically amounts to is that the patrons of literature—no longer Peers with a taste—acting under the censorship of prudery, rigorously exclude from the pages they regulate subjects that have been made, by general approval of the best judges, the bases of the finest imaginative compositions since literature rose to the dignity of an art. The crash of broken commandments is as

9. These selections are from an essay of the same title, which first appeared in *The New Review,* January, 1890.

1. Once an actual street in London (now called Milton Street) inhabited by many needy and inferior writers, Grub Street refers to literary hacks who will write almost anything for money.

necessary an accompaniment to the catastrophe of a tragedy as the noise of drum and cymbals to a triumphal march. But the crash of broken commandments shall not be heard; or, if at all, but gently, like the roaring of Bottom—gently as any sucking dove, or as 'twere any nightingale, less we should fright the ladies out of their wits.[2] More precisely, an arbitrary proclamation has gone forth that certain picked commandments of the ten shall be preserved intact—to wit, the first, third, and seventh; that the ninth shall be infringed but gingerly; the sixth only as much as necessary; and the remainder alone as much as you please, in a genteel manner.

It is in the self-consciousness engendered by interference with spontaneity, and in aims at a compromise to square with circumstances, that the real secret lies of the charlatanry pervading so much of English fiction. It may be urged that abundance of great and profound novels might be written which should require no compromising, contain not an episode deemed questionable by prudes. This I venture to doubt. In a ramification of the profounder passions the treatment of which makes the great style, something 'unsuitable' is sure to arise; and then comes the struggle with the literary conscience. The opening scenes of the would-be great story may, in a rash moment, have been printed in some popular magazine before the remainder is written; as it advances month by month the situations develop, and the writer asks himself, what will his characters do next? What would probably happen to them, given such beginnings? On his life and conscience, though he had not foreseen the thing, only one event could possibly happen, and that therefore he should narrate, as he calls himself a faithful artist. But, though pointing a fine moral, it is just one of those issues which are not to be mentioned in respectable magazines and select libraries. The dilemma then confronts him, he must either whip and scourge those characters into doing something contrary to their natures, to produce the spurious effect of their being in harmony with social forms and ordinances, or, by leaving them alone to act as they will, he must bring down the thunders of respectability upon his head, not to say ruin his editor, his publisher, and himself.

What he often does, indeed can scarcely help doing in such a strait, is, belie his literary conscience, do despite to his best imaginative instincts by arranging a *dénouement* which he knows to be indescribably unreal and meretricious, but dear to the Grundyist[3] and subscriber. If the true artist ever weeps it probably is then,

2. Bottom boasting of his ability to play the part of a lion in Shaksepeare's *Midsummer-Night's Dream* I.ii.

3. Term referring to the narrow-minded censor of both literature and personal conduct, derived from Mrs. Grundy, a character in *Speed the Plough,* a 1798 play by Thomas Morton.

when he first discovers the fearful price that he has to pay for the privilege of writing in the English language—no less a price than the complete extinction, in the mind of every mature and penetrating reader, of sympathetic belief in his personages.

* * *

Whether minors should read unvarnished fiction based on the deeper passions, should listen to the eternal verities in the form of narrative, is somewhat a different question from whether the novel ought to be exclusively addressed to those minors. The first consideration is one which must be passed over here; but it will be conceded by most friends of literature that all fiction should not be shackled by conventions concerning budding womanhood, which may be altogether false. It behoves us then to inquire how best to circumvent the present lording of nonage over maturity, and permit the explicit novel to be more generally written.

* * *

There remain three courses by which the adult may find deliverance. The first would be a system of publication under which books could be bought and not borrowed, when they would naturally resolve themselves into classes instead of being, as now, made to wear a common livery in style and subject, enforced by their supposed necessities in addressing indiscriminately a general audience.

But it is scarcely likely to be convenient to either authors or publishers that the periodical form of publication for the candid story should be entirely forbidden, and in retaining the old system thus far, yet ensuring that the emancipated serial novel should meet the eyes of those for whom it is intended, the plan of publication as a *feuilleton*[4] in newspapers read mainly by adults might be more generally followed, as in France. In default of this, or co-existent with it, there might be adopted what, upon the whole, would perhaps find more favour than any with those who have artistic interests at heart, and that is, magazines for adults; exclusively for adults, if necessary. As an offshot there might be at least one magazine for the middle-aged and old.

There is no foretelling; but this (since the magazine form of publication is so firmly rooted) is at least a promising remedy, if English prudery be really, as we hope, only a parental anxiety. There should be no mistaking the matter, no half measures. *La dignité de la pensée,*[5] in the words of Pascal, might then grow to be recognised in the treatment of fiction as in other things, and untrammelled adult opinion on conduct and theology might be axiomatically assumed and dramatically appealed to. Nothing in

4. A serial story or novel.

5. "The dignity of thought."

such literature should for a moment exhibit lax views of that purity of life upon which the well-being of society depends; but the position of man and woman in nature, and the position of belief in the minds of man and woman—things which everybody is thinking but nobody is saying—might be taken up and treated frankly.

* * *

The Science of Fiction[6]

Since Art is science with an addition, since some science underlies all Art, there is seemingly no paradox in the use of such a phrase as 'the Science of Fiction.' One concludes it to mean that comprehensive and accurate knowledge of realities which must be sought for, or intuitively possessed, to some extent, before anything deserving the name of an artistic performance in narrative can be produced.

The particulars of this science are the generals of almost all others. The materials of Fiction being human nature and circumstances, the science thereof may be dignified by calling it the codified law of things as they really are. No single pen can treat exhaustively of this. The Science of Fiction is contained in that large work, the cyclopædia of life.

In no proper sense can the term 'science' be applied to other than this fundamental matter. It can have no part or share in the construction of a story, however recent speculations may have favoured such an application. We may assume with certainty that directly the constructive stage is entered upon, Art—high or low—begins to exist.

The most devoted apostle of realism, the sheerest naturalist, cannot escape, any more than the withered old gossip over her fire, the exercise of Art in his labour or pleasure of telling a tale. Not until he becomes an automatic reproducer of all impressions whatsoever can he be called purely scientific, or even a manufacturer on scientific principles. If in the exercise of his reason he select or omit, with an eye to being more truthful than truth (the just aim of Art), he transforms himself into a technicist at a move.

* * *

The reasons that make against such conformation of story-writing to scientific processes have been set forth so many times n examining the theories of the realist, that it is not necessary to recapitulate them here. Admitting the desirability, the impossibility of reproducing in its entirety the phantasmagoria of experience

6. This selection is from an essay of the same title, which first appeared in *The New Review*, April, 1891.

with infinite and atomic truth, without shadow, relevancy, or subordination, is not the least of them. The fallacy appears to owe its origin to the just perception that with our widened knowledge of the universe and its forces, and man's position therein, narrative, to be artistically convincing, must adjust itself to the new alignment, as would also artistic works in form and colour, if further spectacles in their sphere could be presented. Nothing but the illusion of truth can permanently please, and when the old illusions begin to be penetrated, a more natural magic has to be supplied.

Creativeness in its full and ancient sense—the making a thing or situation out of nothing that ever was before—is apparently ceasing to satisfy a world which no longer believes in the abnormal—ceasing at least to satisfy the van-couriers of taste; and creative fancy has accordingly to give more and more place to realism, that is, to an artificiality distilled from the fruits of closest observation.

This is the meaning deducible from the work of the realists, however stringently they themselves may define realism in terms. Realism is an unfortunate, an ambiguous word, which has been taken up by literary society like a view-halloo, and has been assumed in some places to mean copyism, and in others pruriency, and has led to two classes of delineators being included in one condemnation.

Just as bad a word is one used to express a consequence of this development, namely 'brutality,' a term which, first applied by French critics, has since spread over the English school like the other. It aptly hits off the immediate impression of the thing meant; but it has the disadvantage of defining impartiality as a passion, and a plan as a caprice. It certainly is very far from truly expressing the aims and methods of conscientious and well-intentioned authors who, notwithstanding their excesses, errors, and rickety theories, attempt to narrate the *vérité vraie*.[7]

To return for a moment to the theories of the scientific realists. Every friend to the novel should and must be in sympathy with their error, even while distinctly perceiving it. Though not true, it is well found. To advance realism as complete copyism, to call the idle trade of story-telling a science, is the hyperbolic flight of an admirable enthusiasm, the exaggerated cry of an honest reaction from the false, in which the truth has been impetuously approached and overleapt in fault of lighted on.

Possibly, if we only wait, the third something, akin to perfection, will exhibit itself on its due pedestal. How that third something

7. "The real truth." Hardy is probably referring to the realistic aims and scientific methods of writers like Emile Zola (1840-1902). Zola, who studied his characters as if in a laboratory, continued the French realistic tradition of Stendahl (1783-1842), Balzac (1799-1850), and Flaubert (1821-1880), but his critics accused him of needless "brutality."

may be induced to hasten its presence, who shall say? Hardly the English critic.

* * *

An accomplished lady once confessed to the writer that she could never be in a room two minutes without knowing every article of furniture it contained and every detail in the attire of the inmates, and, when she left, remembering every remark. Here was a person, one might feel for the moment, who could prime herself to an unlimited extent and at the briefest notice in the scientific data of fiction; one who, assuming her to have some slight artistic power, was a born novelist. To explain why such a keen eye to the superficial does not imply a sensitiveness to the intrinsic is a psychological matter beyond the scope of these notes; but that a blindness to material particulars often accompanies a quick perception of the more ethereal characteristics of humanity, experience continually shows.

A sight for the finer qualities of existence, an ear for the "still sad music of humanity,"[8] are not to be acquired by the outer senses alone, close as their powers in photography may be. What cannot be discerned by eye and ear, what may be apprehended only by the mental tactility that comes from a sympathetic appreciativeness of life in all its manifestations, this is the gift which renders its possessor a more accurate delineator of human nature than many another with twice his powers and means of external observation, but without that sympathy. To see in half and quarter views the whole picture, to catch from a few bars the whole tune, is the intuitive power that supplies the would-be story-writer with the scientific bases for his pursuit. He may not count the dishes at a feast, or accurately estimate the value of the jewels in a lady's diadem; but through the smoke of those dishes, and the rays from these jewels, he sees written on the wall:—

We are such stuff
As dreams are made of, and our little life
Is rounded with a sleep.[9]

Thus, as aforesaid, an attempt to set forth the Science of Fiction in calculable pages is futility; it is to write a whole library of human philosophy, with instructions how to feel.

Once in a crowd a listener heard a needy and illiterate woman saying of another poor and haggard woman who had lost her little son years before: 'You can see the ghost of that child in her face even now.'

That speaker was one who, though she could probably neither read nor write, had the true means towards the 'Science' of Fiction

8. William Wordsworth, "Lines Composed a Few Miles Above Tintern Abbey."

9. *The Tempest* IV.i.

innate within her; a power of observation informed by a living heart. Had she been trained in the technicalities, she might have fashioned her view of mortality with good effect; a reflection which leads to a conjecture that perhaps, true novelists, like poets, are born, not made.

* * *

[On English Marriage Laws][1]

I have already said many times, during the past twenty or thirty years, that I regard Marriage as a union whose terms should be regulated entirely for the happiness of the community, including, primarily, that of the parties themselves.

As the English marriage laws are, to the eyes of anybody who looks around, the gratuitous cause of at least half the misery of the community, that they are allowed to remain in force for a day is, to quote the famous last word of the ceremony itself, an "amazement," and can only be accounted for by the assumption that we live in a barbaric age, and are the slaves of gross superstition.

As to what should be done, in the unlikely event of any amendment of the law being tolerated by bigots, it is rather a question for experts than for me. I can only suppose, in a general way, that a marriage should be dissolvable at the wish of either party, if that party prove it to be a cruelty to him or her, provided (probably) that the maintenance of the children, if any, should be borne by the breadwinner.

[On Writers and the State][2]

Sir,—I daresay it would be very interesting that literature should be honoured by the State. But I don't see how it could be satisfactorily done. The highest flights of the pen are often, indeed mostly, the excursions and revelations of souls unreconciled to life; while the natural tendency of a government would be to encourage acquiescence in life as it is. However, I have not thought much about the matter.

Thomas Hardy

1. This was Hardy's contribution to a symposium on "How Shall We Solve the Divorce Problem?" in *Hearst's Magazine*, June, 1912.

2. Hardy wrote this letter in response to a question from *The Bookman* (London). It was published in December, 1891.

Hardy's Poems†

Although he had written poems early in his career, Hardy wrote poetry almost exclusively for the last thirty-two years of his life. Most modern critics have recognized him, as his contemporaries generally did not, as one of the greatest poets of his time, and many twentieth-century poets, Auden and Spender among them, have spoken of Hardy's enormous influence on the diction and attitudes in their early verse. Florence Emily Hardy, his second wife, wrote: "Speaking generally, there is more autobiography in a hundred lines of Mr. Hardy's poetry than in all the novels."[1] In *Thomas Hardy, a Critical Biography*,[2] Evelyn Hardy skillfully demonstrates how many of the poems fit both Hardy's interests at various periods during his life and his concerns in many of his novels.

I have chosen the following twelve poems[3] as particularly relevant to the background and attitudes expressed in *The Return of the Native*.

By the Barrows

Not far from Mellstock—so tradition saith—
Where barrows, bulging as they bosoms were
Of Multimammia stretched supinely there,
Catch night and noon the tempests's wanton breath,

A battle, desperate doubtless unto death,
Was one time fought. The outlook, lone and bare,
The towering hawk and passing raven share,
And all the upland round is called "The He'th."

Here once a woman, in our modern age,
Fought singlehandedly to shield a child—
One not her own—from a man's senseless rage.
And to my mind no patriots' bones there piled
So consecrate the silence as her deed
Of stoic and devoted self-unheed.

† From *Collected Poems of Thomas Hardy* (1925).

1. Florence Emily Hardy, *The Later Years of Thomas Hardy, 1892-1928* (New York, 1930), p. 196.
2. Published by David Higham Associates, Ltd., London, 1954.
3. From *Collected Poems of Thomas Hardy*, Macmillan, New York, 1925.

The Moth-Signal

(ON EGDON HEATH)

"What are you still, still thinking,"
He asked in vague surmise,
"That you stare at the wick unblinking
With those deep lost luminous eyes?"

"O, I see a poor moth burning
In the candle flame," said she,
"Its wings and legs are turning
To a cinder rapidly."

"Moths fly in from the heather,"
He said, "now the days decline."
"I know," said she. "The weather,
I hope, will at last be fine.

"I think," she added lightly,
"I'll look out at the door.
The ring the moon wears nightly
May be visible now no more."

She rose, and, little heeding,
Her life-mate then went on
With his mute and museful reading
In the annals of ages gone.

Outside the house a figure
Came from the tumulus near,
And speedily waxed bigger,
And clasped and called her Dear.

"I saw the pale-winged token
You sent through the crack," sighed she.
"That moth is burnt and broken
With which you lured out me.

"And were I as the moth is
It might be better far
For one whose marriage troth is
Shattered as potsherds are!"

Then grinned the Ancient Briton
From the tumulus treed with pine:
"So, hearts are thwartly smitten
In these days as in mine!"

The Roman Road

The Roman Road runs straight and bare
As the pale parting-line in hair
Across the heath. And thoughtful men
Contrast its days of Now and Then,
And delve, and measure, and compare;

Visioning on the vacant air
Helmed legionaries, who proudly rear
The Eagle, as they pace again
The Roman Road.

But no tall brass-helmed legionnaire
Haunts it for me. Uprises there
A mother's form upon my ken,
Guiding my infant steps, as when
We walked that ancient thoroughfare,
The Roman Road.

On a Heath

I could hear a gown-skirt rustling
Before I could see her shape,
Rustling through the heather
That wove the common's drape,
On that evening of dark weather
When I hearkened, lips agape.

And the town-shine in the distance
Did but baffle here the sight,
And then a voice flew forward:
"Dear, is't you? I fear the night!"
And the herons flapped to norward
In the firs upon my right.

There was another looming
Whose life we did not see;
There was one stilly blooming
Full nigh to where walked we;
There was a shade entombing
All that was bright of me.

The Sheep Boy

A yawning, sunned concave
Of purple, spread as an ocean wave
Entroughed on a morning of swell and sway
After a night when wind-fiends have been heard to rave:
Thus was the Heath called "Draäts",[4] on an August day.

4. An Anglo-Saxon term for heath.

Suddenly there intunes a hum:
This side, that side, it seems to come.
From the purple in myriads rise the bees
With consternation mid their rapt employ.
So headstrongly each speeds him past, and flees,
As to strike the face of the shepherd-boy.
Awhile he waits, and wonders what they mean:
Till none is left upon the shagged demesne.

To learn what ails, the sheep-boy looks around;
Behind him, out of the sea in swirls
Flexuous and solid, clammy vapour-curls
Are rolling over Pokeswell Hills to the inland ground.
In to the heath they sail,
And travel up the vale
Like the moving pillar of cloud raised by the Israelite:[5]—

In a trice the lonely sheep-boy seen so late ago,
Draäts'-Hollow in gorgeous blow,
And Kite-Hill's regal glow,
Are viewless—folded into those creeping scrolls of white.

On Rainbarrows.

The Bride-Night Fire[6]

(A WESSEX TRADITION)

They had long met o' Zundays—her true love and she—
And at junketings, maypoles, and flings;
But she bode wi' a thirtover[7] uncle, and he
Swore by noon and by night that her goodman should be
Naibour Sweatley—a wight often weak at the knee
From taking o' sommat more cheerful than tea—
Who tranted,[8] and moved people's things.

She cried, "O pray pity me!" Nought would he hear;
Then with wild rainy eyes she obeyed.
She chid when her Love was for clinking off[9] wi' her:
The pa'son was told, as the season drew near,
To throw over pu'pit the names of the pair
As fitting one flesh to be made.

The wedding-day dawned and the morning drew on;
The couple stood bridegroom and bride;

5. Symbol of God's protection in leading the Israelites out of Egypt. Exodus xiii.21-22; xiv.19; xiv.24.
6. Unless otherwise designated, the footnotes in this poem are Thomas Hardy's.
7. Cross.
8. Traded as carrier.
9. Running off. with the connotation of doing so defiantly and noisily [*Editor*].

The evening was passed, and when midnight had gone
The feasters horned,[1] "God save the King," and anon
    The pair took their homealong[2] ride.

The lover Tim Tankens mourned heart-sick and leer[3]
    To be thus of his darling deprived:
He roamed in the dark ath'art field, mound, and mere,
And, a'most without knowing it, found himself near
The house of the tranter, and now of his Dear,
    Where the lantern-light showed 'em arrived.

The bride sought her chamber so calm and so pale
    That a Northern[4] had thought her resigned;
But to eyes that had seen her in tidetimes[5] of weal,
Like the white cloud o'smoke, the red battlefield's vail,[6]
    That look spak' of havoc behind.

The bridegroom yet laitered a beaker to drain,
    Then reeled to the linhay[7] for more,
When the candle-snoff kindled some chaff from his grain—
Flames spread, and red vlankers[8] wi' might and wi' main
    Around beams, thatch, and chimley-tun[9] roar.

Young Tim away yond, rafted[1] up by the light,
    Through brimbles and underwood tears,
Till he comes to the orchet, when crooping[2] from sight
In the lewth[3] of a codlin-tree, bivering[4] wi' fright,
Wi' on'y her night-rail[5] to cover her plight,
    His lonesome young Barbree appears.

Her cwold little figure half-naked he views
    Played about by the frolicsome breeze,
Her light-tripping totties,[6] her ten little tooes,
All bare and besprinkled wi' Fall's[7] chilly dews,
While her great gallied[8] eyes through her hair hanging loose
    Shone as stars through a tardle[9] o' trees.

She eyed him; and, as when a weir-hatch is drawn,
    Her tears, penned by terror afore,

1. Sang loudly.
2. Homeward.
3. Empty-stomached.
4. A person from the North, a stranger [*Editor*].
5. Holidays.
6. Profit or advantage. Here, Hardy is using the term ironically, for the white cloud of smoke really reveals the presence of the "red battlefield" it is supposed to hide [*Editor*].
7. Lean-to building.
8. Fire-flakes.
9. Chimney-stack.
1. Roused.
2. Squatting down.
3. Shelter.
4. With chattering teeth.
5. A loose, thin woman's wrap or dressing gown, not generally worn out of doors [*Editor*].
6. Feet.
7. Autumn.
8. Frightened.
9. Entanglement.

With a rushing of sobs in a shower were strawn,
Till her power to pour 'em seemed wasted and gone
From the heft[1] o' misfortune she bore.

"O Tim, my *own* Tim I must call 'ee—I will!
All the world has turned round on me so!
Can you help her who loved 'ee, though acting so ill?
Can you pity her misery—feel for her still?
When worse than her body so quivering and chill
Is her heart in its winter o' woe!

"I think I mid[2] almost ha' borne it," she said,
"Had my griefs one by one come to hand;
But O, to be slave to thik husbird,[3] for bread,
And then, upon top o' that, driven to wed.
And then, upon top o' that, burnt out o' bed,
Is more than my nater can stand!"

Like a lion 'ithin en Tim's spirit outsprung—
(Tim had a great soul when his feelings were wrung)—
"Feel for 'ee, dear Barbree?" he cried;
And his warm working-jacket then straightway he flung
Round about her, and horsed her by jerks, till she clung
Like a chiel on a gipsy, her figure uphung
By the sleeves that he tightly had tied.

Over piggeries, and mixens,[4] and apples, and hay,
They lumpered[5] straight into the night;
And finding ere long where a halter-path[6] lay,
Sighted Tim's house by dawn, on'y seen on their way
By a naibour or two who were up wi' the day,
But who gathered no clue to the sight.

Then tender Tim Tankens he searched here and there
For some garment to clothe her fair skin;
But though he had breeches and waistcoats to spare,
He had nothing quite seemly for Barbree to wear,
Who, half shrammed[7] to death, stood and cried on a chair
At the caddle[8] she found herself in.

There was one thing to do, and that one thing he did,
He lent her some clothes of his own,
And she took 'em perforce; and while swiftly she slid
Them upon her Tim turned to the winder, as bid,
Thinking, "O that the picter my duty keeps hid
To the sight o' my eyes mid[9] be shown!"

1. Weight.
2. Might.
3. That rascal.
4. Manure-heaps.
5. Stumbled.
6. Bridle-path.
7. Numbed.
8. Quandary.
9. Might.

In the tallet[1] he stowed her; there huddied[2] she lay,
Shortening sleeves, legs, and tails to her limbs;
But most o' the time in a mortal bad way,
Well knowing that there'd be the divel to pay
If 'twere found that, instead o' the element's prey,
She was living in lodgings at Tim's.

"Where's the tranter?" said men and boys; "where can he be?"
"Where is the tranter?" said Barbree alone.
"Where on e'th is the tranter?" said everybod-y:
They sifted the dust of his perished roof-tree,
And all they could find was a bone.

Then the uncle cried, "Lord, pray have mercy on me!"
And in terror began to repent.
But before 'twas complete, and till sure she was free,
Barbree drew up her loft-ladder, tight turned her key—
Tim bringing up breakfast and dinner and tea—
Till the news of her hiding got vent.

Then followed the custom-kept rout, shout, and flare
Of a skimmity-ride[3] through the naibourhood, ere
Folk had proof o' wold[4] Sweatley's decay.
Whereupon decent people all stood in a stare,
Saying Tim and his lodger should risk it, and pair:
So he took her to church. An' some laughing lads there
Cried to Tim, "After Sweatley!" She said, "I declare
I stand as a maiden to-day!"

The Night of the Dance

The cold moon hangs to the sky by its horn,
And centres its gaze on me;
The stars, like eyes in reverie,
Their westering as for a while forborne,
Quiz downward curiously.

Old Robert draws the backbrand[5] in,
The green logs steam and spit;
The half-awakened sparrows flit
From the riddled thatch; and owls begin
To whoo from the gable-slit.

Yes; far and night things seem to know
Sweet scenes are impending here;

1. Loft.
2. Hidden.
3. Satirical procession with effigies.
4. Old.
5. A large log put at the back of a fire.

That all is prepared; that the hour is near
For welcomes, fellowships, and flow
Of sally, song, and cheer;

That spigots are pulled and viols strung;
That soon will arise the sound
Of measures trod to tunes renowned;
That She will return in Love's low tongue
My vows as we wheel around.

The Pedestrian

AN INCIDENT OF 1883

"Sir, will you let me give you a ride?
Nox venit,[6] and the heath is wide."
—My phaeton-lantern shone on one
Young, fair, even fresh,
But burdened with flesh:
A leathern satchel at his side,
His breathings short, his coat undone.

'Twas as if his corpulent figure slopped
With the shake of his walking when he stopped,
And, though the night's pinch grew acute,
He wore but a thin
Wind-thridded suit,
Yet well-shaped shoes for walking in,
Artistic beaver, cane gold-topped.

"Alas, my friend," he said with a smile,
"I am daily bound to foot ten mile—
Wet, dry, or dark—before I rest.
Six months to live
My doctors give
Me as my prospect here, at best,
Unless I vamp my sturdiest!"[7]

His voice was that of a man refined,
A man, one well could feel, of mind,
Quite winning in its musical ease;
But in mould maligned
By some disease;
And I asked again. But he shook his head:
Then, as if more were due, he said:—

"A student was I—of Schopenhauer,
Kant, Hegel,—and the fountained bower

6. Night Comes.

7. Walk as much as I possibly can.

Of the Muses, too, knew my regard:
But ah—I fear me
The grave gapes near me! . . .
Would I could this gross sheath discard,
And rise an ethereal shape, unmarred!"

How I remember him!—his short breath,
His aspect, marked for early death,
As he dropped into the night for ever;
One caught in his prime
Of high endeavour;
From all philosophies soon to sever
Through an unconscienced trick of Time!

A Meeting with Despair

As evening shaped I found me on a moor
Sight shunned to entertain:
The black lean land, of featureless contour,
Was like a tract in pain.

"This scene, like my own life," I said, "is one
Where many glooms abide;
Toned by its fortune to a deadly dun—
Lightless on every side."

I glanced aloft and halted, pleasure-caught
To see the contrast there:
The ray-lit clouds gleamed glory; and I thought,
"There's solace everywhere!"

Then bitter self-reproaches as I stood
I dealt me silently
As one perverse, misrepresenting Good
In graceless mutiny.

Against the horizon's dim-discernèd wheel
A form rose, strange of mould:
That he was hideous, hopeless, I could feel
Rather than could behold.

"'Tis a dead spot, where even the light lies spent
To darkness!" croaked the Thing.
"Not if you look aloft!" said I, intent
On my new reasoning.

"Yea—but await awhile!" he cried. "Ho-ho!—
Now look aloft and see!"
I looked. There, too, sat night: Heaven's radiant show
Had gone that heartened me.

To the Moon

"What have you looked at, Moon,
In your time,
Now long past your prime?"
"O, I have looked at, often looked at
Sweet, sublime.
Sore things, shudderful, night and noon
In my time."

"What have you mused on, Moon,
In your day,
So aloof, so far away?"
"O, I have mused on, often mused on
Growth, decay,
Nations alive, dead, mad, aswoon,
In my day!"

"Have you much wondered, Moon,
On your rounds,
Self-wrapt, beyond Earth's bounds?"
"Yea, I have wondered, often wondered
At the sounds
Reaching me of the human tune
On my rounds."

"What do you think of it, Moon,
As you go?
Is Life much, or no?"
"O, I think of it, often think of it
As a show
God ought surely to shut up soon,
As I go."

At Moonrise and Onwards

I thought you a fire
On Heath-Plantation Hill,
Dealing out mischief the most dire
To the chattels of men of hire
There in their vill.

But by and by
You turned a yellow-green,
Like a large glow-worm in the sky;
And then I could descry
Your mood and mien.

How well I know
Your furtive feminine shape!
As if reluctantly you show
You nude of cloud, and but by favour throw
Aside its drape. . . .

—How many a year
Have you kept pace with me,
Wan Woman of the waste up there,
Behind a hedge, or the bare
Bough of a tree!

No novelty are you,
O Lady of all my time,
Veering unbid into my view
Whether I near Death's mew,
Or Life's top cyme![8]

Nobody Comes

Tree-leaves labour up and down,
And through them the fainting light
Succumbs to the crawl of night.
Outside in the road the telegraph wire
To the town from the darkening land
Intones to travellers like a spectral lyre
Swept by a spectral hand.

A car comes up, with lamps full-glare,
That flash upon a tree:
It has nothing to do with me,
And whangs along in a world of its own,
Leaving a blacker air;
And mute by the gate I stand again alone,
And nobody pulls up there.

October 9, 1924

8. Top sprout of a plant, a single terminal flower.

Hardy and Folklore

Carefully confined by the boundaries of Egdon Heath, the action of *The Return of the Native* reveals Hardy's interest in folk culture even more than do most of his other novels. The rustic characters on the heath believe in omens and primitive superstitions, interpreting their experience in terms of folk customs and beliefs. In addition, Hardy organizes the novel around folk festivals with pagan origins: the principal action of the novel takes a year, from one Guy Fawkes night to the next; the long scene in which Eustacia Vye and Clym Yeobright become acquainted with each other takes place at an ancient mummers' play performed every Christmas; the final section of the novel, the extension of the time scheme required to bring Diggory Venn and Thomasin together, is centered on the communal dance around the maypole.

Folk ceremonies, as Hardy described them and as they existed in Dorset and other counties in southwestern England (the area of Hardy's imaginary Wessex) in the nineteenth century, generally included elements from both the Christian and the pagan traditions. The bonfires of Guy Fawkes night (November 5) commemorate both the saving of the state from Roman Catholic plotters in 1605 and a pre-Christian ceremony that used the fire to appease the force of the coming winter and to memorialize the dead of the past year. Even in Roman Catholic communities in Britain, autumnal bonfires—without burning Guy Fawkes's effigy—are still customary. In *The Return of the Native,* Hardy adds another possible function for the bonfires, that of a gesture of defiance against the harsh environment of the heath. For Eustacia, who uses the fire to lure Wildeve and, by so doing, consumes much of the fuel her grandfather had put away for the winter, the bonfire as rebellion is more important than its ceremonial associations. Eustacia's rebellion, her use of the bonfire for personal reasons, places her outside the normal community on the heath, a community for whom the bonfire is public, ceremonial, and connected with a set of established traditions.

The mummers' play, like the celebration that evolved into Christmas itself, was originally a pagan celebration of the New Year, worshipping the return of the sun and the imminent death of winter. As it survived into the Christian era, the mummers' play incorporated Christian symbols, such as Saint George as the hero and the Turkish Knight or Saracen as the villain, both originating at the time of the medieval Crusades. The central theme common to all versions of the folk drama, including that presented by Hardy, is the revival of the dead, represented either as a revived figure of sun and spring in purely pagan ceremonies or a revived Crusader who is both killed and brought back to life within the play and who symbolizes Christian virtue. Appropriately, a physician, an agent of revival, is an important character in all these dramatizations of human triumph over death. Hardy relates his mummers' play to his other themes in *The Return of the Native,* for he has Eustacia usurp the role of the Turkish Knight, the villain, the character who kills the valiant Crusader but is finally slain by the righteous Saint George, as an indication of Eustacia's role in the traditional community on Egdon Heath.

Like any original and imaginative writer, Hardy adapted the mummers' play for his own novelistic purposes. At the same time, according to Miss Firor,[1] Hardy's version was more traditional, closer to the old folk drama, than were most other nineteenth century versions. Frequently, other versions were corrupted by humorous references to contemporary events (Saint George was changed to King or Prince George, the villainous Turkish Knight became Napoleon) and the various minor characters, like comic rustics, engaged in farce and in knocking each other down. But the mummers' play in *The Return of the Native,* appropriately for the novel, is somber and traditional, the age old assurance that the good and life triumph finally over evil and death. Hardy also carefully describes many of the traditional elements of the mummers' plays: the costumes, the gestures, the set speeches.

One of Hardy's folk ceremonies illustrates no Christian influence whatever. This is the communal dance around the maypole, a pagan celebration of summer and fertility which brings Diggory and Thomasin together at the end of the novel. Characters like Diggory and Thomasin, as well as some of the comic rustics, are lighter, free to live following the ancient world of the seasons without being tortured by guilt, excessive ambition, or the wish to be other than they are. The more central characters, Eustacia and Clym, are deeper and divided by the sometimes uneasy mixture between pagan and Christian worlds. The festivals of Guy Fawkes night and Christmas, more closely connected with the grim influence of the heath than is the more pastoral maypole, suggest the human complexity and mystery that leads Eustacia and Clym to

1. Ruth A. Firor, *Folkways in Thomas Hardy,* Philadelphia, 1931. This is an excellent and comprehensive book, full of information on Hardy's use of local customs and superstitions.

disaster. Other instances of the mixture of pagan and Christian fill the novel. The barrows that mark the heath, originally burial mounds, survive from pre-Christian days and the relics placed in them are sometimes discovered during the course of the novel. Hardy ends by having Clym, once an enthusiastic gatherer of primitive relics, preach his Biblical sermon standing on top of the largest barrow.

Many of the folk customs and superstitions, primitive means of assuaging the forces of evil, survived alongside a proclaimed belief in Christianity. For Hardy's rustics, the primitive beliefs always express all of experience, leaving the Christian doctrine for superficial Sunday observance. The timid Christian Cantle attributes his initial luck in gambling to having been born with a caul, a superstition that goes through and beyond Greek and Roman civilization; Christian also is sure that having been born when there was no moon accounts for his timidity and lack of sexual success, another instance of primitive belief. Almost all of the characters have premonitions: the most notable is Eustacia's foreknowledge that the heath, her enemy, will be her death. But folk belief also provides counter measures, means by which human beings can allay the evil forces that work against them. On the ancient principle of taking "the hair of the dog that bit you" (inversely confirmed by some of the practices of modern vaccination), Hardy's country people apply fried fresh adder's fat to ease Mrs. Yeobright's poisoned adder's bite. Since, according to old superstition, an adder cannot really die until sundown, the two killed that day are almost as useful as the one they catch alive. Johnny Nunsuch values the crooked sixpence Eustacia gives him for tending her fire, because a crooked sixpence was regarded as lucky, the bend in the coin breaking the straight circuit of malign forces and diverting the evil harmlessly away. Johnny's mother, Susan Nunsuch, regards Eustacia as a witch and attempts to break Eustacia's spell by pricking her with a long needle in church, relying on the magical assumption that drawing a witch's blood will also draw away her power. That Eustacia does bleed proves that she is not a particularly malevolent witch (for such witches were supposedly bloodless). Still convinced that Eustacia exercises evil power over her son, Susan finally resorts to the ultimate form of primitive exorcism: she molds a wax image of Eustacia, sticks pins in it, and melts it over the fire—a standard version of the kind of exorcism involved in burning the effigy of Guy Fawkes.

Hardy does not link the effigy Susan makes and the fact that Eustacia drowns the same night together in a chain of cause and effect. Still, the events are placed closely together and create a suggestion that lingers over the novel. Eustacia's fate is given cause in her character—her restlessness, her desire for anything unattainable, her hatred of the heath. At the same time, enough superstitious premonitions are confirmed to make the folk point of view credible for those who hold it. The people on the heath are motivated by their customs and their primitive beliefs, but Hardy provides other reasons more credible to us to explain what happens. That the two ways of examining human nature often reach similar conclusions in the novel underlines Hardy's point that primitive insights can come very close to the central issues of human experience. Hardy contrives his folk perspectives to depict many of the people on the heath (not all of them, however: Mrs. Yeobright neither believes in or is motivated by any folk superstition). For most of the novel Diggory Venn seems a benevolent folk spirit, mysteriously appearing out of the heath whenever he is needed to challenge the forces of evil. Yet, when the novel was expanded in Hardy's "change of intent" and Diggory needed to become a presentable human suitor for Thomasin, Hardy simply eliminated the suggestion of Diggory's supernatural force along with the staining reddle. Hardy always combines an interest in more sophisticated human character and motives with his curiosity about folklore.

Some of the images and names Hardy uses are drawn from folk dialect; the phrase "to work like Diggory," for example, means to work with dogged persistence. Yet Hardy's language is far from a transcription of Dorset dialect. In a reply to a review of *The Return of the Native* in *The Athenaeum* (reprinted elsewhere in this volume), Hardy maintained that he was trying "only to give a general idea of their linguistic peculiarities." And, when the reviewer of a later novel called him a popular dialect novelist, Hardy expanded on his method in a public reply:

> The rule of scrupulously preserving the local idiom, together with the words which have no synonym among those in general use, while printing in the ordinary way most of those local expressions which are but a modified articulation of words in use elsewhere, is the rule I usually follow;
>
> (*The Spectator*, October 15, 1881)

Hardy's language, like his view of human character and his organization of the annual calendar around traditional festivals in *The Return of the Native*, owes something to his interest in and knowledge about folk culture. Yet, at the same time, folk culture cannot provide the origin for all the insights, ideas, and ironies that infuse the novel. Hardy, like other highly talented writers, shaped the background he knew and molded the elements in the culture around him in order to create his fiction.

Hardy's interest in and use of folk culture can be partially explained by his background. Except for several years in London in his twenties, Hardy spent most of his long life near his birthplace in Dorset. And, although most of England became increasingly urban and industrial in the latter half of the nineteenth century, Dorset remained more agricultural and its populace more committed to the popular beliefs and superstitions surviving from earlier ages. Hardy knew the area intimately and his exceptional memory enabled him to recall songs and tales he had not heard since childhood. A number of these folk ballads, psalm tunes, and dances of Dorset appear in *The Return of the Native*. His grandfather, father, and uncle were excellent amateur musicians (well-known in the 1820's and '30's as the Stinsford stringband), playing at country weddings and other festivals. Hardy himself was a skilled violinist. Although he apparently had less talent as an actor than as a musician, Hardy always retained a strong interest in drama. In his later years, he was closely associated with the Dorchester Players, a local amateur dramatic society particularly interested in folk drama. They performed a dramatic version of *The Return of the Native* in 1920. Later that year, Hardy wrote down a full version of the mummers' "Play of Saint George" for them, just as he remembered it from his childhood, and the players performed it at Hardy's house at Christmas. In 1923, Hardy wrote his own version of a legendary folk drama, "The Famous Tragedy of the Queen of Cornwall at Tintagel in Lyonesse," also put on by the Dorchester Players.

Biographical information is also useful in establishing that Hardy's great interest in folk culture was balanced by a clear recognition of its limitations as an expression of the attitudes of country people. To read Hardy's work as just a transcription of folk ceremonies, customs, and attitudes is to simplify the work drastically. In *The Athenaeum* (October 16, 1886), Hardy wrote a long obituary notice for his friend, the Reverend William Barnes, the Dorsetshire poet and philologer (1800-1886). A schoolmaster as well as a minister, Barnes was also an authority on Dorset folk customs, Roman remains in the county, and the Druidical origins of Stonehenge. Hardy details these interests and achievements, but he also, with very gentle irony, adds an account of the obsolete beliefs with which Barnes's "mind was naturally imbued." For example, Barnes lived near and apparently believed in a "white wizard," a man who supplied people who were ill with a toad-bag, a limb of a living toad sewn in a bit of linen and worn around the sufferer's neck. The twitching of the limb would give the wearer's blood a "turn," altering its composition and curing the ailment. Most of Hardy's essay, however, praises Barnes's learning and his poetry. Barnes frequently read his poetry at local town halls and was widely appreciated, especially for his humorous dialect poems. His "Poems in

Dorset Dialect" are, as Hardy points out, accurate transcriptions of the patterns of local speech, fond, unpretentious depictions of provincial life, and as "unaffected and realistic as a Dutch picture." Yet, for all this praise, Hardy felt that Barnes's poetry was limited. In ignoring what Hardy regarded as the basic injustice of human circumstance, Barnes made the Dorset folk too happy, too shallow, and too unaware of their own experience.

Hardy always realized that the local rustic was also generally an agricultural laborer, a social and economic fact not always expressed in the attitudes and beliefs of folk culture. Hardy wrote an essay published in *Longman's Magazine in* July, 1883, called "The Dorsetshire Labourer." He described at length the living conditions of the agricultural workers, the rural hiring fairs, the houses, and the careful economy. Charting the changes during the nineteenth century, Hardy welcomed the rise in real wages in the face of the general agricultural depression in the 1880's, but he lamented that tenancy and steady employment were less secure than they had been earlier. He also wondered about the effect of importing London clothes and customs, and about Dorset's loss of its uniquely local character as its people became less secluded. Yet, Hardy, for all his veneration of the old Dorsetshire simplicity, was not one to sentimentalize:

> But the artistic merit of their old condition is scarcely a reason why they should have continued in it when other communities were marching on so vigorously toward uniformity and mental equality. It is only the old story that progress and picturesqueness do not harmonise. They are losing their individuality, but they are widening the range of their ideas, and gaining in freedom. It is too much to expect them to remain stagnant and old-fashioned for the pleasure of romantic spectators.

An understanding of Hardy's concern with the changing economic aspect of Dorset life and the connection between Dorset and the rest of nineteenth-century England is just as important for understanding *The Return of the Native*, for Eustacia, for Clym, for Mrs. Yeobright, even for the transformed Diggory in the final episode, as is a knowledge of witchcraft and the mummers' play. Hardy knew and respected the real Dorset too well ever to succumb, in his novels, his poems, or in his essays, to a condescending quaintness. He was interested in the folk customs, the superstitions, the beliefs, the primitive simplicity, but he also always saw beyond the provinciality. Fascinated by what was curious and local, Hardy always worked through the curio to a fuller and more general sense of humanity.

James Gindin

Criticism

Hardy's Contemporary Critics

From *The Athenaeum*

November 23, 1878

Where are we to turn for a novelist? * * * Mr. Hardy, who at one time seemed as promising as any of the younger generation of story-tellers, has published a book distinctly inferior to anything of his which we have yet read. It is not that the story is ill-conceived—on the contrary, there are the elements of a good novel in it; but there is just that fault which would appear in the pictures of a person who has a keen eye for the picturesque without having learnt to draw. One sees what he means, and is all the more disappointed at the clumsy way in which the meaning is expressed. People talk as no people ever talked before, or perhaps we should rather say as no people ever talk now. The language of his peasants may be Elizabethan, but it can hardly be Victorian. Such phrases as "being a man of the mournfullest make, I was scared a little," or "he always had his great indignation ready against anything underhand," are surprising in the mouth of the modern rustic. Indeed, the talk seems pitched throughout in too high a key to suit the talkers. A curious feature in the book is the low social position of the characters. The upper rank is represented by a young man who is assistant to a Paris jeweller, an innkeeper who has served his apprenticeship to a civil engineer, the daughter of a bandsman, and two or three of the small farmer class. These people all speak in a manner suggestive of high cultivation, and some of them intrigue almost like dwellers in Mayfair, while they live on nearly equal terms with the furze-cutting rustics who form a chorus reminding one of "On ne badine pas avec l'amour." All this is mingled with a great deal of description, showing a keen observation of natural things, though disfigured at times by forced allusions and images. The sound of reeds in a wind is likened to "sounds as of a congregation praying humbly." A girl's recollections "stand like gilded uncials upon the dark tablet of her present surroundings." The general plot of the story turns on the old theme of a man who is in love with two women, and a woman who is in love with two men; the man and the woman being both selfish and sensual. We use the last word in its more extended sense; for there is nothing in the book to provoke a comparison with the vagaries of some recent novelists, mostly of the gentler sex. But one cannot help seeing that the two persons in question know no other law than the gratification of their own passion, although this is not carried to a point which would place the book on the "Index" of respectable households. At the same time it is clear that Eustacia Vye belongs essentially to the class of which Madame Bovary is the type; and it is impossible not to regret, since this is a type which English opinion will not allow a novelist to depict in its completeness, that Mr. Hardy should have wasted his powers in giving what after all is an imperfect and to some extent misleading view of it.

Dialect in Novels[1]

A somewhat vexed question is reopened in your criticism of my story, 'The Return of the Native'; namely, the representation in writing of the speech of the peasantry when that writing is intended to show mainly the character of the speakers, and only to give a general idea of their linguistic peculiarities.

An author may be said to fairly convey the spirit of intelligent peasant talk if he retains the idiom, compass, and characteristic expressions, although he may not encumber the page with obsolete pronunciations of the purely English words, and with mispronunciations of those derived from Latin and Greek. In the printing of standard speech hardly any phonetic principle at all is observed; and if a writer attempts to exhibit on paper the precise accents of a rustic speaker he disturbs the proper balance of a true representation by unduly insisting upon the grotesque element; thus directing attention to a point of inferior interest, and diverting it from the speaker's meaning, which is by far the chief concern where the aim is to depict the men and their natures rather than their dialect forms. THOMAS HARDY

From *The Saturday Review*

January 4, 1879

The question is perpetually suggesting itself nowadays whether it is better for a novel-writer to be clever or entertaining. Personally we have no doubt on the matter, but then the feelings of even a professional critic are apt to get the better of his principles. Possibly, in the interests of the highest art, we ought to hold up to the discriminating admiration of our readers the talent which we are compelled to recognize, although it has impressed more than

1. Hardy answered a point made in the *Athenaeum* review. His reply was printed in *The Athenaeum*, November 30, 1878.

delighted us. But we fear that if we took that sublime view of our vocation we should fail to carry our readers along with us; and, on the whole, it may be more advisable to be absolutely frank and speak out all we have upon our minds. We may appreciate the depth and brilliancy of George Eliot's later writings; but somehow we cannot fall into the same kindly and familiar companionship with *Middlemarch* and *Daniel Deronda* as with *Adam Bede* or *the Mill on the Floss*; and there is a rising school of novelists, of which Mr. Hardy is one of the ablest members, who seem to construct their fictions for themselves rather than for other people. It would be scarcely fair to say that they are dull; and they give us the fullest persuasion of a latent power which would enable them, as our ideas go, to write infinitely more agreeably if it pleased them. In one respect they resemble those fashionable and self-opinionated artists who embody their personal conceptions of art in forms that scandalize traditional opinions. In another respect, as we are glad to think, they differ from them very widely. For, whatever may be our estimate of their manner in the main, there is no denying the care they bestow upon their workmanship, and this is a thing to be grateful for in these days of slovenly writing. After all, however, we are brought round again to the point we started from. We maintain that the primary object of a story is to amuse, and in the attempt to amuse us Mr. Hardy, in our opinion, breaks down. In his case it has not been always so; but he would seem to be steadily subordinating interest to the rules by which he regulates his art. His *Under the Greenwood Tree* and *Pair of Blue Eyes*, partly perhaps because of rather unpromising names, were books that received less attention than they deserved. But his *Far from the Madding Crowd* was launched under favourable circumstances in a leading magazine, and—with reason—it won him a host of admirers. There may have been too much of the recurrence of marked mannerisms in it; with a good deal of what was hardly to be distinguished from affectation. But its characters were made living and breathing realities; there was a powerful love tale ingeniously worked out; the author showed a most intimate knowledge of the rural scenes he sympathetically described; and, above all, as is almost invariably his habit, he was quaintly humorous in the talk which he put into the mouths of his rustics. In this *Return of the Native* he has been less happy. The faults of *Far from the Madding Crowd* are exaggerated, and in the rugged and studied simplicity of its subject the story strikes us as intensely artificial. We are in England all the time, but in a world of which we seem to be absolutely ignorant; even a vague uncertainty hangs over the chronology. Every one of the people we meet is worked in as more or less of "a character"; and such a coincidence of "originals," under conditions more or less fantastic, must inevitably be repugnant to our sense of the probable. Originality may very easily be overdone, especially when it is often more apparent than genuine. We need not say that Mr. Hardy's descriptions are always vivid and often most picturesque. But he weakens rather than increases their force by going out of his way for eccentric forms of expression which are far less suggestive of his meanings than the everyday words he carefully avoids. His similes and metaphors are often strained and far-fetched; and his style gives one the idea of a literary gymnast who is always striving after sensation in the form of some *tour de force.* In his very names he is unreal and unlifelike; so much so that we doubt whether nine in ten of them are to be met with in the pages of the London Directory. It is true that they may possibly be local for all we know to the contrary; and, if so, we may praise them as being in happy harmony with the theatrically local colouring of his fiction.

At the same time, having decided to write a story which should be out of the common, Mr. Hardy has shown both discretion and self-knowledge in the choice of its scene. It gives him ample opportunity for the display of his peculiar gifts and for the gratification of his very pronounced inclinations. Egdon Heath is one of the wildest spots in all England, and is situated among some of the most sequestered of parishes. The people seem to know nothing of high-roads or stage-coaches; there is nothing of a market-town in the immediate vicinity where the men might brush up their bucolical brains by weekly gossip on a market day; there is not a good-sized village, and hardly even a hamlet. The inhabitants live chiefly in lonely dwellings, where the snow heaps itself round the doors in the dreary winter-time, and where they lie listening in their tempestuous weather to the melancholy howling of the winds. The very public-house stands by itself, and bears the quaint sign of "The Quiet Woman," who is a lady carrying her head under her arm. So that naturally we have the unadorned simplicity of nature in every shape. There must have been landed proprietors, we presume, and yet we hear nothing of a squire; while there is only incidental notice of a parson when some of the natives are joined together in matrimony. The people above the class of labourers or paupers are still in very humble stations, and for the most part extremely eccentric in their habits. There is a veteran captain of the merchant service who has come to moorings in his old age in a solitary cottage in the middle of those desolate wastes, which give every convenient facility for assignations to his beautiful granddaughter, who is one of a pair of heroines. There is a Mrs. Yeobright, who is tolerably well-to-do and the mother of "the Native" whose return is chronicled; and there is the innkeeper, Mr. Wildeve, who is comparatively rich, and who figures relatively as a man of the world and a gay and fascinating Lothario. It is of these somewhat unpromising materials that Mr. Hardy has undertaken to weave his romance, and he has so far overcome the initial difficulties by making his hero, "the Native," with his leading heroine, superior by their natures to their situation and surroundings. * * * We are given to understand that, had their circumstances been different, or if fortune and ambition had served them better, they might have played a very different part in the grand drama of the world:—

> Eustacia Vye was the raw material of a divinity. On Olympus she would have done well with a little preparation. She had the passions and instincts which make a model goddess—that is, those which make not quite a model woman. Had it been possible for the earth and mankind to be entirely in her grasp for a while, had she handled the distaff, the spindle, and the shears at her own free will, few in the world would have noticed the change of government.

Again, "in Clym Yeobright's face could be dimly seen the typical countenance of the future. Should there be a divine period to art hereafter, its Phidias may produce such faces." Those natures of *élite* tend towards each other instinctively. And when the lovers have one of their meetings, after three short months of acquaintance, "they remained long without a single utterance, for no language could reach the level of their condition. Words were as the rusty implements of a barbarous bygone epoch, and only to be occasionally tolerated." The harmony of ill-tutored minds so highly pitched could hardly fail in a sensational novel to end in discord and tragedy. Clym prevails on Eustacia to marry him; he loses money and health, and sees his dreams of good fortune gradually dissipated, while the brooding shadows of despondency fall thickly on his domestic horizon. For Eustacia is equally disenchanted of her expectations. She had given admiring devotion to her husband, contrasting him with the boors about him; she had recognized the superiority of his manners, acquirements, and intellect; but she had looked, above all, to being introduced by him to some of the wonders of the world, and to the dazzling delights of Parisian society. For before Clym Yeobright is presented to us "the Native" returning to his native wilds he had been serving an apprenticeship as a shopman in Paris. But when Eustacia sees herself shut up with him in a lonely cottage on that Egdon Heath of which she has grown so heartily sick; when she sees him labouring to keep their bodies and souls together by cutting furze and sods like a common day labourer; when she sees him covering up his expressive eyes with spectacles; and, in short, when she is settling down to the monotony of penury, feeling at the same time that she might have done far better for herself, then she decides to take leave of the world. With "her soul in an abyss of desolation seldom plumbed by one so young," she quits her home to strike across the moors, "occasionally stumbling over twisted furze-roots, tufts of rushes, or oozing lumps of fleshy fungi, which at this season lay scattered about the heath like the rotting liver and lungs of some colossal animal," and seeks a refuge from her troubles in a deed of desperation. She and her husband, and her admirer, Damon Wildeve, all have a meeting at last in the gloomy waters; and the crowning horror of a succession of sombre descriptions is in the search for the senseless bodies in Shadwater Weir. Unfortunately, our sympathies have never been strongly enlisted in any of the three. Even the style of Eustacia's beauty is so vaguely and transcendentally described that it neither wins our heart nor takes our fancy. For the rest she is a wayward and impulsive woman, essentially commonplace in her feelings and wishes, who compromises herself by vulgar indiscretions. Thus she bribes a country lad to help her to carry out a whim of hers by permitting him to hold her hand for fifteen minutes, although she knows that he exacts those terms because he has fallen hopelessly in love with her. Damon Wildeve, the innkeeper, although in a measure idealized in a doubtful atmosphere of romance, is in reality an underbred country clodhopper who plumes himself on his substance and gentility, and an education superior to that of his neighbours; while Clym Yeobright is a moon-struck dreamer, who seems singularly out of place among the eminently practical population of Egdon.

Still we would not be misunderstood, nor would we wish to do Mr. Hardy injustice. We think he has been injudicious in his invention of characters, and that he has deliberately prepared disappointment for us in his method of treatment, if he aimed at making his story in any degree realistic. But, as usual, there are dialogues of true and quaint humour, which have never been rivalled by any writer of the present day, and which remind one of Dogberry and Verges; and there are many *tableaux* of wild and powerful picturesqueness. Take, for example, the opening scene, where the whole of the barren country on a dreary November night is kindling to the blaze of the roaring bonfires; when we are introduced to the old-fashioned parishioners of Egdon, crowding round the pyramid of furze, thirty feet in circumference, that crowns the summit of the tumulus of Blackbarrow; and there, in his description of the excited little mob, we have some of Mr. Hardy's most distinctive touches:—

> All was unstable: quivering as leaves, evanescent as lightning. Shadowy eye-sockets, deep as those of a death's head, suddenly turned into pits of lustre; a lantern jaw was cavernous, then it was shining; wrinkles were emphasized to ravines, or obliterated entirely by a changed ray. Nostrils were dark wells; sinews in old necks were gilt mouldings; things with no par-

ticular polish in them were glazed; bright objects—such as the tip of a furze-hook one of the men carried—were as glass; eye-balls glowed like little lanterns. Those whom Nature had depicted as merely quaint became grotesque, the grotesque became preternatural—for all was in extremity.

Or, again, when the fair and stately Eustacia Vye steals through the darkness of the night into the glowing reflection of the balefire to keep an appointment with Wildeve, who was then paying his court to her; or when Wildeve, in his wretchedness and reckless-ness, later in the story, sits down to gamble by lantern-light on the lonely moors with an enemy and rival, who has thrown himself into the game with all the rancour of inveterate hatred. They are scared by spectral shadows falling across the stone table and the dice, which turn out to come from a gang of moorland ponies. When the lantern is extinguished by a great death's-head moth, they replace it with the handful of glowworms that they gather, and the wild game goes on, in its alternations of triumph and despair, till Wildeve loses his last sovereign. This scene has striking vividness and power. There can be no doubt that Mr. Hardy has no ordinary talent; and we regret the more that he should not condescend to human frivolity, and exert his unquestionable powers in trying to be more natural and entertaining. We dare say the effort would soon come easily to him, and then our gratitude might give him less stinted praise.

From *Blackwood's Edinburgh Magazine*

March, 1879

Mr. Hardy is an original thinker and writer, although less original than he appears at first sight. His 'Pair of Blue Eyes,' and 'Under the Greenwood Tree,' prepared the way for his decided success in his 'Far from the Madding Crowd.' But he hardly improves with acquaintance as we should have hoped, and his excessive mannerisms become irksome. In the best things that give their flavour to his succesive books, you recognise some familiar idea that you can trace back to himself. The 'Return of the Native,' which he published the other day, might have been a clever parody of the other novels we have named. In the idea and the development of the plot, as in the style of the writing—from the first page to the last, there is a labouring after originality which has rather the air of affectation. He never serves himself with a plain phrase, if he can find anything more far-fetched; and even those humorous peasants who used sometimes to remind us of Shake-speare's gravediggers and Dogberrys begin to talk like books—that is to say, like Mr. Hardy's books. We can hardly doubt that it would be well for his fame were he to strike out more boldly in fresh directions; but at all events he deserves credit for taking a line of his own, and bestowing all reasonable pains on his execution.

From *Harper's New Monthly Magazine* (New York)

March, 1879

Mr. Hardy's *Return of the Native* is a descriptive and emotional novel of more than average artistic merit, which is chiefly displayed by a succession of powerful scenes and skillful or striking contrasts. His descriptions of the scene of the story, Egdon Heath, as night and mist are settling upon its barren ruggedness, and the surrounding gloom is made to seem blacker and more impenetrable by the huge fires of furze which its denizens have lighted on its central barrow, have many of the features of Rembrandt's paintings of fire-light, camp-light, and torch-light scenes, and, like them, the deep shadows of these artificial lights operate to invest a grim and commonplace reality with a romance that is fruitful of shuddering fancies and creeping half-fears. In this production, as in his *Far from the Madding Crowd*, Mr. Hardy introduces a large body of actors belonging to the class of English peasantry, and their manners, customs, humors, amusements, superstitions, and dialect colloquies are reproduced with picturesque effect. Nearly all the characters belong to these primitive people, one of the exceptions being the admirably painted heroine Eustacia Vye, an exotic from a more advanced state of society, who has been planted on this unattractive wild and among its simple folk by circumstances which she could not control, and against which she unceasingly rebels, and whose nature is a singular compound of contradictions—of fierceness and gentleness, resolution and vacillation, love and inconstancy, coldness and passion, strength and weakness. The other exception is one of her lovers, Wildeve, another waif from the outside world, who is a bundle of petty attractions and foibles, sufficient, however, to find grace in her eyes. The subordinate figures, especially those of Mrs. Yeobright, Diggory Venn, and "Charley," are scarcely less engaging than the central ones. The story is powerfully scenic rather than regularly and continuously dramatic. While many of its scenes might be represented upon the stage singly with great effectiveness, they are not knit closely enough together by the tie of a controlling interest, they contribute too slightly to the progress of the plot, and the influence which they exert upon the catastrophe is too remote or inconsiderable to render the story, as a whole, capable of successful dramatization or representation. Nevertheless, it is delightful reading.

Critical Essays

During his career as a novelist Hardy received little genuine criticism or analysis, for reviews were apt to be only quick judgments. Two exceptions were an essay by Havelock Ellis (printed in *The Westminster Review*, June 1, 1883) and an erudite book, *The Art of Thomas Hardy* (1895), by Lionel Johnson. Although acknowledging that his own Roman Catholicism made him disagree strongly with Hardy's view of experience, Johnson appreciated the power of the novelist's art and attempted to define his ideas. After Hardy stopped writing novels, appreciative studies of his fiction began to appear; the most distinguished of these were by Lascelles Abercrombie (1912), H. C. Duffin (1916), and Virginia Woolf (1928). Mrs. Woolf's, in particular, demonstrated the extraordinary power and excitement in Hardy's fiction.

Much of this early criticism concentrated on Hardy's skill in depicting character. D. H. Lawrence's essay, published posthumously in 1936, was one of the first to examine Hardy's characters psychologically. If, as always in Lawrence's criticism, some of the analyses seem to explain Lawrence's characters more fully than Hardy's, the essay is still provocative and perceptive. This approach to Hardy is still used, for a contemporary critic, Charles C. Walcutt, devotes most of his essay (1966) to discussing the psychological nature of the characters and their relationships in *The Return of the Native*.

Critics also explored Hardy's intensely dramatic quality. In 1922, Joseph Warren Beach carefully examined the structure of *The Return of the Native*, illustrating how Hardy shaped dramatic conflict. More recently, R. W. Stallman, in an essay published in 1947, minutely schematized the reversals of plot in the novel. But this critical interest in the dramatic structure of the novel, valid and important as it was, could descend to pettiness, as it did in a controversy carried on in several journals in 1938 and 1939, as to whether Hardy's chronology of the year in *The Return of the Native* was accurate in every particular.

Early critics of Hardy's work were often interested in the philosophical basis for his ideas. To label him a "pessimist," a "determinist," or a "meliorist" often seemed more important than to examine his fiction comprehensively. As if to justify the critics' search for accurate classification, some of Hardy's own statements and observations in his autobiography indicate he was anxious to set his intellectual position straight. In 1911, Helen Garwood published a book[1] arguing that Hardy's ideas were drawn from Schopenhauer's philosophy. Other writers connected Hardy with the works of Nietzsche and Spengler. One of the most accurate

1. *Thomas Hardy: An Illustration of the Philosophy of Schopenhauer*.

and sensible treatments of Hardy's ideas on man and nature was Ernest Brennecke Jr.'s *Thomas Hardy's Universe* (1924). Although most contemporary critics do not regard Hardy as a consistent philosopher and deplore the inaccurate rigidity of the attempt to define the novelist by his reading alone, Hardy did speculate on philosophy and cosmology, and his ideas are worth discussing. One fairly recent book on the subject is Harvey Curtis Webster's,[2] published in 1947. Webster's book is helpful and relevant, although written from a perspective somewhat too literal-minded to account for the range of Hardy's intellectual apprehension of his world.

When in the 1930's, critics saw that Hardy the novelist was not a profound or consistent philosopher, derogatory articles began to appear. For the followers of F. R. Leavis, who praised George Eliot's fiction and revived interest in it, Hardy's reputation suffered because patterns of moral statement could not be traced in his work. One of the least dogmatic of these critics reevaluating Hardy was Frank Chapman. Chapman, like some other critics, emphasized Hardy's faults—his lack of consistent ideology, his clumsiness, his reliance on coincidence—yet in a 1934 essay[3] he grudgingly acknowledged that the power of Hardy's fiction transcended these faults. If Chapman and critics like him did not account for Hardy's greatness, they at least asked important questions about the relationship between character and theme, questions still echoed by more recent critics like George Wing (1963). More strident was the objection to Hardy evident in T. S. Eliot's *After Strange Gods* (1934). Eliot criticized Hardy's fiction as an example of the "diabolic," the evil passions that lead man away from the truth of orthodoxy. In this work, which is far from typical of his literary criticism, Eliot sounds something like the reviewers of fifty years earlier who had called Hardy immoral and arrogantly labeled his characters inferior creatures.

During the decade or so after Hardy's death, scholarship about Hardy and his work grew rapidly. The two volumes of the autobiography were published in 1928 and 1930. W. R. Rutland published *Thomas Hardy: A Study of his Writings and Their Background* in 1938, a book that adds information about Hardy's life and reading. Carl J. Weber, a scholar who devoted his career to Hardy, published his major work, *Hardy of Wessex,* in 1940, and followed this with biographical studies and an edition of Hardy's letters. Scholarly work on Hardy has continued. Additional biographies have been written; the best recent ones are those by Edmund Blunden (1952) and Evelyn Hardy (1954). The definitive bibliography has been written by Richard L. Purdy (1954).[4]

A 1940 issue of *The Southern Review,* marking the centenary of Hardy's birth, created a change in Hardy criticism. The issue was devoted to essays on Hardy by distinguished poets, novelists, and critics. Excerpts from three of the essays are reprinted here: one by Allen Tate relating Hardy's folk background to his poetry and fiction, one by Katherine Anne Porter answering T. S. Eliot's objections, and one by Donald Davidson tracing the

2. *On A Darkling Plain: The Art and Thought of Thomas Hardy.*
3. "Hardy the Novelist," *Scrutiny,* June, 1934.
4. *Thomas Hardy: A Bibliographical Study.*

background of Hardy's fiction to traditional folk attitudes and concerns. Although Ruth Firor had published her excellent book, *Folkways in Thomas Hardy*, nine years earlier, the Hardy centennial issue of *The Southern Review* finally directed critical attention away from Hardy's philosophy and toward the influence of Hardy's Dorset background. A few years later, Lord David Cecil, the English critic, expanded the range of literary background relevant to Hardy's work by demonstrating how much Hardy's fiction owed to traditional elements in Elizabethan drama and eighteenth-century fiction.

The traditional element in Hardy's fiction, as Donald Davidson warns, can be overstated. Not all the critical problems in Hardy's work can be solved by attributing them to folk or literary traditions, because Hardy did not simply reflect the attitudes and perspectives of his background but consciously used and shaped it. A fully adequate and comprehensive critical work on Hardy's fiction has yet to be written. Hardy's ideas cannot be placed in a consistent theological or metaphysical system, but they can be described more fully and coherently than any critic has yet done. Hardy's characters, the ways in which he moves them and plays them against one another, can be examined more thoroughly from a psychological point of view. Hardy's social ideas and their relevance to his fiction have hardly been discussed at all, perhaps only by Arnold Kettle in *An Introduction to the English Novel* (1951), and he does not deal with *The Return of the Native*. Even Hardy's style—conventionally called uneven or clumsy, but powerful—needs further analysis. John Holloway has done some excellent work on Hardy's use of metaphorical language and has defended the apparent reliance on coincidence in Hardy's fiction. But Holloway has devoted only one chapter to Hardy in each of his books, *The Victorian Sage* (1953) and *The Charted Mirror* (1960). Perhaps the most thorough contemporary treatment of Hardy's fiction is Albert J. Guerard's *Thomas Hardy: The Novels and Stories* (1949). Guerard's work is knowledgeable and sophisticated, but so much time is spent acknowledging Hardy's flaws and crudities as well as in pointing out that Hardy's vision of the world was different from that of most twentieth-century novelists that the center of Hardy's fiction often seems neglected. A full-scale work, dealing carefully with the texts of the novels and the abundant scholarship, yet sensitive to verbal and artistic structures and to social and psychological ideas, would be a valuable addition to the criticism of Hardy's fiction. As Philip Larkin pointed out in a recent essay,[5] the best contemporary critics have neglected Hardy and many who have written on Hardy's fiction have lacked the sensibility that would provide truly illuminating criticism. This leaves room for the student and the young critic.

The following selections represent most of the principal critical positions on Hardy's fiction that are still generally regarded as relevant and are frequently discussed. I have arranged them in chronological order.

5. "Wanted: Good Hardy Critic," *Critical Quarterly*, Summer, 1966.

D. H. LAWRENCE

[The Psychology of the Characters]†

This is the tragedy of Hardy, always the same: the tragedy of those who, more or less pioneers, have died in the wilderness, whither they had escaped for free action, after having left the walled security, and the comparative imprisonment, of the established convention. This is the theme of novel after novel: remain quite within the convention, and you are good, safe, and happy in the long run, though you never have the vivid pang of sympathy on your side: or, on the other hand, be passionate, individual, wilful, you will find the security of the convention a walled prison, you will escape, and you will die, either of your own lack of strength to bear the isolation and the exposure, or by direct revenge from the community, or from both. This is the tragedy, and only this: it is nothing more metaphysical than the division of a man against himself in such a way: first, that he is a member of the community, and must, upon his honour, in no way move to disintegrate the community, either in its moral or its practical form; second, that the convention of the community is a prison to his natural, individual desire, a desire that compels him, whether he feel justified or not, to break the bounds of the community, lands him outside the pale, there to stand alone, and say: "I was right, my desire was real and inevitable; if I was to be myself I must fulfil it, convention or no convention," or else, there to stand alone, doubting, and saying: "Was I right, was I wrong? If I was wrong, oh, let me die!"—in which case he courts death.

The growth and the development of this tragedy, the deeper and deeper realisation of this division and this problem, the coming towards some conclusion, is the one theme of the Wessex novels.

* * *

The Return of the Native

This is the first tragic and important novel. Eustacia, dark, wild, passionate, quite conscious of her desires and inheriting no tradition which would make her ashamed of them, since she is of a novelistic Italian birth, loves, first, the unstable Wildeve, who does not satisfy her, then casts him aside for the newly returned Clym, whom she marries. What does she want? She does not know, but it is evi-

† From the article entitled "Study of Thomas Hardy" in *Selected Literary Criticism* (edited by Anthony Beal), pp. 166-228. Copyright 1936 by Frieda Lawrence, © 1964 by the Estate of the late Frieda Lawrence Ravagli. All rights reserved. Reprinted by the permission of The Viking Press, Inc.

dently some form of self-realisation; she wants to be herself, to attain herself. But she does not know how, by what means, so romantic imagination says: Paris and the *beau monde.* As if that would have stayed her unsatisfaction.

Clym has found out the vanity of Paris and the *beau monde.* What, then, does he want? He does not know; his imagination tells him he wants to serve the moral system of the community, since the material system is despicable. He wants to teach little Egdon boys in school. There is as much vanity in this, easily, as in Eustacia's Paris. For what is the moral system but the ratified form of the material system? What is Clym's altruism but a deep, very subtle cowardice, that makes him shirk his own being whilst apparently acting nobly; which makes him choose to improve mankind rather than to struggle at the quick of himself into being. He is not able to undertake his own soul, so he will take a commission for society to enlighten the souls of others. It is subtle equivocation. Thus both Eustacia and he sidetrack from themselves, and each leaves the other unconvinced, unsatisfied, unrealised. Eustacia, because she moves outside the convention, must die; Clym, because he identified himself with the community, is transferred from Paris to preaching. He had never become an integral man, because when faced with the demand to produce himself, he remained under cover of the community and excused by his altruism.

His remorse over his mother is adulterated with sentiment; it is exaggerated by the push of tradition behind it. Even in this he does not ring true. He is always according to pattern, producing his feelings more or less on demand, according to the accepted standard. Practically never is he able to act or even feel in his original self; he is always according to the convention. His punishment is his final loss of all his original self: he is left preaching, out of sheer emptiness.

Thomasin and Venn have nothing in them turbulent enough to push them to the bounds of the convention. There is always room for them inside. They are genuine people, and they get the prize within the walls.

Wildeve, shifty and unhappy, attracted always from outside and never driven from within, can neither stand with nor without the established system. He cares nothing for it, because he is unstable, has no positive being. He is an eternal assumption.

The other victim, Clym's mother, is the crashing-down of one of the old, rigid pillars of the system. The pressure on her is too great. She is weakened from the inside also, for her nature is nonconventional; it cannot own the bounds.

So, in this book, all the exceptional people, those with strong feelings and unusual characters, are reduced; only those remain who are steady and genuine, if commonplace. Let a man will for himself, and he is destroyed. He must will according to the established system.

The real sense of tragedy is got from the setting. What is the great, tragic power in the book? It is Egdon Heath. And who are the real spirits of the Heath? First, Eustacia, then Clym's mother, then Wildeve. The natives have little or nothing in common with the place.

What is the real stuff of tragedy in the book? It is the Heath. It is the primitive, primal earth, where the instinctive life heaves up. There, in the deep, rude stirring of the instincts, there was the reality that worked the tragedy. Close to the body of things, there can be heard the stir that makes us and destroys us. The Heath heaved with raw instinct. Egdon, whose dark soil was strong and crude and organic as the body of a beast. Out of the body of this crude earth are born Eustacia, Wildeve, Mistress Yeobright, Clym, and all the others. They are one year's accidental crop. What matters if some are drowned or dead, and others preaching or married: what matter, any more than the withering heath, the reddening berries, the seedy furze, and the dead fern of one autumn of Egdon? The Heath persists. Its body is strong and fecund, it will bear many more crops beside this. Here is the sombre, latent power that will go on producing, no matter what happens to the product. Here is the deep, black source from whence all these little contents of lives are drawn. And the contents of the small lives are spilled and wasted. There is savage satisfaction in it: for so much more remains to come, such a black, powerful fecundity is working there that what does it matter?

Three people die and are taken back into the Heath; they mingle their strong earth again with its powerful soil, having been broken off at their stem. It is very good. Not Egdon is futile, sending forth life on the powerful heave of passion. It cannot be futile, for it is eternal. What is futile is the purpose of man.

Man has a purpose which he has divorced from the passionate purpose that issued him out of the earth into being. The Heath threw forth its shaggy heather and furze and fern, clean into being. It threw forth Eustacia and Wildeve and Mistress Yeobright and Clym, but to what purpose? Eustacia thought she wanted the hats and bonnets of Paris. Perhaps she was right. The heavy, strong soil of Egdon, breeding original native beings, is under Paris as well as under Wessex, and Eustacia sought herself in the gay city. She thought life there, in Paris, would be tropical, and all her energy and passion out of Egdon would there come into handsome flower. And if Paris real had been Paris as she imagined it, no doubt she was right, and her instinct was soundly expressed. But Paris real was not Eustacia's imagined Paris. Where was her imagined Paris, the place where her powerful nature could come to blossom? Beside some strong-passioned, unconfined man, her mate.

Which mate Clym might have been. He was born out of passionate Egdon to live as a passionate being whose strong feelings moved him ever further into being. But quite early his life became narrowed down to a small purpose: he must of necessity go into business, and submit his whole being, body and soul as well as mind, to the business and to the greater system it represented. His feelings, that should have produced the man, were suppressed and contained, he worked according to a system imposed from without. The dark struggle of Egdon, a struggle into being as the furze struggles into flower, went on in him, but could not burst the enclosure of the idea, the system which contained him. Impotent to *be*, he must transform himself, and live in an abstraction, in a generalisation, he must identify himself with the system. He must live as Man or Humanity, or as the Community, or as Society, or as Civilisation.

* * *

He came back to Egdon—what for? To reunite himself with the strong, free flow of life that rose out of Egdon as from a source? No—"to preach to the Egdon eremites that they might rise to a serene comprehensiveness without going through the process of enriching themselves." As if the Egdon eremites had not already far more serene comprehensiveness than ever he had himself, rooted as they were in the soil of all things, and living from the root! What did it matter how they enriched themselves, so long as they kept this strong, deep root in the primal soil, so long as their instincts moved out to action and to expression? The system was big enough for them, and had no power over their instincts. They should have taught him rather than he them.

And Egdon made him marry Eustacia. Here was action and life, here was a move into being on his part. But as soon as he got her, she became an idea to him, she had to fit in his system of ideas. According to his way of living, he knew her already, she was labelled and classed and fixed down. He had got into this way of living, and he could not get out of it. He had identified himself with the system, and he could not extricate himself. He did not know that Eustacia had her being beyond his. He did not know that she existed untouched by his system and his mind, where no system had sway and where no consciousness had risen to the surface. He did not know that she was Egdon, the powerful, eternal origin seething with production. He thought he knew. Egdon to him was the tract of common land, producing familiar rough herbage, and having some few unenlightened inhabitants. So he skated over heaven and hell, and having made a map of the surface, thought he knew all. But underneath and among his mapped world, the eternal powerful fecundity worked on heedless of him and his arrogance. His preaching, his superficiality made no difference. What did it matter if he had calculated a moral chart from the surface of life? Could that affect life, any more than a chart of the heavens affects the stars, affects the whole stellar universe which exists behind our knowledge? Could the sound of his words affect the working of the body of Egdon, where in the unfathomable womb was begot and conceived all that would ever come forth? Did not his own heart beat far removed and immune from his thinking and talking? Had he been able to put even his own heart's mysterious resonance upon his map, from which he charted the course of lives in his moral system? And how much more completely, then, had he left out, in utter ignorance, the dark, powerful source whence all things rise into being, whence they will always continue to rise, to struggle forward to further being? A little of the static surface he could see, and map out. Then he thought his map was the thing itself. How blind he was, how utterly blind to the tremendous movement carrying and producing the surface. He did not know that the greater part of every life is underground, like roots in the dark in contract with the beyond. He preached, thinking lives could be moved like hen-houses from here to there. His blindness indeed brought on the calamity. * * *

This is a constant revelation in Hardy's novels: that there exists a great background, vital and vivid, which matters more than the people who move upon it. Against the background of dark, passionate Egdon, of the leafy, sappy passion and sentiment of the woodlands, of the unfathomed stars, is drawn the lesser scheme of lives: *The Return of the Native*, *The Woodlanders*, or *Two on a Tower*. Upon the vast, incomprehensible pattern of some primal morality greater than ever the human mind can grasp, is drawn the little, pathetic pattern of man's moral life and struggle, pathetic, almost ridiculous. The little fold of law and order, the little walled city within which man has to defend himself from the waste enormity of nature, becomes always too small, and the pioneers venturing out with the code of the walled city upon them, die in the bonds of that code, free and yet unfree, preaching the walled city and looking to the waste.

This is the wonder of Hardy's novels, and gives them their beauty. The vast, unexplored morality of life itself, what we call the immorality of nature, surrounds us in its eternal incomprehensibility, and in its midst goes on the little human morality play, with its queer frame of morality and its mechanised movement; seriously, portentously, till some one of the protagonists chances to look out of the charmed circle, weary of the stage, to look into the wilderness raging round. Then he is lost, his little drama falls to pieces, or becomes mere repetition, but the stupendous theatre outside goes on enacting its own incomprehensible drama, untouched. There is this quality in almost all Hardy's work, and this is the magnificent irony it all contains, the challenge, the contempt. Not the deliberate ironies, little tales of widows or widowers, contain the irony of human life as we live it in our self-aggrandised gravity, but the big novels, *The Return of the Native*, and the others.

And this is the quality Hardy shares with the great writers, Shakespeare or Sophocles or Tolstoi, this setting behind the small action of his protagonists the terrific action of unfathomed nature; setting a smaller system of morality, the one grasped and formulated by the human consciousness within the vast, uncomprehended and incomprehensible morality of nature or of life itself, surpassing human consciousness. The difference is, that whereas in Shakespeare or Sophocles the greater, uncomprehended morality, or fate, is actively transgressed and gives active punishment, in Hardy and Tolstoi the lesser, human morality, the mechanical system is actively transgressed, and holds, and punishes the protagonist, whilst the greater morality is only passively, negatively transgressed, it is represented merely as being present in background, in scenery, not taking any active part, having no direct connexion with the protagonist. Œdipus, Hamlet, Macbeth set themselves up against, or find themselves set up against, the unfathomed moral forces of nature, and out of this unfathomed force comes their death. Whereas Anna Karenina, Eustacia, Tess, Sue, and Jude find themselves up against the established system of human government and morality, they cannot detach themselves, and are brought down. Their real tragedy is that they are unfaithful to the greater unwritten morality, which would have bidden Anna Karenina be patient and wait until she, by virtue of greater right, could take what she needed from society; would have bidden Vronsky detach himself from the system, become an individual, creating a new colony of morality with Anna; would have bidden Eustacia fight Clym for his own soul, and Tess take and claim her Angel, since she had the greater light; would have bidden Jude and Sue endure for very honour's sake, since one must bide by the best that one has known, and not succumb to the lesser good.

Had Œdipus, Hamlet, Macbeth been weaker, less full of real, potent life, they would have made no tragedy; they would have comprehended and contrived some arrangement of their affairs, sheltering in the human morality from the great stress and attack of the unknown morality. But being, as they are, men to the fullest capacity, when they find themselves, daggers drawn, with the very forces of life itself, they can only fight till they themselves are killed, since the morality of life, the greater morality, is eternally unalterable and invincible. It can be dodged for some time, but not opposed. On the other hand, Anna, Eustacia, Tess or Sue—what was there in their position that was necessarily tragic? Necessarily painful it was, but they were not at war with God, only with Society. Yet they were all cowed by the mere judgment of man upon them, and all the while by their own souls they were right. And the judgment of man killed them, not the judgment of their own souls or the judgment of Eternal God.

Which is the weakness of modern tragedy, where transgression against the social code is made to bring destruction, as though the social code worked our irrevocable fate. Like Clym, the map appears to us more real than the land. Shortsighted almost to blindness, we pore over the chart, map our journeys, and confirm them: and we cannot see life itself giving us the lie the whole time.

D. H. LAWRENCE

Why the Novel Matters†

Now I absolutely flatly deny that I am a soul, or a body, or a mind, or an intelligence, or a brain, or a nervous system, or a bunch of glands, or any of the rest of these bits of me. The whole is greater than the part. And therefore, I, who am man alive, am greater than my soul, or spirit, or body, or mind, or consciousness, or anything else that is merely a part of me. I am a man, and alive. I am man alive, and as long as I can, I intend to go on being man alive.

For this reason I am a novelist. And being a novelist, I consider myself superior to the saint, the scientist, the philosopher, and the poet, who are all great masters of different bits of man alive, but never get the whole hog.

The novel is the one bright book of life. Books are not life. They are only tremulations on the ether. But the novel as a tremulation can make the whole man alive tremble. Which is more than poetry, philosophy, science, or any other book-tremulation can do.

The novel is the book of life. In this sense, the Bible is a great confused novel. You may say, it is about God. But it is really about man alive. Adam, Eve, Sarai, Abraham, Isaac, Jacob, Samuel,

† From *Selected Literary Criticism* (edited by Anthony Beal), pp. 102-08.

David, Bath-Sheba, Ruth, Esther, Solomon, Job, Isaiah, Jesus, Mark, Judas, Paul, Peter: what is it but man alive, from start to finish? Man alive, not mere bits. Even the Lord is another man alive, in a burning bush, throwing the tablets of stone at Moses's head.

I do hope you begin to get my idea, why the novel is supremely important, as a tremulation on the ether. Plato makes the perfect ideal being tremble in me. But that's only a bit of me. Perfection is only a bit, in the strange make-up of man alive. The Sermon on the Mount makes the selfless spirit of me quiver. But that, too, is only a bit of me. The Ten Commandments set the old Adam shivering in me, warning me that I am a thief and a murderer, unless I watch it. But even the old Adam is only a bit of me.

* * *

Let us learn from the novel. In the novel, the characters can do nothing but *live*. If they keep on being good, according to pattern, or bad, according to pattern, or even volatile, according to pattern, they cease to live, and the novel falls dead. A character in a novel has got to live, or it is nothing.

We, likewise, in life have got to live, or we are nothing.

What we mean by living is, of course, just as indescribable as what we mean by *being*. Men get ideas into their heads, of what they mean by Life, and they proceed to cut life out to pattern. Sometimes they go into the desert to seek God, sometimes they go into the desert to seek cash, sometimes it is wine, woman, and song, and again it is water, political reform, and votes. You never know what it will be next: from killing your neighbour with hideous bombs and gas that tears the lungs, to supporting a Foundlings' Home and preaching infinite Love, and being co-respondent in a divorce.

In all this wild welter, we need some sort of guide. It's no good inventing Thou Shalt Nots!

What then? Turn truly, honoroubly to the novel, and see wherein you are man alive, and wherein you are dead man in life. You may love a woman as man alive, and you may be making love to a woman as sheer dead man in life. You may eat your dinner as man alive, or as a mere masticating corpse. As man alive you may have a shot at your enemy. But as a ghastly simulacrum of life you may be firing bombs into men who are neither your enemies nor your friends, but just things you are dead to. Which is criminal, when the things happen to be alive.

To be alive, to be man alive, to be whole man alive: that is the point. And at its best, the novel, and the novel supremely, can help you. It can help you not to be dead man in life. So much of a man walks about dead and a carcass in the street and house, to-day: so much of women is merely dead. Like a pianoforte with half the notes mute.

But in the novel you can see, plainly, when the man goes dead, the woman goes inert. You can develop an instinct for life, if you will, instead of a theory of right and wrong, good and bad.

JOSEPH WARREN BEACH

[The Structure of *The Return of the Native*]†

In his early novels we might say that Mr. Hardy was treating a subject, but not a theme. In *Far from the Madding Crowd,* for instance, he took up the subject of Wessex country life; and his characters and plot were so chosen as to introduce the typical incidents in the business of shepherd and farmer. It is these incidents that stand out most prominently, and make the most vivid appeal to the reader's imagination. * * *

But with *The Return of the Native,* Hardy has taken up a theme which involves a clear-cut issue in the minds of the leading characters, and especially in the mind of Eustacia, which is the main stage of the drama. It is her stifled longing for spiritual expansion which leads her to play with the love of Wildeve, which causes her later to throw him over for the greater promise of Clym, which leads her back again to Wildeve, and at last—with the loss of all hope—to suicide. In every case it requires but the smallest outlay of incident to provoke the most lively play of feeling; and the play of feeling—the opposition of desires—is embodied here, in true dramatic fashion, in talk rather than in acts. It takes nothing more than the return of Thomasin from town unwed to set going the whole series of dialogues which make up the substance of the first book, dialogues in which Wildeve and Mrs. Yeobright, Venn and Eustacia, Eustacia and Wildeve do nothing more than fence with one another, each maneuvering for position in a breathless game of well-matched antagonists. These are scenes in the true dramatic sense, not in the popular sense that calls for violence and surprising action.

In the third book the main thing that happens is a quarrel between Clym and his mother over Eustacia. The wedding itself is not presented, having no dramatic value. The dramatic value of the book is indicated in its caption, "The Fascination," the drama

† From Joseph Warren Beach, *The Technique of Thomas Hardy* (New York, 1922), pp. 90-97, 101-05, 228-29. Reprinted by permission of the publishers, Russell & Russell.

lying in the resistless attraction to one another of two persons so far apart in mind.

In the fourth book we have the major incident of Mrs. Yeobright's death on the day when she was turned away from Eustacia's door. But there is none of the bustle of action about this narrative; and, especially at the end, it is the *feeling,* the pathos, the spiritual significance, of the events that is rendered. There is one scene of special impressiveness. It consists in the talk between Mrs. Yeobright, as she plods wearily homeward across the heath on a stifling August day, and little Johnny Nunsuch trotting beside her and plying her with the cruel naïve questions of a child. This is all done, in the weird, intense manner of symbolistic drama—something of Ibsen or Maeterlinck—in which the characters are children and old women, gifted with preternatural vision. Objective facts are but as objects seen in some magic crystal, whereof the meaning is mystic, and deeper than material reality. * * *

Never before in Hardy had the machinery of action been so masked and subordinated. Never again perhaps was it to occupy a place of so little prominence in his work. It is only once or twice in Meredith, and more generally in the later novels of James, that we find so great a volume of emotional energy released by events of so little objective importance. Only in them is found a greater economy of incident; and many more readers will testify to the dramatic intensity of *The Native* than to that of *The Egoist* or *The Golden Bowl.*

The whole course of the story was conceived by the author in terms suggestive of physics and dynamics. Each step in the plot represents the balance and reaction of forces expressible almost in algebraic formulas. Many readers have been impressed with the strong scientific coloring of Hardy's mind: with his tendency to view both external nature and the human heart with the sharpness and hard precision of a naturalist, and to record the phenomena observed with some of the abstractness of the summarizing philosopher.

Nowhere was this latter tendency exhibited in more striking fashion than in the brief arguments or abstracts prefixed to the several books in the original magazine version of *The Native.* The first book, we read, "depicts the scenes which result from *an antagonism between the hopes of four persons.* . . . By reason of this strife of wishes, a happy consummation to all concerned is impossible, as matters stand; but *an easing of the situation* is begun by *the inevitable decadence of a too capricious love,* and rumors of a new arrival." In the second book, the stranger's arrival, "by *giving a new bias to emotions* in one quarter, *precipitates affairs* in another with unexpected rapidity." In the next book, Clym's passion for Eustacia "hampers his plans, and *causes a sharp divergence of opinion, committing him to an irretrievable step.*" In the fourth book we read how "the old affection between mother and son reasserts itself"; how "a critical juncture ensues, truly the *turning point* in the lives of all concerned—*Eustacia has the move*, and she makes it; but not till the sun has set does she suspect the *consequences involved in her choice of courses.*" In the argument of the fifth book are briefly listed "*the natural effects* of the foregoing misadventures."

In these abstract statements of the action is suggested how the situation is made up of a succession of tensions, gradually tightening and relaxing, and how steady and continuous is the pull, throughout each book taken by itself, and through the history as a whole. The story as a whole is a continuous record of Eustacia's vain attempt to escape the limitations of Egdon through the means of love; and this is the key to all her tug-of-war with Wildeve and with Clym. In the first book the particular pull is between Eustacia on the one hand and Thomasin and her friends on the other, with Wildeve for the bone of contention. It becomes more and more intense to the point of Eustacia's triumph, and then lets up with her growing sense of Wildeve's mediocrity. The second book shows us Eustacia drawn to Clym, and Wildeve consequently repelled in the direction of Thomasin. The third book is wholly taken up with the fascination of Clym and the resulting disagreement and break with his mother. The fourth book records the growth of misunderstanding between man and wife on the one side, between son and mother on the other, with the resultant tragedy. The fifth book carries the strain between Clym and Eustacia to the breaking-point, and shows us Eustacia driven by Clym and drawn by Wildeve to her death. * * *

The philosophical arguments to the several parts were not retained when the story was published in book form; but in their place the author has supplied the more artistic and not less pregnant headings or titles, which so aptly describe the subject-matter of the several "books." The division of a novel into parts is always a significant indication of an author's interest in the logical massing of his material, in the larger architectonics of his work. It is very little used by novelists like Dickens; very much used by novelists like George Eliot, Victor Hugo, Henry James, and—in our own time—Mr. Walpole. It generally implies a bias for the "dramatic," in so far as it involves the grouping of the subject-matter around certain characters or great moments in the action, as that of a play is grouped in the several acts. In *The Native* this is especially notable. The first book is entitled "The Three Women," which characterizes the single situation involving on the one hand Eustacia and on the other Thomasin and Mrs. Yeobright. The second book is "The Arrival," signalizing the new dramatic alignment caused by the first appearance of the hero. "The Fascination" vividly describes the following situation between Eustacia and Clym as viewed by Mrs. Yeobright. "The Closed Door" is the terse dramatic label for the combination of events which issued in the death of Mrs. Yeobright. And "The Discovery" is the slightly less effective word for the climax between Clym and Eustacia, leading to the tragic dénouement.

These five books are like the five acts of a classic play. And in each book the scenes are largely grouped around certain points in time so as to suggest the classic continuity within the several acts. In the first book, for example, all the scenes take place on the fifth and sixth of November and closely follow upon the Guy Fawkes celebration. In the second book the scenes lead up to and center about the Christmas mumming where first the hero and heroine "stand face to face." The fourth book centers about, and half the scenes take place upon, the thirty-first of August, the day of the "closed door" and Mrs. Yeobright's death. * * *

What we are concerned with here is the unity of tone—the steadiness with which the heath makes us feel its dark and overshadowing presence, so that men and women are but slight figures in a giant landscape, the insect-fauna of its somber flora. Mr. Hardy was bold enough to begin this grave history with an entire chapter devoted to a description of the heath at twilight; and his choice of a title for the second chapter but serves to signalize the littleness and frailty of man upon the great stage of inhospitable nature: "Humanity appears upon the scene, hand in hand with trouble." It is very quietly and without word or gesture that humanity makes its appearance, like a slow-moving shadow. "Along the road walked an old man. He was white-headed as a mountain, bowed in the shoulders, and faded in general aspect. . . . Before him stretched the long, laborious road, dry, empty, and white."

The effect is obtained at this point by means too subtle for analysis. It may be that the gravely cadenced rhythm itself plays a mysterious part in rightly affecting the imagination. More often the effect can be traced largely to figures of speech of definite connotation. The sights and sounds of man's activity the author is forever comparing to those of extra-human nature, assimilating them to the concert of natural sights and sounds. In one place he has been describing the strange whispering emitted by the myriad, mummied heath bells of the past summer played upon by plaintive November winds. It was like the voice of a single person, of a spirit, speaking through each in turn. And then . . .

> . . . Suddenly, on the barrow, there mingled with all this wild rhetoric of night a sound which modulated so naturally with the rest that its beginning and ending were hardly to be distinguished. The bluffs, and the bushes, and the heather-bells had broken silence; at last, so did the woman; and her articulation was but as another phrase of the same discourse as theirs.

The movements of human beings are sometimes described as seen upon the horizon by someone watching, and in terms that suggest the motions and forms of the lower organic, or even of the inorganic, world. Diggory Venn, for example, has been eavesdropping at a meeting of Eustacia and Wildeve, and at a certain point he loses sight of them. "Their black figures sank and disappeared from against the sky. They were as two horns which the sluggish heath had put forth from its crown like a mollusc, and had now again drawn in." By various means the people of the story are made to seem, like the heath-croppers or wild ponies dimly discerned in the dusk, but as creatures of the heath. * * *

It is thus that Egdon takes its place as the dominating force of the tragedy, as well as its appropriate and impressive setting. So that the unity of place, in itself an artistic value, is but the counterpart of a unity of action rooted and bedded in a precious oneness of theme. Instead of being, as in *Far from the Madding Crowd*, brought together arbitrarily to make out the prescribed materials of a novel, plot and setting here are one, growing equally and simultaneously out of the dramatic idea expressed in the title. For the first—and almost for the last—time in the work of Hardy, the discriminating reader is delighted with the complete absence of mechanical contrivance. Contrivance there is as never before in his work, the loving contrivance of an artist bent on making everything right in an orderly composition; the long-range contrivance of an architect concerned to have every part in place in an edifice that shall stand well based and well proportioned, with meaning in every line.

* * *

The determinist may be equally impressed with the helplessness of man in the grip of strange forces, physical and psychical. But he is distinguished from the fatalist by his concern with the causes that are the links in the chain of necessity. Determinism is the scientific counterpart of fatalism, and throws more light on destiny by virtue of its diligence in the searching out of natural law. Mr. Hardy is rather a determinist than a fatalist. When he speaks most directly and unmistakably for himself, it is to insist on the universal working of the laws of cause and effect. "That she had chosen for her afternoon walk the road along which she had returned to Casterbridge three hours earlier in a carriage was curious—if anything should be called curious in a *concatenation of phenomena wherein each is known to have its accounting cause.*"

The point in which determinism and fatalism agree is the helplessness of the individual will against the will in things. Only the determinist conceives the will in things as the sum of the natural forces with which we have to cope, whereas the fatalist tends to a more religious interpretation of that will as truly and literally a *will*, an arbitrary power, a personal force like our own. Sometimes Mr. Hardy allows his characters the bitter comfort of that personal interpretation. "Henchard, like all his kind, was superstitious, and he could not help thinking that the concatenation of events this evening had produced was *the scheme of some sinister intelligence bent on punishing him. Yet they had developed naturally.*" It was so that Eustacia Vye, wishing to escape the responsibility for the shutting out of Mrs. Yeobright, imagines a spiritual power upon whom to put it. "Instead of blaming herself for the issue she laid the fault upon the shoulders of some indistinct, colossal Prince of the World, who had framed her situation and ruled her lot."

What gives rise to such notions is the ironic discrepancy between what we seek and what we secure, between what we do and what follows from it. We have control of so very few of the factors that go to determine our fortunes that we can hardly help imagining behind the scene a capricious and malignant contriver of contretemps. * * *

FRANK CHAPMAN

[Hardy's Faults as a Novelist]†

* * * Unlike other established reputations, he [Hardy] is regarded on the Continent as an English fad; that he was never awarded the Nobel Prize is significant—he would seem to have been an obvious choice in comparison with some of the prizewinners.

This lack of Continental standing should provide an excuse, if one is needed, for enquiring into the reasons for his English status, and considering how far it is justified. Judging by the writings on Hardy, the attribution of greatness is to be justified under two main heads—firstly, his philosophy of life and tragic world-outlook and secondly, his powers of characterization, exemplified chiefly in the rustics. Although some critics have found these 'period peasants, so pleasing to the metropolitan imagination'[1] blots on the

† From Frank Chapman, "Hardy the Novelist," *Scrutiny,* June, 1934; Volume III in the reissue of *Scrutiny* by Cambridge University Press, 1963, pp. 22-23, 26-29, 32-37. Reprinted by permission of the publishers.

1. T. S. Eliot, *After Strange Gods.*

seriousness of his art, nearly all have agreed on the impressiveness of the philosophy, and the grandeur of the tragedy. * * * For the most part, the prose has the clumsy aiming at impressiveness.

* * * The description of Egdon Heath, at the beginning of *The Return of the Native* is a representative example. Extracts will serve as illustration—anyone interested will find that it is all of the same material:

> The heaven being spread with this pallid screen and the earth with the darkest vegetation, their meeting-line at the horizon was clearly marked. In such contrast the heath wore the appearance of an instalment of night which had taken up its place before its astronomical hour was come; darkness had to a great extent arrived hereon, while day stood distinct in the sky.

The second sentence merely amplifies the first, needlessly, and says the same thing in two equally stilted ways. An evident desire to impress results in mere verbosity and redundance, which continues for the rest of the paragraph. In the next one we are told that the Heath is only itself at night in this language:

> The spot was, indeed, a near relation of night, and, when night showed itself, an apparent tendency to gravitate together could be perceived in its shades and the scene. The sombre stretch of rounds and hollows seemed to rise and meet the evening gloom in pure sympathy, the heath exhaling darkness as rapidly as the heavens precipitated it.

Obviously to be impressive is, for Hardy, to be 'literary'—to use the erudite word in preference to the simple one; there is no real feeling for words in these passages. Often this attempted impressiveness overflows from the style into a display of knowledge, classical, geographical and historical. There is an instance of this a few paragraphs further on, where Hardy discusses the possibility of a new ideal of beauty:

> Indeed, it is a question if the exclusive reign of this orthodox beauty is not approaching its last quarter. The new Vale of Tempe may be a gaunt waste in Thule : . . . And ultimately, to the commonest tourist, spots like Iceland may become what the vineyards and myrtle-gardens of South Europe are to him now; and Heidelberg and Baden be passed unheeded as he hastens from the Alps to the sand-dunes of Scheveningen.

These shows of erudition often occur with more disastrous effect than in the present instance—for example, the much-admired ending of *Tess*: 'The President of the Immortals, in Aeschylean phrase, had ended his sport with Tess.' This seems to me grossly theatrical. Hardy, in his endeavour to be impressive, deserts his own conception of the 'Immanent Will' to drag in literary references.

* * *

Hardy's dialogue is successful only with the ordinary villagers. His chief characters, even when of village origin, speak in precisely the same style that he uses for narration or description—this is, presumably, to give them added dignity, for we are always aware of a patronizing attitude towards the rustics. * * * For an example of the speech of educated people an extract from the quarrel of Clym and Eustacia will serve (*The Return of the Native*, Book V, Chapter 3). Clym is at the height of passion, Eustacia resigned to misery:

> "Phew—I shall not kill you" he said contemptuously, as if under a sudden change of purpose. "I did think of it, but—I shall not. That would be making a martyr of you, and sending you to where she is; and I would keep you away from her till the universe come to an end, if I could."
>
> "I almost wish you would kill me," said she, with gloomy bitterness. "It is with no strong desire, I assure you, that I play the part I have lately played on earth. You are no blessing, my husband."

And later, when Clym has almost lost control of himself, he erupts into:

> "Do you brave me? do you stand me out, mistress? Answer. Don't look at me with those eyes as if you would bewitch me again! Sooner than that I die. You refuse to answer?"

Their ordinary conversation is in a similar style.

The rustic dialogue is very different. It is, undoubtedly, highly stylized, but the stylization is intentional and carefully done, whilst the dialogue of the other characters, compounded of the same elements as the narrative style, is unintentional in its stiltedness (it is significant that Hardy was a great admirer of Scott—there is a similar comparison between the speech of such characters as Bailie Nicol Jarvie, and Scott's narrative style).[2] The rustic speech was founded on direct experience and observation and, in its nature, was more vivid than 'polite' speech.

* * * There is some actual way of life behind the rustic speech, whilst that of Clym, Eustacia and the others, represents nothing but a decadent literary tradition.

* * *

2. Bailie Nicol Jarvie is a character in *Rob Roy*, an 1818 novel by Sir Walter Scott (1771-1832) [*Editor*].

The bulk of *The Dynasts*[3] looks impressive, but only a few scenes in this ponderous work possess any kind of vitality, and those deal with the familiar people and life of Wessex. *The Dynasts*, which is the direct expression of Hardy's beliefs and outlook, does more than anything to show that his was not a truly philosophical mind, and that he was incapable of any real thinking. His concept of a blind 'Immanent Will,' controlling all human action to disastrous ends, is just as obvious at the beginning of this lengthy work, as it is at the end. Near the beginning, the Spirit of the Years reveals to the Pities, the feelers and tentacles of the Will, pushing human beings to war and disaster. This occurs several times in the course of the work, and on the last occasion, nothing has been added since the first. The hundreds of intervening pages contain nothing but a long series of battles and conferences made up of incredibly bad blank verse, and dull prose descriptions, in the form of stage-directions. The vision of the Will serves to jog the reader's attention now and then, to remind him that there is a moral to be drawn from this versified history. There is no question of the genuineness of the habit of mind expressed by the 'philosophy,' but this 'philosophy' is far from adequate to the function assigned it in the construction of an epic.

We may see the same thing in novels. As long as the habitual 'philosophic' attitude remains in the background, it gives atmosphere and unity to the book; it stands for Hardy's essential character, his constancy of bent, the sense of fate, and the level of seriousness at which he contemplates human life. But directly, he obtrudes it on our attention, it becomes tedious and unconvincing. Often, to point his moral and bring about the tragic climax, he has to resort to a long chain of improbable coincidences, Tess's confession, slipped under Angel's door, goes under the carpet, Winterborne's team meets Mrs. Charmond's carriage in a narrow lane, and forces it to turn back: these are well-known instances. But there are even more flagrant examples, as in *The Return of the Native*. Here, most of all, we get the impression that Hardy thought of his tragedy, but had difficulty in bringing it about. First, Mrs. Yeobright sends Christian Cantle—almost the village idiot—with the money to be divided between Clym and Thomasin. On the way he meets the heathmen going to a raffle, accompanies them, wins the raffle, and is so elated with his success that he gambles with Wildeve and loses all his money, and Mrs. Yeobright's, to him. But Venn is watching, and regains it all. He, however, gives it all to Thomasin by mistake, and it is not divided until after Mrs. Yeobright and Eustacia have met and quarrelled. It is then too late, for this

3. *The Dynasts* was Hardy's dramatic epic on the Napoleonic Wars, published in three parts, 1903, 1906, and 1908 [*Editor*].

quarrel leads to Eustacia being unwilling to open the door to Mrs. Yeobright when she calls. By another completely incredible coincidence, Eustacia thinks Clym has opened the door, when he is really asleep, and Mrs. Yeobright goes away (having seen Eustacia looking at her, and knowing Clym to be inside), and is killed by an adder's bite. Her words before her death lead to the violent quarrel between Clym and Eustacia, which, eventually leads to the final tragedy. In *The Mayor of Casterbridge*, we are told—'But the ingenious machinery contrived by the Gods for reducing human possibilities of amelioration to a minimum . . . stood in the way of all that.' In such instances as this, the machinery is too obviously contrived by Hardy himself.

* * *

Hardy saw the attendant ills of the institution of marriage in a way his contemporaries did not but, as *Jude* shows, he was almost as opposed to—though more understanding of—any form of sensuality, as they were. Arabella is the incarnation of sensuality and Jude's marriage with her results in poverty, suffering and the loss of his hopes, and, when he appears to have reached happiness, Father Time, the fruit of this marriage, appears, to bring about disaster. Similarly, Jude and Sue live together in an unbelievably Platonic manner—it is only when their union becomes physical, and children are born, that the catastrophe is made possible. Hardy never loses sympathy with Jude and Sue, but his opinions on physical love are obvious—'the wages of sin is death.' Both here and in *The Woodlanders*, his protest against marriage-laws becomes a protest against sensuality. The bishops' horror is all the more understandable, when we consider that Hardy was attacking the marriage-laws to promote virtue.

* * *

This Victorianism is part of Hardy's strength; it stands for the solid, static environment, and his own, the simple, taking-for-granted stolidity—like Dorchester and the country round, it forms his essential background, and the necessary code and framework in which he was to work. Thirty years later, he could not have been so sure of himself, and, I think, could not have formulated any satisfactory response to contemporary problems. * * * Just as his style in verse and prose remained unaltered throughout his literary career, so his outlook remained static. His very pessimism implies firm and solid positions—there is none of the agonizing doubt and conflict that we find in a man like Lawrence. And though he felt some sympathy and admiration for the passionate Eustacias, it is always the Thomasins and Venns who fare best, and have the most amiable qualities.

The prose of the novels must, in some way, be an expression of Hardy's sensibility, its ponderous 'literary' quality notwithstanding. But any effect it achieves must depend peculiarly on cumulative processes; indeed, the analysis of any isolated paragraph will yield only the faults we have seen. These faults, naturally, stand out clearly, when the urgency of the writing relaxes, and the attitude becomes '*voulu*.'[4] Where we shall find the prose taking on real impressiveness will be in some portion of a book where all Hardy's most vital interests and attitudes are engaged. The greater part of *The Mayor of Casterbridge* and Parts One and Two of *Jude the Obscure* are both good examples, and anyone interested should turn to these books. We become aware that this clumsy, polysyllabic style is not ordinary journalese, but stands for real character. It is easy to regard it as a suitable medium, in its 'literary' impressiveness, for the record of Jude's striving for knowledge, and attempts at self-education. It is obviously the product of a mind which was as firmly convinced about the question of style, as about everything else, and its Victorianism has just the same virtues and limitations as Hardy's Victorian attitudes. Detailed analysis is impossible, and would probably defeat its own ends. But, whatever its faults, Hardy's medium is individual, and unlike that of any of his contemporaries. His style could never lend itself to the indecent bathos of the death of Little Nell—it is as unyielding as his attitude. In the novels we feel his greatness as the greatness of the Victorian age, in its solidity and its sureness of what it really valued, yet Hardy is above the Victorian ethos, and did not share the limitations that made tragedy impossible and was responsible for the unpleasant sentimentality of Dickens and Thackeray. The life he describes is still in touch with primary production.

His is a curiously qualified greatness, and is not what it is conventionally taken to be—a vaguely metaphysical one. But the greatness is there, and both the rural environment and the 'philosophy'—which, at least, represents a serious outlook—have their essential significance.

ALLEN TATE

Hardy's Philosophic Metaphors†

* * * We have here in the case of Hardy—though for no doubt quite different reasons—the figure of the poet-sage not

4. What the situation requires, what is deliberate or intentional [*Editor*].

† From Allen Tate, "Hardy's Philosophic Metaphors," *Southern Review*, VI (Summer, 1940), 100-04. Reprinted by permission of Louisiana State University Press.

unlike that of Mr. Robert Frost, whose admirers will not permit the critics to dissociate the poetry from the wise man who wrote it. When without permission a critic like Mr. R. P. Blackmur assumes that his task is to discuss Mr. Frost's language, he suffers the ignorant obloquy of a popular spellbinder, Mr. Bernard DeVoto, who promptly calls Mr. Blackmur a fool.

Now very much this same sort of thing went on towards the end of Thomas Hardy's life, and one must suspect very strongly, from all the evidence, that he liked it, and that he liked it because, like most critically naïve minds, he accepted the personal tribute as tribute to the power of his message, which was the message of a philosopher. Hardy was a great poet, but I arrive at that conclusion after disposing of a strong prejudice against the personal qualities that have led his admirers to believe him great. I see him as a somewhat complacent and tiresome old gentleman, mellow and wise; a man who in his youth had set about conquering a career; who married a woman his inferior but above him socially, and could never forget it[1]—a fact that forbids us to forget it; who permitted his literary reputation to lead him into the tow of society hostesses who could have seen in him only his fame and from whom, as he frequently confessed, he got nothing; yet he continued until late in life to appear as the literary lion. Why did he do it? It is useless to pretend that Thomas Hardy's social sense was distinguished, or that he was not lacking in a certain knowledge of the world that would have been valuable even to the historian of a yeoman society: in so far as historical and biographical criticism will illuminate Hardy's poetry, it is important to keep his defects steadily in mind, for he never overcame them. Shakespeare's origins were humbler than Hardy's, yet they are irrelevant in the criticism of Shakespeare, because the confusion of feeling that one finds in Hardy cannot be found in Shakespeare. Hardy's background and education, like other backgrounds and other educations for poetry, will give us a clue to the defects of the work, but not to its merits, and it is with the merits that criticism must be specifically occupied. Literature can be written from any background and Hardy wrote literature.

Mr. Weber[2] quotes from Hardy's famous description of Clym Yeobright the following passage, and applies it to Hardy's own young manhood:

> Mentally he was in a provincial future, that is, he was in many points abreast with the central town thinkers of his date. Much of this development he may have owed to his studious life in

1. Tate refers here to Hardy's first wife, Emma Lavinia Gifford (1840-1912) [*Editor*].
2. The critic Carl J. Weber from whose book *Hardy of Wessex: His Life and Literary Career* a selection is reprinted elsewhere in this volume [*Editor*].

> Paris, where he had become acquainted with ethical systems popular at the time. In consequence of this relatively advanced position, Yeobright might have been called unfortunate. The rural world was not ripe for him.

From this and other passages in the novels, in which Hardy presents himself in the disguise of certain characters, we get a portrait of the young Hardy against the background from which he sprang. He was a young man "educated" out of the folk culture of his region: he had read Darwin, Huxley, Hume, Gibbon—the Victorian agnostics and their rationalist predecessors of the eighteenth century. He began to see the world in terms of "ethical systems popular at the time"; more than that, he began to see the people of Dorset in terms of the metaphysical basis of these systems; so that when he came back to Dorset from his studies in London he must have felt that his "advanced position" cut him off from his people.

There can be no doubt that, if this situation actually confronted Hardy at the outset of his literary career, it offered him tremendous advantages. He had had in him from birth an immense, almost instinctive knowledge of the life of a people rooted in ancient folk-traditions and fixed, also, in the objective patterns of nature and of the occupations close to nature. This knowledge of a provincial scene, where "life had bared its bones" to him, must have toughened his skepticism against the cruder aspects of Victorian thought, liberalism, optimism, and the doctrine of progress, and he could concentrate with a sort of classical purity upon the permanent human experiences. He did not see his characters as they ought to be or were going to be, but as they were.

Yet he did have a philosophical view of the significance of the human situation: he maintained, as William R. Rutland indicates in his *Thomas Hardy* (the best book on the subject), from the beginning of his literary career a steady philosophical attitude. The attitude did not change. Mr. Rutland makes an astute analysis of it (p 112):

> It is an interesting paradox that Hardy should have placed so high a value upon intellectual reason, while his own mental life was almost entirely governed by emotion. . . . he criticized J. H. Newman for failing to provide logical support for his beliefs. The outlook upon life of his mature manhood was almost wholly due to emotional reactions against suffering and injustice; but he sought for intellectual explanations of the universe in the writing of the philosophers. He went on reading philosophy till he was old, but he never advanced beyond what had been in the forefront of thought during his early manhood. When, in 1915, he read that no modern philosopher subscribes to Herbert Spencer's doctrine of "the Unknowable" (which had greatly influenced him) he declared himself "utterly bewildered."

How much this philosophical reading did towards making the young Hardy, like Clym Yeobright, partially an outsider in his own region, nobody could calculate accurately; but that it did affect him in this manner I believe no one will deny. His "advanced position" is only another way of saying that he had very early come to be both inside and outside his background, which was to be the material of his art: an ambivalent point of view that in its infinite variations from any formula that we may state for it, is at the center of the ironic consciousness. While Hardy had a direct "emotional reaction" to his Wessex people, who were the human substance of the only world he knew, he nevertheless tried to philosophize about them in the terms of Victorian materialism.

This, I think, was his intellectual situation, and Mr. Rutland has given us a clue to its meaning that ought to receive at some future time a more detailed analysis than I can give it here. In setting forth the experiences of people deeply involved with the cycle of the earth and "conditioned" in their emotional relations by close familiarity with the processes of nature, he had constantly before him a kind of "naturalism" that only an astute philosophical mind could have kept, in that period, distinct from a naturalism of a wholly different order: the philosophic naturalism of Huxley and Spencer which according to Mr. Rutland he tended to look upon as "explanations" of the world, not as theories. When he was shocked in 1915 by the decline of Spencer's reputation, he doubtless felt that a final conclusion had been upset; his outlook was not philosophical but brooding and ruminative; and I believe that here, again, we get the image of Clym Yeobright, the young man ill-prepared to digest the learning of the great world, the provincial amateur who sees farther than his neighbors but who, if he had seen still farther, might not have accepted, in an act of faith, the Darwinian naturalism of his time. As late as 1922 he wrote in the "Apology" to *Late Lyrics and Earlier* that "when belief in witches of Endor is displacing the Darwinian theory and 'the truth that shall make you free,' men's minds appear, as above noted, to be moving backwards rather than on." The witches of Endor were doubtless presiding over the irrational passions of the War; but at any rate the going backwards instead of forwards indicates, I believe, a somewhat greater belief in one of the leading Victorian ideas, Progress, than is usually attributed to Hardy.

Perhaps Hardy's intense awareness of the folk realism of his people modified the liberal optimism of his time, and checked his assent to the enthusiasm of his age at a stage which he described as evolutionary meliorism. Nevertheless, the reader of Hardy's novels gets a total impression in which this doctrine of "meliorism" is occasionally stated but in which it plays little part in terms of the characters and their plots. It has often been said that Hardy's two leading ideas, Necessity and Chance, Fate and "Crass Casualty," continue the Greek tradition; but it seems more likely that his Necessity is only Victorian mechanism, and that Chance represents the occasional intercession into the mechanical routine of the universe, of Spencer's Unknowable. It is a curious feature of Hardy's treatment of the Dorchester peasantry that not one of them is permitted to have a religious experience: their religious emotions are thoroughly "psychologized" and naturalistic. It would seem then that Hardy, like Clym, had reached an "advanced position" which forbade him to take seriously the religious life of his people, and that the peculiar compound of pagan superstition and Christianity which issued in a simple miraculism, as opposed to Hardy's mechanism of Fate interrupted by blind chance, he tended from the first to look at from the outside, where it seemed quaint and picturesque. This, of course, is not quite the whole story of Hardy's profound insight into human character, nor of his mastery of dramatic form which he achieved in spite of technical limitations and of a highfalutin prose style in the manner of the uncertain amateur. (He once said that while poetry requires technique, prose writes itself—perhaps a British as well as a personal blindness.) * * *

KATHERINE ANNE PORTER

[Hardy and T. S. Eliot]†

The Bishop of Wakefield, after reading Thomas Hardy's latest (and as it proved, his last) novel, *Jude the Obscure*, threw it in the fire, or said he did. It was a warm midsummer, and Hardy suggested that the bishop may have been speaking figuratively, heresy and bonfires being traditionally associated in his mind, or that he may have gone to the kitchen stove. The bishop wrote to the papers that he had burned the book, in any case, and he wrote also to a local M.P. who caused the horrid work to be withdrawn from the public library, promising besides to examine any other novels of Mr. Hardy carefully before allowing them to circulate among the bishop's flock. It was a good day's work; added to the protests of the reviewers for the press, and twenty-five years of snubbing and nagging from the professional moralists of his time, Thomas Hardy resigned as novelist for good. As in the case of the criticism presently to be noted, the attack on his book included also an attack on his personal character, and the bishop's action wounded Thomas

† From Katherine Anne Porter, "Notes on a Criticism of Thomas Hardy," *Southern Review*, VI (Summer, 1940), 150-54, 157-61. Reprinted by permission of Louisiana State University Press.

Hardy. He seems to have remarked in effect "that if the bishop could have known him as he was, he would have found a man whose personal conduct, views of morality, and of vital facts of religion, hardly differed from his own."

This is an indirect quotation by his second wife, devoted apologist and biographer, and it exposes almost to the point of pathos the basic, unteachable charity of Hardy's mind. Of all evil emotions generated in the snake-pit of human nature, theological hatred is perhaps the most savage, being based on intellectual concepts and disguised in the highest spiritual motives. And what could rouse this hatred in a theologian like the sight of a moral, virtuous, well-conducted man who presumed to agree with him in the "vital facts of religion," at the same time refusing to sign the articles of faith? It was long ago agreed among the Inquisitors that these are the dangerous men.

The bishop threw the book in the fire in 1896. In 1928, Mrs. Hardy was happy to record that another "eminent clergyman of the church" had advised any priest preparing to become a village rector to make first a good retreat and then a careful study of Thomas Hardy's novels. "From Thomas Hardy," concluded this amiable man, "he would learn the essential dignity of country people and what deep and passionate interest belongs to every individual life. You cannot treat them in the mass: each single soul is to be the object of your special and peculiar prayer."

Aside from the comment on the social point of view which made it necessary thus to warn prospective rectors that country people were also human entities, each possessed of a soul important, however rural, to God, and the extraordinary fact that an agnostic novelist could teach them what the church and their own hearts could not, it is worth noting again that churchmen differ even as the laymen on questions of morality, and can preach opposing doctrine from the same text. The history of these differences, indeed, is largely the calamitous history of institutional religion. In 1934, a layman turned preacher almost like a character in a Hardy novel, runs true to his later form by siding with the bishop. Since his spectacular conversion to the theology and politics of the Church of England, Mr. T. S. Eliot's great gifts as a critic have been deflected into channels where they do not flow with their old splendor and depth. More and more his literary judgments have assumed the tone of lay sermons by a parochial visitor, and his newer style is perhaps at its most typical in his criticism of Thomas Hardy:

> The work of the late Thomas Hardy represents an interesting example of a powerful personality uncurbed by any institutional attachment or by submission to any objective beliefs; unhampered by any ideas, or even by what sometimes acts as a partial restraint upon inferior writers, the desire to please a large public.

> He seems to me to have written as nearly for the sake of "self-expression" as a man well can, and the self which he had to express does not strike me as a particularly wholesome or edifying matter of communication. He was indifferent even to the prescripts of good writing: he wrote sometimes overpoweringly well, but always very carelessly; at times his style touches sublimity without ever having passed through the stage of being good. In consequence of his self-absorption, he makes a great deal of landscape; for landscape is a passive creature which lends itself to an author's mood. Landscape is fitted, too, for the purposes of an author who is interested not at all in men's minds, but only in their emotions, and perhaps only in men as vehicles for emotions.[1]

After some useful general reflections on the moral undesirability of extreme emotionalism, meant as a rebuke to Hardy * * * Mr. Eliot proceeds:

> I was [in a previous lecture] . . . concerned with illustrating the limiting and crippling effect of a separation from tradition and orthodoxy upon certain writers whom I nevertheless hold up for admiration for what they have attempted against great obstacles. Here I am concerned with the intrusion of the *diabolic* into modern literature in consequence of the same lamentable state of affairs; . . . I am afraid that even if you can entertain the notion of a positive power for evil working through human agency, you may still have a very inaccurate notion of what Evil is, and will find it difficult to believe that it may operate through men of genius of the most excellent character. I doubt whether what I am saying can convey very much to anyone for whom the doctrine of Original Sin is not a very real and tremendous thing.

Granting the premises with extreme reservations, Thomas Hardy was a visible proof of the validity of this disturbing doctrine. He had received early religious training in the Established Church, and by precept and example in a household of the most sincere piety, and of the most aggressive respectability. He remarked once, that of all the names he had been called, such as agnostic (which tag he adopted later, ruefully) atheist, immoralist, pessimist, and so on, a properly fitting one had been overlooked altogether: "churchy." He had once meant to be a parson. His relations with the church of his childhood had been of the homely, intimate, almost filial sort. His grandfather, his father, his uncle, all apt in music, had been for forty years the mainstay of the village choir. He felt at home in the place, as to its customs, feasts, services. He had a great love for the ancient churches, and as a young architect his aesthetic sense was

1. T. S. Eliot's attack on Hardy was published in *After Strange Gods* (London, 1934). The material in the book was originally delivered as the Page-Barbour lectures at the University of Virginia in 1933. [*Editor*].

outraged by the fashionable and silly "restorations" amounting to systematic destruction which overtook some of the loveliest examples of medieval church architecture in England during the nineteenth century. His devotion to the past, and to the history and character of his native Wessex became at times a kind of antiquarian fustiness. His personal morals were irreproachable, he had an almost queasy sense of the awful and permanent effects of wrong doing on the human soul and destiny. Most of his novels deal with these consequences; his most stupendous tragedies are the result of one false step on the part of his hero or heroine. Genius aside, he had all the makings of a good, honest, church-going country squire; but the worm of original sin was settled in his mind, of all fatal places; and his mind led him out of the tradition of orthodoxy into another tradition of equal antiquity, equal importance, equal seriousness, a body of opinion running parallel throughout history to the body of law in church and state: the great tradition of dissent. He went, perhaps not so much by choice as by compulsion of *belief*, with the Inquirers rather than the Believers. His mind, not the greatest, certainly not the most flexible, but a good, candid, strong mind, asked simply the oldest, most terrifying questions, and the traditional, orthodox answers of the church did not satisfy it. It is easy to see how this, from the churchly point of view, is diabolic. But the yawning abyss between question and answer remains the same, and until this abyss is closed, the dissent will remain, persistent, obdurate, a kind of church itself, with its leaders, teachers, saints, martyrs, heroes; a thorn in the flesh of orthodoxy, but I think not necessarily of the Devil on that account, unless the intellect and all its questions are really from the Devil, as the Eden myth states explicitly, as the Church seems to teach, and Mr. Eliot tends to confirm.

There is a great deal to examine in the paragraphs quoted above, but two words in their context illustrate perfectly the unbridgable abyss between Hardy's question and Mr. Eliot's answer. One is, of course, the word *diabolic*. The other is *edifying*. That struck and held my eye in a maze, for a moment. With no disrespect I hope to conventional piety, may I venture that in the regions of art, as of religion, edification is not the highest form of intellectual or spiritual experience. It is a happy truth that Hardy's novels are really not edifying. The mental and emotional states roused and maintained in the reader of *The Mayor of Casterbridge* or *The Return of the Native* are considerably richer, invoked out of deeper sources in the whole human consciousness, more substantially nourishing, than this lukewarm word can express. A novel by Thomas Hardy can be a chastening experience, an appalling one, there is great and sober pleasure to be got out of those novels, the mind can be disturbed and the heart made extremely uneasy, but the complacency of edification is absent, as it is apt to be from any true tragedy.

* * *

He [Hardy] did believe that there is "a power that rules the world" though he did not name it, nor could he accept the names that had been given it, or any explanation of its motives. He could only watch its operations, and to me it seems he concluded that both malevolence and benevolence originated in the mind of man, and the warring forces were within him alone; such plan as existed in regard to him he had created for himself, his Good and his Evil were alike the mysterious inventions of his own mind; and why this was so, Hardy could not pretend to say. He knew there was an element in human nature not subject to mathematical equation or the water-tight theories of dogma, and this intransigent, measureless force, divided against itself, in conflict alike with its own system of laws and the unknown laws of the universe, was the real theme of Hardy's novels; a genuinely tragic theme in the grand manner, of sufficient weight and shapelessness to try the powers of any artist. Generally so reluctant to admit any influence, Hardy admits to a study of the Greek dramatists, and with his curious sense of proportion, he decided that the Wessex countryside was also the dwelling place of the spirit of tragedy; that the histories of certain obscure persons in that limited locality bore a strong family resemblance to those of the great, the ancient, and the legendary. Mr. Eliot finds Hardy's beloved Wessex a "stage setting," such as the Anglo-Saxon heart loves; and Hardy's Wessex farmers "period peasants pleasing to the metropolitan imagination." Hardy was Anglo-Saxon; that landscape was in his blood. Those period peasants were people he had known all his life, and I think that in this passage Mr. Eliot simply speaks as a man of the town, like those young vicars who need to be reminded of the individual dignity and importance of the country people. Further, taking all the Hardy characters in a lump, he finds in them only blind animal emotionalism, and remarks: ". . . strong passion is only interesting or significant in strong men; those who abandon themselves without resistance to excitements which tend to deprive them of reason become merely instruments of feeling and lose their humanity; and unless there is moral resistance and conflict there is no meaning." True in part: and to disagree in detail would lead to an endless discussion of *what* exactly constitutes interest in the work of a writer; *what* gives importance to his characters, their intrinsic value as human beings or the value their creator is able to give them by his own imaginative view of them. * * *

Hardy's characters are full of moral conflicts and of decisions arrived at by mental processes, certainly. Jude, Gabriel Oak, Clem

Yeobright, above all, Henchard, are men who have decisions to make, and if they do not make them entirely on the plane of reason, it is because Hardy was interested most in that hairline dividing the rational from the instinctive, the opposition, we might call it, between nature, and second nature; that is, between instinct and the habits of thought fixed upon the individual by his education and his environment. Such characters of his as are led by their emotions come to tragedy; he seems to say that following the emotions blindly leads to disaster. Romantic miscalculation of the possibilities of life, of love, of the situation; of refusing to reason their way out of their predicament; these are the causes of disaster in Hardy's novels. Angel Clare is a man of the highest principles, trained in belief, religion, observance of moral law. His failure to understand the real nature of Christianity makes a monster of him at the great crisis of his life. The Mayor of Casterbridge spends the balance of his life in atonement and reparation for a brutal wrong committed in drunkenness and anger; his past overtakes and destroys him. Hardy had an observing eye, a remembering mind; he did not need the Greeks to teach him that the Furies do arrive punctually, and that neither act, nor will, nor intention will serve to deflect a man's destiny from him, once he has taken the step which decides it.

A word about that style which Mr. Eliot condemns as touching "sublimity without ever having passed through the stage of being good." Hardy has often been called by critics who love him, the good simple man of no ideas, the careless workman of genius who never learned to write, who cared nothing for the way of saying a thing.

His own testimony is that he cared a great deal for *what* he said: "My art is to intensify the expression of things, as is done by Crivelli, Bellini, etc., so that the heart and inner meaning is made vividly visible." Again: "The Realities to be the true realities of life, hitherto called abstractions. The old material realities to be placed behind the former, as shadowy accessories." His notebooks are dry, reluctant, unmethodical; he seems to have spent his time and energies in actual labor at his task rather than theorizing about it, but he remarks once: "Looking around on a well selected shelf of fiction, how few stories of any length does one recognize as well told from beginning to end! The first half of this story, the last half of that, the middle of another . . . the modern art of narration is yet in its infancy." He made few comments on technical procedure, but one or two are valuable as a clue to his directions: "A story must be exceptional enough to justify its telling. We tale tellers are all Ancient Mariners, and none of us is warranted in stopping Wedding Guests . . . unless he has something more unusual to relate than the ordinary experiences of every average man and woman." Again: "The whole secret of fiction and drama—in the constructional part—lies in the adjustment of things unusual to things eternal and universal. The writer who knows exactly how exceptional, and how non-exceptional, his events should be made, possesses the key to the art."

So much for theory. Not much about the importance of style, the care for the word, the just and perfect construction of a paragraph. But Hardy was not a careless writer. The difference between his first and last editions proves this, in matters of style aside from his painful reconstruction of his manuscripts mutilated for serial publication. He wrote and wrote again, and he never found it easy. He lacked elegance, he never learned the trick of the whip-lash phrase, the complicated lariat twirling of the professed stylists. His prose lumbers along, it jogs, it creaks, it hesitates, he is as dull as certain long passages in the Tolstoy of *War and Peace*, for example. That celebrated first scene on Egdon Heath, in *The Return of the Native*. Who does not remember it? And in actual re-reading, what could be duller? What could be more labored than his introduction of the widow Yeobright at the heath fire among the dancers, or more unconvincing than the fears of the timid boy that the assembly are literally raising the Devil? Except for this; in my memory of that episode, as in dozens of others in many of Hardy's novels, I have seen it, I was there. When I read it, it almost disappears from view, and afterward comes back, phraseless, living in its sombre clearness, as Hardy meant it to do, I feel certain. This to my view is the chief quality of good prose as distinguished from poetry. By his own testimony, he limited his territory by choice, set boundaries to his material, focused his point of view like a burning glass down on a definite aspect of things. He practiced a stringent discipline, severely excised and eliminated all that seemed to him not useful or appropriate to his plan. In the end his work was the sum of his experience, he arrived at his particular true testimony; along the way, sometimes, many times, he wrote sublimely.

DONALD DAVIDSON

The Traditional Basis of Thomas Hardy's Fiction†

* * * There was a real intellectual distance between Hardy and the critics—indeed, between Hardy and almost three generations of critics. The critics had not so much underrated—or

† From Donald Davidson, "The Traditional Basis of Thomas Hardy's Fiction," *Southern Review*, VI (Summer, 1940), 163-78. Reprinted by permission of Louisiana State University Press.

overrated—Hardy as missed him, in somewhat the same way as, in our opinion, Dr. Johnson missed John Donne. When we look over the impressive list of those who have made literary pronouncements in Hardy's time and ours, they do not seem to be the kind of people who would have affinity with Hardy. From George Meredith, his first literary adviser, up to T. S. Eliot, one can hardly think of a critic whose view of Hardy's work, however well-intentioned, would not be so external as to set up a gross incongrunity like what we find in Marxian criticisms of Shakespeare.

Possibly the critics have been most in error in not realizing the comparative isolation of Hardy in modern literary history. Misled by the superficial resemblance between his work and the product current in their day, they have invariably attempted to treat him as a current author—or at least as a queer blend of tendencies receding and tendencies coming on. They have been further misled by Hardy's own attempt (not always happy) to shape his work into a marketable form or to bring it up to what he conceived to be a good current literary standard. For Hardy seems to have had little idea of being an innovator or an iconoclast. He sought to please and entertain, and perhaps to instruct, and he must have been amazed to find himself now acclaimed, now condemned, as heretic.

The appearance of Thomas Hardy among the temporal phenomena of the England of 1870 to 1928—that is the amazing, the confusing thing. I believe we ought to begin consideration by admitting that though Hardy was *in* that time, and was affected by its thought and art, he was not really *of* that time whenever he was his essential self. It is not enough to say that Hardy is "old-fashioned" or "quaint." Certainly he did not try consciously to be old-fashioned. Although there are archaisms of language in his poetry and prose, and much general display of the antique in subject matter, there is nowhere in Hardy the affectation of archaism (found in such ironic romanticists as Cabell[1]) or the deliberate exploitation of archaism (found in a great many of the literary specialties offered in America). The old-fashioned quality in Hardy is not in the obvious places, but lies deeper. It is in the habit of Hardy's mind rather than in "folk-lore" or the phenomena of language and style.

Hardy wrote, or tried to write, more or less as a modern—modern, for him, being late nineteenth century. But he thought, or artistically conceived, like a man of another century—indeed, of a century that we should be hard put to name. It might be better to say that he wrote like a creator of tales and poems who is a little embarrassed at having to adapt the creation of tales and poems to the conditions of a written, or printed, literature, and yet tries to do

1. James Branch Cabell (1879-1958) was a distinguished American novelist, most famous for *Jurgen* (1919) [*Editor*].

his faithful best under the regrettable circumstances. He is not in any sense a "folk author," and yet he does approach his tale-telling and poem-making as if three centuries of Renaissance effort had worked only upon the outward form of tale and poem without changing its essential character. He wrote as a ballad-maker would write if a ballad-maker were to have to write novels; or as a bardic or epic poet would write if faced with the necessity of performing in the quasi-lyrical but non-singable strains of the nineteenth century and later.

Hardy is the only specimen of his genus in modern English literature, and I do not know how to account for him. He has no immediate predecessors; and though he has some imitators, no real followers as yet. For his habit of mind has seemingly disappeared in England, and threatens to disappear in America; and without the habit of mind to begin with no real following can be done. I am almost ready to characterize Hardy (if he must be "placed") as an American whose ancestors failed to migrate at the proper time and who accordingly found himself stranded, a couple of centuries later, in the wrong literary climate. In this connection it is amusing to remember that Hardy has been charged with borrowing a description from Augustus Baldwin Longstreet's *Georgia Scenes*[2] for use in *The Trumpet Major*. The truth is that his general affiliation with the frontier humorists of the Old Southwest is a good deal more discernible than his affiliation with Victorian romantic-realists or with French Naturalists. It is an organic affiliation, not a literary attachment, because the Southwestern humorists drew their art, such as it was, from the same kind of source that Hardy used, and wrote (when they had to write) under the same embarrassment. If Hardy's distant seventeenth-century progenitor had migrated to America at the time of the Monmouth Rebellion[3]—as some of his progenitor's relatives and many of his neighbors did, in all haste, migrate, then Thomas Hardy might easily have been a frontier humorist of the Longstreet school. And then he would never have been accused of pessimism, though he might, to be sure, have caused eyebrows to lift in Boston.

* * *

Hardy was born early enough—and far enough away from looming Arnoldian or Marxian influences—to receive a conception of art as something homely, natural, functional, and in short traditional.

2. Augustus Baldwin Longstreet (1790-1870) was an American regional author, jurist, and college president. *Georgia Scenes* (1840) was a series of broadly humorous sketches [*Editor*].

3. James Scott, Duke of Monmouth (1649-1685), led an unsuccessful rebellion against the new king, James II, in 1685. He was widely believed to be the bastard son of the old king, Charles II. He claimed the throne and had considerable support in Cornwall, Devon, and Dorset [*Editor*].

He grew up in a Dorset where fiction was a tale told or sung; and where the art of music, always important to him, was primarily for worship or merriment.

* * *

For what it may be worth I note that Hardy first conceived *The Dynasts* as a ballad, or group of ballads. In May, 1875, he wrote in his journal:

> Mem: A Ballad of the Hundred Days. Then another of Moscow. Others of earlier campaigns—forming altogether an Iliad of Europe from 1789 to 1815.

This, Mrs. Hardy says, is the first mention in Hardy's memoranda of the conception later to take shape in the epic drama. Again, on March 27, 1881, Hardy referred to his scheme: "A Homeric Ballad, in which Napoleon is a sort of Achilles, to be written."

To evidence of this kind I should naturally add the following facts: that Hardy wrote a number of ballads, like "The Bride-Night Fire," and ballad-like poems; that his poems like his novels are full of references to old singers, tunes, and dances, and that many of the poems proceed from the same sources as his novels; that he is fond of inserting in his journals, among philosophizings and other memoranda, summaries of anecdotes or stories he has heard. Of the latter sort is the following entry:

> Conjurer Mynterne when consulted by Patt P. (a strapping handsome young woman), told her that her husband would die on a certain day, and showed her the funeral in a glass of water. . . . She used to impress all this on her inoffensive husband, and assure him that he would go to hell if he made the conjurer a liar. He didn't, but died on the day foretold.

Such notations should not be unduly emphasized. Yet they appear in his journal with such frequency that we are justified in assuming Hardy's special interest in such material. On the other hand, in the record of Hardy's life thus far available to us, there is little evidence to indicate that, in devising the greater stories, he had some specific literary model before him, or was trying out some theory of fiction, or had, at the beginning of his conception, a particular philosophical or social thesis. Critics may show that such and such a literary influence reached him, or that a theory or philosophy ultimately engaged his mind; but I cannot believe that such elements controlled the original conception or determined the essential character of the greater novels and stories. * * *

My thesis is that the characteristic Hardy novel is conceived as a *told* (or *sung*) story, or at least not as a literary story; that it is an extension, in the form of a modern prose fiction, of a traditional ballad or an oral tale—a tale of the kind which Hardy reproduces with great skill in *A Few Crusted Characters* and less successfully in *A Group of Noble Dames*; but, furthermore, that this habit of mind is a rather unconscious element in Hardy's art. The conscious side of his art manifests itself in two ways: first, he "works up" his core of traditional, or nonliterary narrative into a literary form; but, second, at the same time he labors to establish, in his "Wessex," the kind of artistic climate and environment which will enable him to handle his traditional story with conviction—a world in which typical ballad heroes and heroines can flourish with a thoroughly rationalized "mythology" to sustain them. The novels that support this thesis are the great Hardy novels: *Under the Greenwood Tree, Far from the Madding Crowd, The Mayor of Casterbridge, The Return of the Native, The Woodlanders,* and *Tess of the D'Urbervilles*—in other words, the Wessex novels proper. *Jude the Obscure* and *The Trumpet Major* can be included, with some reservations, in the same list. The novels that do not support this thesis are commonly held to be, by comparison with those named above, of inferior quality: *The Hand of Ethelberta* and *A Laodicean,* for example. These are Hardy's attempt to be a fully modern—and literary—novelist.

The fictions that result from Hardy's habit of mind resemble traditional, or nonliterary, types of narrative in many ways. They are always conceived of as stories primarily, with the narrative always of foremost interest. They have the rounded, often intricate plot and the balance and antithesis of characters associated with traditional fiction from ancient times. It is natural, of course, that they should in such respects resemble classic drama. But that does not mean that Hardy thought in terms of dramatic composition. His studies in Greek (like his experience in architecture) simply reinforced an original tendency. The interspersed descriptive elements—always important, but not overwhelmingly important, in a Hardy novel—do not encumber the narrative, as they invariably do in the works of novelists who conceive their task in wholly literary terms; but they blend rather quickly into the narrative. Action, not description, is always foremost; the event dominates, rather than motive, or psychology, or comment. There is no loose episodic structure. Hardy does not write the chronicle novel or the biographical novel. Nor does he build up circumstantial detail like a Zola or a Flaubert.

Hardy has an evident fondness for what we might call the "country story"—the kind of story *told* by the passengers in the van in *A Few Crusted Characters;* or *sung* in ballads of the type attributed by scholars to the seventeenth and eighteenth century and sometimes called "vulgar" ballads to distinguish them from the supposedly more genuine "popular" ballads of an earlier day. * * *

The Return of the Native gives us far more complexity, but many of its focal incidents are of the stuff in which tale-tellers and ballad-makers delight. Mrs. Yeobright is bitten by a snake; Eustacia and Wildeve are drowned in one pool, to make a simultaneous romantic death, and we almost expect to learn that they were buried in the old churchyard and presently sprouted—a rose from her breast, a briar from his. We should not forget that Eustacia disguises herself in man's clothing (as heroines of traditional stories have long done) for the mummer's play. * * * Coincidence in Hardy's narratives represents a conviction about the nature of story as such. Hardy's world is of course not the world of the most antique ballads and folk tales—where devils, demons, fairies, and mermaids intervene in human affairs, and ghosts, witches, and revenants are commonplace. It is a world like that of later balladry and folk tale, from which old beliefs have receded, leaving a residue of the merely strange. Improbability and accident have replaced the miraculous. * * * He felt that the unlikely (or quasi-miraculous) element belonged in any proper story—especially a Wessex story; but he would go only so far as the late ballads and country tales went, in substituting improbabilities for supernaturalisms. Never does he concoct a pseudo-folk tale like Stephen V. Benet's "The Devil and Daniel Webster." Superstitions are used in the background of his narrative; coincidence, in the actual mechanics. Tess hears the legend of the D'Urberville phantom coach, but does not actually see it, though the moment is appropriate for its appearance. In *The Return of the Native* Susan Nonesuch pricks Eustacia Vye for a witch and later makes a waxen image of her, just before her drowning; but coincidence, not superstition, dominates the action. Henchard visits the conjurer just before his great speculation in grain, but only out of habit and in half-belief; and it is coincidence that makes Farfrae a winner just at the moment when Henchard is a loser. The supernatural, in Hardy, is allowed in the narrative, but in a subordinate position; the quasi-miraculous takes its place in the main position.

If we use a similar approach to the problem of Hardy's pessimism, it is easy to see why he was irritated by insensitive and obtuse critics. Are the ballad stories of "Edward," "Little Musgrave," and "Johnnie Armstrong" pessimistic? Were their unknown authors convinced of the fatal indifference of the Universe toward human beings? Should we, reading such stories, take the next step in the context of modern critical realism and advocate psychoanalysis for Edward's mother and social security for Johnnie Armstrong? In formal doctrine Hardy professed himself to be an "evolutionary meliorist," or almost a conventional modern. But that had nothing to do with the stories that started up in his head. The charge of pessimism has about the same relevance as the charge of indelicacy which Hardy encountered when he first began to publish. An age of polite literature, which had lost touch with the oral arts—except so far as they might survive in chit-chat, gossip, and risqué stories—could not believe that an author who embodied in his serious stories the typical seductions, rapes, murders, and lusty lovemakings of the old tradition intended anything but a breach of decorum. Even today, I suppose, a group gathered for tea might be a little astonished if a respectable old gentleman in spats suddenly began to warble the outrageous ballad of Little Musgrave. But Hardy did not know he was being rough, and had no more notion than a ballad-maker of turning out a story to be either pessimistic or optimistic.

To be sure, Hardy is a little to blame, since he does moralize at times. But the passage about the President of the Immortals in *Tess* and about the persistence of the unforeseen in *The Mayor of Casterbridge* probably came to him like such ballad tags as "Better they'd never been born" or "Young men, take warning from me."

* * *

The most striking feature of Hardy's habit of mind, as traditional narrator, is in his creation of characters. The characters of the Wessex novels, with certain important exceptions, are fixed or "non-developing" characters. Their fortunes may change, but they do not change with their fortunes. Once fully established as characters, they move unchanged through the narrative and at the end are what they were at the beginning. They have the changelessness of the figures of traditional narrative from epic, saga, and romance to broadside balladry and its prose parallels. In this respect they differ fundamentally from the typical characters of modern literary fiction. Our story-writers have learned how to exploit the possibilities of the changing, or changeful, or "developing" character. The theory of progress has seemed to influence them to apply an analogical generalization to the heroes of their stories: to wit, the only good hero in a serious novel is one that *changes* in some important respect during the course of the narrative; and the essence of the story is the change. This has become almost an aesthetic axiom. It is assumed that a story has no merit unless it is based on a changing character. If the modern author uses the changeless character, it is only in a minor rôle, or as a foil; or he may appear as a caricature.

But we have forgotten a truth that Hardy must have known from the time when, as a child, he heard at the harvest home the ballad of the outlandish knight. The changeless character has as much aesthetic richness as the changeful character. Traditional narrative of every sort is built upon the changeless character. It is a defect in modern fiction that the value of the changeless character is apparently not even suspected. But since the human desire for the changeless character is after all insatiable, we do have our changeless characters—in the comic strips, the movies, the detective story. Perhaps all is not well with a literary art that leaves the rôle of Achilles to be filled by Pop-Eye.

At any rate Hardy made extensive use of the changeless character. The habit of his mind probably forbade him to do otherwise; or at least he could not with complete success build his stories upon the changeful character. And so his novels of manners and genteel society are failures. At the same time, Hardy was no untutored child of the folk but a great author who learned by trial and error how to utilize self-consciously the rich material which by unself-conscious habit crowded his mind. He was thinking of his problem, I believe, when he wrote: "The uncommonness must be in the events, not in the characters." He did not make the mistake of exploiting his material for its mere picturesqueness—its *special* quality. He did not write dialect poems like William Barnes or romantic reconstructions like Blackmore's *Lorna Doone.*

What Hardy did is, in its astonishing completeness and verity, a rebuke to superficial quasi-regionalists and to all who attempt to exploit "folk material" with the shallow assumption that the "folkishness" of the material is alone enough to dignify it. Hardy rationalizes the changeless characters by creating in highest circumstantiality not only the local environment in which they move, but the entire social order—the tradition itself, and the basis of the tradition—which will accommodate them. The basis of the tradition is a natural environment—a nature not very much despoiled or exploited, a town life neither wholly antique nor wholly modern, and the whole removed a little in time from the strictly contemporary, but not so far removed as to seem like a historical reconstruction. The antiquities, the local color, the folk customs are not decorative or merely picturesque; they are organic with the total scheme. They are no less essential and no more decorative than the occupations, ambitions, and interrelationships of the changeless characters. He accepts the assumptions of the society that he depicts, and neither apologizes for it nor condescends to it. The stories are stories of human beings, not of peasants or moor-dwellers as such.

The scheme is somewhat more complex than it might appear to be. The changeless characters of the Wessex world are of both minor and major order; and they are generally set in juxtaposition with one or two characters of a more changeful or modern type. The interplay between the two kinds of characters is the focus of the struggle that makes the story. Hardy is almost the only modern novelist who makes serious use of this conflict and at the same time preserves full and equal respect for both sets of characters. His great art lies in not setting up too great or obvious a distance between his changeless and his changeful characters. * * *

Such a conflict is found in *The Return of the Native*. Here the rustics are Timothy Fairway, Grandfer Cantle, Christian Cantle, Susan Nonesuch and her son Johnny, and the mummers. It would be wrong to regard these persons as curiosities, or as interesting literary fossils planted in the environment for the verisimilitude that they give. They not only take part in the series of festivals that provide a symbolic chronological pattern for the novel; but they also participate in the critical action itself, as agents of destiny. Timothy carries the letter which was so fatally not delivered at last. Johnny Nonesuch is liaison agent between Eustacia and Wildeve. Christian Cantle carries the guineas, and gambles them away. Susan Nonesuch and her son intervene actively in the lives of both Eustacia and Clym. Their part is organic, not decorative; they are much more than the "Greek chorus" that they have been called. They are, in fact, the basic pattern to which other characters conform or from which they differ. Diggory Venn and Thomasin, at a slightly higher level, conform more or less; they are changeless characters who venture near the danger line of changefulness but do not pass over it. Eustacia and Clym have passed over the line, though not beyond the possibility of retraction. They are changeful characters, strongly touched by Promethean influences—as Wildeve, in a vulgar way, is also touched. Modernism has worked on Eustacia to lure her away from Egdon Heath; but Clym, who has already lived in Paris, has reached a second stage of revulsion against modernism. Yet when this native returns he brings with him a characteristically modern program of education and evangelism. Eustacia and Clym, as changeful characters, do not diverge extravagantly from the changeless pattern, but their rebellion is great enough to render their life-courses inconstant and tragic.

Hardy has taken some pains to mark the essential nature of Clym's character. The motto for the chapter that describes Clym is: "My mind to me a kingdom is." Clym is a Renaissance, or non-traditional, man. His face, already marked with disillusionment, foreshadows "the typical countenance of the future." * * *

Perhaps these are dangerous simplifications. I do not offer them as definitive explanations of Hardy's fictions, but rather as possibilities not yet explored. Hardy's habit of mind, and his method of using his habit of mind in fiction, seem to me the least discussed of the aspects of his work. I have found no other approach that does not seem to impose a critical explanation from without, with an arbitrariness that often seems to do violence to the art work itself.

There is surely no other example in modern English fiction of an author who, while reaching the highest levels of sophisticated artistic performance, comes bringing his tradition with him, not only the mechanics of the tradition but the inner conception that is often lacking. The admonitions we hear so often nowadays about the relation of the artist and his tradition seem dry and academic when we look closely at Hardy's actual performance. He seems to illustrate what we might think the ideal way of realizing and activating a tradition, for he did, without admonition, what the admonishers are always claiming ought to be done; and yet for that particular achievement he got no thanks, or even a notice. The achievement is the more extraordinary when we consider that he worked (if I read his career rightly) against the dominant pattern of his day. He did what the modern critic (despite his concern about tradition) is always implying to be impossible. That is, Hardy accepted the assumptions of a society which in England was already being condemned to death, and he wrote in terms of those assumptions, almost as if Wessex, and perhaps Wessex only, would understand. From his work I get few of the meanings, pessimistic or otherwise, that are commonly ascribed to him. His purpose seems to have been to tell about human life in the terms that would present it as most recognizably, and validly, and completely human. That he succeeded best when he wrote of rural Wessex is significant. He probably had strong convictions on one point—convictions that had little to do with his official inquiries into Darwinism and the nature of Deity.

LORD DAVID CECIL

[Hardy's Use of Literary Convention]†

Hardy's characters linger in our imagination as grand typical figures silhouetted against the huge horizon of the universe. Here they resemble characters of epic and tragedy. Indeed, alike in his themes and his treatment of them, Hardy has less in common with the typical novelist than with the typical author of tragedy and epic. And we must adjust our mental eye to envisage life in the tragic and epic focus if we are to see his vision in the right perspective.

† From Lord David Cecil, *Hardy the Novelist (An Essay in Criticism)*, pp. 36-42, 56-58, 93-95, 111, 116-17, 128-29, 148-51, 156-57. Reprinted by permission of David Higham Associates, Ltd. These are the Clark Lectures given at Cambridge in 1942.

We are assisted to do this by the convention he adopts. For our preparations for judging him are not complete when we have realised his range. We must also acquaint ourselves with the conventions within which he elected to compose his pictures. We should in criticising any writer. Every artist constructs his work within certain conventions, which we must accept before we are in a position to estimate his success. Some of the most famous ineptitudes of criticism are due to a failure to realise this obligation. Macaulay read Racine without understanding the conventions of French classical tragedy; he expected all good tragedies to be like Shakespeare's. The consequence was that Racine's subtle and passionate presentation of the drama of the human heart struck him as intolerably stilted and artificial. Voltaire, on the other hand, read Shakespeare's plays expecting them to be like Racine's. He thought, therefore, that Shakespeare was a barbarian. That two persons of this eminence should talk such nonsense should be a warning to the ordinary reader to be careful to acquaint himself with an author's convention before starting to criticise him. He should be particularly careful with Hardy. For Hardy does not write in the convention that one might expect.

Hardy's convention was that of an earlier age, the convention invented by Fielding. The novel is a new form, as forms go, and it was some time before it discovered the convention most appropriate to its matter. It aimed at giving a realistic picture of actual life. How was this to be given a shapely form? Various writers experimented to solve the problem in various ways. Defoe put his tales in the form of autobiography, Richardson in the form of a correspondence. Fielding, who had begun his career as a dramatist, turned to the drama for help. The English novel, as created by Fielding, descends directly from the English drama. Now, that drama was unrealistic. In Shakespeare's day it did not even try to be realistic. It aimed at entertaining its audiences by showing them a world as little like their own as possible: a world in which heroic and dramatic personages took part in picturesque, sensational adventures. The writers of Restoration comedy modified this convention a little. They set their scene in contemporary England and made their characters talk in something approaching the language of real conversation. But essentially their plays remained unrealistic; their plots were highly artificial, their dialogue stiff with ornament and their characters stylised.

Bred to this tradition, Fielding and his followers took for granted that a mere accurate chronicle of ordinary life would be intolerably dull to the reader. So they evolved a working compromise. The setting and characters of their stories were carefully realistic, but they were fitted into a framework of non-realistic plot derived from the drama, consisting of an intrigue enlivened by all sorts of sensational events—conspiracies, children changed at birth, mistakes of identity—centring round a handsome ideal hero and heorine and a sinister villain, and solved neatly in the last chapter. As in the drama, the characters revealed themselves mainly through speech and action—there is not much analysis of them by the author—and the serious tension is relieved by a number of specifically comic characters drawn in a convention of slight caricature.

In one respect this type of novel was even more limited than the drama had been. It was intended as light reading. It might point a moral—it generally did—but it did not deal with those profounder and more impersonal aspects of life which were the subject of serious poetry. It was not supposed to be an intellectual strain, and themes that would set its reader's intellect seriously to work were, except in a few instances, avoided.

This convention was a loose makeshift affair. But it proved less clumsy and more effective than any other hitherto proposed. And, though it gradually discarded its more artificial devices, some elements at least of it were accepted by most English novelists until the time of George Eliot. She was a revolutionary in her sober way. In her books we are presented for the first time with a form of fiction freed from the last vestiges of the dramatic tradition—novels without romantic heroes and villains, with lengthy analysis of motive and character, and in which action is determined by no conventions of plot, but solely by the logical demands of character and situation. In addition, George Eliot, extremely intellectual and uncompromisingly serious, employed her books to expound her most considered reflections on human conduct.

The next generation of novelists carried this change still further. With Henry James, Meredith and George Moore, the novel showed itself as fully entered on a new phase.

Now, Hardy has been looked on usually as part of this new phase. It is natural. For one thing, he was the contemporary of the new novelists; and for another, his books do have some elements in common with theirs. Intellectually, Hardy was a man of the new age—a so-called advanced thinker, in open rebellion against traditional orthodox views about religion, sex and so on—and he used his novels to preach these heretical opinions. Drawing his inspiration largely, as we have seen, from his vision of man's relation to ultimate Fate, he welcomed the movement to deepen and elevate the subject-matter of the novel. Since he wanted to write about tragic and epic subjects, he was pleased that the novel should be regarded as a form capable of achieving tragic and epic dignity. Enthusiastically he discarded the happy ending and made his stories the mouthpieces of his most serious views.

But although intellectually Hardy was a man of the future,

aesthetically he was a man of the past. His broad conception of the novel form was much more like that of Fielding than it was like that of Henry James. Circumstances were partly responsible for this. His taste in story-telling was that of the simple rural society in which he had been brought up. He liked a story to be a story. It should have a beginning and an end. It should be full of action. And, above all, it should be sufficiently unusual to arouse the interest of its hearers. * * *

There was also a more serious motive in his adopting the old convention. It harmonised with the peculiar nature of his inspiration. The presentation of any special vision of reality must involve a process of elimination. The artist, in order to bring out the distinguishing characteristics of his vision of the world, must select and emphasise these features in the real world which illustrate his view. * * * But the nature of their vision requires some artists to be much more careful than others to give an illusion of ordinary reality. Jane Austen, for instance, who is out to show us the comedy that lies in the everyday life of the average person, must not allow us to doubt for a moment that we are reading about such a life. We must be under the impression that we are getting a genuine glimpse of an ordinary drawing-room, and listening to the conversations there. Any obvious discrepancy between what she shows us and what we should expect to find in such a drawing-room will destroy this illusion, and with it our belief in her comic vision of life.

Hardy, concerned not with the everyday surface of things but with the deeper principles and forces that lie behind them, does not need to do this. On the contrary, too much preoccupation with the surface of things would distract our attention from the facts which he wishes to emphasise. If our eyes are always being directed to superficial details they will not penetrate below them to perceive fundamental causes: we shall not notice the pattern, to use his phrase, in the carpet of experience which his idiosyncrasy moves him to observe. In consequence, it would be mistaken for him to adopt a realistic convention. As he says, "My Art is to intensify the expression of things so that the heart and inner meaning is made vividly visible," and "Art is a disproportioning—(i.e. distorting, throwing out of proportion)—of realities, to show more clearly the features that matter in those realities, which, if merely copied, might possibly be observed, but would more probably be overlooked. Hence 'realism' is not Art." He required a convention that would give full scope for the expression of the spiritual and imaginative aspects of experience, and would eliminate the necessity for describing the mere superficial features of its appearance. Naturally the greater realism, to which the go-ahead novelists of his time were turning, held no attraction for him.

So far from disliking the dramatic intensity and regularity which the first novelists had taken on from the playwrights, he found it necessary for the expression of his vision. He turned backwards, not forwards, in order to discover the most appropriate mode for his art. If he had masters, they are Shakespeare and that British novelist who learnt most from Shakespeare, Sir Walter Scott.

I do not know if you have remarked how often I have mentioned Scott when seeking for a parallel to Hardy. It was inevitable that I should; for Hardy has more in common with Scott than with any other British novelist. Intellectually, of course, they were poles apart. Their kinship is aesthetic. Scott, like Hardy, was inspired by rural life, country humours, traditional customs. His imagination was also fired by ancient stories, ballads and superstitions, and, even more strongly than Hardy, he saw the life of his own day in terms of its history, with every house, every landmark stamped all over by the associations of its past. Further, Scott also envisaged human beings simply and epically—as grand, tragic figures fired by elemental passions. Hardy, therefore, searching for an appropriate form through which to express his inspiration, turned away from his contemporaries—turned away even from George Eliot—to the Waverley novels.

* * *

Before he does anything else, Hardy wants to make you see with your mind's eye the action of the tale he is telling. Indeed his creative impulse seems to have instinctively expressed itself in picture. He, as it were, begins by drawing the curtain aside and giving you something to look at. Of course, all novelists do this in some degree or other, but many—in particular, those who make their characters real by the accuracy with which they portray their conversation or the workings of their minds—do it only slightly. No other English novelist has so great a power of visualisation: it is Hardy's most important weapon, and it is the basis of his whole method. He constructs his book in a series of scenes. We are always told what we are looking at. His technique, oddly enough, is that of the modern director of films. We watch the story. The scene opens; we take it in with our eyes; then someone begins to speak, and the action gradually unfolds itself. Let me take an example:

> Along the road walked an old man. He was white-headed as a mountain, bowed in the shoulders, and faded in general aspect. He wore a glazed hat, an ancient boat-cloak, and shoes; his brass buttons bearing an anchor upon their face. In his hand was a silver-headed walking-stick, which he used as a veritable third leg, perseveringly dotting the ground with its point at every few inches' interval. One would have said that he had been in his day, a naval officer of some sort or other.
>
> Before him stretched the long, laborious road, dry, empty, and

> white. It was quite open to the heath on each side, and bisected that vast dark surface like the parting-line on a head of black hair, diminishing and bending away on the furthest horizon.
>
> The old man frequently stretched his eyes ahead to gaze over the tract that he had yet to traverse. At length he discerned, a long distance in front of him, a moving spot, which appeared to be a vehicle, and it proved to be going the same way as that in which he himself was journeying. It was the single atom of life that the scene contained, and it only served to render the general loneliness more evident. Its rate of advance was slow, and the old man gained upon it sensibly.

It is only after this, when the road and the old man are clearly before us, that Hardy tells us who is he and what he is doing.

This passage, of course, occurs early in the book, but he continues the same method all the way through. One clear picture succeeds another. When the plot rises to its crisis, Hardy's visualising power burns all the brighter. Once more like a film producer, he often makes his climax a silent one. The dramatic moment expresses itself in action rather than words. Consider that great scene between husband and wife, which is the turning-point in the action of "The Return of the Native." Hardy wishes to indicate that although Clym Yeobright has broken—so he thinks—finally with Eustacia, he is still passionately in love with her:

> She hastily dressed herself, Yeobright moodily walking up and down the room the whole of the time. At last all her things were on. Her little hands quivered so violently as she held them to her chin to fasten her bonnet that she could not tie the strings, and after a few moments she relinquished the attempt. Seeing this he moved forward and said, "Let me tie them."
>
> She assented in silence, and lifted her chin. For once at least in her life she was totally oblivious of the charm of her attitude. But he was not, and he turned his eyes aside, that he might not be tempted to softness.
>
> The strings were tied; she turned from him.
>
> "Do you still prefer going away yourself to my leaving you?" he inquired again.
>
> "I do."
>
> "Very well—let it be. And when you will confess to the man I may pity you."
>
> She flung her shawl about her and went downstairs leaving him standing in the room.

It is not the dialogue that makes this scene so moving. The dialogue, as a matter of fact, is rather stilted and inexpressive. But the emotion comes through to us; for it is incarnate in every movement and gesture that Clym and Eustacia are represented as making: the quivering of her hands, his involuntary movement forward, the way he turns aside his eyes lest the spectacle of her beauty should compel him to weaken.

* * *

The chorus is the symbol of the great majority of humdrum mortals, who go on living through their uneventful day, whatever catastrophes may overtake the finer spirits placed among them. Henchard and Eustacia may love and suffer and die; but the rustics go on. It is they who bring the children to birth, dance at the wedding, mourn at the graveyard, and speak the epitaph over the tomb. They are eternal as the earth by which they live. And their very prosaicness anchors the story to reality. It gives the reader a standard of normality by which he can gauge the tremendous heights and depths to which the main characters rise and fall. In his last two big novels, "Tess" and "Jude," he leaves them out. And they lose by it. We feel them to give a distorted picture of life, as his greatest works do not. Nor, for all that they are drawn in so stylised a convention, are these figures unreal. Taken individually, they may seem exaggerated, but taken—as they are meant to be taken—in a corporate mass, they build up a picture of average mankind in its rural manifestation that is carved out of the bedrock of life.

This chorus provides also the chief occasion for Hardy's humour. Humour is not the quality that one might expect to find in him, so grand and so gloomy as he is. But it is there all right. Nor is it incongruous with the rest of his achievement. It is rustic, it is elemental, it is grotesque, it is Gothic, it is traditional. Like the characters who are its subject, it descends directly from Shakespeare and the Elizabethans. Here, again, it differentiates his picture of the rural scene from that of the George Eliot school. In the first place, it is not satirical. Hardy does not make us laugh by the brilliant penetration with which he exposes his characters' foibles and follies. His are the jokes and anecdotes that enliven the evenings in cottage and village inn, and, like theirs, his primary aim is simply to make us laugh. The mood which inspires them is simple, genial enjoyment—the countryman's slow relish of the absurd for its own sake. The main themes are the themes of most country humours—the naïve credulity of yokels and of crusted old eccentrics. We are made to laugh at the immemorial butts of village life—garrulous, reminiscent old grandfathers, henpecked husbands, ludicrous, timid simpletons, and the incongruity between the facts of life and the countryman's ignorant comment on them. Hardy's mode of conveying this humour is also Elizabethan. It is leisurely—there is nothing sharp or slick about it—and it is adorned with a flourish of whimsical fancy. Now and again there is a touch of the grave-diggers in "Hamlet" about it—of the Elizabethan taste for the macabre.

* * *

The Athenians, it is said, grew weary of hearing Aristides called "The Just."[1] And you may, I fear, have grown weary of hearing me call Hardy a creative genius. If so, the following pages may bring you relief; in them I propose to examine Hardy's faults. For he was a faulty writer—so faulty that, in spite of all his gifts, his most successful works are stained by noticeable blemishes, and his least successful are among the worst books that ever came from the pen of a great writer. His genius works in flashes. When the flash comes it is dazzling, but out it goes, and then the reader is left in the dark, groping about, bothered and bewildered. Like Dickens or Scott, Hardy is liable at any moment to let us down. The reason for this is that his equipment for the task was as defective on one side as it was rich on another. The creative gift, the power to apprehend his material aesthetically, he possessed in the highest degree; but, for complete success, a writer cannot rely on the aesthetic qualities alone. He must know how to present his imaginative conceptions to best advantage. For this he needs the critical qualities—the qualities of craft. Hardy was a great artist, but not a great craftsman.

This appears, first of all, in the design of his books. A craftsman's gift shows primarily in his ability to construct a fitting form in which to incarnate his inspiration. Hardy took trouble to do this: and indeed there are many worse designers. His plots are clear; and he sticks to them. All the same, his hold on design is slack and clumsy.

* * *

His creative power is so much stronger than his critical sense that he always disregards probability if it stands in the way of the emotional impression he wishes to make. As a matter of fact, he was not a good judge of probability. The plot of "The Return of the Native" in the form we possess it concludes with the marriage of Venn and Thomasin. But Hardy did not originally intend to end it like this. He had conceived Venn as a sort of benevolent, mysterious spirit, who appears, from no one knows where, to save Thomasin at the crises of her fortunes, and then, once more, vanishes into obscurity. This, however, would have meant that the book ended sadly for everyone concerned in it. Not only Clym and Eustacia, but the virtuous Venn and Thomasin would fail to attain happiness. His publishers told Hardy that the public would not stand for this; and in deference to his publishers Hardy modified his plan. He regretted doing so, because a happy end conflicted with the aesthetic image he had formed of Venn. But the publisher was right, if the claims of probability were to be respected. Venn did want to marry Thomasin. Once she was free, he would cer-

1. Aristides (530?-468? B.C.), Athenian statesman and general [*Editor*].

tainly have asked her, and Thomasin—a clinging, timid woman, left alone when still young—would almost certainly have accepted a lover so attractive and who had treated her so nobly. Hardy does not seem to have considered this. If an idea pleased his imagination, that was good enough for him.

Alas! Hardy did not always have the luck to be saved from himself in this way. We see this in two of his most famous books—"Tess" and "Jude." Here his lawless imagination, unchecked by a publisher's wise hand, bolted with him.

* * *

Again, Hardy is liable to over-emphasize the part played by chance in producing catastrophe. That it should play such a part is, of course, an essential element in his view of life. Chance is the incarnation of the blind forces controlling human destiny. The smallest incident may help to determine a great event. But no author should make chance condition action too often, or he will strain the reader's credulity. For, even if man is not a free agent, the powers that direct his fortunes—his general circumstances, his inherited disposition—are too constant to be diverted at every turn from achieving their ends by some trivial accident. If we are really in love with someone, we shall not be stopped from declaring it just by missing a train. Blind chance must only be introduced in fiction as a determining element at some crucial moment when time is everything, as when Mrs. Yeobright's visit of reconciliation coincides with Eustacia's visit from her lover. In such an instance, Hardy's use of chance is legitimate.

* * *

Further, we ought not to be required to believe that so many unfortunate accidents happened in a short space of time. Once again, let me ask you to consider the catastrophe in "The Return of the Native." We can believe that Mrs. Yeobright called on Eustacia and Clym at the wrong moment. We can also just believe that she was bitten by a poisonous snake on the way home. This double calamity does answer Hardy's purpose by giving the effect of a hostile Fate, driving the characters to destruction, despite all their efforts to save themselves. But when, two chapters later, Eustacia's letter of appeal to Clym goes astray because her messenger forgets to post it, scepticism begins to creep in. Hardy seems to be twisting his plot to suit his purpose. The characters seem puppets all right; but puppets not in the hands of Fate but of the author.

There is another reason for this failure than a mere indiscretion of taste. Hardy insists on this aggregation of evil chances the better to illustrate his doctrine that man is the sport of an indifferent

Destiny. The most fatal error into which he was led by his lack of critical sense was preaching. At moments, obsessed by his views about the universe, he turns from an imaginative creator into a propagandist.

* * *

Here at last we come to the central significance of the truth about his genius, the key to his riddle, the figure in his carpet. This is the fact that strikes us, now that his figure has receded far enough into the past for its true place in the perspective of English literature to be visible. Hardy was a man born after his time—the last lonely representative of an ancient race, strayed, by some accident of Destiny, into the alien world of the later nineteenth century. His circumstances were peculiar. The society in which he was brought up was that in which the ancient mode of life lingered longest. Rural Wessex was still feudal pre-industrial Wessex, with its villages clustering round the great houses and church, with its long-established families and time-hallowed customs, its whole habit of mind moulded by the tradition of the past. Further, this life found in Hardy a subject especially susceptible to its influence. He was the typical child of such a society—simple, unselfconscious, passionate, instinctively turning for his imaginative nourishment to the fundamental drama and comedy of human life, responsive to the basic joys and sorrows of mankind, to the love of home, to the beauty of spring and sunshine, the charm of innocence; to fun and conviviality and the grandeur of heroism; to the horror of death and the terrors of superstition. His talent was of a piece with the rest of him—naïve and epic, massive and careless, quaint and majestic, ignorant of the niceties of craft, delighting shamelessly in a sensational tale, but able to rise to the boldest flights of imagination. So far from being the first of the modern school of novelists, Hardy is the last representative of the tradition and spirit of the Elizabethan drama.

The last—but with a difference; for the age in which he lived made it impossible for him to perceive in that human life which is his subject, the same significance as the Elizabethans did. They saw man against a religious background, as a Lord of Creation, a Child of God, a soul born to immortality. The scientific and rationalist view of the universe which Hardy found himself reluctantly forced to accept made him unable to take such a view. To him, man was the late and transient product of some automatic principle of life which had cast him into a universe of which he knew nothing, and to whom—as far as he could see—his hopes and fears were of no significance whatever. The consequence of this is that Hardy's picture differs profoundly from that of his ancestors. The old world seems very changed when we look at it in the sunless light of the new science. Hardy's England may have the same features as the old England; but, surveyed against the new cosmic background, it has shrunk to a tiny ephemeral fragment of matter, lost in a measureless universe and dissolving swiftly to extinction. Hardy's characters may be the Elizabethan characters; but how different they look when we realise that the fierce passions animating them are ineffectual to influence their destiny, that their ideal beliefs and fantasies fleet but for a moment across a background of nothingness. A profound irony shadows Hardy's figures. Though we enter with heartfelt sympathy into their hopes and joys and fears and agonies, yet always we are aware that soon they will be gone for ever, and that behind them stands the indifferent universe, working out its inscrutable purpose, careless whether they live or die. It is still the Elizabethan world, but the Elizabethan world with the lights going down; and gathering round it the dusk that heralds its final oblivion.

Such a view entails a loss; dusk is darker and colder than noonday. And, obscured by its encroaching shadow, Clym and Henchard loom somehow dimmer than Othello. Bereft of their power to control their fates, the Elizabethan figures dwindle in vitality. And not only in vitality: Hardy's characters retain the Elizabethan grandeur, but not the Elizabethan glory. For that glory was the reflected radiance of their spiritual significance. Immortal souls, they towered over mortal matter, proud of their stature. How they dominate circumstance! how their spirit rises to resist the challenge of catastrophe! Even the moment of their death is irradiated by a terrible splendour. Is not death the culmination of their lives, the assertion of the victory of their spirit over mortality? For Hardy's characters, on the other hand, death is only the same meaningless and haphazard extinction as must in the end overtake alike the greatest hero and the meanest insect. They confront it with outward fortitude or outward resignation, they may even welcome it as a release from the intolerable agony of living, but always they meet it with despair in their hearts. Shakespeare's tragic emotion is a blazing flame; Hardy's broods like a thundercloud.

Yet we cannot regret his darker interpretation of the ancient scene. For in it lies the originality of his vision. We learn to see the old England as we have not seen it before, just because it is presented to us in the light of Hardy's disillusionment. And what his vision loses in splendour, it gains in poignancy. The tragic intensity of Hardy's work is increased by his conviction that there is a fundamental dissonance between man and his environment, by the ironical contrast he draws between poor striving humanity and the ruthless omnipotent Destiny with which he vainly contends. On the other hand, this contrast could not achieve its tension if

Hardy's temperament and talent had not been of the old type. So many pessimists fail to dishearten us because we feel them to be persons with a weak stomach for life, who feel gloomy because they are congenitally unable to appreciate the normal satisfactions of human existence. But Hardy had more than the normal zest for life, more than the normal fellow-feeling for other men. He shared their hopes and their pleasures; he appreciated to the full the dignity of their virtue. Coming from such a man, this considered and despairing judgement on life has a terrifying power.

The fact, too, that his talent was of the old kind enabled him to achieve effects unattainable by most modern rationalist writers. Though he may have disbelieved in the ultimate significance of the spirit, his imagination continued to express itself in spiritual terms. It is striking that at the climax of his drama he often sounds a supernatural note. Henchard's neglect of the weather doctor's warning is a contributing cause of his catastrophe; Eustacia goes to her death the very moment that her waxen effigy is wasting away before the fire of the avenging Susan. Even in "Tess," where Hardy is openly in rebellion against the old creeds, he strikes the supernatural chord. As Tess starts on her ill-fated marriage journey the evil omens gather round her as thickly as though she were the heroine of a saga. And when Hardy comes forward to draw his final moral, he does it in strange terms for an atheist—"The President of the Immortals (in Aeschylean phrase) had ended his sport with Tess." He was careful afterwards to explain that this was a metaphor. He also remarks in another place: "Half my time—particularly when writing verse—I 'believe' (in the modern sense of the term) in spectres, mysterious voices, intuitions, omens, dreams, haunted places, etc. But I do not believe in them in the old sense of the word for all that." No doubt he was perfectly sincere in these statements; but the fact remains that his breeding made him so incurably anthropomorphic that when his creative genius begins working, it instinctively embodies the forces conditioning human life in anthropomorphic terms.

* * *

The Christian virtues—fidelity, compassion, humility—were the most beautiful to him; and the same integrity that compelled him to accept the grim view of life which his reason told him was the true one, kept him also faithful to what his instinct told him was the highest ideal of virtue. These virtues might be of no avail in the universe; they might be born only to strive and suffer and be defeated; all the same, he ranged himself under their banner. Indeed, whatever may be said to the contrary by Mr. Eliot and Mr. Chesterton[2] and other professional champions of orthodoxy, Hardy

2. Gilbert Keith Chesterton (1874-1936), well-known English critic, biographer, and poet [*Editor*].

was one of the most Christian spirits that ever lived. The ideal of character he presents to us—in Diggory and Tess, Marty and Giles—is, far more than that presented by many officially orthodox writers, a specifically Christian ideal: the ideal set up in the Beatitudes, meek, merciful, pure in heart and peace-making, its highest virtue a self-sacrificing love for others. Hardy's very pessimism is of a kind only possible to one indissolubly wedded to Christian standards of value. Christian teachers have always said that there was no alternative to Christianity but pessimism, that if Christian doctrine was not true, life was a tragedy. Hardy quite agreed with them. But he could not think the doctrine true, all the same. He found it impossible to believe the Christian hope.

He may have been mistaken in this. Myself, I think he was. But he can only be respected for the honesty which compelled him to accept a philosophy of the universe so repugnant to the deepest instincts of his heart. And still more must he be honoured for that elevation of soul which enabled him to maintain the Christian temper without the help of the Christian consolation. Bitter and hard as he conceived life to be, Hardy himself was never hard, nor, save in a rare impulse of exasperation, was he bitter. The burning flame of his charity blazed all the higher for the infinite and unrelieved blackness of the universe, in which it was the solitary gleam of light.

HARVEY CURTIS WEBSTER

[Pessimism in *The Return of the Native*]†

At any rate, it is unquestionable that *The Return of the Native* is the most pessimistic of the early novels. From the first description of Egdon Heath until the close of the story, this dreary and unfertile waste seems to symbolize the indifference with which Nature views the pathetic fate of human beings. Occasionally the reader is likely to look upon the long-enduring barrenness and apparent purposelessness of the heath as a sign of its kinship to man, to feel that it is like man, slighted and enduring. More frequently, its somber beauty, which, Hardy tells us, is the only kind of beauty that thinking mankind can any longer appreciate, reminds us that man is of no more significance than an insect against its far-extending barrenness. It is the unsympathetic background for the human scene. What happens to man is not its concern. Like the forces of Nature, it has participated passively in

† From Harvey Curtis Webster, *On A Darkling Plain: The Art and Thought of Thomas Hardy* (1964), pp. 120-25. Reprinted by permission of Archon Books and the author.

man's slow and unhappy progress through disillusive centuries, unconcerned with the joys or sorrows of petty humankind.

What the dreary atmosphere of Egdon Heath makes us feel, the author's interpolations emphasize. The modern facial expression portrays a "view of life as a thing to be put up with." A long train of disillusive centuries have shown the defects of natural law and the quandary in which their operation has placed man. Life causes one to set aside the vision of what ought to be and induces a listless making the best of the world as it is.

More than in any other Hardy novel, we feel the power of the forces that control man's destiny. Heartless Circumstance, this time *not* viewed as an environment that can be contended against, has placed Eustacia Vye in a situation in which her gifts are a plague rather than a blessing. Natural law leads man from one mistake to another. Chance, in the shape of accident and coincidence, joins itself with these other unsympathetic powers to assure man's unhappiness. Diggory Venn accidentally misunderstands the terms of Mrs. Yeobright's bequest to Clym and Thomasin. As a consequence, Eustacia and Mrs. Yeobright misunderstand each other, and Clym and his mother quarrel openly. Mrs. Yeobright comes to see Clym to attempt a reconciliation. When she knocks at his door, Eustacia hears Clym say "mother" and does not know that he is talking in his sleep. Mrs. Yeobright believes her son refuses her entrance and starts her weary journey home. She tells of her son's treatment to the passing Johnny Nonsuch, who later tells Clym of her bitter reproaches—which no one would have known otherwise, for she lies down to rest, is bitten by an adder, and dies before reaching her home. Clym's feeling that he and Eustacia are guilty of what a chain of coincidences actually caused is responsible for the estrangement of the two. And when a letter that might have ended their misunderstanding comes to Eustacia, she does not find it but goes to her unhappy and accidental death. Undoubtedly Hardy believes that there is nothing actively malign in Egdon Heath, in natural law, or in the play of Circumstance or accident; but the very indifference of these forces to the fate of human beings results in such unhappiness that we are likely to assume that sinister gods control the action.

Against the somber atmosphere of an indifferent and Chance-guided universe, the characters move in accordance with natural law. Eustacia's physical attractiveness compels the love of Charley, Clym, and Wildeve. By a similar force Eustacia is drawn to Wildeve and Clym. None of them is fitted for each other, but their imaginations cause them to believe that their ideas of each other are real. Disillusionment and pain result.

* * *

In addition to the pains consequent upon love, the two most intelligent characters, Clym and Eustacia, feel the antilogy of making figments feel. Eustacia's view of life was begot by her situation on her nature. Partly because of the swift change from the gay society of Budmouth to the Egdon region, more importantly because of her innate tendency to seek the impossible, she is always yearning for what she cannot have. She is "eternally unreconciled" to Egdon Heath. She longs for a grand passion. She wishes to find a great hero to whom she can give her love wholeheartedly. She wants what is called "life": music, poetry, passion, war. Like so many Hardyan characters, she has unrealizable desires that she would realize. Inevitably she discovers none of the things she wants. In this "ill-conceived" world, "cruel" heaven makes sport with her, until, tired with its play, it kills her.

Eustacia's predicament is an exaggerated form of the quandary in which Hardy believes intelligent human beings find themselves. Clym is in many respects like Hardy himself. He has reached the stage where the grimness of the general situation first becomes clear. He realizes the antilogy which exists between man's emotional longings and the possibility of their realization. Yet, just as Hardy did when he wrote *The Poor Man and the Lady*, he wants to make the world over so that it will suit him, and—again like Hardy—he hates to find finiteness in his Eden. Because of his knowledge that realization is impossible, he is discontented. Thought upon the "general situation" has even affected his physical appearance, for thought is a disease of the flesh, incompatible with emotional development and the perception of the evil in things. So Clym is, in the same limited sense that Hardy is, a pessimist. He would like to die and get rid of the horror of existence. It is better not to have been born; but, being born, one should strive to get out of life with as little shame as possible.

This philosophy, however, does not keep Clym from having a distinct desire to ameliorate. He does not acquiesce any more than Eustacia. But, as he finds nothing very great in the highest walks of life or very low in the lowest, he is primarily interested in bettering the way of life of the peasants. He combats such superstitions as those of Susan Nonsuch. He is a moral preacher, an advocate of high thinking and plain living. He wishes to teach men that the knowledge of wisdom is more important than the knowledge of wealth. He hopes to raise the peasant class as a whole, not the individual at the expense of the class. He is not intent upon cramming unnecessary knowledge of any creed down the throats of the peasants. But he does hope to teach them an ethic, from which creeds and philosophies are omitted, that is based upon the Sermon on the Mount, the eleventh commandment, and those moral ideas that are common to all good men. Clym does not succeed any more than Hardy did with *The Poor Man and the Lady* and *The Hand of Ethelberta,* for, as the author comments, Clym is too far in advance of his age, and the peasants wish material before spiritual comfort. Again, like Hardy, his failure to effect any notable change in social circumstance throws him back upon a pessimism as deep as that which pervades the novel in which he is a character. But his philosophy is never blankly pessimistic, for, while recognizing the defects in the general plan, he still continues to advocate the elimination of remediable ills. He is ahead of his time, not all times. Like his creator, he continues to see grounds for future hope even in moods of the most unrelieved depression.

Hardy, then, like his character, sees some hope in the future. But his perception of the consolation which may be found for evil times does not stop at the same point the perceptions of his chief character do, for he inserts in his story two illustrations of a way of life that makes living endurable even when it is faced by the worst contingencies. Neither Diggory Venn nor Thomasin Yeobright expects much of life. They lack both the infinite aspirations and the discontent of the major characters in the book. When Venn is disappointed a second time in his love for Thomasin, he suffers only a limited pain because he does not expect much. For him, disappointments seem the natural preface to realization. Similarly Thomasin, though her circumstances cause her somewhat more unhappiness, is able to attain a measure of content because of her willingness to accept the inevitable. It is this quality in her, Hardy tells us, that accounts for her becoming reasonably happy, while Clym, Wildeve, and Eustacia find little but suffering during the course of their lives. These two characters who do not rebel unnecessarily achieve in the end a content impossible for those who refuse to accept their lot. * * *

Even in *The Return of the Native,* then, one does see some basis for hope. Those who accept the inevitable are at least not *un*happy, and it is possible that efforts to change things will succeed eventually. But the book is in the main illustrative of the more somber side of Hardy's outlook. Tortured by natural law, unrealizable desires, Circumstance, and Chance, against a background inimical to man, in a time out of joint, man is an unhappy creature. The reader feels convinced that the author, in common with Clym and Sophocles, believes that not to be born is best.

R. W. STALLMAN

Hardy's Hour-Glass Novel†

I[n] the commonwealth I would by contraries Execute all things.
—THE TEMPEST: II, 1, 147-148

The ground-plan of *The Return of the Native*, the only novel in which Hardy consciously attempted to observe the Unities * * * is contrived with the symmetry of an architect's blueprint. Its geography reads like a surveyor's map. Its chronology seems plotted by an almanac-maker. Its architectonics of Time, Space, and Action are diagrammatic. The narrative, running the cycle of a year and a day, is spaced by the two signal fires of November fifth, 1842 and 1843; these are its poles of Time and Action. The axis of Space is Rainbarrow, for within the immediate radii of Rainbarrow all action is located. The plot is a piece of geometry. The key to it is a geometric pattern. My critical interest is this structural interest: to discover the geometric pattern and to diagram the structure of the novel.

The geometric pattern is the figure of an hour-glass.

The structure of Hardy's hour-glass novel can be summed up in this one diagrammatic symbol.

* * *

In Hardy's design, furthermore, the structural symbol is represented in an actual hour-glass, the hour-glass of Eustacia Vye. She discovers it the first time we meet her, where she stands fixed "as the pivot of this circle of the heath-country" beside a fire of illuminating coals. What those coals revealed, you recall, was "a small object, *which turned out to be an hour-glass, though she wore a watch*. She blew long enough to show that the sand had all slipped through." Why does Eustacia, you ask, require an hour-glass *and* a watch? Is it not that Eustacia with her watch *tells* Time and with her hour-glass *perceives* Time? That she requires both hour-glass and watch is indicative not only of her own philosophical mind but also of her creator's. Hardy is making a double use, a structural and a philosophical use, of Eustacia's hour-glass. Even as her telescope is the symbol of Space, so her hour-glass is the symbol of Time, of Hardy's time-consciousness and of his concern with the time-motif. But the hour-glass itself is also the emblem—the aesthetic pattern—of Time's turnabout of events.

† From R. W. Stallman, "Hardy's Hour-Glass Novel," *Sewanee Review*, Volume LV, Number 2 (April-June, 1947), pp. 283-94, 296.

Let us begin with Hardy's philosophical use of the symbol (the hour-glass as the symbol of Time). Eustacia in her slow walks to recover from depression of spirits "carried her grandfather's telescope and her grandmother's hour-glass—the latter because of *a peculiar pleasure she derived from watching a material representation of time's gradual glide away*." The sands that clock the Moment Now are the "material representation" of Time, of "real-time" in the Bergsonian sense. In her hypnotic gazing upon the sands of Time, Eustacia seeks to penetrate beyond mere "clock-time" into the secret of "real-time." Like the author of *Tess*, Eustacia is intensely conscious of "the flux and reflux, the rhythm of change [that] alternate and persist in everything under the sky." Her time-sense is telescoped. Hence "To dance with a man is to concentrate a twelve-month's regulation fire upon him in the fragment of an hour." Her point-present awareness is intensified: "The actual moment of a thing is soon gone," she remarks. And the Past, apart from its possible consequences upon the Present, is dead, is unreal.

> "Wait, let it go—see how our time is slipping, slipping, slipping!" She pointed towards the half-eclipsed moon.
>
> "You are too mournful."
>
> "No. *Only I dread to think of anything beyond the present.* What is [the Present], we know. We are together now, and it is unknown how long we shall be so . . ." (III, iii).

Since real existence for Eustacia is in the Present, the only "real-time" for her is Now; hence her rapt attention to Time's hurried flight, and her despairing attempts to check it. "The sand has nearly slipped away, I see, and the eclipse is creeping on more and more. Don't go yet! Stop till the hour has run itself out." Eustacia's time-sense of "real-time" is to be contrasted with Thomasin's time-sense of "clock-time." Eustacia in her point-present time-sense, in her pained awareness of this transitory Moment Now, is the opposite of Thomasin, who "is impressed with a sense of the intolerable slowness of time" and who braids her hair "according to a calendric system."

Eustacia's questioning delight in peering into hour-glass Time and telescopic Space identifies her with her creator—with Hardy's own probing into these two basic forms of philosophic thought. Witness his use of Time as an instrument of Fate (as in *Far from the Madding Crowd:* "the moment was the turning-point of a career"), his ironic commentaries on Time in the Wessex world (as in *Tess of the D'Urbervilles*: "The man to love rarely coincides with the hour of loving"), and his repetitious personification of the time-motif now as "dicing Time," now as "Time's Laughing-stocks," again as "Father Time," or again as "Time the archsatirist." Witness his frontispiece to the Wessex Poems: a sketch of an hour-glass drawn in Hardy's own hand.

* * *

I suppose an uncommon event is at its most exceptional, contrived in its most geometric form, when initial circumstances are ironically reversed. What is unique about *The Return of the Native* is its schematic figuring of reversed events whereby the fortunes of the lovers are again and again turned upside down. The human pair, fixed in Time like glass, are simultaneously turned contrariwise, their crisscross fortunes inverted with each shift of the hour-glass sands. From start to finish, Fate or Chance or Coincidence or Time keep tumbling the hour-glass over and over.

The Return of the Native resolves structurally into a mechanical concatenation of seven hour-glass plots. The species of diagram for this geometric counter-turning is a sequence of seven crisscross designs:

(1)⧗ (2)⧗ (3)⧗ (4)⧗ (5)⧗ (6)⧗ (7)⧗

The first two hour-glass reversals are caused by a single chance happening; a single fateful incident causes the third and fourth; initial circumstances of the third are determined by the issue of the second; the last two turnabouts are determined by the issue of the fifth, which has been prepared for by the ill-falling out of preceding events. Each reversed situation is thus logically located in a rigid system of causation. Double turnabouts (occurring in 1 and 4, 2 and 5, 3 and 6) contrive three full revolutions of the glass. Irony upon irony, Hardy's deterministic machinery grinds on to its appointed end.

The first reversal turns upon the accidental hitch in the marriage of Thomasin and Wildeve: their marriage license is made out for the wrong place. Wildeve, by taking advantage of this slip, reverses his position both to Thomasin and to her aunt. *Where earlier Mrs. Yeobright by forbidding the banns had Wildeve in her power, Wildeve by evading the marriage has Mrs. Yeobright at last in his.*

* * *

The reversal of initial positions resulting from this chance miscalculation in their marriage-license constitutes the second hour-glass plot. *Thomasin, who was once the pursued and who is now the pursuer, is given over by Wildeve for Eustacia, who before had been given over for Thomasin.* It is because of Eustacia that Wildeve goes "further in the business"; their relationship forms the third turnabout.

The hour-glass of this third turnabout is weighed first against

Eustacia, then against Wildeve. She has drawn the still unmated moth to her signal fire:

> "I determined you should come; and you have come! *I have shown my power*. A mile and half hither, and a mile and half back again to your home—three miles in the dark for me. *Have I not shown my power?*" (I, vi).

But Eustacia—an irony again—counts upon a power she does not now possess. By the scant facts that Chance has provided her (by the highway encounter of Diggory Venn and Captain Vye), she misinterprets Wildeve's motives. Chance, not love for Eustacia, brings Wildeve to her yet unwed. Even now, like Thomasin, she is his pursuer. The choice is his: "The scales are balanced so nicely," Wildeve observes, "that a feather would turn them." "Wildeve's backward and forward play," as Diggory Venn calls it, only increases his attraction and intensifies her desire; now that another favors him, Eustacia desires him most. For Wildeve, conversely, Eustacia's preciousness increases "in geometrical progression" with each advance in another's desire for her. This device of injecting situations with a drop of irony ("Often a drop of irony into an indifferent situation," Hardy remarks, "renders the whole piquant") is a fundamental in Hardy's artistic code. The intervention of the reddleman forces Wildeve to make his choice. And this shifts the hour-glass sands and shapes the third reversal: *Eustacia, who before pursued Wildeve, is now pursued by him.*

Diggory Venn's proposal to Thomasin is the stick by which Mrs. Yeobright beats Wildeve into marriage with her niece. And thus the fourth hour-glass situation results: *Whereas Mrs. Yeobright,* without this weapon of Venn's proposal, *had been in Wildeve's power, she now in turn has him in her power*. One full revolution of the glass is charted by this double reversal in their relationship.

(1) Wildeve in the power of Mrs. Yeobright;
Mrs. Yeobright in the power of Wildeve.

(2) Mrs. Yeobright in the power of Wildeve;
Wildeve in the power of Mrs. Yeobright.

Again, as the third consequence of the reddleman's proposal, the fifth turnabout is framed: *The jilted suitor is forced to pursue the woman who before pursued him*. For to lose both women "was too ironical an issue to be endured. He could only decently save himself by Thomasin." Once more the hour-glass has been turned full cycle:

(2) Wildeve in the power of Thomasin;
Thomasin in the power of Wildeve.

(5) Thomasin in the power of Wildeve;
Wildeve in the power of Thomasin.

That Wildeve's bride should be given away by her former rival is a final ironic climax.

By the casual confluence of untoward events, from Wildeve's fantastic dice-game and its issue in Eustacia's quarrel with Mrs. Yeobright to the fateful incident of the closed door and the resulting divorce between Eustacia and Clym, once more Eustacia is forced to pursue Wildeve. This situation shapes the sixth hour-glass: *Wildeve, who before pursued Eustacia, is now pursued by her.* The hour-glass of their courtship has been turned completely upside down. For in the situation which shaped the third reversal, Eustacia, who before pursued Wildeve, was in turn pursued by him. This double reversal is the third and final full revolution of the glass:

(3) Eustacia in the power of Wildeve;
Wildeve in the power of Eustacia.

(6) Wildeve in the power of Eustacia;
Eustacia in the power of Wildeve.

Coalescing with this sixth turnabout is the inverted relationship between Eustacia and Clym. *In the beginning Eustacia,* while Wildeve pursued her, *was the pursuer of Clym.* Yet *in the end,* when the deterministic interlocking of coincidences that first brought them together finally thrusts them apart, *Clym is the pursuer of Eustacia.* In this reversal, the seventh in Hardy's chain of inverted plots, the sands of Fate (Time and Chance) are against Clym. Time, in Clym's undelivered letter, and Chance, in Eustacia's mishap at Shadwater Weir, hasten on the last pyramiding of the hour-glass sands. No wonder Eustacia has dreaded "to think of anything beyond the present," when everything in her future has been so tool-marked and pinned down upon this blueprint of her hour-glass world.

This analysis reduces *The Return of the Native* to seven structural hour-glass plots. But extra-structural hour-glass patterns recur throughout the book. The "ru-um-tum-tum" turnabout in the relationship between Wildeve and Diggory Venn suggests that pattern. On reading Eustacia's letter of rejection, Wildeve asks:

> "Do you know what is in this letter?"
> The reddleman hummed a tune.
> "Can't you answer me?" asked Wildeve warmly.
> "*Ru-um-tum-tum,*" *sang the reddleman.*
>
> . . . .
>
> "But of all the odd things that ever I knew, the oddest is that you should so run counter to your own interests as to bring this to me."
>
> "My interests?"

"Certainly. 'Twas your interest not to do anything which would send me courting Thomasin again, now she has accepted you—or something like it. Mrs. Yeobright says you are to marry her. 'Tisn't true, then?"

"Good Lord! I heard of this before, but didn't believe it. When did she say so?"

Wildeve began humming as the reddleman had done.

"I don't believe it now," cried Venn.

"Ru-um-tum-tum," sang Wildeve.

A second extra-structural hour-glass pattern is framed by the two dice-games between Wildeve and Christian Cantle and between Wildeve and Diggory Venn, in which by chance counterturns Mrs. Yeobright is outwitted by Wildeve, who in turn is outwitted by Venn.

* * *

The union of Eustacia and Clym was ill-fated from the start; but then, any love she might win was destined, as Eustacia surmised, *to "sink simultaneously with the sand in the glass."* For the missed opportunities involved in the counter-journeys across the heath by Mrs. Yeobright and by her son, Eustacia is at fault; yet instead of blaming herself she blames some "colossal Prince of the World, who had framed her situation and ruled her lot."

* * *

"Take all the varying hates felt by Eustacia Vye toward the heath, and translate them into loves, and you have the heart of Clym." Or diagram this symmetrical antithesis by an hour-glass pattern: Eustacia's hatred of the heath simultaneously shifts to love of Paris as Clym's hatred of Paris shifts to love of the heath. The disparity of opposing tensions between them increases as their schematic lines converge and their ill-conceived desires crisscross. Again, equally diagrammatic is the extra-structural hour-glass pattern of those crisscross-journeys over the heath—Clym going off towards his mother's house for the same purpose for which she has just come to his. The heath is at the center of the hour-glass of *The Return of the Native.*

* * *

My point is that the single coincidence, *because it has been prepared for,* is neither illegitimate nor incredible. Critical scrutiny should focus, not upon the single incredible coincidence, but upon the entire incredible machine. I conclude that what is incredible about that machine is the fact that its resultant tragedy becomes so wholly credible.

* * *

Its mechanics are integral to the total aesthetic effect, even as its coincidence is integral to the mechanics. In the very novel which most consistently geometrizes its mechanics the triumph over mere mechanics is at its greatest. In this triumph of total aesthetic effect lies the wonder of Hardy's art.

JOHN HOLLOWAY

[Philosophy, Image, and Language in Hardy's Fiction]†

The sages themselves throw light here, and their own statements do something to resolve the difficulties. They all knew that what they had to offer was special in kind; and they take trouble to show how it is confirmed and given meaning in its own way, or how, to grasp it properly, the reader requires a special insight or sense. It is interesting to trace, at a rather earlier time, this preoccupation with how a 'philosophy of life' is understood and confirmed in Coleridge's prose. 'I assume a something, the proof of which no man can *give* to another, yet every man can *find* for himself. If any man assert, that he *can* not find it, I am *bound* to disbelieve him! I cannot do otherwise without unsettling the very foundations of my own moral Nature.' Coleridge might almost be called the founder in modern England of this kind of thought, and his influence on both Newman and Carlyle was very great. Carlyle takes this attitude further. He emphasizes that he has answers to ultimate questions; that his answers offer themselves to imagination rather than logic; that they are not recondite, for everyone can read them in his own heart, from 'a felt indubitable certainty of Experience'; and finally that failure to do so is a kind of blindness and a kind of viciousness. This is how he brings home that what he calls 'Life-Philosophy' has its own mode of confirmation. He is aware, too, that a difficulty remains to be overcome about its meaning. 'To *know*; to get into the truth of anything, is ever a mystic act,—of which the best logics can but babble on the surface.' Hence he constantly invites the reader to meditate humbly and carefully on some assertion that he admits is essentially simple. The kind of understanding that he has at heart is a kind which merely supervenes upon dutiful attentiveness.

Newman's discussion of this sort of knowledge was so full that it must be left until last. But the other writers in the list give a picture much like Carlyle's, though usually more sketchily. Disraeli often conveys a sense of the matter through the characters of his heroes: they are concerned about ultimate questions; they learn by a kind of trustful meditation that supplements reason with imagi-

† From John Holloway, *The Victorian Sage: Studies in Argument* (Archon Books, 1962), pp. 5-6, 246-47, 250-53, 258-61, 264-66, 277, 279-83, 286-87. Reprinted by permission of the publishers.

nation; and the understanding to which they finally come is something concrete and particular, which abstract formulae cannot express. Utilitarian abstractions are his constant butt, and his remark, 'the fallacy of the great Utilitarian scheme consists in confounding wisdom with knowledge' indicates just the distinction all these writers were trying to draw. Arnold says less than the others, but even he mentions the essential simplicity of the knowledge that matters to him, and how it is something which cannot be learnt off like an abstract formula, but most come gradually alive in our minds, through a right disposition chiefly. George Eliot says enough to show that her idea of what a 'solution' to 'life' was like, and how it could be known, closely followed Carlyle's. The contrast she draws between 'feeling the truth of a commonplace' and merely 'knowing' is worth a mention in passing.

Perhaps Hardy's insistence that the more general meaning of what he wrote did not really stand or fall by logical consistency was self-defence, and not entirely relevant here. But an interesting passage in *The Return of the Native* shows him fully conscious that there is something special about the proof and the meaning of what Disraeli calls 'wisdom'. Shortly after Clym Yeobright's return in this novel to the village of his childhood, he and his mother argue about what is meant by 'doing well'. Clearly, this is just the sort of point upon which the sage, in his rôle as moralist, has something to say. Hardy writes that Clym found he could not prove his point by 'a logic that, even under favouring circumstances, is almost too coarse a vehicle for the subtlety of the argument'. But he is able to convey a sense of his outlook by more intangible methods. Because Clym had inherited some of his view from his mother he 'could not fail to awaken a reciprocity in her through her feelings, if not by arguments'; and later on Hardy supplements this: 'he had despaired of reaching her by argument, and it was almost a discovery to him that he could reach her by a magnetism which was as superior to words as words are to yells'. The disparagement of logic as not subtle enough, the emphasis on feelings and on reawakening dormant understanding to a new life, the use of a word like 'magnetism', and the suggestion that this is proof of a higher kind, are all typical of the sage's notion of his own insights and how to communicate them.

* * *

A recent penetrating study of Hardy, A. J. Guerard's *Thomas Hardy, the Novels and Stories*, has suggested that much is lost through excessive interest in Hardy's philosophy. 'Academic schematizing . . . has . . . fastened on certain structural and didactic aspects of the major Wessex novels to the neglect of much else which remains readable and can even be useful to the novelist writing today.' One should not, Guerard continues, 'reduce . . . a novel's meaning to some philosophy of life . . . theorize oneself quite away from the living complex of the work of art, and the impression it actually makes'. Hardy would have welcomed Guerard's approach. Several times he denies that he is advancing any general theory of things, anything that can be tested by its abstract consistency; and the word 'impression' is his own favourite term for whatever sense of life his novels convey. 'Like former productions of this pen', he writes, '*Jude the Obscure* is simply an endeavour to give shape and coherence to a series of seemings, or personal impressions, the question of their consistency or . . . their permanence . . . being regarded as not of the first moment'; or again, 'a novel is an impression, not an argument'. But one can easily see that Hardy's attitude is not wholly clear; in the General Preface to the Wessex Edition of the novels he writes 'that these impressions have been condemned as "pessimistic" shows a curious muddle-headedness . . . it must be obvious that there is a higher characteristic of philosophy than pessimism, or . . . optimism . . .—which is truth'. He writes elsewhere that since some 'philosophy of life' was necessary in an epic work like *The Dynasts,* he used that which he had 'denoted' in the early verse and also to some extent in the prose. * * * Plainly we must strike some sort of balance between Hardy's desire not to be seen as a theorizing philosopher, and his clear conception of himself as somehow giving expression to a 'philosophy' all the same.

This can be done. A Hardy novel is not an argument, because it *is* an impression: not idle romance, but the work 'in all sincerity of purpose' of one who though modestly 'a mere tale-teller' is nevertheless a thinker and a realist, and 'writes down how the things of the world strike him'. Wessex was, for him, not a place simply of picturesque oddity, a colourful geographical freak. Its people 'were meant to be typically and essentially those of any and every place where

Thought's the slave of life, and life time's fool,[1]

[that is, *every* place]—beings in whose hearts and minds that which is apparently local should be really universal'. It imposed no limitations on an author interested in the central realities of life; its humble dramas could rise to 'a grandeur and unity truly Sophoclean'. Surely, in view of these assertions, Guerard's warning is not a discouragement but an encouragement to apply to Hardy our present method. If anything can do justice to its dual aspect, as embodying a considered view of the world, and as in essence

1. Shakespeare, *King Henry IV, Part I.V.iv* [*Editor*].

remote from theorizing abstractions, it will be an attempt to recreate the author's 'idiosyncratic mode of regard' by studying the whole texture of his work. * * *

* * * It should be recognized, in the first place, that Hardy's major novels rarely or perhaps never actually turn on their improbabilities. They develop through basic and abiding factors of character and environment; and it is usually clear that if the incident Hardy describes had not occurred, some other detail could soon enough have brought about the same ultimate result. There is no real feeling that had Angel Clare received Tess's letter and read it, he would have torn it up and cheerfully married her; no real possibility that Clym and Eustacia would have lived happily ever after, had his mother's knocking at the door only wakened him as he slept; no life of success for the Mayor of Casterbridge, had he not read his wife's last letter too soon because it had been faultily sealed. It is a mistake to think that Hardy's novels move through arbitrary accidents to a sad end, in the way that for example the novels of Fielding or Dickens often move through accidents to a happy end. The potentialities of change are in the people, and Hardy merely waits until what in *The Dynasts* he calls the 'listless sequence' of events produces something that moves the action a step further on.

There are, in Hardy, unexpected or apparently unlikely incidents of rather another kind. These are incidents which do not advance the story, but illustrate its significances more or less symbolically. * * * When Mrs. Yeobright, exhausted and at the point of death, sits on the lonely Heath after her futile visit to Clym, she sees a heron flying above her into the sunset, gleaming like silver as his body catches the light, and seeming to symbolize the happy release from earth to heaven that she has begun to long for. Incidents like these raise a point of some interest. At first, they may seem improbable: but on reflection, it seems likely that something of the kind could well have occurred each time, provided only that we have regard, as Hardy has, to a wider range of fact than most people normally consider. And for these symbolic incidents not to seem vain and artificial, Hardy must in some way persuade his readers that this wider range of observation is not fanciful, but justified seriously. He must, in the given cases, persuade them that the lives of humans and of birds are related by more than whimsical significances. Hardy's success or failure in these incidents can only be judged against his whole view of the quality of human life and the human environment.

* * *

The very word 'Nature' can confuse Hardy's view of things. A shallow and uncomprehending reading of Wordsworth, for example—a reading which ignores the deeper significance of his poetry—has by now made it difficult to use this word except for scenery, for vistas and panoramas that in one way or another can please the observer's eye, and that may provide the novelist with a picturesque static backcloth which his characters may adorn, and ignore. 'Nature' for Hardy is scarcely picturesque, clearly not static, and above all not a backcloth. It is the working and changing system of the whole world—Nature in the older sense of Chaucer or Spenser or Pope (for they had one sense in common), though with a detailed knowledge of its operations which none of these displayed or perhaps possessed. Nor is it a backcloth against which to see human activity; it is a system which includes that activity, profoundly modifies it, and ultimately controls it. But this impress of the system of Nature on man's life must be seen as following from the life that Hardy sees in nature itself. To explore this is therefore the next problem.

As always, this cannot be tidily expressed in a simple formula, because it is a sense of something, an imaginative insight. But in tracing how Hardy mediated his insight to the reader, it may help to distinguish four of its most distinctive and prominent aspects:

First, Nature is an organic living whole, and its constituent parts, even the inanimate parts, have a life and personality of their own.

Second, it is unified on a great scale through both time and space.

Third, it is exceedingly complex and varied, full of unexpected details of many different kinds—details that are sometimes even quaint or bizarre.

Fourth, for all that, these heterogeneous things are integrated, however obscurely, into a system of rigid and undeviating law.

All these aspects may to some extent be traced through Hardy's account, in *The Woodlanders*, of Giles' and Marty's special understanding of their native woodland country:

> The casual glimpses which the ordinary population bestowed upon that wondrous world of sap and leaves called the Hintock woods had been with those two . . . a clear gaze . . . to them the sights and sounds of night, winter, wind, storm, amid those dense boughs were simple occurrences whose origin, continuance and laws they foreknew . . . together they had, with the run of the years, mentally collected those remoter signs and symbols which seen in few were of runic obscurity, but all together made an alphabet. From the light lashing of the twigs on their faces when brushing through them in the dark either could pronounce on the species of the tree whence they stretched; from the quality of the wind's murmur through a bough either could . . . name its sort afar off. They knew by a glance at a trunk if its heart were sound, or tainted with incipient decay, and by the state of its upper twigs the stratum that had been reached by its roots. The artifices of the seasons were seen by them from the conjurer's own point of view and not from that of the spectator.

Had the whole argument of this section to stand or fall by one quotation, this would perhaps be enough to make it stand.

The personality in and behind nature is something that Hardy often stresses explicitly. When the wind sweeps over Egdon Heath (which is often called the chief character in *The Return of the Native,* though this obscures how Hardy's method here is typical of him through many novels) it makes three distinct sounds, of which one comes from the myriads of dead heath-bells as it blows through them. Now comes the salient point. Hardy adds that the sound is not like something simply from the florets themselves; it is 'the single person of something else speaking through each at once'. * * *

* * * The most interesting examples of figurative language conveying this part of Hardy's view are all variations on one theme. When it is bonfire night on Egdon Heath, the fires of twigs or timber are 'steady unaltering *eyes* like planets'; elsewhere, bonfires are 'like wounds in a black hide', while in other books a grove of beechtrees can form 'a line over the crest, fringing its arched curve against the sky, like a mane', and meadow-grass is 'the grey beard of the hill'. These comparisons have little real basis in visual resemblance, and they operate chiefly to make us fancy a resemblance by conveying a doctrine which would justify and explain a closer resemblance than we can actually see. The doctrine—it is an old one—is simply that the earth itself is a great living creature. Hardy has one even bolder comparison of this sort: after having described the sky becoming overcast and foggy, he writes 'the air was as an eye suddenly struck blind'. This only seems not forced if we incline a little to the implicit assertion at which it hints, but for which it is not evidence: an assertion which would account for a resemblance that is not, in fact, to be seen.

So much for how Hardy conveys that Nature is alive beyond our ordinary knowledge; but we could have very different impressions of this life, and Hardy wants to present one quite distinctive impression. For him, the life of Nature is such that the smaller unity lies always under the impress of the larger. Nothing is cosily self-contained, nothing can be seen in isolation. Hardy's view always quickly expands until it depicts something of a whole landscape, of the varied integration of a region. For him the proper expression of Nature's active principle tends always to lie in geography, in an organization that runs on mile after mile through a massive and abiding English countryside. * * *

Hardy is particularly careful to spread his scene to its full extent towards the opening of a novel. Of this, Egdon Heath—'vast tract of unenclosed wild'—is the familiar example. But the method is the same elsewhere: Norcombe Hill in *Far from the Madding*

Crowd, bare chalk and soil, so open to the sky that the rotation of the earth makes itself felt at night. * * *

Hardy's system of Nature not only spreads through space, but is also vast in time. Clym looks over the ferny valleys and hillocks of Egdon Heath, and the landscape seems to belong to the world of the Carboniferous period; to this the Heath goes back in a slow, obscure continuity, through the Middle Ages, the Roman period, pre-historic times. Mrs. Yeobright, finding a colony of ants on the Heath, recalls how they have been steadily there, generation after generation, for many years.

* * *

It is not difficult to see, then, how Hardy creates a developed sense of what the world is like and how it functions; and that he does so much more vividly and sensitively through particular scenes and incidents than through the abstractions which from time to time accompany them. Hardy has a corresponding picture of human society; and this proves to show the life of mankind as, sometimes at least, a microcosm of Nature as a whole. The correspondence is integral to Hardy's work, for the former, in his opinion, is properly no more than a part of the latter, and moulded by it totally and without intermission.

That human life, and indeed human consciousness itself, is wholly subject to the control of Nature is something which the people in Hardy's novels illustrate everywhere. It is his constant care to make the reader visualize them encompassed by a landscape to which they are subordinate. Clym, in his furze-cutting days, is 'a brown spot in the midst of an expanse of olive-green, and nothing more'; when Tess and her companions are out walking in the meadow, Hardy writes 'thus they all moved on, encompassed by the vast flat mead which extended to either slope of the valley—a level landscape compounded of old landscapes long forgotten'. One cannot overlook his haste, even, to subdue the particular to its general context here, nor the distinctive quality which he gives the scene. The opening passages of his novels very often depict a solitary figure moving over a landscape or submerged in it: *Under the Greenwood Tree, A Pair of Blue Eyes* (the second scene), *The Return of the Native, Two on a Tower, The Mayor of Casterbridge, The Woodlanders*, all exemplify this. * * *

A hint of the same thing lies in the numerous cases where a figure is silhouetted against a landscape—of which Eustacia motionless on the summit of the Rainbarrow is the obvious example.

But that Hardy shows people as merely situated within a wider and spreading landscape is not the full story. They are not simply in, but governed by and subdued to their environment. * * * Clym Yeobright was 'inwoven with the heath'; he was 'permeated with its scenes, with its substance . . . his estimate of life had been coloured by it'. The Heath limits Eustacia in the same way, though she is a newcomer to it. Mrs. Yeobright, Clym's mother, is also 'limited by circumstances'. But what brings these assertions to life and gives them their nuance is such a scene as Clym watching Eustacia while she goes away over Egdon on a sunny day. 'Clym watched her as she retired towards the sun. The luminous rays wrapped her up with her increasing distance. . . . As he watched, the dead flat of the scene overpowered him . . . there was something in its oppressive horizontality which too much reminded him of the arena of life; it gave him a sense of bare equality with, and no superiority to, a single living thing under the sun.' And later in the novel, as he crosses the Heath himself, this time passionately angry with Eustacia, his anger is silently frustrated and annulled by his environment; 'this overpowering of the fervid by the inanimate' is what Hardy calls it.

* * *

The varied, the unexpected, the bizarre in human life has been often noticed in Hardy; it could scarcely have been overlooked. Much that in a cursory or light reading might please by its quaint charm is taken from the fanciful customs or superstitions of Wessex peasantry. But these fanciful incidents prove on more serious reading to have a deeper meaning. Hardy is not exploiting them as oddities pure and simple; each is odd if thought of by itself, but all together they are the kind of things which for him largely constitutes the day-to-day pattern of life. They are integral to Hardy's general picture, and they are analogous to that element of the bizarre which he traces outside human life in the complexity of nature. This well illustrates how the outlook of a writer is not the sum of his abstractions, but how he interprets them. The abstractions of George Eliot and Hardy about the general course of things are to some extent similar. But their picture of life is totally different. In one Necessity suggests a bracing drabness; in the other a sometimes dreamlike inconsequentiality.

In most of the 'Novels of Character and Environment', odd customs, occupations, superstitions and so on are common. In *The Return of the Native* there is the strange figure of the reddleman, the heath bonfires of 5th November and their scarcely human attendants, the mummers' play, Eustacia pricked with a needle in church as a witch, an eclipse of the moon, the extraordinary scene where Wildeve and the reddleman, surrounded by a ring of heath ponies, gamble at night on the heath by glow-worm-light, the village gipsying, the incident of the wax image and the pins, and the picturesque Maypole scene. * * *

Quite frequently, though for the most part only in a passing phrase, Hardy suggests that all these events make up one great system of necessity. 'The next slight touch in the shaping of Clym's destiny occurred a few days later', he writes. * * *

The sense that human events move on slowly but irresistibly to their appointed conclusion is important in Hardy, because it produces one of the two rather different kinds of irony in things which he portrays. Ironical situations—the faded weather-vane in the Miller's garden, Tess's vow on the roadside stone, Fitzpiers happening to meet Suke Damson's wedding procession, Tess wringing the necks of the wounded pheasants—are a reflection in Hardy's work of the bizarre variety of things. But much more important, because having to do with the whole span of one novel after another, is the irony that lies in the long-term consequences of human actions. * * * Eustacia marries Clym to escape the Heath, and finds that he is devoted to it; while Clym in part marries her because he thinks she could help in his projected school, which is the last thing she would or could do. * * * One novel after another testifies over its whole development to the existence, and to the quality, of a determined system of things which ultimately controls human affairs without regard for human wishes.

* * * George Eliot and Disraeli were both novelists who in one form or another believed in heroic actions. For Hardy the heroic deed is barely possible; and since this is so, the moral outlook he expresses is a good deal less overt and emphatic than theirs. In his view, wise or right conduct can never be spectacular, and dramatic exhortations to pursue it simply fail to recognize life's major determinants. His values tend as a result not usually to be obtrusive in the novels; but all the same one book after another quietly embodies them. The single abstraction which does most to summarize Hardy's view is simple enough: *it is right to live naturally*. But this is the abstraction central to any number of moralities; Hardy glosses it by showing how to live naturally is to live in continuity with one's whole biological and geographical environment.

Hardy does not portray any great range of admirable characters, and makes no attempt to portray what many people regard as the more complex or sophisticated kinds of excellence. There are plenty of approximations to Caleb Garth in his work, but no Maggies, no Dorotheas, no Ladislaws, no Felix Holts.[2] Perhaps Hardy saw things in unrealistically simple terms; but it seems truer to say that he had the more formed (and controversial) view of what was basi-

2. These are all characters from the novels of George Eliot (1819-80). Caleb Garth, Dorothea, and Ladislaw are in *Middlemarch* (1871-72); Maggie is in *The Mill on the Floss* (1860); Felix Holt is in *Felix Holt, Radical* (1866). [*Editor*].

cally the ideal mode of life for man, while George Eliot was more definite about the principles of moral choice valid within any life one happened to be leading. Hardy's admiration is really wholehearted for one kind of life and one only. It is fairly clear that he saw intellectual culture as at root a trouble to human happiness (though he seems to have regarded its growth as inevitable in his own time). Clym Yeobright's features 'showed that thought is a disease of the flesh'.

The people whom Hardy presents in an altogether sympathetic light are like Gabriel Oak, Diggory Venn and Giles Winterbourne—all solid sterling characters completely satisfied with their position in life and at one with it. Their only misfortunes are in love, and they endure them with resignation and calm. They all have a sense of humour and they all have simple country pleasures—Gabriel his flute, Diggory his practical jokes, Giles his little 'randy' for the Melburys. * * * The minor rustic characters in what have been called Hardy's 'choruses' are the same too—genial, kindly, content with their station in life, resigned to disappointments, and never without a touch of humour. Hardy calls them 'the philosophic party'. * * * All these characters live in that continuity with their environment which for Hardy is the one root of a right life.

His whole concept of good and bad follows these lines, and is perfectly simple: people are to be admired as they have continuity with nature more or less completely, and those whom he stresses as on a false track in life are those who have lost it, and pursue some private self-generated dream instead. * * *

[For example, Clym Yeobright pursues] impossible ideals. Clym's notion of a night-school to raise the heath-dwellers at one step to the heights of philosophical cultivation is the result of a 'disproportion' of mind. ''Tis good-hearted of the young man', a rustic neighbour observes, 'but, for my part, I think he had better mind his business.' Jude, a village boy and a stone-mason's assistant, dreams of becoming an Oxford scholar; he and Clym make just the same mistake, one for others, and one for himself. * * *

Finally, it is true that the whole trend of one novel after another portrays this same scale of values. To adapt one's life to one's traditional situation is good, to uproot oneself for material ends is bad, to do so for romantic passion or an abstract ideal is if anything worse. *Under the Greenwood Tree* has a happy conclusion along these lines. *Far from the Madding Crowd* shows a return to stability after abandoning these values has brought tragedy. Throughout *The Well-Beloved*, Jocelyn's right course is to return to his island world; though this he can never do until at the very end he marries Marcia—his infatuation for whom in youth was what cut him off from home. Most of the novels recount how tragedy sooner or later results from the attempt to abandon the natural pattern of things in pursuit of the dream. In *A Pair of Blue Eyes*, the disaster comes because both Elfride and Henry are infatuated with empty intellectual ideals; in *Two on a Tower* the tragic situation is implicit in Swithin, the country lad who wants to be Astronomer Royal. *The Return of the Native*, *The Woodlanders*, *Tess* and *Jude* are all novels where the catastrophe comes through evading the established and natural order for the sake of one illusion or another; and whatever is saved from the wreck—the marriage of Thomasin and Venn, for example, though contrary to Hardy's own original plan, or Angel's union with Tess's sister, though forced and hurried—is in one way or another a reversion to that natural order.

GEORGE WING

[Clym Yeobright and Egdon Heath]†

The background is less frequently sunlit in *The Return of the Native*, and, to my mind, there are two unfortunate exaggerations about this novel: one is the character of Clym Yeobright and the other is the nature of Egdon Heath. Neither come to full fruition of artistry or entertainment in a deeply moving tale which has great power. With Clym, Hardy tried an experiment in characterisation. He wanted to produce a new man (complementary to the new woman?), and he turned out a dull dog. There is a dramatic build-up to his introduction, which is structurally delayed, and we anticipate a man of heroic proportions. Alas the clay of the character is refractory, and it refuses to assume a final triumphant form. Here is an intelligent rustic whose peasant ruggedness has been gold-plated by his experience in the jewellery trade in Paris, but no catalyst can be found to hasten a fusion of incompatibilities, and the native returns to his peasant superstition-bedevilled village, and there is an Aeneastic charge of glamour about him. He is virile and, to some extent, sophisticatedly moulded, although Hardy does his best to make a Frankenstein out of him. His features were unusual—"in Clym Yeobright's face could be dimly seen the typical countenance of the future." No doubt to Eustacia in her first ecstasy of passion, he was strikingly handsome, but Hardy still insists on oddness: "the observer's eye was arrested, not by his face as a picture, but by his face as a page: not by what it was, but by what it recorded." Of course Clym *was* odd. Surely this is an earlier

† From George Wing, *Hardy* (Edinburgh and London, 1963), Writers and Critics Series, pp. 52-56. Reprinted by permission of the publishers, Oliver and Boyd Ltd., and of the author.

masculine attempt at a Sue Bridehead.[1] Hardy seems derisively to throw as many antipathies as possible into one personality and then watch it writhe. From the very start the inimical is postulated:

> He grew up and was helped out in life. That waggery of fate which started Clive as a writing clerk, Gay as a linen-draper, Keats as a surgeon, and a thousand others in a thousand other odd ways banished the wild and ascetic heath lad to a trade whose sole concern was with the especial symbols of self-indulgence and vainglory.

The ironical thing is that this ascetic heath lad was, in an access of passion, to forget all his asceticism (which included an overall plan to do good to mankind—a sort of atonement for making diamond pendants), and to marry that very sort of woman for whom the "symbols of self-indulgence and vainglory" were made. The fact is that Clym's vague evangelism, his martyrdom to an unspecific cause, his undefined discontent with the worldly and fleshly, will just not be even contrivedly compatible with his hot-bloodedness, his grand passion, his physical love for Eustacia (for indeed there was little that was ethereal about it). The picture will not hold together. At times his gormlessness cannot be credited. Having won the passionately wild Eustacia, eagerly anticipating a metropolitan and civilised life, he dumps her in the back of the beyond she hates. Having gratuitously contracted a disease of the eyes—and this was wretched luck indeed—he intensifies the insult to his young bride by adopting the garb and way of life of a furze-cutter, the meanest of labourers. He stretches out on the floor, like a beast, to sleep after his swink.[2] It is under these circumstances that Eustacia is accused of infidelity and mother-in-law murder. What is surprising is that she is not guilty of either. The "ascetic heath lad," with a boorish prodigality, with, in view of his Parisian background, an incredible bush lack of delicacy, heaps indignity after indignity upon his new wife.

Hardy wrote novels and stories which had as their situation every corner of his nominated Wessex, and generally the changing landscapes are felicitously compounded into the tale. The harmony between plot and background is so prevalent that it is felt that the story could not have been told with any other geography. * * * But in *The Return of the Native* there is a suspicion that Hardy devised a story and then tried to hang Egdon on to it. There are, in this case, unwoven pieces. The physical geographical area known as Egdon (although for the purpose of fictive convenience it was a number of real heaths put together) undoubtedly meant much to Hardy. He extols it in fine passages, and it would seem that for him it existed as a personality, as a monstrous livingness which is more often

1. A character in Hardy's novel, *Jude the Obscure* (1896) [*Editor*].
2. Anglo-Saxon word for work [*Editor*].

Satanic than benevolent. People die of snake-bite on it; primitive witchcraft is practised there; there are violent drownings in weirs; and throughout Hardy wants us to feel that the spirit of the heath is at malicious and derisive work. * * * The case is not that Egdon is not at times magnificently presented. It is not that Hardy fails in conveying the notion of threatening personalised power. It is just that it is overdone in its "tragic possibility," in its evocation as a protagonist in this dark love-story. A heath cannot be a player. No amount of constriction of contingency or arrangement of plausible incident will effect the necessary artistic harmony. When Eustacia struggles against the hostility of the heath, she is boxing shadows.

If, through over-complexity and too much contrivance, Clym and Egdon are not artistically solvent, there is no doubt about the supreme success of the character of Eustacia. This queen of the night, this bundle of neuroses tingling in a body of great physical beauty, was too Shelleyean a thing for the didactic but earthbound Clym. Wildeve was paltry beside her. Her ancestry—a Corfu bandmaster's daughter—did not detract from her regality. "To be loved to madness—such was her great desire," but there was nobody mad or great enough to do so. She was ever in a spring of discontent, and one can never conjecture a phase or situation of anything like a permanent nature in which she would ever be contented. There was an insatiability about Eustacia, a restlessness, an unceasing demanding. She had to live at a hotter pace: she had to burn up quicker than anybody else. Because of her sultry grandeur, because of her disdain for the Egdon peasants, she incurred the enmity of the women especially. Mrs. Yeobright considered her as good or as bad as a whore: in her prosaic eyes Eustacia is cut down to less than life size: she is "lazy and dissatisfied"; she is "that woman—a hussy." Susan Nonsuch stabs her in church with a long stocking-needle, and later, as if signing her death-warrant, thrusts pins into her wax image. But the attitudes of these women, both fundamentally and for special causes, are jaundiced, and, despite them, Eustacia queens it over the Egdon she despises, and over the novel she fires. The countrified and narrow-minded pathos of Mrs. Yeobright; the ancient concupiscence of Granfer Cantle, the ribald ex-serviceman of the Bang-up Locals; the long-suffering passivity of the humanly unexplained Diggory Venn, the original Mephistophelean visitant; Thomasin's Cytherea[3]-like meekness: these are all, indeed, lively attributes of this brooding tale of applied misfortune. But its mainspring, its imaginative centrality, its energy, lie in the grand, tormented Eustacia, about whom most men would dream, but whom they would never dare to win.

3. A surname of Aphrodite or Venus [*Editor*].

CHARLES CHILD WALCUTT

[Action and Character in *The Return of the Native*]†

In the opening pages of *The Return of the Native* (1878), Thomas Hardy elaborates a theme with a series of symbolic images which he modulates so that, by the time he has got to the end of his first chapter, the theme has been considerably enriched and qualified. At first the bright sky and the dark heath seem to be bold images of two sharply distinguished principles: ". . .their meeting line at the horizon was clearly marked. . . . the heath wore the appearance of an instalment of night which had taken up its place before its astronomical hour was come . . . while day stood distinct in the sky. . . . The distant rims of the world and of the firmament [at the horizon] seemed to be a division in time no less than a division in matter." (Book I Chapter 1.)

The bright sky and the dark heath seem to be two aspects of life—aspiration contrasted with ability, freedom or will against fate, or intelligence against the dark compulsions of instinct. The glowing sky stands for the potential, the hope, the release; the dark heath for the forces of character and fate that oppress and defeat them. Thus the first statement; but Hardy presently introduces a suggestion of dark power and *life* in the heath which reach up in concord and sympathy toward the darkening sky: "And so the obscurity in the air and the obscurity in the land closed together in a black fraternization towards which each advanced half-way." Here are mystery and conspiracy in the unfolding of which the lucid candors of the sky have been endowed with a demonic intent. The sharp line of the horizon, between aspiration and defeat, has vanished. And with such words as "prison," "dignity," and "sublimity" Hardy goes on to suggest that the nighttime of the heath is indeed the most fitting symbol of the condition of man, ". . . a place perfectly accordant with man's nature—neither ghastly, hateful, nor ugly . . . but, like man, slighted and enduring; and withal singularly colossal and mysterious in its swarthy monotony." It is beautiful, because "Men have oftener suffered from the mockery of a place too smiling for their reason than from the oppression of surroundings oversadly tinged." (I,1.)

At this point the duality or balance between good and evil has been veiled by "the obscurity in the land," which represents man and rises up to fuse with the growing darkness of the sky. This sym-

† From Charles Child Walcutt, *Man's Changing Mask: Modes and Methods of Characterization in Fiction* (Minneapolis, 1966), pp. 159-60, 162-74. Copyright 1966 by the University of Minnesota. Reprinted by permission of the publishers, the University of Minnesota Press.

bolic setting in preparation for the action suggests a union of human and fatal darknesses that should guide us in understanding the relation between character and coincidence in the story.

As soon as these patterns of light and dark have been established, a further change is wrought upon them. The natives appear with their burdens of furze and light a huge bonfire on top of the Rainbarrow, against the skyline. A dozen other fires are in sight, at various places on the heath, each with its particular color and shape. Thus when the light of the bright sky, which I have identified with reason, freedom, and hope, fades, it is replaced by a darker light from human hands. The darker light has the wild character that the author has already attributed to the heath, and it is tempting to see in it a further symbol of the groping dark purposes by which humanity makes its way toward its puzzling ends. They might be the purposes declared by the passions, which certainly make constant use of the intelligence although they use it to irrational and frequently destructive ends. Eustacia Vye, first seen silhouetted against the darkening sky, then by her fire, described as "Queen of Night," with hair that "closed over her forehead like nightfall extinguishing the western glow" (I, 7), is literally and figuratively associated with darkness.

* * *

It would seem that it is time to take a fresh look at the role of coincidence in *The Return of the Native*. Accident will move an action that depends upon malign cosmic powers or upon pure nothing. In either event the characters will not control their fates and will therefore shrink as characters.

The first coincidence is the fact that the marriage license procured by Damon Wildeve for himself and Thomasin Yeobright was made out for Budmouth instead of for Anglebury. This error causes Thomasin to flee in shame both from the town and from Wildeve (and we recall that she has cause for anxiety in the fact that her aunt had already forbidden the banns, inflicting a mortal insult on Wildeve). She meets Diggory Venn; the event is also the occasion for Wildeve's returning to Eustacia when she lights her signal fire that evening. Very much depends upon this accident. Yet it is not really an accident; it is the purest example of that expression of an unconscious motive that we now call a Freudian error—and at least two characters recognize it as such: " 'Such things don't happen for nothing,' " said the aunt. " 'It is a great slight to me and my family.' " (I, 5). Diggory Venn has the same reaction: "After what had happened it was impossible that he should not doubt the honesty of Wildeve's intentions" toward Thomasin. (I, 9.) Eustacia goes even further, trying to make Wildeve admit that he intentionally delayed the marriage because of his passion for her. Wildeve's attachment to Eustacia and his desire for revenge on Mrs. Yeobright are abundant motivation for his "mistake," and the skillful manner in which he exploits both interpretations of his conduct is further evidence that such use was not entirely unforeseen by him. Although he later rather neutralizes these insights into his subconscious motivation by telling Eustacia plainly that the error with the marriage license was an accident, he does not radically alter the reader's impression of him. Mrs. Yeobright's contribution to the "coincidence," likewise, is a substantial expression of her pride, her inflexibility, and her determination to keep Thomasin from Wildeve. She inflicted the original insult; she now carries Thomasin away from the Quiet Woman by the back window while Wildeve is serving mead to the singing natives in the front room.

The character of Eustacia Vye is something of a puzzle because we expect Victorian reticence in a Victorian novel—and Hardy is so unreticent that many readers are unable to believe what is written on the page. Eustacia is not presented in the very act of love, but she is described in quite unequivocal terms as a sophisticated, promiscuous sensualist who is willing to take almost any risk to attain new intensities of passion. Yet she is also beautiful, dignified, intelligent, and noble. Vulgarity, Hardy writes, would be impossible for her. "It would have been as easy for the heath-ponies, bats, and snakes to be vulgar as for her." (I, 7.) Her dignity and taste are partly natural, partly absorbed by her from the austerity of the heath country, where the remembered glitter of Budmouth is transformed by her romantic imagination into a fairyland instead of transforming her into something tawdry, as it might have done if she had stayed on there.

Her dignity survives her liaison with Wildeve—and even the ignobility of being jilted by him. She can still be imperious in saying, " 'you may tempt me, but I won't give myself to you any more' " and thus rekindle his desire. When she has spurned his caress and sent him away, "Eustacia sighed; it was no fragile maiden sigh, but a sigh which shook her like a shiver." (I, 6.) Physical desire impels her: "she seemed to long for the abstraction called passionate love more than for any particular lover." Her sense of the flight of passion "tended to breed actions of reckless unconventionality, framed to snatch a year's, a week's, even an hour's passion from anywhere while it could be won. . . . Her loneliness deepened her desire." (I, 7.)

Eustacia is innocent and pagan in her sensuality. Hardy seems to attach no moral stigma whatsoever to the simple fact of her eager quest for sexual sensation. We are led to pity her isolation, admire her intelligence and spirit, deprecate her fierce pride, and perhaps contemn her snobbish sense of class (although we cannot be sure that an Englishman would completely agree on this last point). If she is to become implicated in a tragic web, it will be through no simple moral retribution for her physical sins—but perhaps because her life has confused her endowments into a strange mixture of innocence and sophistication: "As far as social ethics were concerned Eustacia approached the savage state, though in emotion she was all the while an epicure. She had advanced to the secret recesses of sensuousness, yet had hardly crossed the threshold of conventionality." (I, 7.)

The qualities noted above have been established through conduct—a word that may be taken here to designate purposeful, committed actions that *cost* something and presumably have consequences. Wildeve has defied Mrs. Yeobright, he has proposed to Thomasin, he has made his fateful error with the marriage license, and he has been deeply involved with Eustacia. She in turn has taken Wildeve, rejected him, and then on this critical evening lighted her passionate little fire to draw him back again. The plot that is launched by these early actions does not seem to express a deterministic view of causation. Here are not people swayed by chemistry or social forces but by their own strong natures. They think, choose, and act. The wild setting that surrounds the Victorian proprieties suggests these personal elements that brood or explode around them. The plot moves among circumstance, ignorance, folly, and the characters' powerful dispositions of mind and temperament in a tragic pattern—to which pity and terror rather than blind indignation against fatal coincidence are the proper aesthetic reactions.

* * *

Eustacia is offered by Diggory Venn the opportunity to escape to Budmouth, with employment that would not demean her. This she instantly rejects; and with this rejection—carefully placed before the return of the native, Clym Yeobright—she has freely chosen to stay in the lonely country that she detests.

"Accidents" continue to thicken the plot: Mrs. Yeobright in attempting to fan the dying embers of Wildeve's passion for Thomasin sends him straight back to Eustacia. Yet there is more than accident; there is complex irony in the sequence that shows Mrs. Yeobright pridefully rejecting Diggory Venn's renewed suit for Thomasin's hand, thanking "God for the weapon which the reddleman had put into her hands," straightway lying to Wildeve to make him fear that Thomasin will accept Diggory Venn—in order to provoke his jealousy—and withal turning the subsequent events in a direction utterly counter to her intentions: "By far the greatest effect of her simple strategy on that day was, as often happens, in a quarter quite outside her view when arranging it. In the first place, her visit sent Wildeve the same evening after dark to Eustacia's house at Mistover." (I, 11.) This is not the pitiless meddling of a cruel Fate in human affairs, but the quite probable outcome of human pride, mixed with folly and ignorance, attempting after the most superficial analysis to control a complicated pattern of people, situations, and motives. The inadequacy of Mrs. Yeobright's understanding is at this point abundantly obvious.

There are two plain reasons why Mrs. Yeobright's plan to manipulate Wildeve into marrying Thomasin misfires. She is ignorant of the fact that what Wildeve wants most is to marry Eustacia and leave Egdon Heath. And, obviously because she is engaged in the symbolic action of enacting the situation which she wishes were the fact, she overplays her hand and gives Wildeve the impression that he is being triumphantly rejected in favor of a new suitor: " 'The woman, now she no longer needs me, actually shows off!' Wildeve's vexation had escaped him in spite of himself." (I, 11.) This result of the interview is precisely what Mrs. Yeobright did *not* want. Headstrong pride and miscalculation have achieved it, not malign or blind Fate. Human motives are seldom so expertly laid bare in the novel. If the ensuing interview, in which Eustacia rejects Wildeve because she believes Thomasin has rejected him, is based on an utterly false premise, that is, after all, life. Nor should we forget that Eustacia and Wildeve have been quarreling and at cross-purposes for some time, and that her "supersubtle, epicurean heart" is never titillated by certainties. Passion flares brightest when she is uncertain or frustrated. Novelty is her goal, fidelity her abhorrence. The stage is set.

Thus we come to the end of Book I, with all except one of the major characters introduced and their lives tangled by passions and errors that have been fully accounted for. It is not an indifferent or incompetent God who is responsible but human qualities that are almost as old as Egdon Heath. I see the superstitious stupidity of the natives—which Hardy pushes past the grotesque almost to the absurd—as his grim background reminder of the frailty of human reason.

As we move into Book II, what looks in the accumulation like coincidence appears in the detail to be something else—personal frustration or the reversal of expectations. It strikes Eustacia with painful force that she has set the stage for an attachment between Clym and Thomasin by her part in preventing the latter's marriage to Wildeve. This reversal horrifies her selfish heart: " 'Oh that she had been married to Damon [Wildeve] before this!' she said. 'And she would if it hadn't been for me. If I had only known—if I had only known!' " (II, 7.) The reader doubtless stands by this time on

Thomasin's side, but whatever his reaction to Eustacia's consternation it cannot fail to add a mite to his sense of human purposes gone awry: once again a character has brewed a plot only to discover that there were elements in the mixture that produced a result quite contrary to his taste. Yet the headstrong and selfish plans of Eustacia could hardly be expected to work out along the simple axis of her yearnings, not when her sight is so blinded by passion. * * *

The character of Clym Yeobright, withheld for 150 pages, destined to be central to the story, demands careful scrutiny. The unhappy force of coincidence seems to mount as we draw into the main action. Could he not have worked out a satisfactory life with Eustacia if it had not been for these misfortunes and accidents he could not control? Hardy writes that Clym is "unfortunate" in being intellectually advanced beyond the readiness of the rural world to respond to his visions: "To argue upon the possibility of culture before luxury to the bucolic world may be to argue truly, but it is an attempt to disturb a sequence to which humanity has been long accustomed. Yeobright preaching to the Egdon eremites that they might rise to a serene comprehensiveness without going through the process of enriching themselves, was not unlike arguing to ancient Chaldeans that in ascending from earth to the pure empyrean it was not necessary to pass first into the intervening heaven of ether." (III, 2.) To announce that Clym lives by a high order of idealism and then introduce these considerations in this language would seem to display an ironic attitude toward him; to label the stupid natives "Egdon eremites" passes the ironic, even borders on the derisive; the notion of preaching a "serene comprehensiveness" to such yokels is ridiculed in the telling. Hardy proceeds, somewhat more gently, to explain that Clym's mind is not well proportioned, that well-proportioned minds do not make heroes and prophets. But he does not say that Clym is the stuff of greatness: here he leaves the reader to look at the facts and judge for himself.

What the facts show is a deep vein of self-destructiveness that runs right through the Yeobright family. * * * Reading stubbornly on until he has ruined his vision is the act of a man who is subconsciously bent on self-destruction. One may argue against judging too harshly his original venture of making eremites of the yokels, but here the evidence cannot be gainsaid. He is challenged, of course, by the nagging reproach of his disappointed mother, but alas he has inherited a broad stripe of her character. Like Eustacia, he has also a generous share of the endowments that enable mortals to cope with their frailties, namely, intelligence and cultivation, and like her he will not use these unique aids.

An extraordinary bit of evidence to this effect slips in so quietly that one is tempted to see in it a glimpse of Hardy's unconscious mind as he develops the more obvious motives of his hero. Although arguments do not prevail with his mother, Clym finds that feelings do—that Mrs. Yeobright shares his contempt for mere physical comforts and will, in spite of her ambitions for him to rise through the world of business, intuitively participate in his contempt for the great world. Then comes a strange sentence: "From every provident point of view his mother was so undoubtedly right, that he was not without a sickness of heart in finding he could shake her." (III, 3.) It seems to reveal Clym *wants* his mother to disapprove of what he is doing. Could there be a more expressive demonstration of his rebellious and self-destructive motives? His silver cord must vibrate when, finding that he has given an exhumed urn full of bones to Eustacia, his mother only comments, " 'The urn you had meant for me you gave away.' " Her disapproval of Eustacia is so fierce, and her expression of it so ominous, that Clym's growing passion is almost matched by the emotional force of his conflict with his mother. After his evening on the heath with Eustacia's kisses, mother and son glare at each other over tea. This doubles his emotional involvement in the wooing.

It might almost be argued that the glowering contest over Eustacia has allowed Clym to modify the original plan of opening a simple school for the natives. That is, his destructive attachment to his mother is satisfied by the new issue, so that now he can please Eustacia by planning a much more impressive operation which will ultimately put him "at the head of one of the best schools in the county!" Thus easily are his ideals accommodated while the basic destructive drives are kept strong and tense. The images of light and dark, introduced early in the book, are fused in a complex of symbolism by Mrs. Yeobright's flashing reply: " 'You are blinded, Clym,' she said warmly. 'It was a bad day for you when you first set eyes on her. And your scheme is merely a castle in the air built on purpose to justify this folly which has seized you, and to salve your conscience on the irrational situation you are in.' " (III, 3.) Seldom has reason been so expertly used in the cause of emotion. In the following scene, when Clym becomes engaged to Eustacia, he sets up a second version—like the subplot in *Lear*—of his destructive relation with his mother. Now he will have two women raging, for Eustacia cannot remain content on Egdon Heath, and Mrs. Yeobright's blazing antipathy for Eustacia is almost completely without basis in observed fact. The fact that she is entirely correct in her estimation of both Eustacia and Wildeve should not be pressed too severely: people respond to others' expectations of them; Mrs. Yeobright gives them no sign of the affection or trust that people commonly repay with good conduct. She expects the worst; they oblige.

The ensuing quarrel between Eustacia and Mrs. Yeobright, in which she says words about Eustacia that can never be unsaid, guarantees a permanent hostility between her and the girl. This hostility, which is perhaps the major cause in the tragic action, has grown from deep psychological roots carefully traced by the author. Here is no coincidence, no accident at all. And it will appear that the passions thus generated are strong enough to create all the "accidents" that follow.

Mrs. Yeobright first offends Wildeve by not entrusting Thomasin's inheritance of golden guineas to him—and then makes the error of choosing a dolt like Christian Cantle to deliver them. Thus she has incited Wildeve and played into his hands. Why should he not take revenge by winning the money from Christian? And in the confusion that follows it is not surprising that Diggory Venn, having won the money back, should give it all to Thomasin. The sequence is melodramatic and theatrical in the extreme, but not the result of accident. Hardy says that Venn's error "afterwards helped to cause more misfortune than treble the loss in money value could have done." (III, 8.)

Well, perhaps, but here Hardy is not letting the facts speak for themselves. The estrangement between Eustacia and Mrs. Yeobright has already been effected, as we have seen. It feeds on incidents that could be explained in a moment between people who did not question each other's good will. But Mrs. Yeobright's tone and phrasing in asking Eustacia whether she has received a gift of money from Wildeve are mortally insulting. They fully account for Eustacia's tearful recriminations. Mrs. Yeobright's question, moreover, is based on pure hostile suspicion which leads her to imagine events that have not occurred—as she has done before. If Hardy had not interpreted this action with the discourse on ill-chance that I have just quoted, the reader might well believe that the quarrel he has witnessed was provoked by Mrs. Yeobright's ungovernable temper and animus. With such a woman, no accident is required. She makes the trouble, prevents the "accident" from being explained away, is determined to quarrel with all of her young kinsfolk, and does.

In this interview, a boiling masterpiece of charges and countercharges, the two women pour out their accumulated grievances. In view of their explosive hostility, it is hard to imagine their maintaining a friendly conversation under any auspices. The guineas are the flimsiest pretext for Mrs. Yeobright to search out Eustacia and blame her for everything. Without that pretext, she would plainly have soon found another. * * *

When Clym's eyes fail, he deserts Eustacia for sixteen hours of furze-cutting a day. He abases himself to the ranks of the meanest, returning home to fall exhausted on his bed. This is not philosophy; it is—however unconscious—a cruel assault on Eustacia and doubtless on his mother too. It is an extravagant neglect, a virtuoso piece of folly by a man with so luscious and moody a wife. He is tempting her to quarrel with him, so that he can suffer more, and of course she does. * * *

The self-destructive impulses, which seem to account for the tragedy far more significantly than coincidence can, make *The Return of the Native* a novel of the greatest insight into character and motivation. The lacerations of the Yeobrights are set forth with such penetration and perspicacity that they reward careful study and repeated perusal. But the question nevertheless reasserts itself: is this a tragedy or a despairing indictment of Fate?

Coming late into the tragic arena, Hardy has penetrated further into the subconscious than Shakespeare, for example, generally had to do. Hamlet moves on a great stage. The Yeobrights move, really, among their psychological complexities, which Hardy fully accepts as inseparable from the nature and plight of man. They are not "abnormal"; they are not to be eliminated by manipulation of the patient's environment; they are the condition of man. Among them grow aspiration, fortitude, loyalty, and devotion, which Hardy also accepts as realities. Revealing so many destructive flaws among the nobilities of his characters, he makes their contests against error and mischance seem more inevitably doomed to failure than those, say, of Othello. Hardy's tragedy is brought on, perforce, by more ignoble mischances, more petty failings, than those of past heroes. Feelings of bafflement and indignation therefore constantly threaten to divert, replace, or obscure the tragic emotions of pity and fear. Hardy, it appears, participated in such a division of feelings toward his subject—and the confusion may have been nourished by a projection into the novel of insights and experiences with which he was too personally involved to achieve for them the aesthetic distance essential to high tragedy. This is one's judgment as the novel sags, occasionally, among the dreary quarreling or morbid self-pity of the characters. It moves back to a far nobler plane when Eustacia makes her fatal attempt to be a magnificent woman.

A bold reinterpretation is suggested: perhaps the coincidences are introduced and stressed to make the tragedy seem *less* due to human frailty! Without them, the defects of the Yeobrights and Eustacia would seem to make their defeats inevitable. The coincidences make them appear less due to the qualities inherent in the characters and therefore more due to tragic flaws in the universe.

Hardy, in short, is not blaming coincidence but rather using it to take some of the "blame" from his characters. But the trouble is that the flaws in the universe do not remove the flaws in the characters, and so the tension in the novel is sometimes painful rather than tragic.

This shifting of "blame" appears signally in the extraordinary circumstances by which Mrs. Yeobright is left standing before her son's door because he is fast asleep on the floor and Eustacia is talking to Wildeve at the back. The mother has built so strong a case against herself that some such device is essential to reclaim the reader's pity for her. Yet it would not be completely reclaimed—Eustacia's uneasiness and fear of meeting Mrs. Yeobright are too thoroughly justified—if it were not for the older woman's anguish and death. The coincidences and her suffering go a long way toward recalling the tragic emotions; yet they do not, finally. There is too much indignation, too cruel a sense of man's inadequacies, too complete an absence of the tragic recognition and insight by which a suffering character is ennobled. Hardy's universe is ignoble, flawed, almost repulsive—"like the white of an eye without its pupil."

Few novels, however, so grandly demonstrate the force of the plot in determining character. In a lesser action, these people could seem to be a set of stupid fools. In Hardy's plot they have great occasions for the making of their perverse decisions. What they do affects fatal destinies and shattering passions. Their various decisions do not admit of reconsiderations or corrections. Each step taken moves the entire person, with a stately and fearful tread. The movement toward doom is grand. And so the characters are con-
motives in a sordid urban setting might reduce them. Protected
stantly raised, by the action, above the pettiness to which the same
from triviality, they are often grand in the simplicity of their fatal drives.

The balance in the novel is between the tragic grandeur of the action and the self-destructiveness of the characters. The former is of a Grecian majesty, the latter expresses itself sometimes with Aeschylean nobility, sometimes with neurotic perversity.

Selected Bibliography

[Note: Articles and books from which excerpts have been reprinted in this edition are not included.]

BIBLIOGRAPHIES

Beebe, M., B. Culotta, and E. Marcus. "Criticism of Thomas Hardy: A Selected Checklist," *Modern Fiction Studies*, VI (Fall, 1960), 258–79.

Fayen, George S., Jr. "Thomas Hardy," in *Victorian Fiction, A Guide to Research* (ed., Lionel Stevenson, Cambridge, Mass., 1964), 349–87.

Weber, Carl J., *The First Hundred Years of Thomas Hardy, 1840–1940: A Centenary Bibliography of Hardiana* (Waterville, Maine: Colby College Library, 1942).

THOMAS HARDY AND *THE RETURN OF THE NATIVE*

Abercrombie, Lascelles. *Thomas Hardy: A Critical Study* (London, 1912).

Allen, Walter, *The English Novel* (London, 1954).

Anderson, Carol R. "Time, Space, and Perspective in Thomas Hardy," *Nineteenth-Century Fiction*, IX (1954), 192–208.

Blunden, Edmund. *Thomas Hardy*, (New York, 1952).

Brennecke, Ernest, Jr. *Thomas Hardy's Universe*, (London, 1924).

Brown, Douglas. *Thomas Hardy*, (London and New York, 1954; revised edition, London, 1961).

Chase, Mary Ellen. *Thomas Hardy from Serial to Novel*, (Minneapolis, 1927).

Chew, Samuel C. *Thomas Hardy, Poet and Novelist*, (New York, 1928).

Child, H. H. *Thomas Hardy*, (New York, 1916).

Duffin, Henry Charles. *Thomas Hardy: A Study of the Wessex Novels*, (Manchester, 1916; second edition, revised and enlarged, 1921; third edition, with further additions and revisions, 1937; reprinted, 1962).

Eliot, T. S. *After Strange Gods*, (New York, 1934).

Ellis, Havelock. "Hardy," in *From Marlowe to Shaw* (ed. John Gawsworth, London, 1950, 203–90. Three essays which appeared in 1883, 1896, and 1930).

Emery, John. "Chronology in Hardy's *The Return of the Native*," *PMLA*, LIV (June, 1939), 618–20.

d'Exideuil, Pierre. *The Human Pair in The Works of Thomas Hardy*, trans. Felix W. Crosse, introduction by Havelock Ellis, London, 1930).

Firor, Ruth. *Folkways in Thomas Hardy*, (Philadelphia, 1931; reprinted New York, 1962).

Garwood, Helen. *Thomas Hardy: An Illustration of The Philosophy of Schopenhauer* (Philadelphia, 1911).

Guerard, Albert J. *Thomas Hardy: The Novels and Stories* (Cambridge, Mass., 1949).

Guerard, Albert J., ed. *Hardy: A Collection of Critical Essays: Twentieth-Century Views* (Englewood Cliffs, N. J., 1963).

Hardy, Evelyn. *Thomas Hardy, A Critical Biography* (London, 1954).

Hawkins, Desmond. *Thomas Hardy* (London, 1951).

Holloway, John. "Hardy's Major Fiction" in *The Charted Mirror: Literary and Critical Essays* (London, 1960).

Johnson, Lionel. *The Art of Thomas Hardy* (London, 1895; reprinted New York, 1923, and New York, 1964).

Loomis, Roger. *The Play of Saint George* (New York, 1928).

Mc Dowell, Arthur. *Thomas Hardy: A Critical Study* (London, 1931).

Modern Fiction Studies, Thomas Hardy issue, VI (Fall, 1960).

Moore, George. *Conversations in Ebury Street* (New York, 1924).

Muller, Herbert. "Thomas Hardy," in *Modern Fiction* (New York, 1937).

Murphree, Albert A. and Carl F. Strauch. "The Chronology of *The Return of the Native*," *MLN*, LIV (November, 1939), 491–97.

Rutland, W. R. *Thomas Hardy: A Study of His Writings and Their Background* (Oxford, 1938; reprinted New York, 1962).

The Southern Review, Thomas Hardy Centennial Issue, VI (Summer, 1940).

Stevenson, Lionel. *The English Novel: A Panorama* (Boston, 1960).

Stewart, J. I. M. "Hardy," in *Eight Modern Writers* (Oxford, 1963).

Symons, Arthur. *A Study of Thomas Hardy* (London, 1927).

Weber, Carl J. "Hardy's Chronology in *The Return of the Native*," *PMLA*, LIII (1938).

Weber, Carl J. *Hardy in America* (New York, 1952).

Weber, Carl J., ed. *Hardy's Letters* (Waterville, Maine: Colby College Library, 1954).

Woolf, Virginia, "The Novels of Thomas Hardy," in *The Second Common Reader* (New York, 1932; first published in *The Times Literary Supplement*, January 19, 1928).